PERILOUS DESTINY

"I have to go north to Gravenfist Keep," Grace said. "I'm supposed to stop the Pale King from riding forth when the Rune Gate opens. But I don't know how I'm possibly going to do that. All I have is an old sword and five hundred men. And this." She drew out the rune of hope.

Mirda studied the rune but did not touch it. "It seems you have much to me. Remember that you do not need to defeat the Pale King, but only to hold him back until the Runebreaker can fulfill his destiny."

A shiver coursed through Grace. "Until he breaks the world, you mean."

"Or saves it," Mirda said, meeting her gaze.

How could it be both? Grace still didn't understand that. But there was one thing she did know—there was no person on any world kinder or truer than Travis Wilder. He would not harm Eldh; she would not believe that he could.

"He's gone, you know." Grace leaned her head against the back of the musty chair.

"He will return," Mirda said.

"But how can you know that?"

"Because prophecy demands it. The Runebreaker will be there at the end."

"But what if it's not Travis? What if it's the other Runebreaker who's there at the end?"

"Then," Mirda said, her words as hard as stones, "all the world is doomed."

ALSO BY MARK ANTHONY

Beyond the Pale
The Keep of Fire
The Dark Remains
Blood of Mystery

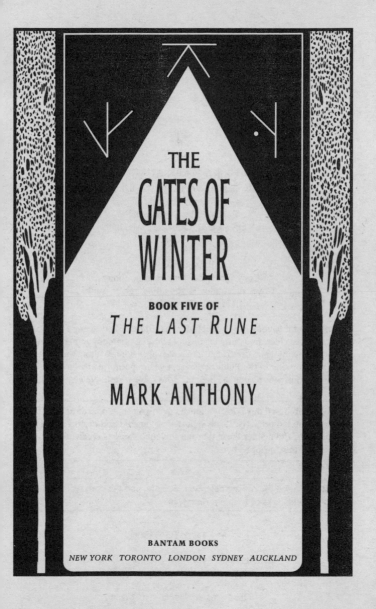

THE GATES OF WINTER

BOOK FIVE OF
THE LAST RUNE

MARK ANTHONY

BANTAM BOOKS
NEW YORK TORONTO LONDON SYDNEY AUCKLAND

THE GATES OF WINTER
A Bantam Spectra Book / August 2003

Published by Bantam Dell
A Division of Random House, Inc.
New York, New York

ISBN 0-553-58333-6

Manufactured in the United States of America
Published simultaneously in Canada

OPM 10 9 8 7 6 5 4 3 2 1

For Carl, Carla, Aurora, and Aidan—
With warm memories of our own winter adventure together
in Salt Lake 2002

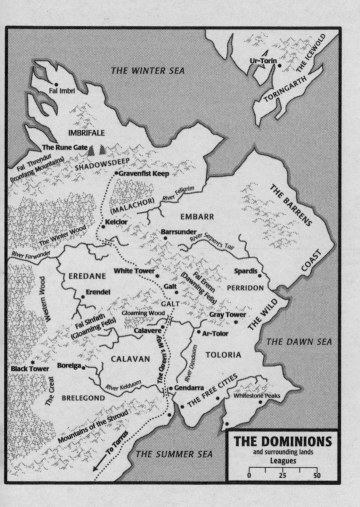

THE WINTER SEA

Ur-Torin

THE ICEWOLD

Fal Imbri

TORINGARTH

IMBRIFALE

The Rune Gate

Fal Threndur
(Ironfang Mountains)

SHADOWSDEEP

Gravenfist Keep

THE BARRENS

River Felgrim

(MALACHOR)

EMBARR

Keldor

The Winter Wood

Barrsunder

River Serpent's Tail

River Farwander

EREDANE

White Tower

Spardis

Fal Erenn
(Dawning Fells)

PERRIDON

THE WILD COAST

Erendel

Galt

GALT

Gloaming Wood

Gray Tower

THE DAWN SEA

Western Wood

Fal Sinfath
(Gloaming Fells)

Calavere

Ar-Tolor

The Queen's Way

TOLORIA

River Dimduorn

The Great

Black Tower

Boreiga

CALAVAN

River Kelduorn

Gendarra

THE FREE CITIES

Whitestone Peaks

BRELEGOND

Mountains of the Shroud

To Toras

THE SUMMER SEA

THE DOMINIONS
and surrounding lands
Leagues

0   25   50

"Love shall yet defy you."

PART ONE

THE QUEEN OF SUMMER

1.

It was the dead of winter when he reached Ar-tolor.

Dusk was falling, and gold lights shone from the windows of the castle on the hill above, beckoning with the promise of crackling fires and steaming cups of wine. He could not remember the last time he had been warm—truly warm—and these last few leagues had been the coldest yet. His feet might as well have been lumps of stone, and despite the rags he had wrapped around them, his fingers were raw and bleeding. All he craved was to ride up to the gates and beg hospitality.

Instead, he turned his gelding away from the road and urged the beast toward a grove of trees that clung, feathery as fog, to the slope beneath the castle. That was where he would find her—not in the bright halls of Ar-tolor, but here, where blue shadows gathered.

He brought the horse to a halt at the edge of the trees, climbed from the saddle with clumsy motions, and threw the reins over a branch. The horse snorted, breath ghosting on the air, and dug at the snow with a hoof. It was Geldath now, the Ice Month; the beast would find nothing to eat. He left the gelding and trudged deeper into the grove, boots crunching on new-fallen snow.

Branches wove themselves overhead, sharp and black as ink on parchment, making a broken mosaic of the colorless sky— just as the webwork of scars made of his face. Here and there, where branches intersected, he fancied he could make out the familiar shape of a rune. There was *Lir*. Light. And over there, three twigs that sketched *Krond*, the rune of fire. He imagined stretching his fingers toward dancing flames....

Those were foolish thoughts; the cold had frozen his mind as it had his hands and feet. However, he knew he had to thaw his wits, for if he did not choose his words with care, they would betray him. Just as he meant to betray her. He muttered *Ber*, the rune of strength, and kept walking.

It was the silence that warned him. Somewhere off in the grove, a mourning dove had been singing. The music ceased. He turned around, and his heart became a lump of ice in his chest. A figure in a black robe stood next to a tree. The hem of the robe fluttered, though there was not a breath of wind. Only one set of footprints marred the snow: his own.

He shivered, and not simply from the chill. Every instinct told him to flee. Instead he willed his stiff legs to move, bearing him toward the other. He clutched a hard bundle beneath his cloak as he came to a halt an arm's reach away. At her feet lay a dove, its neck twisted. Blood spattered the snow like winter berries.

A voice emanated from within the robe's hood, sharp as breaking sticks. "Why has it taken you so long to come?"

"It is a long journey from the Black Tower." His lips seemed molded of clay; it was an effort to speak. "I rode with all possible haste."

"Is that so? Your steed did not seem overly exhausted when I came upon it."

He peered back the way he had come. Through the trees, he could just make out a large form sprawled on the snow, slender legs splayed. "That was my third mount. The last dropped beneath me in eastern Calavan."

"What fragile things they are. I would not tolerate such weakness in my servants."

He said nothing, and she drew closer, drifting over the snow. A precipitate of frost dusted the fabric of his tunic.

"Are you certain," she said, "you did not stop at the fortress of your brethren before coming here? It is not so far away from Ar-tolor. Perhaps you desired to show them what you've found."

"They are my brethren no longer. I am forbidden ever to return to my home—a condition I believe is familiar to you."

Within the cowl, he caught the glint of a milky eye. "Be careful, mortal man!"

He laughed, no less surprised by this reaction than she. "Don't you think it's far too late for that, Shemal?"

She clucked her tongue. "So, do you have it?"

"I do."

"Quickly—show it to me!"

He drew out the cloth bundle he had kept next to his heart all these leagues. *Forgive me, my friend.* Hoping she thought his trembling due to cold alone, he unwrapped the cloth, revealing a disk of creamy stone as large as his splayed hand. Inlaid in its surface was a silvery rune. *Tal.* Sky.

She reached out hands as pale as the disk.

"Do you want to hold it, then?"

A hiss escaped her, and she snatched her hands back. "Do you mock me?"

He kept his tone disinterested. "I shouldn't think so." However, as he wrapped the bundle again, he felt a spark of triumph. He had guessed she would not dare touch the rune; surely its magic was at odds with her own. She needed him still, to bear the rune. And to break it.

True, there were two others in the world Shemal might have used to break the rune of sky. However, the runelord Kelephon served the Pale King, not her. And the man the Witches believed was the Runebreaker of prophecy, Travis Wilder, was a tool of her foe Melindora Nightsilver. So Shemal had sought out another Runebreaker, one she could make her slave, and she had found him. She had made him bow before her, and he had done so eagerly, pledging himself to her.

In all, the plan was nearly perfect. There was just one problem. He did not know how to break runes. And if she discovered that fact before he found a way to break the rune of sky, all hope was lost.

"You're thinking of something," she said. "I see it in your eyes. Tell me what it is."

"I was thinking of our master," he lied quickly, trying not to look at the dead dove as he spoke. "He has been banished for more than an eon. Will he truly have the strength to do what he seeks?"

"Such petty thoughts! I had not believed you to be as weak as Liendra. How can you doubt the power of the Lord of Nightfall?"

"He was defeated once. He was banished beyond the circle of the world by the elder gods and the deities of Tarras, just as you and I were banished ourselves."

"Yet we will all have our victories in the end. And those who dared to cast us out will prostrate themselves at our feet before we destroy them." She brushed slender fingers against the trunk of the tree, and its bark turned black where she touched it.

"You will see," Shemal said, her words soft now. "I confess, not long ago, I felt doubts such as yours. The Great Stones Krondisar and Sinfathisar were lost, and the sorcerers of Scirath proved as worthless as insects. So powerful they claimed to be. They would open a gate between worlds, letting Mohg step through. All I had to do was show them how to dig up some dead city lost in the sands of the south." A sharp laugh escaped her. "Of course, I knew nothing of this city they sought, but I told them I would reveal it to them if they did what they said. I knew it wouldn't matter, that once the Lord of Nightfall returned to Eldh the Scirathi would be his slaves or be annihilated."

He stamped his feet, trying in vain to warm them inside his boots. She had deceived the sorcerers, just as he was trying to deceive her. Could he really hope to best her at her own game? Look what had happened to the Scirathi.

"The sorcerers were destroyed," he murmured.

Fear gripped him. He had not meant to speak that last thought aloud. However, she seemed not to notice the slip.

"Melindora Nightsilver saw to that, blast that bitch! She and the fool bard and that Runebreaker whelp of hers. How I wish them dead! I would forge their cadavers into shambling husks and make them serve me." Her hood slipped a fraction, revealing the curved corner of a mouth, lips as black as bruises against snowy skin. "But that will come soon enough. The raven you sent found me, and the news it carried changes everything. Krondisar and Sinfathisar have returned to Eldh. The Pale King's minions failed to gain them at the Black Tower, but Berash will soon ride forth himself to retrieve them, and he will place them beside Gelthisar in the iron necklace Imsaridur. When that happens, you will break the rune of sky—"

"—and Mohg will return to Eldh," he said, his breath a fog of dread and wonder. "He will take the Imsari from the Pale King, and with them he will break the First Rune. He'll destroy the world, then remake it in his own dark image."

Never, since the first day she had come to him in twilight at the ruins of the White Tower of the Runebinders, had she been so talkative as this; the message he had given to the raven must have intoxicated her indeed. "What of the Dominions?" he dared to ask. "What if they stand together and wage war against the Pale King, preventing him from gaining the Imsari? The queen of Malachor has been revealed. Will she not unite the Dominions?"

Shemal laughed, a sound like icicles shattering. "What Dominions? Eredane and Brelegond lie under the fist of Kelephon and his Onyx Knights. Much as I loathe him, he has done well in his task. Embarr shall soon follow, and Perridon and Galt are weak and worthless."

"And what of Toloria and Calavan?"

The black hood turned, facing up toward the castle on the hill. "Do not concern yourself with them. I have seen to it they will never stand together. And as for your little Malachorian queen—the Pale King will take care of her. Even Berash should be able to accomplish that much."

He should not ask more questions; surely she would grow suspicious. However, the cold had numbed his fear. "And once the Pale King does gain the Imsari, what if he decides not to surrender the Stones to Mohg, but instead to wield them and rule Eldh himself?"

It was getting darker now; her robe merged with the dusk. "What you speak is possible, and it is why I trust neither him nor his slave Kelephon. For a thousand years, Berash has ruled alone in Imbrifale. He believes he is the dark lord whom we all serve. But once Mohg returns, the Pale King shall recall who is the master and who the slave. Or he shall perish like the others."

He tried to speak again. However, his lips would not seem to move right.

"Hush," Shemal said. "The cold has nearly made a corpse of you. I have seen the rune of sky, and that is all I need for now. Go to the castle. I have told Liendra to receive you, and even she cannot fail to comprehend such simple instructions."

"What of Ivalaine?" he managed to croak. By Olrig, he was not a corpse yet.

"Don't concern yourself with the Witch Queen. She spends most of her time pacing in her chamber, muttering and pulling out her pretty flaxen hair. But you must take care what you speak in earshot of Ivalaine's counselor, Tressa. That witch still has her wits, and I fear Liendra has not always been prudent around her. I would crush Liendra like a gnat if I did not need her to make the Witches do my bidding."

With a noise no louder than the sound of snow falling, Shemal was gone. A full moon had risen, setting the world aglow, but there was no point searching the night for her. He would not see the Necromancer again. Not until she wished to find him.

With stiff motions, he bent and picked up the dove. Its little body was frozen solid. He let it fall back to the ground, then started trudging toward the road. However, after only a dozen steps, he stumbled and dropped to his knees. He couldn't make it to the castle on foot; he was too cold.

"Hey there, get up! This is no time for napping."

The voice was a croak, harsh and commanding, yet not without kindness. Light encapsulated him, too soft and golden to be that of the moon. A delicious warmth seeped into his flesh and bones, making his joints ache. He was lying on the ground; he must have fallen into the snow to die. Only he hadn't. Shivering, he pushed himself up to his knees.

An ancient woman stood above him. Her body was a shapeless lump inside myriad layers of rags, and her humped back was nearly bent double.

"Is that the best you can do?" she said, a sour expression on her withered face. "Some Runebreaker you are."

Clenching his jaw, he gained his feet. He was still stiff, but his hands and feet tingled with pinpricks of fire. He was going to live.

"I'm not a Runebreaker." He wasn't certain why he told her this; if Shemal knew the truth, he would be dead in an instant, his neck twisted just like the dove's. However, there was something queer about the old hag. The golden light welled forth from somewhere behind her. It was tinged with green and made him think of a forest in summer.

She let out a snort and peered at him with her one bulbous eye. "Well, if you're not a Runebreaker, you should be. You have the face for it."

Without thinking, he reached up and touched the fine scars that crisscrossed his visage. He had gotten them as a boy, after he had shown a talent for runespeaking. As a reward, his father had tried to cut out his tongue.

"So," she said, jabbing a bony finger at his chest, "are you keeping him safe?"

He moved his hand to the bundle of the rune, and as he touched it, he understood. The light, the warmth—it had to be. "You're the one he served, aren't you? Sky. You're the one who created him."

"You mean the Ones," she said, and for a moment it wasn't a crone who stood before him, but a gray-bearded man. He was tall and powerful, with a storm in his eyes and wisdom on his brow. On his right hand shone *O'rn*, the rune of runes. His left wrist ended in a stump.

Before he could speak, the hag stood before him once more.

"Do you truly mean to break it?" she said.

Despite the warmth, he could not stop shivering. He felt weak, sick, and stupid. All the same, he nodded. "It's the only answer."

The old woman clucked her tongue, but there was sorrow in her lone eye. "I suppose it is, lad. I suppose it is at that. But you'll never do it, you know. Not as you are now."

"I have to," he said, trying to sound confident. "I'll find a way."

She let out a cackling laugh. "I think the way's found you, lad."

As she reached out, he saw the symbol shining on her bony hand: three crossed lines. *O'rn*.

"Go, runelord," she said. "Break the sky."

Before he could pull away from her, she gripped his right hand in her own. Light split the darkness, pain sizzled up his arm, and Master Larad—runespeaker, outcast, traitor—threw his head back and screamed as power coursed into him.

2.

On another world, Deirdre Falling Hawk sat in a claw-footed chair that was older than she by a good four centuries and stared at the closed mahogany door across the hallway.

All right, Deirdre—blink already. You don't have X-ray vision. And even if you did, the room is probably encased with lead shielding. Gods know, the Philosophers always think of everything.

With a sigh, she leaned her head back against glossy wood paneling. She wasn't certain she believed in fate. All the same, she had a feeling hers was being decided on the other side of that door right now. She reached up and touched the polished bear claw that hung around her neck, wishing she could muster some kind of true vision. Wishing she knew what Hadrian Farr was telling them.

She wasn't surprised they had asked to see her and Farr separately. That was standard procedure in interrogation, wasn't it? Divide and conquer. Nor was she surprised the Philosophers themselves had wished to conduct this final *interview*, as they termed it. The fact was, compared to what she had witnessed on the weathered asphalt of Highway 121 outside of Boulder, Colorado, nothing in the three months since—the midnight phone calls, the endless question-and-answer sessions, the surprise early-morning visits to the South Kensington flat they had granted her—could possibly have come as a surprise.

If she closed her eyes, Deirdre could still see it: the window rimmed with crackling blue fire, hanging in midair. It was what she and Farr had joined the Seekers in hopes of finding—a gateway to another world. They had watched as Travis Wilder and Grace Beckett stepped through the gate, along with the wounded man Beltan and the spindly gray being that was, impossibly, a fairy. Then the window collapsed in on itself, and they were gone. Not two hundred yards away, the Seekers were waiting to pick the rest of them up. So much for the policy of not interfering with those who had otherwordly connections.

No doubt the Seekers had desired to intercept them before the arrival of the police, whose sirens had already wailed on the air.

Besides, the otherworldly beings with which Deirdre and Farr had been connected were gone—vanished through a gate to another world. In the days before, she and Farr had been cut off from the Seekers for becoming too closely involved in the Wilder-Beckett case. They had been allowed to break Desiderata left and right just so the Seekers could see what they would do. They had gone from being watchers to being the watched. Only with Grace Beckett and Travis Wilder now far out of reach, the rules had changed again. Silently, they had climbed into the waiting black sedans.

The Seekers had taken Travis's friends, Davis and Mitchell Burke-Favor, into custody as well. Deirdre had not been allowed to talk to them, though she learned later from Sasha that they had been released after intensive debriefing. And also that, in exchange for signing an affidavit of secrecy—something Deirdre suspected was not an option if the cowboys wanted to avoid being turned over to the police to be prosecuted for aiding and abetting known fugitives—they received substantial compensation from the Seekers' deep coffers. Deirdre knew that the two men could use the money; ranching was not an easy business. So maybe, in the end, some good had come out of all this.

Twelve hours after the Seekers picked them up, they had touched down in London; to Deirdre, it felt like traveling to another world. In the time since, she and Farr had both written detailed reports about their activities in Denver. They had been questioned and questioned again by Seekers at nearly every level in the organization. Deirdre was no psychologist, but she knew enough to be sure the subtle repetition was conceived to reveal any inconsistencies in their stories. However, she simply told them the truth; she guessed Farr did as well.

But maybe not all of the truth, Deirdre. Do you think he told them he really is following in the footsteps of the famed Seeker Marius Lucius Albrecht, who fell in love with the woman he had been sent to observe? Do you think Farr told the Philosophers what he feels for Dr. Grace Beckett?

Regardless, it was almost over. Deirdre knew that the only ones left to talk to were the Philosophers themselves—if they even existed.

Evidently they did; the summons had come that morning.

Deirdre actually dressed up for the occasion, donning a simple but tasteful skirt suit of black wool. However, she had kept her bear claw necklace, and she had been forced to grab her leather biker jacket against the chill January drizzle that slicked the London streets.

She had spent perhaps an hour in the room beyond that mahogany door. It had been dark and empty except for a single chair carefully placed in a circle of gold light. Then the voices had started, and she had seen the row of dim silhouettes just beyond the light. For a moment she thought they were really there. Only that wouldn't be nearly mysterious enough for the Philosophers, would it? After a minute, a crackle of static passed in front of the figures. It was a projection, that was all—their electronically altered voices coming through speakers, her replies returning to them by hidden microphone. They could have been a thousand miles from that room.

All the same, these were the dread Philosophers she was speaking to—the secret governing body of the Seekers, whose number and identities were unknown. This fact had registered on her, but distantly. She had seen a gold-masked sorcerer from another world use magic to control savage monsters; she had seen a fairy. In the end, nothing could shock her anymore. They had asked all the same questions the others had, and she had answered them mechanically.

It was only at the end of the interview, after a long pause, that a different question finally came.

"Please tell us one last thing, Ms. Falling Hawk. If you were given the opportunity, would you go there?"

She stiffened in the chair. "Go there?"

"To AU-3, the world some call Eldh. Would you go there, if you could?"

She leaned back and touched the silver ring she wore on her right hand. It was the ring Glinda had given to her at Surrender Dorothy—the London nightclub that had been a secret haven for people with fairy blood in their veins. Duratek had been controlling the folk of Surrender Dorothy, supplying them with the drug Electria, hoping to use their blood to open a gateway to Eldh. Only then Duratek had captured a true fairy; it had needed the others no longer. The nightclub had burned to the ground, but not before Deirdre had managed to talk to Glinda.

As she had a thousand times since that night, she thought of Glinda's purple eyes and the impossible forest she had glimpsed when they kissed. A forest she was certain had not been anywhere in the nightclub, or anywhere in London.

"Please answer the question, Ms. Falling Hawk. If given the opportunity, would you go to Eldh?"

She twirled the ring on her finger and smiled. "I think maybe I already have."

The lights came up, and it was over. She had gone into the hall to wait while Farr took his turn.

Once again Deirdre sighed. How long had he been in there? There was no clock in sight—nothing that would mar the precisely engineered patina of age and tradition that permeated the London Charterhouse. The only concessions to modernity were an Exit sign at the end of the hallway and electric bulbs in the brass sconces that had once burned oil.

Built just before Shakespeare's time, the Charterhouse had originally been the guild lodge of some of London's most notorious alchemists. These days, passersby thought it some exclusive club. They weren't that far off. The Seekers weren't so very different from the geographic societies of Victorian times, planning trips to exotic locales. That these locales resided not on other continents, but on other worlds, was merely a matter of degree.

Acquired by the Seekers just after the Restoration to be their first Charterhouse, the structure had been modified almost continuously, including the addition of a vast maze of offices, laboratories, and computing facilities beneath the ground floor, as well as tunnels that connected to several surrounding buildings.

Just as Deirdre contemplated getting up and pounding on the door, it swung open. Farr stood half in the darkness beyond, so that she could see him only in stark black and white. With his chinos, rumpled white shirt, and before-noon five o'clock shadow, he looked as if he had been digitized right out of a Humphrey Bogart movie.

"Well?" Deirdre stood.

Without looking back, Farr shut the door and stepped into the light. "I wouldn't have thought it would go like that."

"Go like what?"

A camel hair jacket drooped over Farr's arm. He unfolded the garment and shook it out, but this only seemed to encourage the wrinkles. Farr slung the jacket over slouched shoulders.

"Do you know how many of the Nine Desiderata we broke?"

"Yes, actually. Numbers One, Three, Four, Six, and Seven. Although I never could see the difference between Desideratum One and Desideratum Three. Do you think something was lost in the translation from the Latin?"

"And do you know how many other directives and regulations we ignored in our actions?" Farr went on.

"Let's see. There was the Vow, of course. Plus a dozen or so local, state, and federal laws applicable in Colorado. And as I recall, Hadrian, you only flossed once the entire time we were in the States."

He ran a hand through his dark hair, as if it could be any more perfectly mussed than it already was. "It doesn't make one whit of sense."

"No, Farr, you don't make one whit of sense." She plucked a bit of lint off his coat, noticed it had been covering a spot, and gently replaced it. "And nobody says *whit* anymore. Now tell me what happened. They've taken three months to decide what to do with us. Are we to be censured? Exiled? What?"

Farr's brown eyes finally focused on her. Even dazed and disheveled, he was handsome. He should have been a poet or an artist a hundred years ago; he would have looked absolutely beautiful dying of tuberculosis.

"They've invited us to rejoin the Seekers. All privileges and benefits restored. And at a higher rank."

Deirdre gaped, surprised at last.

"So what do we do?" she managed to say.

Farr stuck his gray fedora atop his head. "We go downstairs. The Philosophers have politely requested we stop by the main office before leaving the building."

"And what if we don't?" Deirdre said. She felt light-headed, as if the air all around her had gone thin.

"What, Deirdre? How could you possibly think to disobey the wise and benevolent Philosophers?"

Farr's voice was strangely soft; nor was he looking at her. Instead he gazed down the corridor, brown eyes haunted.

Deirdre started to reach toward him. "Hadrian?"

He turned his back and moved out of reach. "Be a good Seeker, Deirdre, and come along. We'd best see what wonders the Philosophers have in store for us."

Three minutes later, they stepped off the elevator into the brightly lit warren of offices beneath the Charterhouse to find Sasha waiting for them, two manila packets in hand. She smacked them idly against her cocked hip as her red lips twisted in a smirk.

"So, Hadrian Farr does it once again. He breaks all the rules and gets all the rewards." She sauntered forward and kissed Deirdre's cheek.

"It's good to see you," Deirdre said, squeezing her hand.

"You, too." Sasha stepped back and rolled her eyes. "Good Lord, Farr, could you quit staring? They're just boobs. I'm sure women on every world have them."

"Not like . . . that is, I wasn't . . ." Farr cleared his throat and looked away.

Deirdre couldn't blame Farr for staring. Sasha was fashion model gorgeous—tall and lanky, curved in all the right places and sleekly muscled everywhere else. Her skin was coffee with cream, her eyes black opal. Nor did the severe bun into which she had pulled her hair, or the faux secretary outfit—prim gray skirt, white blouse buttoned low, and reading glasses dangling on a rhinestone chain—do much to hide her beauty.

Sasha regarded Deirdre. "Some days it's a complete nuisance being hot, isn't it?"

"I wouldn't know," Deirdre said with a laugh.

Sasha grinned. "Don't tell me you're just fine with the girl in the mirror."

Deirdre shrugged. "I can't say I talk to her much, but I suppose she's all right. Although her nose is a little crooked, and I do keep telling her she needs a better haircut, but she doesn't seem to listen."

"I hope she never does," Sasha said, the words wistful. Then she turned her attention on Farr. "Why so quiet, Golden Boy? I would have thought you'd be crowing over your victory." Only Sasha could make disgust seem so impersonal and boring.

"News travels fast in this place," Deirdre said.

"You know our motto," Sasha said with a wink, tarting up her West End accent. "To Watch, To Wait, To Believe."

"And, evidently, To Spring On People When They're At Their Most Defenseless," Farr grumbled, hands in his pockets.

"I hate to destroy your fantasies, Farr, but I'm not your stalker. I was simply instructed to give these to you."

Sasha held out the large envelopes. Deirdre took the one with her name on it. Farr hesitated, then took the other.

"What is it?" he said.

"I'm letting myself hope it's a good dose of humility," Sasha said.

"Thanks, Sasha," Deirdre said.

"So, when will you be back at work?"

Deirdre fingered the envelope. It wasn't very thick or heavy. "I don't know. Soon, I hope. Hadrian?"

She looked at Farr, but he had turned back toward the elevator.

Sasha held a hand to her forehead. "I think I actually liked him better when he was an arrogant git. Would you go get him a stiff drink? Alcohol should reinflate his false sense of superiority."

Deirdre nodded. "I'll make it my first mission."

"Good girl."

Sasha stalked away through the offices, and Deirdre followed Farr to the elevator.

"Sasha's right. What's going on, Hadrian? You won, didn't you?"

"Let's get that drink," Farr said as the elevator whooshed open.

3

A quarter of an hour later they stepped through the door of the Merry Executioner, a pub three blocks from the Charterhouse, and their haunt of old.

Over the last few years, a shocking number of London's centuries-old drinking houses had been quietly replaced by chain-owned franchises—establishments that were not genuine English pubs but rather deftly manufactured replicas of what an American tourist thought a pub should be. Deirdre had mistakenly walked into one not long after their return to London. The too-bright brass railing on the bar and the random coats of arms on the walls couldn't hide the fact that the steak-and-kidney pie came out of a microwave and the bartender didn't know the difference between a black-and-tan and a half-and-half.

In a way, the bland commercialization of London's pubs reminded Deirdre of the workings of Duratek Corporation. That kind of thing was right up their alley—take something true and good, and turn it into a crass mockery in order to make a tidy profit. Wasn't that what they wanted to do to AU-3, to the world called Eldh? She could see it now: roller coasters surrounding the medieval stone keeps, and indigenous peasants in the castle market hocking cotton candy and plastic swords imported from Taiwan in order to keep sticky-fingered Earther tourists from noticing the smokestacks rising in the distance.

Luckily, the M.E. hadn't succumbed to the scourge of commercialization in Deirdre's absence. The dingy stone exterior and grimy windows were just unsanitary-looking enough to ensure foreigners would hastily pass by, shrieking children in tow. Inside, things were as dim and warmly shabby as Deirdre remembered. A drone of conversation rose on the air from a scattering of locals. She and Farr slipped into a corner booth and caught the bartender's eye. Scant minutes later they sipped their pints.

Deirdre gave Farr a speculative look over the rim of her glass. "Better now?"

He leaned back. "Marginally. However, I'm not sure just one pint will be antidote enough for an encounter with Sasha."

"You know, she doesn't really hate you," Deirdre said, not entirely convinced that was the case.

Farr must not have heard her. He gazed at the pair of manila envelopes Sasha had given them.

"So, are you going to open it, Hadrian?"

"Maybe. I suppose I really haven't decided."

Deirdre let out a groan. "Please spare me the I'm-too-cool-to-care routine. You know as well as I do that for all the rules we broke, and for all the havoc we caused, we're the first Seekers in centuries—maybe even the first since Marius Lucius Albrecht himself—to report real, verifiable, and multiple Class One Encounters. We've done the one thing the Seekers have always wanted to do: We've met travelers from other worlds." She leaned over the table. "Admit it. You want to know what the Philosophers have planned for us as much as I do."

Farr's expression was unreadable. He flicked a hand toward the envelopes. "Ladies first."

He had called her on this one. Deirdre picked up the envelope marked with her name, tore off one end, and turned it over.

A plastic card fell to the table. On the card was a picture of herself, her name, her signature, and the sigil of the Seekers: a hand holding three flames. So it was a new ID card, that was all, a replacement for the one they had taken from her at the first debriefing months ago. She turned it over to look at the reverse side.

Farr sat up straight and drew in a sharp breath. Deirdre raised an eyebrow.

"What is it, Farr?"

"Those bastards. Those cunning, diabolical bastards."

Deirdre frowned and followed Farr's gaze to the back of the card. It bore her thumbprint—no doubt in ink laced with her DNA, taken from blood samples the Seekers had on file. The DNA signature in the ink could be read with an ultraviolet scanner, providing a level of authentication that was virtually impossible to counterfeit. However, as interesting as the technology was, that couldn't be the source of Farr's outburst.

Then, in the lower corner of the card, she saw the small series of dots and lines—a computer code printed in the same DNA ink. Next to the code was a single, recognizable symbol: a crimson numeral seven.

A jolt of understanding sizzled through Deirdre. She looked up at Farr, her eyes wide. When she spoke, it was in a whisper of wonder. Or perhaps dread.

"Echelon 7 . . ."

Farr grabbed the other envelope, shredded it, and snatched his new ID card from the debris. He flipped the card over, then tossed it on the table with a grunt. Like Deirdre's, his card was marked with a red seven.

He slumped back in the booth, his expression stricken. "Now," he murmured. "After all these years, they finally give it to me now. Damn them to hell."

Deirdre didn't understand. Why was Farr so upset? Energy crackled through her. She turned the ID card over and over in her hands. "I'd heard stories, of course. Echelon 7—a superhigh level of clearance, a type of access far beyond anything else granted by the Philosophers. But I always thought it was just a rumor—a legend told to new recruits. The highest level of clearance I've ever seen is yours, Hadrian, and that's Echelon 5. I didn't think anyone who wasn't a Philosopher could go any further."

"No, Echelon 7 is quite real. I know because I've been working for years to gain it." He hunched over the table, voice hoarse. "Do you understand what this means? With this card, you can access every file, every artifact, every document and bit of data. The deepest secrets of the Seekers will be at your disposal—everything but the private files of the Philosophers themselves is yours."

"And yours, too, Hadrian."

"I don't think so."

Deirdre gave an exasperated sigh. "What are you talking about? You said you've been working for this for years. And now you're just going to throw it away?"

Farr shrugged, running a thumb over his card. "I suppose I did want this once. But I can't say I really know what I want anymore. Except maybe that's not true, either. Maybe I do know what I want, only it isn't this." He flicked the card away from him across the table.

Deirdre snatched it up. Sasha was right; Farr at his most coy and arrogant was vastly preferable to this maudlin version. "This is ridiculous, Hadrian. You're one of the most important agents the Seekers have, and they've rewarded you for your work. Why is that so hard to bear?"

Farr let out a bitter laugh. "Come now, Deirdre, surely you're not that guileless, not after what we've witnessed. This is no reward. It's simply another ploy to control us. Think of what we've seen, what we know. And think of who besides the Seekers might want that knowledge for themselves."

"Duratek," she said on reflex.

"Exactly. The Philosophers will do anything to keep us out of the hands of Duratek—even if it means giving us what we've always wanted. But that doesn't mean we're anything more than the puppets we were in Colorado."

Anger bubbled up inside Deirdre, at Farr—and, she had to admit, at the machinations of the Philosophers. Much as she would have liked to deny it, there was a ring of truth to Farr's words. But it didn't matter.

"So what?" she said. "So the Philosophers are trying to manipulate us. No matter why we have them, these cards still work." She reached across the table and took his hand. "Think of what we can do with them, Hadrian, what we can learn. We never knew until last year that the Graystone and Beckett cases were connected. What other connections will we find with access to all of the files of the Seekers?"

Farr winced, and Deirdre knew her words had stung him. It was cruel to mention Dr. Grace Beckett—whom he loved, and who was now a world away from him. However, Deirdre didn't care; he had to listen to her.

"If the Philosophers really think we're their puppets," she said, "then the joke's on them. We'll be reinstated and—"

He pulled his hand from hers. "I'm not resuming my work with the Seekers, Deirdre. I'm resigning from the order as of this moment."

This was ridiculous. She glared at him. "You can't quit, Hadrian. I know; I tried it once. And you were the one who told me that leaving the Seekers isn't an option."

"It seems I was mistaken."

Deirdre hardly believed what she was hearing.

Farr's face was haggard but not unsympathetic. "I'm sorry, Deirdre, I truly am. I know it's difficult. But you have to face the fact that we've lost."

"Lost what?"

"Our belief."

She sat back, staring as if slapped. In all the years she had known him, Farr had never wavered in his quest for other worlds, had never stopped believing in them. "I don't understand. You were there, Hadrian, on the highway to Boulder. You saw it all with your own eyes."

"You misunderstand me. I haven't lost my belief in other worlds. It's my belief in the Seekers I've lost. And from everything you're telling me, you have as well."

She struggled for words but could find none.

"To Watch, To Wait, To Believe—that was our motto. We thought all we had to do was keep our eyes open, be patient, and one day it would happen. One day the Philosophers would reveal everything, and the door would open for us. Well, the door did open, only it wasn't the Philosophers who did it." He laughed, and the cold sound of it made her shiver.

"Stop it, Hadrian."

"I used to believe the Philosophers knew everything, that they were infallible. But it turns out they're not. They make mistakes just as the rest of us do. Do you think our mission in Denver went even remotely as they had planned?"

"I said stop it."

"We don't have to be their playthings, Deirdre. And we don't need them or the magic of their little plastic cards in order to find other—"

"Stop!"

She hit the table with a hand. Beer sloshed, and patrons turned their heads. Deirdre hunkered deeper into the dimness of the booth; the eyes turned away.

Farr was watching her, one eyebrow raised. She drew a breath, willing the spirits to grant her strength. She was going to need it.

"Don't even think about it," she said, her voice low and dangerous. "I mean it, Hadrian. Leaving the Seekers is one thing. If you want to start a nice quiet life as a shopkeeper or an accountant, that's fine. But leaving the Seekers and continuing your . . . work is something else altogether."

He started to speak, but she held up a hand.

"No—shut up for once in your life and listen to me. The Seekers have eyes everywhere; you know that better than anybody. And you also know how the Philosophers feel about renegades. If they can't be sure of your allegiance, they'll make sure no one else can, either."

She locked her eyes on his and listened to the thudding of her own heart. For a moment she thought she had him, that he had finally seen reason. Then a smile touched his lips—it was a fond expression, sad—and he stood up.

So it was over; the words escaped her anyway. "Please, Hadrian. Don't go like this."

He held out a hand. "Come with me, Deirdre. You're too good for them."

She pressed her lips together and shook her head. Farr was wrong. It wasn't just their belief they had lost. He had lost Grace Beckett to another world. And Deirdre had lost Glinda to the fire in the Brixton nightclub. To Duratek.

All the same, Deirdre hadn't lost her faith. There was still so much to learn, and with the new card the Seekers had given her—with Echelon 7—there was no telling what she might discover.

Deirdre gripped the silver ring on her right hand. "I can't go with you, Hadrian. I have to stay here. It's the only chance I have to learn what I need to."

"And that's the reason I have to go."

Despite his grim expression, there was something about him—a fey light in his eyes—that made him seem eager. He had always taken risks—that was how he had risen so high so quickly in the Seekers—but he had never been one recklessly to thrust himself into danger. Now Deirdre wasn't so sure. In the past, she had been angry with Farr, awed by him, even envious of him. Now, for the first time, she was afraid for him.

"What are you going to do?"

He shrugged on his rumpled coat. "You're a smart girl, Deirdre, and you've got good instincts. That's why I requested you for my partner. But you're wrong about something. You said we've done the one thing the Seekers have always wanted to do. Except that's not quite true." Farr put on his hat, casting his face into shadow. "You see, there's still one class of encounter we haven't had yet. Good-bye, Deirdre."

He bent to kiss her cheek, then turned and made for the door of the pub. There was a flash of gray light and a puff of rain-scented air.

Then he was gone.

4.

They came home to Calavere on a cold, brilliant day late in the month of Geldath.

Grace Beckett smiled as the familiar silhouettes of the castle's nine towers hove into view, banners snapping atop their turrets, as blue as the winter sky. All her life, she had lived in places she had not chosen, houses in which she had not belonged—the orphanage, an endless rotation of foster homes, countless drab apartments where she had never bothered to hang a picture on the wall. But she belonged in Calavere; she knew it by the beating of her heart. If ever she had a home, on any world, it was here.

A small form wriggled in the saddle in front of Grace. She wrapped her arms around the girl and rested her chin atop Tira's curly red head.

"Do you see the castle on the hill over there?" Grace murmured. "That's where I live."

Tira reached out her hands and laughed.

Grace stroked the girl's hair, smoothing tangles she knew would reappear in an eyeblink. In moments like this, it was possible to believe Tira was a normal child. Possible, if Grace didn't think about how she ran around in the frigid air wearing just her thin smock, yet was always warm to the touch. Possible, if Grace forgot how she had once risen into the sky like a star to become a goddess.

Tira had not spoken a word since Midwinter's Eve, since she

appeared at the Black Tower without warning, handed the Stone of Fire to Travis, and called him *Runebreaker*. There was so much Grace wanted to ask her—where she had been, how she had come back, and why she had brought Krondisar to Travis—only there was no point. Tira wouldn't—perhaps couldn't—answer. And Grace did not for a moment let herself believe she wouldn't be leaving again soon.

"I love you," Grace said, tightening her arms around the girl's tiny body.

Tira gazed up with a placid expression, one side of her face soft and pretty, the other a blank mask of scar tissue. On Midwinter's Day, when they had set out from the Tower of the Runebreakers, Grace had wondered about Tira's face. Krondisar had turned her into a goddess. So why hadn't the transformation made her whole? However, as the leagues passed by, Grace understood. Tira *was* whole. This was what the Stone of Fire had made her.

Grace kissed her forehead—the scarred half—and Tira looked again at the looming castle.

"That is a sight I feared we would never see again," said a deep voice, comforting in its gloominess.

Grace looked up to see Durge guide his horse close to hers. She smiled again. "I don't believe you, Durge. I think you've known all along we would make it back here. Why else would you have set out on the journey in the first place?"

"To be by your side, my lady. Where I belong."

Grace couldn't help feeling a note of pleasure. She loved the craggy-faced knight; he was truer than any person she had ever met. Travis had told her Durge had been a sheriff's deputy in Castle City, in the year 1883, to which they had traveled and returned from with the magic of the gate artifact. It wasn't difficult to see Durge as a frontier lawmen; no matter where he went, no matter what century he was in, he would always be a knight. Her knight. However, she doubted loyalty was his only reason for returning with her to Calavere.

We're coming, Aryn. Grace cast the words across the thread of the Weirding, not knowing if her thoughts could be heard from so far away. Several times, as they journeyed east, the baroness had contacted Grace over the Weirding, the web of life and power that wove itself among all things in the world. Aryn had spoken of affairs in Calavere and the Dominions, and Grace had recounted their own harrowing encounters at the Black Tower. However, each time Grace tried to contact Aryn herself, she had failed. She did not have the ability to reach out with her thoughts over such long distances as Aryn seemed able to do.

Grace stole a glance at Durge's somber profile. His eyes were focused on the castle as he rode, his left hand pressed against his chest. She wasn't certain when she had first begun to suspect the truth. Maybe it was the way, each time she told the others Aryn had contacted her over the Weirding, Durge seemed to take particular interest. At the same time, Lirith would cast frequent glances at the knight, her dark eyes troubled.

One night, as they lay on the frozen ground near the feet of the Gloaming Fells, Grace had asked Lirith if there was something about Aryn and Durge she ought to know. Lirith had tried desperately to hide the truth, but Grace was a doctor; she knew precisely where to make an incision. At last, over the secret strands of the Weirding, Lirith had told her what she had learned by accident in the Barrens last summer, when she and Durge had traveled with Falken to find the Keep of Fire. In that desolate place, the witch had tried to lend a bit of her own life power to the weary knight, but in the process she had unwittingly stolen some of Durge's memories.

He loves her with all his heart, Grace, Lirith's anguished voice had sounded in Grace's mind. *But he says she must never know, that she is too young and good to be bothered by one as old and derelict as he, and he made me vow never to tell anyone. Only now I have, and so I've betrayed him again.*

No, Lirith, you haven't betrayed Durge—he's betraying himself. If he loves Aryn, he owes it to her to tell her the truth. Just because he didn't want to trouble Aryn was not reason enough to hide his feelings from her. Grace always gave her patients the true diagnosis, even if it was something they didn't want to hear.

The wind blew Durge's hair from his brow and tugged at the mustaches that drooped beneath his hawkish nose. Durge wasn't handsome. All the same, there was a kindness to his craggy visage, a nobility that went beyond mere beauty. She didn't know if Aryn could return Durge's love, but the young woman deserved the chance.

Durge glanced at her. "Is something amiss, my lady? We must look our best to greet King Boreas and Lady Aryn, and I suppose there's a bit of this morning's porridge stuck in my mustaches."

Grace laughed. "No, Durge. You're absolutely perfect."

This statement appeared to confound the knight. He opened his mouth, shut it again, gave her an odd look, then spurred his mount ahead, toward Falken's horse.

"What did you do to him?" Travis said, veering his horse toward Grace's. "It looks like his brain just went *bonk*."

"I told him the truth."

"That'll do it," Travis said with a nod. "I used to complain that no one ever told me what was really going on. Only then they did, and I realized how much happier I was not knowing."

"And would you go back if you could? To not knowing?"

Travis smiled, only there was a look in his eyes—sorrow? resignation?—she couldn't quite name. His hair was coming in now, thick and red as his beard. After Krondisar destroyed and remade him last summer, he had taken to shaving his head, hating the way his hair had changed from sand to flame. However since the Black Tower, he had been letting it grow. It was as if he didn't mind anymore seeing the outward reflection of what he really was. And maybe that meant he had answered her after all.

Travis gazed at the castle, bouncing in the saddle like a sack of turnips. After all these leagues, he was still a terrible rider. Grace sat on her own mount straight and tall, rising and falling with its gait as if she had done it all her life. Of course, the horses were only a recent luxury. For most of the journey they had traveled on foot. Grace, Falken, Beltan, and Vani had had no horses; they had taken the fairy ship as far as they could up the River Farwander, then had marched the rest of the way to the Black Tower. And the horses Travis, Durge, Sareth, and Lirith had ridden there had been left over a century in the past.

It was nearly a hundred leagues from the Black Tower of the Runebreakers to Calavere. The idea of walking the entire way had filled Grace with despair, but with little other choice they had set out on foot on Midwinter's Day, and much to their surprise, they made good time. Perhaps *too* good. After they made camp each night, Falken would judge the landmarks, and by his estimates they would have covered more leagues than seemed possible.

"Something's not right about this," Falken said the third night of their trek, and Grace agreed. As they walked, she would keep her eyes fixed on a distant hill, measuring their progress toward it. Then they would pass through a copse of trees or descend into a ravine, and when she caught sight of the hill again it would suddenly loom close, as if it had leapfrogged over the intervening miles when she wasn't looking.

"That's just not possible," Beltan said, scratching his head after one such instance, and Tira had laughed, as if he had told a marvelous joke.

Grace looked at Tira, but the girl only bent her head over the half-burnt pinecone she had plucked from the campfire, and around which she had wrapped a rag, as if it were a doll.

Soon they left the wild reaches of the western Fal Sinfath and moved along the borders of Brelegond. Several times they caught sight of a troop of knights in black armor riding heavy warhorses, their shields marked with a silver tower and red crown. Durge and Beltan would draw their swords, Vani would vanish into the shadows, and Lirith and Grace would use the Touch to weave illusions to divert the eye.

They needn't have bothered. Each time, the knights rode on without getting close. The runelord Kelephon—whom the Onyx Knights knew as their supreme general Gorandon—wanted both Grace's blood and the magical sword Fellring, which he had failed to wrest from her in the dead kingdom Toringarth. What would he have done if he had known his knights had come within a half a mile of her more than once? Only he wouldn't know.

"You're keeping them from seeing us, aren't you?" she whispered to Tira one night as they curled together on the ground. The girl's little body was so warm Grace hardly needed her cloak, which she had thrown over them as a blanket. The snow curled into steam as it landed on them. "Just like you're helping us walk faster than we should be able to."

Tira snuggled against her and went to sleep.

The Onyx knights were not the only peril they encountered on the road. Sometimes, those first few nights after they left the Black Tower, whoever was standing watch—Beltan or Durge or Vani—would see a pale glow atop a distant hill or ridge. The Pale King had failed to gain Sinfathisar and Krondisar at the Tower of the Runebreakers, but his minions still searched for the Stones.

However, before they left the tower, Travis had taken a rusted iron pot he found—their old cooking pot from a hundred years before—and had held it in his hands while he spoke the rune *Dur*. The pot shone with blue radiance, and when the light dimmed, in its place was an iron box. The box was surprisingly delicate and perfectly formed; whether or not he cared to use his power, his ability was growing. Travis slipped the Stones into the box and shut it. On its lid were angular symbols.

"What are they?" Grace asked, touching the runes on the box.

"A warning," he said, and tucked the box inside his tunic.

The Pale King's wraithlings could see the trail of magic the Imsari left on the air—but not if the Stones were encased in iron. The eerie glow never drew close to their camp, and after a few nights they did not see the lights again.

At last they crossed the headwaters of the Dimduorn and entered into Calavan. They saw no more Onyx Knights, and when they came to a town, they dared to stop and buy horses with some of the gold Grace had left. After that, the leagues had flown by more quickly yet.

"Our journey's almost over." Grace only realized she had said the words aloud when Travis gave her a sharp look.

"Is it really over, Grace?" He reached inside his cloak, as if for the iron box he kept hidden there.

Grace touched the sword belted at her hip. Fellring. It felt heavy and good at her side, as if she had always worn it. "No, I suppose it isn't."

"Well, at least we've made it this far."

They rode in silence until they reached the track that spiraled up the hill toward the castle. Falken and Durge still rode ahead. Grace turned in the saddle to see how the others fared.

Lirith and Sareth rode not far behind, their horses close, their heads bent toward one another. As she had many times on the journey, Grace found herself wondering what exactly had happened to Travis and the others in Castle City. They had told the story of course—how they had found themselves in the Colorado town in the year 1883, and how a sorcerer had followed them through the gate—but Grace suspected there were some things they didn't speak of. For one thing, Lirith and Sareth's love was clear; they made no attempt to hide it anymore. Yet it was fragile, like a bauble made of spun glass.

We can never be as one, Lirith had told Grace. But was the witch talking about the laws of Sareth's people—the Mournish—which forbid a man to marry outside the clan? Or was something else keeping her and Sareth apart?

Behind Lirith and Sareth, Beltan and Vani brought up the rear of the party. Here was another mystery. While there was still an uneasiness between the blond knight and the golden-eyed assassin, they had left their animosity behind on Sindar's ship. Something had happened to them there. Only what?

On the voyage to Toringarth, it had been all Grace could do to keep Beltan and Vani from throttling one another. Now the big knight seemed curiously, awkwardly protective of her. More than once Grace had seen him bring Vani a cup of *maddok* when he thought the others weren't looking, or lay a cloak over her as she slept. Nor did she seem to resist such gestures.

After a while, it occurred to Grace that Vani might be ill. While the rest of them were always ravenous after a long day of walking, devouring what scant foodstuffs they had scrounged, the *T'gol* seemed to have little appetite, and often her coppery skin was tinged with green. However, one night when she asked Vani if she could examine her, the assassin had stared, a look of horror on her face, and had told Grace to leave her alone.

As they journeyed, both Vani and Beltan cast frequent glances at Travis, their expressions fond and longing. All the same, both of them seemed unwilling to spend too much time near him. Each time Travis tried to draw close to Beltan, the blond knight would retreat, and Vani did the same. Travis would smile at them, but Grace knew by the slump of his shoulders that their behavior wounded and confused him.

Then again, Travis spent much of his time lost in thought, head bowed over the box that held the Stones. Like Grace, he had other things to worry about. She coiled her hand around Fellring's hilt, enjoying the way her fingers fit against the grip the Little People had fashioned for the sword.

Grace sighed, as she always did when she thought of the silver-eyed man, Sindar. Except he hadn't really been a man. Once he regained his memories, he had remembered his true nature and purpose; he transformed into a being of light—a fairy—and threw himself upon the blade Fellring, his blood making it whole once more.

A thousand years ago, King Ulther had wielded the sword against the Pale King, cleaving Berash's iron heart and defeating him, even as the sword itself was shattered. Now the Pale King gathered his power once again, and Fellring had been forged anew. Grace tightened her fingers around the hilt. According to Falken, only one descended of Ulther and the royal line of Malachor could wield the sword.

You know what he's going to ask you to do, Grace.

And could she? Before she could answer that question, there was a whinny ahead as Falken's horse reared onto its hind legs. What had spooked it? The road to the castle was empty save for a few peasants trudging up the slope, pushing carts of peat or carrying bundles of firewood. Except one of the peasants—a man in a grimy tunic—was heading down the road, moving as if in a great hurry.

Durge gripped the bridle of Falken's horse, helping the bard regain control. "Watch where you're going, man!" Falken shouted after the peasant. "You might have been trampled."

If the man had heard Falken, he didn't show it. Grace caught a glimpse of him as he passed by. He was taller than most peasants she had seen on Eldh—their growth was usually stunted by malnutrition—and given his clear skin he seemed to have escaped the usual childhood diseases. The man hurried past and was gone.

"Are you all right?" Grace said as she caught up to Falken and Durge.

"I am, thanks to Durge," Falken said. "I wonder where that fellow was going in such a hurry."

"The poor man was probably just trying to make his escape,"

Beltan said with a laugh as he and Vani rode up, along with Lirith and Sareth.

The blond knight pointed up the road. A group of people had appeared before the castle gate. There were five of them standing in front of a small band of knights: a powerful, black-bearded man, a diminutive woman in a blue kirtle, a taller woman with eyes the same blue as the banners that flew above the keep, a slender young man with a bored look on his face, and a red-haired man who wore no armor but carried himself like a knight all the same.

Travis glanced at Grace. "It looks as if someone in the castle knew we were coming."

"No wonder that man was fleeing," Beltan said with a grin. "I doubt he expected to run into the king."

Falken scratched his beard. He had let it grow on the journey; it was half-silver. "My guess is he's been hunting on the king's lands without permission. Then he gets to the castle gates and finds the king waiting for him. One look, and the poor man turned and ran in fright."

Grace nodded. King Boreas had that sort of effect on people. Herself included. While the other peasants weren't running, they had all stopped dead in their tracks and were kneeling in the muck.

"Let's go say hello," Beltan said.

"Wait a moment." Durge climbed down, retrieved something from the muck, and mounted his horse again. "I believe that peasant dropped this." He held a small leather sack about the size of a money pouch.

"That could be his life savings," Lirith said. "He could be working to buy his freedom."

Sareth gave her a concerned look. "Do you really think so, *beshala*? If so, it would be a crime not to return it."

"I agree," Durge rumbled. However, the peasant man had vanished.

"You'll have to return it to him later," Beltan said. "I really don't think we should keep my uncle waiting."

"Or Melia," Falken said.

They urged their horses into a trot. Grace's heart soared as she saw the faces of her friends. Aryn looked more beautiful than ever, and older as well. She stood beside Melia, who appeared as regal and ageless as ever, though she clapped her hands together in a display of youthful enthusiasm as the riders drew near. Sir Tarus wore a broad grin, and even King Boreas looked fiercely happy, a toothy smile showing through his black beard.

The only one who wasn't smiling was the slender young man clad all in black. Grace had never seen him before, but all the same she recognized him. Teravian would never be powerfully built like his father, the king of Calavan, and his features were finer, but there was the same sharp, compelling look to his face. At the moment, though, that face was marred by a sullen look. Teravian let out a bored sigh and started to look away—then stopped. His eyes shone, locked on Lirith.

They brought their horses to a halt. Grace didn't wait for Durge to help her, but instead slid from the saddle and raced forward.

"Aryn!" She caught the baroness in a tight hug. The young woman returned the embrace with her left arm.

"Grace, you're here—you're really here!"

Talking long distance over the Weirding had been wonderful, but it couldn't compare to this—the real, living touch of someone she loved.

Grace was aware of the others crowding around. Falken was whirling Melia in an embrace, and Melia was actually laughing. She heard Boreas's booming voice, and out of the corner of her eye she saw Sir Tarus hesitate, then grip Beltan's arms, his expression full of warmth.

For so long they had all been apart, lost in different lands and on different worlds. Now, at last, they were all where they belonged—here, together. For that moment, Grace let herself believe they would never be apart again.

At last, reluctantly, she pulled away from Aryn and turned to greet the king.

"It's about time you paid your obeisance, my lady," Boreas said with a snort, hands on his hips.

"Greetings, Your Majesty." Grace curtsied, and with only a slight wobble. When she rose, she was surprised to see the king's smile gone and a thoughtful look in his eyes. "What is it, Your Majesty?"

"Nothing," he said, his voice gruff, "save that I'm not certain it's you who should be paying obeisance. Your Majesty." He started to move, as if he would kneel before her.

Grace stared, horror flooding her. Boreas was so bold, so proud. He was a king, and she didn't believe there was a stronger man on this or any world. He should never bow before her, no matter what dead kingdom she was supposedly the queen of.

She opened her mouth to stop him, but her words were lost in a peal of thunder.

A shock wave hit her, and a ringing sounded in her ears, shrill as a siren, transporting her for a moment back to the Emergency Department at Denver Memorial Hospital. How many times had she heard that wail approaching as she stood in the ambulance entrance, waiting to put broken people back together? The lightning must have hit close.

Except, last she noticed, the sky had been clear.

Another deafening *boom* ripped through the air, and it wasn't thunder. She heard cries of dismay, and Beltan swore an oath as he pointed. However, by then Grace already saw it: A white cloud of dust and smoke billowed up from the base of the castle's southeastern tower. It shuddered once, then with beautiful slowness slumped and fell over, sliding down the hill in a heap of rubble.

5.

Travis couldn't hear.

People were shouting all around him, but their mouths moved in silence. A suffocating pall enveloped him, like the time he was bound to the null stone outside the Gray Tower of the Runespeakers, and ancient magic had kept him from speaking the runes that would free him.

Beltan and Durge grabbed for the reins of the horses, which were stamping and bucking. Lirith hurried over, moving among the animals, pressing a hand against their necks. As she touched them, the horses grew calmer, though their eyes were still wild. Boreas seemed to be shouting at the guardsmen. Travis couldn't hear what he was saying, though it seemed the men did, for they turned and dashed back through the castle gate, Sir Tarus with them. The king turned around, and his expression was not one of confusion or shock, but one of fury.

The rest of them watched, motionless, as the remains of the stone tower careened down the slope of the hill on which Calavere was built. Although he appeared as surprised as anyone, there was a look of fascination on Prince Teravian's face. Aryn's eyes were shut, but whether it was because she could not bear to witness this sight, or for some other purpose, Travis didn't know.

Like a rockslide in the Colorado mountains, the wreckage of the tower poured over a stretch of the road that led up to the castle. As far as Travis could tell, no one was caught in its path. A few stray blocks of stone spun down the hillside, then all was still. Travis felt a sharp pang in his gut. He had once studied with the runespeakers Rin and Jemis in that tower. Now it was gone.

The others began moving toward the gates, following after Tarus and the guards, and Beltan pulled at Travis's arm. He was saying something, though Travis couldn't make out the knight's words over the ringing in his ears. The sound of the explosion must have deafened him, along with the crash of the wreckage. Only now his hearing was returning, and when Beltan spoke again Travis barely made out his shouted words.

"I've got to go with Tarus to see what happened. Do you want to stay out here?"

Travis shook his head. "I'm coming with you."

So was everyone else. Travis found himself next to Grace as they jogged beneath the raised portcullis, through a tunnel, and into the castle's lower bailey. Lords, ladies, peasants, and merchants alike stood frozen in the midst of their comings and goings, staring at the column of smoke and dust that rose into the sky where a tower had stood moments ago.

"What's happening, Grace?" Travis said, trying not to shout even though it was hard to hear his own words.

"I don't know." Tira's arms seemed welded around her neck.

"As far as I know, castles don't just blow up. What could cause that kind of explosion?"

"Grain?" Travis said, trying to think over the ringing in his ears. "Back when I was a kid in Illinois, a silo exploded at the farm down the road. The grain dust hanging on the air was so thick it was combustible. A spark from a frayed wire set it off." Except the fallen spire had been the tower of the castle's rune-speakers, not a grain tower. And he doubted there had been any electrical wiring inside.

Grace's face was pale, determined. "It doesn't matter what caused it. There could be people injured. I've got to go see." Gently, deliberately, she set Tira on the ground. "Stay close to Melia."

Travis gripped her arm. "It could be dangerous. There could still be falling stones."

Before Grace could protest, a stooped figure limped across the bailey toward them, white hair fluttering. "Your Majesty! You must come quickly! There's been—"

"I know, Lord Farvel," Boreas growled. "I have eyes—I saw the tower fall. Do you know anything about it?"

"No, Your Majesty. I've sent guards to investigate."

"As have I, and Sir Tarus is with them. We will get to the bottom of this." The king turned toward Beltan. "Nephew, I want you and Sir Durge to see if—"

The king's words were lost as another explosion sundered air and stone. The concussion was instantaneous, slapping Travis to the ground next to Grace. The sky went dark, then sharp fragments of stone began falling in a deadly hail. Before he could scramble to his feet, a crushing weight landed on top of him.

At first he thought it was a rock, pressing the life out of him. Then he groped, feeling hard muscles, and realized it was Durge. The Embarran had thrown his body over Travis and Grace, protecting them from the falling stone.

Travis clenched his jaw, waiting for the second explosion. Hadn't there been two when the runespeakers' spire fell? However, the second report never came. The sound of thunder rolled away; the *ping* of falling stones slowed and ceased. For an awful moment there was silence. Then a new sound rose on the air all around: wails of pain and confusion.

Travis couldn't breathe. Durge wasn't a rock, but he was every bit as solid as one.

"Durge," Grace said. "Off."

The knight scrambled up, then reached down to help Grace stand; her riding gown was caked with mud. She searched around, looking for Tira, but the girl was safe, clinging to Melia's skirt. Travis staggered to his feet. He might have fallen back down, but strong hands gripped him.

"Are you injured?" Vani said, her gold eyes holding him as surely as her hands. Her black leathers were spotless, as if she had simply dodged the falling debris.

"I'm fine. What about everyone else?"

Travis turned. One of the blocky guard towers that stood above the castle gate tilted at an odd angle. A hole yawned in its side like a mouth full of broken teeth; black smoke poured out its upper windows as if it were a chimney. The tunnel through which all of them had run just moments ago was now half-filled with rubble. If they had been in there . . .

He tried not to think about it. Most of them were scuffed and battered, and Lord Farvel was trembling and could not keep his feet without Falken's assistance. However, after a moment, it became clear the only one who was actually hurt was King Boreas.

"It's nothing," the king said with a grunt as Grace probed the rapidly growing lump on the top of his head. Blood matted his black hair. "It was a pebble, that's all. You needn't fuss."

The king's credibility was immediately countered by the way his knees buckled. Beltan caught him under the armpits to keep him from falling.

"You could have a concussion," Grace said, and Travis doubted she noticed that she had forgotten to call him *Your Majesty*. She shut her eyes, then opened them again. "In fact, you do. It's mild. You're not in serious danger—as long as you lie still and do nothing."

Boreas started to protest, only then he doubled over and vomited into the muck.

"You there!" Beltan called to a trio of guardsmen running toward them. "Help the king return to the keep." Beltan turned toward Teravian, who stood nearby, shoulders hunched. "Your Highness, there are likely to be intruders in the castle. You must guard the king. Take him to his chamber, summon more men. Whatever you do, protect him with your life."

These words seemed to astonish the young prince, but after a moment he nodded and squared his shoulders, and it seemed a light ignited in his dark eyes. "I'll protect him, cousin." He moved to Boreas, taking Beltan's place. "Come, Father."

"Away, boy. I must see to my people."

"This is a matter for your warriors now. You must leave it to them."

"Yes, my warriors . . ." His eyelids fluttered.

"Keep close watch on him, Your Highness," Grace said. "Make him drink water. And don't let him fall asleep."

Teravian nodded, and Boreas did not protest further as the prince led him toward the arch to the upper bailey. The men-at-arms followed, bearing Lord Farvel with them.

Grace glanced at Melia. "Will you watch Tira?"

The amber-eyed lady picked up the girl, and Tira laid her head on Melia's shoulder. Grace moved toward the ruined gates, threading her way through the crowd. Castle folk ran every which way, their faces white with dust, some of them smeared with blood.

"There could be another explosion," Durge sputtered, staring after Grace, brown eyes wide. "What is she doing?"

"Helping," Travis said. "Come on."

He started after Grace. Dimly, he was aware of the others hesitating, then following after him.

Travis lost sight of her, then a knot of peasants broke apart, and he saw her kneeling over a crumpled form, blood on her hands. It was a young woman in a serving maid's gray dress. Travis started to move to Grace, wondering if he could help. Grace stood, shaking her head. Much of the young woman's lower body was gone; she must have been close to the blast.

"Sir Tarus!" Beltan called out behind Travis. "What news do you have?"

The red-haired knight ran toward them, several men-at-arms on his heels. "The southeastern tower was abandoned," Tarus said, breathless, as he reached them. "And it broke away clean. There were a few minor injuries, that was all, but the castle wall has been breached—there's a hole in it you could march an army through."

"What of this tower?" Durge said. "Surely it was not abandoned. It is too much to hope any within might yet live, yet we must try."

Beltan exchanged grim looks with Durge and Tarus. "We'll get them out of there."

"And I will see if any intruders yet remain within the castle," Vani said.

Travis felt a twinge in his heart. Beltan and Vani were each so strong, so brave. What had he done to deserve the love of one of them, let alone both? Except maybe they didn't care for him after all. Both had avoided him on the journey back to Calavere. Had he done something to drive them away? But it didn't matter. Whether or not they loved him, he loved them. That was the one thing in this fabulous disaster of a life of which he was certain.

"I can't possibly do this alone," Grace said, taking in the sight of the wounded. Her words weren't despairing, but rather factual, frustrated.

"I'm here, sister," Lirith said, touching her arm. "I'm not so skilled a healer as you, but I'll do what I can."

Grace met the witch's dark eyes. "I'll also need help with triage—someone to sort and prioritize the wounded."

"Tell me how, and I'll do it," Sareth said.

Falken nodded. "And I."

Moments later the two men picked among the wounded, determining who was alive, who was dying, and who was already dead. Grace bent over a blackened form, and Lirith grabbed a guardsman, instructing him to fetch supplies they needed—cloth, water, needle, thread, and wine. Melia, holding Tira, rushed after the guard to make sure the order was filled swiftly.

Travis hesitated, unsure what to do. This wasn't a task he could help with. After all, his power was not about healing, but about breaking. To his surprise, he found he was not alone. Aryn stood beside him, her blue eyes filled with sorrow, but with conviction as well.

"If there are men trapped beneath the rubble of the guard

tower, they will be difficult to find," she said. "Beltan, Durge, and the others will need help sensing where they are."

Travis understood. Healing wasn't Aryn's strength either, but she had other abilities, just as he did. He exchanged a look with the young witch, then together they raced toward the listing tower and into the archway where Beltan, Durge, and Tarus had vanished minutes earlier.

Dust and smoke closed around them, blinding and choking them. After three steps, Travis lost all sense of direction. He groped, trying to find a wall to guide him, then a slender hand closed around his wrist, and a shimmering green net of light appeared, outlining floor, walls, ceiling.

This way, said a voice in his mind.

Next to him, the green threads spun themselves brightly around the slim figure of a young woman. Aryn. Was this how she and the other witches saw the world with their Touch?

After a dozen paces, they reached a cavernous space. The smoke was thinner here, escaping through the large breach in the tower's shell, and Travis was able to see even after Aryn released his wrist. All of the tower's upper floors had collapsed into a mountain of rubble rising up from the cellar. Beams stuck out from the wreckage at odd angles like broken bones.

Beltan, Durge, and Tarus had heaved one of the fallen beams into place, creating a makeshift bridge to the mountain of debris, and now they picked at the rubble.

"They're looking in the wrong place," Aryn said, opening her eyes, her face white with dust. "The men are trapped beneath the other side of the pile, down deep. I can see their threads, but they're already getting dimmer."

"Beltan!" Travis called, cupping his hands around his mouth. "Stop!"

The blond man stopped and turned. Travis and Aryn scrambled to the beam the knights had wedged into place. Travis edged over slowly, trying not to look down—there was a deep crevice between the mountain of rubble and the cellar walls—but Aryn raced across lightly, holding her gown up around her ankles.

"What are you doing here?" Beltan said when they reached the other side.

Travis glanced at Aryn. "You're digging in the wrong place."

"You have to get to them," the young witch said. "They're trapped in a—Durge!"

Stones shifted beneath the knight's feet and he lost his footing. He would have gone tumbling down the slope along with several tons of rock if not for Tarus's grip on his arm.

Travis bent and laid his hands on the stones. "*Sar*," he murmured, and the rubble shuddered to an uneasy halt. The stones knew their ancient name.

He could feel it—the broken stones wanted to sink down, to rest against the ground. However, there was a hollow space within the mound—that must be where the survivors Aryn had sensed were trapped. Crossed beams pushed the rocks up, while the rocks sought to crush the beams.

"*Sar*," Travis said again, willing the stones to obey him. Then he gripped the end of a broken beam that protruded from the wreckage. "*Meleq*." Power resonated through the wood. *Hold strong, bind together, do not break.*

Tarus gave him a curious look. "What are you doing?"

"I think I've stabilized the debris." Travis leaned back, wiping sweat from his brow. "For now at least."

Beltan gazed at him, only what his look contained—love? pride? fear?—Travis couldn't say. "Where do we dig?" the knight said to Aryn.

She scrambled around the side of the rubble heap. "Here. They're under here. Six of them. You have to hurry."

Some of the guards had fetched shovels and picks, but they were worthless against the heavy stones. Instead the men used bare hands to push aside the rocks, as well as levers fashioned from broken planks. It was dreadful work. Acrid smoke rose from the still-smoldering beams, and dust caked their faces and filtered into their lungs until all of them were coughing.

Travis was awed by the tirelessness of the three knights. Beltan and Tarus stood shoulder to shoulder, working together to move stones that had to weigh a quarter ton or more. Durge moved stones nearly as heavy on his own. Soon the dusty mask of Durge's face was creased from effort, and his knuckles were raw and bleeding, but he didn't stop. None of them did.

As Aryn guided the diggers, Travis kept his hands on the debris, speaking *Sar* and *Meleq* under his breath. He felt every vibration through the beams, every shift in the blocks of stone. The more wreckage the men removed, the more unstable the heap became.

You must hold on, Travis. He wasn't sure if the voice that spoke in his mind was his own, or that of Jack Graystone and the other runelords whose power flowed in his veins. *If you cease speaking the runes, the stones will come crashing down, taking all of you with it. It will be your burial mound.*

Travis kept muttering runes.

It was only when Beltan called out "I need light!" that Travis realized it was growing dark.

"*Lir*," he croaked, his lips cracked and dry from his endless litany of runes.

Silver radiance sprang into being, shining into the gap in the rubble the men had made. Frightened eyes peered out. Beltan and Tarus reached in and pulled out a guardsman, scraped and battered but alive. Five more times they reached in, and five more men came out. Some held broken limbs or clutched the stumps of missing fingers, but all were alive.

A groan rose up through the debris mound. Travis felt terribly heavy. "You have to get out of here," he gritted the words through his teeth. "I can't hold on much longer."

Tarus barked orders. The guardsmen who had been digging helped their wounded brethren over the beam and down the passage that led outside. Tarus and Durge accompanied Aryn, then it was only Beltan and Travis.

Travis was so weary. All he wanted was to sink to the ground with the stones, to let them bury him. It would be cool beneath, and still. He could never hurt anyone there, he could never break an entire world. "Go, Beltan. I'll hold the stones back until you reach the other side."

"That's not how it works, Travis. We're going together or not at all."

Travis looked up, and the light in Beltan's eyes was so fierce and so tender that his breath caught on his lips, and he could speak neither runes nor mundane words. The magic he had forged with *Sar* and *Meleq* shattered. The mound slumped in on itself.

Beltan grabbed Travis's arm and hauled him across the beam. They reached the other side just as the beam slid backward, pulled in by the cascade of stone. Hand in hand, Travis and Beltan pounded down the passage and burst into the lower bailey along with a cloud of pulverized rock. He staggered around in time to see the walls of the guard tower sheet downward, sending a gray plume into the sky.

"I couldn't save it," Travis said. His mouth was full of dust. "I tried, but in the end I couldn't stop the tower from falling down."

Beltan wrapped a strong arm around his shoulder. "It was beyond saving, Travis. And this way it can be rebuilt. Sometimes, when something's ruined, the only way to repair it is to destroy it first."

These words sent a chill through Travis, only he couldn't say why. He tried to speak, but his tongue was dry as chalk.

6.

They gathered in Calavere's great hall for a late supper, though no one had much of an appetite. However, Grace knew it was important that they eat; they had to keep up their strength. She gagged down a bite of cold venison to set a good example, though only a generous swallow of wine kept it from coming right back up.

She surveyed the familiar faces around the high table, and it was easy to make a diagnosis: exhaustion and emotional trauma. They had all witnessed terrible sights in their journeys over the last year. *Feydrim* and wraithlings. Dragons and plagues. Demons and sorcerers. But it was different when the perils followed you back to the place you called home. If the darkness could reach them here, then no place was safe.

Grace knew she should feel every bit as exhausted as the others; instead she felt strangely, keenly alive. Not since her days in the Emergency Department at Denver Memorial Hospital had she worked so hard and for so long to save so many lives. She had labored on nearly twenty patients that day, though she could never have done it without help. Sareth and Falken had made excellent triage nurses, and Lirith was able to set broken bones and stitch wounds, allowing Grace to see to the worst cases. More than that, the dark-eyed witch was able to soothe away fear and pain with the cool touch of her hand in a way Grace had never been able to do.

Grace had kept Melia and several guards constantly running for supplies, and soon even Tira would come dashing back into the bailey, her small arms filled with bandages. By the time the sun sank behind the castle walls, it was over. Grace had lost just three of her patients—though there were nine more who had died in the explosion and whose bodies had been pulled from the rubble. A dozen in all. Still, when she thought of the crowded castle, it was hard to believe it hadn't been worse.

It would have been, if people hadn't run into the middle of the bailey after the first explosion to try to see what had happened. But what exactly *had* happened? In the aftermath of the explosions, all of their energy had gone into plucking people from the debris and treating their wounds. Only what had caused the explosions in the first place?

Just as she opened her mouth to ask the others what they thought, a tapestry fluttered, and Vani was there. She stalked toward the high table, silent in her form-fitting black leathers. She carried a small cloth sack. Grace hadn't seen her since just after the last explosion. Where had she been?

Travis smiled at Vani, a look that was weary but warm. "It's good to see you," he said, and at the same time Beltan said, "Did you find anything?"

Vani gazed at Travis, and for a moment her face softened. Grace often forgot how beautiful the *T'gol* was. Intertwining tattoos accentuated the graceful line of her neck, and thirteen gold earrings glittered on her left ear. Then Vani looked at Beltan, and her features sharpened. "Yes, we did find something."

"We?" Durge said, stroking his mustaches; they were gray with dust. "Who else was with you?"

Vani glanced at the wall. Grace saw only blank gray stones. Then the stones rippled, and a man stepped away from the wall. He was slightly built, with a pointed blond beard, and flicked back a shimmering gray cloak that had blended seamlessly with the wall.

"There you are, Aldeth," Aryn said, setting down her wine goblet. "I was wondering if you would show yourself."

"Actually, I wasn't really planning on it, Your Highness. However, it seems someone had other ideas." He cast a sidelong glance at Vani.

The *T'gol* shrugged. "I cannot be blamed because you did a poor job of hiding."

"I let you find me in the north tower," the Spider said hotly.

"You mean in the same way a sheep graciously allows a wolf to catch it?"

The Spider glared at the assassin but seemed unable to formulate a rejoinder. Grace shot Aryn a questioning look. How had the baroness known Aldeth was here in Calavere? The last time they had seen him had been many months ago in Castle Spardis. He was a Spider, one of Queen Inara's personal spies; surely he was a long way from home. It seemed Aryn had not told Grace everything in their conversations over the Weirding.

"I'd like to know what you uncovered," Falken said. "That is, if you two can stop hissing and spitting long enough to tell us." The bard held his lute but had yet to play a note. As usual, a black glove covered his right hand. Melia sat next to him, amber eyes thoughtful, Tira on her lap. The girl hugged a black kitten with eyes the same color as Melia's.

"We found this," Vani said, setting the sack on the table.

Aldeth rubbed his neck. "Actually, I found it, and you shook it off of me like a common cutpurse."

Despite all that had happened, Grace found herself smiling. Something told her two shadowy types were one more than a single castle could comfortably contain.

"What is it?" Tarus said.

Vani untied the sack and turned it over. Fine black dust poured out in a steady stream.

Durge shoved back his chair and leaped to his feet. "Get the candles away!"

Lirith and Sareth hastily snatched a pair of candles from the table and snuffed them out. Most of the others looked at Durge in confusion, but Grace understood. She had smelled the sharp, acrid odor on countless gunshot victims in the ED.

"It's gunpowder," she said.

Durge nodded. "I worked with black powder such as this in Castle City. It is a perilous alchemy, one used to power dangerous weapons called guns. There is enough powder here to kill many men."

"Or to destroy two towers?" said a booming voice.

They all looked up to see Boreas striding across the hall toward the high table. Behind him came a pair of guards and Prince Teravian. All those around the table leaped to their feet. Aldeth wove first one way then another, hunting for a path of escape.

"Don't act as if I don't see you there, Spider," Boreas said as he ascended the dais. "No matter what you might believe, I'm not that dense. Besides, Queen Inara told me in her last missive you were here."

Aldeth stopped in his tracks and stared at the king. Aryn stared as well.

Boreas gave them a smug smile. "I'm not the only one around here who has secrets."

"You should be resting, Your Majesty," Grace said.

Teravian rolled his eyes. "That's what I tried to tell him."

"And when you're king, if you should be so fortunate, people will obey you," Boreas snapped, and the young man turned away, his shoulders crunching in.

Lirith gave the young prince a worried look, and Grace agreed that the king's words seemed harsh. Then again, it had been anything but a good day for Boreas. Grace moved to him, probing the bandage on his head. Belatedly she realized she should have begged his permission to touch him, but it was too late now, so she finished her examination.

"You're going to be fine," she said. "I imagine you'll live forever."

"That's an ill curse for a warrior, my lady," Boreas growled. "I'm not familiar with this *g'hun* powder you speak of, Sir Durge, but it's capable of working great deviltry, as we saw today. I wonder how it got into my castle."

"Perhaps we should ask the one who brought it," Aldeth said, and all eyes were instantly on the spy.

Vani advanced on the Spider. "Did you see someone? Why did you not tell me?"

"It's surprisingly difficult to talk when you're being strangled," Aldeth said, giving her a sour look. "I saw him not long before the explosions, leaving the room where we later discovered the sack of black powder. Several guardsmen were passing nearby, making a good deal of noise, and the fellow ran off. I suppose he left the powder in his haste."

Beltan stole the uneaten venison from Lirith's trencher. "So that's why there was only one explosion in the guard tower instead of two. He hadn't finished his work."

"It seems to me he did well enough," Sareth said, gazing at his hands. He had washed them clean, but the sleeves of his shirt were still spotted with blood.

Grace rubbed her aching temples. There was something peculiar about Aldeth's story, and not just the fact that someone in a medieval castle had managed to acquire large quantities of gunpowder and fashion it into bombs.

"This man you saw," she said to Aldeth. "Do you remember what he looked like?"

The Spider stroked his beard. "Vaguely. There was nothing remarkable about him. He was dressed like a peasant."

"Was he tall? And with good skin?"

"Now that you mention it, yes. Why?"

Grace moved to Durge and gripped his arm. "The bundle you found on the road—the one that peasant who ran into you dropped. Do you still have it?"

"I had forgotten about it, my lady. But I believe so." He rummaged inside his tunic and drew out the small leather purse the man had dropped in his haste.

"Open it," she said.

Durge fumbled with the strings and upended the purse. Something sleek and black clattered on the table.

"What is it?" Lirith said, drawing closer.

Grace picked it up. It was smooth and hard, shaped like a river pebble, but made of plastic, and fit easily into her hand.

There were two buttons on one edge, and a circle of small holes on one side. Her finger brushed the topmost button.

There was a hiss of static, then a man's voice—tinny but clear—said, "Base here. Is that you, Hudson? Over."

Grace flung the device down as if it had stung her. It lay on the table, silent now. She looked up and met Travis's startled eyes.

"It's some kind of radio, Grace."

The torches had burned low, making a shadowed cave of the great hall, by the time Grace and Travis finished explaining what a radio was, what it could do, and how such things were common on Earth. As they spoke, Grace cast frequent glances at Boreas and his son. All of the others knew about Earth, but she had never told the king she had spent most of her life on a world other than Eldh, or that Travis was not from Eldh at all. However, Boreas listened with interest rather than surprise. Prince Teravian, in contrast, was obviously shocked—but only for a minute, and after that he watched in narrow-eyed fascination.

"This makes little sense to me," Durge said in his somber voice. "Surely the intruder could have caused more damage if he had placed the incendiaries in the castle's main keep."

Beltan shook his head. "There are more guards in the main keep. Someone would have seen him."

"No, that's not the reason," Aryn said. The young woman's blue eyes were strangely hard. "His goal wasn't to destroy the castle."

Beltan gave her a puzzled look. "Then what is his goal, cousin?"

"Fear."

A cold needle pierced Grace's heart. Yes, she understood, but Travis voiced it before she could.

"If we're frightened, we won't fight," he said, his words soft, so that they all had to lean in to catch them. "That's what they want. They're trying to distract us, to make us afraid so we won't fight."

The king gave him a sharp look. "Whom do you speak of, Goodman Wilder? Who is trying to do these things?"

Travis stared at the communication device on the table, then picked it up. He clenched his fingers around it and whispered a word. *"Reth."*

Travis opened his hand; like the shell of a walnut, the black plastic had been shattered. He picked through the black shards and pulled out a green circuit board covered with transistors. A sharp laugh escaped him. Printed on the circuit board, white on green, was the shape of a crescent moon merging with a capital D.

"Duratek," Beltan said as if he were chewing stones. He seemed not to notice as he pressed a hand to the inside of his left elbow.

That's where they would have attached the IVs, Grace, the ones that infused him with the blood of the fairy.

Boreas gave Beltan a keen look. "You have encountered this enemy before, Nephew? Then you know how we can fight them."

"No," Travis said, letting the shards of plastic slip through his fingers. "You don't understand, you can't fight them. They have everything—weapons, technology—things you can't even imagine, things that would seem like magic to you. They could take this Dominion apart stone by stone. And they will. They want to take everything they can from Eldh and sell it on Earth at a profit."

Boreas fingered the knife tucked into his belt. "Whatever weapons they might have, these men of the kingdom of Duratek sound like bandits. I do not know how things are on your world, Goodman Wilder, but here we know what to do with bandits."

Travis shook his head, and Grace gave him what she hoped was a look of understanding. She could talk to Boreas tomorrow, but not right now. She felt so terribly heavy.

A small form crawled into her lap. Tira. The girl looked up and yawned, and Grace yawned back.

"We can speak more of this in the morning," Melia said, rising. "It has been a dark day."

Lirith met the lady's eyes. "I can concoct a tea for anyone who wishes for sleep...without dreams."

"I believe we could all do with a cup, dear."

As they rose from the table, Aldeth cast a look at Vani. "I'm sure you're thinking what I'm thinking, so we might as well go together."

She rested her hands on lean hips. "The intruder you saw will not have gone far. The voice that spoke through the device implied that the one called Hudson had not yet returned to their base, wherever it is. No doubt he wishes to stay close to the castle to see the result of his handiwork."

The Spider and the *T'gol* exchanged looks, then both vanished into the dim air.

"Who else thinks their habit of disappearing is getting a little annoying?" Falken said.

A number of hands went up around the table.

The bard sighed. "Come on, Melia, let's do our own vanishing act."

The two rose and departed the hall, along with Sir Tarus. Boreas was asking Travis more questions about Earth as they walked from the hall, with Beltan, Durge, and Teravian following behind. Grace picked up Tira's limp form and headed after them, along with Sareth, Lirith, and Aryn.

Grace had just reached the doors of the great hall—the others had already passed through—when she heard a snarl echo off stone. It was like the feral sound of a wolf, but higher-pitched, and full of malice. There were shouts, and the ringing of a sword being drawn.

"Travis, get back!" came Beltan's voice through the doors.

Grace set Tira down. "Keep her safe," she said to Lirith, then dashed through the doors.

She turned to her left and saw Travis and King Boreas with their backs to the wall. A spindly gray form wove toward them, maw open. Boreas slashed with his knife, and Travis gripped his stiletto before him, the gem in its hilt blazing crimson. They were holding the *feydrim* off, but just barely; the knives were pitifully small.

On the other side of the broad corridor, Durge, Beltan, and Teravian had been cornered by two more of the monsters. Beltan stood in front of Teravian, pressing the prince back against the wall. Like Boreas, he had only a small knife, but Durge gripped his Embarran greatsword in his hands. Only there wasn't enough room to get a proper swing. The two *feydrim* hissed and spat, looking for an opening.

Grace knew she should feel fear. Instead outrage rose within her. Before she thought about what she was doing, she had drawn Fellring from the scabbard belted at her side. The slender blade gleamed in the dim light, the runes on the flat undulating like things alive.

"Get away from them," she commanded.

Snarling, the two *feydrim* closest to her turned, glaring at her with yellow eyes. Her hand sweated around the sword's grip. Maybe that hadn't been such a good idea after all.

Before she could move, Durge let out a roar. The two *feydrim* had scuttled a few feet toward Grace, and now he had room for a proper swing. The beasts tried to leap aside, but Durge's sword caught one of them on the neck, and the thing's head flew across the corridor. The blade continued its arc, cutting a deep gash in the other *feydrim's* belly. Its black guts spilled onto the floor. The thing kicked and whined, then went still.

The last remaining beast lunged at Boreas, going for his throat. Travis thrust with his stiletto. The move was unskilled, but the blade was sharp, and it pricked the *feydrim*. The beast hissed and turned on Travis. By then Durge had crossed the corridor in three strides. He lunged, and his sword pierced the *feydrim*, passing entirely through its body. The light flickered in its eyes, then went dark.

Grace thrust Fellring into its scabbard and hurried to the king. "Your Majesty, are you all right?"

"I am, but that stone hit me harder on the head than I thought. I didn't even see the beast leap at me from that doorway there. Luckily Goodman Wilder did. He drew his blade and kept its jaws from closing around my neck." He gave Travis a solemn look. "I owe you my life."

Travis took a step back. "Not me. It was Durge who killed them. He was the one who—Durge?"

Grace turned around, and her blood froze. Durge's face was pallid and lined with pain, and he was gasping for breath. He leaned on his sword and clutched at his chest with his left hand.

"Durge, what's wrong?" Grace said, rushing to him.

"A pain in my chest, my lady. But it's nothing—it's already passing."

His breathing was growing easier, and color was returning to his face. All the same, Grace grabbed his wrist with a thumb and two fingers, checking his pulse. Durge was in his mid-forties, and he had exerted himself strenuously that day, first digging through the wreckage of the tower and now fighting the *feydrim*. He was in excellent physical shape for his age, but that didn't mean he couldn't be having a heart attack.

Except he wasn't. His pulse was rapid, but not erratic, and it was already beginning to slow, as was his respiration. He wasn't just being stoic; the pain had passed. All the same, she should be certain. She pressed a hand to his chest and shut her eyes. Yes, his heart was strong and healthy, beating at a regular pace. She started to let go, then halted. There was something else in his chest, small and shadowy...

"Travis, you're bleeding," Beltan said.

Grace opened her eyes and turned around. Travis held up his left hand, staring at it with a look of confusion. Blood streamed from a long gouge in his forearm where the *feydrim* had clawed him. She hesitated.

"Do not concern yourself with me, my lady," Durge said, standing straight now. "I am getting old, that is all. Go see to Travis."

She nodded, then hurried to Travis. The wound was not deep, and it was bleeding freely, which was good, as that would clean away any contaminants from the *feydrim*'s talon. She pulled a kerchief from her pocket and started to bind it around his arm.

He pulled away from her.

"Keep still, Travis."

"You have to be careful, Grace."

She frowned at him. "What are you talking about?"

"It was in Castle City. I . . ." He glanced at the others. Boreas was bellowing for his guards, demanding to know how the *feydrim* had gotten into the castle, and Teravian knelt, examining one of the dead creatures, but all of the others were nearby, watching.

Grace touched his hand. *What is it, Travis? You can tell me anything.*

Surprise registered in his gray eyes, then he nodded. *It's about the scarab's blood.*

What about it, Travis? You used the last drop to open the gate to the Black Tower.

No, Grace. I didn't.

She didn't understand. *But if you didn't use it, how did you get here? And where's the last drop of blood?*

It's in me, Grace.

An image formed in his mind, and she saw everything: Travis's final encounter with the sorcerer in Castle City, and the way the last drop of blood in the scarab—the blood of the god-king Orú—had fallen on his hand and had entered a wound, merging with his own blood, changing him.

Stunned, she let go. "Oh, Travis . . ."

"First Jack made me into a runelord. Then Krondisar destroyed and made me again. Now this." He shook his head. "I don't know who I am anymore, Grace. I don't know even know *what* I am."

Shock melted away, replaced by a fierce resolve. She took his arm and deftly bound the handkerchief around his wound, then took his hand in her own. "You are and always will be the man we love."

Travis smiled at her, but the expression was as sad as it was beautiful. "Sometimes I don't know if I'm cursed, or if I'm the luckiest man alive."

Grace felt a tingling and looked up. Beltan stood a ways off, but his green eyes were locked on Travis.

"Lucky," she said.

7.

Three days later, Travis sat on a wall in the lower bailey, soaking up the scant warmth of the winter sun. Across the bailey, fifty men—peasants impressed into labor by the king—swarmed over the wreckage of the guard tower. They had been working since the day after the explosions. Already they had cleared the castle gates and shored up the tunnel with beams. All of the debris had been removed from the yard of the bailey, but the guard tower itself was still a heap of shattered stone.

In another corner of the bailey, more men worked to repair the breach in the wall where the tower of the castle's runespeakers had stood. From his vantage, Travis could see through the outer wall of the castle, across the snowy landscape. Dark clouds hovered on the horizon, not approaching yet, but gathering all the same.

It was no use; the workmen would need many months to repair the gap in the castle wall. Only they didn't have months. Travis didn't know when the dark clouds would start marching toward them. Only that it would be soon. After all, winter was his time.

Except it's not just the Pale King that's coming, Travis.

Vani and Aldeth had returned to the castle at dawn the day after the explosions. They had not found the Duratek agent, the one named Hudson. However, the *T'gol* and the Spider had discovered an empty hut in the town beneath Calavere that contained signs of a hasty departure, as well as an item they could not identify, but which Travis recognized as a roll of black electrical tape. Aldeth had found three distinct sets of footprints on the dirt floor.

But how had Duratek gotten three of its agents from Earth to Eldh? Maybe they had learned something in their workings with the sorcerer on Earth. They had possessed one of the gate artifacts—albeit an incomplete one—for a time. No doubt they had studied it closely, and who knew how much of the fairy's blood they had taken? They could have gallons of it frozen in a vault somewhere.

They're smart, Travis, and they're learning. First they were able to send guns through. Now people. What's next, entire armies?

No, they couldn't have perfected the technology yet. Otherwise, they would already be here in force. However, they were getting ready for a full-scale invasion, that much was clear. Yesterday, Boreas had received a missive from Queen Inara in which she described a mysterious concussion that had destroyed one of Perridon's border keeps. That meant the Duratek agents who had blown up Calavere's towers weren't the only advance team sent to Eldh. There were others here, and their job was to sow strife and confusion, to weaken the Dominions and its peoples, so that when Duratek's main force arrived they would be assured an easy victory.

Except Duratek was going to find itself fighting over the spoils. The Pale King gathered his strength again, preparing for the coming of his master, the Old God Mohg, Lord of Nightfall. At the Black Tower, the man in the dark robe—the one they believed to be another Runebreaker—had gained the rune of sky. If he broke the rune, he would shatter the borders of the world, allowing Mohg to return to Eldh. Then all Mohg would need were the three Great Stones. With them, he could break the First Rune and forge the world anew in his own image.

The Pale King already possessed one of the Imsari—Gelthisar, the Stone of Ice. At the Black Tower, he had tried to wrest Sinfathisar, the Stone of Twilight, from Travis, but his minions had failed—though just barely. Then Tira had appeared, and she had given Krondisar, the Stone of Fire, to Travis.

As long as the child goddess had guarded Krondisar in the heavens, there was no way the Pale King could have gained it, and no way Mohg could break the First Rune. Only now all three of the Imsari were on Eldh; all the Pale King had to do was come and take them.

"Why did you give me the Stone?" he had asked Tira last night in Grace's chamber. "What am I supposed to do with it?"

She had only given him a shy smile, then had run off and buried her half-scarred face in Grace's skirts.

Some things ought to be broken, a raspy voice echoed in his mind.

Brother Cy. That was what the strange preacher had said in Castle City. Travis knew now that Cy and Samanda and Mirrim were all Old Gods. They had helped lure Mohg beyond the circle of Eldh a thousand years ago, and they were trapped there with him when the way was shut. Only then Travis had traveled back to Castle City, to the year 1883, and his Sinfathisar came in contact with the version carried by Jack Graystone. Two copies of the Stone couldn't be in the same place at the same time, and a rift was opened, allowing Mohg and Cy to slip into

Earth. And, decades later, the Pale King's forces as well, along with the infant who would grow to be Grace Beckett.

Travis rubbed his aching neck. What had Brother Cy meant? He found himself thinking of Beltan's words from a few days earlier. *Sometimes, when something's ruined, the only way to repair it is to destroy it first.*

But a world wasn't the same thing as a building, and Travis was not going to destroy Eldh, no matter what the prophecies of witches and dragons said.

He watched the men work for a while more. One thing was certain: The attack on Calavere meant that war was no longer coming; it had already begun. King Boreas had sent messengers all over his Dominion, calling for a muster. Even now, his barons, dukes, earls, and knights would be readying for battle and preparing to march to Calavere. Boreas had sent messengers to the rulers of the other Dominions as well, reminding them of the pact they had made over a year ago at the Council of Kings. He had even sent word to Tarras.

Travis shivered. The sun had edged close to the top of the castle wall. He slipped down from his perch and started back toward the keep. Near the archway that led to the upper bailey, he ran into Aryn.

"Hello," he said, startling her. She had been absorbed, watching the men work as he had. She blinked and turned toward him.

"Travis, I'm sorry. I didn't see you there."

Her gaze moved again to the broken wall and the workers, and a frown shadowed her face.

"What is it?" he said.

"Have you ever had the feeling you've seen something before, even when you know you haven't?"

"We call it déjà vu where I come from. What is it you feel like you've seen before?"

"This." She gestured to the ruined towers. "It all seems so familiar to me. I'm sure I've seen it before, or something like it. Only that's impossible, isn't it?"

Travis ran a hand through his short red-brown hair. "Since I came to Eldh, I've learned that *impossible* only means *just hasn't happened yet.*"

That won a soft laugh. "I imagine you're right. We've seen so many things I would have thought impossible a year ago." She smiled at him, only then the expression fled, and her eyes turned a deeper shade of blue, like the darkening sky. "Sometimes it's so hard to believe that you would..."

Travis swallowed the lump in his throat. "That I would what?"

"We should be going inside."

He moved closer to her. "You have to tell them I'm here, don't you? Ivalaine and the Witches. They think I'm going to destroy Eldh, that I'm Runebreaker—the one they've been looking for—and now you have to tell them you've found me."

Her face was an ivory mask of determination, but she was trembling, and something told him it was not only because of the cold.

"So you aren't going to tell them about me." His words fogged on the air. "The dragon was right. He said you would betray your sisters."

"Maybe I already have." She crossed her arms, hunching her shoulders. "Did not Falken say dragons always speak truth?"

Yes, and the dragon had also said Travis was doomed to destroy the world.

"I heard Grace and Lirith talking yesterday," he said after a moment. "I heard them say you're powerful. Maybe more powerful than any other witch alive."

"What does that mean?" she murmured, and he had the feeling the question was not for him.

He started to reach out, to touch her shoulder, then pulled his hand back. "Neither of us asked for this. This power. We're not really all that different, you and I."

She turned around, her eyes startled. "No, I don't believe we are."

"It's good not to want it, Aryn. That's the one thing I've learned. Because if you want the power, then there's nothing to stop you from becoming like them."

She nodded. "Except sometimes I do want it."

"You're right," he said, shivering. "We should go inside."

The next few days were strangely empty. It was too cold to venture outside the castle, and inside there was little for Travis to do. Grace and Beltan spent much of the time in conference with King Boreas, as did Melia and Falken, Durge and Sir Tarus, and the Spider Aldeth. Aryn was often busy with Lord Farvel, who was planning her wedding to Teravian, though the prince himself was usually as scarce as shadows at noon.

Vani was scarce herself. Travis knew she was busy patrolling the castle and the surrounding lands, watching for *feydrim* and other intruders. All the same, he would have liked to see her, to talk to her. Or to Beltan. However, both continued to avoid him.

When he wasn't alone, Travis most often spent his time with Lirith and Sareth, who were keeping an eye on Tira while Grace was in council with the king. Unlike the rest of them, the dark-eyed witch and the Mournish man rarely spoke of the coming storm. Instead they seemed content to dwell in the fragile peace of the moment. The laws of the Mournish people forbid him to marry Lirith, but except for his sister Vani, Sareth's people were a hundred leagues away. For a time, at least, he and Lirith could be together.

Given that, it was strange and tender how fleeting their expressions of love for one another were. They did not share a chamber at night, and Travis had never seen them kiss. However, their emotion was clear when they gazed at one another, though there was often a sadness in their eyes as well.

They frequently spent afternoons in Lirith's chamber. The witch would work on her embroidery, and Tira would play quietly with a doll Sareth had carved for her from a fir branch, while Sareth and Travis played a Mournish game using *T'hot* cards. To Travis's surprise, he usually won.

"I should know better than to play *An'hot* with one of the Fateless," Sareth grumbled one day, scooping up the cards. Hard crystals of snow scoured the chamber's window, and they all huddled close to the fire. All except Tira, who padded about barefoot, clad only in her simple shift.

Travis rubbed the palm of his hand. The skin was still smooth—burned away and re-formed in the fires of Krondisar— but lines were beginning to appear again. Were they his fate, forming anew? He was aware of Lirith's eyes on him.

"I'm sorry, Travis," Sareth said, concern in his coppery eyes. "I wasn't thinking. You know I didn't mean anything by it. It's only a card game."

He shrugged. "I just hope it's true. I hope I don't have a fate." He couldn't help glancing at Lirith. Was the witch of the same mind as Aryn? Or had she already penned a missive to Queen Ivalaine saying he was here in Calavere?

"I think I'll send to the kitchens for some *maddok*," she said, setting down her embroidery.

Tira laughed and danced before the fire. Travis touched the iron box tucked inside his tunic. He could sense them, nestled in the box, quiescent but craving release. He didn't dare. If he opened the box, wraithlings would see the glow of their magic; they would know where he was.

At first, after the attack of the *feydrim*, he had feared the Pale King's minions already knew he was here. Only when Beltan had referred to the attack as an assassination attempt had Travis realized the truth. The *feydrim* hadn't been after him; they had been after King Boreas. What better way to plunge Calavan into chaos? They must have crept through the gap in the castle walls unseen. It was all part of the plot to sow strife in the Dominions.

Except it was Duratek who had engineered the destruction of the castle's towers, not the Pale King.

"Duratek's allied with the Pale King," Grace said that night at supper when Travis voiced these thoughts. "I've suspected it for a while now, and this only confirms it."

"But they want to get to Eldh to exploit its resources, to make a profit."

Grace shook her head. "I think that's just a happy side effect. The real reason they want to open a gate is to help Mohg get back to Eldh."

"I believe you're right," Sareth said. He and Lirith sat close by. "The sorcerer who held me captive in Castle City—his kind are ancient enemies of the Mournish, and he could not resist gloating as he held me in thrall. He said the Scirathi were allied with people from the world Earth, that these people wished to open a gate to let their master return to Eldh. While he did not name Mohg, it can only be he."

Lirith touched Sareth's hand. "But why did the sorcerers ally themselves with this Duratek?"

Sareth closed his hand around hers. "They were promised knowledge of Morindu the Dark. My ancestors destroyed their own city, burying it beneath the sands of Amún, rather than let the Scirathi gain the secrets of their magic. The sorcerer told me their reward for helping Duratek would be the key to finding Morindu the Dark."

Lirith shook her head. "But you said before Morindu has been lost for eons. Who could tell them where it was?"

"Shemal," Melia said, her small hand clenched into a fist. "All of this bears the mark of her meddling. And I felt her presence near here not long ago."

"But would this Shemal person know where to find Morindu the Dark?" Sareth said.

Melia sighed. "Shemal is a Necromancer, not a person. She was once a goddess of the south, as was I, but Morindu was lost well before our time. I imagine she was simply lying to the sorcerers in order to make them do her bidding."

Travis was stunned—not so much by this new knowledge, but rather by the fact that he hadn't seen it sooner. He gave Grace a shaky grin. "You and your logical mind."

"Don't be too impressed." She stared into her wine goblet, and she lowered her voice so only he could hear. "If I was that smart, I would be able to figure out a way to keep Falken from asking me to fight the Pale King."

Travis glanced at the bard, who sat at the far end of the table. "You think he'll ask you?"

"He does with every look. I'm only waiting for him to speak the words. It won't be long now. Once the army of the Dominions gathers in response to Boreas's call to muster, Falken will ask me to lead them."

"And will you?"

She looked up, her green-gold eyes frightened. "I can't. I'm not that strong."

Travis took her hands in his. "You are, Grace. You're stronger than anyone. You'll do what you have to do to save Eldh."

And so would he. Why hadn't he seen it before? That was why Tira had given him the Stone of Fire.

"Travis, what is it?"

He smiled at her. "I love you, Grace. More than anyone, I think. I never would have made it this far without you."

Questions shone in her eyes, but all she said was, "I love you, too, Travis. No matter what happens."

He couldn't think of any more words, so he nodded.

"Your wound," she said, her tone brisk now, a doctor's voice. "How is it?"

He lifted his arm. "There's a little blood still, but it's healing. Thanks to you."

"You should probably let it breathe now," she said, and before he could protest she deftly removed the dressing from his wound and spirited it away. A long scab was forming on his arm. "It's going to leave a scar."

"Everything does," he said.

It was after midnight, and moonlight streamed through high windows, as he made his way through an empty hall, back toward his chamber. He had spent the hours since supper roaming the castle; he had needed time to think, to make sure what he was going to do was the right thing.

Except it was, and the real reason he had been wandering was in hope he would see one of them. Neither Beltan nor Vani had been at supper. However, which was the one he hoped to find?

It didn't matter. He hadn't found either of them, and maybe that was a good thing. It would only make what he had to do harder. With a sigh, he headed down a corridor.

He rounded a corner, and a laugh escaped him. Why was it you always found something the moment you stopped looking for it? A tall figure was just turning away from the door to Travis's room.

"Beltan," he called out softly.

The big knight looked up, and he smiled. As always, the expression transformed his plain face, making him as handsome as his uncle. However, while King Boreas was dark, Beltan's thinning hair was so blond it was almost white, and the scruffy beard on his chin and cheeks was gold. A light shone in his green eyes, but it flickered as his smile vanished.

"I came to be sure you were safe tonight," Beltan said. "Now that I've seen you're well, I'll go. Be sure to lock your chamber door behind you."

He started to move away, but Travis caught his arm. He fel

Beltan's muscles tense, but he didn't let go. Instead, he pulled the knight closer to him, surprised at his own strength.

"Have I done something wrong?" Travis said.

"There is no ill you are capable of doing."

Travis felt a pang in his chest. If only that were true. "If that's so, why have you been avoiding me?" He smiled, a bitter expression. "Not that I can really blame you. After all, I am the one who's supposed to destroy the world."

Beltan did not relax, but nor did he pull away. "I don't care what the prophecies say, Travis. You've saved the world, not harmed it. It's just . . ."

"It's Vani."

Beltan looked away.

Travis drew in a deep breath. Hadn't he known this was going to happen sooner or later? It was as inevitable as the coming of the Pale King. "You want me to choose, don't you? You want me to choose between you and Vani."

"No," Beltan said, still looking away. "I don't."

"Why?" Travis said, more confused than ever.

The knight looked at him, his eyes stricken. "Because I'm afraid you'll choose her."

Travis pressed his hand against Beltan's chest, feeling the rhythm of the knight's heart. "I won't lie to you, Beltan. I do love her. And not just because she saved my life, and Grace's. And yours. And not because she's strong or beautiful, though she is." He shook his head. "I'm not really sure why I love her. Except that maybe it's because she needs love so much, and she doesn't even see it. But I can."

Beltan nodded. "I'll leave you then."

"No, you won't." Travis moved closer, preventing the knight from pulling away. "I love Vani, but I loved you first, Beltan—I loved you when I didn't even know that was something I was capable of, and I won't let you go. If I had to choose, then I'd choose you."

"You might not, Travis. You might not choose me if you knew."

"If I knew what?"

The knight only shook his head. Travis could feel Beltan trembling. It seemed strange and amazing that one so brave, so strong, could need comfort. All the same, Travis circled his arms around the knight and pulled him close. Beltan resisted, but only for a moment. Then he let his head rest against Travis's shoulder. A sigh escaped him.

Travis was suddenly, keenly aware of the clean smell that rose from Beltan, of the warmth and hardness of his body. Never in his life had he needed someone as he needed Beltan at that moment. Maybe, until then, he had never been ready. Before he even thought about it, they kissed, pressing close together.

Beltan pulled away. Travis stared, too stunned for words.

"I'm sorry, Travis." Beltan's face was anguished. "I promised Vani I'd help her keep watch over the castle. I've got to go find her. I'm sorry."

Before Travis could speak, Beltan turned and hurried down the corridor, disappearing around a corner.

Sweat evaporated from Travis's skin, leaving him feeling clammy and sick. Was he really so horrible that Beltan would rather help Vani than stay with him? Only that couldn't be right. Beltan had said he was afraid Travis would choose Vani. And Travis had felt Beltan's passion when they kissed; there was no mistaking that.

You might not choose me if you knew. . . .

What had Beltan meant by those words?

It didn't matter. Beltan had made his own choice, and cruel as it was, it made Travis's choice that much easier to bear. He opened the door and stepped into his room. It was cold and dank, but he didn't bother to stir up the fire. Instead he pulled the iron box from his tunic. He could feel it like a hum: the Stones wanted to be released from their prison, only he couldn't open the box, not yet. He didn't want to draw the wraithlings to Calavere. But once he was a world away . . .

For so long Travis had run from his power, afraid of it, but he was done running. Aryn had said that sometimes she wanted power, and maybe that wasn't so wrong. He knew now why Tira had brought him Krondisar: because the time for guarding it was over. It was time to use it—to use all his power. Duratek Corporation had sent its agents to Eldh to sow chaos and destruction. Travis intended to return the favor. In the past,

Sinfathisar had granted him the power to speak runes on Earth. What might two of the Great Stones enable him to do there? He didn't know, but he was going to find out.

And so was Duratek.

And if you manage to destroy Duratek and their gate, then what will you do? spoke Jack Graystone's familiar voice in his mind. *Your magic is needed here on Eldh, Travis, and so is the magic of the Great Stones.*

Travis ignored the voice. It was still dim, but the spark of another idea had begun to smolder in his mind. Even on Earth, the Great Stones weren't safe from the Pale King. But what if there was a way to make sure neither Berash nor Mohg ever gained control of Sinfathisar and Krondisar?

Some things ought to be broken. . . .

It was time. He tucked his stiletto into his belt, along with a small money purse. He would have liked to raid Melia's stash for more gold, but he had enough to last him a while, and asking Melia for money might have aroused her suspicion. The others would want to search for him, of course. He had to let them know there was no use. There was no parchment to write on, so he scribbled a note on the smooth surface of the hearthstone with a piece of charcoal, then rose.

He picked up the iron box in his left hand, and with his right he fished into a pocket and pulled out the silver half-coin Brother Cy had given him what seemed an age ago. At the Black Tower, he had gathered the slivers of the coin he had given to Lirith, Durge, and Sareth on Earth. When he spoke *Eru*, the rune of binding, the slivers had joined back together without visible seam.

Travis turned the half-coin in his hand, looking at the fragmentary runes on each side: Eldh and Earth. The coin was a bound rune, he knew that now, and a powerful one, for its magic functioned even when it was fragmented. He wouldn't have been surprised if Olrig himself had created this rune.

He tightened his fingers around the half-coin. *What if Grace uses her piece of the coin to follow you?*

She wouldn't. As much as she feared what Falken was going to ask her to do, Travis knew she wouldn't refuse the bard. Besides, Travis was certain now that the half-coin wouldn't work for her as it did for him. It had the power to return you to your world. Eldh *was* Grace's world. But not Travis's.

He made sure he had a good grip on the iron box, then he raised the hand with the half-coin before him.

"Good-bye, everyone," he whispered.

Silver light welled between Travis's fingers, and the world faded away.

8.

Grace stood on the ramparts, huddled inside her fur-lined cape, and watched the Tarrasian soldiers march in rigid formation toward the castle. Sunlight glinted off spears and breastplates; black horses pranced, tails and heads held high. Grace's heart soared. Perhaps they really would stand against the Pale King. She gazed past the first company of soldiers and saw . . .

. . . empty road stretching as far as she could see.

"One company," Sir Tarus said beside her, his words a growl of disgust. "He calls himself an emperor, yet all he sends is one single company."

Trumpets blared. The castle gates opened, and the soldiers passed through—eighty on foot, twenty mounted. All too soon the gates closed behind them.

Grace sighed, her breath white on the air. It was the tenth of Durdath, what common folk called Iron Month. Three weeks had passed since their return to Calavere, and over a month since Boreas had called for a muster. The Tarrasians were the last to come, but they were hardly the least.

"We should go down and see him," Grace said, not relishing the idea.

Tarus stamped his boots. "He's not going to be happy."

"No," Grace said, her smile as wan as the late-afternoon light, "I don't suppose he is."

It turned out *not-happy* was something of an understatement. They heard the king's bellowing three halls away. As they neared his chamber, they crossed paths with the captain of the Tarrasian company. He was a short, powerful man with black eyes and a smooth-shaven face set in lines so hard it seemed cast of bronze. His red cloak snapped as he strode past them.

"I'd say he's fairly *not-happy* as well," Grace said. "Just in case you were wondering."

Tarus took her elbow. "Come, my lady. We've already got one hole in the castle wall. We don't need him opening another with his bare fists. Perhaps you can calm him down."

Grace tried to tell Tarus that it was Lirith who had a way with wild beasts, but by then it was too late. They had already crossed the threshold into the king's chamber.

"What is the meaning of this, my lady?" Boreas said, advancing on her before she could draw a breath, shaking a wadded-up parchment in his hand.

Melia glided from the corner of the room. "Perhaps if you stopped waving it at her and let her read it, she might be able to tell you, Your Majesty."

The king grunted and held the paper out. Grace took it and smoothed it out so she could read the words penned in a flowery hand. She scanned the missive.

"Does that say what I think it does?" the king said in a dangerous voice.

Grace nodded. "As long as you think it says that this one company is all Tarras can spare. Emperor Ephesian offers his regrets, but he says that the present state of affairs in the empire do not allow him to send more."

"I don't need regrets, I need men!" Boreas snatched the parchment from Grace and tossed it into the fire.

Falken glanced at Melia. "The 'present state of affairs.' What does that mean?"

"The usual, I imagine," Melia said, coiling a hand beneath her chin. "If Ephesian were to send a large portion of his army north to the Dominions, his position would be greatly weakened, and his enemies wouldn't be able to resist taking the opportunity to depose and execute him."

Falken scratched his beard. "If you can never do anything with your army, what good is being emperor?"

"I'll have to get back to you on that one, dear."

Grace glanced around the room, but there was no sign of Beltan. That was unfortunate. He had a deft manner with his uncle, and she could have used his assistance. However, she had seen little of Beltan these last few weeks. She knew he still blamed himself. Beltan was the last one to see Travis, and the knight believed he could have done something to stop Travis from leaving.

Only there was nothing any of them could have done. Grace had learned over the course of this last year that Travis could be as stubborn as he was kind. She had read his message—badly scrawled in charcoal on the hearth in his room—through the tears in her eyes.

> Dear Everyone,
>   I've gone to stop Duratek. You can't follow me, but
> even if you could, promise me you won't. This is
> something I have to do alone. I love you all.
>   —Travis

It was so foolish, and so selfless and brave. Just like Travis. If he could face such an impossible task, Grace could face this.

She stepped forward and laid a hand on Boreas's arm. "Your Majesty, we must work with the tools we have been given."

"And what will we be able to forge with such poor tools as these, my lady? I need to build a wall to defend the Dominions, and in answer to my call I am sent a handful of sticks and stones."

Grace sighed. She hated to admit it, but Boreas was right; his call to muster had yielded only an army of disappointments. The Order of Malachor, founded just over a year ago at the Council of Kings, was in shambles. King Sorrin of Embarr had recalled his knights from the Order months ago. The knights from Brelegond had vanished without word not long after, and now that Dominion had become as silent as Eredane.

Some knights had come from Toloria, sent by Queen Ivalaine, and Grace wasn't certain whether to be surprised or not. From what Lirith and Aryn had told her, the Witches intended to work against the Warriors of Vathris. However, Ivalaine was a queen as well as a witch, and Toloria was Calavan's most ancient ally. Surely she had had no choice but to send some of her knights—though their number was few, only thirty.

Galt had sent a similar number of knights. *We are hard-pressed to guard the passes through the highlands,* King Kylar wrote in his missive to the king. *The dark knights of Eredane grow restless, and they seek a way south. Would that we could spare more men for you, but to speak the truth, we cannot spare even these I do send.*

Queen Inara's news was just as bleak. She wrote of dark clouds gathering to the north in Embarr, and of unrest in her own Dominion. As a result, she had sent just twenty knights, though she also granted Boreas five of her Spiders in addition to Aldeth. *May they help you in ways a warrior cannot,* Inara wrote.

Grace appreciated Queen Inara's gesture, but she wondered if it was really a good idea to have so many spies in one castle; there was no telling what they were up to. The Spiders were as hard to pin down and bring together as drops from a spilled bottle of mercury.

Then again, if the Spiders could discover the location of the Duratek agents who had destroyed the castle's towers, then Inara's gift would be great indeed. Except one of Inara's own keeps had blown up, and the Spiders hadn't been able to stop it.

Then maybe Travis will, Grace. If anyone has the power to keep Duratek from reaching Eldh, he does.

But even if Travis succeeded, Duratek was hardly the only peril facing the Dominions. The Raven Cult had been reborn stronger than before. The Onyx Knights still controlled Brelegond and Eredane, and surely they would make their move on Embarr soon. *Feydrim* and wraithlings stalked the land. All the signs pointed to one thing: The Pale King would soon ride again.

Amid all this cold and gloom, one spark of unexpected hope had come a few days ago, when a band of twenty men in gray robes arrived at the gates of the castle. They were runespeakers from the Gray Tower, and while they seemed either woefully young or overly wizened, they were led by All-master Oragien himself.

Oragien was a tall and surprisingly hale man despite being

well into his eighth decade. His blue eyes were keen beneath shaggy white brows as he greeted King Boreas in the great hall.

"We are not what we once were," Oragien had said in his resonant voice. "But we have been learning since Master Wilder left us. Our forebears created the Rune Gate that bound the Pale King in Imbrifale. It is only right that we stand in Shadowsdeep when that gate opens once more."

"I welcome you and your runespeakers, Oragien," Boreas had said in a gruff voice. "Would that more remembered their call to duty as you do."

Even with the addition of the runespeakers, it was a small and motley force that had gathered in answer to Boreas's call to war: some eighty knights, the single Tarrasian company, plus the handful of Spiders and the twenty runespeakers. As she watched the missive from the emperor burn, Grace searched for something, anything cheerful she could say.

"What of your own men, Your Majesty?" she said, hitting on the first topic that came to mind. "How many men has Calavan been able to raise?"

Once again, she had miscalculated. Boreas's visage darkened, and his hands became fists. "It seems even my own barons grow stingy these days. They think they can fulfill their oaths of fealty by sending me but seventy knights and two hundred foot. All the more reason my son and Lady Aryn must wed quickly. I would have at least one baron who is loyal to me."

Grace had at least hoped for good news from Calavan. Even with these new forces, that gave them fewer than five hundred men. Five hundred to stand against the entire army of the Pale King. It was like throwing a pebble at a river in an effort to dam it.

Her thoughts must have been plain to see, for Boreas moved close and touched her cheek. His hand was rough and warm.

"Do not despair yet, my lady." His voice was low, rumbling through her chest. "The muster I called as king has yielded us little, but I have sent out another call to war, one I believe will be heeded by far many more."

Grace gazed into his eyes, then a gasp escaped her. "The Warriors—the followers of Vathris Bullslayer. You're summoning them here."

She saw the king and Sir Tarus exchange a fleeting look. So Tarus already knew. No doubt Beltan did as well.

"Can you really expect them to come?" Falken said. "What if their kings and queens command them otherwise?"

Boreas gave the bard a sharp look. "There are powers even higher than kings and queens, Falken Blackhand. And there are vows that bind more tightly than vows of fealty. Throughout the centuries, the followers of Vathris have waited for one day to come. For one thing."

"The Final Battle," Grace murmured.

Boreas bared his teeth. "Can the war that comes be any other? The men of Vathris will heed the call. If they believe, then they must."

"Forgive me, Your Majesty," Melia said, smoothing her blue kirtle, "but I know something of the temple of Vathris in Tarras. I do not imagine the high priests will appreciate a call to war issuing from the north. And while there are many worshippers of Vathris in the Dominions, surely there are ten times that number in the lands of the south."

Boreas let out a grunt of disgust. "The high priests of Tarras are fanatics and fools. They have forgotten their true purpose and do naught but scheme to find ways to bring men under their power, and to use that power for their own ends."

"Is it true," Tarus said, a pained expression on his face, "that the priests in Tarras are forced to offer up the jewels of their manhood in a golden bowl on the altar of Vathris?"

"That and their sanity," Boreas rumbled. "I doubt an army of eunuchs is what Vathris had in mind when he foretold the coming of the Final Battle." He stalked toward Melia. "The priests may have forgotten the legends, but the men of Vathris have not. It may take some time for the men of Tarras to come, and even longer for the men of Al-Amún across the Summer Sea. But they will come."

Melia's amber eyes were thoughtful. "Yes, I believe they will."

Grace felt hot; she had been standing too close to the fire. Dizzying visions of warriors and *feydrim* and iron gates swirled in her mind, and she herself stood at the center of it all, holding a shining sword. She had to get out of here, away from the fire, and talk to Lirith and Aryn.

But to talk to them of what? The Witches, and how they sought to stop the Warriors, who they feared would fight on the side of Runebreaker in the Final Battle? Grace wasn't sure. One thing she *was* sure of was that Aryn was still hiding something—not just from her, but from Lirith as well.

Grace had hardly had a chance to speak to Aryn these last weeks, occupied as the baroness was by Lord Farvel's endless questions regarding her coming wedding. Grace wished the young woman was here now. Or perhaps it was better she wasn't, with all this discussion of the Warriors and the Final Battle.

You don't really believe Aryn would betray Boreas, do you, Grace? She loves him like a father.

And what of herself? She was a witch, too. Not so powerful as Aryn, nor so experienced as Lirith, but a witch all the same. Was she bound to betray Boreas as well?

She struggled for something to say, something that would distract Boreas from the guilt she was certain shone on her face. However, before she could speak, Falken moved to her.

"It's time, Grace," he said in a soft voice.

She wanted to believe she didn't know what he was talking about, but she did. Slowly, she drew Fellring from the scabbard at her side and held the blade before her. The runes on its flat caught the firelight, gleaming red as if writ in fire.

Falken's eyes were locked on her. "The Warriors of Vathris gather, but it will take time for them to come together. Time we may not have. The Rune Gate could open any day. We need to take what men we have and march north to Gravenfist Keep."

"Gravenfist Keep?"

"It is an ancient fortress, the greatest ever raised by Malachor. The keep sits atop a narrow pass, guarding the only way out of Shadowsdeep—and out of Imbrifale. If the Rune Gate opens, Gravenfist Keep is all that stands between the Pale King and the rest of Falengarth."

No, it wasn't nearly enough. What good was a ruined keep manned by five hundred men and one skinny woman with a too-big sword against all the vast hordes at the Pale King's command?

"I can't do it," she croaked.

Falken actually laughed. "Yes you can, Grace. You're Ulther's heir. Everyone knows it. You don't see the light in the eyes of the men when they see you holding that sword, but the rest of us have."

Boreas, Tarus, and Melia all nodded, and Grace felt her knees go weak.

"But the keep—what if it isn't even standing anymore?"

"It yet stands," Falken said. "I saw it myself when I dared to venture into Shadowsdeep over a year ago. It is in disrepair, but it is still strong. It was said both runelords and witches had a hand in the building of Gravenfist, and that they wove its very stones with enchantments of power. If you could find a way to awaken those ancient defenses, you could hold the Pale King's army at bay with just ten men, or even by yourself. Five hundred will be enough to hold back the Pale King until the Warriors of Vathris can reach you."

Her stomach clenched into a hard knot. "Defenses? What kind of defenses?"

"I honestly don't know," Falken said.

A groan escaped her. "Well, that's just great. I don't suppose there's a button on the wall labeled 'Push here for magic'? What if I can't find a way to turn on these defenses you're talking about?"

Her words didn't rattle Falken in the least. His eyes shone as he wrapped his gloved fingers around her sword hand. "You will, Grace. You will because you have to."

No, she tried to say. *I can't do it. I won't.*

Instead she met the bard's eyes and gave a grim nod.

9.

That afternoon, Grace ventured down the winding paths of Calavere's garden. She wasn't certain what she was looking for. If it was solitude, then she found it in abundance. In winter, the garden was a half-wild thicket—the hedges untended, the paths all but obscured by dried leaves—as if a section of primeval forest had been transported from Gloaming Wood to the middle of the castle's upper bailey.

If it was signs of spring stirring she had come looking for, then the effort was in vain. Here and there, Grace stooped down to dig through the loam with her fingers. On Earth it would be the middle of February; crocus would already be poking up through the snow. However, she could do no more than pry away a thin sheet of soil; beneath, the ground was frozen hard as iron.

Falken had said the bitter weather was the work of the Pale King and the one Imsari he possessed—Gelthisar, the Stone of Ice. Was this what Berash had planned for Falengarth? A land of frost and snow, where springtime never came?

Grace stood, shivering inside her fur-lined cape. After their meeting that morning, Boreas had begun giving orders; what forces they had were to prepare to march north in three days. There was no point in delaying, the king had said. The journey would be a long one, since they would be forced to avoid Eredane and its Onyx Knights, and instead travel through Toloria, then follow the eastern edge of the Fal Erenn north through Perridon and Embarr to Shadowsdeep.

Grace hadn't bothered mentioning that, by the time they reached Embarr, it could be under the sway of the Onyx Knights as well, and even if it wasn't, the Raven Cult was rampant there. However, none of that mattered. Much as she wanted to find an escape, she knew there wasn't one.

She touched the hilt of Fellring, belted at her side. *You sacrificed yourself to reforge this sword, Sindar. Am I supposed to sacrifice myself to reforge the Dominions?*

Only sacrificing herself wasn't what she was afraid of. At Denver Memorial, she had always given of herself without limits to heal the wounds of others. No, it was sacrificing the hundreds who were to march with her, and the thousands more that would follow after with Boreas, that terrified her.

If there's no way to stop these things from happening, Grace, then you can't let it all be for nothing. You have to get to Gravenfist Keep, and you have to find a way to hold the Pale King back.

Only how was she supposed to discover the key to unlocking the magical defenses of a centuries-old fortress? Falken always seemed to know about everything, but even the bard didn't know how she was supposed to accomplish this. It was hopeless. She sighed and turned to walk from the garden.

Music chimed on the cold air, high and distant—the sound of bells.

Grace froze, listening. She could hear wind over branches and the thudding of her own heart. Then it came again, faint but clear, like sleigh bells on a winter's night.

She turned and ran farther down a path. Why hadn't she thought of it before? They were more ancient than anyone. If anyone knew what she had to do, the Little People would. Clutching her cape, she raced around a bend in the path—

—and came to a halt. The path ended in a grotto; there was no way to continue on. Yet Grace was sure this was the direction the sound of the bells had come from.

"Are you searching for something, Grace?"

A lithe form separated itself from a shadow and stalked forward.

"Vani," Grace said the name like a gasp. "I didn't see you there."

The *T'gol* shrugged, as if to say this was only to be expected. Grace knew Vani hated the cold. What was she doing out here?

"Did you hear them?" Grace said.

"Hear what?"

"The bells. I was following the sound of them when I ran into you."

Vani frowned. Dark circles hung underneath her eyes, as if she had not slept well lately. "I heard no such sound. The only noise was the sound of your approach."

The sound of the bells had been distant, but the *T'gol* had keen ears. Surely if Grace had been able to hear it, Vani should have as well. Unless the music had been meant only for Grace. But if so, why had they led her to this place? She doubted Vani knew anything about Gravenfist Keep or its ancient magic.

Not that she was sorry to run into Vani. Grace had seen little of the *T'gol* lately. Ever since their time on the fairy ship, Vani had been acting every bit as strangely as Beltan had, and things had only gotten worse since Travis left them three weeks ago.

"You miss him, don't you?" Grace said the words when she had only meant to think them.

Vani stiffened. "As we all do."

"No, not as we all do." Grace knew she should leave the *T'gol* alone with her pain. Instead, she closed the gap between them. "You love him, Vani. And so does Beltan. Travis's leaving has been hard for you. For both of you."

Vani crossed her arms over her stomach. "It is for the best that he's gone. This way he will not see . . ."

"He won't see what?"

Vani only looked away.

Grace studied her, searching for signs and symptoms, things she could assemble into a diagnosis. She listed everything unusual she had noticed about the *T'gol* in the last two months. There was her sudden bout of seasickness on the white ship, her unusual weariness on the journey to Calavere. Then there was the way she often folded her arms over her stomach, and the fact that her cheeks were flushed despite the cold.

Think, Grace. Nausea, fatigue, abdominal cramps, and a slightly elevated temp. It could be something viral, or maybe an infection, or—

Grace's eyes went wide. "You're pregnant, aren't you?"

Vani did not look at her. "Yes."

It took a moment for Grace to gather her wits. Vani was an assassin, a highly skilled killer. However, while it was difficult to see Vani as a mother, it was not impossible. Some of Grace's shock was replaced by warmth.

"How far along are you?"

"Two cycles of the moon."

"And is Travis the father?"

"In my heart he is."

What did that mean? Grace took a step closer. "I don't understand."

Vani turned back, a bitter smile on her lips. "You are not alone in that."

What was Vani talking about? She couldn't be two months along already. It had only been six weeks since Midwinter's, when they met Travis at the Black Tower. Two months ago they had been on the fairy ship...

Like a needle, knowledge pierced Grace's brain. The odd looks, the strangely tender gestures. It was impossible, and yet it was the only answer. "It's Beltan. He's the father."

Vani said nothing, and that was confirmation enough.

Grace gripped her arm. "But how? Beltan is—"

"I know what Beltan is. He was tricked just as I was."

"Tricked?"

Vani pulled away. "It was the Little People. They drew us below the ship, into a garden like this, only in full bloom. And they caused each of us to believe that the other was..."

"Travis," Grace said, seeing it clearly, as if through magic. "They made each of you think the other was really Travis."

Vani nodded, her gold eyes haunted.

"But why would they do such a thing?"

"I would that you could tell me."

Grace couldn't. As Falken had often said, the Little People were queer and ancient, and while they were not the enemies of mankind, they were not friends either. Their ways were a mystery, and their purposes unknown.

"Does Beltan know?"

"I'm not sure. If not, he soon will." Vani pressed a hand to her stomach.

Grace examined the options. Vani was two months along. It was too late for a tea brewed of mistmallow seeds. And a surgical procedure was out of the question here, in these conditions. "So you're keeping the baby."

"It is not the child's fault how it was made. And who knows? Perhaps Travis Wilder was not my true fate. Perhaps I was only meant to pursue him, to be led to this." Vani turned away, but not before Grace saw the tears roll from her eyes.

Since Grace had known her, Vani had always been fierce and strong, but now she seemed slender and surprisingly delicate, alone and frightened. So often in her life, Grace didn't know how to respond to people. But this she understood.

Grace wrapped her arms around Vani and held her close. Vani resisted, but only for a moment, then she let herself weep.

After a minute she was done, and gently but deliberately she pulled away.

"You have to talk to Beltan," Grace said.

"I know. But not yet." Vani wiped the moisture from her cheeks with a rough gesture. "I wish only that there was a way I could tell both Beltan and Travis together, so that I would have to speak these words but once."

"Maybe there is a way," Grace murmured, startled at her own words.

Vani gave her a curious look, but Grace shook her head. She would have to think about it later. Right now she needed to perform a thorough examination on Vani, to make sure everything was progressing as it should be.

"Come on," she said. "Let's go back in where it's warm."

Grace held out her arm. Vani stared at it a moment, as if unsure what she was supposed to do with it. Then, tentatively, she hooked her elbow around Grace's.

"I am not good at this," Vani said.

Grace glanced at her. "Not good at what?"

"Sharing secrets with another."

Grace smiled. "That's what friends are for."

"A *T'gol* has no friends."

"This one does," Grace said, tightening her hold on Vani's arm, and they walked that way back to the keep.

10.

It was evening by the time Grace returned to her chamber. She had spent over an hour in Vani's room. The *T'gol* had been reluctant to allow herself to be examined, but Grace was a queen *and* a doctor. She was not about to take no for an answer. Realizing this, Vani had submitted.

As far as Grace was able to tell—without blood tests or an amniocentesis—Vani's pregnancy was progressing normally. At first Grace wished for an ultrasound machine, only then she realized she had an even better tool. She pressed her hands to

Vani's bare, flat stomach, shut her eyes, and reached out with the Touch.

Instantly she saw the fetus. It was tiny, its life thread a wisp of light attached to Vani's own shining strand. While Vani's thread was brilliant gold, the fetus's thread had a green tinge to it, like sunlight on leaves. Had that come from Beltan? Grace probed gently with her thoughts; small as it was, everything was in order.

"It's a girl," Grace said, smiling, eyes still shut. "I'd say you're a little ahead of—"

Hello, Aunt Grace, a piping voice said in her mind, faint but clear.

A gasp escaped her, and her eyes flew open.

"Is something wrong?" Vani said, her brow furrowed.

Grace shook her head. "No, everything looks fine. I was just saying you seem to be a little further along than I would have expected at eight weeks. But everyone's different." She shut her eyes again, listening, but this time she heard only the beating of two hearts. She had to have imagined it.

When she opened her eyes, she saw Vani watching her. Grace rose and spoke in a brisk tone.

"There's nothing to worry about. You and the baby are both in excellent health. You should try to keep the *maddok* and wine to a minimum. I'll fix you a simple that will help with the morning sickness."

"Thank you," Vani said, pulling her jerkin back down over her stomach.

"You know, I have a feeling it's going to be hard to find maternity leathers," Grace said with a laugh. Vani smiled, and for the first time that day it seemed like things really might be all right.

Now, as she opened the door to her chamber, Grace wasn't so certain. The events of that morning came rushing back, as did the enormity of the task that lay before her. She pushed through the door, wanting nothing more than to stir up the fire and flop into bed.

Aryn and Lirith stood from two chairs by the hearth.

"Oh, sister," Aryn said, rushing forward and throwing her left arm around Grace.

"Aryn," Grace said, stunned. "What's wrong?"

"It can't be true. You can't be leaving us."

Grace sighed. So they had heard the news of what she was to do. Gently, she pushed Aryn away.

"I have to go," she said. If she acted like this was something she actually wanted to do—rather than an idea that turned her knees to rubber—it might make it a little easier for the others. "If we can man Gravenfist Keep, we might have a chance of holding the Pale King back."

Lirith moved forward with a whisper of russet wool. "Do you truly believe that, sister?"

"I'm trying to," Grace said with a wan smile.

"You're tired," Aryn said, pulling Grace toward the fire and making her sit in one of the chairs. Lirith poured them all cups of wine and took the other chair, while Aryn sat on the floor and rested her arms and chin on Grace's knee.

"Let's stay like this forever," Aryn murmured, gazing into the fire. "Just the three of us, together. Let's pretend there's nothing in the world we have to do except stay here, and drink wine, and talk about foolish things."

"That's a fine fancy, sister," Lirith said. The firelight gilded her dark skin like gold on wood. "I wish that it could be so. But we each have our tasks."

Grace clutched her wine cup. "What tasks do you mean?"

Aryn and Lirith exchanged a look, and the fire went cold. Grace knew the two witches had attended a High Coven in Ar-tolor last summer, when Grace was in Denver. Grace didn't know exactly what had happened at the coven, but over the months she had gleaned bits and pieces. Enough to be afraid.

"Boreas has sent a call out to the Warriors of Vathris," Lirith said. "The men of the bull prepare for the Final Battle."

Grace's lungs were too tight; she couldn't breathe. "You can't, Lirith. You can't ask me to defy him. I know the Witches are the enemies of the Warriors, but I gave King Boreas my word, and nothing can make me work against him."

"No, nothing can," Lirith murmured, gazing into her cup. "You're not part of the Pattern as Aryn and I are. There are no threads to bind your actions, but Aryn and I must do as the Pattern commands. And it commands us to bring the Warriors and Travis Runebreaker under our control, lest they work together to destroy the world."

Grace shook her head. "You can't believe that, Lirith. King Boreas is anything but evil. And Travis would never do anything to harm Eldh. That's the one thing in all of this lunacy I can believe."

Lirith sighed. "I agree, sister. I have seen firsthand how kind he is, but I have also seen the power he wields, and how it is not always under his command. Even so, I would not choose to work against Travis or King Boreas, but there is no way to escape the Pattern."

"Actually," Aryn said softly, "there might be."

Grace stared at the baroness. Lirith set down her cup, slipped from the chair, and knelt on the rug beside Aryn. "What do you mean, sister?"

Aryn leaned back. Her blue eyes were haunted, yet there was a resolve to them. "I've joined a shadow coven," she said.

Lirith gasped, and her brown eyes went wide. Grace didn't understand what these words meant, not as Lirith clearly did, but all the same they sent a thrill through her.

"Sister," Lirith said, reaching out as if to touch Aryn's arm, "what have you done? The shadow covens were forbidden long ago, and for good reason. Many of the witches who belonged to them were cruel of spirit and deed."

"But not all of them," Aryn said, her tone defiant. "Do you remember Sister Mirda?"

Grace didn't recognize the name, but Lirith nodded. "She was at the High Coven. We never learned where she came from, but it was her words that softened the Pattern. Were it not for her, the Witches would be seeking, not to control Travis Wilder, but to slay him."

"She came to Calavere before Midwinter," Aryn said. "When Queen Ivalaine brought Prince Teravian back."

Connections crackled in Grace's brain. "So that's who was with you," she said to Aryn. "The time you spoke to me across the Weirding, when we were being held prisoner on Kelephon's ship, I felt another presence with you. It was this Mirda, wasn't it?"

"It was," Aryn said.

As the fire burned low, they listened as Aryn spoke about the shadow coven, and about what Sister Mirda had told her. While the prophecies of the Witches told that one they called Runebreaker would destroy Eldh, there were other prophecies, ones just as deep and ancient, that spoke how Runebreaker would save Eldh as well. Because this idea was anathema to most—how could the world be at once destroyed and saved?—the Witches chose to ignore the second set of prophecies.

However, over the years, a few witches remembered. It was the purpose of the shadow coven to which Mirda belonged to work for the cause of Runebreaker, to make sure his destiny came to pass. And the Warriors of Vathris were part of that destiny.

"I knew it," Grace said, her cheeks hot from wine and fire and excitement. "I knew Travis would never destroy Eldh."

"But he *will* destroy it, sister," Lirith said. "If one prophecy is true, then so is the other. How that can be, I do not know, but the crones of old were wise, and their vision far-reaching, and I believe they saw truth."

Aryn gripped Lirith's hand. "So you'll join the shadow coven?"

Lirith didn't hesitate. "I will, but I do not see how it helps us. We are still bound by the Pattern."

"Yes," Aryn said, "but does the Pattern truly require what you think it does?"

"What do you mean?"

Aryn rose, standing before the hearth. "Sister Mirda left Calavere a few days before you returned. She told me she had to meet in person with the other witches who are part of the shadow coven—that they did not dare speak across the Weirding for fear of who might overhear. Before she left, she showed me a way to look deeper into the Pattern.

"On the surface, the weave of the threads seems to say we must work against the Warriors of Vathris and Travis Runebreaker, but if you look beneath, to the warp of the loom from which the Pattern was woven, what it really says is that we must work against them to save Eldh. Yet if working against them would somehow prevent Eldh from being saved—"

"—then the Pattern will allow us to work *with* them," Lirith said, leaping to her feet. "The Pattern will allow us to do whatever would save the world in the end." Her dark eyes shone. "You have given us hope where there was none, sister."

Aryn looked at Grace. "Will you join us?"

Grace couldn't help smiling. "I think I already have," she said. Aryn's words were a great relief, but one question nagged at the back of her brain.

"Lirith," she said, "you mentioned that the shadow covens were forbidden long ago. What would happen if Ivalaine discovered us?"

It was Aryn who answered. "We have no fear on that account. If Ivalaine and Tressa are not members of the shadow coven, they are at least sympathetic to its cause. Although, as Matron, she dares not reveal it."

"And what of Sister Liendra?" Lirith said. "She was at the center of the Pattern, and she seeks to be Matron in Ivalaine's stead. Most of the Witches follow her lead. What would happen if Liendra were to discover us?"

Aryn turned away. "Then our threads would be plucked from the Pattern, and a spell would be woven over us, so that we would never be able to use the Touch or the magic of the Weirding again."

Grace shuddered, and Lirith's face went gray. Being cut off from the Weirding would be like a walking death—alive, but unable to feel any of the light or warmth all around them.

"I've got just one more question," Grace said as Lirith and Aryn made ready to leave. "Lirith, you said the shadow covens were forbidden for working cruel spells."

The witch nodded. "They brought the hatred of the common folk upon the Witches. That's why they were all disbanded."

"Only they weren't," Aryn said, shaking her head. "Mirda's shadow coven survived."

"And that's my question," Grace said, crossing her arms. "If this one shadow coven endured, others might also have survived. And if so, what if they aren't ones that work for good, like Mirda's coven? What if they're the wicked shadow covens, the ones that gave the Witches a bad name?"

Silence pressed close. The coals settled on the hearth, and sparks crackled up the chimney.

"Come, sister," Lirith said at last, taking Aryn's good left arm. "It is time we all went to bed."

11.

Grace woke to the sound of bells.

She sat up in bed, the shards of a dream falling away from her like broken pieces of glass. Her hair was snarled, and her nightclothes clung to her, cold and clammy with sweat. The space beside her in the bed was empty and cold; Tira had spent last night in Melia's chamber. Frigid air poured through the chamber window, along with hard granules of snow. The wind must have pushed it open.

Grace scrambled from the bed and reached to pull the window shut. She halted. Twenty feet below, at the base of the castle's north wall, prints dented the crust of new snow. She couldn't be certain, but it looked as if the prints had been pressed into the snow by small, cloven hooves. She lifted her gaze, toward a feathery smudge hovering in the distance. The hoofprints made a line pointing straight toward it. Gloaming Wood.

Shivering, Grace shut the window and moved to the fireplace. She stirred up the coals, threw on several sticks, and as flames leaped up she shucked off her nightclothes and pulled on a wool gown the same frosty purple as the predawn sky.

As she dressed, her mind raced. It was the sound of bells that had roused her from her dream, and she had heard bells yesterday in the castle garden. The Little People were trying to communicate with her, she was certain of it. But what was the message?

Grace tried to remember the dream the bells had awakened her from, but it was already growing fuzzy. She had been alone in some sort of castle or keep, running down empty halls, searching in shadowed chambers for something. Searching for a key. But the key to what?

To hope, she thought, only she didn't know why. Was that what the Little People were trying to tell her?

She grabbed her cape, tossed it around her shoulders, and threw open the chamber door, to the round-mouthed surprise of the serving maid standing on the other side. She carried a tray with a pot of *maddok.*

"Perfect timing," Grace said, pouring a steaming cup and setting the pot back on the tray. "I wouldn't have made it far without this."

The serving maid stared, slack-jawed, as Grace hurried down the corridor, sipping *maddok* as she went.

This is mad, Grace. Completely mad.

Which was precisely why she needed help. She stopped in front of a door and knocked. It opened after a scant second—by all the gods, didn't the man ever sleep?—and Durge gazed at her with somber brown eyes.

"Good morrow, my lady." He wore a tunic as gray as the keep Grace had seen in her dream. "Though I suppose it isn't morrow yet, as the sun is not yet up."

"But you are, Durge. And I'm glad, because I need your help."

"As you wish, my lady." He eyed her fur-lined cape. "We are going out, then?"

"We are."

"Then allow me to fetch my cloak." He retrieved the garment, which was warming on a chair by the fire—that was Durge, always at the ready—and threw it about his thick shoulders.

"Don't you even want to know where we're going, Durge?"

"I imagine I'll find out when we get there, my lady."

Grace winced. She didn't deserve this kind of loyalty, but all the same she was grateful.

"We'll need our horses," she said.

They rode away from the castle just as the sun crested the horizon. The cold air pinched the soft flesh inside Grace's nostrils and made her jaw ache, but she was warm inside her heavy gown and cloak, and it felt good to be free from the castle's stone walls.

Beneath her, Shandis cantered lightly over the frozen

ground. Last summer, Grace had left the honey-colored mare in Castle Spardis, and she had believed she would never see the horse again. However, a few days after their return to Calavere, she was thrilled to discover Shandis was in fact housed in King Boreas's stable. Aryn and Durge had brought the mare with them when they journeyed from Spardis to Ar-tolor last Krondath, and Ivalaine had returned Shandis—along with Durge's gigantic charger, Blackalock—when she visited just before Midwinter. Durge rode Blackalock now, following Grace as she led the way north, away from the castle.

After an hour, they crossed the old Tarrasian bridge over the River Darkwine. Chunks of ice floated on the water below. Once on the other side, they were no longer in Calavan. Gloaming Wood was closer now. Grace could make out the wispy branches of bare trees; she leaned against Shandis's neck and urged the young horse into a full gallop. She knew Durge would warn her it was reckless to ride so fast over the snow, but first he would have to catch her.

Icy wind numbed her cheeks as the snowy landscape rushed past. Grace risked a glance over her shoulder; she was right—Blackalock pounded furiously after Shandis, and Durge wore a glower of disapproval. That was good. Durge needed something to worry about, and this way he wouldn't stop to think about where they were headed.

Many stories were told in the castle of Gloaming Wood. For as long as anyone could remember, the patch of primeval forest had been a place of shadow and rumor. Folk spoke of lights that shone among the trees late at night—lights that would draw a man into the wood, only to disappear once he was deep among the trees, leaving him lost and alone. Some whispered of hearing queer music or eerie laughter when they passed near the eaves of the wood, and it was said a man could not come within a hundred paces of the forest with an axe in his hand. A terrible fear would come upon him, leaving him shaking and pissing.

When Grace first heard such stories, she had dismissed them as fabrications of the castle's common folk. Then she had met Trifkin Mossberry and his peculiar troupe of actors, and she had been forced to adjust her thinking. The Little People were not products of a fantastical imagination, at least not on this world.

Elfs and dwarfs and greenmen—all of them were real. And at least some of them dwelled in the shadows of Gloaming Wood.

By the time Durge caught up with her, they had reached the edge of the forest. Grace brought Shandis to a halt and waited for Durge to dismount and offer his hand to her. In these heavy clothes, she would never make it to the ground by herself without falling facefirst in the snow.

"Thank you, my lord," she said with what she hoped was a winning smile as Durge helped her down. "You're every bit as strong as you are courteous."

The knight scowled at her, his mustaches twitching. "Do not try to distract me with idle flatteries, my lady. I can see quite well where you've led us, and I must say I am not pleased. This is a queer and perilous place, and while it is not for a knight to question his mistress, I must wonder all the same why you've brought us here."

She gripped his hand. "I've come to ask the Little People for help."

"My lady, you must do no such a thing!" The knight pulled his hand from hers, his brown eyes wide. "The Little People might have aided us in the past, but it was done of their own will and for their own purposes. Surely this is a dangerous scheme. We should return to the castle at once."

She was not surprised by his outburst. Durge was a man of logic; he did not like meddling with magic. Grace understood how he felt, for she was a scientist herself. However, if she was going to face the Pale King and his army, she needed help from any source—illogical as it might seem. She moved toward the line of trees. Though they were bare, she could see no more than a dozen paces into the wood.

"It can't be so dangerous, Durge," she said. "Otherwise, you never would have ridden through the wood that day over a year ago, and you never would have found me, lying there in the snow."

Durge let out a foggy sigh. "That I came upon you here is something for which I will ever be grateful, my lady. Still, it is my duty to question this deed. Even that day I found you, I was riding only through the eaves of Gloaming Wood, following a game track no more than a hundred paces in. I could still glimpse the plains through the trees. If we would find whom you seek, we would be forced to venture deep into the forest, and surely it is impossible for mortals to go there."

"No, I don't think so." She touched the papery bark of a tree. "I think I've been in there once before."

Durge gave her an odd look, and she thought of the time when she and Travis had gone looking for Trifkin Mossberry in Calavere. They had entered the little man's chamber only to find themselves, not in the castle, but in an impossible forest. Even then, with Trifkin Mossberry to protect them, she and Travis had not dared to linger. Durge was right; this forest was perilous for mortals. However, the Little People were trying to tell her something, and Grace was going to find out what it was.

"I'm going in," she said, gathering her courage. "You can wait here with the horses."

Durge gave her a sharp look out of the corner of his eye. "I should think not, my lady."

Grace knew better than to argue. She took Durge's hand, and together they stepped into the wood.

As the trees closed around them, so did a quietness. There were no birds flitting among the bare branches overhead, no small animals scurrying through the underbrush. The only sound was the crunch of snow beneath their feet.

While it was dawn in the world outside, here it was as if the sun had not yet risen. The air was a misty gray, and the trees crowded together, so at first it was difficult to pick a route among them. However, they soon came to a path, most likely worn by deer and boar. As best Grace could tell, the path headed toward the heart of the wood, and they started down it.

"I do not like this," Durge rumbled. "It seems too easy to come upon a path so quickly."

"Maybe this is our lucky day," Grace said. She was going to say something more, but their voices, low as they kept them, rang out unnervingly on the still air.

Durge shook his head. "Mark my words, this path is surely cursed. It will lead us down into a ravine, or over a cliff, or to some other unseemly demise."

Despite her trepidation, Grace almost laughed. She knew it wasn't his intent, but somehow Durge's gloomy admonitions always seemed to cheer her up. She tightened her grip on his hand, and as they walked she tried not to think of fairy tales in which children met with bad ends in dark forests.

Soon Grace lost track of time. She expected the air to lighten as the sun rose higher into the sky, but if anything the light grew grayer yet. The trees all looked the same to her—tall and slender, with pale bark—and the path wove left and right but on the whole kept leading them deeper into the wood. Despite her heavy garments and the exertion, the cold began to creep into her joints, and ice collected on Durge's mustaches.

At last Grace realized they would have to turn back. She was shivering so violently she could hardly walk in a straight line, and, while Durge was making a valiant effort, he could not keep his teeth from chattering. They had not seen so much as a squirrel, let alone a dwarf or greenman. If the Little People truly dwelled here, then they did not wish to be found. Grace started to tell Durge it was no use, that they had to turn back.

A high, trilling note rang out on the air. The sound echoed away among the trees.

"What was that?" Grace whispered. It had not been the music of bells.

"That was the call of a trumpet," Durge said.

The sound came again, and it was closer this time—a note so high and pure and wild it caused Grace's heart to beat in a swift, unfamiliar cadence.

"It sounds to me like a hunting call," Durge said, gazing around. The path had widened into a small clearing.

Grace hugged her arms around herself. "The king's huntsman wouldn't come so far into the forest, would he?"

"He might, if he were on the trail of a fat roe," Durge said, though he sounded doubtful.

Grace hoped it was indeed the king's huntsman, and that he had blankets with him, and a flask of spiced wine.

The trumpet sounded again, so close the sound set Grace's ears ringing. At the same moment, a bank of evergreen bushes on one side of the clearing shuddered and burst apart, and something large and sleek and white bounded through. It paused, standing no more than five paces away, and Grace found herself gazing into dark, liquid eyes.

It was a stag. The beast was tall and muscled, its coat a silvery white that blended with the trees. It held its neck arched and proud, and its head was crowned by an enormous pair of antlers whose points were too numerous for Grace to count quickly. The stag let out a snort, then sprang away to their left, vanishing among the trees.

"May steel break and stone splinter," Durge swore. "I've never seen so magnificent a beast." He reached over his shoulder to grip the hilt of the greatsword strapped to his back and took a step forward.

Grace grabbed his arm. "No, Durge. Don't go after it."

He frowned at her. "Why not, my lady? It would make a fine prize to offer the king."

She struggled for words. She didn't know why it was wrong to hunt this animal—only that it was too proud, too fabulous to be pursued by mortals such as they. However, before she could speak, another trumpet call rang out, followed by the pounding of hooves. Grace and Durge turned to see a horse leap over the bushes from which the stag had burst moments ago.

The horse was every bit as beautiful as the stag, though in an entirely different way. It was short of stature—no larger than a pony—its legs delicate, its coat pure jet. A silver star marked its forehead.

Riding the horse, without benefit of either saddle or bridle, was a boy. He appeared to be ten or eleven years old, and he was lean and lanky, with a shock of red hair that stuck up from his head. A bow was slung on his back, along with a quiver of arrows fletched with green feathers. Despite the cold, he wore only a pair of leather breeches, leaving his chest and feet bare. His skin was brown as *maddok*.

In the boy's hand was a small silver trumpet. He blew it again, then called out in a piping voice, "This way! The king has come this way!" He touched his horse's neck, and the beast spun around, ready to lunge into a gallop.

Grace and Durge stood in its path. Before they could leap out of the way, the horse skittered to a halt. Its rider glared down with malachite eyes, and only then did Grace see the stubby horns that protruded from his brow. This was no boy.

"What is this?" the rider said, a sneer crossing his freckled face. "Mortals? A kind of quarry, to be sure, but none so noble as that we hunt. How did you get here?"

Grace was so startled she could only answer with the simple truth. "We came by the path."

"The path?" the rider snapped. "And who gave you permission to tread upon it?"

Durge cleared his throat. "The path is here for all. We need no permission to follow it."

Ire flashed in the rider's eyes. "You are wrong, mortal. The path belongs to us, as does everything in this wood. You are trespassing here."

"Then we'll leave at once," Grace said. Like a candle burned to a stump, the desire to talk to the Little People had sputtered and died within her. In spite of his boyish appearance, there was a predatory air about the rider. His eyebrows slanted over his green eyes, lending his face a cruel aspect. "Let's go," she said, tugging Durge's arm.

"Not so quickly," the rider said, guiding his horse in a quick circle around them. Other figures stole into the glade. Some slunk on four legs while some pranced on two; some slithered on their bellies, and others flitted on wings as delicately woven as a spider's web. Grace had glimpsed such creatures on Sindar's ship, but only fleetingly, out of the corner of her eye. Here they gathered in plain view.

It was hard to be sure how many of them there were, given the way they kept weaving in and out among the trees. There were greenmen with round bellies and beards of oak leaves, prancing goat-men with shaggy legs and curving horns, and swan-necked women who wore gowns of white feathers—or were the feathers part of them? Tiny beings with butterfly wings and ugly, long-nosed faces darted about on the air, and golems made of sticks bound together by vines stared at Grace and Durge with hard pebble eyes.

"Stay close to me, my lady," Durge rumbled as he reached up to grip the hilt of his greatsword.

The strange beings formed a circle around the two mortals. Like the boy on the horse, the goat-men and swan-women carried bows with arrows ready, and the butterfly creatures carried tiny bows as well, fitted with darts no larger than toothpicks.

The greenmen carried wooden cudgels, and the other beings bore stone-pointed spears or wielded long thorns like knives.

"Tell me quickly," said the one on the horse. "Which way did the king go?"

Grace shook her head. "But he didn't go anywhere. King Boreas is in the castle."

Even in anger, the rider's boyish face was beautiful. "Not him, you dolt. I couldn't care less for the comings and goings of some foolish mortal who dares call himself a king. I speak of the true king—the forest king. Which way did he go? Tell me, and perhaps we will spare your wretched, finite lives."

Like a ray of light, understanding pierced the fog in Grace's brain. "The stag. That's who you're hunting."

The boy's eyes sparked with green fire. "We are always hunting him. Every year we slay him and spill his blood upon the ground. And every year he comes again, so we may begin the hunt anew. Now speak up, or it's your blood that we'll spill. Which way did he go?"

"That way," Grace said, pointing to a gap in the trees directly opposite the place where the stag had vanished. Durge turned to stare at her, but she gave her head a slight shake. She didn't know why she had done it; only that the stag had been so majestic, so beautiful.

The rider grinned and lifted the silver trumpet, blowing a ringing note. "This way!" he said, motioning to the others, and urged his horse in the direction Grace had pointed. Grace dared to breathe a sigh.

Two greenmen bounded into the clearing, coming from the direction the stag had gone. The rider whirled his horse around, a frown on his elfin face. He leaned over in the saddle, and one of the greenmen jumped up to whisper something in his ear. The boy sat up at once, his face a mask of fury.

"You lied to me, mortal. The king did not go the way you pointed."

Grace shook her head, searching for words. Durge pressed close against her.

"You are a fool to protect the forest king," the rider said. He climbed down from his horse and advanced on them. "Don you know it is his fate to fall to our arrows? You will pay for your deception."

"Hold right there!" Durge roared, and in a swift motion he drew his greatsword, holding it before him.

Laughter rose from the strange beings, a sound like falling water. The boy threw his head back as peals of mirth escaped him. Durge frowned, then his expression turned to shock. His sword writhed back and forth in his hands. With a cry he dropped the blade, and Grace saw it wasn't a sword at all, but rather a great silvery snake. It slithered away across the snow and vanished into the forest.

Durge stared at his empty hands, then clenched them into fists. "Stay back," he said, standing before Grace. "You cannot harm her."

"You're right about that, mortal, I can't." He gazed past Durge at Grace. "The light of the forest is in your eyes. It's faint, but even your mundane blood cannot sully it. You shall be spared." His gaze moved back to Durge. "But this beast is mortal through and through. Since we have been denied our true quarry for today, we will make sport of this one instead and hunt him like the animal he is."

"No!" Grace said, her voice rising in panic. "It wasn't his fault. It was I—I was the one who lied to you!"

It was no use. The hunters were already moving. The queer beings shoved Grace aside and swarmed around Durge. He swatted several of the things away, but they kept coming. A root tripped Grace—or was it the limb of some creature?—and she fell to her knees. She heard Durge let out a roar, but the sound was drowned out by laughter. She crawled until she found a tree, then used it to gain her feet.

There were too many of the beings for Durge to fend off. They had pinned his arms and legs, and though cords of effort stood out on his neck, he could not break away. The creatures tore at his clothes with twisted hands, leaving him standing naked in the cold. A pair of antlers was placed on his brow and fastened in place with ropes woven of vines.

"Durge!" Grace cried out.

He could not turn his head, but he met her gaze with wide

eyes. "My lady, you must flee this place! Take the path back the way we came. Go now!"

No, she couldn't leave him. If she had told them the truth about the stag, this wouldn't be happening. She gathered what remained of her will and hurried to the boy.

"Let him go," she commanded.

"That I will," the boy said. "It would make for poor sport if he didn't have a head start."

He gave a flick of his hand, and the creatures moved away from Durge. The knight staggered and caught his balance. He was hairy in his nakedness, and with the antlers he looked not unlike one of the goat-men. A queer expression crossed his face—not pain exactly. Rather, it was the face one would make if something precious were being torn away.

"My lady," he said, but the words were oddly slurred.

A spasm passed through him, and Durge hunched over. When he looked up again, his eyes were dull and wild, and his lips pulled back from his teeth. The rope that had tied the antlers to his head were gone. Instead, the things sprang from his brow, curving and growing longer even as Grace watched.

She stared at the boy. "What have you done to him?"

"Nothing so very great," the boy said with a smirk. "A man is but an animal at heart. All we've done is to help him remember that fact."

Durge let out a snarl, crouching and spinning around, the whites of his eyes showing. The fey beings laughed and raised their weapons.

A wave of terror crested in Grace. "Run, Durge!" she screamed. Could he even still understand her words? "Run!"

For a moment it seemed dim recognition shone in his eyes, then with a roar Durge sprang forward, running across the snow on bare feet, and vanished into the trees.

"You said you'd give him a head start," Grace said, turning toward the red-haired boy. "How long?"

The boy laughed. "I'd say he's already had more than long enough." He lifted the trumpet and blew a shrill note. "Let the hunt begin!"

12.

Grace ducked as a hail of arrows hissed through the air. They stuck quivering into trees or sank deep into the ground. A tiny arrow shot from the bow of one of the butterfly creatures caught in Grace's cloak. She plucked it out; the tip was sticky with green sap. A brief examination using the Touch confirmed her fear: The green substance was some kind of toxin.

The red-haired boy leaped onto his horse and urged it into the forest after Durge. The fey hunters bounded or flitted or scuttled after, fitting new arrows to their bows as they went. They seemed to have forgotten Grace in their glee for the hunt, and in moments all of them were gone. Grace reeled, gathering her wits, then she picked up the hem of her gown and dashed into the trees after the hunters.

There should have been a trail where the fey folk had trampled the ground, but instead she saw only Durge's footprints in the thin layer of snow. She followed them. The trumpet rang out again, and it already sounded alarmingly far off. Grace ran faster. Branches scratched at her face and tore her clothes. At some point she lost her cloak, but she didn't stop for it. Despite the cold she was sweating, and her breath came in ragged gasps.

Several more times Grace heard the call of the trumpet, and each time it was fainter than the last. She lost Durge's trail on a stony patch of ground, and when she heard the trumpet call again, it was off to her left, and so distant she could hardly make out the sound over the thudding of her heart.

Grace staggered in that direction, but after that she did not hear the sound of the trumpet again. The sweat froze her dress stiff as her pace slowed, and she grew clumsy with the cold. At last she could go no farther, and she leaned against the trunk of a gigantic tree. She listened, but there was no trumpet call, no trilling of high laughter; the forest air was still and silent.

"I've lost him," she mumbled with numb lips.

Pain stabbed at her heart. Durge was gone—the kindest, truest, and dearest friend she had on this or any world—and it was her fault. The agony of that thought was too much to bear.

Grace threw her arms around the tree, pressed her face to its trunk, and wept.

"Are you well, daughter?" said a kindly voice behind her.

Grace pushed herself from the tree. A moment ago the forest had been gray and bleak, but now green-gold light sparkled through her tears. She wiped her eyes and gasped.

"Whyever do you weep so?" said the old woman who stood before her. "Is it for this great father of trees you embrace? If so, then dry your tears, for he is not dead. When spring comes, he will be green and full of life again."

Grace stared, sorrow and shock receding. Like the light, a feeling of peace radiated from the old woman. She was tiny and withered and beautiful, her skin as delicate as flower petals, her hair as fine as spider's silk. She wore a robe the color of snow, and in her hands was a wooden staff every bit as gnarled as the fingers that gripped it.

"Who are you?" Grace said.

The old woman smiled, and her eyes—the same color as the light—sparkled. "I suppose you may say I am the queen here, even as you are queen out there." She made a sweeping gesture with the staff. "Of course, my reign is nearly at an end, and yours is only about to begin, daughter."

Grace struggled to comprehend these words, but she couldn't, not quite. Her brain was dull and slow from fear and cold. "I'm not crying for the tree."

"Then for whom is it you weep?"

The words tumbled out of her in a rush. "It's Durge. The boy—the one with red hair—he and the other hunters are chasing him through the forest. And they've done something to him. They tied a pair of antlers to his head, only they aren't just tied in place anymore. They're real. The hunters are going to kill him, and it's all my fault."

The old woman cocked her head. "Your fault, daughter? Now how can that be?"

Grace felt more tears welling up. "I lied about the white stag. I told them he ran one way when he ran the other. But he was so beautiful. I didn't want them to kill him."

The other shut her eyes and gripped her staff. "Yes," she murmured. "I see it now, and I should have known that Quellior was part of all this." She opened her eyes. "That was kind and selfless of you to help my husband escape."

Grace shook her head. "Your husband?"

"As I said, I am the queen of this place. And is he not the king?"

Yes, that was what the red-haired boy had called the stag—the forest king. "So he's safe, then?" Grace said. "The stag? I mean, the king?"

The old woman nodded. "For now. But in time Quellior and his hunters will catch him, and they will slay him."

"No!" Grace said, cold with horror. "They can't!"

The old woman gave a soft sigh. "It is the way of the wood, daughter. Every year Quellior and his hunters pursue the forest king, every year they slay him, and every year he returns again. However, the king is newly risen. It is not yet time for them to catch him, and it is because of you that he escaped. So for your good-hearted deed, I will help you."

"What can you do?" However, before Grace finished uttering the words, the old woman moved her staff, and a thicket of trees parted like a curtain. Beyond was a glade, and a scene that made Grace's heart stop.

The red-haired boy—Quellior—sat on his black horse, an arrow fitted to his bow. The other hunters gathered around him. Like a fallen beast on the ground, Durge lay below them. His eyes were shut, his hair tangled with leaves and twigs, the antlers jutting from his brow. A dozen tiny darts pierced his skin. Quellior laughed and pulled the arrow back to his ear, ready to send it flying down into Durge's heart.

"Stop!" Grace cried out, tripping over roots as she dashed forward. She fell to her knees beside Durge, covering his body with her arms. "Leave him alone!"

"Wood and bone, how did you get here?" Quellior sneered in his high voice. "But it's no matter. My arrow can pierce two as easily as one."

"I should think it will pierce none at all," said a sharp voice, and at the same moment the arrow in Quellior's bow sprouted leaves and tendrils. The tendrils coiled around the boy's hands like green snakes, binding them. The other hunters gasped and chattered and fluttered their wings.

Quellior glared at the old woman. "Blood and stone, Mother! I nearly had him!"

Grace blinked in astonishment. Mother?

The old woman marched into the glade, staff in hand. "Shame on you, Quellior." She cast a stern eye at all of the hunters, and they quailed under her ire. "Shame on all of you. Is this mortal man the quarry you are bound to hunt?"

"She denied us our quarry," the red-haired boy said, glaring at Grace. "So we were hunting this one instead."

The forest queen's eyes flashed. "Answer my question. Is this mortal your true quarry?"

Quellior hung his head and sighed. "No, Mother."

"I should think not. Now off with you." She gave a flick of her staff. "All of you. You shall find the forest king again when summer comes and is in its waning days."

Quellior lifted his head, and there was a queer look in his eyes. "If summer ever comes again, Mother." He cast one hateful glance at Grace, then his horse bounded away through the trees, and the other fey hunters followed.

Grace cradled Durge's head in her lap. She smoothed his mousy hair from his brow, and she could not help marveling at the way the antlers melded with his skin and skull. She touched a tiny arrow that jutted from the skin just above his collarbone but could not bring herself to check his pulse.

"Is he dead?"

"No, daughter," said the forest queen, standing above her. "The darts of the winged ones bring sleep, not death."

"Then how can I wake him up?"

"Are you sure you wish to, daughter?"

Grace stared in blank confusion.

Sorrow lined the old woman's face. "A mortal man is not a beast, but he may be made to act like one. I fear Quellior has played a wicked trick upon your friend. If he were to wake now, he would not remember he was a man at all, but rather would think himself an animal."

In a way he did look like a beast—naked, dirty, and wild. But Grace knew the true man that lay beneath. Her tears fell on his face, washing away some of the dirt. "He's not a beast. He is the kindest, bravest, and truest man in the world."

"If you can see that in him, then perhaps there is a way you can help him."

Grace looked up, hope surging in her. "How?"

"You must join your spirit with his. You must show him how you see him—not as a beast, but as a man. If you do, he may remember himself."

For a moment Grace trembled. All her life she had kept others at a distance, afraid that if they drew too close they would see what she really was and would recoil in horror. But Durge was her friend; if she could see good in him, she had to believe he would see it in her as well.

She steeled her will and ran her fingers over Durge, plucking out the darts where she found them. A groan escaped him, and he stirred, eyelids fluttering. He was waking up. If he did, he would run from her, she was sure of it; she had to hurry.

Grace pressed her hands against Durge's chest and shut her eyes. Instantly she saw his life thread. It was somber gray, as she remembered it, only marked with a wild streak of crimson. He let out a grunt, moving beneath her, but before he could twist away she reached out and gripped his thread, bringing it close to her own shimmering strand. In her mind she pictured Durge as she knew him: kind, strong. Good. Then, with a thought, she braided the two strands together.

I love you Durge! she called out. *Come back to me!*

For a single moment she could not discern Durge's thread as a separate thing from her own. They were a single strand, gleaming and perfect.

No, not perfect. There was something else there. Something sharp and dark and terrible, pressing dangerously close. What was it? Before Grace could tell, a gold light welled forth, encapsulating her, and she knew no more.

She must have fallen asleep. Grace pushed herself up to her elbow and used her fingers to comb leaves from her hair. The gold light was dimmer now, but still comforting, and she felt warm. Durge lay beside her, his chest rising and falling in a steady rhythm. The antlers had fallen away to either side. She laid a hand on his forehead; the skin of his brow was unblemished, save for the lines of worry that furrowed it even in repose.

Grace smiled, then rose. Her cloak, which she had lost earlier, now hung on a nearby branch. She cast it over Durge, covering his nakedness, then knelt beside him. Her smile faded as
she touched the center of his chest. When their threads were
one, she had sensed something inside him—like a shadow, but
different. Harder, colder.

"So you've seen it within him, daughter. I thought you
might."

Grace looked up. The old woman—the forest queen—stood
above her.

"You can see it, too?" Grace said.

The old woman nodded. "It was clear to my eyes the first
moment I saw him. But then, ever have we hated the cruel touch
of iron, and we know it when it comes near us."

Grace was no longer warm. "What are you talking about?"

"There is a splinter of iron in his chest. It lies dangerously
near his heart. And it works its way nearer each day."

No, it was impossible. Durge couldn't be one of *them*. Then
Grace remembered the pains he had felt in his chest the night of
the attack on Calavere. She examined his chest. A dozen scars
traced white lines beneath dark hair, but she recognized them as
the remnants of the wounds he had received on Midwinter's Eve
over a year ago, when he was attacked by a band of *feydrim*.

Durge was a marvelous warrior, but all the same she had
been amazed he had been able to fend off so many *feydrim* by
himself. Grace had always wondered how he had managed to
get away from the creatures. . . .

*But what if he didn't, Grace? What if he didn't get away—at
least not until they let him go?*

She shut her eyes, and though dread filled her at what she
might see, she reached out with the Touch, gazing into Durge's
body. Now that she knew what to look for, she saw it immediately, an inch from his heart. The splinter was no bigger than the
tip of her little finger, but it was cold, so terribly cold.

She opened her eyes. "Oh, Durge, what did they do to you?"

She could see it clearly, as if the memory had lingered in his
flesh and she had glimpsed it like a ghost image on an X ray.
Even his greatsword was not enough to keep so many *feydrim*
away. They swarmed over the brave Embarran, dragging him

down, knocking him unconscious. Only they did not kill him. Instead they fell back as a figure strode into the chamber, clad in a bloodred gown, a smile on her pale face. It was Lady Kyrene, who had been Grace's first teacher as a witch, and who had traded her living heart for one of iron. Kyrene knelt, taking something small and dark, and pressing it deep into a wound in Durge's left side. He cried out, a sound of despair and agony, only by the time his eyes opened, the others were gone. He couldn't have known what they had done to him, why they let him survive.

"They wanted to turn him into a traitor," Grace said, and it felt like a splinter of metal had pierced her own heart. "Only they wanted to do it without us knowing."

"Yes," the old woman said above her. "But his heart is far stronger than they believed. Evil always underestimates the power of good—that is its greatest weakness. All this while, he has resisted."

"Then he can keep resisting it," Grace said, grasping for hope.

The forest queen shook her head. "He is mortal, daughter. Even a man so strong as he cannot resist forever. Soon now, the splinter will reach his heart."

Grace could barely speak the words. "What will happen when it does?"

The old woman met her eyes. "His heart will turn to ice, and he will become the willing slave of the Lord of Winter—the one whom you call the Pale King."

A moan escaped Grace. "I have to get it out of him. I have to operate before it's too late."

"It's already too late, daughter. He should have perished that night. It is only the enchantment of the splinter that has kept him alive. If you remove it, he will die."

Grace couldn't believe it. She wouldn't. Except she had to. She wiped tears from her cheeks and looked up. "You do it, then. You can help him with your magic."

"I fear that is not so," the forest queen said, sorrow on her wizened visage. "Iron is a thing whose touch none of us can bear. I have no power over it."

Anger boiled up in Grace, and she seized on it as she stood, because it was so much easier to endure than despair. "I came here to find Trifkin Mossberry and the Little People. I wanted to ask them for help in standing against the Pale King, and I found you. But you're no help at all. You don't even care. You ran away from the world to hide here in your forest, and now I can see why. Your magic is old and weak and useless."

For a moment, anger touched the old woman's face, and her eyes blazed like the noonday sun. It was a terrible sight, but such was Grace's own rage that she did not flinch.

At last the forest queen shook her head, and her eyes dimmed. "Perhaps you are right, perhaps we have grown too distant from the world outside. Yet you are wrong if you think we do not care. Quellior is brash and foolish, but he was right— if you cannot stop the Lord of Winter from riding forth, summer will never come again. And while we cannot stand beside you in the way you hoped, perhaps I can help you discover a way to help yourself." She met Grace's eyes. "You seek a key, do you not, one that can aid you in the war you must fight? Sit in the chair that is forbidden to all others, and the key shall be revealed to you."

It wasn't enough, Grace wanted to say. She wanted the Little People to fight beside her when the Rune Gate opened. And she wanted Durge to be solid and whole, to be there for her as he always was. All the same, Grace felt her anger melting. She turned away.

"Do not lose all hope, daughter," the old woman said behind her. "The splinter has not yet reached his heart. You will yet have time with your knight before the end." Her voice was receding now. "Farewell. And remember the chair."

Grace turned around, but the gold light filled the forest, and she couldn't see the old woman. Then the light dimmed, and she turned back to see a silver snake slither up against Durge's side. Only it wasn't a snake at all, but his greatsword. He was clothed again, his garments bearing no sign of rip or stain.

"My lady, what has happened?" Durge sat up, blinking gentle brown eyes as he stared in all directions.

Grace knelt beside him and gripped his hand. Her breath fogged on the air; the bitter cold had returned. "What do you remember?"

"I'm not entirely certain." His mustaches pulled down into a frown. "I recall riding to the forest with you. And then..." He shook his head, his expression one of wonder. "I fear the Little People must have been at work, my lady, even if we never saw them, for I had the most peculiar dream. I dreamed I was a stag running through the forest, and that hunters wanted to slay me. Only a beautiful maiden threw herself upon me, protecting me from their arrows. It was all most queer."

Relief flooded Grace. He didn't remember what had really happened. "Don't think about it, Durge. You're fine now." Only that wasn't true, was it? Even now the splinter of iron was working its way nearer his heart.

Grace didn't even realize she was crying until he wiped the tears from her cheek.

"What is this, my lady?" he said in a chiding tone. "You must not weep. After all, there was never any hope the Little People would help us. Nor does it matter. I can't imagine we'll ever find a way to stop the Pale King from riding forth, but at least we'll not find it together."

"Oh, Durge," Grace said, and to his clear astonishment she threw her arms around him and wept.

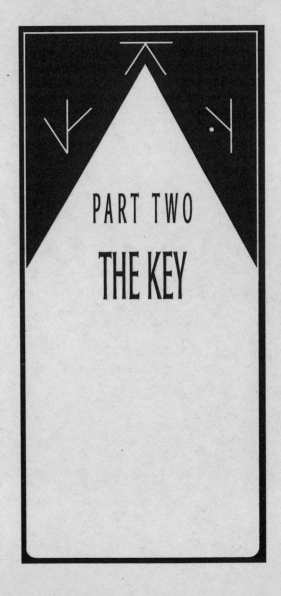

PART TWO
THE KEY

13.

There was a package from the Seekers waiting for Deirdre Falling Hawk when she stepped through the door of her flat. She set her keys next to the cardboard box on the Formica dinette table. The landlady must have let them in.

Or maybe the Seekers have a skeleton key that works for all of London.

Regardless, the package could wait. She squeezed into the closet with a stove and a sink that served for a kitchen, put on a pot for tea, then headed to the adjoining bathroom. She took a shower, letting the hot water pound her, as if it had the power to wake her when she knew perfectly well she wasn't sleeping.

She toweled off, wrapped herself in a terry robe, and padded back to the kitchen to fix a cup of Earl Grey with lemon. Cup in hand, she curled on the threadbare sofa. She sipped tea, watching the day drizzle away outside the window, and wondered if she would ever see Hadrian Farr again. Over and over, she thought through their conversation at the pub earlier that day. It was no use; nothing she could have said would have stopped him from leaving.

It rained until night fell. Deirdre rose and switched on a tasseled floor lamp. Whoever decorated this place for the Seekers had clearly possessed a penchant for vintage stores—along with a fierce and single-minded need to make sure every object in the flat was a completely different color.

She donned jeans, a lamb's wool sweater she had picked up in Oslo a few years ago, and her leather jacket. She left the flat, walking down streets made black mirrors by the rain. After a few blocks she passed a neon-lit nightclub. Pounding music spilled out the door, running down the gutters like rainwater. Laughter floated on the moist air. Hands in pockets, she walked on.

She bought Indian takeout at a small shop and headed back to the flat. The Seekers' box took up almost the entire table, so she moved it to the floor. There was no mark on it, not even a mailing label—only a small symbol stamped in one corner: a hand with three flames.

Deirdre sat at the dinette and ate slowly, breathing in the heady aromas of cardamom and clove. As she ate, she looked at the newspaper she had bought from a box, only noticing after she had nearly finished going through it that it was yesterday's edition. Not that it mattered. These days, the news was always the same: more fear and unrest, more shootings and suicide bombings, more rumors of war.

Things had gotten better for a while last fall, after the plague of fire had ended as suddenly as it began. Now troubled times were back, darker than ever. Things seemed particularly bad in the United States. People were afraid, and the economy was crashing as a result. At the same time, the government's rhetoric was growing increasingly hard-line. Basic civil liberties were being suspended, and some senators were actually talking about closing the borders. Only that would accomplish nothing. Hiding in a locked room didn't do any good when the whole house was falling down around you.

Appetite gone, she folded up the paper and tossed it in the recycle bin, then took the leftovers and dishes to the kitchen. Finished, she went back to the sofa and sat. The box from the Seekers lurked in the corner, sinister in its blankness.

Deliberately, she pulled her gaze from the box and reached for the wooden case that held her mandolin. It was too quiet in this place; every thought was like a shout in her head. Maybe a little music would help. She strummed the mandolin and winced. The poor thing could never seem to hold a tune in the damp London air. She tightened the strings, then strummed again. This time she smiled at the warm tone that rose from the instrument, a sound as welcome and familiar as the greeting of an old friend.

She plucked out a lilting Irish air. It was the first tune she had learned to play as a girl at her grandmother's house. She supposed she had been no more than eight or nine, and small for her age, so that she had barely been able to finger chords and strum at the same time. Now the mandolin nestled perfectly against the curve of her body, as if it had been fashioned just for her.

More songs came to her fingertips, bright and thrumming, or slow and deep as a dreaming ocean. Her mind drifted as she played, back to the days when she had been a bard, wandering to a new place, earning a little money with her music, then moving on. That was before she had ever heard of Jack Graystone or Grace Beckett. Before Travis Wilder was anything other than a gentle saloonkeeper in a small Colorado town with whom she had almost had an affair. Before she met Hadrian Farr in that smoky pub in Edinburgh, fell like countless other foolish women for the mystery in his dark eyes, and found her way into the Seekers.

It was only as she thought how strange and unexpected were the journeys on which life could lead one that she realized it was a song about journeys she was playing. In a low voice, she sang along with the final notes.

> *We live our lives a circle,*
> *And wander where we can.*
> *Then after fire and wonder,*
> *We end where we began.*

Her fingers slipped from the strings, and the music faded away. A chill stole over her, and she shivered. What had made her choose that song?

She had found the music and lyrics two years ago in the Seekers' file on James Sarsin. Sarsin had been the focus of one of the Seekers' most famous cases. He had lived in and around London for several centuries before abruptly disappearing in the 1880s after his bookshop burned. After that, the Seekers lost track of him. It was only recently, through Deirdre's work, that they discovered James Sarsin was in fact one and the same with Travis Wilder's antique dealer friend Jack Graystone.

Among the few papers recovered from Sarsin's burnt bookshop were several sheaves of music. One of them was "Fire and Wonder." The music had been transcribed in a manner Deirdre had never seen before, but at last she had managed to decipher the code and learn the song. She had played it in Travis Wilder's saloon, curious to see if it would get a reaction from him.

And it did, Deirdre, though not for the reason you thought.

He didn't hear it from Jack Graystone. He heard it from a bard on another world.

She hadn't played the song since that day. It was a simple tune, pretty, yet there was a sadness to it that made her heart ache. Again she strummed the last few chords. The words reminded her of something. Something that had happened in Castle City, something she had forgotten.

She set down the mandolin and moved over to the trunk where she had stowed her few belongings. After a bit of rummaging, she pulled out a leather-bound book—one of her journals. Farr had taught her early in her career as a Seeker to take notes. Lots of them. She checked the label on the spine to make sure it was the right volume and headed back to the sofa. She flipped through the pages, trying to remember. Then three words caught her eye, and her heart fluttered in her chest.

Fire and wonder. . . .

Quickly, she read the entire entry. She remembered now. It was the day she had ridden alone into the canyon above Castle City, to make a satellite phone call to Farr. There, by the side of a deserted road, she had encountered a pale girl in an archaic black dress. Only later did she learn that both Grace Beckett and Travis Wilder had encountered this same girl, that her name was Child Samanda, and that there were two others she seemed to travel with: a preacher named Brother Cy, and a red-haired woman named Sister Mirrim.

The Seekers had never been able to locate any trace of these three individuals, but that didn't surprise Deirdre. Maybe Marji, the West Colfax Avenue psychic, had been right. Maybe Deirdre did have some ability as a shaman. Because Deirdre had known in an instant this was no normal child.

Cradling the journal, Deirdre ran her finger over the conversation she had transcribed over a year ago.

Seek them as you journey, the child had said.

What do you mean? Deirdre had asked. *Seek what?*

Fire and wonder.

At the time, there had been so much going on—the Burned Man, the illness of Travis's friend Max Bayfield, Duratek's agents in Castle City—that Deirdre hadn't noticed the connection. Now, at last, she did. What was the significance of the ghostly child's words? And why had she appeared to Deirdre?

She set the journal down and found herself staring once more at the box in the corner. Maybe it was a hunch. Or maybe it was what Marji would have called her gift. Either way, Deirdre moved to the box and knelt beside it. She broke the tape with a key, dug through layers of packing peanuts, and pulled out something cool and hard. It was a notebook computer. The machine was sleek and light, encased in brushed metal.

She took the computer to the dinette table, opened it, and pressed the power button. A chime sounded as it whirred to life. A login screen appeared, but there was no place to type her agent name or password.

She turned the computer, studying it. Inserted into the side was a silvery expansion module. The module bore a thin slit, about the width and thickness of a credit card. Deirdre reached into the pocket of her jeans and pulled out her new ID card. It slid into place with a soft *snick*.

The login screen vanished, replaced by a spinning wheel. Just as Deirdre was thinking she should have plugged the computer into a phone jack, the screen went black. Then words scrolled into being, as if typed by invisible hands:

> DNA authentication scan accepted. Seeker Agent
> Deirdre Falling Hawk—identity confirmed.
> Working . . .

Deirdre let out a low whistle. So this thing was wireless. More glowing words scrolled across the screen.

> Welcome to Echelon 7.
> What do you want to do?
> >

The cursor blinked on and off, expectant. Deirdre sat back in the chair and ran a hand through her red-black hair.

"Damn," she said.

What was she supposed to do? There were no menus on the

screen, no windows to explore, no buttons to click. Just the glowing words.

It asked you a question, Deirdre. So why not answer it?

She swallowed a nervous laugh, then leaned forward and tapped out words on the keyboard.

    I want to find something.

She pressed *Enter*. A moment later new words appeared on the screen.

    What do you want to find?
    >

Deirdre hesitated, fingers hovering over the keys. Then, quickly, she typed three words.

    Fire and wonder.

Again she pressed *Enter*. The words flashed, then vanished. Deirdre chewed her lip. Had she done something wrong? She reached out to press another key.

Before her finger touched the keyboard, the screen exploded into a riot of motion and color. Dozens of session windows popped into being. Text poured through some of the windows like green rain, while in others images flashed by so quickly they were superimposed into a single blurred montage of stones covered with runes, medieval swords, pages of illuminated manuscripts, and ancient coins.

Deirdre leaned closer to the screen. Some of the data windows contained menus and commands she recognized; they belonged to various systems in the Seeker network she had accessed in the past. However, most of the windows contained unfamiliar interfaces, their indecipherable menus composed in glowing alien symbols. Atop everything was a single flashing crimson word: *Seeking*... Trembling, she reached out to touch the computer.

The screen went dark. Deirdre jerked her hand back. Had she

damaged it somehow? Then her heart began to beat once more as glowing emerald words scrolled across the screen.

```
Search completed.
1 match(es) located:
/albion/archive/case999-1/mla1684a.arch
>
```

So it had found something. But where? Deirdre didn't recognize the server name; wherever this file was located, it wasn't in a database she had ever searched before.

And why should it be? This is Echelon 7. And if Hadrian is right, this file is something just about no one in the Seekers has access to.

She drew in a breath, then typed a quick command.

```
Display search file. [Enter]
```

The cursor flashed, and the computer let out a beep.

```
Error. Unable to access file mla1684a.arch.
File does not exist.
>
```

Deirdre swore. "What do you mean the file doesn't exist? You just found it, you stupid computer."

She forced herself to take a breath. It was not a good sign when one started berating inanimate objects. Forcing her hands to hold steady, she typed another command.

```
What happened to search file? [Enter]
```

```
File mla1684a.arch has been deleted from the
system.
>
```

That made even less sense. How could the query have found the file in the first place if it had been deleted? Deirdre typed with furious intensity.

```
When was file mla1684a.arch deleted? [Enter]

File mla1684a.arch was deleted from the system at
time stamp: Today, 22:10:13
>
```

A coldness stole over her. She forced her eyes to focus on the wall clock—10:12 P.M. Two minutes ago. The file had been deleted from the system two minutes ago. But that had to be . . .

"Just a few seconds after your search query located it," Deirdre whispered.

She pushed back from the table and reached for the phone on the wall. Fumbling, she punched the number of the flat where Farr had been staying. One ring, two.

Someone had deleted the file the moment after she found it. Why? To keep her from reading it, of course. But then why leave the file on the server where she could find it in the first place? Her mind whirred like the computer.

Maybe deleting the file would have drawn attention to it, Deirdre. Maybe whoever erased it didn't want to do so until they absolutely had to—until the file was found. So how were they watching it?

She had to talk to Farr; he would know what to do.

Three rings, four. "Come on, Hadrian, answer. Bloody hell—come on."

A click. The ringing ended, and a robotic voice spoke in her ear. "The number you have reached has been disconnected. If you feel you have reached this recording in error—"

Deirdre slammed the phone back onto the wall. No, it was no error. Farr had left. But where was he going? There had been something about him earlier—a power, a peril—she had never seen before. Then, with a shiver, she remembered his last words to her.

You see, there's still one class of encounter we haven't had yet. . . .

Deirdre sank back into the chair, staring at the computer screen. It was the first thing every Seeker learned upon joining the order: the classification of otherworldly encounters. Class Three Encounters were common—rumors and stories of otherworldly nature. Class Two Encounters were rarer, but well represented in the history of the Seekers—encounters with objects and locations that bore residual traces of otherworldly forces. And Class One Encounters were the rarest—direct interaction with otherworldly beings and travelers.

But Farr was right. There was one more class of encounter, one that had never been recorded in all the five centuries of the Seekers' existence. A Class Zero Encounter. Translocation to another world oneself.

Deirdre clenched her hands into fists. "What are you doing, Hadrian? By all the gods, what are you doing?"

The only answer was the ceaseless hum of the computer.

14.

Deirdre fumbled with her sunglasses as she climbed the stairs of the Blackfriars tube station and stepped onto the bustling sidewalk.

Never before had she believed it possible for the sun to be too bright in London. After all, she had lived most of her life in the cloudless American West; the sun in England was a sixty-watt bulb compared to the brilliant floodlight that hung above Colorado three hundred-plus days a year. However, after staring all night at the phosphorescent screen of the computer the Seekers had sent her, even the weak morning light (which, frankly, was as much haze as sun) seemed to jab at her eyes.

She started down the sidewalk and immediately stepped in gum. Leaning against a lamppost, she lifted her foot. Gooey strings stretched from the cement to the sole of her boot. She tried to pull off the wad of chewed gum, but it only stuck to her fingers.

"That doesn't look at all sanitary," volunteered an elderly woman in a cheerful voice. She took a tissue from her purse and held it out.

Deirdre gave her a wan smile, took the tissue, and wiped her hand as the woman strolled away. The gum didn't come off, but bits of tissue adhered to it, reducing the stickiness.

Twenty minutes later she stepped from a mahogany-paneled elevator into the main office below the Charterhouse.

"You're late," Sasha said. "Nakamura was expecting you ten minutes ago."

Deirdre raised an eyebrow. Maybe Farr was on to something; Sasha did have a propensity for springing on people. Today she wore a clingy white sweater and black slacks. A saffron scarf was draped around her neck with a carefree air so perfect the thing could only have been pinned in place.

"I had a problem at the gate," Deirdre said. "The card reader wouldn't take my new ID card."

She had inserted the card into the reader a half dozen times. However, each time the light flashed red, and the last time a sickly buzzing noise had emanated from the reader. At that point a security guard had rushed out of a side gate, eager to clap her in irons, but a fingerprint scan had confirmed her identity, and he had grudgingly escorted her in.

Sasha raised a dark hand to her chin. "That's right. I forgot about your new card. Are you having any fun with it yet?"

Deirdre tried not to look shocked. Did Sasha know about her new clearance for Echelon 7? Deirdre would have imagined that was restricted knowledge.

"Why does the assistant director want to see me?" she said.

"Because you're a wicked girl and already plotting mischief, and Nakamura means to nip it in the bud. All right, that's just speculation. All the same, you'd better get moving." Sasha prowled away like a runway model, then paused to glance over her shoulder. "By the way, where's Sir Mopesalot today?"

Deirdre did her best to keep her voice neutral. "I honestly have no idea where Farr is."

Sasha nodded, as if Deirdre had confirmed something she already knew. The elevator doors opened and shut, and she was gone. Deirdre headed for the front desk, behind which a receptionist typed at Mach speed. She was middle-aged, with tortoiseshell-rimmed glasses and a sensible haircut. Deirdre didn't recognize her; the nameplate atop the counter read *Madeleine*.

"Excuse me," Deirdre said when the receptionist did not look up from her work.

"You're a Seeker, Miss Falling Hawk. I'm absolutely certain

you're capable of reading." The receptionist didn't miss a key as she typed.

Deirdre stared, then noticed the small sign resting next to a clipboard. *Please sign in before proceeding.*

"I'm sorry." Deirdre groped for the pen attached to the clipboard. "We didn't use to have to sign in."

"I have every confidence you'll make the adjustment."

Deirdre didn't know how to interpret that, so she scribbled her name and headed down a hallway to the assistant director's office. Nakamura stood and smiled when she entered, and some of her fear that she was going to be scolded faded a bit.

"Close the door, will you, Agent Falling Hawk? And please, take a seat."

She pulled the door shut and perched on the edge of a leather chair as the assistant director sat once more behind his desk.

Richard Nakamura was, as far as Deirdre knew, the highest-ranking American in the entire order of the Seekers. He was a short, compactly built man with white hair and an oval face that was surprisingly smooth given his seventy years. He had been born in San Francisco to Japanese immigrants, and as a child during World War II he and his family had been forced to spend time in Amache, an internment camp in eastern Colorado. Deirdre didn't know if it was ironic or fitting that Nakamura was one of the most patriotic men she knew. A U.S. flag stood in one corner of the room, opposite the Union Jack, and a picture of the American president decorated the mahogany wall, along with Roman death masks, medieval tapestries, and samurai swords.

Nakamura had entered the Seekers as a young man in the late 1950s, and if his rise was not meteoric, like Hadrian Farr's, it had certainly been steady. He had made solid progress in his laboratory research over the decades, especially in the area of detecting and classifying trace energy signatures. Five years ago, he had been promoted to the assistant director level.

That made Nakamura one of the dozen most powerful men and women in the Seekers—apart from the Philosophers. The assistant directors answered only to the directors of Research, Operations, and Security. And the directors answered only to the Philosophers themselves.

Deirdre fidgeted on the edge of her chair, knew she should stop, and couldn't. Why did Nakamura want to see her? Did he want to question her further about what happened in Colorado? He folded his hands on the desk and said nothing.

Deirdre couldn't stand it any longer. "Farr is gone," she said.

Nakamura's placid expression didn't change. "Yes, we know. He couriered a letter to us just before his departure. I'm sure you did your best to convince him to stay."

Deirdre's throat ached. "I don't know where he is."

"Of course you don't, Miss Falling Hawk. No one does. Agent Farr's talents are such that we won't find him until he wishes to be found."

The pace of Deirdre's heart slowed, and belatedly she realized Nakamura's silence had been deliberate. He had wanted her to speak first, to see what she would say. But she didn't care if he knew what was on her mind. She had nothing to hide.

And don't you? What about Glinda? What about the forest you saw when you kissed her?

She folded her hands in her lap, covering the silver circle on her right ring finger. "What will happen to him?" she said.

Nakamura's brown eyes were serious, and perhaps sad. "I suppose in the end that's up to Mr. Farr."

Deirdre nodded, though she wasn't certain she agreed. Once you opened a door, could you really control what came through? Maybe Farr was the last person who could decide what would happen to him.

"I read everything," she said. "All of the files about Hadrian and me. The reports, the assessments, the observations. Everything that was written about us. My new ID card . . ."

"Gave you access." Nakamura nodded. "Yes, of course you read the files. We imagined you would do so immediately once you were granted Echelon 7. Would you care for some tea?"

Deirdre licked her lips. "No, thank you."

"I'll have Lucas bring a second cup just in case you change your mind." He touched a button on the telephone. "Lucas, two cups of tea, please. With honey and lemon. And some of those shortbread biscuits—you know, the ones Abby says will give me another heart attack. Thank you."

Light spilled through the window, illuminating Nakamura's

white hair. He seemed kind and grandfatherly, but Deirdre dismissed that image. One did not rise so high in the Seekers by doling out cookies and tea. All of the orders about how to handle her and Farr in Denver had come from this desk.

"You were using us," she said.

He peered over a pair of bifocals. "Certainly, Miss Falling Hawk. We gained a great deal of knowledge from observing your actions in Colorado. I know you were placed in some degree of peril. However, you and Farr were willing participants in the experiment, were you not?"

Deirdre didn't know what to say. She hadn't expected this level of honesty. Maybe her new rank had brought her more than just Echelon 7 access.

"I believe you gained a valuable experience," Nakamura went on. "It's useful for the observer to know what it feels like to be the subject. I know it changed my own perspective. Good, here's Lucas with our tea."

A white-haired man shuffled into the room carrying a silver tray. It was said Lucas had served the Seekers since the time of the Great Depression. He certainly looked old enough for the story to be true; he was stoop-shouldered and hawk-nosed, and he seemed lost inside a dusty black suit that had obviously been worn by a much larger man years ago.

Lucas set the tray down on Nakamura's desk, porcelain teacups rattling. Deirdre hardly noticed as, with a trembling, white-gloved hand, he set a steaming cup of tea before her. What had Nakamura just told her?

I know it changed my own perspective. . . .

Had Nakamura once been the subject of observation by the Seekers, just as she and Farr had been in Denver?

"Thank you, Lucas," Nakamura said with a smile.

The old man bowed stiffly, remaining bent over for such a long time Deirdre grew alarmed he was having a stroke. However, he finally straightened again, shuffled from the room, and shut the door.

"I'm sure you're curious about your new assignment, Miss Falling Hawk, so I won't keep you in the dark any longer. While it's not quite as glamorous as your most recent assignments, I think you'll agree it's important work."

Nakamura handed her a manila folder. Deirdre opened it and scanned the directive clipped to a slim bundle of papers, then shut the folder.

She had guessed as much. It looked to be an exercise in cross-database cataloging. It was just the kind of work she had been doing two years ago when she discovered the link between the Graystone and Beckett cases. Important? Yes. Dull? Yes again. It was just as Sasha had said. The Seekers wanted to make sure she stayed out of trouble.

Only it doesn't make sense, Deirdre. Why give you a promotion and Echelon 7 clearance if all they intend for you to do is a safe and boring desk job?

Then again, with Echelon 7, there was a whole new world of files and information open to her. Maybe it wouldn't be so tedious after all.

"Thank you," Deirdre said, holding the folder on her lap. "I'm sure it will be interesting work."

Nakamura sighed. "Well, I suppose I shouldn't have expected an outburst of excitement." He sipped his tea, then regarded her over the cup. "This isn't a punishment, you know. You're very important to the Seekers, and I don't mean as a subject with otherworldly connections. You have a gift for seeing pattern, symbol, and meaning others can't. You're one of our finest agents—now more than ever."

Deirdre's heart ached. It would be so easy to let herself think Nakamura didn't mean what he said, that it was nothing more than a cynical ploy intended to engender her loyalty to the organization. Except somehow she couldn't make herself believe that.

"You can let yourself out, Miss Falling Hawk."

Only as he spoke did she realize she had been staring. "Of course," she said, clutching the folder and standing. She hurried to the door.

"By Hermes himself, I nearly forgot." Nakamura removed his glasses. "It will take him a day or two to wrap up his previous assignment, but he'll be contacting you very soon."

Deirdre shook her head. "What?"

Nakamura picked up his teacup. "It's simply our standard procedure. We really prefer Seekers to work in tandem. And don't worry—he isn't your superior. In fact, with your promotion, you'll be the senior agent this time."

Deirdre's mind buzzed; this was important, she was sure of it, but she couldn't quite grasp why. "I don't understand. Who are you talking about?"

"Your new partner, of course."

Deirdre's jaw dropped open.

"Good day, Miss Falling Hawk," Nakamura said as he took another sip of tea.

15.

It quickly became evident Deirdre wasn't going to get any work done that day.

After her conversation with Nakamura, she stopped by her office—the same one she had shared with Farr for the last three years. It was a dank space, with only a single iron-barred window looking out at sidewalk level. However, it was huge, which was the reason they had chosen it. Bookshelves and filing cabinets lurked in countless alcoves, and in between the two gunmetal gray desks was a battered claw-footed table which Deirdre had often used for spreading out maps, facsimiles of manuscripts, and other documents.

When she stepped through the office door, she found a workman in blue overalls just folding up a stepladder.

"I've replaced all the lightbulbs for you, Miss Falling Hawk. They were beginning to flicker. And I used natural light fluorescents. That should help make it a bit less like a dungeon in here." A grin showed through his curly red beard. "Unless you're into that sort of thing, in which case I could switch them back."

She smiled. "No, the lights are wonderful. Thank you, Fergus."

Whistling, he carried his stepladder out the door. Deirdre walked around the office, exploring, and soon realized the lightbulbs weren't all that had been changed. The filing cabinets and bookshelves were empty. So were the drawers in each of the desks. All of the books, papers, notes, and drawings she and

Farr had accumulated over the years were gone. But why had the Seekers taken their files?

To pick them apart, Deirdre. To analyze them and see if there was anything in them about your otherworldly connections which you hadn't mentioned.

A crushing weight filled her. It had taken years to accumulate, index, and cross-reference all of the information in those files. Now she was going to have to start over completely from scratch.

Or was she? Deirdre reached into her pocket and pulled out her new ID card, turning it over. The crimson number 7 shone like wet blood. Maybe everything she had had before was right here in her hand—everything and more.

She slipped the card back into her pocket and moved to one of the desks. There was a working phone, a stapler, a pencil holder filled with sharpened pencils, and a box of paper clips. That was all. She had left her new computer at her flat. There was nothing she could do here; she might as well go home.

On her way out she looked for Sasha, but Madeleine the receptionist said she was in a meeting. Deirdre didn't really know what Sasha did for the Seekers. She didn't conduct research or perform investigations. All Deirdre knew was that Sasha was some sort of attaché to the director of Operations. Whatever her job description was, she always seemed to know far more about what went on around here than Deirdre did. Deirdre had hoped Sasha could tell her what happened to Deirdre and Farr's files. It could wait.

"Will we see you tomorrow, Miss Falling Hawk?" Madeleine asked, glancing up from her computer.

Deirdre stepped into the elevator, then turned around. "I'll be in by nine," she said, and the silver doors whooshed shut.

As she walked through the gate in front of the Charterhouse, she noticed a pair of technicians in white shirts huddled over the security card reader. The front of the card reader was open, and the men picked at its innards with needle-nosed pliers. The technicians spoke in annoyed voices, and Deirdre caught the words *gum* and *tissue*. She stuck her hands in her pockets and quickened her pace.

She walked along the iron fence that surrounded the Seeker

complex and in her mind went over her conversation with Nakamura. Why had they assigned her a new partner? She didn't buy the line that it was simply standard procedure.

Stop it, Deirdre. Farr was the one obsessed with conspiracy theories. Nakamura said you're the senior partner, so it's probably just some neophyte they want you to train, that's all.

A rough croak sounded above her, and Deirdre looked up. A raven perched on top of the fence, staring down at her with eyes like onyx beads. A breeze ruffled black feathers as it opened its beak, letting out another raucous call.

Deirdre halted on the sidewalk. In many Native American myths, Raven was a trickster—often a troublemaker, but sometimes a creator and even occasionally a hero. In one story, it was Raven who rescued the Sun when it was stolen, and who restored its light to the world.

Ravens were also important in Norse mythology, in which they were symbols of battle and wisdom. It was said two ravens named Hugin and Munin—Thought and Memory—sat on the god Odin's shoulders. They flew out over Midgard each day, searching for fallen warriors worthy enough to be brought back to Odin's great hall, Valhalla.

Yet Deirdre knew that in many myths and cultures of old, ravens were not such noble creatures. Instead they were seen as carrion eaters—harbingers of death and decay, followers of strife and destruction. For some reason it was these myths and stories that came to her as she gazed up at the bird. It cocked its head, watching her.

"Go away," she whispered.

With a loud croak, the bird spread its wings and swooped down to a patch of scarlet-stained fur in the middle of the street. It was a dead squirrel, or perhaps even a cat; it was too flattened for Deirdre to tell. The bird hopped toward the dead thing and picked at it.

A shrill sound pierced the air, and Deirdre stumbled back a step. A van as black as the raven's feathers sped down the street. The shadowy driver behind the windshield honked again. The bird spread its wings and sprang off the pavement.

It was too slow. The van struck the raven. There was a wet thud, and black feathers flew in all directions. Without slowing, the van cruised past Deirdre. On its side was painted a capital letter D merging with a white crescent moon.

Duratek. It seemed as if they were everywhere. They were constantly in the news, and a dozen times a day Deirdre saw the ghostly crescent emblazoned on cars, T-shirts, cell phones, computer screens, and store windows. Every time she turned on the TV, one of their commercials was blaring—a pageant of surreal landscapes, perfect houses, and blankly smiling people that advertised nothing and everything at once.

The van rounded a corner and was gone. In the street lay a small black heap. Feathers fluttered in the wind, but otherwise the thing was motionless. Deirdre forced her eyes away from the dead raven and continued on.

When she reached the Blackfriars tube station, she didn't descend the steps. It was a good three miles back to her flat on the south side of Hyde Park, but what reason did she have to hurry? She kept walking, her boots scuffing out a steady rhythm on the sidewalk. Near Charing Cross, a cozy-looking coffee shop caught her eye, and she stopped in for some late breakfast. To her chagrin, the shop turned out to be a chain restaurant. It only annoyed her further that the coffee was rich and perfectly bitter, and the pancakes set before her were flavored with just a touch of real vanilla and melted in her mouth.

That was the danger of big corporate chains. Not that they were often so horrible—but rather that sometimes they were disturbingly good.

That's how Duratek will win in the end. Even those of us who know better will be seduced. We'll drink their perfect coffee, drive their luxurious cars, and wear their fashionable clothes, and in our satisfaction we'll forget to think about the people—the whole worlds—that were exploited to bring those things to us.

She cleaned her plate, emptied her cup, and left a large tip for the khaki-clad waiter. On her way out she passed a newspaper box, and the headline caught her eye. The U.S. stock market was continuing to crash, dragging the world economy with it. However, a subheading noted, one stock was defying the trend and continuing to surge upward: Duratek. Deirdre turned and walked on.

Something more than an hour later, she stepped through the

oor of her flat and saw the light blinking on the answering ma-
hine. Even as she punched the PLAY button, she knew it would
e Hadrian Farr's accentless voice that would emanate from the
nachine.

"I'm sorry I missed you, Deirdre. I suppose you're at the
Charterhouse, being a good little Seeker just as they want. Do
ne a favor, however, and don't be too good. Somebody has to
eep giving the Philosophers conniptions, and I think you're up
o the job. You have to be your own Philosopher, Deirdre. You're
ne only one you can trust now."

Deirdre pressed her hand to her heart and leaned her head
gainst the wall. She tried to imagine where he was. New York?
1adrid? Istanbul?

"I'm not anywhere you might think I'd be," Farr's voice con-
nued as if to answer her question. "So don't try to find me. My
ourney has begun more quickly than I could ever have guessed.
m not sure when I might be able to contact you again, or if I'll
ave time, but I'll do my best. I owe you that much and—"

A click sounded in the background.

"Well, I believe that's my signal to go. Even if I could tell
ou more, I'm afraid there isn't time. According to my watch, in
ven more seconds the Seekers will know exactly where I am.
ood-bye, Deirdre."

The synthesized voice of the answering machine spoke, in-
rming her there were no more messages. Deirdre hesitated,
en picked up the phone, listening to the steady sound of the
al tone. Then she caught it: a clicking noise, just like the one
ne had heard while Farr was talking.

"Who's there?" she said.

Another click. She slammed down the phone and moved
vay. So her line was tapped. Nakamura had lied—they were
ill watching her.

*No, Deirdre. It's not you they're watching. It's Hadrian. They
new he was likely to call here. You can't blame them, can you?
u would have done the same.*

Her outrage cooled. Wherever he was, Farr had his quest,
d so did she. Deirdre sat at the table and turned on the com-
ter. She pulled her ID card from her pocket, wiped it off, and

inserted it. The screen flickered, then glowing green words appeared.

Welcome to Echelon 7.
What do you want to do?
>

Deirdre's fingers hovered above the keyboard. What did she want to do? Search for something—but what? There was no point in doing another search on the words Child Samanda had spoken. The only file that query returned had been deleted the moment she found it.

She still wondered what that file had contained. It had to be important—so important the watcher would do anything, even risk drawing notice, to keep the file's contents from being discovered. However, right now there was something else that weighed on her mind.

She gazed at the ring on her right hand—the ring Glinda had given her at Surrender Dorothy, just before the fire. Deirdre had never been able to decipher the writing engraved inside the band. She thought for a moment, then began to type.

Identify all cases that include samples of nonhuman
DNA. Cross-reference with cases that contain
instances of written inscriptions of unknown language
affinity. Display linked files.
[Enter]

The computer emitted a chime as a dozen session windows sprang into being. Deirdre leaned closer as a single word pulsed at the top of the screen. *Seeking*...

It was only when she realized the glow of the computer was the brightest thing in the room that the passage of time finally impinged upon her. She leaned back from the table and stretched, causing her spine to emit a distinct *crunch*. Outside the flat's windows, dusk had fallen. Dead leaves swirled by the glass, causing the lights of the city to flicker like stars. Her stomach growled; the pancakes had been a long time ago.

She stood and switched on the lamp by the sofa, bathing the

om in amber light, then glanced again at the computer screen.
he still wasn't certain exactly what it was she had found, only
at all of her instincts as an investigator told her it was impor-
nt.

In one of the open session windows, a chromosome map
rolled by. The map was from a mitochondrial DNA sequence,
banded series of genes delineated in blues, oranges, and pur-
es. In another window was the scanned photo of a marble key-
one, removed from an arched doorway. An inscription was
graved on the keystone; however, the stone was chipped and
ttered, its surface stained with soot and some other dark sub-
ance, so that the inscription was almost completely illegible.

Almost. The writing on the stone was too incomplete to have
en transcribed into the Seekers' language files. That was why
match had come up months ago, when Deirdre first per-
rmed a search on the writing on Glinda's ring. However, once
e magnified and enhanced the image, the similarities were ap-
rent to her eye despite the fragmentary nature of the inscrip-
n. The writing on Glinda's ring and the keystone were exactly
same—the same symbols written in the same order.

That wasn't the only similarity. Just like the inscription on
keystone, the DNA sequence was fragmentary. It was taken
m a sample that had been collected nearly two centuries ago,
the same London location from which the keystone was re-
ved. The sample had been analyzed only recently, as part of
ongoing effort to sequence all biological matter—hair, blood,
ne—contained in the Seeker vaults before time took its toll
d any hope of doing so was lost.

Despite the poor quality of the sample, computer analysis
termined there was significant similarity between the partial
A sequence and the sequence Deirdre had performed on the
mple of Glinda's blood she had collected. The case to which
keystone and the partial DNA sequence were related had
en closed in 1816. Now, once again, Deirdre had found a con-
ction between a long-forgotten case and a modern investiga-
n. Without doubt, the 1816 case was linked to Glinda. But
w?

"Maybe it's simpler than you think." She sat at the computer
d quickly typed a query.

Identify the location where the biological sample and
keystone from the case 1816-11a were collected.
Superimpose result on a map of present-day London.
[Enter]

The computer chimed, and a new window opened, covering
the others. It showed a map of London. A red star blinked in th
center of the map. Deirdre leaned closer, reading the word o
the map just below the star: Brixton.

Surrender Dorothy. It had to be; it made too much sense. I
1816, the Seekers had collected samples with otherworldly con
nections from a building in Brixton—the same building tha
nearly two centuries later, housed the nightclub.

*So the Seekers were aware of Surrender Dorothy. At least a
one time they were.*

Or was it the other way around? Maybe it wasn't chance th
Deirdre had met Glinda that day in the Sign of the Green Fair

*They knew about the Seekers—Glinda, Arion the doorma
all of them—and they were desperate for help. Duratek was u
ing them, hoping their blood might open a gate to Eldh. Wh
else could they turn to?*

Only it had been too late. Deirdre hadn't been able to he
them. That night, Surrender Dorothy had burned, taking i
strange denizens with it.

Deirdre twirled the silver ring on her finger. "Who were yo
Glinda? You and the others. You weren't quite fairies. But yo
weren't quite human, either. So where did you come from? Ar
why were you in London?"

She opened a new session window on the computer. The
had to be more answers in the Seekers' files. And with Echelo
7, she was going to find them. She started a new query, one
call up all otherworldly cases located in London in the last fo
hundred years, but before she could finish typing the scre
went blank.

Deirdre frowned. Was the battery dead? She started to che
it, then froze. Words scrolled across the screen.

> You'll never find it that way.

She stared at the computer. She hadn't done that; her hands weren't even on the keyboard. The words pulsed slowly, like a slow laugh. Deirdre moistened her lips, then touched her fingers to the keys.

Find what? [Enter]

> What you're seeking.

The reply had come quickly, as if the person on the other end had been waiting for it. If it was even a person at all. Deirdre thought a moment, then typed.

Who are you? [Enter]

> A friend.
> Make that a secret friend.

Again the reply came quickly, but somehow these words were not comforting.

If you're a friend, where can I find you? [Enter]

> Look out your window, Miss Falling Hawk.

Dread spilled into Deirdre's chest. Her body seemed to move of its own volition as she rose from the chair and moved to the window. Outside, full night had fallen. A few cars passed down the quiet side street; a cat ran along the sidewalk. Then she saw it across the way: a dark figure standing just on the edge of a pool of light beneath a streetlamp. The figure moved. Had it nodded? There was something in its hands.

"Why are you watching me?" she whispered. "What do you want?"

A chime sounded behind her. She turned and glanced at the computer screen.

> I want the same thing you do.
> To understand.

So the other was listening as well as watching. Later she would tear the flat apart and find the bug. Now she kept her back to the window. "I don't believe you," she said, the words sharp and angry this time.

More words scrolled across the computer screen.

> He's coming.
> You should be careful of what other eyes see.

A knock sounded at the door. Deirdre had to bite her tongue to keep from letting out a cry. At the same moment, the computer screen flickered; the words vanished, and the results of Deirdre's previous searches reappeared—the keystone and the DNA analysis. She glanced again out the window. The pool of light beneath the streetlamp was empty.

Another knock sounded at the door, this one more impatient than the last.

"Coming!" Deirdre called out. She slammed the computer shut, then headed for the door. Her hands were shaking, and she fumbled with the dead bolt before jerking the door open.

A man she had never seen before stood in the hallway. At first she wondered if he was the one she had glimpsed beneath the streetlamp. But she had seen the other just seconds before the knock came at her door; he couldn't have gotten all the way up to her third-floor flat so quickly. Besides, the dark silhouette she had seen had been tall and slender, almost willowy.

In contrast, the man before her was not particularly tall and anything but willowy. The elegant lines of his Italian suit were mostly defeated by the muscles that bulged beneath, straining the fabric. His white-blond hair was cropped close to his head; nor was its color natural, given his short, dark beard. His eyes were shockingly blue above craggy, pitted cheeks.

Deirdre was too startled to say anything but, "Can I help you?"

The man smiled, his blue eyes crinkling. The effect was quite riveting.

"I'm Anders," he said in a voice at once gravelly and offensively cheerful. She couldn't quite place the accent. New Zealand? Australia? "I'm sure Nakamura told you about me. I blew into town earlier than I expected. You weren't at the office, so I thought I'd stop by."

Deirdre tried to comprehend these words but failed utterly. "Excuse me, but who the hell are you?"

Still smiling, he held out a large hand.

"Come now, Deirdre. That's no way to greet your new partner."

16.

If Travis had thought returning to Denver would be like coming home again, then he was wrong. All of those thoughts and feelings that might occur to one when considering the word *home*—things like warmth and comfort and safety—were only shadows here. They were thin and vaporous things, haunting every street corner, fogging every bright shop window: reminders of what was lost and could never be regained. No, this was not his home, and he was anything but safe.

Travis shoved raw hands into the pockets of his battered parka as he trudged down Sixteenth Street. He kept watch out of the corners of his eyes, glancing left and right, staying vigilant as he always must. The sky was as gray as the cement beneath his duct-taped sneakers, and hard bits of ice fell from above like shards of glass. He hunched his shoulders toward his ears. The kindly Chinook winds of January had blown east across the plains weeks ago, and the fast-melting snows of spring were still a month away. It was February, it was cold, and he had nowhere to stay for the coming night.

He peered into brightly lit stores as he passed by. The people in them smiled as they purchased designer shoes or sipped steaming coffee drinks. When they were ready, they would dash out to cars already warmed by waiting valets and speed away home. No one lingered out on the street; no one, that was, except those who had nowhere else to go. Travis's feet scuffed to a halt, and he stared into a men's clothing store, thinking how he might go in and get warm for a moment.

But only a moment. Then a clerk, or possibly two, would

hurry up to him and speak in low voices that he had to leave, that if he didn't, they would call the police. Travis knew from experience they would do just that. Then he would be back outside, and the brief flirtation with warmth would only make the cold more bitter. It was better not to go in at all.

As he turned away, he caught a reflection of himself in the store window. His beard and hair were shaggy and unkempt: copper flecked with more gray than he ever would have guessed. His face was haggard beyond his thirty-four years, and dirt smudged his coat and ill-fitting jeans. But it was the eyes that would truly startle the clerks: gray, set deep into his face, and as haunted as the streets of this city. They were the eyes of a man with nowhere left to go.

He hadn't planned on being homeless in Denver in February. Then again, he supposed no one did. However, the gold coins he had brought from Eldh had fetched far less than he had hoped they would at the pawnshop on East Colfax where he had finally been able to sell them.

At first, all of the pawnbrokers he approached had seemed suspicious of the coins. He and Grace had sold Eldhish coins for money once before in Denver. Had agents from Duratek visited the area pawnshops, telling their proprietors to be on the lookout for a man or woman selling strange coins?

Travis didn't know. All the same, he went into a hardware store and, in a back aisle, used a file to smooth away the writing on the coins. After that he managed to sell them, but for less than a third of what he had been counting on. Still, it had been enough money to last several weeks if he was careful. He didn't need much—just enough to find out where in the country Duratek had hidden the gate and to get himself there.

However, focused as he was on Duratek Corporation, he had forgotten to worry about more mundane dangers. He would never know who they were or how they found out about the money. Maybe they had seen him selling the coins at the pawnshop earlier that day, or maybe the shop owner himself had told them. It didn't matter. That night he rented a room in a cheap motel. He left to get some food, and when he returned he found the door of his room ajar, the lock broken. Inside, the bed and dresser had been torn apart. The money, which he had placed beneath the Gideon Bible in the nightstand, was gone. All he had were the few dollars in his pocket left over from buying dinner.

After Travis told the motel's manager of the break-in, she had called the police. By the time the black-and-white cruiser pulled into the parking lot, Travis was already walking away down Colfax, head down. He didn't dare let himself believe the police had stopped looking for him and Grace. Without money and with nowhere to go, he had spent the night wandering the cold streets of Denver.

Tonight was going to be no different.

Travis put his back to the store window and started down the street. He supposed he could walk the ten blocks to the home-less shelter, though there was little point. By this late in the day all of the beds would be claimed. He had planned to head over to the shelter earlier, but he had gotten caught up in the books he had been reading at the Denver Public Library, and he had lost track of time.

The library was a neoclassical fortress of cast stone guarding the south edge of downtown, and it was one establishment people like him weren't automatically thrown out of—at least not if they followed the rules. On the coldest days, when he couldn't stand to be outside, he would clean himself up as best he could in the public rest room, and if he sat at a table and quietly read books, he could stay there as long as he wanted.

Of course, the security guards patrolled by frequently and cast hard looks at him, and he knew no matter how tired he was—no matter how much he wanted to lay his head on the table or, better yet, curl up on the carpet that was softer than anything he had slept on in weeks—he knew he didn't risk it. The moment he slept instead of read, he would be loitering, and the guards would toss him out, and maybe write him up so he could never come back. So he read book after book, and when his brain could no longer force the dancing letters into compre-hensible order, he would simply stare with his eyes open and turn a page every few minutes. Then, after that poor facsimile of rest, he would blink, get up, and find another book.

Usually when he was at the library he spent his time in the Western history collection. It was there, just that afternoon, in a bound book of crackling yellow newspapers, that he finally found what he had been searching for. It was a copy of the Castle City Clarion from December 26, 1883. His eyes blurred as he read the title of the first entry in the Obituaries section:

Maude Carlyle, aged 35, hosteller, of consumption

Beneath that was a second entry:

Bartholomew Tanner, aged 37, former sheriff, by his own hand, of a revolver wound to the head

Travis ran a shaking finger over the page as he read the obituaries, but they were short and offered little information, and there were no pictures. Which of them had gone first? Only he knew. Tanner had wanted to spend Maude's last days together with her. And when she was done with this life, so was he. Travis stared, not understanding, as dark blots spread over the page, and only after a while did he realize they were his own tears.

He was still staring at the book when a security guard touched him on the shoulder and told him he had to leave. At first Travis thought he must have fallen asleep in his reverie, that he was being kicked out. Then the announcement came over the loudspeaker that the library was closing. He had hastily shelved the book and hurried out into the failing day.

Travis was right. By the time he made it to the homeless shelter there was already a cluster of men waiting outside the door for any last bed that might become available. Some of the men looked at him through narrowed eyes, and he hurried on; he would find no shelter there tonight.

He supposed he could try one of the churches, but most were a long walk away, and they were likely to be filled as well on a night as cold as this—what few still offered shelter for the homeless. Every day, the newspapers Travis retrieved from waste bins bore news darker than the last. More company closures and layoffs, more bombs planted in shopping malls and random shootings, more strange new diseases without cause or cure. The flood of charity had thinned to a trickle; most churches had been forced to shut their doors to the needy and had become beggars themselves.

Most, but not all. As he walked, Travis looked up. It loomed against the skyline north of downtown, on the other side of the river, as sharp and imposing as a mountain. Only this mountain was not made of stone, but rather of steel and glass. The first time he had seen it, the structure had still been under construction. Now light welled forth from within, like the radiance of heaven spilling through bleak clouds, gold and hard—beautiful but forbidding.

Some of the other men Travis had spoken with from time to time said that you could still get charity at the Steel Cathedral. All you had to do was fall on your knees, confess your sins, and pledge your soul, and you'd get a soft bed and all the hot food you could eat. Only if that was true, why was there a line outside the homeless shelter? Maybe it was just that most people didn't want or need to be saved. All they wanted was some food and a safe place to sleep. Because being poor wasn't a sin, and offering up one's soul seemed like an awfully high price to pay for a bunk and a bowl of soup.

Or maybe souls were cheaper than he thought these days—another side effect of the faltering economy.

He kept walking, not sure where he was going, only knowing it would be colder if he stopped moving. His belly rumbled, but he still had three dollars—money earned from collecting bottles and cans out of trash bins—and that would be enough to buy him a hamburger and a cup of coffee. The garish sign of a fast-food establishment loomed in the night. He would eat—slowly, lingering in the harsh fluorescent warmth as long as possible—then he would decide where to go after that.

The glowing yellow sign filled his vision, and he thought of Calavere's great hall, of the fire that would be roaring even now in the massive fireplace, and of the roasted venison and flagons of wine that would lade the tables. However, it wasn't the thought of food and warmth that caused his breath to fog on the air. It was the faces he could picture sitting at the high table.

Grace and Aryn on either side of a blustering King Boreas. Lirith, Sareth, and good, solid Durge. Melia and Falken, speaking in mysterious whispers as always. And on opposite ends of the table, a fair-haired knight with green eyes, and a woman in sleek black leather, her eyes as gold as moons....

He clenched his jaw and stared at the fluorescent interior of the fast-food restaurant, letting the light burn away the visions. He couldn't let himself think about them. It would only lead to despair. Or worse yet, to madness. Besides, both Beltan and Vani had made it clear that they no longer needed him. Somehow he had won their love, then just as inexplicably lost it. Only why should he be surprised? He had lost Alice, and Max, and the saloon. When in his life had he ever been able to hold on to anything good?

You don't preserve things, Travis. Not like a doctor, like Grace. You break them, and it's time to quit denying it. Besides, some things need to be broken. That's what Brother Cy said— and Beltan, too.

Only Travis wasn't going to break a world, not like the Witches and the dragon Sfithrisir believed. He was going to break Duratek Corporation and the gate they had created to get to Eldh. And when he was finished, there was something else he was going to break. Some things...

He felt a note of curiosity in his mind. The presence of his old friend Jack Graystone was always there, listening to his every thought. But Travis couldn't let Jack know what he was thinking; Jack would only try to stop him. Travis forced the thoughts from his mind, then stepped off the sidewalk and started across the street.

He froze as a black van cruised silently around a corner just ahead. The crescent moon on the side of the van glowed a sickly orange color in the illumination of sodium streetlights. Travis stumbled back, folding himself into the shadow of an empty atrium, and watched.

The vehicle pulled into the parking lot of the fast-food joint. The door opened, and the driver climbed out, a young man in a black uniform, the same crescent moon emblazoned on the back of his nylon jacket. In his hands was a black plastic tablet with a shimmering green screen. The driver looked around, then headed into the restaurant.

Travis had seen them use the tablets before. The man was a technician, coming to check on the electronic systems installed in the restaurant. It seemed as if almost every store these days used Duratek systems for inventory, communication, and security. No one used a credit card, accessed a computer, or made a phone call without Duratek knowing about it—Travis had learned that quickly enough.

The morning after he fled the police at the motel, he fished a newspaper out of a trash can and read about the contract the city of Denver had signed with Duratek Corporation. Despite the positive spin presented in the article, Travis could only imagine it had been a desperate act, one intended to pacify the anxious populace of Denver. Or had the mayor been compelled by other factors—by money or threats?

Whatever the reason, the city had hired Duratek Corporation and their technology to assist the police in maintaining security. And while that might have made the people of Denver feel safer, no doubt that security came with a price beyond mere dollars. Travis could not bring himself to believe the well-being of Denver's citizens was truly Duratek's primary concern.

After that, he had thought about getting out of Denver as quickly as possible. His goal was to find the gate Duratek was using to send its agents across the Void to Eldh. Just where the gate was located, Travis didn't know. Duratek was a multinational conglomerate; it could be anywhere in the world. All he knew was that, somehow, he would find it—and then he would destroy it, along with any hopes they might have of creating another.

A grand plan began to form in his mind. He would seek out their corporate headquarters, he would blast open the polished doors of their boardroom with the power of the Great Stones, and Duratek's highest executives would cower before him. They would tell him where the gate was located, or they would suffer the wrath of his runes.

There was just one problem with the plan: It was utterly hopeless.

When Travis ventured into the bus terminal, he saw sleek

Duratek computer systems poised on the ticketing counter. It was the same at the train station, and no doubt at the airport as well. They were monitoring all ways out of the city, keeping watch. Keeping watch for him and Grace.

Not that it made a difference. After the robbery at the motel, he didn't have the money for a cab ride, let alone a trip on a bus or airplane. Nor was getting a job to earn more money an option. Thanks to the new security contract, every business in Denver was required to screen new employees using Duratek's systems.

The plan crumbled in Travis's mind. Wracking his brain, he tried to concoct an alternative, but he came up with nothing. He couldn't use the Stones to destroy the gate if he couldn't get to it. And tempting as the thought was, he couldn't use the Imsari to return to Eldh, because that would only make it easier for the Pale King to gain them and surrender them to Mohg.

As the days passed, it grew increasingly difficult to think about how to destroy the gate and stop Duratek, and his thoughts became occupied instead with more basic concerns, like keeping warm, and wondering how he could get some food in his aching stomach, and where he could find shelter when blue night fell over the city. Duratek wasn't his only enemy now. So were cold, and hunger, and the danger of living on the street.

And those enemies were winning.

Inside the restaurant, the technician pulled a stylus from the tablet and began writing on its screen as he spoke to the clerk behind the counter. There would be no going into the burger place now. The technician wouldn't be so caught up in his work that he wouldn't notice a homeless man come in, and Travis had no doubt his photo and description—as well as Grace's—had been distributed to every employee who worked for Duratek Corporation. Much as he wanted to, he couldn't believe they had given up searching for him. What would they do if they found him and the two Stones in his pocket?

Travis had no desire to find out. Despite his growling stomach, he turned and hurried away down the street.

17

Half an hour later, cold and stiff from walking, Travis pushed through the door of a bar in an industrial neighborhood just far enough from downtown to have rebuffed any encroaching gentrification. The air was sour with smoke and disinfectant, and the decor was not so much cozy as claustrophobic. However, the establishment had one compelling feature; on the bar, rather than a sleek computer unit, was a cash register that looked like it hadn't been wiped off once in its decade-spanning history. This bar didn't use Duratek systems, and that was why Travis came here from time to time.

That, and the fact that the beer was cheap and they served free peanuts.

The place was all but deserted, and what few patrons there were seemed more intent on their glasses than on Travis. He sat at the bar, showed his money to the bartender, and ordered a beer. The man plunked down a glass in front of him, pale brew slopping over the edge and onto the scarred wood of the bar. In this place, they didn't bother with niceties like cocktail napkins.

The bartender halfheartedly dabbed at the spill with a grimy rag, then started to turn away.

Travis cleared his throat. "Peanuts?"

The bartender glared at him, then grabbed a big bowl from behind the bar and pushed it across the bar. "Only as long as you're drinking."

Travis nodded. He could drink slowly.

He took a sip of the beer—it was none too fresh—then shelled and ate boiled peanuts with deliberate motions. It wasn't much of a meal, but it was better than nothing, and better than he had gotten some days. When the bartender wasn't looking, he shoved a handful of peanuts into a coat pocket.

I must say, this is absolute madness, Travis, Jack's voice spoke in his mind. *You shouldn't be here, scrounging for crumbs. You're a runelord, by Olrig—you should be back on Eldh, standing with Queen Grace against the Pale King.*

These words pricked at Travis's heart; he hated feeling like he had abandoned Grace to face her fate alone. However, Jack was wrong. Eldh was Grace's world; she belonged there. But this was his world, and if it was up to her to fight the Pale King on Eldh, then it was up to him to stop Duratek here on Earth.

Only he didn't see how he could. Even after everything he had learned since returning to Denver, up until tonight he had still clung to a fragment of hope. However, it was as if being forced to run from the burger joint had leeched the last drops of resolve from him. He was tired and cold and trapped, and if he couldn't get out of Denver, there was nothing he could do to stop Duratek.

Yet that didn't mean there was nothing at all he could do. Maybe he could help Grace and Eldh after all. Because if Plan A wasn't going to work, there was always Plan B. . . .

What are you intending, Travis? An anxious note sounded in Jack's voice. *You're not hiding something from me, are you? I gather that destroying Duratek's gate was your Plan A. So what in the world is this Plan B?*

"Never mind, Jack," Travis said.

The bartender shot him a dark look, then turned up the sound on the television above the bar. The local news was on—the usual parade of unrest, violence, and disaster.

Travis ignored it, gazing down at his hands. A thin scar that ran across the back of his right hand—the only trace left of the wound through which a drop of the scarab's blood had entered. The power of blood sorcery flowed in him now, along with the power of rune magic. Travis didn't know what that meant, only that there had to be a way to use that power. Blood sorcery had its source in the *morndari*, the ravenous, bodiless spirits who inhabited the Void between worlds. Their power was that of consuming, of destruction; he had learned that when he faced the demon—one of the *morndari* bound in rock—in the Etherion. Could there be a way to use sorcery to do what he intended?

"—and her report on more rumored disappearances among the homeless," blared a tinny male voice.

Travis glanced up. The bartender had turned up the volume on the TV another notch. Doe-eyed local reporter Anna Ferraro was on-screen, standing in front of Union Station downtown. Travis had noticed before how men tended to stop and stare vacantly every time Anna Ferraro appeared on TV, though he couldn't quite understand the attraction. She was pretty in a thin and fawnish way, but there was something about her—a calculating air—that left him cold. She reported about death and disaster with a glint in her eye, as if she could see the ratings going up even as she spoke. The bartender remained fixated on the screen, and Travis took the opportunity to sneak another handful of peanuts into his coat pocket, cleaning out the bowl.

On the TV, Anna Ferraro launched into her report with apparent relish. "That's right, Dirk. I'm here in downtown Denver tonight, where I've been speaking with people who don't have homes as you or I do, and who actually live on the streets." She wrinkled her nose in an expression that was at once sympathetic and repulsed. "But it's not just the cold that these men and woman are worrying about tonight. Many of the homeless are telling stories about how others who live on the street have vanished without a trace in recent days. There are unconfirmed reports of at least seven missing, and the number may be higher. However, the Denver police have yet to take any action."

She lowered her microphone and looked out of the TV expectantly. After an awkwardly long moment, the report cut to videotape of a police officer—a Sergeant Otero, according to the text at the bottom of the screen—standing outside the Denver police station, a microphone jammed in his face. "—and we're not taking action because no official missing person reports have been filed," he said.

A cutaway to Anna Ferraro, a coy expression on her heavily madeup face. "But isn't it true that an address and telephone number are required to file such a report? And homeless people, as I'm sure you know, don't have addresses."

The sergeant squinted, obviously annoyed. "We take all reports seriously. However, right now there is no evidence that anyone is actually missing—"

From the way his lips moved, the sergeant had gone on to say something more, but his words were muted, and the scene cut back to Anna Ferraro in front of Union Station.

"There you have it," she said triumphantly. "Right now the police are refusing to help in this matter, so the homeless of

Denver can do nothing but wonder tonight." She gave the camera a long look. "And fear. This is Anna Ferraro reporting in downtown Denver. Back to you at the station, Dirk."

Dirk the anchorman looked startled, then smiled blankly at the camera. "Thanks for that fascinating report, Anna. Coming up next, we have an exclusive interview with Denver's deputy mayor. She's going to tell us how the test of the new security program, launched last month in association with Duratek Corporation, is making our city safer than ever. After that, we've got the latest weather forecast. It looks like it's going to be cold, cold, cold over the next few days, so—"

The bartender turned the sound back down. He turned around and gave the empty bowl of peanuts in front of Travis a suspicious look, then swapped it out with a full one. Travis smiled and took another sip of his tasteless beer.

He didn't know if the reports of disappearances among the homeless had any truth to them. At the shelter the other day, he had overheard a group of men talking in whispers about others who had vanished, but the stories were second- and third-hand. Whether the rumors were true or not, one thing Travis did know was that he wasn't safe in Denver. Nobody was.

Every day the newspaper headlines blared word of the latest shootings, wars, and biological scares. People were constantly afraid—afraid of anything and anyone that was at all strange or unfamiliar. When people were afraid, they were all too willing to give up their freedom in exchange for the illusion of feeling safe. Just as the people of Denver had done by inking that contract with Duratek. They believed they were safe from the monsters now, but they were wrong. They had locked the monster in the room with them.

Travis's gaze focused back on the television. The news was over, and now the image on the screen was that of a man in a white suit. His black hair swept up from his forehead, shellacked into a glistening wave. The volume was too low to hear what he was saying, but he prowled back and forth on the stage, gesticulating with stiff energy. A choir of bland-faced young men and women was arranged behind him, though they weren't singing.

The scene cut to a shot of a rapt audience. Mouths hung

pen, and tears streamed down faces. The camera panned across
he seated crowd, and Travis saw glass and sculpted metal soar-
ng to a ceiling so dizzying it made him think of the Dome of the
Etherion in Tarras.

So it was the Steel Cathedral, only seen from the inside.
Travis hadn't realized just how big it really was. There must
have been two thousand people in that audience. The scene cut
back to the man onstage, pulling in so tight that Travis could see
he way his pancake makeup cracked as he spoke. The man
eemed at once excited, angry, and exultant. A computer-
generated title appeared at the bottom of the screen:

Sage Carson, Pastor of the Steel Cathedral

In a way, the pastor reminded Travis of Brother Cy. Both
were tall, edging toward lanky, and both obviously knew how to
old an audience in thrall. However, Sage Carson's white attire
was modern and well tailored, unlike Brother Cy's dusty black
coffin suit. And while Brother Cy's angry preaching had always
een softened by sorrow, even without being able to hear him,
Travis could tell this Sage Carson exuded only do-as-I-say-or-
e-damned righteousness. By the looks on their faces, the audi-
nce was eating it up. But then, deep down, most people liked
eing told what to do. It was so much easier than thinking.

"So are you going to buy another round or not?" The bar-
ender's growling voice startled Travis.

"No, sorry," he muttered.

His glass was empty. He must have finished the last sip with-
ut thinking. He stood and shoved his hands in his coat pockets.
A stray peanut fell out, and the bartender glared at him. Travis
hurried toward the door.

"Don't come back, you hear?" the bartender called out after
im.

Travis headed out into the frigid night. The door of the bar
ut behind him: one more way that was barred to him.

*But the way's not barred, Travis. You could go back to Eldh.
All you have to do is use the Stones. They have the power to take
ou there. Jack said they do.*

For a moment he let the image of Calavere's great hall fill

him. He imagined Grace smiling, drawing him close to the fire, handing him a cup of spiced wine.

Then a different vision rose up within him, blotting out the image of friends and fire like a black cloud: the sun went dark, the ground shook and cracked apart, the walls of Calavere came tumbling down, and darkness swallowed the world.

No, he wouldn't let that happen. Maybe he couldn't get to Duratek, but he would keep Mohg from getting the Great Stones. He gripped the iron box in his pocket and headed into the frosty night.

Ten minutes later, he stood at the top of an embankment. Below, the half-frozen waters of the Platte River oozed among small islands of sand and gravel. There was no place in downtown where it was safe to start a fire; lighting one was guaranteed to bring the police—along with fingerprint scanners networked to Duratek databases. However, there were a pair of cement-and-steel viaducts here. If he started a fire underneath one of the viaducts, no one would be able to see it from above.

He climbed over a cement barrier and half walked, half slid down the weed-covered embankment. As he reached the bottom, the sounds of the city receded, and the sluggish murmur of water rose on the air. Gravel and ice crunched under his sneakers as he walked toward one of the viaducts. The space under the bridge was veiled by a curtain of shadow even his preternaturally sensitive eyes could not penetrate.

That was good; if there wasn't already a fire beneath the viaduct, it meant no one else had already staked out the place. Hands clamped under his armpits, he trudged across weeds and gravel, then passed into the darkness beneath the viaduct.

The darkness moved. Before Travis could react, an arm coiled around his throat, and a hand clamped over his mouth, muffling his cry of surprise as well as any runes he might have spoken. He reached up, to try to pull away the hands of his unseen attacker, then froze as something glinted in front of his face.

It was a knife, gleaming in a stray beam of moonlight.

"You don't belong here," hissed a man's voice, and the arm tightened around his neck as the knife moved closer.

18.

They must have been waiting for him to step into the shadows. They would have been able to see him walking toward them in the cast-off cityglow, while he had not seen them in the blackness of the viaduct. However, now that he was in the darkness, his eyes—made anew and keener than before in the fires of Krondisar—were starting to adjust. He could just make out the silhouette of the man who held the knife. Travis jerked hard, half-breaking the grip of the other who held him.

"Keep him still!"

"I'm trying," came a voice from behind. "He's stronger than he looks."

Despite the powerful arms that gripped him, Travis might have broken free, except his shoes hit a patch of gravel, skittering out from beneath him. He started to fall, but strong hands hauled him back to his feet. A crunching sound filled Travis's skull as all of the vertebrae in his neck popped.

"Didn't you hear me, you big moron? I said hold him still!"

"You're not going to kill him, are you?"

"Why not? He isn't a cop or anything. He's one of us. I've seen the news—the police could care less what happens to people like us. What's one more disappearance to them?"

"What will we do with the body?"

"I say we cut it up. There are plenty of stray dogs down here by the river. They should take care of the pieces."

Travis's heart lurched as he felt the touch of metal against his cheek. Frantic, he twisted his head, and for a second one of the hands flailed, trying to clamp back down on his mouth.

A second was all Travis needed. *"Dur!"* he said through clenched teeth. There was a cry of pain as the knife went flying away into the dark, followed by a *plop* as it landed in the icy waters of the Platte.

"What the hell . . . ?" The shadow in front of him shook a hand as if it had been stung.

Travis felt the arms holding him go slack. This was his chance. He drove backward with his elbows and was rewarded with an exhalation of pain and surprise. A forward lunge broke him free, but his legs were shakier than he thought. He stumbled and fell to his knees.

"*Sar!*" he gasped, pressing both of his hands against the ground.

The rune was weak, like the rune of iron. The Stones were sealed in the iron box; their power could not help him. However, the magic was enough to lift a dozen pebbles from the ground and send them whizzing through the air. Soft thuds sounded as rocks pelted skin, and yelps of pain rang out.

Travis gained his feet. His eyes had finally adjusted, and he could see the two men. The one who had held the knife spun in circles, yowling; he was a small, pudgy man with rounded shoulders. The other, the one who had grabbed Travis from behind, was tall and scarecrow thin, his long arms waving like the blades of a windmill as he tried to bat away the flying stones. Travis knew he should run, but he found himself laughing instead.

"Stop it!" The shorter man shouted, his voice high-pitched and rasping. "Stop throwing stones!"

"I have," Travis said. The magic had faded away, leaving only an itch in his right hand.

"Oh." The small man stopped spinning.

"How did you do that?" the other man said, his long arms falling back at his sides. His voice had a halting yet musical cadence to it. "You weren't throwing the stones. You said something, and they started flying."

Travis took a step back. He should get out of here; these men were killers. "Why did you pull a knife on me?"

The little one spat a wad of phlegm. "Get a clue, dipstick. We were playing with you, that's all—giving you a little scare for invading our place, and maybe making you think you were going to be the next guy to disappear."

"I told you it was a bad idea," the tall man said.

"Well it's not my fault this jerk doesn't have a sense of humor." The little one glared at Travis. "You didn't have to go all psycho on us."

Travis shoved his right hand into his pocket. "Sorry. I didn't mean to..." There was no use trying to explain. "Sorry." He turned around and started across the gravel.

"Wait!" Heavy boots sounded on gravel behind him. "Wait a minute. You don't have to go."

Travis hesitated, then turned back. The tall man gazed at him with placid brown eyes. His long black hair was streaked with gray. "It's cold tonight, but the viaduct blocks most of the wind. You should stay here with us."

The other man danced a jig of anger on the gravel. "Holy crap, what did you go and do that for, Marty?"

"Maybe he can start a fire," the tall one, Marty, called back. He smiled at Travis. "We haven't had any luck. The wood is so cold it won't catch."

"What makes you think I can do it?"

"You look like a man who can start fires," Marty said, then turned and started back toward the viaduct.

Travis stood still, not sure what to make of those words.

You should leave. You can't trust anybody—you can't know who's working for Duratek.

Even as he thought this, a chill wind whistled over the river, slicing through his thrift-store parka. He drew in a breath, then ducked his head and trudged back toward the dimness of the viaduct.

There was a niche in the cement retaining wall beneath the bridge where the men had set up their makeshift camp. However, it was anything but warm; their breath formed frozen ghosts on the air. Marty introduced himself, along with his associate. The short man's name was Jay, and his sparse black beard framed what seemed to be a permanent scowl. Travis gave them his first name and shook Marty's big hand, but Jay turned his back when Travis tried to repeat the gesture.

"Never mind him," Marty said. "He has a thing about certain kinds of people."

Travis pulled his hand back. "What kinds of people do you mean?"

"The living kind." Marty squatted down beside a pile of unburned sticks. "So, you can get it going, can't you?"

Travis gazed down at the wood. "I suppose I can."

Despite the darkness and his turned back, it was impossible to hide what he was doing. He held a hand toward the sticks and whispered the rune of fire. A tendril of smoke curled up from the wood, but that was it. His rune magic was pathetically weak here on Earth, and while it would have been far stronger if he opened the iron box, he didn't dare. He might end up setting them all on fire. Instead, he spoke the rune with greater force.

"Krond!" Flames leaped up, bright and consuming.

Marty grinned, the sharp planes of his face illuminated by golden light.

"How did you do that?" Jay stood above Travis. "You didn't even use a match. Marty's right—all you've got to do is say some mumbo jumbo and stuff happens. What was that word you said? Tell it to me so I can start a fire."

Travis stared into the flames. "It's not that simple."

"You mean you just don't want to tell me," Jay said, his scowl deepening. "You want to keep the secret for yourself, don't you, you greedy bastard?"

"Believe me, if I could give it to you, I would."

Those words seemed to startle Jay. He opened his mouth, closed it again, then sat next to the fire.

Marty laughed. "You really must be able to do magic, Travis. I've never seen anyone put Jay at a loss for words."

The little man glared at Marty. "And I've never heard you be such a big blabbermouth before, so maybe it *is* voodoo." He turned his hot gaze on Travis. "You're pretty good with the fire stuff. Got any words that'll magic up some food?"

Travis shook his head.

"Well, then what good are you?" Jay's tone was disgusted, but a trace of a smile showed inside his beard as he held his stubby hands toward the fire and rubbed them together.

"My uncle told a story," Marty said, "of a man he knew who could use sticks to find lost jewelry, and I knew a pretty woman who could see the future in a deck of cards. But I've never heard of making a fire with a word."

"I didn't make the fire," Travis said. "Fire is just a transformation. When something burns, all it's doing is moving from one state to another. The heat and light were locked inside the wood all along. All I did was release them."

Jay let out a snort. "Good grief, that sounds like the kind of crap old Sparky is always dumping on anyone stupid enough to listen to him. Still the professor, even though the college gave him the boot years ago. It's all something is nothing, and nothing is everything, and the universe was once the size of a walnut, only now it's flying apart. It makes my brain hurt." He pulled off his stocking cap and rubbed his bald head.

Travis felt a tightness in his chest. "Who is this Sparky person?"

"A smart man," Marty said before Jay could say anything. "He's usually in Civic Center Park in the morning. Although if it snows tonight, he might not be there. His chair gets stuck in the drifts. We can take you to him in the morning, if you'd like."

"What do you mean we?" Jay snapped. "I'm not going near that freak. He makes me feel . . . weird."

"Why is that?" Travis said.

Jay shook his head. "Lots of reasons. All the junk he says. Like the universe is so freaking big, and we're just stupid little specks. But mostly it's his eyes. It's like he's seen things nobody else has. Things maybe no one shouldn't see." Jay licked his lips. "Kind of like your eyes."

Travis opened his mouth, but he had no reply.

"We should get some more wood for the fire," Marty said, standing. "We don't want it to go out on a night like this."

They returned to the viaduct with two pilfered loading pallets to break up for wood—Travis helped Jay with one, while Marty carried the other by himself—and spent a cold but bearable night huddled close to the fire. For a while they spoke in low voices, and Travis learned that Marty and Jay had both come to Denver that summer on a train from Topeka. The two men had met a couple of years ago in Ohio and had been traveling together ever since, slowly making their way west. Travis asked them how long they would keep traveling.

"Until we run out of country to cross," Jay said, firelight shining in his eyes. "Then we'll spend our days on a California beach lying in the sand, eating oysters, and watching the ladies walk by. That's our plan, isn't it, Marty?"

Marty said nothing and used his big hands to break off more wood from one of the pallets. Finally, it grew too late and too cold for talking. At Jay's suggestion, each took a turn keeping watch while the others dozed.

"No creep is going to get us like those other guys who disappeared," Jay said. "That's why Marty and I travel together. It's safer that way." He thrust a finger at Travis. "It's a bad idea to try to go it alone in this world. If that's what you were thinking, then you need to think again."

"I'll take the first watch," Travis said.

While the two men slept on ragged blankets by the fire, Travis pressed a hand to the cement viaduct and whispered *Krond* over and over, until waves of heat radiated from the retaining wall, pushing back the frigid air a few more inches.

After midnight he woke Marty, whose turn it was to keep watch, then he curled up next to the fire, wishing he hadn't sold his old mistcloak in Tarras over a century ago.

The world was filled with gray light when Travis opened his eyes.

"Well, well, it looks like the wizard is finally awake," said a sardonic voice.

For a moment Travis was confused. Everything was the soft color of fog. Was he back in the Gray Tower of the Runespeakers? Master Larad was always mocking him and his power, his scarred face at once disgusted and amused. Except that couldn't be right. All-master Oragien had banished Larad from the Gray Tower for his treachery, and Travis hadn't seen the sharp-tongued runespeaker since.

The sound of thunder rumbled above. Travis sat up and rubbed his eyes, and the world smeared into focus. Marty was rolling up the blankets, and Jay poked at the ashes of the fire with a stick. Sunlight turned the icy-clogged water of the Platte a soft pink, and flakes of cement fell like snow as another truck hurtled over the viaduct above.

"I don't suppose you could get the fire started again, Mr. Wizard," Jay said.

Travis shook his head. "The wood's all gone." It was hard to speak; his jaw was stiff as a rusty hinge.

"What about what you did to the cement wall?" Marty said.

Travis winced. The tall man must not have been asleep after all when Travis worked that magic.

"What do you mean, what he did to the wall?" Jay said, glaring at Marty.

"He means this." Travis pressed his hand against the retaining wall and muttered *Krond* several times, until a comforting warmth radiated from the hot cement.

Jay's eyes bulged from their sockets. "For the love of Pete, how did you do that?"

"The same way I started the fire last night."

"I thought that was just a trick. You know, like a magician pulling a rabbit out of his hat." Jay clamped his hat tighter on his head, as if the force of his surprise might send it flying. "I didn't know you really could do magic."

Travis glanced at Marty, but the tall man appeared as placid as ever. "Now you do."

"Man, that feels good." Jay held his bare hands close to the wall. "I've got to tell someone about this."

"Don't," Travis said.

He hadn't meant the word to sound so harsh. However, Jay took a startled step back. Even Marty raised his eyebrows.

"Sure, man," Jay said, holding up his hands. "Whatever you want. Just don't do anything crazy."

Travis cringed. "No, I didn't mean it like that. I won't do anything to . . . I won't hurt you."

"I know you won't," Jay said, but all the while as they finished gathering their things, his small eyes kept flicking in Travis's direction.

"It didn't snow last night," Marty said, shouldering his frayed backpack. "Sparky will be at Civic Center."

"This early?" Travis said.

"He likes to watch the sunrise."

"Like I told you, he's a goddamn loon," Jay said. The little man wasn't carrying anything; he had stowed his blanket in Marty's pack. "But if we're going to go, then let's go. Do you have any money, Mr. Wizard?"

Travis shook his head. He had spent his last three dollars at the bar.

Jay snorted. "Now why doesn't that surprise me? Well, you provided the heater last night, so I'll buy us all a cup of coffee on the way. Then we'll call it even."

Despite his weariness, Travis couldn't help grinning. He didn't know these men, and he doubted they were trustworthy, but all the same it was good not to be alone in the world. In *this* world. The two men started up the embankment, Jay taking two steps for each one of Marty's lanky strides, and Travis followed after them.

19.

As promised, Jay bought them all Styrofoam cups of coffee at a street vendor's cart at Colfax and Broadway, and they walked beneath a neoclassical colonnade into the broad circle of Civic Center Park just as the sun set fire to the gold-plated dome of the Capitol building.

"It looks like Tarras," Travis murmured, shading his eyes against the fiery glare of the dome.

"It looks like what?" Jay said, squinting at him.

Travis shook his head. "Nothing." He glanced at Marty. "Do you see your friend?"

"Hell's bells, I told you he's not our friend," Jay said. His pudgy hand tightened around his cup, so that coffee shot out the hole in the lid.

"I think he's over there," Marty said. He started across the brown grass, moving fast on his scarecrow legs, so that Travis had to march briskly to keep up, while Jay was forced to break into a terrier-like trot.

Travis saw him when they were halfway across the park. He had positioned his wheelchair in a patch of sunlight, and he basked in the morning radiance, eyes closed. They came to a stop before him, but he didn't open his eyes. He was a grizzled man, about fifty years old. His body was a shapeless lump wrapped in a canvas coat over multiple sweaters, and his legs were short stumps ending at mid thigh, each one covered with a Denver Broncos knit ski cap that matched the one on his head. A metal box with a profusion of dials and knobs rested on his lap. It emitted a low hiss of static.

"Hey, Sparky," Jay said. "What's up?"

"The sun," the man in the wheelchair said, a crooked-toothed grin showing through his matted beard.

Jay scowled at him. "So I noticed."

"Did you?" the man replied, his eyes still shut. "Then you're a smart man, Jay. It took the writings of Galileo to finally convince the world once and for all that it was not the sun that rose in the sky, but rather the Earth that was turning as it revolved around the sun. And even then poor Galileo was arrested by the pope for the crime of heresy. Tell me, would you suffer the same—going to prison for refusing to disavow something you know to be true?"

Jay snorted. "Crap on a cracker, I told you he makes my brain hurt."

The man in the wheelchair laughed and opened his eyes. "That's a good sign, Jay. It means it's working. Hello, Marty. It's nice to see you—you always remind me silence is the better part of wisdom. Who's your friend here?"

"This is Travis," Marty said. "He wants to talk to you."

"Nice to meet you, Travis." He held out a gloved hand. "My name is Caleb Sparkman."

Jay snorted. "Sparkman, Sparky—what's the difference?"

Travis shook his hand. "I hope we're not bothering you."

"Not in the least. Rather, you're a fine distraction."

Travis glanced around the deserted park. "Distraction? From what?"

"From the voices," Marty said.

Travis pulled his hand back. Sparkman smiled up at him. "Don't worry, friend. They're not real. Although they can be quite annoying."

Jay let out a bark of laughter. "A little more than just annoying." He circled behind the wheelchair and leaned on the handles. "See, here's the story, Travis. The professor here used to teach at some of the community colleges around town. Physics and math and crap like that. Only then the voices started talking in his head, and they told him to do stuff."

Sparkman folded his hands and nodded, listening to the story right along with the others.

Jay kept talking, rolling the chair forward a few inches, then back a few. "At first it was just weird little stuff, you know, like shredding all of his files so no one could know what he was thinking, and setting up a machine to make some kind of radio interference so the security cameras in his classroom wouldn't work. Only then it got worse, and the voices told him parts of his own body were being used to track him. Isn't that right, Sparky?"

"It is," he said in an agreeable tone.

"So you know what he did next?" Jay said, eyes glittering. "He cinched a belt around each of his thighs for a tourniquet. Then he took a hatchet, just like the voices told him to do, and he chopped off his own legs."

Travis staggered back a step. He should have tried to hide the horror he knew was written across his face, but he couldn't.

"That's not quite accurate, Jay," Sparkman said, his tone pleasantly argumentative. "The hatchet was too small for the job, as it turned out—I was a good mathematician but a poor carpenter. I lost consciousness before I completed the task the voices gave me. One of my students came upon me in my office, and I was taken to a hospital, where doctors completed the amputations."

Jay laughed and clapped his hands. Marty was silent, gazing at the gold dome of the Capitol.

The bitter coffee churned in Travis's stomach. "You were ill, weren't you?"

Sparkman nodded. "Very much so. But the doctors helped me understand the effects of my psychosis. Knowledge is a powerful thing—a tool that can help you accomplish any task—and it helped me control my illness."

Jay clapped him on the shoulders. "But you still hear the voices, don't you, Sparky?"

"I always will. But I've learned not to listen." He smiled up at Travis. "Still, even after all these years, it's hard to ignore them. They hate not being listened to, and they can get rather vociferous. Which is why the distraction of conversation is most welcome."

Travis turned his head, letting the morning light blind him. Shock melted into sorrow and understanding, and he let out a sigh. What would they think if they knew he heard voices in his head as well—the voices of Jack and all the runelords who had gone before him?

Marty touched Travis's arm. "You should tell Sparkman about your magic."

"That's right," Jay chimed in. "You should have seen it, Sparky. It was freaking amazing. He started a fire just by saying a word."

"Really?" Sparkman appeared interested but not surprised. He looked up at Travis. "You're a magician, then. Were you employing some sort of legerdemain?"

Jay's eyebrows drew together in a thick scowl. "It was no trick, Sparky. I saw it with my own eyes."

"I'm afraid our eyes can deceive us right along with any of our senses," Sparkman said.

Travis sighed. It was wrong, he shouldn't do magic without grave need. Except maybe this was important after all. He held out his hand, palm up, and whispered a rune. *"Lir."*

It condensed instantly from thin air to hover above the palm of his hand: a small orb of light, not gold like the morning sun, but silver-blue. With a flick of his finger, he sent it whizzing through the air. The orb flew between Marty and Jay as the little man swore. It made several orbits around Sparkman's head, then returned to Travis's hand. He squeezed his fingers around it, and the light vanished.

Sparkman's eyes were wide now. He wheeled his chair closer to Travis. "Absolutely fascinating. It looked holographic, only you could move it at will. And unless you've hidden a laser up your sleeve, I have no idea how you created it."

Travis shrugged. "I'm not sure I know, either. But it doesn't matter right now. That's not what I want to talk to you about."

"And what do you want to talk about?"

Travis licked his lips. "Destroying something."

Jay cast a startled look at Marty and Sparkman. "Hell, Travis—you're not going to go and try to blow something up, are you? People could get hurt."

"No," Travis said, holding a hand to his head. It ached from the cheap caffeine, and from fear. "I don't want anyone to get hurt. That's what I'm trying to keep from happening. And that's why I've got to destroy them."

"Destroy what?" Marty said.

Travis wrapped his fingers around the iron box in his pocket. "I can't tell you."

Marty's face was solemn. "Are they something evil?"

Travis shook his head. "No, not in and of themselves. But they could be used to create great evil if the Pale ... if they fell into the wrong hands."

Jay gave him a cockeyed look. "That sounds like something old Sparky here would say. Are you sure you're not hearing voices, too?"

Travis almost laughed. He was quite certain Jack would not want him to do what he intended.

And just what are you intending to do, may I ask? came Jack's testy voice. *You've been awfully secretive lately.*

Travis ignored him.

Sparkman stroked his beard, his expression thoughtful. "Destroying things is a perilous profession. Einstein showed us that a small amount of mass is equivalent to an enormous amount of energy. For example, did you know the nucleus of an atom has less mass than the sum of all the particles within it?"

Travis was beginning to agree with Jay. Talking to Sparkman made his head hurt. "But that seems impossible. Where is the missing mass?"

"It's not missing at all," Sparkman said, smiling as he clapped his gloved hands together. "You see, breaking apart matter releases the force that binds that matter together. The difference in mass is the potential energy that would be released if the nucleus was broken apart." He pulled his hands away from one another. "Of course, you would never be able to break apart just one nucleus. Free particles would strike adjacent atoms causing a chain reaction. And if that reaction is uncontrolled you have—"

"—a nuclear bomb," Travis said.

Sparkman nodded. "At the very least. But then, even today nuclear weapons create imperfect chain reactions. If the reaction was perfect, there would be nothing to stop it from destroying the world. Or even all the universe."

Travis felt sick. There was something important here, something about what Sparkman had just said. However, before h could grasp the answer, a sharp crackle of static broke the silence, followed by a series of beeps and clicks.

"Oh, good," Sparkman said, eyes lighting up. "Here they are now." He fiddled with several knobs on the metal box in his lap. The static faded, and the beeps and clicks grew clearer. "They've been quiet all morning. I was beginning to think they'd gone, but they must still be here."

Travis shook his head. "Who must still be here?"

"Why, the aliens of course."

"The aliens?"

"The ones who've been abducting homeless people for their experiments." Sparkman patted the metal box. "I put together this special radio so I could monitor their transmissions, and I've been listening to them for weeks now. But don't worry— I've made sure they can't track this receiver. Or my thoughts." He pulled off his stocking cap. His bald head was covered with a crinkled dome of aluminum foil.

Jay let out a crowing laugh. "See, Travis? I told you old Sparky was a nut."

"What are the aliens talking about now?" Marty said, his brown eyes serious.

Sparkman bent his head over the receiver, listening. "I'm not certain. This seems to be some sort of encoded data transmission."

Travis's mouth had gone dry. He knelt beside the wheelchair. "If they communicate in code, how do you know they're the ones who are abducting people in Denver?"

"This receiver is rather low power," Sparkman said. "It's range is quite limited, so I know the aliens can't be more than a few miles away. What's more, I've been able to understand some of what they say. They must have collaborators here, because often they speak in English, though even then they use code words in their alien tongue. Still, I've heard enough to be certain the aliens are the ones behind the abductions."

Travis wanted to tell Jay and Marty it was time to go, but before he could speak muffled voices emanated from the receiver.

Sparkman's eyes lit up. "Here we go! Listen."

He turned a knob, and the words grew clearer. "—and have been ordered back to base. Report there as soon as you can. I believe we're to receive new—" The man's voice was lost in another crackle of interference.

"There," Sparkman looked up, smiling. "Did you hear that?"

Jay rolled his eyes. "Hear what? Half of that was gibberish. Did you understand it, Marty?"

The tall man shook his head. "Only a little. They used words I've never heard before."

"That's their alien language," Sparkman said, nodding.

Travis stared at the receiver. If half of that had been spoken in an alien tongue, why had all of it made sense to him? He dug into his pocket, pulled out the silver half-coin, and set it on the ground.

Jay frowned at him. "What are you doing, Mr. Wizard?"

"Turn it up," Travis said.

Sparkman fiddled with the knobs. Again static phased into words, only this time Travis didn't understand all of them.

"—and heading to the *taldaka* location now."

Another voice, a woman's, replied. "Any indication that the *senlath* has—?"

The words were lost in a low hiss. However, it had been enough. Travis picked up the half-coin and slipped it into his pocket as he stood. He hadn't understood the non-English words; he hadn't made an effort to learn the language, unlike Grace. Yet even without the magic of the half-coin, they had sounded familiar—familiar enough to know they were Eldhish. But who would use Eldhish words on Earth?

You heard Sparkman. They're using the words for a code. And what better code than a language from another world? No one would ever be able to decipher it.

Only Travis was certain the voices didn't belong to aliens. They belonged to people from Earth. They had sent operatives to the Dominions; surely they had learned much about the culture and language there.

It's Duratek, Travis. They're the ones Sparkman has been hearing. They're the ones who are abducting people.

But that didn't make any sense. What would a multinational corporation need with a bunch of homeless people? Besides, no matter how smart he was, Sparkman was surely crazy. Travis tried to think, but before he could Marty spoke.

"We should go to the shelter," the tall man said. "If we don't go now, they'll run out of breakfast."

Jay pawed at the sleeve of his jacket to bare a Timex watch, its face barely visible beneath the fogged crystal. "Damn, we've got to go. Come on, Travis."

The idea of food made Travis's stomach churn, but he didn't have the energy to resist as Jay tugged at his sleeve. "What about you, Professor Sparkman?" he said.

Sparkman reached into his pocket and pulled out a bagel. "I'm all set. And look." He stuck a finger though the hole. "It's just like the missing mass in an atom's nucleus."

Travis clamped his jaw shut, and Jay started pulling him across the park after Marty. Sparkman waved after them, then took a bite of his bagel and bent his head over the receiver.

"Put a move on it," Jay snapped. "I can't believe we wasted so much time talking to Sparky. All of that thinking puts me in a bad mood."

"It makes me hungry," Marty said.

Jay punched his arm. "Everything makes you hungry."

20.

Dawn was still an hour off, and the castle was silent as Grace made her way down empty corridors. Cold poured off the stone walls, and she had thrown only a shawl over her nightgown before stealing from her chamber.

This is stupid, Doctor. How are you supposed to lead an army if you catch pneumonia?

She was to ride forth from Calavere later that morning to begin the journey north to Gravenfist Keep. Behind her would follow the woefully small force that had come in answer to Boreas's call for war. As if Grace knew the first thing about commanding an army.

Maybe it's better so few answered the call to muster, Grace. At least this way you're only leading five hundred men to certain death, rather than five thousand.

All night she had lain awake in bed, and she had thought it

simply fear of the task that lay before her that made sleep an impossibility. However, as gray light seeped beneath the shutters, she realized it was something else that weighed on her mind, something that had to do with her trek into Gloaming Wood three days ago. Then, as the light changed from gray to silver, it came to her.

You seek a key, do you not, the forest queen had said, *one that can aid you in the war you must fight? Sit in the chair that is forbidden to all others, and the key shall be revealed to you....*

She had slipped from the bed, careful not to wake Tira, who was curled in a tight ball under the covers, and without making a sound had opened then shut the chamber door.

Now she padded through the castle's entry hall and down a passage until she reached an enormous oaken door carved with the crest of Calavere: a pair of swords crossed beneath a crown with nine points. Only the crown shouldn't have nine points anymore, it occurred to Grace. Two of the castle's towers were gone, fallen to rubble. Would there ever be a time to repair them?

There wouldn't be if she didn't do this. Grace pushed against the door and opened it just enough to slip into the space beyond. Once in, she leaned against the door to shut it, grateful that some servant must have oiled the hinges in the recent past.

Enough light came through the high windows to let her make out the rows of raised seats that ringed the chamber, as well as the circular table that dominated the center. This was the place where the Council of Kings had been held over a year ago. The space had been used little since then, and the air was frigid and musty. Grace hurried to the table, then glanced over her shoulder. She felt like a teenager sneaking into school after hours.

That's ridiculous, Grace. If the forest queen was right, then you belong here.

She walked around the table. Inlaid in the center was the rune of hope, which Travis had bound there after he broke the rune of peace. Eight ornate wooden chairs surrounded the table, royal crests carved into the back of each one. There was Chair Calavan next to Chair Toloria, and chairs for the rest of the seven Dominions.

Grace came to a halt behind the final chair. It was newer in appearance than the others, glossier. But then, over the centuries, it had never been sat in, had it? Legend told that a witch had cast a spell on this chair, and that only the true heir to the throne of Malachor might dare sit in it, for one who was false would surely be struck dead.

Mad mirth bubbled up inside Grace. Falken and the others were absolutely convinced she was the last descendant of the royal house of Malachor. What if she sat in this seat and ended up getting fried to a crisp?

"That would certainly show them, wouldn't it?" she murmured, and had to bite her lip to keep from laughing.

Grace brushed the symbol carved on the back of the chair: a stylized knot with four loops surrounding a four-pointed star. There was no jolt of magic. Her fingers came away dusty, not burnt. She edged around to the front of the chair.

"Well, here goes nothing."

Grace sat down. If Chair Malachor had a curse, it was simply that it was extremely uncomfortable. The seat was hard, and the carvings in the back poked her from behind. Other than that—and the fact that the chair seemed to have been constructed for someone three feet taller than she—there seemed to be nothing special about it.

But there had to be something here. *Sit in the chair that is forbidden to all others,* the forest queen had said, *and the key shall be revealed to you.*

Grace didn't see anything sticking out of the chair that looked remotely keylike, and all of the knobs and protrusions were firmly attached. Perhaps it was a riddle of some sort—perhaps there was something that could be seen only when sitting in this chair. Except the chamber looked the same from this angle as it did from any other.

All right, so maybe there was something about the table in front of the chair. She groped along the underside of the table with a hand, half-expecting to encounter a chewed piece of gum someone had stuck there, but there was nothing. Grace sighed, feeling cold and tired and more than a little sick. What had she really expected? It was just a chair, and she doubted that the story of the witch who had cursed it was true.

"Tell that to the Earl of Wetterly," said a croaking voice. "He fancied himself descended of King Ulther, and he tried sitting in the chair a few centuries ago. All they found of him the next morning were his teeth. No one's touched the chair since. Until now."

Grace gasped and looked around, but she could not see the speaker. "Who's there? Show yourself!"

"Why, I'm right here, Your Majesty." A lumpy form clad in gray rags shambled around from behind the chair.

"Vayla," Grace said. She cocked her head, thinking of the hag she had met in King Kel's camp. "Or is it Grisla?"

The crone shrugged knife-edged shoulders. "Why don't you decide, Your Majesty?"

"Let's stick with Vayla for now. She's a bit less . . ."

"Fun?" the old woman said.

Grace smiled. "I was going to say impertinent."

Vayla let out a snort. "Suit yourself, Your Majesty. But maybe it would be better if it was Grisla who was here and not me. You see, she wouldn't hesitate for a second to tell you what an enormous dolt you are."

"What do you mean?"

"You know what I mean." Vayla jabbed a bony finger at her chest. "You're always so sure there's no hope. After all you've seen, do you really think so little of magic? So little of life? By the first and the last, sometimes you make that Embarran fellow look like a ray of sunshine. Perhaps you should change your name to Lady Lamentsalot?"

Grace's eyes narrowed. "Are you sure you aren't really Grisla?"

"We all have different faces. It's just a matter of which face we choose to wear at any given moment." The crone peered at Grace with her one bulbous eye. "So which face are you going to put on today?"

Grace started to say that she didn't have different faces, but that wasn't true, was it? She was a doctor and a witch. And, whether she wanted it or not, a queen. She was a woman as well, frightened and alone. But which of them was really her?

"I don't know what I'm going to be."

"Humph," Vayla said, hands on her shapeless hips. "You'd better decide."

"What will happen if I don't?"

"Madness, that's what. Doom and death." The crone leaned into the chair; she smelled like old leaves. "We have many faces, but we can wear only one at a time. If you try to be everything to everyone, then you'll end up being nothing at all. So pick one and stick with it."

"Even if it's not the right one?"

"And if what you choose comes from within you, daughter, how can it possibly be wrong?"

These words startled Grace—and filled her with a strange excitement as well. Ever since her heritage was revealed, she had resisted the idea that she was a queen. But what was the true reason for that?

Queens are supposed to be proud and regal and fearless, Grace. They order people about with a flick of a finger. And they always know exactly what they're doing.

Or was that just some silly notion of what a queen was supposed to be—something culled from books and movies? Maybe Grace didn't have to be any of those things to be a queen. Maybe all she had to do was put those unattainable ideas aside and be her own sort of royalty—one with a bad haircut, a serious *maddok* addiction, and a complete inability to curtsy. And one blessed with wondrous friends who could help her through just about anything. Maybe, just maybe, she really could be a queen.

A gasp escaped her—a sound of realization, and of letting go.

Vayla patted Grace's cheek with a crooked hand. "That's it, daughter—no one can tell you who you're going to be. Not bards or gods or pale kings. That's for you to decide."

The old crone turned and shuffled toward the chamber door.

Grace stared, then panic gripped her. "Wait! I need you. I have to find the key!"

"You don't need me for that!" the old woman called over her shoulder in a surly voice. "It's been right under your thumb all this time."

Under her thumb? Grace looked down at her hands, which rested on the arms of the chair. The wood was smooth beneath both thumbs, though next to the right was a small carving of—what? She bent closer, and her heart leaped into her throat.

It was a carving of a walled fortress atop a high mountain. Her thumb gave an involuntary twitch against the carving. There was a click, and a small section of wood beneath her thumb pressed inward. Startled, she pulled her hand away, and a small drawer popped out of the arm of the chair.

Once her heart decided to start beating again, Grace peered into the drawer. Inside was a creamy disk of stone about the size of a quarter, but many times thicker. She hesitated, then picked it up. Immediately she saw it was a rune. Three parallel lines incised the surface of the disk, identical to the rune in the center of the council table. Grace recognized the symbol. It was hope.

Of course. Wasn't hope always the key? With hope, anything was possible.

"So how do I use it?"

Silence. She looked up. Vayla was nowhere in sight. However, there was only one way the crone could have gone. Grace rose and tucked the rune into a pocket, then slipped through the crack in the door. Shawl flapping, she ran down the passage until she came to an intersection. Which way?

Grace caught motion out of the corner of her eye and turned in time to see a flutter of gray cloth vanishing around a bend. She sprinted down the corridor and rounded the corner. A lumpy shadow was just passing into an archway ahead. Grace hurried after.

She found herself in a dim hall lined with suits of armor. At the other end was a doorway, glowing with gold light. For a moment a shapeless silhouette was outlined in the doorway, then it passed through. Grace leaned forward, raced down the hall, and ran through the doorway.

"Going somewhere?" said a voice. It was gentle and serene but slightly bemused, a woman's voice.

Grace skidded on her heels, halting just short of a spear that a suit of armor gripped at a decidedly perilous angle. She was in a small antechamber. There were a few chairs, and several time-darkened portraits of dukes, earls, and princes adorned the walls. Saffron-colored light spilled through the window; outside, the sun had just risen.

"Are you well, sister?"

Grace turned. The woman was not tall, but she was elegant all the same, clad in a gown that seemed to catch the morning light and spin it into a dozen different hues of purple, green, and peacock blue. Her black hair was marked by a single streak of white, and wise lines accented her almond-shaped eyes. Was she a noblewoman? Perhaps, though her dress seemed a bit unusual.

Realizing she should probably say something, Grace drew in a breath. "I'm looking for someone. She came in here."

"Really?" The woman raised an eyebrow. "That's curious. For as you can see, I am the only one here besides yourself, and there are no doors to this chamber other than the one you came through."

Grace frowned. Where could Vayla have gone?

Probably anywhere. There's no telling who Vayla really is. Or Grisla, or whatever she calls herself. But there's certainly more to her than meets the eye. You won't see her again until she wants you to.

"I ask again, are you well, sister?" the woman said in a motherly voice, taking a step closer.

Grace nodded. "I'm fine, really. I just have a lot on my mind, that's all. I'm sorry to have bothered you." She started toward the door.

The woman smiled. "It's no bother. I arrived at the castle early this morning, and I've simply been waiting for people to wake up."

Grace hesitated. "What people?"

The other's smile deepened. "Why, people like you, sister."

Grace took a step back into the room. For some reason the woman reminded her of Vayla, though the other was certainly no hag. Instead, she was beautiful and mature, a woman in the prime of life.

"Excuse me," Grace said, "but have we met before?"

The other nodded. "In spirit, yes, if not in person."

Grace stared, then it hit her. On the white ship, when she had struggled against the runelord Kelephon, Aryn had reached across countless leagues to help her weave a spell. But there had been another presence along with Aryn's, one that was deep, calm, and wise. It was . . .

"You!" Grace said with a gasp. "Aryn and Lirith told me all about you. Your name is Sister Mirda, and you're the witch who helped change the weaving of the Pattern at Ar-tolor. And you were the one who convinced Aryn to join the—" Grace dropped her voice to a whisper. "—to join the shadow coven."

Mirda nodded, her expression knowing. "I see Sister Aryn has told you much."

"No, don't worry," Grace said, moving forward. "You see, we've joined the shadow coven, too. Lirith and I."

Mirda pressed a hand to her chest. "I know not whether to be glad for myself, sister, or afraid for you. It is no simple thing to join a coven such as ours. The shadow covens were forbidden over a century ago, and if we are ever discovered, we shall all be cut off from the Weirding forever."

"Aryn told us the risks," Grace said, trying to sound confident. "But we've joined, and what's done is done."

Mirda's smile returned, then in an action that surprised Grace, the elder witch glided forward and caught her in an embrace. Despite her shock, Grace found herself smiling as well.

"We are lucky," Mirda said, stepping back, "to be joined by three witches such as you and your sisters. Each of you is so talented in your own way."

Grace stiffened and tried to pull away, but Mirda held her hands tight.

"No, sister, you must not deny your gifts, not now when they are most needed. You are a great healer, and you have skill such as I have never seen before. You weave the Weirding in new and wondrous ways."

At least Grace freed her hands. "I'm nothing compared to Lirith and Aryn."

"I would hardly say that. But it is true that Sister Lirith is strong in the Sight, and Sister Aryn's power is deep—deeper than any other's, I think. With you three, perhaps there is hope for our impossible task after all."

Hope. Grace touched the pocket where she had slipped the rune.

"Where have you been, Mirda?" Grace asked. "Aryn said you left just before we arrived in Calavere."

Mirda turned toward one of the windows. "I'm afraid an urgent task called me away. But it is done, and I've returned, and I'll not be leaving again." She turned back. "Unlike yourself, sister."

Grace sank into one of the chairs. "I have to go north, to Gravenfist Keep. I'm supposed to stop the Pale King from riding forth when the Rune Gate opens. But I don't know how I'm possibly going to do that. All I have is an old sword and five hundred men. And this." She drew out the rune.

Mirda studied the rune but did not touch it. "It seems you have much to me. Remember that you do not need to defeat the Pale King. Your part in this shadow coven is to hold him back until the Runebreaker can fulfill his destiny."

A shiver coursed through Grace. "Until he breaks the world, you mean."

"Or saves it," Mirda said, meeting her gaze.

How could it be both? Grace still didn't understand that. But there was one thing she did know—there was no person on any world kinder or truer than Travis Wilder. He would not harm Eldh; she would not believe that he could.

"He's gone, you know." Grace leaned her head against the back of the musty chair.

"He will return," Mirda said.

Grace shut her eyes. "But how can you know that?"

"Because prophecy demands it. The Runebreaker will be there at the end."

"But what if it's not Travis? What if it's the other Runebreaker who's there at the end?"

"Then," Mirda said, her words hard as stones, "all the world is doomed."

Grace sighed and opened her eyes. She couldn't know who was going to reach the First Rune first—Travis or Mohg or the other Runebreaker. However, even if Travis did manage to save the world, there would be nothing left to save if the Pale King had already ridden across it and enslaved all of its people. She had to face Berash. Not because she was better than anyone else, or stronger. Simply because someone had to stand against the Pale King, so it might as well be her.

Her thoughts must have been clear upon her face.

"Is it not time for you to go, sister?"

Grace stood, feeling a bit shaky, but surprisingly strong. "I suppose it is."

Mirda touched her cheek. "Do not fear. We will keep watch here while you are gone. Sister Liendra and the other Witches would work to hinder the Warriors of Vathris, so it is the task of Sister Aryn, Sister Lirith, and myself to make certain that does not come to pass. Once the Warriors have answered King Boreas's call to muster, they will march north, and you will have a vast force at your command."

Grace didn't know whether to be reassured by that thought or terrified. She started to pull away, then a thought occurred to her. Mirda's knowledge seemed to run so deep. Perhaps she would have an answer to the other shadow that weighed upon Grace.

"Sister Mirda," she said. "My friend, the knight Durge—there's something wrong with him."

"There is none whose skills at healing are greater than your own, sister," Mirda said. "Can you not care for him?"

Grace felt a sob rising in her chest, but she swallowed it down. "No, I can't. At least, I don't know how, but maybe you can help me. You see, it's his heart." Forcing herself to speak in a clinical tone, Grace described what had been done to Durge.

Mirda was silent for a moment, then a sigh escaped her. "That is how evil works—by taking what is good and true and corrupting it. That your friend has resisted so long tells me his spirit is one of unsurpassed strength and goodness."

"Then there's hope for him," Grace said, her words hoarse.

Mirda shook her head. "I fear not, sister. In the end, the splinter will work its magic. All the goodness in his heart, all the loyalty and kindness, will be replaced by shadow. There is nothing that can be done for him. Except for one thing."

Grace staggered back. "What are you talking about?"

"Take this." Mirda pressed a small vial into her hand. "It is a tincture of barrow root. A single drop brings an end, swift and painless. Keep watch on your friend, and before it is too late, you must give it to him."

Grace stared, cold horror spilling into her chest. "I can't," she said, choking. "I won't."

Mirda closed Grace's fingers around the vial. "You must, sister, if you love him as you say you do. He would never want to become what the splinter will make of him."

It was too much. Grace couldn't breathe. She staggered toward the door. "I have to go."

"So you do, sister," Mirda said, nodding. "I will be there to see you off when you ride from the castle."

Grace hardly heard her. Her head swam, and she was shaking. She wanted to throw the vial down, only somehow her hand wouldn't let go of it. *A single drop brings an end, swift and painless.* . . .

She pushed through the door and ran down the hall, past the suits of armor. They seemed to stare at her, like specters forged of cruel metal. Her nightgown tangled around her feet, tripping her, and she started to fall.

Strong arms gripped her, holding her upright.

"My lady, what is wrong?" spoke a deep, familiar voice.

She blinked and saw Durge's craggy face in the gloom. The knight wore riding gear and a mail shirt. Panic seized her. How long had he been out here in the hall? Had he heard what she and Mirda had been talking about? She gripped the vial so hard she thought it must shatter, but it didn't.

"Durge," she managed to croak. "What are you doing here?"

"Looking for you, my lady. And I'm lucky to have found you, as I was just passing by the door to this hall when I saw you come running this way."

Grace tried not to breathe too obvious a sigh of relief. He hadn't entered the hall until after she had left the antechamber. That meant there was no way he could have heard her conversation with Mirda.

"I came to your chamber at dawn," Durge went on. "However, I found only Tira playing a game with a serving maid, so I came in search of you. Your army gathers even now in the lower bailey. We are to ride forth in an hour." His mustaches descended in a frown as he took in her tangled nightgown. "I must say, my lady, this is hardly proper riding attire. You will freeze to death before we travel a league."

"Sorry," she said. "I'll change."

And despite her fear, she found herself laughing. Whatever the iron splinter would make of him, right now he was still Durge—good, dear, gloomy Durge. As long as she had the Embarran by her side, she was going to enjoy every moment of it. She threw her arms around his stooped shoulders, much to his obvious surprise.

"Thank you, Durge."

He hesitated, then wrapped his strong arms around her. "Whatever for, my lady?"

"For being you."

He let out a rumbling breath. "Well, I can't say I give being me very much thought or effort. But all the same, you're welcome, my lady."

21.

An hour later, Grace glanced out the window of her chamber to see the sun cresting the castle's battlements. In the last few minutes Durge had checked on her twice and Sir Tarus once, and the servants had already taken her things. Everyone would be waiting for her in the lower bailey.

"I have to go now, Tira," she said.

The girl sat in front of the fire, playing with one of her half-burnt dolls. Grace knelt beside her, though the action was made awkward by the scabbard belted at her side. Fellring's hilt jabbed her in the kidney, and she grimaced as she readjusted the sword. How did Beltan wear one of these blasted things all the time?

"Tira, do you understand what I'm saying?"

It was always so hard to know if she was getting through. Tira still hadn't spoken a word since they left the Black Tower. Grace smoothed back the girl's tangled red hair and touched her chin, so that she stopped her playing and looked up.

"I'm going to be going on a journey, to a place very far away from here, and I'm afraid you can't come. It's not that I don't want you to." Grace drew in a breath, shocked at how difficult this was. "I'm going to miss you so much. But where I'm going is too...that is, it's not a place for children. It's all right, though—you'll have Aryn and Lirith and Sareth here to take care of you, so you'll be safe. And I'll come back to you soon. I promise."

Tira smiled—though the expression did not touch the scarred side of her face—then bent back over her doll. Grace sighed, hoping it had been enough. She caught the girl in a tight hug, rocking her, kissing her head. At last, fearing she would weep, she rose quickly and left the room.

Waiting outside was a slender man with a pointed blond beard and a silver-gray cloak.

"Aldeth," she gasped, clutching a hand to her chest. "You startled me."

The Spider smiled, revealing rotten teeth. "I may have been discarded by Queen Inara like a soiled handkerchief, but it seems I've still got the touch."

Grace frowned at him. "Durge sent you, didn't he?"

"Tarus, actually. Durge was too busy having an apoplectic seizure. Something about how if we don't leave immediately, the army won't get a league from the castle before it's time to set up camp. I didn't catch the rest. He was too busy swelling up and turning red. Do you think Embarrans can burst?"

"We'd better not find out," Grace said, wincing. "I'm ready now. I just had to say good-bye to someone."

The Spider let out a snort. "You should do what I do, my lady, and avoid getting to like other people. That way it's never hard to say good-bye."

Somehow those were the saddest words Grace had ever heard. Maybe because they reminded her of herself not long ago.

"Oh, Aldeth," she said and touched his cheek.

When they reached the castle's lower bailey, they found it empty save for a scattering of sheep and peasants. For an absurd moment Grace wondered if she had missed the departure of her own army. But no, there were Durge and Tarus, both walking swiftly toward her.

"Your force awaits you below the castle, my lady," Durge

said. Aldeth was right. His cheeks and neck were red as holly berries.

"I prefer to think of the army as being all of ours, Durge," she said with a wry smile.

He glowered and grew a touch redder.

Tarus took her arm and steered her toward the castle gate. "If you don't mind my saying, my queen, I'd lay off the jests. At least until we're well on the road."

"Understood," Grace said with a nod.

They passed by the remains of the ruined guard tower—the rebuilding had only barely begun—and through the castle gate. As they reached the other side, Grace's heart skipped in her chest. Perhaps Aldeth was right; perhaps growing to love people was not worth the pain of saying good-bye.

Except it was, no matter how much it hurt. Lirith and Aryn rushed up to her, catching her in a fierce embrace.

Sisters, she spoke in her mind.

Hush, Grace, came Aryn's voice over the threads of the Weirding. *You don't have to speak. We just came here to let you know how proud of you we are.*

You are brave, sister, Lirith spoke, her voice as true and warm as sunlight. *Braver than any of us. We will think of you every moment while you're away, and we will speak prayers to Sia for your safety.*

And we'll speak to you, too, Aryn said. *I know I'll always be able to find you now, no matter where you go. The Weirding will guide me to you.*

Grace laughed despite her tears. *Then I'll never be alone, will I?*

At last, reluctantly, she stepped back from the two witches. Tarus was giving them a wary look.

"Did they just cast some sort of spell?" the red-haired knight said.

Sareth grinned. "Almost certainly." The Mournish man approached and kissed Grace's cheek. He smelled of spices. "Let Fate guide you."

She met his dark eyes and nodded. "I'll try."

"My brother is right," Vani said, drawing close. "Fate will lead you where you must go, if you will let it."

Grace smiled and gripped the *T'gol'*s hand. Then, over her shoulder, she saw a tall, rangy figure. Beltan.

Talk to him, Vani, she spun the words over the Weirding, and by the *T'gol'*s wide gold eyes Grace knew she heard.

Vani said nothing, but she nodded before she turned away. Then Beltan was there, hugging Grace so tightly it hurt, but she didn't care, and she hugged him back as hard as she could.

"This feels wrong," he said. "I don't care what King Boreas says. I should be coming with you now, not waiting until the rest of the Warriors of Vathris answer the call to war."

"Boreas needs you as a commander."

"My place is with you, Grace."

She thought about it only a moment. "Is that really true, Beltan? Isn't your place with someone else?"

She felt him tense. Was this right? Was she working toward Fate, or against it? She didn't know; all she knew was that she had to do this.

Grace moved her lips close to his ear. "There's a way you and Vani can go to him. You have to find him and bring him back. Eldh needs him. We all need him."

Beltan was trembling now. "Travis," he whispered. "You mean Travis."

"Yes. You see, I kept—"

"That's quite enough, Beltan," said a blustering voice. "I'd say it's my turn now."

Grace and Beltan broke apart as King Boreas strode toward them. Beltan's expression was one of wonder and confusion. Vani gave him a sharp look, and Beltan met her gold eyes, but the king seemed not to notice this exchange.

"My lady," King Boreas said to Grace. "Or, I should say, my queen—it is a brave thing you do this day, for the Dominions, and for all of Eldh. Nor will I insult you by pretending it is not a most perilous thing as well."

She managed a weak smile. "You know, that's not really all that comforting, Your Majesty."

He flashed a toothy grin. "Isn't it? Well, take heart, my lady. While it will be difficult, you need only hold Gravenfist Keep for a short time. The men of Vathris have heard my call. It will not be long until a great host assembles here. When they do, the

Warriors of Vathris will march north with all haste to relieve you."

Grace nodded, hoping the terror wasn't too apparent in her eyes. Perhaps it was, for he moved in close and took her right hand in his.

"It was a lucky day when Sir Durge found you in Gloaming Wood, Lady Grace." His voice was low and gruff, so that only she could hear. "Lucky for Eldh. And for me as well."

He smiled, and this time the expression was only slightly fierce. "I loved Queen Narenya, and when I lost her I thought I had no more need of women, that ruling a Dominion was enough to occupy me. But last winter, when you came into this castle and brightened its halls, I realized how mistaken I was. There are times when I occupy myself with a fancy, my lady. And a most beguiling fancy it is. For in it, you and I sit side by side on the thrones of Calavere, ruling wisely. Together."

Grace could do nothing to hide her astonishment as all words, all motion, fled her. The king bent his head, and his lips passed near hers, almost brushing them. She did not retreat. However, at the last, he turned his head and kissed her cheek—gently, chastely—before stepping back.

Grace trembled. In that moment she was struck by how like Boreas was to the god he followed. Like Vathris, he was a man so strong, so powerful, no one could deny his wishes. How would she ever resist him if he desired to make her his own? Only he had let her go, and was that not more powerful than even the sternest command?

Grace lifted her chin and met his eyes. "Your Majesty, I am in your debt for the kindness you have shown me. More than that, I care for you, so I won't lie to you. The fact is, I don't know if it's possible for me to love someone as you loved Queen Narenya. And I'm fairly sure I wouldn't be much of a wife. But if you ever have need of a queen by your side, you have only to ask, and I will be there."

Her own words astonished Grace, but she knew they were true. However, the king did not accept her offer. Instead his smile faded, and a strange light shone in his eyes, though what it was—joy? regret?—Grace couldn't be sure.

He touched her cheek with a rough hand. "May the gods go

with you, my lady." Then he strode away. He paused to raise a fist for the benefit of the small army below, this action eliciting a cheer, then the bullish king of Calavan vanished through the castle gate.

"What was that all about?" Falken said. The bard drew close, along with Melia. Both wore thick riding cloaks.

"He wished me luck, that's all." Grace gathered her own cloak about herself. The sun was bright, but the air was bitter. The Feast of Quickening was only a month away, but winter had not loosened its grip on the world.

"Tell me, dear," Melia said. "Did you see Prince Teravian on your way out of the castle?"

"I'm afraid not. I suppose he's lurking somewhere."

"Almost certainly." The amber-eyed lady sighed. "That's unfortunate. I had hoped to say good-bye to him."

The cold must have numbed Grace's brain. "What do you mean, Melia? Teravian isn't going anywhere."

"No, dear," Melia said, "but we are."

Grace stared at the bard and the lady. "You mean you're coming with us to Gravenfist Keep?" Hope soared in her chest, but was dashed as Falken shook his head.

"We have our own journey to make. Shemal is still loose in the world, and so is the other Runebreaker. I'm guessing that if we find one, we'll likely find the other."

Melia took Grace's hands in her own. "I'm sorry we can't come with you, Ralena. But you have your task, and we have ours. Now that my dear brother Tome is no more, I am the last of my kind, and Shemal is the last of hers. It is right that we face each other as the end approaches, and Falken has been good enough to agree to come with me."

Grace didn't know what to say, so she settled for, "I'll miss you both so much." Then she flung herself into their arms.

"Don't weep, dear," Melia said as she hugged Grace tight. "We'll meet again before the end. I'm certain of it."

"Remember your heritage, Grace," Falken said, kissing her brow. "You are the queen of Malachor. Gravenfist Keep will know you."

Durge approached and cleared his throat; it was time to go. Reluctantly, Grace pulled away from Melia and Falken, then turned, searching for Beltan and Vani. However, before she could start toward them, a woman in a multihued cloak glided forward. She nodded to Lirith and Aryn, then halted before Grace.

"I could not let you go without a blessing from Sia," Mirda said in her calm voice. "May she guide you in all of her guises: Maiden, Matron, and Crone."

A sense of peace radiated from the elegant witch, soothing Grace's frazzled nerves. Then Grace remembered the small vial Mirda had given her, and which now rested in the leather pouch belted at her waist, and the sense of peace vanished.

"Excuse me, but do I know you?" Falken said, tilting his head as he gazed at Mirda.

She turned her wise gaze toward him. "I cannot say, Falken Blackhand. Do you?"

He glanced down at his black-gloved hand. "You remind me of her, in a way. Only that's impossible, isn't it?"

"Perhaps," Mirda said. "But tell me, what was she like, this one I remind you of?"

Falken's voice was soft. "She was barely more than a maiden, though her power was deep. Her hair was gold, and her eyes like blue cornflowers."

Mirda smiled. "Well, that doesn't sound much like me."

"No, I suppose it doesn't." He glanced again at the mature, dark-haired witch. "Though I must confess, you're a bit more my style. I never went for the girlish type."

Melia shot the bard an outraged look. "Falken!"

The bard gave her a sheepish grin, then the expression faded. "I never did get a chance to thank her. I think she saved my life."

Mirda touched his gloved hand. "If you wish to thank her, then do not hide the gift she made for you."

"How did you—?" Falken shook his head. "But you're right. I think it's time I stopped trying to hide my past and started living up to it." He stripped off the black glove, and his right hand gleamed in the morning light. "From now on, my name is Falken Silverhand."

Mirda smiled. "She would be glad to know." The witch gazed at Grace. "Remember you are never alone, sister. Look for help on the road—it will find you as you journey."

"Thank you," Grace managed.

Mirda nodded, then, cloak fluttering, she moved to stand by Lirith and Grace.

Melia arched an eyebrow. "That was curious."

Falken said nothing as he flexed his silver hand.

A coldness crept into Grace's chest. So that was it, then. There were no more good-byes to make. Durge spoke to Tarus, and the red-haired knight mounted his horse and rode down the hill. The Spider Aldeth followed on a horse as gray as his mist-cloak. Durge climbed into the saddle of his charger, Blackalock, and Melia and Falken mounted their own horses. Nearby, a guardsman held the reins of Shandis, Grace's honey-colored mare. Heart heavy, Grace turned to mount the horse—

—and stopped. A small figure sat in Shandis's saddle, the wind tangling her flame-colored hair. She wore only a thin smock, and her feet were bare.

"Tira," Grace gasped. "How did you get there?"

By the guardsman's stunned look, he wondered the same. He nearly dropped Shandis's reins. However, the mare was non-plussed, and she gave a soft whicker as Tira laughed, burying her hands in Shandis's mane.

Falken gave Grace a sharp look. "I think somebody wants to come with you."

Grace thought her heart would shatter. "But she can't. It's too dangerous. She's just a child."

"No," Melia said carefully, "she's not."

It was true. Krondisar had transformed Tira into a goddess. What her purpose was, Grace didn't know, but she had the feeling that, even if she wanted to, she could not prevent Tira from coming. Nor could Grace say she was sorry.

With the guardsman's help, Grace climbed into the saddle behind Tira. The girl snuggled close.

"Grace!" said a hoarse voice.

Beltan stood beside her horse. The knight's green eyes were desperate, questioning. Hastily, Grace reached into the pouch at her side and drew out a wadded piece of cloth. It was blotched with dark brown stains.

"Take this."

He fumbled with the cloth. "What is it?"

"A bandage. I took it from Travis's arm."

Shock flickered across his face, then understanding. There was only a small amount of Travis's blood contained in the cloth, but it was enough. And Vani still had the gate artifact.

"Bring him back to us, Beltan. To Eldh."

The knight looked up at her, his face determined. "I will. We both will."

"Now, my lady!" Durge said, wheeling Blackalock around.

Grace had done everything she could; it was time to ride. On impulse, she drew Fellring and raised it above her head. The morning sun glinted off the blade, setting it afire.

"To Gravenfist Keep!" called a bold voice, and Grace was amazed to realize it was her own.

Tira laughed. "Blademender," she said.

And a cheer rose on the bitter air as Grace rode down to meet her army.

22.

They marched east, following the same road Grace had traveled on the way to the Gray Tower last summer. She rode at the head of the small force, Durge to her right and Tarus to her left. Behind came the knights of the Dominions, followed by the Calavaner foot soldiers and the band of runespeakers upon sturdy mules. Last of all came the one Tarrasian company, bronze breastplates gleaming. As for Queen Inara's Spiders, Grace could never be certain where they were, though she had little doubt that they were keeping up—and keeping watch.

The weather was crisp and brilliant. Sunlight splintered into rainbows as it struck prisms of ice, and the jingle of chain mail rose like bells on the frigid air. Despite the cold, Grace was warm in her fur-lined cloak as she rode Shandis. Although she supposed it was neither garment nor horse that accounted for her comfort.

"Thank you," she said as the castle vanished from sight behind them. She pressed her cheek against Tira's unruly red hair.

As always, the girl was warm despite her bare arms and legs. "For keeping me warm."

Tira ignored Grace as she made her doll dance along Shandis's mane, as if running through fields of wheat.

After that, Grace gave her first order as commander of the army. She told Tarus that if at any time as they traveled, any man—or woman, for there were the two lady Spiders—found the cold too unbearable, he was to come walk or ride near Grace.

Tarus gave her an odd look. "And how will that help, Your Majesty?"

"You haven't been cold riding beside me, have you?"

"Now that you mention it, I haven't."

She hugged Tira and smiled. "I didn't think so."

Tarus shot her a puzzled look, then wheeled his horse around to give the order.

Grace knew she shouldn't be enjoying this—they were riding off to war, not a picnic in the countryside—but all the same it was difficult not to feel her spirits soaring. Maybe after they had marched a hundred leagues they would look weary and bedraggled, and things would seem different, but right then she was struck by the grandeur of the army. All of the men looked hard and capable and brave, their helms gleaming in the sun. Bright banners snapped overhead: white on blue for Calavan, gold on green for Toloria, dark violet for Perridon, and russet for the men of Galt. The Tarrasian force carried the standard of the empire—five stars over three trees—and the gray robes of the runespeakers were like their own kind of banner.

Grace let out a foggy breath. "It seems I'm the only one without a flag."

Durge smacked a hand to his forehead. "Forgive me, Your Majesty, in all the haste to depart I quite forgot to give you this. Senility must be setting in already."

She gave him a fond smile. "I rather doubt that, Durge."

The Embarran rummaged in a saddlebag and drew out a bundle wrapped in waxed cloth. He handed it to her.

"What is it?"

"A gift from Falken and Melia. They asked me to give it to you once we were on the road."

Grace opened the bundle, and inside was a folded piece of cloth. Grasping two corners, she shook it out.

It was a banner. The colors were like those of Calavan, though the blue was deeper, and the symbol embroidered in silver thread was not the crown and swords of Calavan. Instead it was a star surrounded by a knot with four loops. Grace knew the symbol well. Falken always clasped his cloak with a brooch that bore the same design.

"It's the emblem of Malachor," she said in wonder.

"You must select a man to be your standard-bearer, Your Majesty," Durge said, his brown eyes thoughtful. "He must be a man you trust above all others, one whose heart will never fail you. For if your standard ever falls, then all is lost."

Grace didn't even need to think about it. "You, Durge. I want you to carry it." She held the banner toward him.

His hesitation was visible. "My lady, I can . . . that is, surely there is another better suited."

For a moment an icicle of fear stabbed at Grace's heart. Durge had never avoided any duty she had ever asked of him. Why would he resist this? She thought of his words, how the standard must be carried by one whose heart would never fail . . .

But he can't know about the iron splinter, Grace. He's being modest, that's all.

She nudged Shandis close to Blackalock and pressed the banner into his hands. "Please, Durge. For me."

He drew in a breath, then took the banner from her. "As you wish, Your Majesty. I will guard it with my life."

Durge called for a lance to be brought to him. He fastened the banner to the end, then turned it upright, planting the butt of the lance in his stirrup. At that moment a gust of wind raced over the river, and the banner leaped to attention, embroidered star gleaming. Grace heard a murmur rise from the men behind her. She kept her gaze forward, but she knew if she looked back she would see wonder in their eyes. To these men, all their lives, Malachor had been a legend—a story of a golden age long lost. By unfurling this banner, she had just brought the legend to life.

"Don't look now, Your Majesty," Tarus said softly, leaning in his saddle toward her, "but everyone's staring at you."

"Then I'd better not fall off my horse."

It was in the late afternoon of that first day out from the castle when All-master Oragien brought his dun-colored mule close to Shandis.

"Excuse me, Your Majesty, but may I take you up on your offer and ride near you for a time?"

Grace winced at the reverence in his voice. Everyone was taking this whole queen thing far too seriously, but she supposed there was no way around it.

"You may ride with me anytime you wish, All-master."

"Thank you, Your Majesty. I fear the cold makes a cruel companion to these old bones, despite young Master Graedin's diligence in speaking the rune of fire. Have you met him? I have not seen such a promising student in all my years at the Gray Tower. Except for Master Wilder, of course."

"I look forward to meeting him," Grace said.

Oragien laughed. "Then you are in luck, Your Majesty, for here comes Master Graedin now. I imagine he's thrilled at the prospect of meeting you, and no doubt he saw my riding beside you as an opportunity. He's nothing if not bold."

"Then he'll go far, I'm sure." *If I don't get him killed first, that is,* Grace added to herself.

The man who bounced on the back of a mule toward them was so young-looking that on Earth Grace would hardly have taken him for a college student. His beard was no more than a light fuzz on his cheeks, and his gangly legs and arms flapped wildly as he rode. For a moment Grace feared his mule would crash into her and Shandis, but at the last second the young man managed to slow the beast down.

"I do trust you have better control over runes than you do over beasts, Master Graedin," she said, her voice sharp, though she couldn't help smiling as his boyish face turned red.

"Forgive me, Your Majesty," he said, his tone one of chagrin. "I've just learned today there is no rune for *mule*. And now I know why. This beast is completely uncontrollable."

Actually, now that Graedin was no longer yanking at its reins, Grace thought the mule looked placid, even relieved. "I find it's usually best to let Shandis decide where to go and how fast to get there. You might try the same, Master Graedin."

The young runespeaker grinned. "A remarkable idea, Your Majesty. You are wise indeed."

"No, I just prefer to worry about the things I can control rather than the things I can't."

"That's a lesson Master Graedin would be wise to heed," Oragien said, giving the young runespeaker a pointed look. "He has a tendency to try for runes that are beyond his reach."

"But how do you know they're beyond your reach unless you try?" Graedin said.

Grace bit her lip but couldn't stifle a laugh. "I'm afraid he has you there, All-master."

Oragien shook his head. It was clear the elder runespeaker was very fond of his student.

"I wish we had more time, Your Majesty," Oragien said. "We've learned much since you and Master Wilder left us last summer—more than I ever would have believed we could. We've managed to reunite several shards of the runestone, thanks in large part to the efforts of Master Graedin here. Yet there's so much we still don't know."

"We'll just have to keep learning as we go," the young runespeaker said.

Grace smiled at him. "I like that idea. I think we're all going to be learning on this trip."

They rode in silence for a time as their shadows lengthened before them.

"So, are you truly a witch, Your Majesty?" Graedin said without warning as they passed through a stand of leafless trees.

"Master Graedin!" Oragien exclaimed, blue eyes flashing.

Grace held up a hand. "It's all right." She imagined many of the men in her army had been whispering about her power. She might as well set the rumors to rest. "I suppose you could say I'm a witch, though not a terribly good one, I'm afraid."

"I doubt that, Your Majesty," Graedin said, eyes gleaming. "Could you do a spell? I've always been curious about the magic of witches, and if there are any similarities between it and runespeaking. You see, I have a theory about—"

"That's quite enough, Master Graedin," Oragien said sternly. "It's time we returned to our brethren. We thank you for your indulgence, Your Majesty."

The All-master shot Graedin a meaningful look, then turned his mule around and started back toward the other runespeakers. Graedin waved at Grace, then kicked his mule, so that the beast gave a buck before starting after the All-master. Grace was sorry to see him go. She liked the young runespeaker, and she was intrigued to know about his theory concerning rune magic and witch magic. She had thought the two irreconcilable, only then she had seen the hag Grisla—who was surely a witch—work a spell with runes in King Kel's camp.

"By Jorus, I thought those two would never leave."

Grace nearly jumped from the saddle at the sound of a man's voice to her right. She glanced that direction. The tangle of bare branches overhead wove a premature gloom on the air, and it was a moment before she saw Aldeth riding not six feet away. His horse was as gray as his mistcloak, causing them both to blend into the twilight, and bits of soft felt were wrapped around every buckle and ring, so that the horse made hardly a sound as it walked over the mossy turf.

"Aldeth, I didn't see you there."

"That was sort of the point, Your Majesty."

She gave him what she hoped was a piercing look. "You're my spy, Aldeth. You don't have to hide from me, just everyone else."

"I find it's best not to make exceptions. That way I'm always covered."

Grace gave up. "What's going on? Is something wrong?"

"It's quite the opposite, Your Majesty. I had a camping site in mind for this evening, only I was afraid our late departure would prevent us from reaching it. But we've made good time, and we're nearly there. Just around this bend is a large dell surrounded by trees. There's a spring, and it's protected from the wind. Samatha and Leris—two of my cohorts—are off scouting it now to make sure it's safe."

That was welcome news. Grace's legs and back ached; it would be a relief to stop for the night. "Thank you, Aldeth. Inform Sir Tarus that we'll be making camp."

The dell was long and narrow, walled on either side by tree-covered ridges, and large enough to accommodate the entire force. Commander Paladus—leader of the Tarrasian company—

voiced his approval. Like all of the Tarrasians, he was short, olive-skinned, and muscular, with stern brown eyes above sharp cheekbones. Although she stood half a head taller than he, Grace found Paladus intimidating, though he followed any suggestion she made as if it were a command. Then again, Emperor Ephesian did consider her a cousin, so no doubt Paladus had been ordered to obey her without question.

Grace stood around feeling generally useless while Tarus barked orders and the men went to work unloading the wagons and packhorses, setting up tents and a mess area.

"We will place your tent here, Your Majesty," Durge said, planting the standard of Malachor in the soil between a pair of graceful *valsindar* trees.

As night fell, Tarus informed her that dinner would be brought to her tent, and while the thought of privacy was tempting—it felt as if she had been on display all day, like a piece of jewelry rotating in a shop window—Grace decided to take dinner with the troops. Silence fell as she approached the mess area with Tira, and Grace had the feeling a number of tongues had been bitten halfway through the telling of bawdy jokes.

"Don't let me spoil the fun," Grace said with a smile. "I just came for a drink."

A goblet of wine was hastily filled and offered to her, but instead Grace picked up a wooden cup filled with gritty, watery ale and quaffed a good part of it down in a long draught. This brought roars of approval from the gathered men, and many hundred cups were raised in Grace's direction, along with hearty calls of "Your Majesty!" and "Health to the Queen!"

Grace raised her own cup in return, then tilted her head toward Tarus. "They won't be drinking like this every night, will they?"

"Don't worry, Your Majesty. The ale will all be gone in another day or two, but let them have their cheer for now. It's a hard road that lies ahead of them."

Grace couldn't disagree with that.

Dinner was an informal affair. Each soldier carried his own cup and knife, and stood in line to get a helping of salted meat and cheese on a trencher of hard bread, which was eaten sitting on the ground. Grace did consent to taking a seat on a flat rock and let Durge fetch her meal, but she ate the same food as the rest of them.

"That was well-done, Your Majesty," Durge said quietly as he took her empty cup. "If there was a man whose loyalty you did not have before tonight, you have it now."

"I hope I deserve it, Durge."

Grace gazed out over the men, who laughed and sang songs by the light of fires. Would any of them still be laughing after they reached Gravenfist Keep?

"Come, my lady. It is time for sleep."

Durge led her back to her tent, which was a little on the grand side, but Grace didn't complain as she lay down on a cot, snuggling close to Tira's warm body.

It was dark in the tent when a hand touched her shoulder, waking her. Grace sat up, staring, but she could see nothing in the gloom. Then the tin screen of a lantern was moved aside, and a shard of light spilled forth. A woman stood over Grace's bed. She wore a gray cloak.

"Who are you?" Grace whispered, so as not to wake Tira.

"My name is Samatha, Your Majesty." The woman's face was long and narrow, her features sharp-edged. She made Grace think of a gray ferret—small, sleek, and dangerous. "Aldeth bid me come and wake you."

So she was one of the Spiders. Grace pushed tangled hair from her eyes and forced her groggy brain to function. "Is something the matter?"

"There are . . . intruders in the camp."

A cold needle injected fear into Grace's heart. Images flashed through her mind: snarling *feydrim* and the ghostly forms of wraithlings. "Get Durge and Tarus," she said, groping for her sword. "We have to wake the army and fight them."

"No, Your Majesty. These intruders are not servants of the Pale King. They have not come to fight."

Fear gave way to confusion. "Then what do they want?"

"To speak to you, Your Majesty."

Minutes later, her cloak thrown hastily over her nightgown, Grace followed Samatha toward a grove of leafless *valsindar*. The pale bark of the trees glowed like bones in the moonlight. Durge and Tarus fell in step beside her.

"What is this all about, my lady?" Durge rumbled, but before she could answer, Aldeth stepped out of a pool of shadow.

"They await you in the grove, Your Majesty."

"Who?" she managed. It was cold, and her teeth chattered.

"I think you'd best go see for yourself."

"You must not go alone," Durge said.

Grace nodded—she would hardly argue that point.

"We'll keep watch out here." Tarus gripped the hilt of his sword. "If you need help, you have only to call out, and we'll be at your side."

Grace gave the knight what she hoped was a brave smile, then moved toward the grove. Durge followed at her side as she stepped between two trees.

She has come, sisters, spoke a voice in Grace's mind.

Grace halted. Next to her, Durge let out a low oath. Within the grove was a small clearing, and in it stood a group of women—it was hard to be certain how many. Balls of green light hung among the branches, flickering and casting strange shadows. Dimly, Grace was aware that it was not cold in the grove; instead, the air was as warm as springtime.

The women were a queer lot. There were crones with matted gray hair clad in baggy dresses to which bits of moss and dried leaves clung, and motherly women who wore practical cloaks and homespun gowns. Others were more of an age with Grace, holding staves of wood or wicker baskets. And there were at least two who were barely more than girls, gazing at Grace with eyes that seemed too wise and knowing for their round faces.

Grace knew at once that the women were witches. A coven? Not quite—as her eyes adjusted, she counted only twelve. Did not a full coven require thirteen?

"So it does, mistress," said one of the younger women. "That is why we've come."

Grace blinked. "Excuse me?"

One of the eldest witches hobbled forward, leaning on a crooked stick. "You travel a long road, one that leads into the very heart of shadow."

Durge took a step forward, scowling. "What business is it of yours where we are traveling, woman?"

The crone laughed. She was quite toothless. "It is the business of all of us, Sir Knight. Do not think we do not see, for our vision is clear. Even now you march to the Final Battle, and soon all the Warriors of Vathris will follow you."

Durge crossed his arms. "And do you mean to try to stop us? For know that you have little chance of doing so."

The young witch who had spoken approached. She was dressed in the drab browns of a peasant, and her long face was plain, yet there was an elegance to her bearing. "We do not wish to stop you, Sir Knight."

"But don't you have to?" Grace licked her lips. "Aren't you part of the Pattern?"

Murmurs rose from the witches, and the crone cast a sly glance at the maiden. "We have made our own Pattern, weaving it in secret these last years."

Excitement coursed through Grace, and dread. "You're a shadow coven."

Durge frowned at Grace—he couldn't possibly know what that meant—but both crone and maiden nodded.

The words tumbled out of Grace. "The shadow covens were forbidden. If you're discovered, your threads will be cut off from the Weirding."

The crone's weathered face was sorrowful but resolute. "So they shall. All the same, we have come together. You see, we have not ignored the eldest prophecies as the other witches have. We know Runebreaker will destroy the world, and also that he will save it. We know also that the Warriors of Vathris have a part to play in this before all is done, and that you, sister, are linked to both the Warriors and the Runebreaker himself."

Durge's eyes narrowed. "I do not care for these witches, my lady. If they have betrayed their own sisters, how can we trust anything they say? We should run them out of the camp before they spin a spell upon us."

"Hush, Durge," Grace said, laying a hand on his arm, and he fell silent, though he still glared at the witches. Grace approached the two women, young and old. "Why have you come here?"

"Our coven is not complete," the younger witch said. "We need one more if we are to be thirteen and our secret Pattern complete."

Grace shook her head. "I'm sorry, but I have to go north. I can't go with you."

The crone laughed, a sound like the call of a crow. "Of course not, sister. That is why we shall go with you."

23.

Two days later, the makeshift army reached the bridge over the River Darkwine and the borders of Toloria. "That bridge can't possibly be there."

Grace sat up straight in the saddle. "Actually, it looks fairly solid to me."

Tarus ran a hand through his red hair. "That's not what I meant, Your Majesty. I know this landscape well. I spent much time patrolling here when I was in the Order of Malachor. It's a week's journey from Calavere to Ar-tolor, which lies just a few leagues beyond that bridge. But it's only been three days since we set out from King Boreas's castle."

"Then we've made exceptionally good time, haven't we?" Grace said with a smile.

"But, Your Majesty—"

Grace gave him a sharp look. "Sometimes it's best not to question good fortune, Sir Tarus."

The knight bit his lip, then nodded. "Very well, Your Majesty. I'll instruct the army to cross the bridge. We'll make camp on the other side." He rode away.

"Thank you for speeding up our journey," Grace murmured, enfolding Tira in her arms as they approached the bridge. The girl wriggled in her arms, making a low sound like a moan. What was the matter? Then, as Shandis's hooves clattered against the bridge, Grace understood.

Glancing down, she saw the footprints melted into the stones of the bridge. It was here at this very bridge that the *krondrim*, the Burnt Ones, had trapped them on their journey east last year. Only the spell Grace wove with the help of Aryn and Lirith— along with the fatal bravery of Sir Meridar—had saved them. Even then, Tira and the blind boy Daynen had been trapped on

he bridge, its stones half-molten from the touch of the fiery be-
ngs. Both children would have perished. But then, as Grace and
he others watched in helpless horror, Daynen had carried Tira
cross the glowing stones of the bridge, saving her—and sacri-
icing himself.

Grace let out a breath when they reached the other side of the
ridge, and Tira grew still in her arms.

Silver twilight was falling by the time they reached the other
ide. Grace was barely able to pick Durge out of the gloom as he
eered his charger Blackalock close to Shandis. Both Embarran
nd warhorse looked like shadows.

"I do not like this," Durge rumbled.

She followed his gaze and saw that the witches who had
ined them two days ago were just coming across the bridge—
ie younger ones walking, the eldest sitting astride shaggy
onies.

"We ride now into the lands of the Witch Queen of Toloria,"
urge said, his eyes glinting. "Will not they betray us to her?
ou yourself, Your Majesty, have said the Witches seek to pre-
ent the Final Battle from coming about."

Grace watched the witches approach. "No, Durge. They
on't betray us to Ivalaine. Besides, I think you may have mis-
dged the queen. Some of her own knights ride with us. Be-
ides, no matter what side she stands on, all laws require that I
quest her permission to ride through her lands."

Durge couldn't argue with that; the Embarran was a staunch
pporter of laws. All the same, he glowered at the witches. "I
ill don't like it. We know nothing about these women. It would
better if we had sent them on their way."

"Nonsense," Grace said crisply. "There are far too many men
out. A few women will do this army good."

Over the last two days, Grace had learned that, while she
dn't know these witches, they knew her. The coven's Crone
as named Senrael, while the Maiden was called Lursa; they
ere the two women Grace had first spoken to. It turned out
th Senrael and Lursa had taken part in the High Coven in Ar-
lor last year. Both had met Aryn and Lirith there, and it was
rough Lirith and Aryn that they had come to know of Grace.
So that explained how they knew who Grace was. But that

didn't explain how the witches had known to find Grace on the road outside Calavere, or where she was going. Only they *had* known. Which meant one among them had the Sight.

Senrael had confirmed it last night, when she and Lursa paid a visit to Grace's tent. The two explained how, after the High Coven allied with the witch Liendra and those who sought to destroy Runebreaker, they had formed a shadow coven and had searched for a role they might play in the Final Battle, something they could do to aid Runebreaker in fulfilling his destiny. Then, a fortnight ago, it had come to Lursa as she gazed at a candle.

"I didn't even know I had the Sight," the young Embarran woman said. She was soft-spoken and unassuming, but there was intelligence and humor in her brown eyes.

"Sometimes power only reveals itself in times of great need," Senrael said. "And I'd say these times certainly qualify." The toothless old woman was at once feisty and grandmotherly. Grace liked her instantly.

Lursa nodded. "It wasn't at all like a dream—it was clear, as if I was living it. I knew we would join you, and that we would travel with you to Shadowsdeep."

Grace gave the young woman a wan smile. "You didn't happen to see how things would go once we got there, did you?"

Lursa shook her head and smiled back. "Magic never seems to be that convenient, does it?"

"No," Grace said, "it doesn't."

Before the two women left the tent, they had asked if Grace would accept the role of Matron in their coven.

"I'm the oldest and crabbiest," Senrael said, "so I get to be Crone. And Lursa has made for a fine Maiden."

Lursa frowned. "I'm too old for the role, you know. I'm four-and-twenty winters."

"Yet you were the best choice, and you know it," Senrael said. "And fear not for your status as Maiden. I'll make certain none of the men in this army dare lay a hand on you. If one does he'll discover his private bits have shriveled up like raisins."

Grace doubted untoward advances would be a problem. She had seen the dark glances the men cast at the witches, as well a

he signs they made with their hands behind their backs. Durge
vas not the only one who was suspicious.

"I'll do it, if you need me to," Grace said, then grimaced.
But I don't really know what being Matron involves. I'm afraid
'm not much of a mother figure."

"And aren't you?" Senrael said, casting a glance at the cot
vhere Tira lay curled up, one of her half-burnt dolls tucked un-
ler her arm.

Now Grace watched as the last of her army marched across
ae bridge. Sir Tarus shouted orders, as did Commander
aladus, and camp was quickly set up near the banks of the
iver. Night fell, clear and cold, and Master Graedin and the
ther runespeakers moved through the camp, touching stones
nd speaking the rune of fire. Dawn seemed to come mere mo-
aents after Grace lay down on her cot, and it was time to rise
nd continue the journey.

It was midmorning when the seven towers of Ar-tolor hove
ato view, green banners snapping. Grace imagined she would
ave to enter the castle in order to meet with Ivalaine, but as
aey approached she saw a pavilion had been set up outside the
astle walls. The canvas of the pavilion was striped green and
old, and atop the center post flew the royal banner of Toloria.
o the queen had come to meet her. But why?

*Perhaps to avoid prying eyes and ears, Grace. Isn't Sister
iendra still in Ar-tolor?*

A pony trotted toward Grace, a drab bundle on its back
hich, a moment later, Grace realized was Senrael.

"The queen must not see my sisters and me," the old witch
iid. She pointed to a distant knot of trees. "We will wait for
ou in that grove."

Grace gazed at the pavilion and sighed. "You know, I believe
at in her heart she supports us."

"That may well be," Senrael said. "All the same, she was Main of the High Coven, and until she renounces that role she is
ound by the Pattern woven there. If she were to see us riding
ith you, she would know we have betrayed the Witches."

"What about me?" Grace said. "Won't she know I've be-
ayed the Witches as well?"

Senrael let out a cackle. "You cannot betray them, deary, for you were not part of the Pattern."

Grace lifted a hand to her chest, trying to quell the sudden ache there. "What pattern am I part of, then?"

"That's for you yourself to weave," the old woman said, then she turned the pony around and rode off to join the other witches. Together, the twelve women headed for the leafless grove of trees. However, before they had gone a furlong, the air shimmered around them, and their forms faded away, vanishing into the dun-colored landscape.

"Your Majesty," Durge called, riding toward her. "The queen awaits."

Despite their many previous interactions, Queen Ivalaine greeted Grace coolly, formally—not as one woman or one witch to another, but rather as ruler to ruler. They did not touch and remained always a distance apart. The queen sat in a folding chair of gilded, intricately carved wood, and she indicated that Grace should sit in a chair that was only slightly less ornate. Grace made her request to ride with her army through the queen's lands. After that, servants brought them steaming goblets of spiced wine and stoked the braziers that warmed the pavilion, then retreated, leaving the two women alone. Even Tressa, the queen's closest advisor, was nowhere to be seen.

Maybe she's back in the castle, Grace, keeping an eye on Sister Liendra.

"You must guard your thoughts," Ivalaine said, her ice-colored eyes fixed on Grace. "It is not only words spoken aloud that may be overheard."

Grace clutched her goblet. "And who might hear us?"

"I would give much to know the answer to that question, sister. I simply know I am being watched. The feeling comes and goes, like clouds on a summer day. But the clouds come more often than light now. The storm approaches, and I fear it will wash us all away."

Grace didn't know how to reply to that, though she noted Ivalaine had called her *sister*. Were they no longer speaking as queens, then, but as witches? There was one way to find out.

"You have not asked me why I ride through your lands with an army, sister."

Ivalaine made a dismissive gesture. "Your business is your own."

Grace set down her goblet. "No, this business is all of ours. Everyone I talk to tells me the Final Battle is coming, and I really have no reason to think they're wrong. So I'm riding to Gravenfist Keep, which lies in Shadowsdeep, right at the gates of Imbrifale. Once I'm there, I'll wait for the coming of the Warriors of Vathris, led by King Boreas."

The queen made no exclamation of shock or surprise. She sat motionless in her chair. However, there was a light in her eyes—a glow that in the ED Grace would have taken as a sign of fever—and blotches of color blossomed on her pale cheeks.

"What of my...what of Prince Teravian?" Ivalaine said softly. "Will he ride with his father?"

"I believe so."

"But of course he will." Ivalaine muttered the words under her breath, as if speaking to herself rather than Grace. "He has to go, does he not? For it is not the father who will fight this battle, but the son."

Grace frowned. "Sister?"

Ivalaine stood, and her goblet fell to the rushes that strewed the ground. Wine spilled, staining the rushes the color of blood. The queen stared at the crimson pool.

"An omen," Ivalaine said, her words hoarse. "Blood will spill. Royal blood. But I will go to him before the end. I will see him before that bull can break him like a sword. I will be queen no longer. Nor will I be Matron. I care not what happens—all is beyond me now. There is but one last role for me to play."

Grace could do nothing to hide the horror on her face. In all the time she had known Ivalaine, the Witch Queen of Toloria had been a figure of authority and cool control. Always Ivalaine had seemed to float above the events that weighed down other mortals, proud and beautiful, untouched by fear or worry. However, the woman who stood before Grace now seemed diminished. She hunched over, her flaxen hair tangled, her beauty shattered by fear, like cracks crazing once-flawless crystal.

"Sister?" Grace said, rising, but still the queen stared at the spilled wine. "Your Majesty?"

Ivalaine's head snapped up. "Go!" she said, her voice a hiss, her eyes wide and shot with red. "This one last thing I will do as queen—you have my permission to ride through my lands. But go quickly, before you and your shadow coven are seen. Their spells of illusion will not hide them for long, not from those who keep watch. And if you are discovered, I can and will do nothing to protect you."

With that, Ivalaine turned her back and vanished through a slit in the canvas wall. Grace stared after her, trying to comprehend what had just happened. *There is but one last role for me to play,* Ivalaine had said. But what role did she mean? And where was it she intended to go?

"Your Majesty?" said a deep voice behind her.

She turned around and let out a breath. "Durge."

The Embarran stood in the entrance of the pavilion. "We spied the queen riding back to the castle with her servants, and we assumed your audience was over. Do we have her permission to ride through Toloria?"

Grace managed a stiff nod. She staggered a bit and caught the back of the chair for support.

Durge hurried to her side, steadying her with a strong hand. "Are you well, my lady?"

A shard of pain lodged in her chest. He wasn't the one who should be asking her that, not with what worked its way toward his own heart. However, Grace forced herself to stand straight. Like Queen Ivalaine, she had just one role to play.

"Come on, Durge. Let's get out of here."

24.

They continued to make impossibly good time as they marched eastward over the rolling hills of Toloria. By late afternoon of their second day after crossing the river, the spire of the Gray Tower soared into view. Much as Oragien and the other rune-speakers might have liked to see how their brethren fared, the army did not stop. By the evening of the next day, they had reached the edge of the wilderness that lay between Toloria and Perridon.

"Tomorrow we turn north," Tarus said as Grace and her commanders took supper by the fire.

Paladus looked up at the frosty stars. "I have never seen an army march so quickly as this. Surely the gods must favor us."

Grace gave Tira a hug. "I'm pretty sure there's at least one who does, Commander."

The next morning they left Toloria behind and marched into the wilderness. Last summer, when they had journeyed through this region on the way to Castle Spardis, Falken had called it Dun-Dordurun, which meant *In-Between-Land* in the language of the Maugrim. Only the Maugrim had vanished an eon ago, and no one lived here now.

The landscape was achingly lonely: a series of misty valleys and scrub-covered ridges that stretched as far as the eye could see. The only sound that broke the silence was the occasional call of a hawk, and the army passed no human habitations, though a few times Grace glimpsed a ragged circle of stones crowning a distant hill.

The sun was sinking low in the west when they reached the gigantic drawing of Mohg on the side of a hill.

"So it's still there," Grace murmured as Shandis came to a halt on a ridge opposite the drawing. But then, it had been there for centuries. She shivered despite the warmth that radiated from Tira's body.

"What is it?" Master Graedin said. The voluble young runespeaker had been bouncing on his mule alongside Grace for the last few leagues, chatting eagerly in response to her questions concerning what the Runespeakers had learned in their effort to repair the runestone.

"It's Mohg," Grace said, only the cold wind snatched her breath away so that the words were barely a whisper.

Graedin's cheerful expression vanished. "The Lord of Nightfall. Most dreaded of all the Old Gods, and above all in power, save perhaps for Olrig himself."

Tarus let out a low whistle. "He's not a terribly pleasant-looking fellow, is he?"

Grace couldn't take her eyes from the crude but expressive figure outlined in stones on the side of the hill. Jagged teeth filled the open maw, and the single eye seemed to stare straight into her heart. It was at least a hundred feet high.

"It's different than when we saw it last," Durge said, a frown on his face. "Some of the stones have been changed. Do you see? He no longer holds men in his right hand. Instead there are only three large rocks on his palm. And all of the stones that make up the drawing are changed. They used to be white."

Durge was right. Grace remembered the gigantic figure as being outlined in white stones. However, now most of the stones were a rusty color.

"Blood," she said, and by their wide eyes the others had come to the same conclusion. "The stones have been painted with blood. Someone must have—"

A distant cry sounded on the air, and Grace's words fell short. At first she thought it to be the call of a hawk again, but the sky was empty, and the sound was different—it was a cry of suffering. Or perhaps of hunger.

"It's just the call of a beast, Your Majesty," Master Graedin said, giving her a reassuring smile.

"Yes, but what sort of beast?" Durge said, gazing around.

Grace swallowed the lump in her throat. "Let's ride."

"Forgive me, Your Majesty," Tarus said, "but the sun is close to setting. We need to make camp, and there is a spring in this vale. It seems an ideal place."

"No," Grace said, her voice sharp. "We're not staying here. Not in the dark. We have to go—now."

The army marched on as shadows lengthened across the land. They crested another rise, then descended into a rocky valley. As they did, the sun vanished behind the wall of the ridge, casting the valley into premature gloom. The sigh of the wind through dry grass was the only sound.

"Something is wrong," Durge said in a low voice to Grace. "Night will fall soon. There should be birds singing, but I hear nothing at all."

This was one time Grace didn't think the Embarran was being overly gloomy. Something *was* wrong—she could feel it in the Weirding.

As do we, sister, spoke Senrael's voice in her mind. Grace glanced over her shoulder; not far behind, the old woman rode with Lursa and the other witches. *It as if the threads of the Weirding recoil in loathing.*

At that moment another cry pierced the air—shrill, trilling. Hateful.

"Did you hear that?" Tarus said as they brought their nervous horses to a halt. "That is no normal beast."

Master Graedin glanced around. "Then what is it?"

"You mean, what are *they*," Aldeth said, casting back his silvery cloak as he stepped from a pool of shadow.

Tarus lowered his sword. "May I suggest you not sneak up on us again—at least not if you don't want a sword in your gut."

The Spider glared up at him. "Don't sheathe that blade just yet, Knight of Calavan. You may yet need it."

Grace swallowed the scream rising in her throat. "What's out there, Aldeth?"

"*Feydrim*, Your Majesty. I'm not sure how many, but they're coming up the ridge behind us."

Grace could see nothing in the gathering twilight, but another cry sounded, and it was echoed by several more, some farther, some nearer. In the saddle in front of her, Tira let out a whimper.

"Why aren't they attacking?" Grace said, holding on to the girl.

Aldeth shook his head. "I'm not sure. It's almost as if they're waiting for something."

"But for what?" Master Graedin said, face pale in the gloom.

Even as he spoke, a light crested the ridge behind them, cold as moonlight. Only the moon would not rise for hours, and when it did it would be in the east, not the west.

"Wraithlings," Grace said.

They gazed at each other for a moment, the whites of their eyes showing in the dimness. Then they were riding.

"We must make for the summit," Durge shouted over the pounding of hooves. "We cannot let them surround us in this lowland."

Tarus fell back, shouting orders. The army fell into precise formation as it marched double time across the valley floor and up the far ridge. Grace clung to the saddle as Shandis cantered up the rocky slope.

By the time they reached the top of the ridge, the sun had slipped beneath the rim of the world, and purple twilight fell from the sky. Grace turned Shandis around and gazed into the shadowed valley. Dozens of yellow sparks wove back and forth. They looked like a swarm of fireflies, but Grace knew they were the glowing eyes of *feydrim*.

"Look," Aldeth said, his voice a hoarse whisper.

The sea of yellow sparks parted as a ghostly light drifted over the valley floor. Grace could just make out the spindly figure moving in the center of the pale globe. On his horse, Durge clutched a hand to his chest, his face lined in pain.

Grace started to reach toward him, but at that moment Sir Tarus spurred his charger forward. "Your Majesty, we have little time. What do you wish to do?"

She opened her mouth, but no words came out. In that moment Grace realized what folly this was, pretending to be a queen. She was a doctor, not a military commander; she had no idea what to do.

"How many are there?" she managed to croak.

"There are at least thirty of the *maltheru* down there," Commander Paladus said as he brought his elegant Tarrasian horse to a halt beside her.

"Make that fifty," said Samatha, stepping out of a nearby shadow. The Spider's silvery cloak shimmered as if it were woven of starlight. "And that's not all, either."

Aldeth stalked toward her. "What have you seen, Sam?"

"It was Leris. He reports that another twenty *feydrim* approach from the north. And I hate to say it, but it sounds like they've got another wraithling with them."

Paladus clenched a fist. "We could fight fifty *maltheru* without loss of our own were it not for the *siltheri*. I have read the ancient accounts of the battles in the north. The touch of the Pale Ones means death, cold and swift."

Master Graedin trembled visibly aback his mule. "But why are they here at all, so far into the Dominions?"

"It's not a large force," Samatha said, stroking her pointed jaw. "My guess is they came south through the Fal Erenn, picking their way along the mountains."

"Your Majesty," Durge said, moving Blackalock close to

Shandis, "you must give us your commands. What would you have us do?"

Either the pain in his chest had passed, or he was doing a good job of hiding it. Below, the pale lights moved closer, the yellow sparks close behind.

"My lady," Durge said, his brown eyes intent upon her. "Your orders."

A rushing sound filled Grace's head. She tried to speak, but words escaped her.

"We must stand and fight," Paladus said. "There is no way we can outpace them, not with half our force on foot, and we cannot hope they'll miss us in the dark. What say you, Your Majesty?"

Grace held a hand to her forehead. It was so hard to think.

Tarus whirled his horse around. "We're at the highest point of the ridge. That should give us some advantage. We'll place the foot soldiers with pikes in the center, the mounted on either flank, and the archers above. At all costs, we must protect the queen." He looked to Grace. "You have only to say the word, Your Majesty, and it will be done."

She tried to speak the word, *yes*. They were military men; they knew what to do. However, even this one word seemed beyond her.

Tarus's horse pranced nervously. "Your Majesty, there is no more time. Give us your assent so we may proceed."

The lights, pale silver and yellow, began to weave up the near slope.

"Surely the queen sees the reason of this plan," Paladus said. "Her silence is her assent. Let it be so."

Tarus nodded. "Give the commands to your company, Paladus. I'll take the orders to the knights of the Dominions. We'll take up the positions as—"

"No," a commanding voice spoke. Grace's voice.

Tarus and Paladus gaped as one.

"Your Majesty?" Tarus said, confusion writ across his face.

"I said no." Fear crystallized into hard resolve. She was only a doctor, but this was just another sort of operation, and she knew with the certainty of a correct diagnosis that what Tarus and Paladus had decided to do was wrong.

There was no way they could fight the wraithlings, not directly; even a single pale one was enough to lay waste to an entire host, and there were two of the things coming. Grace knew they had to find another tactic, and it was Paladus's own words that had shown it to her. Her mind raced, fitting the last pieces into place.

"We won't stand here. Instead, we'll ride over the top of the ridge and down the other side."

Tarus's eyes went wide. "Your Majesty, we must not do such a thing. Higher ground is our only advantage."

Grace waved his words away. There was no time to explain. "Master Graedin," she said, turning toward the young rune-speaker, "how skilled are you and your brothers at speaking the runes of stone and light?"

The hardness of her words seemed to snap him out of his fear. He sat up straight. "Those are two of our very best runes, Your Majesty. Speaking together, we can cast a bright light and command even a large stone."

"You're going to have to command more than one." Grace turned to summon the others she needed, but twelve women clad in brown and gray already rode toward her.

"We are here, sister," Lursa said, resolve on her plain face. "What would you have us do?"

"You must weave a spell," Grace said. "A spell of illusion." Words were too slow. She gathered up all of her thoughts and sent them humming along the strands of the Weirding.

Senrael let out a cackle. "And a fine spell that will be, sister. But our coven must be complete in order to weave it. You must join us as Matron."

"I will." She glanced at Tarus and Paladus. "Gather all the men and go a hundred yards down the other side of the ridge. You must get them all, mounted and foot, to stand in as tight a circle as possible."

"But that is no proper formation," Paladus said, sputtering. "We'll be flanked in moments."

Tarus shook his head. "Your Majesty, I—"

"You heard the queen," Durge growled, maneuvering Blackalock between Grace and the two soldiers. "Carry out her orders. Now."

Tarus and Paladus stared at Durge, then at her, then at one another. For a terrified moment Grace thought they would defy her. Then both whirled their horses around and began barking orders.

"Down the other side of the ridge!" Tarus shouted.

"Keep close together!" came Paladus's stern voice. "I don't care if you have to stand on top of each other—let there be not space enough to slide the blade of a knife between you."

Grace wavered in the saddle, but a strong hand steadied her. "Durge," she said, her voice thick with gratitude.

"What are my orders, Your Majesty?"

"Keep Tira safe." She slipped from the saddle, took the small girl, and held her up toward Durge, who caught her in his arms.

"I will guard her with my life," Durge said.

He placed Tira in the saddle before him and caught Shandis's reins, then Blackalock pounded down the far side of the ridge, Shandis following. Grace found herself atop the ridge with only twenty runespeakers and twelve witches, all of them on foot.

"I must admit, this seems an interesting tactic, Your Majesty," Oragien said, leaning on his staff. He surveyed the small band of men and women—some elderly like himself, others woefully young.

"We're not going to fight them, All-master." Grace drew in a breath. "At least, not with swords."

Snarls rose on the air, along with a metallic humming. Grace saw a gleam of light to the north, coming up the line of the ridge. They had mere moments.

"Follow me, everyone," she said, moving just over the top of the ridge to a bare patch of granite.

"What are we to do, Your Majesty?" Graedin said, panting.

Grace touched his shoulder with one hand and rested the other hand on Oragien's arm. Words flowed from her, along the threads of the Weirding. By their startled eyes, both runespeakers—young and old—heard her.

"Instruct your brothers," she said. They turned to murmur swift words to the other gray-robed men.

What of us, sister? asked Lursa's voice in her mind.

Weave with me, Grace said.

She shut her eyes, and twelve glimmering threads entwined

with her own. There was no time to explain what to do, and nor was there need. Grace began weaving the threads of the Weirding into a new pattern, and as if they were extensions of her own body, twelve pairs of shining hands followed suit.

For a moment, the sense of closeness, of connection, was almost overwhelming. Grace had woven spells with Aryn and Lirith before, but never with an entire coven. An intoxicating warmth filled her. . . .

The threads—they're slipping through my fingers! said the frightened voice of one of the younger witches, snapping Grace back to herself.

Be strong, sisters, came Senrael's wise, rasping voice. *The presence of the Pale King's servants befouls the Weirding and tangles its threads, but even the wraithlings are not so strong as the magic of life. The Weirding will remain true, if only you weave without fear.*

Grace wove with renewed swiftness and certainty, and she felt the other witches do the same. Then a tone like a bell sounded in her mind. The new pattern shone on the air, shimmering and perfect. Grace opened her eyes.

Twenty yards away, the first of the *feydrim* were just cresting the ridge, prowling over the stones on spindly limbs. The twisted creatures hissed, their yellow eyes flashing, as they caught sight of their prey. Grace risked a glance over her shoulder. A hundred yards down the slope, where the army had gathered moments ago, there now stood a dense grove of trees, bare branches gleaming in the half-light.

Our spell of illusion is complete! Lursa wove the words over the Weirding. *The creatures do not see the army.*

But they see us, Grace wove. *Keep back.*

She drew Fellring in one hand, then stooped and grabbed two pebbles from the ground with the other. With a thought, she wove one last illusion. The pebbles on her hand began to glow—one fiery red and one silver as the fading twilight. Grace moved in front of the witches and runespeakers and held the two glowing stones before her.

The *feydrim* hissed with glee and started to lunge for her. Grace beat back the first wave with a swing of Fellring, but more of them came behind. The rest of the creatures had reached the top of the ridge. Carefully this time, avoiding her sword, the *feydrim* began to close in—

—then squealed and fell back, cowering and pissing on the ground. A pair of ghostly lights crested the summit and drifted toward Grace. Spindly figures moved within the lights, gazing at the stones on Grace's hand with lidless eyes, reaching out with slender fingers.

"That's right, you bastards," Grace said through clenched teeth. "Come get your precious Stones. That's what you think they are, don't you? The two Great Stones your master seeks. But I've got another kind of stone in store for you."

The metallic hum rose to a whine, and the scent of lightning filled Grace's nostrils. All instincts told her to throw down the stones, to turn and run. However, she could still sense the twelve threads that were entwined with her own, lending hers strength. The wraithlings drifted past the sniveling *feydrim*, heading straight for Grace.

"Now," she whispered.

Twenty male voices chanted a single word, blending together in deep and perfect harmony. *"Sar!"*

Grace felt the rush of magic as a gust of wind. There was a sound like thunder, and a crack ten feet long and five wide opened in the granite beneath the two wraithlings. Focused as they were on the pebbles in Grace's hand, the beings did not see what was happening until too late. The stone vanished beneath their feet, and like a great maw the crack swallowed the Pale Ones. Two high-pitched shrieks pierced the air—then were cut short as the runespeakers ceased their chant. With a grinding noise, the crack snapped shut.

Snarls and grunts of confusion rose from the *feydrim*. They milled about, pawing at the ground. Then their hungry eyes fell upon Grace and the others. Now that the Pale Ones they feared were gone, their hunger ruled them again.

Grace threw down the pebbles—dull and lifeless now. "Now, Oragien!"

"Lir!" the runespeakers chanted, and a half dozen spheres of light burst into being behind the *feydrim*. The spheres were large and silvery—just like the orbs of lights in which the wraithlings always came.

The runespeakers continued their chant, and the spheres of light drifted closer. Fresh squeals of terror rose from the *feydrim*. The creatures scrambled away from the lights, coursing on all fours down the hill, running past Grace and the witches. Still the lights followed, driving them on, though Grace saw that the spheres were starting to flicker.

"Don't stop!" she called to the runespeakers, and despite their haggard faces they kept up their harmony, chanting the rune of light.

The shining spheres drove the terrified *feydrim* on, down the slope and past the grove of trees. Grace waited until the last of the creatures had passed the grove, then she gave the signal. The runespeakers ceased their chant at the same time the witches plucked apart the threads of the spell they had woven. The illusion unraveled, and the trees vanished, replaced by an army of nearly five hundred men.

Grace was so tired, she had no more strength to shout. Instead, she sent a single word spinning along the Weirding, hoping it would be enough. *Attack!*

With the call of trumpets, the army rushed forward, attacking the fleeing *feydrim* from behind. Scattered and terrified as they were, the creatures had no chance. Warhorses pounded over them, trampling them into the ground. Others fell with arrows in their humped backs, and more squealed on the ends of pikes.

It was over in moments—fifty *feydrim* lay dead and broken on the ground, their bodies gray as ghosts in the twilight. Grace shut her eyes, probing along the Weirding, then opened her eyes again. A feeling of elation rose within her, and she gave a satisfied nod. Not only had her army not lost a single man, none bore a wound greater than a scratch.

Below, the men let out cheers. Tarus raised his sword in the air, and Paladus let out a victory call on his trumpet. A black charger pounded up the slope toward Grace. It was Durge, Tira on the saddle before him. Shandis pounded behind.

"That was well-done, Your Majesty," the Embarran said as he reined Blackalock to a halt before her, and to her astonishment, the consistently solemn knight grinned. "Well-done indeed. These men will follow you anywhere now, even into the dark gates of Imbrifale itself."

His words sent a chill through Grace, but they couldn't completely counter the jubilant feeling of victory. True, this had been but a small force, but they had faced it, and they had survived.

Grace sheathed Fellring and swung herself up into Shandis's saddle. The stars were bright, and she was not ready to stop for the night.

"Come on, Durge," she said, returning his grin. "Let's ride to Shadowsdeep."

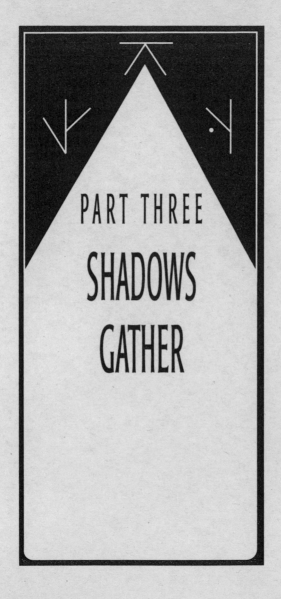

PART THREE

SHADOWS GATHER

25.

The next morning, for her official first act as a newly reinstated Seeker, Deirdre was late to work.

She shielded her eyes from the glare of the fluorescent lights and glanced at the wall clock as she stepped out of the elevator—9:32 A.M. That wasn't so bad, especially given the scotch-induced headache she had awakened with. After all, it wasn't as if anyone would be expecting her.

"Director Nakamura is expecting you," Madeleine said, peering over the top of her computer. "Didn't you say you'd be in by nine?"

Deirdre worked her face into what she hoped was a jaunty smile. "My train was hijacked by tube gnomes."

"I thought as much." Madeleine picked up a pencil that looked sharp enough to pierce Kevlar and made a precise tick on a sheet of paper.

"What are you doing?" Deirdre said.

"Putting you on my list."

The receptionist turned her attention to her computer and began typing as if she were trying to start a fire by generating friction with the keyboard. Deirdre slung her satchel over her shoulder and hurried down the corridor to Nakamura's office. Why did he want to see her again? He had given her an assignment just yesterday. She found him behind his desk, face furrowed in concentration as he tried to make a wooden puppet walk across the blotter. However, the strings tangled, and the puppet collapsed as if it had suffered a seizure.

"Deirdre, there you are," Nakamura said, looking up.

She couldn't take her eyes off the crumpled puppet.

The assistant director sighed. "The man in the store made it look so easy. But I suppose controlling another person—even one made out of wood—isn't a simple affair."

Deirdre sank into one of the chairs in front of the desk. "Is that supposed to be a lesson?"

"Everything's a lesson, Miss Falling Hawk, if we look hard enough. However, this is merely a plaything. I can put it away when I grow tired of it." He opened a drawer, scooped up the tangled puppet, and dropped it in.

Deirdre sank deeper into the chair and mulled over these words. Were they meant to comfort or caution her? Maybe Nakamura was telling her not to worry, that the Seekers wouldn't try to control her as Farr feared they would. Or maybe Nakamura was just a curious and eccentric elderly gentleman who had bought a new toy. Either way, he was right. You could find a message in anything if you looked hard enough, even if there wasn't really one there.

Except there is a message. It's on Glinda's ring, and it's on that old keystone taken from a building that centuries later housed Surrender Dorothy.

Whoever the stranger was last night—the one who had stood outside her window and communicated through her computer—he knew what the message was. Or at least had an idea how to find out. But who was the other? And why did he—or she—want to interfere in the first place?

One thing was certain—this person was a Seeker, and high up in the order. How else would the other be able to send messages to her computer? What's more, the fact that contact had been made so soon after she was granted Echelon 7 clearance couldn't be a coincidence. Perhaps the shadowy Seeker was the same one who had deleted the file she had found. Except that didn't make sense. Why delete the file to avoid discovery, only to approach her the next day?

Deirdre considered telling Nakamura about it. The assistant director knew far more about the workings of the Seekers than she did. He might have an idea who would make contact with her in such a peculiar way. However, even as she opened her mouth, she found herself unable to speak the words.

"What was that, Deirdre? I didn't quite catch you."

"I met Anders last night," she said, blurting the first words that came to mind.

Nakamura smiled. "Yes, Agent Anders. I ran into him first thing this morning. That's why I asked Madeleine to send you my way when you came in."

Deirdre clenched her jaw. Anders's visit last night had been brief—and unbearably upbeat. He had pumped her arm, crushing her fingers in his grip, had said repeatedly how much he was looking forward to working with her, and managed to use the word *crikey* on at least two occasions. After he left, it had taken an entire tumbler of scotch to stop her nerves from buzzing.

"He's no Hadrian Farr, of course," Nakamura went on. "But I think he could learn a great deal from you. I do hope you'll give him a chance."

"Of course," she said, feeling suddenly guilty. Why was she so quick to damn someone she had just met? No doubt Anders was a good man who was just a bit overeager. Still, it was hard not to think of the words that had flashed on the computer screen just before the knock sounded on her door.

He's coming....

Not, *Someone's coming*, or even, *A man is coming*. But rather, *He's coming*. It was as if the shadowy one had specifically meant Anders.

"Deirdre?"

She sat up straight in the chair. "I'm sorry. My head's a bit cloudy this morning, that's all."

"Not to worry. We'll start you off slow. You can forget that assignment I gave you yesterday. Anders already started on it this morning. Take this instead, and let me know if you need anything. Good day, Miss Falling Hawk."

She stared at the folder Nakamura placed in her hand, then with all the grace and self-determination of the assistant director's puppet, she rose and tottered out the door.

When she reached her office, Anders sat at one of the desks, typing on a notebook computer so hard she wondered that the keys didn't fly off. He looked up as she entered, his blue eyes as jolting as before, then smiled, an action that deepened the pits in his cheeks.

"Good morning, Deirdre."

He pronounced her name *DEER-dree*. She might have found it slightly charming if there had been any caffeine in her system; there wasn't.

"Hello, Anders."

She slung her briefcase onto her desk and shrugged her

leather jacket off, then looked down at the baggy sweater and faded jeans she had donned in a mad rush to get out the door. Anders wore another dark, elegant suit that could barely contain his shoulders.

"I hope you don't mind—I started on that cross-indexing assignment Nakamura gave you. I didn't know which desk was whose, and the assignment was sitting here, so I thought, bugger, maybe I'd better get to it."

Deirdre forced a smile and held up the folder Nakamura had given her. "Don't worry about it. I'm all set."

Anders kept typing. "I'll tell you, I never thought I'd be much into computer work. I was a bit worried about that when I decided to join up. But crikey, it turns out I'm a fiend for it. I got here at quarter to seven just to get a jump on things."

She held a hand to her pounding temple. "I'm sure you did."

"There's coffee over on the filing cabinet there. Help yourself."

Deirdre couldn't resist the lure of caffeine and went over to investigate. There was a stainless-steel carafe, several mugs, and a carton of real cream. She filled a mug from the carafe, laced it with a generous dollop of cream, and took a sip. The coffee was superior.

She raised an eyebrow and gazed at Anders over the mug. "Who brewed this?"

"I did. The beans are Kenya Double-A. I got them on my last trip home. That coffee came from the best field in my family's plantation."

So that was the source of the accent she couldn't quite place. He was Kenyan, descended of British colonials. As she moved back to her desk, she noticed the bouquet of flowers in the center of the claw-footed table.

"Someone sent you flowers?" she said, then took another vitalizing sip.

"Not bloody likely," Anders said with a gravely laugh. "In case you haven't noticed, I've got a mug only a mother could love. And even my mum squints when she looks at me. I brought those in myself. I thought they might cheer up the place."

Deirdre sat at her desk. For some reason it bothered her to

drink Anders's coffee, but it was a matter of survival. By the third cup her brain finally kicked into gear, and she was able to focus on the papers Nakamura had given her.

She didn't know if it was ironic or simply fitting, but her assignment was to perform a survey of historical cases from the seventeenth and eighteenth centuries and determine if any of the Nine Desiderata had been broken in the course of each case. The goal of the study was to determine if the modern definitions of the Desiderata were in any way at odds with how the rules were applied in the first two centuries of the Seekers' history. Deirdre had to admit, it was an interesting topic. All the same, it was a bit on the academic side.

Be glad you have work to do at all, Deirdre. They could have ousted you from the order. Besides, research is exactly what you need to be doing right now.

However, as the day wore on, there was no opportunity to perform any more searches about the message on the keystone and Glinda's ring. The way the desks were arranged, Anders only had to turn his head slightly to see her—as well as the contents of her computer screen.

He did this what seemed like every ten minutes, asking her some question or another about how best to construct search queries, or what were her favorite indexing techniques. Deirdre did her best to answer his questions, and each time he'd respond with an outpouring of gratitude that made her cringe before he turned his broad back to punish his computer some more.

By afternoon, despite the warning of the shadowy stranger last night, she could only think that Anders really was nothing more than a chipper tyro. True, he did seem a little old for a fresh recruit. She guessed him to be somewhere in his late thirties. Then again, people came into the Seekers at all ages, and from all different backgrounds. The only thing they had in common was an unquenchable curiosity—and a belief that there were worlds other than Earth.

At five o'clock, Deirdre couldn't take it any longer. Her desk looked like the aftermath of a battle between two libraries; papers and open books were heaped in chaotic piles. She took one last slug of coffee and grimaced; it was ice cold. Her headache had returned—the result of too much caffeine this time. The only thing that would get rid of it was a pint of beer.

And so one vice leads smoothly into another. Maybe hitting the pub isn't such a good idea.

Then again, knowing you had a problem was the first step in ignoring it. She shut her computer, stuffed it into her satchel, and stood.

"I'll see you tomorrow, Anders. Thanks for the coffee."

Anders looked up from his computer and grinned. "No problem, mate. See you."

Deirdre noticed that all of the papers on his desk were arranged in neat stacks. She turned before he could see her grimace and headed out the door. Belatedly, she realized she should have invited Anders to the pub. With Farr, it had been an unspoken agreement that they would go out for a pint after a day at the office. However, before she could go back, Sasha appeared from around a corner and hooked her elbow around Deirdre's, guiding her down the corridor.

"So, who's the Neanderthal with the bottle blond hair?" Sasha said, dark eyes gleaming. Today she was dressed like a ski resort vixen, from her too-tight sweater to the pink leg warmers.

"What?" Deirdre feigned mock surprise. "You don't already know? He's my new partner, Anders."

Sasha scowled. "Is that his last or first name?"

"I honestly don't know."

"You'll have to try to peek at his ID card. I bet his first name is Leslie or Carol. You know, something that doesn't go with the rough and rugged image."

"Like designer suits, flowers, and gourmet coffee?" Deirdre mused with a sharp smile.

Sasha didn't seem to hear her. "He's a bit scary-looking, to say the least. The baby blues work, though. And the muscles, of course, but that goes without saying."

"He's my new partner, Sasha, not my motorcycle daddy."

"Oh, yes, I bet he's got a black leather getup in his closet," Sasha went on eagerly, on a roll now. "You know, chaps, studs, whips—the whole scene. If you like that sort of thing. Oh, Deirdre, you don't like that, do you?"

Deirdre gaped at the other woman. *"No!"*

"Too bad," Sasha purred. "Farr was way too vanilla in my opinion. I think you could do with a little danger. It's good for the complexion." She patted Deirdre's cheek. "See you, darling."

26.

Travis, Jay, and Marty reached the homeless shelter just in time to get the last few scoops of half-burnt oatmeal and reconstituted eggs. They ate it ravenously, even Travis. He had to eat to stay warm, and to have the energy to do what he intended to do.

Except that thought brought a wave of nausea with it, and he wished he hadn't drunk so much of the bitter, black coffee they served at the shelter. Something Professor Sparkman had said in the park that morning was important, Travis was sure of it, but his head throbbed, making it impossible to think. It had to do with matter and energy, and the missing mass in an atom. . . .

"That tasted like crap," Jay said, pushing back his paper plate, which he had wiped clean of every speck of food.

"What are we going to do today?" Marty said.

Jay let out a belch. "We need money. I think it's time for a little can collecting. What do you say, Travis?"

He stood up. "I can't. I've got to . . . there's something I need to do."

Jay gave him a suspicious look. "It's not something voices are telling you to do, is it?"

Despite the buzzing in his head, Travis grinned. "No, I came up with this all on my own. How about if I meet you guys later back at the park?"

"Just so long as we don't have to talk to Sparkman again," Jay said. "Let's meet there before dark. The shelter still has a waiting list a mile long, so maybe we can find another place tonight where you can do your little hot cement gimmick."

Marty gave an enthusiastic nod. "I liked that."

Travis promised them he would. The two men waved goodbye, then headed out the door. Travis stared at his empty plate, then dumped it in the trash and ventured out.

He spent the day wandering the gray streets of downtown, trying to gather courage enough to go through with his plan.

And just what is this plan that requires so much courage? came Jack's inquisitive voice. *I've never been able to fathom you, Travis, but I have to say, your current behavior is more confounding than usual.*

Travis started to tell Jack to be quiet, but he forgot the words as something caught his eye: a red piece of paper taped to a newspaper box. He moved to the box and tore off the paper. On it was the photocopied picture of a man. He was handsome, smiling in his tuxedo jacket—a wedding photo. There was a name and address below the picture, but it was the word above, printed in large type, that Travis read over and over. *Missing.*

The wind snatched the paper from his hand, and it fluttered away. He squatted, peering at the headline through the scuffed window of the newspaper box, but the lead story was about how the crime rate had gone down 32 percent since Denver began its contract with Duratek Corporation.

They control everything in this city, Travis. That has to include the newspapers. You won't read any news stories about the abductions.

Yet Anna Ferraro had done a story about the disappearances on TV. Maybe Duratek didn't control everything.

Not yet, anyway. Travis stood, shivering in his parka. He had no idea why Duratek was abducting people, but it was hardly out of character. What was the life of a homeless person to them if they could gain from it?

Except it wasn't just the homeless who were vanishing now. The man on the flier had been happy, loved. Someone missed him. Travis didn't know what that meant. He turned his back on the newspaper box and trudged on.

At last, as the late-afternoon sun angled toward the mountains, he found himself in Confluence Park. It was here, at the point Cherry Creek flowed into the Platte, where gold was first found in 1858. Maybe Travis would find what he was looking for here as well. He headed down a bike path and found a shadowed nook beneath the Speer Boulevard bridge. On the other side of the river rose the spires of the Steel Cathedral, and they looked sharp enough to cut the sky.

He glanced down. The iron box rested in his hands. He didn't remember pulling it out.

Was this really the right thing to do? Maybe not, but it seemed to be the only option. He didn't know where in the world Duratek's gate was hidden, and even if he did, there was no way to get out of Denver and go there. Yet there was still something he could do for Eldh. He could destroy any chance Mohg had of breaking the First Rune.

He could destroy Krondisar and Sinfathisar.

I knew you were scheming something, Jack said, his words thrumming angrily in Travis's mind. *And I must say, this is most rash indeed. I wish you had brought this foolish idea up earlier. For you see—*

Travis envisioned *Sirith*, the rune of silence, and Jack's voice was cut short. He had known Jack would object to his plan, but Travis couldn't let anything stop him.

He opened the box, took out the Stones, and held them in his right hand, feeling the hum of power against his skin. It would be so easy. He was a runelord—all he had to do was invoke their power and he could do anything he imagined. The wall between the worlds would fall down like a curtain, and he would see his friends standing before him, smiling, arms outstretched...

No. That was precisely why it was so dangerous to use the Stones. Because it *was* easy.

I won't become like Mohg. I won't.

Travis sensed Jack's muffled protest, but he ignored it. Tightening his fingers around the Stones, he spoke the one word that could save him.

"*Reth.*"

Power condensed out of thin air, striking him, racing along bone and flesh, as if his body was a lightning rod. He went rigid, unable to blink, to breathe, as the magic coursed through him—down his arm, into his hand, crackling around the two Stones like the vengeful blue fires of heaven.

The flames burned themselves out. Sweating, trembling, Travis slumped against a cement column and looked down. He expected to see a charred stump, but his hand was whole, unmarked save for the thin white scar on its back. Stiffly, he turned his hand over and unclenched his fingers.

The Stones glistened on his palm, smooth and perfect. Krondisar seemed small and dull in the gloom beneath the bridge, while Sinfathisar shone with soft gray-green light. For a time he simply stared. At last a laugh rose within him, only when it reached his lips it emerged as a sob. Nothing had happened. The Stones weren't so much as scratched.

"Maybe it's because I'm on Earth," he said. A passing bicyclist glanced at him, then pedaled hard down the path. "Rune magic is weak here. That has to be it."

You're wrong, Travis.

Travis tried to shut out Jack's angry voice. "Magic doesn't work right in Denver. It's dangerous, but I'll have to risk going back to Eldh to destroy the Stones."

But you can't destroy them. That's what I was trying to tell you, only you were too hardheaded to listen.

"I won't believe that. There's got to be a way."

There isn't. The Stones cannot be destroyed.

Travis felt his own anger rising. "And how would you know?"

Because we already tried long ago to destroy them.

Travis's anger sublimated into a soft breath, white on the cold air, and melted away. "What?"

It was in the years following the War of the Stones, Jack spoke in his mind. *In the first days of Malachor. After Ulther wrested them from the Pale King, the Great Stones were given to the Runelords.*

"For safekeeping," Travis managed to croak.

No, not for safekeeping. With the Stones, the Pale King might have gained dominion over all of Eldh, and his master, Mohg, would have used them to break the First Rune. It was decided that it was best for the world if the Stones were no more, so the first mission of the Runelords—the very purpose for which the order came into being—was to destroy the Great Stones so that they could never again be used for evil.

Travis couldn't believe what he was hearing. The Great Stones made the wonders of runic magic possible. Would the Runelords really have given that power up so readily?

There was some dissent, Jack's voice said in answer to these thoughts. *A few said that rather than destroy the Stones, we* should use them for good. Kelephon was chief among them. I imagine even then he was scheming a way to gain the Stones for himself. However, though he was the most powerful among us, even he dared not stand against the will of King Ulther and Empress Elsara. For years we labored, exerting all our skill and effort in an attempt to destroy the Great Stones. But no matter how many of us came together, no matter what runes we chanted or sundered, we could do no harm to the Stones.

In the end, the only way we were able to damage the Stones was by seeking out blood sorcerers in the far south. Three came back with us to Malachor, enticed by gold, and working together they were able to remove a single grain from Gelthisar. However, in the process, all three were slain. And when the grain they had removed came in contact with Gelthisar, it bound itself to the Stone, becoming one with it again.

Travis squeezed his fingers around the Stones. So that was how Dakarreth had managed to remove two grains from Krondisar. The Necromancer's magic—like the magic of all the New Gods—was of the south, and born ultimately of blood sorcery.

Do you see it's no use, Travis? The Stones are greater than any of us. There is nothing you can do to destroy them.

Could that really be true? Travis remembered a story he had read long ago, about terrible rings of power that only a dragon's breath could destroy.

No, Travis—the dragons ever loathed to come near the Great Stones. The Gordrim are older than the world, but the Imsari are older yet. The dragons have no power over them. And it's a good thing. You heard what the scholar you spoke with this morning said. Breaking apart things is dangerous, and there is nothing more primal, more powerful than the Imsari. What if you really were somehow to break them?

A jolt of fear coursed through Travis. What had Professor Sparkman said? Something about how a chain reaction, if nothing stopped it, could go on forever....

Travis swallowed the sickness in his throat, then put the Stones back into their iron box and shoved it into his pocket. He started trudging down the bike path.

What are you going to do now, Travis?

"I don't know, Jack." He felt tired and hollow. "I can't destroy the Stones, and I can't take them back to Eldh. And if I try to leave Denver to find the gate they've created, Duratek will catch me."

By Durnach's Hammer, what are you talking about, Travis? Didn't you hear the voices on the contraption your scholar friend was listening to this morning?

Travis shook his head. What was Jack talking about? The voices on Sparkman's receiver hadn't said anything that could help him, though they had belonged to Duratek agents—he was sure of that. No one else on Earth would make a communications code out of Eldhish words—

He stopped in his tracks.

Eldhish words. He had set the silver half-coin down, then had listened to them speak something in a mixture of English and Eldhish. He wracked his brain, trying to remember.

They said they were heading to the taldaka *location,* Jack said. *And they also made mention of a* senlath.

The silver half-coin, in his pocket now, worked its magic, translating the Eldhish words. *Senlath* meant priest. And *taldaka* was . . .

"Gate," Travis murmured. "They were talking about the gate. It's not somewhere else in the world. It's here in Denver."

Which meant there was a way to stop Duratek after all.

Hope rekindled in Travis, bringing with it new energy. He started moving once more, jogging along the river path. "I have to go see Sparkman again, Jack. I have to listen to his receiver and monitor their transmissions. If I do, maybe I can learn exactly where in Denver they've hidden the gate."

Very well, Travis. But do be careful. Night is coming soon, and it's not safe to be out alone in this city.

"It's all right, Jack. I'll be meeting up with . . ." What were Jay and Marty? He had only met them last night, so they couldn't be friends, could they? ". . . with some guys I know. We'll stick together."

This seemed to satisfy the voice in Travis's mind, and it stayed quiet as he headed back downtown and caught the free shuttle up Sixteenth Street. Dusk was falling by the time he reached Civic Center Park. Columns glowed in the half-light like the bones of a ruined Greek temple. He searched around and saw two figures—one tall, one short—near the center of the park. Travis hurried over to them.

"Dammit!" Jay jumped around. "You shouldn't sneak up on a guy like that. Especially not when people have been disappearing. I practically shot out of my skin."

"Sorry," Travis mumbled. He always forgot others didn't see so well in gloom as he did.

"So," Jay said, "did you get your thing done today, whatever the hell it was?"

"Not exactly." Travis looked around. "Where's Professor Sparkman?"

Jay shoved his hands in his pockets. "I don't give a rat's ass where that nut job is. Maybe the voices told him to whack his head off this time. Anyway, it's going to be a cold night, so let's get a move on before all the good spots are taken."

Travis gazed around the shadowed park, but he saw no sign of a wheelchair.

"We can come find him tomorrow," Marty said in his slow voice. "He'll be here once the sun is up."

They headed back to the viaduct by the river where they had spent the previous night but found it already taken—though the new occupants were having no better luck starting a fire than Jay and Marty had. Travis started to move forward, to help, but Jay grabbed his arm.

"You don't know those guys, Travis. They could pull something on you."

"You mean like a knife?" Travis said, giving the little man a pointed look.

Marty shook his head. "I told you it was a bad joke."

"Both of you maggots shut up," Jay said, and he stamped back up the embankment.

They ended up in a narrow alley between two warehouses off Kalamath Street. They built a fire from more pilfered loading pallets, and Travis pressed his hands to the cinder-block wall, muttering *Krond* over and over, until waves of warmth radiated forth. Jay let out a laugh and pressed his back to the wall. Marty opened his knapsack and pulled out a loaf of white bread and packages of bologna and American cheese—all bought at a

7-Eleven with proceeds from the day's bottle-collecting venture.

Travis tried not to eye the food as Marty put together a thick sandwich, then to his surprise and delight Marty held the sandwich out toward him.

"You provide the heat, we'll provide the food," he said, grinning.

"You got that right," Jay said, rubbing his hands together in front of the fire. "Having a wizard around is damn handy."

Travis accepted the sandwich in shaking hands—he hadn't eaten since the shelter that morning—and managed to wait until Jay and Marty had sandwiches themselves before greedily eating it. They talked and ate until all the food was gone, then lay close to the fire on ragged blankets as Travis whispered *Krond* again and again. Before long the food and heat did their work, and he drifted into a dream in which Anna Ferraro stood over him, her TV reporter smile firmly affixed to red lips.

"So how does it feel to know you're going to destroy the world?" she said, jamming a microphone into his face.

Travis fought for words. "I . . . I don't want to destroy it."

"So that means you believe you will," she said with a gleam in her eyes.

"No, I didn't mean . . ."

"That's all we have time for." She pulled the microphone away. "You know, you shouldn't all go to sleep at the same time. That is, unless you want to be the next ones to vanish. It's dangerous out here."

Travis jerked awake, and after that he kept watch for several hours, staring into the dark until he couldn't keep his eyes open any longer. At that point he woke Marty with a gentle shake. The tall man agreed to keep a lookout, then wake Jay to take the last watch. Travis curled up next to the dying fire and whispered *Krond* until sleep took him once again.

When he woke, the sky was as flat and white as a sheet of paper, and Jay and Marty were already rolling up their blankets. The fire was out, and it was bitterly cold.

"I don't want to be the last ones to breakfast today," Jay said, "and I figured you'd be dragging us by the park again to see old Sparky. So let's get moving."

Despite all they had eaten last night, the idea of food set Travis's stomach to growling. Trying to keep warm took a lot of energy. Or was it using magic that made him so hungry?

Civic Center Park was on the way as they headed back to downtown. The gold dome of the Capitol blazed to life as they walked between the library and the art museum into the park. Sunrise. Sparkman should be there.

Travis searched around, then saw it not far off—a wheelchair, angled away from them. Only it was sitting in a patch of shadow by a tree. That was odd. He hurried over, Jay and Marty behind him.

"Professor Sparkman," he said as he approached the chair, "I need to listen again to your—"

He came to a halt, staring at the wheelchair. It was empty. For a moment Travis thought it wasn't his. Then he saw the faded bumper sticker slapped on the back of the seat. $E=mc^2$. There was no sign of the receiver.

Jay clamped his wool hat down on his cranium. "Hell, I was only kidding about him chopping off his head."

"He didn't chop off his head," Marty said, brown eyes sad.

Travis shuddered. It was just like his dream about the TV reporter. *It's dangerous out here,* she had said. He touched Professor Sparkman's empty wheelchair and breathed a foggy sigh. "They took him."

"The aliens," Marty said.

Travis didn't have the energy to disagree. He leaned on the handles of the wheelchair. Now how would he learn where in Denver they were hiding the gate?

"Well," Jay said with a shrug, "since we're not going to talk to Sparky, we might as well go get breakfast."

27.

Aryn stood atop the battlements of Calavere and watched the band of horsemen ride toward the castle.

She had first spied them when they crested a hill more than a league from Calavere, and now they moved along the road like a dark cloud. She wondered what land they hailed from. One of the Free Cities? The Dominion of Embarr? She would find out soon, and anyway it was a small band—no more than twenty.

Then again, if one was patient, even a large bucket could be filled a drop at a time.

They had begun arriving the day after Grace left Calavere. The first was a band of thirty men who rode shaggy horses across the Darkwine Bridge. They were brutish and half-wild, clad in leather and mismatched armor. However, to Aryn's surprise, when their leader presented himself to Boreas in the lower bailey, he spoke in the well-mannered tones of a nobleman. He was a duke of Eredane, and those who followed him earls and knights. They had been driven from their keeps by the Onyx Knights over a year ago, and had spent the time since living on the edges of the Dominion, hiding from their enemies, and harrying them when they could.

"Things are worse in Eredane than you know," the duke said after he gripped Boreas's arms in greeting. "The dark knights rule by sword and flame, but even they do not dare stand against the Raven Cult. More fall under the shadow of the Raven each day—entire villages are branded with its sign, and they take to the roads, abandoning field and home, marching I know not where. On some terrible pilgrimage, I fear."

Each day more men arrived at the castle, some on horses, some on foot. They came alone, or in small bands, or in companies of a hundred or more. A few of them were nobles, like the duke and his men, but many more were farmers and freemen, or merchants and traders and craftsmen. Some, given their rough looks and even rougher manners, were little better than mercenaries and thieves. Boreas welcomed them all.

They hailed from every direction. Some spoke of daring escapes from Brelegond, which—like Eredane—was ruled by the Onyx Knights and plagued by the Raven Cult. Others had abandoned farms and families in Calavan, Galt, Toloria, and Perridon. They had put down hoes and spades and had traded them for old swords that had lain in chests, forgotten for years.

The only Dominion not represented so far was Embarr, which boded ill for that land. However, of all the Dominions, Embarr was farthest from Calavan. Perhaps men would yet come from there. Besides, it was not from the Dominions that most of the men would come. Like all the Mystery Cults, the Cult of Vathris Bullslayer had its origins in the ancient lands of the south, and it was to the south that King Boreas looked.

The first men from Gendarra and the other Free Cities had arrived several days ago. They were equipped with fine armor and swords, for some of the wealthiest merchants in the Free Cities were patrons of Vathris. Men from Tarras had begun to arrive as well, and yesterday the first band of men from Al-Amún had reached the castle, riding white horses with arched necks.

The men were as proud and exotic as the horses they rode. Their hair was long and black, and gold and lapis lazuli gleamed against their dark skin. Aryn thought them as fierce as they were beautiful. They saluted King Boreas with curved swords, and he invited them into the castle to speak.

Women were not welcome in the great hall when the king was meeting with his warriors, and Aryn imagined that was doubly true for witches. Nor did she have Aldeth to spy for her any longer. However, she had other ways to observe. She had cast a spell on a small amethyst, and she had left it in a niche near the king's throne at an opportune moment.

Late last night, when she was certain she wouldn't be seen, she stole back into the great hall to retrieve the gem. Once in her chamber, she held the gem in front of a candle, and in its many facets she saw reflections not of herself, but of the great hall. She watched as the men of Al-Amún approached the throne, and the gem seemed to hum in her hand as the words they and the king exchanged sounded in her mind.

You have answered my call more quickly than I could have hoped, King Boreas had said.

One of the men bowed before him, then spoke in a richly accented voice. *I must confess, Great Man of Vathris, it was not in answer to your call for war that we first set out on the road to the north.*

Boreas raised an eyebrow, and another of the men stepped forward.

A vision came to some of us in our dreams, he said. *In it, Vathris appeared and told us the Final Battle drew near, and that it would be fought not in the south, but in the icy lands of the north. So we began our journey, and it was only as we were about to set sail across the Summer Sea that your message reached us, and by it we knew our visions were true.*

And how many more are behind you? Boreas said.

The man who had first spoken laughed. *We are but the first of many. Already they gather at the ports faster than ships can bear them across the sea, and so they build more ships. A great host comes behind us, a host larger than any this world has ever seen. The end of all things comes, and any true man of Vathris would die before he would ignore the call to war. So what if it is our destiny to fail? At least in fighting, we will know a glory greater than any other.*

These words filled Aryn with awe and dread, and the amethyst tumbled from her hands, cracking as it struck the floor. It didn't matter; she had heard enough. The prophecies were true. The Warriors of Vathris would come, they would march to the Final Battle. And they would be defeated.

But how can any of this possibly make a difference if they're doomed to lose?

"There you are, sister," said a warm voice, snapping her back to the present. "I thought I might find you here."

Aryn looked up to see Mirda walking along the battlement. The witch wore only a light cloak against the cold, and her multihued gown fluttered in the wind. Aryn smiled as the elder witch halted beside her, then her smile faded.

"What is it, sister?" Mirda said.

"I don't know. I think, despite everything that's happened, I still wanted to believe it was all just a story. But it's not a story, is it? The Final Battle is coming, if it hasn't already begun." Aryn pointed. "Look—more warriors ride to the castle even now."

Mirda sighed. "You're right, sister. It isn't simply a story, much as you or I might wish it were. There are dark times ahead of us, but there is yet hope that we will find light on the other side." A smile touched her lips. "And are you so certain it is a group of warriors who rides to the castle now? Your eyes are keen, but you have sharper senses."

Aryn shut her eyes and reached out with the Touch. Swift as

a sparrow, she let her consciousness fly along the threads of the Weirding toward the band of riders. She could see them far more clearly than before, outlined in shimmering green...

Aryn gasped as her eyes flew open. "We have to find Lirith at once."

Mirda nodded, her smile gone.

As it turned out, Lirith found them first, coming upon them as they rushed down a corridor. Aryn met her dark eyes and saw the knowledge in them.

"You already know," Aryn said. "You've had a vision, haven't you?"

Lirith nodded. "It's Queen Ivalaine. I saw her in my mind. She'll reach the castle in minutes."

Aryn's chest grew tight. "Do you think she knows about us? About our—?" She didn't dare speak the words *shadow coven*.

Mirda started down the corridor. "Come, sisters. Let us hope we can meet the queen before she takes an audience with King Boreas."

When they reached the massive set of doors that led to the great hall, Aryn let out a breath of relief. The doors were open. She picked up the hem of her gown and started toward them.

"Now that's a funny sight," said a sardonic voice just to Aryn's left. "I thought witches were supposed to be so mysterious and powerful, but you look more like three field mice who've just seen the shadow of a hawk."

Aryn pressed a hand to her chest. A shadow separated itself from the dimness of an alcove and stalked toward her.

"Prince Teravian!" she said, and surprise gave way to annoyance.

A smirk crossed his face, marring its handsomeness. "That was fabulous. I thought you were going to faint."

She gave him a stiff bow. "Anything to please you, Your Highness. Shall I fall and crack my head open on the stones for your further amusement?"

He rolled his eyes. "Gods, Aryn. I thought you had learned how to take a joke."

"Perhaps it would help if you actually learned how to tell one, Your Highness," Lirith said, moving closer. "You seem to subscribe to a rather abnormal definition of humor. I can mix a potion that will cure you of that affliction, if you like."

Teravian grinned. "Now *that's* funny."

Aryn gave Lirith a grateful look. The dark-eyed witch had a deft way with the prince. Of course, the fact that he had a crush on her certainly helped. Aryn wished she was as good at dealing with him, especially since he was soon to be her husband. True, they had made strides in their relationship—Teravian had even helped her on one occasion. However, conversations like this were still the norm rather than the exception, and in the last week he had seemed more sullen and solitary than usual.

Aryn decided to start over. "What are you doing here, Your Highness?"

He scowled. "You know perfectly well why I'm here. Queen Ivalaine will ask to see me—she always does. I was fostered at her court, after all."

Mirda gave him a sharp look. "And how did you know the queen was coming?"

A startled look crossed his face, but it was replaced so quickly by anger that Aryn wasn't certain she had seen it.

"Why bother asking me?" he said, glaring at the elder witch. "Can't you just use a spell to pick apart my brain and find the answer for yourself?"

Mirda gazed at him with her wise eyes.

Teravian looked away first. "I'm going to wait with my father." He turned and strode into the great hall—so swiftly he didn't notice as something fell to the floor. Aryn bent to retrieve it. It was a glove; he must have had a pair tucked into his belt. Except why had he been carrying gloves inside the castle?

Aryn didn't care. She would return it to him later. "Every time I think maybe he's not so awful as I thought, he does something to prove me wrong."

"Do not judge him too harshly, sister," Mirda said, touching Aryn's shoulder. "There is much that troubles him."

"Yes, but what? He's been acting strangely lately. More strangely, I mean. I often see him riding out of the castle alone. I think he's up to something."

Lirith gave a rich laugh. "I believe the prince is always up to something. It's his nature." She glanced at Mirda. "But Aryn is right. He is changed of late, and his power is growing. He seems able to disappear into shadows at will, and I would wager a month of *maddok* he's weaving a spell of illusion to do it."

Mirda gazed after the prince. "In the end, he may be stronger than all of us." She glanced at Aryn. "Or nearly all. However, he will not come into the true fullness of his power until he is a man."

Aryn frowned. "But the prince is eighteen now. Surely that's old enough to be considered a man."

"I do not speak of his age," Mirda said.

Lirith raised an eyebrow. "I see. But he is a prince. Any number of bold young women in the castle would be glad to make themselves available to him. I'm surprised he has not already lost his maidenhead."

"Perhaps he knows what it will make of him," Mirda said.

Before Aryn could ask what that meant, one of the king's guards pounded down the corridor and dashed into the great hall. Moments later, Queen Ivalaine appeared around a corner, accompanied by a pair of knights. She still wore her mud-stained riding gown, and her flaxen hair was tangled from wind. Whatever her business here was, it must be urgent indeed.

Ivalaine strode swiftly down the corridor, her pale eyes fixed on the doors of the great hall. It seemed she would walk right by the three women.

"Your Majesty, please!" Aryn gasped.

Ivalaine hesitated, then turned to look at her. The queen's eyes were feverish, and they darted about, not focusing on anything for more than a moment.

"Do not approach me again," Ivalaine said, her voice flat and cold. Her hands twitched against her gown; her fingernails were dirty, worried down to the quick. "I have nothing to say to any of you. I come here for one and for one only."

Aryn felt Lirith go stiff beside her. "But, sister, we ask only that—"

"Do not call me that ever again," Ivalaine hissed. "I am no one's sister anymore. Nor am I Matron. Though perhaps, if it is not too late, if I have not ruined everything with my folly, I may still be a mother."

With that the queen strode into the great hall. The doors shut with a boom like thunder, leaving the three women to stare in astonishment.

That night, Aryn hoped to get another chance to speak with Ivalaine at supper. However, the seat at the high table to King Boreas's left remained empty; there was no sign of the queen anywhere in the great hall. Or of Prince Teravian, not that his absence was a surprise. He rarely took the seat to Boreas's right these days, though it was always reserved for him.

The king sat in the center of the high table, glowering at no one in particular. Despite the many warriors who streamed into the rapidly growing camp below the castle, Boreas had been in a bleak mood ever since the day of Lady Grace's departure. And it wasn't just Grace's absence that troubled him, for it was later that same day that Beltan had disappeared, along with Vani. No doubt Boreas missed having his nephew for a commander.

"They've gone to find Runebreaker," Mirda had said. "They're going to bring him back to Eldh."

The gate artifact had gone missing with Vani and Beltan. Somehow they had found a way to activate it, and they had left without telling anyone, though where they had gone was not in question. Both loved Travis Wilder. Surely they had gone to him as Mirda said.

Aryn sighed, and such was her own bleak mood that she had little appetite. Lirith and Sareth had opted for a quiet supper alone, and Aryn wished she had followed suit. When the servants brought out the subtleties—usually her favorite dessert—she stared at them without relish. The sugary confections were molded into various shapes. Aryn had gotten a dragon.

Remembered words hissed again in her mind. *And here are two daughters of Sia, both doomed to betray their sisters and their mistress. . . .*

Did Ivalaine know of their betrayal of the Pattern? Was that why she had spurned them? Aryn smashed the dragon with a spoon, then excused herself from the table.

She walked the castle corridors for a time, then found herself before the door to Sareth's chamber.

You shouldn't bother them, Aryn.

However, even as she thought this, the door opened, and she found herself facing Lirith.

"What is it, sister?" the witch said. "Is something amiss?"

"No, nothing." Aryn grimaced. "Except that Grace has ridden off to the Final Battle, Beltan and Vani have gone to bring Travis Runebreaker back to Eldh, and Queen Ivalaine won't even talk to us. Oh, and I'm going to be married to a prince who abhors me. Other than that, things are just fine."

Sareth—who sat next to the fire—let out a bell-like laugh. "Well, you might as well come in and have a cup of *maddok*. It doesn't sound like you're going to be getting any sleep tonight."

Aryn imagined not. She gazed around as she stepped into the room. "I'm not . . . interrupting anything, am I?"

"Only my departure for the evening," Lirith said briskly. "But you know me—I can always be persuaded to take another cup of *maddok*."

It turned out to be two cups, not one, and Aryn was glad of the company. Sareth relinquished the chair by the fire, and Aryn sat in it, sipping the hot, spicy liquid. The last things Aryn wished to speak about were current events, so instead Sareth told stories of ancient Amún and the fabled city of his ancestors, Morindu the Dark. Aryn tried to imagine what it would be like—an entire city of sorcerers. What a strange, shadowed, and wonderful place it must have been.

At last the hour grew late. The women bid Sareth farewell, then walked together back to their own chambers. However, Aryn found it odd that Lirith didn't stay behind.

Her thoughts must have been louder than she intended.

"There is no reason for me to stay with him," Lirith said softly.

Aryn glanced at her, shocked. "I don't understand. Don't you love him as he loves you?"

"I do, but . . ." Lirith hesitated, then took Aryn's hand in her own. *There is no hope for us, sister. I cannot give him a child as a woman should. And ever since the demon took his leg, he cannot do what a man would do with a woman in his bed.*

Anguish squeezed Aryn's heart. *But is there no spell that can help you?*

I have tried with all my skill, but if there is a magic that can help either of us, it is beyond me.

It doesn't matter, Lirith. You love each other, and surely love is more than lying down together, or making children between you. It has to be.

Lirith pulled her hand from Aryn's and let out a bitter laugh. "Love doesn't matter to his people. Their laws forbid him to wed outside his clan. One day he will return to them. And on that day he will leave me. Good night, sister."

Lirith stepped into her chamber and shut the door. There was nothing for Aryn to do but continue to her own room.

She chided herself as she walked. *You are small and selfish, Aryn of Elsandry. Your problems are nothing to what Lirith and Sareth are suffering. So what if you are to marry Prince Teravian? He's sullen, yes, but you could do far worse. Besides, it's not as if there's another whom you love.*

Except for some reason that last thought left her feeling strange and weak, and her hand shook as she fumbled with the latch on her door. It was the *maddok*, of course. She shouldn't have drunk so much; she would never be able to fall asleep.

Her room was dark—the fire had burned low—but a sliver of moonlight fell through a crack in the curtains. She stumbled her way to the window and pulled back the curtains to let more of the silvery light into the room.

Aryn froze. Below, a slim figure clad all in black stalked across the courtyard of the upper bailey. The figure stepped into a pool of shadow and vanished, but Aryn had seen enough to know who it was.

"Where are you going, Teravian?" she whispered. There was no way to find out without following him, but by the time Aryn got all the way down to the bailey, he would be long gone.

Maybe there's a swifter way, sister.

Aryn didn't give herself a moment to think about it, afraid she would change her mind. She moved to the sideboard and picked up the glove Teravian had dropped earlier that day, then she sat in a chair.

This was foolish and dangerous. Once, when performing a spell like this, Grace had nearly lost her spirit forever. If Ivalaine had not intervened, Grace would have died. Aryn knew she should go fetch Lirith.

No, there isn't time. They always keep saying how strong

your talent is, Aryn. Well, now's the time to prove it. If they're right, you can do this.

She gripped the glove with both hands, then she reached out with the Touch, spinning a thread along the Weirding and weaving it around the glove.

An instant later she was flying. Aryn glanced over her shoulder and saw herself through the window of her chamber, sitting in a pool of moonlight, eyes open and staring. A silver strand stretched back to her body. She knew if the thread was severed, she would die. Forcing away the thought, she faced forward and let the magic draw her on.

The spell led her down into the upper bailey. She passed through the shadow of the keep, then feathery shapes rose before her, frosted by the light of the moon. Aryn felt a tug as the spell pulled her through a wrought-iron archway and into the castle's garden.

A dizziness came over her as she flew along twisting paths, and she was terribly cold. Was she dying? She glanced back, but the thread still stretched behind her. The spell led her onward, deeper into the garden.

"I knew you would come to me," said a woman's voice.

If she could have, Aryn would have let out a scream. Had she been seen somehow?

"It's not as if I really had a choice," sneered another voice, which Aryn instantly recognized as Teravian's. It was not Aryn the woman had addressed, but the prince.

Aryn drifted around a curve in the path and came to halt. Before her was a grotto sheltered by *valsindar* trees. Teravian stood in the center, his dark attire blending with the night, his face pale in the moonlight. The woman who had spoken stood a few feet from him, though who she was Aryn couldn't say, as she was clad from head to toe in a dark cloak.

"You are dutiful," the woman said to Teravian, her voice hoarse. "Just as a son should be."

He let out a sharp laugh. "I'm his son, too, aren't I? But here I am all the same."

Confusion filled Aryn. What were they talking about? Teravian was son only to King Boreas. His mother, Queen Narenya, had died long years ago.

"You know what you will be asked to do, don't you?" the woman said.

He stared into the darkness. "I've seen it. Bits of it, anyway. It comes in flashes. There's a battlefield, and two armies face each other. Both of the armies carry banners bearing the crown and swords of Calavan, only one is green and yellow instead of silver and blue."

The woman drew closer. "And what else do you see? Which army will prevail?"

"I don't know. It's all a fog after that—I can't see it." His eyes narrowed. "And what do you care, anyway? You've cut yourself off from them, haven't you?"

"Care? What do I care?" The woman muttered the words, as if trying to fathom their meaning. "I suppose I care for nothing now, save to keep him from using you."

His lip curled into a sneer. "What, so you can use me yourself, is that what you mean? I know you've been watching me all these years, prodding me, trying to figure out a way to use me for your own ends."

The woman pressed a hand to her chest. "You know much. And yet so much less than you think. Perhaps once I did seek to use you, though my intentions were good. But no more. My thoughts are for you only. I would have you do this thing not for them, but for yourself. That's why I've come."

"I wish I could believe that."

She reached a hand toward him. "You must trust me."

"Trust you?" Anger twisted his face, and he clenched a fist. "How can I trust you when you've lied to me all these years about who you really are, who I really am? You're no better than he is. Why should I trust either of you, Mother?"

Shock coursed through Aryn. Mother? What was he talking about? Before she could wonder more, the woman reached up with shaking hands and pushed back the hood of her cloak. Her flaxen hair was colorless in the moonlight, and tears streamed down her smooth cheeks.

"Trust me because I love you, my son," Queen Ivalaine said. "As I have always loved you, even when I could not tell you the truth."

Teravian laughed. "Now you're lying again. But I'm not a child anymore. You can't trick me as you used to."

"Please," Ivalaine said. "Please don't turn from me, Teravian. You're all I have left."

He gazed at her, his eyes calculating. "Then you have nothing, Mother."

The prince turned and walked from the grotto. He moved right past Aryn, but he did not pause. The shadows took him, and he was gone.

"Go," Ivalaine hissed, the tears drying on her cheeks.

She was staring right at Aryn. Only that was impossible. She must have meant the word for Teravian.

"I see you there, witch," Ivalaine said, her face a white mask of rage. She pointed a trembling finger at Aryn. "Go spin your evil threads with your shadow coven and leave me alone!"

Horror flooded Aryn. The world became a dark blur, and she felt a wrenching inside. Her eyes snapped open. The garden was gone; she was back in her chamber, and she was terribly cold.

Aryn forced her stiff muscles to move, pushing herself out of the chair. She had to find Lirith and Mirda and tell them Queen Ivalaine had gone mad.

28.

After the battle against the *feydrim* and wraithlings, the army turned north. They kept close to the rugged foothills of the Fal Erenn, marching just outside the borders of Perridon to avoid having to beg Queen Inara for permission to travel across her Dominion.

Not that Grace would have minded seeing how the young queen and her son were faring. Grace had not seen them since last summer, when all of them had faced the Necromancer Dakarreth in Castle Spardis. However, though they continued to make good time thanks to clear weather and Tira's meddling with distances, they could ill afford a detour all the way to Spardis.

The excitement they had felt at the start of the journey was forgotten now. What little of it had remained had died along with the *feydrim* and wraithlings in the rocky hills of the Dun-Dordurun. The camp was quiet at night; the ale had run out over a week ago, and the supplies of food were being rationed carefully. They had many days yet to Gravenfist Keep, and once there, who knew how long their supplies would have to last?

Perhaps not long at all, Grace, if we don't find a way to restore the keep's defenses.

But they still had hope. She touched the leather pouch at her waist which contained the small disk of white stone she had found in the arm of Chair Malachor. The men around her were grimmer than before, hardened by the road but not yet made weary by it. Their victory against the forces of the Pale King in Dun-Dordurun had lent them a confidence they had lacked before. They knew now they could stand against this enemy.

Don't get cocky, Grace. Winning that battle was an accomplishment, but fifty feydrim *and two wraithlings are just a drop in the bucket. How many thousands more will be waiting when we get to Shadowsdeep?*

She gazed at the dark clouds that rose up from the northern horizon. They pulsed with a sickly, yellow-green glow, as if lit from behind by sulfurous fires.

"What is it, Your Majesty?" Durge said.

Only as he spoke did she realize she had sighed. She glanced at the knight, who rode nearby.

"We've turned north, Durge. Every step brings us closer to Imbrifale now. Closer to *his* Dominion."

"Journeys have a way of doing that."

She shook her head. "Of doing what?"

"Taking one to a final destination." Durge started to lift a hand to his chest, then lowered it back to his thigh.

Grace licked her lips. "It's the pain again."

"It is nothing, my lady."

She opened her mouth to say more, but at that moment Sir Tarus's charger pounded up to them.

"I just thought I'd let you know we'll be making camp soon, Your Majesty," the red-haired knight said. "Aldeth tells me the Spiders are scouting for a suitable place even now."

Grace wrapped her arms around Tira's warm body in the saddle before her. "I don't think anyplace around here is really suitable, Tarus."

The land around them was broken and barren, a series of featureless plains scarred by deep gorges. All that day, a cruel wind had rushed down from the mountains to their left, slicing through wool and leather like a cold knife. Grace looked forward to sitting as close to a crackling fire as she could without becoming kindling herself.

Aldeth appeared out of a shadow a short while later to let them know a place to make camp had been found. They reached it just as the sun sank behind the mountains: a flat area beneath a cliff that offered good protection from the wind. Already the men were beginning to pitch tents and dig latrines. A group stopped in their work and raised their fists, cheering, as Grace rode by. The men had being doing that a lot lately, ever since the battle, and Grace never knew quite how to respond. She settled for a crooked smile and an awkward little wave.

Durge helped Grace down from Shandis's back, and Tarus lifted Tira from the saddle. He started to set her down, but the girl threw her arms around his neck, gripping him tightly.

"I believe she likes you, Sir Tarus," Durge said.

Grace moved closer. "No, look at her. She's frightened—that's why she doesn't want to get down." She touched Tira's cheek. "What is it, sweetheart?" But the mute girl couldn't—wouldn't—answer. She only buried her face against Tarus's shoulder and held on tighter.

Grace met Durge's eyes. "Something's wrong."

"I think you're right in that, Your Majesty," said a woman's voice.

Grace gasped as, with a flick of her silvery cloak, Samatha appeared out of thin air.

"What is it, Sam?" Grace said, doing her best to swallow her heart back down.

The Spider's mousy face was pinched with concern. "Two of our brothers are missing. We all went ahead a few hours ago to seek a place to stop for the night, but Henrin and Wulther never returned."

That was strange news. It wasn't like a Spider to get lost,

even in rugged country such as this, and Grace would hardly expect one to fall into a ravine.

"Where's Aldeth?" Grace said.

"He's gone off in search of the missing Spiders. Leris and Karthi are helping him. I wanted to inform you what's happened, but now I must help Aldeth in the search."

Grace nodded, and Samatha started to move away, but before she could wrap her mistcloak around herself, a cry rose up from the far side of the camp. Several of the men gathered around, shouting. Grace cast glances at the others, then they were running across the camp.

The knot of men parted when Grace approached. She hurried forward, Tarus and Durge at her heels, then clasped a hand to her mouth as she lurched to a halt.

The two men lay in a patch of brambles, staring upward with dead eyes, silver-gray cloaks tangled, limbs entwined as if in a final embrace. A knife protruded from one's chest. Another had bled out from a long gash in the throat.

"Sweet Jorus, no," Samatha gasped, her face white. She fell to her knees, clutching their bloodied cloaks.

Tarus clenched his hands into fists. "By all the gods, who did this to them?"

"They did," Paladus said.

The others stared at the Tarrasian commander. He had been in the group of men gathered around the bodies.

"Do you not see it?" Paladus pointed to the bodies. "Look at the way they have fallen, and how this one grips a knife still. These men murdered each other."

"But why would they have done such a terrible thing?" Tarus said, shielding Tira's eyes with a hand.

"Maybe they accepted what we've all been denying," Samatha said, rocking back and forth in her grief. "Maybe they knew we're all doomed."

"Yes," Durge said softly, gazing at the dead men. His hand crept up to his chest. "Doomed."

Paladus spun around, his face flushed. "I might expect that kind of talk from a weasel and spy like her, but not from a man of war. Speak that way again, sir, and I will show you doom." His hand moved to the hilt of his sword.

Tarus advanced on the commander. "Hold your tongue, Paladus. You have no right to talk to a knight of the Dominions in such a coarse manner."

Tira wriggled free of Tarus and ran to Grace, clutching her skirts. Grace picked the girl up, staring, unable to believe what was happening.

Paladus's eyes narrowed. "I'll say what I know to be true. You northerners are a lot of weaklings and cowards. You'd be dead already without us."

Tarus bared his teeth. "We're not going to stand for talk like that, are we, Durge?" Durge only stared at the corpses, but Tarus seemed not to notice. He advanced on the commander. "We don't need help from a bunch of mangy southern dogs."

Paladus's face darkened, but before he could speak Samatha leaped to her feet. "Go away!" Her voice rose into a shriek. "All of you, go away! My brothers are dead, and you're like vultures circling the bodies."

Aldeth stepped out of a swirl of mist; a fog had begun to rise from the ground, its touch clammy and chilling. He took in the fallen men, the angry faces, and his eyes went wide. "By the Seven, what's going on here?"

That was a good question. Grace shut her eyes and reached out with the Touch.

It yawned like a mouth in the Weirding, black and hungry, swallowing all light, all life that came near it.

She was a fool. It was in western Perridon where they had first encountered such a thing. She should have known they might come upon another. Her eyes flew open.

"Durge," she said, pointing a trembling finger toward the thicket of brambles. "In there."

Her voice seemed to snap the knight out of his torpor. He stepped over the bodies, using gloved hands to push aside the brambles. His work revealed a stone column about five feet high, the three planes of its sides glossy and black, carved with jagged symbols.

Durge looked back at Grace, his face gray. "It's a pylon, Your Majesty."

Paladus and Samatha stared in confusion. Tarus held a hand to his head and staggered. "What's a pylon?"

"Evil," Grace said through clenched teeth. "Get away from it—all of you. We can't make camp here. We have to leave this place. Now!"

As if they were a spell—and indeed, she wasn't certain she hadn't unconsciously woven some magic into them—her words seemed to dispel the dark cloud that fogged their minds. Paladus and Tarus exchanged stunned looks, then both were striding toward the camp, shouting orders. Aldeth helped Samatha to her feet.

"We have to bury them," Aldeth said, gazing at the fallen Spiders.

Samatha looked at Grace, her cheeks wet with tears. "Only we can't, can we?"

Grace hesitated, then shook her head. "Their bodies are tainted with the magic of the pylon. We must not touch them. I'm so sorry, Sam."

"Then we'll use fire," Aldeth said, eyeing the dry bushes surrounding the dead men and the pylon.

Samatha gave a grim nod. "I'll get torches."

"Come, my lady," Durge said, his voice hoarse. "Let us get away from this thing."

They pressed on as night cloaked the world. Thankfully it was clear and there was a quarter moon; otherwise, they would have ridden right into one of the ravines that crisscrossed the landscape. As it was, they went slowly, stumbling their way over heath and stone, relying on the Spiders for their eyes.

As they rode, Grace could not stop thinking of the pylon, and how it had spun its black tendrils out over the world. Last year, they had unwittingly camped near a pylon, and it had driven them all to the brink of despair and madness. However, that stone had taken hours to affect them, while this pylon had seemed to work its terrible effect in mere moments.

It's no longer dormant like the other was, Grace. It's awake, and it's working.

Falken had said the pylons were created during the War of the Stones a thousand years ago, and that the Pale King had used them to communicate with his slaves. Had this one been watching them even as they argued before it?

The horizon had begun to glow with faint silver light when

Durge rode close and told her they had to stop. The foot soldiers were exhausted from marching so long without rest and food, and some of the horses were on the verge of collapse. Grace was so tired herself she couldn't manage spoken words, so she simply nodded her assent.

It was dawn by the time they had finished setting up camp, and much as she hated the delay, Grace knew the army would not be going anywhere that day. After a cold breakfast, Durge stopped by her tent to report that all was well, though tempers had been flaring. There was some fighting among the men, and a few had even come to blows, but without serious injury.

The violence was a residual effect of the pylon, Grace knew. She could still feel its presence, like a slick of oil on her skin she couldn't wash off. Leaving Tira in their tent, Grace went in search of Senrael and Lursa, and together they wove a spell that allowed them to gaze for leagues along the Weirding, but they sensed no trace of another pylon.

After that, Grace paid a visit to All-master Oragien and young Master Graedin, and in short order all of the runespeakers were wandering through the camp, speaking the rune of peace. This had the calming effect Grace hoped, and after that the camp grew quiet as the men finally rested.

When she returned to her tent, she found Durge waiting for her with a handful of men. Some stared at the ground, their faces blank, while others could not stop sobbing.

"These foot soldiers were the ones working closest to the pylon," Durge said quietly to Grace.

She nodded, then examined each of them in turn.

"I don't know what's wrong with me, Your Majesty," one of the men said as she touched his brow. "I've never been one to tuck my tail and run from a fight."

Grace smiled. "I imagine not." He was a burly fellow with big, scarred hands.

Those hands were trembling now. "By Vathris, look at me. I'm shaking like a frightened lamb, and there's nary a wolf in sight. It's foolish, Your Majesty, what with you being such a fierce warrior, and a great sorceress as well—but I feel all cold and watery inside, as if we haven't a hope in the world."

"There's always hope," she said briskly. "And don't worry

about how you're feeling. It's an effect of the pylon. In fact, you're remarkably brave. Most people who stood near it as long as you did would have been reduced to jelly."

Or would murder each other in a blind rage. But she didn't say that, and her words seemed to hearten the fellow. She spoke similar words of encouragement to the others, and she examined each of their threads. However, she could see no signs of permanent damage. She discharged the men, giving them each a simple to help them sleep, and excused them from any duties that day so they could rest.

"Yours is a healing touch, Your Majesty," Durge said after they had gone.

Then why can't I excise the iron splinter from your chest? Only those were more words she could not speak.

"Get some rest, Durge," she said instead.

"As you wish, Your Majesty," he said and left her tent. However, she knew he wouldn't. The tireless knight would keep on working so others could rest in his stead. Grace didn't know how he did it. A crushing weariness descended upon her, and she curled on her cot next to Tira, who was fast asleep.

Grace, can you hear me?

The voice was familiar, comforting. Grace must have been dreaming.

Please, Grace. Are you there?

Grace's eyes opened, and she sat up. "Aryn?"

Yes, Grace, it's me. Thank Sia I've found you. There's a shadow in the Weirding not far from here. I had to follow other threads far around it. Lirith had a terrible feeling that something had happened. Are you all right?

Grace sighed. *We are now. At least, most of us.*

Quickly, she explained what had happened: the dead Spiders and the pylon. She spoke also of the battle in Dun-Dordurun and her strange meeting with Queen Ivalaine.

Oh, Grace, I'm so sorry. I shouldn't have waited so long to reach out to you. I think I was afraid talking to you would only make your being so far away harder to bear.

Grace smiled, her weariness lifting as the bright energy of her friend filled her. *How are things in Caluvere?*

The Warriors are arriving in droves now, even from the far south. Soon Boreas will march north with a great host. But there's something else, and hearing your story helps me understand it a little better. Still, I have to think she's going mad.

A chill passed through Grace. *What are you talking about, Aryn? Who's going mad?*

Queen Ivalaine. . . .

Grace wrapped a shawl around herself as Aryn spoke of Ivalaine's unexpected arrival at Calavere, and of the way the queen had spurned Aryn, Lirith, and Mirda.

She said she'd have nothing to do with us, that she had come here for one only. I couldn't imagine what she meant. Then, last night, I wove a spell. It was dangerous, I know, but I saw Prince Teravian in the garden talking with Ivalaine.

Grace shivered. *But what on Eldh does she want with the prince?*

The words flew along the Weirding in a rush. *He's her son, Grace. Queen Ivalaine is Prince Teravian's mother.*

They spoke for another few minutes across the web of the Weirding, until at last the effort was too much for Aryn.

I have to go, Grace. I'm getting tired, and I can't guard our thread any longer. I can't be certain that she . . . that someone isn't listening to us. We all love you, and I'll contact you again soon. Sia be with you.

Good-bye! Grace called out in her mind. Only Aryn was already gone, and Grace was shivering, alone in the tent save for Tira, who was still fast asleep.

Grace was glad to know the men of Vathris were answering the call to war. But what was Ivalaine doing, and how could the prince be her son? Before she could think of an answer, the tent flap opened.

"Forgive me, Your Majesty," Samatha said, ducking her head inside the tent. "But you must come with me at once."

Grace met her gray eyes, then she grabbed her cloak and headed outside. The sun was at its zenith, and the day was bright and cold. She instructed the guard posted by her tent to keep an eye on Tira, then followed the Spider across the camp.

"What's going on, Sam?"

"I found the signs not far from here, and Leris and Aldeth were able to come upon them unaware. However, they reacted swiftly. They had some magic that monitored their hideout. One of them was slain, but we caught the other alive."

Grace grabbed the Spider's arm. "What are you talking about? Whom did you capture?"

The Spider held out her hand. On her palm, a small, black object absorbed the sunlight. A hiss of static issued from the speaker embedded in the plastic device. Grace snatched it from the Spider's hand, then they were both running.

They came to a tent on the edge of the camp. Leris stood outside. The Spider was so slight Grace would have taken him for a twelve-year-old boy on Earth. That would have been a deadly mistake. Leris nodded, and they slipped inside.

The tent was dark. Grace concentrated, touching the threads of the Weirding, and a ball of green witchlight sprang into being above her, pushing back the shadows. The man sat on the ground, his hands and legs bound with ropes, blood trickling from a scrape on his cheek. She recognized him. He was dressed in the rags of a peasant, but his skin was clear of disease, and standing he would have been tall.

"Your mission is over," Grace said. "Your only purpose now is to answer my questions. You will speak precisely, truthfully, and without hesitation. Do you understand?"

The man squinted against the glare of the witchlight, and Grace knew he couldn't see her. "Please, my lady." His voice quavered. "I'm but a simple farmer. I know not what you speak. I ask only that you let me return to my village."

The performance was convincing. He was speaking in Eldhish, and his accent was that of a commoner. They had learned more these last months than she would have thought; no wonder they had managed to blend in so well.

"I know who you are," she said in English.

The man snapped his head up, and his eyes went wide—but only for a moment before they narrowed again.

"And now I know who you are as well," he said, his voice hoarse but defiant. "It's hopeless, Dr. Beckett. We're close now— closer than you can possibly imagine. There's nothing you can do to stop us from getting what we want."

"Really? It seems I've done pretty well so far."

He glared at her, straining against the ropes; they creaked but held fast.

"The pleasantries are over," Grace said, speaking in Eldhish again. "Now it's time for you to talk. You'll tell me what your mission is, who sent you, and how you got here."

He shifted back to Eldhish as well, his accent that of a groveling peasant once more, only mocking this time. "You'll get nothing from me, my lady. Your only choice is to kill me as your slaves killed my partner."

Aldeth stepped from the shadowed corner of the tent and knelt, pressing a knife to the man's throat. "I can arrange that, if you'd like."

"That's not fair, Aldeth," Samatha said, moving forward, her own knife drawn. "You and Leris got to kill the last one. This one's mine, and I'm going to savor every moment of it."

Grace made a sharp motion with her hand. "No, Sam, Aldeth—no knives. I'll deal with this."

The two Spiders reluctantly sheathed their weapons and stepped back.

Grace stood above the prisoner. "If you won't speak of your own free will, I have other options at my disposal."

"Like what?" he sneered.

She had no time for games. "Like this."

Grace reached out with the Touch and gripped his thread. He resisted, but his will quickly crumbled before her own. No doubt his training had inured him to any sort of physical torture, but nothing could have prepared him for this. She probed deep into his mind, searching for whatever knowledge she could excise.

The prisoner screamed. "Get out! Get out of my head!"

Grace let go of his thread. The prisoner slumped over, sobbing and shaking. Snot ran from his nose.

"So that was what Duratek was doing at the facility in Denver," Grace said, feeling cold and sick. "They were creating a gate. First they found a way to send messages through, then objects. That was how you communicated with the Scirathi, how you got them guns. Now Duratek has finally figured out the last step. They've learned how to send people through the gate. People like you, Agent Hudson."

The prisoner rolled back and forth on the ground, speaking shrilly. She knew the hole she had left in his mind would soon drive him mad.

"The first ones . . . they died. They were ripped to shreds the moment they stepped through the gate. But the scientists kept working, and after that others made it through, and they sent a few reports from the other side, reports about the languages and cultures and geography. Only something went wrong in the process of translocation. The scientists called it cellular disruption. All I know is their bodies . . . they dissolved into sludge in a few days. All the same, I volunteered when I had the chance, along with Meeks and Stocker. We were the first to make it through and survive." A shudder coursed through him. "Only Meeks caught something a while back—a disease the meds couldn't stop. He died last week. And your men killed Stocker. I'm the only one left. I'm the only one. . . ."

Grace staggered, and she might have fallen except for Samatha's steadying hand. "Only more are coming. I saw it. They think they can break the gate wide open now."

The prisoner's shaking eased, and his lips twisted into a smile. "That's right, Dr. Beckett. We made it through, and we lived. That means the scientists have finally gotten the calibration of the gate right. All they need now is more of whatever fluid it is that powers it, and I hear soon they'll have it by the gallon."

"Yes," Grace said, sifting through the information she had ripped from his mind. "Fairy blood. They're trying to synthesize it in their labs. And they're close. But what's their plan once they have it?"

The prisoner looked up, his eyes full of hate. "No more answers for you, Dr. Beckett."

He clenched down hard on his jaw. Even as Grace heard the sharp sound of porcelain breaking, she knew what he had done. His eyes rolled up into his head, and his body went limp.

"Dammit, no!" Grace flung herself down beside him.

"What is it, Your Majesty?" Aldeth said.

She pried open his mouth. "He had a false tooth. He broke it when he bit down."

Samatha nodded. "Often a spy is given poison to use if he is caught by his enemies."

His breathing was growing shallow, and his thread grew dim. The poison had already spread through him. His heart rate was slowing. It would be a quick death, and painless.

Not if I can help it.

Grace studied the poison flowing through his veins. As if her mind were a microscope, she looked closer, until she could see its molecular structure like a series of colored spheres. It was simpler than she would have thought. A flick of a thought, and the structure was altered. Like a chain reaction, the change spread through his blood.

Hudson screamed, a bubbling sound of agony. His body went rigid as convulsions wracked him. His back arched, the cords of his neck standing out. Purple blotches mottled his skin, and yellow foam boiled out of his mouth.

His screaming phased into words. "Help me! Oh, God, it burns!"

For a moment sympathy pricked Grace's heart. She was a doctor, or at least she had been once. However, she was more than a doctor now. She was a witch, a queen, a woman. And this man had set the bombs that destroyed Calavere's towers.

"Please!" he raved. "Please help me!"

She bent over him, touching his hot forehead with a gentle hand. "No," she murmured.

He was beyond words now, thrashing on the floor. His tongue, black and swollen, jutted from his mouth. It took several long minutes. Then one last scream ripped itself from him, followed by the sudden stillness of death.

Grace stood and turned away from the corpse. Samatha's face was pale, and Aldeth stared with wide gray eyes.

The Spider rubbed his throat. "Remind me never to disobey your orders, Your Majesty."

"I imagine you'll remember all on your own, Aldeth," Grace said, then stepped out of the tent into the failing day.

29

By the time she made it out of the Seeker complex, Deirdre craved quiet and solitude rather than the public clamor of a pub. She took the tube back to South Kensington, picked up a bottle of stout at a shop a block from her flat, and holed up for the rest of the evening.

Midnight found her at the dinette table in front of the phosphorescent screen of the computer. Unfortunately, hours of searching had yielded no more information than she had discovered the night before. Despite its incompleteness, the message on the battered keystone was certainly identical to that inscribed on Glinda's ring. However, what language the message was written in remained a mystery. The Seeker database contained shape and pattern information for all known written languages, modern and ancient, but all of her searches resulted in no matches. Not even the runic language of AU-3—of Eldh—was similar.

If she had hoped the mysterious Seeker would make his presence known to her again that night, then she was disappointed. The pool of light beneath the streetlamp opposite her window remained empty, and the only text that appeared on the computer screen was what she typed herself. When she finally went to bed, she slept fitfully, dreaming of words that shimmered and danced before her. The words comprised an urgent message, she was sure of it, but she couldn't read what they said.

The next morning was better than the previous, if only slightly. Her head still ached, but less, and she made it to work by five minutes to nine. Anders was already there. He must have been feeling more at ease, as he had taken off his suit coat and rolled up the sleeves of his silvery shirt.

He kept pounding away at the keyboard as he glanced up. "Coffee's waiting."

Deirdre sighed as she poured a steaming cup. Maybe she could get used to this whole new partner thing.

She was able to focus better on her task that day, and by noon she had actually started to collect data. According to the official histories, the earliest recorded violation of one of the Desiderata came in 1637, when a Master Seeker was proven to be an opium addict—a clear violation of the Sixth Desideratum: *A Seeker shall not allow his judgment to be compromised*. However, in an old Seeker journal, Deirdre had come upon an even earlier case that, by today's standards, would almost surely have violated the Seventh Desideratum: *The word of the Philosophers is the will of the Seekers*.

It was in 1619, just four years after the founding of the Seekers. A young journeyman by the name of Thomas Atwater was ordered by the Philosophers never to return to the business where he had worked prior to joining the Seekers. Later it was discovered that the young man had indeed visited the forbidden establishment, yet as far as Deirdre could tell, there was no record of reprimand following the incident. Nor was it clear why he had been told not to visit his former place of work.

The documents she had found so far regarding the case were fragmentary and difficult to read. Modern English was coming into focus by the early seventeenth century, but spelling was still a highly creative art, and there was much in the facsimiles Deirdre couldn't decipher. Still, it was an interesting start, so she decided to celebrate by inviting Anders to lunch.

"Have you been to the Merry Executioner?" she asked, pulling on her jacket.

"Never heard of it," Anders said. "Sounds ominous. What is it?"

"It's a pub."

"It's not the food that does the executing, is it?"

"There's only one way to find out, partner," Deirdre said with a smile that surprised her.

They headed out the door—Anders stopped to lock it, which was probably a smart idea, though Deirdre had never bothered herself—then made for the pub.

The Merry Executioner was comforting, though it felt strange to be there with someone other than Farr. Deirdre had steak-and-kidney pie, and Anders got a salad. She had never suspected they served green leafy things in this place, but Anders's salad was large and fresh-looking.

Determined to be a bad influence, she made him get a second pint to keep her company, and as they sipped them she listened to his stories of growing up in Kenya, working in the coffee fields as a boy. Her favorite story was one he told about the day a troupe of monkeys got into one of the warehouses. She could only imagine the chaos wrought by a dozen caffeine-hyped primates.

"Tell me one thing," Deirdre said. "If Kenya is so wonderful, why leave it to join the Seekers?"

Anders quaffed the last of his beer. "We'd better get back to it, hadn't we?"

He rose and headed out the door, moving so quickly she was forced to jog to keep up. By the time they walked down the corridor to their office, she was panting for breath.

"I'm in worse shape than I—"

Anders held up a hand, cutting her off. She gave him a puzzled glance. He nodded toward the door of their office, then she saw it: The door was cracked open an inch.

Who would have a key to their office? Nakamura, she supposed. And Fergus and Madeleine, of course. Perhaps the receptionist had needed some form or requisition one of them had forgotten about and had let herself in. Deirdre would ask her about it when—

Anders reached inside his suit jacket and pulled out a sleek pistol. He pressed his back to the wall and peered through the gap in the door, the pistol next to his cheek. Deirdre stared. What was Anders doing with a gun? Agents were forbidden by Seeker law to carry weapons. That's why they used security guards on dangerous missions.

Anders nudged open the door. He slipped through with a fluid motion, sweeping the gun left, toward the room's nearest corner. Then he opened the door wider, turned his back to the corner he had just examined, and moved farther into the office.

Deirdre watched from her position by the door. Despite his bulk, Anders moved with a leonine stealth, sweeping with the pistol, always keeping his back toward a part of the room he had already cleared. Finally, he lowered the gun.

"Whoever was in here, he's gone now."

Deirdre approached and gave him a critical look. "Not many Seekers I know are that handy with a gun. Or know exactly how to clear a room."

Anders tucked the pistol back into his jacket, a guilty light in his blue eyes. "Crikey, I thought I could keep it a secret longer than two days."

Deirdre crossed her arms. "Who are you really?"

"Now, now, Deirdre. They told me that to be a Seeker, I'd have to work on my deductive reasoning skills. Haven't you gotten it yet?"

Even as he said this, she did. "You're not a Seeker agent. You're a security guard."

He put his hands in his pockets, looking suddenly boyish. "Well, you're almost right. For ten years, I did work security for the Seekers. But security doesn't get to ask questions. You're just there to take a bullet if Duratek or some other unfriendly type decides to start shooting. But I did have questions—so many of them. I couldn't just stand by and watch anymore."

Anders moved to his desk. "A few months ago, I finally got up the nerve to talk to Nakamura. At first he didn't take me seriously, but I kept after him. He finally gave me an exam—some kind of logic test—and I suppose he thought I'd fail it, and that would be the last of me."

He laughed. "It turns out I pretty well aced the test. I guess it takes a bit more brains to work security than most people think. So Nakamura admitted me as a journeyman agent. Only provisionally, though. He said he was going to put me with one of his best agents, and that after three months it was going to be up to her whether I got to stay or not." He looked at her. "I suppose that's you, mate."

Deirdre crossed her arms. It was a good story. Almost too good. It provided a neat way to keep a security guard close to her when normally she would have rejected such an action.

"What about the gun?" she said.

Anders gave her a sheepish look. "I was supposed to keep that a secret, too. I told Nakamura that, after carrying one for ten years, I'd feel a little naked without it. Since I've got the training to use it, he's letting me keep it. For the moment, anyway, until final word comes down from the Philosophers."

Deirdre searched his face for any hint that he wasn't telling her the truth. She didn't see it, but that could simply mean he was a good liar.

You can't live like this, Deirdre. Anders's story is completely plausible, and no doubt Nakamura can verify everything. You can't be suspicious of everyone around you. It will drive you mad if you do.

As it had driven Farr mad? Except the light in his eyes that last time she had seen him had been anything but crazy. No, Farr had been perfectly sane, and that was what terrified her.

Deirdre made a decision. "You can't keep any more secrets from me, Anders." She smiled, hoping the expression was more reassuring than it felt. "Not if we're going to be partners. We have to be able to depend on each other. Understood?"

Astonishment flickered across his face, followed by a broad grin. "You've got it, mate."

"So, is there anything else I should know?"

He scratched his chin, looking uncomfortable. "Well, only that you've still got a bit of your lunch in your teeth. I've been trying not to notice it, but frankly it's driving me bonkers. That was why I rushed us out of the pub."

Deirdre slapped a hand to her mouth. "Thanks a lot," she muttered through her fingers.

Ten minutes later—after a trip to the rest room, toothbrush in hand—Deirdre sat at her desk. Anders was already typing away on his computer, and she supposed the best way to calm her mind was to try focusing on the task at hand. She picked up a pen and started going over the facsimiles from the 1619 case, reminding herself that, four centuries ago, people had had an annoying habit of writing F's that looked like S's, using Y's instead of I's, and putting E's on the end of pretty much everything.

It wasn't until hours later that she noticed the folder. Anders had gotten up to brew another pot of coffee. Deirdre leaned back, rubbing her neck. She had made good progress on deciphering the pages from one of the old Seeker journals and was ready for more. She shifted one of the towering stacks of papers on her desk.

Unlike the manila folders she used, this folder was red, its flap tied shut with a string. She glanced up at Anders, but his back was still turned as he worked on the coffee. Quickly, she unwrapped the string from the clasp and opened the folder.

Inside was a single black-and-white photograph. It showed what looked like a fragment of a clay tablet covered with two rows of writing. The top row looked vaguely familiar. She had seen writing like that before but couldn't remember exactly what it was. Sumerian cuneiform? No, not quite. Phoenician? Maybe. Then her eyes moved down to the second row of writing, and her breathing ceased.

She recognized the lines of queer, angular symbols. She had stared at them so long, how could she not? They were the same as the symbols on Glinda's ring and the keystone.

"More coffee, Deirdre?"

She stared at the photograph. Anders's back was still turned.

"Deirdre?"

"Yes," she said, managing to breathe again. "Please."

She shoved the photograph back into the folder. As Anders turned around, mugs in hand, she slipped the folder into one of the stacks on her desk.

"Found anything interesting yet?" he said, handing her a steaming mug.

"Not really."

She clutched the hot cup; it burned her fingers, but she didn't let go. *I thought you said partners weren't supposed to keep secrets, Deirdre.*

"Well, keep trying," Anders said with a wink.

He returned to his desk. Deirdre ached to pull out the folder again to study the photograph, but she didn't dare. And she didn't need to look at it again to know what it was.

It was her Rosetta Stone.

30.

Travis huddled in the blue shadow of an alley a block from the downtown Denver police station, waiting. Cautious, he peered out around the corner of the alley until he could see the front door of the station, but there was no sign of either Jay or Marty. The sun was already skittering across the tops of the foothills. They had been inside over an hour.

It had been Travis's idea to come to the police station, to file a missing person report about Caleb Sparkman, and while Marty had agreed right away to the plan, it had taken most of the day to convince Jay it was a good idea. Nor would Marty go without Jay; he looked to the smaller man as his leader.

"Why don't you go do it yourself, Mr. Wizard?" Jay had said after the third time Travis asked him to file the report. At the time they were rooting in Dumpsters along Santa Fe, looking for cans and bottles to trade in for money, loading them into a battered shopping cart.

After swallowing the lump in his throat, Travis had explained how his photo had been shown on the local television news last fall. Marty shrugged at this information, while Jay was clearly impressed. He pestered Travis relentlessly to know what he had done to get on the wrong side of the law. All Travis told him was that it was a misunderstanding, which Jay obviously didn't believe.

After that, Jay had agreed to file the report, and they had headed down Thirteenth Avenue to the police station.

"Don't you worry, buddy," Jay said, punching Travis in the shoulder. "We'll tell them about old Sparky, but we won't let it slip about you being here. Right, Marty?"

Marty had nodded vigorously.

From his hiding place in the alley, Travis had watched the two men walk up the steps and disappear into the building. Only it wasn't the thought of their telling the police he was there that worried him. Rather, it was the fact that he could very well be sending them into danger.

According to Grace, there had been at least one ironheart at the police station. What if he hadn't been alone? Last fall, the police had been working with Duratek, and in Calavere they had finally learned that Duratek was allied with the forces of Mohg and the Pale King. What if there were more ironhearts in the police station, and they captured Marty and Jay, tortured the two, and made them talk about Travis?

Now you're being paranoid, Travis. Marty and Jay are just going to talk about Caleb Sparkman. There's no way the police could know you're involved.

Besides, he couldn't believe that every officer in Denver was an ironheart, or in the pocket of Duratek. The detective on the news the other night—despite having his words cut off by Anna Ferraro—had seemed like he genuinely cared about the disappearances among the homeless.

It grew colder. Minutes crystallized into an hour. Then, just when Travis decided Jay and Marty had been captured, that he had to go in and save them, the door of the station opened, and the two men walked down the steps.

"Did you file the report?" Travis asked as they stepped into the alley.

Jay let out a disgusted snort. "Finally. I told the police they needed to get off their cans and do something about all the folks disappearing, and they didn't seem to like that."

"I wonder why," Travis said dryly.

The little man seemed not to notice him. "Anyway, they couldn't rush us out of there fast enough, but I told them we weren't leaving until we got to talk to someone and file a report about Sparky. They agreed and sat us down in a hallway, but I think we'd still be sitting there getting ignored, except I grabbed one of them as he walked by, and he actually listened to us. Sergeant Otero, that was his name."

Marty nodded. "I liked him. He gave us coffee."

Otero. Travis thought back. Wasn't that the name of the officer Anna Ferraro had interviewed on the news the other night?

"What did the sergeant say?"

Jay jerked his head toward the street. "Let's head over to the recycle center before it gets dark. We'll tell you about it on the way."

As Marty pushed the shopping cart down the street, Travis walked with Jay, listening as the small man described what had happened in the police station. Sergeant Otero had taken their report himself, and he had been excited when he learned Caleb Sparkman used to work for various local colleges.

While Marty and Jay drank hot coffee—Travis envied them that—Otero had called several of the colleges until he found one that still had contact information on file for Professor Sparkman. It turned out Sparkman had a sister in Salt Lake City. Otero had called her, and while she hadn't talked to her brother in years, she had agreed to have her name on the report.

That was good. Sparkman's sister was a real person, with a real home and an address. The police would have to take this case seriously now. They would look for Sparkman, and the others who were missing.

Then again, official investigations could be lengthy, and Travis wasn't sure he had time to wait for the police. He had to find Sparkman. Duratek was behind the disappearances in the city. If Travis found the missing people, he would find Duratek. And, he believed, the gate.

"We've got to start speaking to people," Travis said. "People like us, on the street. We have to see if anyone saw Professor Sparkman before he disappeared."

Jay glared up at him. "For crying out loud, you can't be serious. We went to the police like you wanted. Now it's up to them to do their job. We're done with this."

Travis only shook his head, and Jay grumbled about crazy people all the way to the recycle center.

They traded in the cans and bottles, getting over forty dollars in return. To celebrate, they went to a convenience store and indulged in coffee and microwave burritos, then went back to the warehouses off Kalamath where they had been camping out. They had rigged a kind of shelter from loading pallets and a tarp Marty had bought at a thrift store, and once Travis got the fire going, it was almost luxurious, especially when they broke out the chocolate bars they had bought with their new money.

The next morning they woke after dawn, and as they ate powdered donuts out of cellophane packets, Marty suggested they should get an early start talking to people about Sparkman.

Jay let out a groan. "Not you, too, Marty. What's up with you two morons? I could care less about old Sparky."

"That's not true, Jay," Marty said quietly. "He's a human being. You have to care."

"The hell I do." Jay waved a powdered-sugar-covered hand. "I don't give a damn about anyone."

Marty gazed at him a long moment, then stood. "Come on, Travis. I think we should leave Jay alone."

"Cut that crap out," Jay said, jumping to his feet. "You guys aren't ditching me. If anyone is going to ditch anyone, I'm going to ditch you. Only I'm not. So shut up about all this leaving junk and let's get going."

Marty knelt to roll up his and Jay's sleeping bags, but not before Travis noticed a smile on his lips. Travis smiled himself despite the sourness in his stomach. Maybe Jay wasn't the leader of the duo after all.

They walked over to Civic Center Park first, got coffee from the same street vendor as before, and spent most of the day talking to anyone who would let three dirty, unshaven men approach them. However, no one they spoke to had seen Sparkman the day he disappeared. As far as Travis could tell, the three of them were the last people to see the professor.

Finally, the sun was sliding down toward the mountains, and Travis's stomach was growling again. Jay wanted to head to the shelter to see if they could get a handout for dinner and save some of their precious cash. Reluctantly, Travis agreed. However, as they walked through the row of columns at the park's entrance, a man ambled up to them. He was old and stooped, his gray hair and beard stained yellow, his dirty fingers poking out of worn gloves.

"Are you three the ones asking all them questions about some homeless guy in a wheelchair who disappeared?" the old man said.

Travis gave Marty and Jay a startled glance, then looked back at the old man. He reminded Travis a little of Ezekiel Frost, the half-mad old mountain man in Castle City who had died at the hands of the sorcerer. Only that had been over a century ago.

"How do you know that?" Travis said.

The old man pointed a thumb over his shoulder. "A friend of mine said you was here in the park, and that you'd give a dollar to anyone who knew someone who had vanished."

"A dollar?" Jay snorted. "There's not a chance in hell, we'd give you a—"

Travis punched Jay in the shoulder and ignored his yowl of pain.

"That's right," Travis said to the grizzled man. "Did you know Professor Sparkman?"

"No, but I do know Myra. Did you know her?"

Travis shook his head.

"Old gal, wore a pink coat, usually worked Sixteenth Street. Nice as anything, liked to sing hymns. She went missing a couple of nights ago. We were going to meet at the Steel Cathedral, to see if we could get us some charity. Only she didn't show up, and I haven't seen her since." The old man's expression grew wistful.

Jay's eyes lit up, his outrage forgotten. "So how was it? The Steel Cathedral?"

The old man clapped his hands together and smiled. "It was like heaven on Earth. A warm bed, a hot meal. I was sorry Myra didn't see it. I'm going back there tonight." His eyes narrowed. "So where's my dollar?"

"Is that all you know?" Travis said.

He nodded and held out his hand. Travis glanced at Jay, and the little man swore as he fished a dollar out of his pocket and slapped it on the old man's hand.

"That's coming out of your share, Mr. Wizard," Jay said as they walked away.

Travis hardly heard him. Something the old man had said was important, but it was too cold to think.

"Two nights ago," Marty said. "That was probably when the aliens came for Sparky."

Travis halted. That was it. Myra had vanished the same night as Sparkman. If they found her, maybe they'd find Sparkman as well.

Jay glared at him. "What are you stopping for?"

Quickly, he related his thoughts to Jay and Marty. Myra and Sparkman had vanished the same night. Maybe they had been taken together. The old man had said Myra had been heading to the Steel Cathedral. Sparkman could have been going there, too. After all, it was one of the few places he could have gone for shelter.

"Maybe someone saw them on their way to the Steel Cathedral," Travis finished.

Marty grinned. "Good thinking, Travis."

"Fine," Jay said, pulling his knit cap down over his ears. "I've been wanting to check out that place for ages, anyway, only Marty would never let me. So let's hoof it on down there and see if anyone knows anything about old Sparky. We'll probably find him lounging in a soft bed, eating hot food. And I plan on joining him."

"What about his wheelchair?" Marty said. "Why was it still here in the park?"

"Hell, the folks at the Steel Cathedral probably gave him a silver-plated one. They're rich, aren't they? I guess if you're holy enough, all of them prayers for money must really work."

Marty looked up at the sky. "Does that mean if you're poor, you've done something bad?"

Jay's expression softened a fraction. "You aren't capable of being bad, Marty. That's my job. Come on, let's go."

Jay and Marty started walking, but Travis hesitated. The two turned and looked at him. Travis wasn't sure why, but for some reason he didn't want to go to the Steel Cathedral. He couldn't put the feeling into words. Maybe it was just that a place that grand didn't seem for the likes of him.

"You two go ahead and check it out," Travis said. "I'm going to collect some cans so I can make up for the money we had to give that old guy. Okay?"

Marty gazed at him with his thoughtful brown eyes, but Jay shrugged.

"Suit yourself, Mr. Wizard. Come on, Marty. Let's go see if we can get us some good Christian charity."

Travis agreed to meet them later in Confluence Park. He watched the two men walk away, trying to ignore the odd feeling of dread in his stomach. He pilfered a plastic bag from one of the park's trash receptacles and started collecting cans.

"And that was when I saw the light. It was, like, totally blinding, but it didn't hurt to look at it."

Travis's can collecting had taken him to the south side of the park, to the edge of the outdoor amphitheater where plays and concerts were performed in the summer. A dozen or so teenagers were hanging out on the stone benches, some lying on their backs, others grooving as a boom box thumped out a techno beat. Despite the cold, they bared as much flesh as they could to show off their multiple tattoos and body piercings.

The young people were speaking over the music, their voices echoing around the amphitheater. Travis froze in the act of reaching into a trash can as the young woman whose voice he had first heard rang out again.

"So he tells me, 'The Brights are coming, they'll take you away from me, we've got to go.' And he grabs my hand, and we run like crazy, and I swear my heart is going to explode."

For emphasis she pounded the front of her puffy down vest, and the others who watched her raptly let out appreciative gasps. She was pretty, despite being too thin, and despite the bad dye job on her green hair and the thick black lines around her eyes, which gave her pale face a sickly cast.

"Finally, we get to his car, and he floors it, and we get out of there. Only then I look back out the window, and for a second I swear I can see them in the light. The Brights."

"So did they get you, Jessie?" a young man asked, awe on his pimply face, his speech slurred by the multiple rings jutting out of his lower lip.

She put her hands on her hips and glared at him. "I know it's hard for you, Todd, but try thinking. If they got me, would I be here talking to you now?"

The young man tugged on his lip rings; it was going to take him a while to puzzle that one out.

The young woman—Jessie—looked up, her dark eyes glinting. "Hey, up there—grungy old man rooting around in the trash can. I know you're listening to us."

Travis pulled his hand out of the trash can and stood up. "It's sort of hard not to." His own heart was thumping. Had she just been telling a story to impress her friends? Or had she really seen something? Something that came in light. . . .

It can't be, Travis. She's just making it up. You should go meet Jay and Marty. They'll be waiting for you.

He set down his bag of cans and started down the steps of the amphitheater.

"Cool," the young woman said, hopping down off a bench. "A new toy to play with."

She sauntered toward him, cheap black boots scuffing against stone, hands on her hips. She barely came to his shoulder, and she was bony as a bird, but there was a sensuousness to her, a fact she was clearly well aware of. The others watched her with a mixture of adoration and anticipation.

"You should get out of here," she said. "I can do magic."

"Like what."

Like this. Her lips didn't move, but her voice sounded—distant but clear—in his mind.

Travis raised an eyebrow. So she was a witch. Not a very powerful one, given the faintness of her voice in his mind, but a witch all the same. That was interesting.

He knew there was magic on Earth, though it was a shadow of the power that resided on Eldh. Marji, the West Colfax psychic who had helped them last fall, and who had died for her kindness, had certainly possessed true power of vision. And even before she came to Eldh, Grace had used the Touch without knowing it to heal people at Denver Memorial Hospital. All the same, to encounter a young witch here struck Travis as odd. She belonged on that world, not on this one.

Maybe the worlds really are getting closer, just like Brother Cy said.

Travis crossed his arms. "Nice trick. Now tell me about the Brights."

She glared at him, clearly disappointed her little spell hadn't gotten more of a reaction out of him, then fidgeted with the ankh symbol that hung around her throat.

"The Brights take them for Him."

"For who?"

"Don't you know anything? For the One-Eyed Dude, who else?"

He shivered, and her purple lips coiled in a smile. That had gotten a reaction out of him. She reminded Travis of the witch Kyrene, who had tried to use him for her own ends not long after he first journeyed to Eldh. Only Kyrene was the one who had been used in the end. All the same, Travis knew he had better be careful.

"You're right," he said, his voice hoarse. "I don't know anything at all. Tell me about the One-Eyed Dude."

"I know about him," said another young woman, sliding off a bench. She twirled a lock of greasy blond hair. "If you light nine black candles in a circle at midnight and face west and pledge your soul to him, you'll see him."

"And have you ever done it, Tiffany?" Jessie asked, turning on her.

The other young woman stared, then shook her head.

"That's because you're chicken shit," Jessie said. "So shut your face already."

The blond girl slunk back to her bench.

Travis tried to swallow the sick lump in his throat. "So you've seen him, then?"

Jessie flicked her hair back over her shoulder. "Why should I tell you?"

He said nothing. She wanted to tell him; she would speak if he waited.

It didn't take long. "You can't see him anyway, not really. He's like a shadow in the night, that's all." The calculating light fled her eyes, and a haunted expression took its place. She folded her skinny arms over her chest, as if suddenly feeling the cold. "But you can see his eye, burning like fire in the dark. He wanted me to give myself to him."

The others were staring at her, mouths open.

"Did you?" Travis said.

She looked up, the haunted look gone, a fierce grin cutting across her face. "I don't take orders from anybody. My mom told me to stay away from my stepfather, but just like that I had him wrapped around my little finger. She wanted to kick me out of the house when she found out, but I told her I'd go to the police and tell them he touched me. That shut her up. I got out of that pit anyway a few months later, but I still make her give me money when I want it."

Travis sucked in a breath. She was like Kyrene indeed. He chose his next question carefully.

"So what do they want—these Brights, as you call them?"

She shrugged. "How should I know? All I know is that they're looking for something—something He wants. And they'll bring it to Him when they find it."

All warmth fled him. He reached into his right pocket, gripping the iron box.

Her eyes narrowed into dark slits. "You know something, don't you, old man? Don't lie—I can tell. That's part of my power. I think maybe I'll tell them about you. I bet they'll give me something good if I do."

He could hardly speak the words. "Tell who?"

"The Deadies. They work for him like the Brights do. Only they hate the Brights. I did it with one once. He showed me his scar. It was totally awesome." She ran a finger down her chest, between her breasts. "His skin was hot to the touch, but when we were done, I put my head against his chest and listened, and I didn't hear anything. No heartbeat."

The others let out squeals of horror and delight at this story, but Travis hardly heard them. He could only stare at the young woman. Beings who came in light, searching for something precious. Men without hearts. A master who gazed from shadows with one fiery eye...

Cold fingers caressed Travis's spine. It wasn't just Duratek behind the abductions. He was in grave danger.

Jessie eyed him. "Shit, you really do know something, don't you?"

Her fingers fluttered, and he knew she was weaving a spell. A moment later he felt it—a presence pushing against his mind, probing for knowledge.

Travis didn't even have to speak the rune of breaking. He merely thought it and gave his hand a flick. Her spell unraveled like a cheap cloth, and her eyes flew wide as she staggered back, gasping for breath.

He grinned, a fierce expression. "You're not the only one who can do magic."

Rage flashed across her face, followed by fear. Yes, she sensed the power humming on the air. Without even thinking to, Travis had opened the iron box in his pocket. His fingers brushed the Stones. "Go before I hurt you."

"They'll find you," she snarled. "You can't win against them. That's the one thing I do know."

He raised his left hand. Silver-blue light crackled around his fingers. "I said get out of here."

The others let out yelps of fear, then they were running, leaving their boom box behind. Jessie glared at him, her eyes full of hate. She made a hissing, animal sound, then turned and ran after the others.

Travis waited until they were lost to sight, then he sank down to one of the benches. The magic had faded, leaving him weak and empty. He reached into his pocket, pulled out the iron box, and made certain it was tightly shut.

But it was too late, wasn't it? He had opened the box once before, thinking them a world away. Only they were here in Denver. Wraithlings. They would sense the presence of the Great Stones—if Jessie didn't tell the ironhearts about it first. Either way, the result was the same.

Mohg, Lord of Nightfall, knew Travis was here.

31.

A voice woke Aryn in the chill gray before dawn.

Sister, do you hear me?

Aryn flung a hand over her eyes and rolled over. The voice was in her mind. She was dreaming, that was all.

You must listen to me, sister. I have to leave now, and I know not when I shall return.

Aryn's eyes flew open, and she sat up straight in bed. This was no dream. "Mirda, is that you?"

Yes, sister. It is I. Look out your window.

Aryn threw back the covers, slid down from the bed, and padded barefoot across the cold floor. Light seeped into the room as she pushed back the curtain. Below, a figure in a green cape stood in the bailey, gazing upward.

"But I don't understand," Aryn said aloud, forgetting to project her words along the Weirding. Her brain was still dull from sleep. "Where are you going?"

On a journey of great distance. I am needed elsewhere.

"But we need you here!" Aryn said, her breath fogging the window.

Mirda's voice was reassuring but adamant. *No, sister, you do not. You and Lirith are both stronger than you believe. You have all you need to meet the trials ahead of you.*

Despair crushed Aryn's heart. This couldn't be happening. Everyone had left them—Travis, Grace and Durge, Beltan and

Vani—and now Mirda was leaving as well. She pressed her right hand against the chill glass. *But why do you have to go?*

There are others who do need me, and I must go to them at once. But do not fear, sister. I believe we shall see one another again before all is through.

There was so much Aryn wanted to say—how afraid she was of the future, how lost she felt, and how much she would miss Mirda's wisdom and strength. However, sorrow had swelled her throat, and for all her power the only words she could spin across the Weirding were, *May Sia be with you.*

Below, in the bailey, the figure in green lifted a hand.

She will be, sister. She will be.

The figure turned and glided from the bailey, disappearing through the gate just as the sun crested the horizon, transmuting the sky from lead to copper. Aryn gazed at the empty bailey for a long time, then turned to put on her dress and go tell Lirith what had happened.

The dark-haired witch wasn't in her chamber, and Sareth's room was empty as well. The two must already be at breakfast in the great hall. Aryn made her way there, but as she neared the doors she saw a crowd gathered around them. There were several men who were leaders among the Warriors of Vathris, as well as Lord Farvel and other members of the king's court, though there was no sign of Boreas himself. Some of the war leaders were grumbling angrily.

As Aryn approached, Lord Farvel broke away and limped toward her. The elderly seneschal wrung his hands, and his face was lined with worry.

"Lord Farvel, what's going on here?" Aryn said.

"Please, Your Highness, you must not fear. He is quite well—it's a scratch, nothing more. He'll make a swift recovery."

Aryn gripped his arm. "What are you talking about, Lord Farvel? Is something wrong with the king?"

He blinked his watery eyes. "Why, no, Your Highness. It's not the king, it's Prince Teravian. An attempt was made on his life. It happened just minutes ago. But rest assured—we will find the one who lies behind this terrible deed."

Aryn could only stare as if struck. Someone had tried to murder the prince? But who? And why?

A disturbing thought came to her. Mirda had departed the castle with strange haste this morning. Could that have something to do with what had happened to the prince?

No, Aryn had been talking to Mirda a little while ago; the witch hadn't been anywhere near Teravian's chamber or the great hall. And she couldn't imagine that Mirda had any designs against the prince.

Yet the witches are scheming something around Teravian— there can be no doubt about that, not after what Ivalaine said the other night in the garden.

Only in the several days since, Aryn had not been able to get anywhere close to Ivalaine.

"Can I see him, Lord Farvel?"

"Of course, Your Highness," the seneschal said, taking her left arm in a frail hand. "You must be frightfully worried about your husband-to-be."

Aryn winced. She had been thinking about questioning Teravian rather than asking after his well-being, but that was horrible of her.

"Yes," she said, "I am worried about him." And the words were true enough, though it was not necessarily his health that troubled her.

Farvel led her past the gathered warriors to the doors.

"Do not concern yourself, Your Highness," Lord Petryen said, laying a hand on her shoulder. Petryen was the duke from Eredane who had been among the first to arrive in answer to Boreas's call to war. "An attack on the king's son is an attack on all of us. We will not stand for this."

"Surely the prince is blessed by Vathris," said the man who stood next to Petryen. He was one of the men who came from Al-Amún, and Aryn had learned his name was Sai'el Ajhir. To the best of her understanding, *Sai'el* was a noble title, something akin to *duke* or *baron*. Gold gleamed against his dark skin.

Aryn gave Ajhir a sharp look. "Someone tried to kill Teravian. How can you say he is blessed?"

"Because he is, Sai'ana Aryn. The poison was without taste or odor. It would have stolen the life of any other man who drank of that wine. Yet somehow the prince stopped after just one sip. It was as if Vathris himself had warned him there was death in that cup."

Poison—so that was how the attempt on his life was made. However, Aryn doubted it was the bull god who had helped Teravian avoid the fatal brew. He had sensed it with the Touch. Poison was a witch's craft, and as a witch he was able to detect it.

But then what witch had placed the poison in his cup?

You don't know it was a witch at all, Aryn. Anyone could have bought the potion from some hag or hedgewife.

Farvel led her through the doors. The great hall was empty save for several figures gathered below the high table, on the steps of the dais. Teravian sat on the lowest step, Lirith and Sareth beside him. Boreas stood above, glowering, while several guardsmen—swords drawn—encircled the dais. Aryn broke away from Lord Farvel's grasp and hurried forward.

"Your Highness, are you well?"

Teravian glared up at her, his eyebrows knitted into a single dark line. "Of course, I always enjoy a nice cup of poison for breakfast."

Aryn didn't flinch at his caustic tone. Instead, genuine concern rose within her. The prince's face had a greenish cast to it, and he clutched a hand to his stomach. She knelt on the step before him, reached out, and took his free hand. He started to pull back, but she held it tight.

"Is there something we must do?" she said, looking at Lirith.

The dark-eyed witch shook her head. "No, I think it is best at this point to let his body expel the poison on its own. Thank Sia, he did no more than touch the cup to his lips."

The prince shivered, though he was sweating. "I could see it. It was as if the cup was filled with shadows."

Aryn met Lirith's eyes, and the other witch nodded. So they had both had the same thought. Aryn looked again at Teravian. "What do you mean when you say you saw the poison?"

Boreas waved an annoyed hand. "That's enough of that talk. The only question now is who committed this deed."

"It was a subtle concoction," Lirith said. "Brewing it would take great skill with herbs, else the brewer himself might be poisoned simply inhaling the fumes."

Sareth looked at her. "Who would have that kind of craft?"

Aryn bit her lip. Perhaps the witches truly did want Teravian dead. Perhaps they believed killing the king's son would cause Boreas to break. If so, they were wrong. By the sparks in his steely eyes, this had only strengthened his resolve.

"I have no doubt that poison was meant for me," the king said, descending the dais. "An assault on my person I do not fear, but an assault on my son is something that will not go unpunished."

Aryn considered this. Perhaps Boreas was right; perhaps the poisoned cup had been meant for him. Killing the king would have far more effect than murdering his son. "What do you mean to do, Your Majesty?"

"There is treachery in this castle, but I will root it out and destroy it, of that you can be certain, my lady."

His gaze moved to the corner of the great hall, toward a hulking object draped with a white cloth. Aryn pressed her hand to her heart and shuddered.

It began that morning. The prince was escorted to his quarters, where Lirith tended to him with Sareth's help. Meanwhile, Aryn stood in the great hall with King Boreas. On the king's orders, the massive object that had stood in the corner of the great hall was dragged out to the center—a feat which took a dozen men straining together. Then the cover was pulled aside, revealing the artifact of Malachor.

The artifact was a thick ring of black stone, as wide across as the span of a man's arms. It was suspended on a wooden base in such a clever fashion that, despite its weight, it could be turned with only moderate effort so that the circle of stone stood upright, like the frame of a window with no glass.

Aryn had not gazed upon the artifact in over a year—not since the Midwinter's Eve feast when, at Grace's urging, Aryn had helped to align the artifact, and it had ripped the iron heart out of Lord Logren's chest. For that was the artifact's power, fashioned as it was of a great piece of lodestone which fell from the sky eons ago.

By order of the king, all of the folk in the castle—from lowest servant to highest noble—were rounded up and made to march before the artifact. Guards stood beside it, ready to force anyone who refused—though they could neither wear armor nor hold swords because of the power of the artifact.

As the hours passed, and slanting beams of sunlight crept across the hall, Aryn grew tired from standing beside Boreas. However, the king did not call for chairs, but rather stood stiffly, watching in silence, as his subjects passed by. The only excitement came from those who had not followed instructions and had failed to remove all of the metallic items from their person. More than once the guards were forced to grip the hand of a wailing earl and pull it from the stone because he had forgotten to take off his rings.

By afternoon, Aryn's mind had grown so dull that she didn't see how the commotion started. She blinked as a shout rang out, followed by the barked orders of the guardsmen. A peasant man tried to bolt from the great hall, but the guards caught him and dragged him toward the artifact. He looked like any other serf—small, with a pockmarked face, dressed in drab clothes. However, he fought violently, nearly besting the strength of three large men.

"Let me go!" he shrieked, spittle flying from his mouth. "Let me go, or my master will destroy you all!"

King Boreas took a step forward, his expression curious, dangerous. "And am I not your master, knave?"

The peasant man went still. He stared at the king, and his lips pulled back from rotten teeth. "You will be a slave to him, a thing for him to use and break as he wishes."

Aryn shuddered at the venom in the man's voice, but Boreas's face might have been carved of marble. He gestured to the guards, but before they could move, the peasant man twisted out of their grasp. He spun and broke away from them—

—stumbling straight toward the artifact.

"Master!" he gasped.

His body gave a single, violent jerk. In a spray of blood and bone, a dark lump burst out of his chest and flew to the center of the stone circle. The onlookers stared. The only sound was the thud of the man's body as it fell to the floor.

The king returned to his place. "Finish the procession," he said to the guards.

The last few castle folk hurried before the artifact, faces pale as they glanced at the crumpled body at their feet. Then, blessedly, it was over.

Boreas approached the corpse of the peasant. "Here is our would-be murderer. The artifact will now be moved to the entry hall, and any who would enter the castle must pass by it. All other entrances will be sealed. From now on, no slaves of the Pale King will be able to enter this keep." He looked at Aryn. "Is that not well, my lady?"

Aryn tried to turn her gaze away from the body but could not. This man had been a tool of evil; surely he had plotted against the king. Yet something told her this was not the one who had slipped poison into the prince's cup.

All she said was, "It is well, Your Majesty."

Later that afternoon, Aryn paid a visit to Teravian's chamber to see how the prince fared, and to bear the news of what had happened in the great hall.

"How is our patient?" Aryn said when Sareth opened the door.

"Get your grotty hands off of me, witch!" came the prince's voice from inside the room.

Sareth grinned. "He's feeling better."

Aryn stepped inside as Sareth shut the door. Teravian lay in his bed, and Lirith bent over him. A struggle seemed to be in progress. Lirith was trying to pull down the covers, and the prince was steadfastly holding them up.

"You're not going to cast any more spells on me."

"I told you, I just want to listen to your heart. I'm not casting spells."

"You bloody well could have fooled me."

Lirith threw her hands up. "This is absurd. What am I to tell the king? That I let his son perish because he insisted on hiding under his blanket for no reason whatsoever?"

This was getting out of hand. Lirith looked as if she was about to pounce on Teravian, and the young man appeared quite ready to fight back.

Aryn touched her shoulder. "Sister, would you please speak with Sareth and me for a moment?"

Lirith cast one last glare at the prince, then followed Aryn and Sareth into a side chamber. Aryn pressed the door shut.

"What's going on?" she said.

The dark-eyed witch let out a frustrated sound. "The prince has suddenly decided I'm not allowed to touch his person."

"I don't understand. He has a crush on you, Lirith. I should think he'd be happy to have you touch him."

Sareth cleared his throat. "Forgive me, my ladies, but it's clear neither of you know what it's like to be a young man confronted by one whom you admire. At his age, certain reactions might not be entirely under his control."

Aryn shook her head. "What do you mean?"

Sareth stroked the pointed beard on his chin. "Let's just say he might be worried that if Lirith examines him, his excitement might become plain to see."

Aryn clapped a hand to her mouth, though whether to stifle a gasp or a laugh she couldn't decide.

"Oh, I'm terrible," Lirith said, groaning as she flopped into a chair. "I never considered that. He must be utterly mortified. Sareth, can you help?"

Sareth opened the door and poked his head out. "Your Majesty, how about if I listen to your heart while the ladies stay in here, and I report to Lady Lirith what I've heard?"

Teravian nodded—blanket pulled to his chin—giving the Mournish man a look of utter gratitude.

Minutes later, Sareth returned to report that the prince's heart beat steadily. He tapped the rhythm as he had heard it on Lirith's wrist, and she was satisfied that all was well.

"It seems you are on your way to recovery, Your Majesty," Lirith said, touching his brow gently.

Teravian sighed, then after a moment glared at Aryn. "What are you looking at?"

She smiled. "Nothing, Your Majesty."

Her smile vanished. It was still so hard to believe Ivalaine was really the prince's mother. But now that she knew to look for the resemblance, she could see it in his eyes and in the fineness of his features.

"I'll return in the morning," Lirith said to the prince. "Until then, I want you to—"

Faint but clear, trumpets sounded outside the chamber's window. Had more warriors arrived at the castle?

Sareth moved to the window, pulling back the drapes. "Lirith, Aryn—I think you'd better come see this."

The women hurried to the window. Aryn heard Lirith's gasp, then she saw the banner that flew above the small host that rode toward the castle, and dread surged through her.

"She's here," Teravian murmured behind them.

He lay in his bed. There was no way he could have seen out the window, no way he could have glimpsed the yellow-and-green banner that flew above the riders.

It's the banner of Toloria, Aryn. But who rides beneath it? The queen is already here.

For a hopeful moment she believed it was Lady Tressa, the queen's loyal advisor, come to minister to Ivalaine, to soothe her madness. Then Lirith clutched Aryn's arm.

"Liendra," she whispered. "It's Sister Liendra."

Sareth gazed at her. "What does that mean, *beshala*?"

"It means we're in grave danger," Aryn said.

Minutes later, Aryn stood with Lirith in the keep's entry hall. Sareth had remained in Teravian's chamber to keep watch over the prince. It was cold in the cavernous hall, and Aryn couldn't stop shivering.

What has she come here for? Aryn spun the words over the Weirding.

Lirith shook her head. *You know as well as I. But I can only believe her arrival bodes ill for all of us. I can only wonder why the king granted her entry to the castle.*

Aryn wondered the same. There had been no opportunity to speak to Boreas, but she had encountered Lord Farvel.

"The king has nothing to fear from a band of hags and hedgewives," the old seneschal said. "There are but twoscore of them. What harm can they cause?"

Plenty, Aryn knew. She and Lirith had both counted the riders. Their number was not twoscore, but one less than that. Thirty-nine. Thrice thirteen. Liendra had brought three covens with her. But for what purpose?

A pair of guards opened the doors of the keep, and a gust of frigid air blew in, along with three figures clad in green cloaks. They pushed back their hoods. Two of them were young and pretty, their hair carefully braided, their eyes bright and haughty.

The third was a decade older, a woman in full bloom. Her hair was fiery gold, and she would have been beautiful were it not for the look of cunning on her face.

The guards directed the women to walk past the artifact of Malachor, and they did so slowly, with great elegance. Once they were finished, they approached Aryn and Lirith.

"Greetings, sisters," Liendra said, bowing her golden head. "I had hoped I would find you here."

"May Sia bless you," Lirith said in answer.

Liendra gave a flick of her hand. "It is not Sia's blessing we seek any longer."

"And whose blessing do you seek?" Aryn said despite her fear, but Liendra only smiled.

Lirith took a step forward. "Why have you come, sister?"

"Surely you must know," Liendra crooned. "Dark times come to the Dominions, and I must speak with the one who would plunge these lands into war. For is it not the way of all witches to seek an end to violence?"

"Forgive me, sister," Aryn said, choosing her words with great care. "Is that not Queen Ivalaine's duty as Matron of the Witches?"

The two younger witches pressed their hands to their mouths but failed to stifle their cruel laughter.

A smile touched Liendra's coral pink lips. "Ivalaine is no longer Matron. She rescinded that role of her own free will. I am Matron of the Witches now, and these are my Maidens."

Lirith affected a puzzled look. "Your Maidens? Help me, sister, for I am confused. What need have you of two Maidens? And where is your Crone, so that your circle can be completed?"

"We don't need a Crone," one of the younger witches said, her voice as prideful as her gaze. "We don't need any horrible old hags to work against the Warriors."

Liendra made a hissing sound to silence the young woman. Lirith let out a soft laugh. "Youth offers power and beauty, but it is age that brings wisdom, as your Maiden here has so kindly demonstrated for us."

Both young woman cast pretty glares at Lirith.

"You speak of Ivalaine," Liendra said, her words sharp "Where is she?"

"Surely you must know, sister," Lirith said, casting the golden-haired witch's own mocking words back at her.

Liendra's eyes narrowed, and she drew close to Lirith and Aryn, speaking softly.

"Do not think you can toy with me. Sisters. I have no evidence of your treachery, yet I have great suspicion of it. I am your Matron now, and as you are bound to the Pattern, so you must do as I say." She lifted a slender finger. "If I sense any disobedience in you two, if I see even the slightest hesitation in following my orders, I will have your threads plucked from the Pattern. And do not think I cannot do it. I have three covens at my disposal, and powers you cannot even guess at."

Aryn could not catch the gasp that escaped her lips. Next to her, Lirith shuddered.

Liendra smiled again. "I see I have made myself clear. Now I must present myself to the Bull King. I will see to both of you later."

Liendra started after the guards, the two young witches following on her heels, leaning their heads toward one another and whispering. Once they were out of sight, a sudden weakness came upon Aryn; she felt as if her knees were going to give out. However, Lirith gripped her hand, holding her up.

"What do we do now?" Aryn whispered.

"We pray to Sia," Lirith said.

32.

From horseback, Grace watched as the desolate landscape slipped by, and she wondered if they would ever reach their destination.

They had forded the River Serpent's Tail yesterday evening before making camp; Perridon lay behind them, and it was through Embarr they traveled now. All day, the gray line of the mountains had receded to their left as they rode across windswept moor. There was little to break up the monotony of the plains—only the occasional clump of wind-stunted trees and great boulders that stood alone, as if set there by giants.

"Are you glad to be home, Durge?" Grace said when the knight's charger drifted near Shandis.

"Glad, Your Majesty?" he said, raising an eyebrow.

She bit her lip. That probably wasn't the best word. In her experience, Durge hadn't actually ever been glad about anything.

Except that's not true. He was glad to see Aryn when we returned to Calavere. You could see it in his eyes.

But Calavere was leagues and leagues away, and Grace hadn't received any more messages from Aryn. It was too dangerous to speak across the Weirding. Since encountering the pylon three days ago, they had come upon two more of the Pale King's magic stones. However, this time they had been prepared. Senrael, Lursa, and the other witches had sensed the evil of the pylons from a distance, and the Spiders had scouted a trail for the army that gave the stones a wide berth.

Grace glanced at Durge, trying a different tactic. "How long has it been since you've been to your manor?"

He stroked his mustaches with a gloved hand. "It is nearly two years since I have set foot upon the lands of Stonebreak. Nor will I have an opportunity to do so on this journey, as it lies many leagues to the east."

"I'm sorry, Durge," Grace said, and she meant it. "I'm sorry I've kept you so long away from your home."

His look was one of genuine surprise. "Why, Your Majesty? What is tending after a patch of rocky soil compared to serving the queen of Malachor?"

Safe, she wanted to say. But all she could do was nod and try to keep from weeping.

They rode in silence after that, Durge's craggy face turned forward, and Grace lost in her thoughts. Over the last few days, she had gone over her conversation with the Duratek operative a hundred times. Duratek was going to open a gate to Eldh. They had perfected the technology, and they were close to synthesizing the fairy blood they needed. But when was the gate going to open, and what was it going to let into Eldh when it did? An army of Duratek agents, or Mohg?

Maybe both.

"Time," she murmured. "How much more time do we have?"

Durge glanced at her. "What did you say, Your Majesty?"

"I said it's time to start looking for a place to camp."

The knight nodded. "I'll inform Sir Tarus."

There was nowhere on the moors that offered much protection from the wind, but the Spiders managed to find a patch of ground that sat a bit lower than the surrounding landscape, and there were a number of the large boulders—left behind by glaciers rather than giants, Grace supposed—which Oragien and Graedin and the other runespeakers touched while speaking the rune of fire.

Dinner that night was a meager affair. They still had a considerable amount of food, as they continued to make impossibly good time on their march north, but their supplies would have to last them a long while yet, as they would not be stopping in Barrsunder to purchase more.

The course Aldeth had plotted for them would take them no closer than thirty leagues to the Embarran capital, but even that was cause for concern. The last time Grace was in Embarr, the Raven Cult had held sway, and there were the Onyx Knights to contend with as well. If they went to Barrsunder, there was no telling whom they would find in power. As for the rest of the Dominion, it seemed deserted.

"Does anyone live in this place?" Aldeth said that night as they ate hardtack and cheese, huddled close to one of the stones over which Master Graedin had spoken *Krond*. "While Sam and I were out scouting, we came to two keeps, both of which were empty. And Leris and Karthi found an abandoned manor where the cattle had all died of starvation."

Samatha reached her hands toward the hot boulder. "It's as if all the people who lived here have vanished."

"They've gone to Barrsunder," Grace said. "King Sorrin is mad, and he's summoned all of his knights to protect him from death. I think the Onyx Knights may be controlling him, using his position to weaken the Dominion."

Commander Paladus glanced at her. "That explains what happened to his knights. But what about the rest of the people—the folk who work the land? Where have they gone?"

"North," Durge said in his deep voice. "The Raven Cultists

are on a pilgrimage north. Like all the slaves of the Pale King, they must answer his call."

Grace stared at the knight. His eyes were unreadable in the dark, and his right hand was tucked inside his cloak.

"The stone," Tarus said softly. "It's getting cold again. We should find Master Graedin or Master Oragien to—"

Tira broke away from Grace's arms. She pressed her hands against the small boulder and laughed. A moment later they all felt it: waves of heat radiating outward.

The others gaped at the girl, and—shy now—she ran back to Grace, burying her head in Grace's skirt.

"Thank you," Grace said, cradling Tira in her arms.

"Krond," the girl murmured, and shut her eyes.

They began their march again with the dawn. The air was bitter, and the day was bright and clear, without a trace of a cloud. Once Aldeth reported seeing a dark smudge off to the west, but it was gone before the rest of them caught a glimpse of it. At least the wind had blown itself out, and the air was still, which was a blessing.

Or, so Grace thought. For if the easterly wind had still blown, there was a chance the Spiders might have heard the sound of their approach. There might have been time for the witches to weave an illusion, or for the runespeakers to work magics of protection. However, the wind had chosen that day to betray them, and so it was they did not see the company of a hundred knights until they crested a low rise and glimpsed the men below, thundering across the moor on sooty horses.

"Back!" Aldeth hissed. "We must get back before they see us!"

It was already too late. The company of knights veered to the right, pounding up the slope toward them. Grace and Aldeth had ridden a little ahead of the main force, along with Durge, Tarus, Master Graedin, and the young witch Lursa. The rest of the army was two furlongs behind.

Samatha stepped out of thin air, pushing her mistcloak over her shoulders. "I take it you've seen them."

"Are there any more?" Aldeth said.

The Spider put her hands on her hips. "Isn't fivescore enough? But no, I think this troop of knights is alone."

"What do they want?" Master Graedin said, a nervous hand at his throat.

"It looks like we'll find out soon enough," Tarus said. "We can't possibly outrun them. They're all on chargers, and we have three hundred foot soldiers."

Grace glanced down at the Spiders. "Sam, Aldeth—go tell Commander Paladus what's happening. Tell him to be ready."

"Ready for what?" Samatha said.

Grace's mouth was so dry she could hardly speak the word. "Battle."

The two Spiders wrapped their gray cloaks about themselves and vanished, blending into the dull colors of the landscape.

Lursa looked at Grace, a brave expression on her plain face. "Might we perhaps weave a spell of illusion, sister? Or is there some rune magic Master Graedin might perform to conceal us?"

"It's too late to hide," Grace said. "But hold that thought, Lursa. We may well need magic before this is over."

The knights were closer now. She could see their steel helms and the swords at their sides.

Tarus swore a low oath. "According to Aldeth, we're over twenty leagues from Barrsunder. What is a troop of Onyx Knights doing so far out?"

"They are not Onyx Knights," Durge said in his rumbling voice.

Grace reached out to grip his arm. "Are you sure?"

Durge nodded. "Their armor is dark, but it does not bear the crown and tower of Eversea, and I can see they are Embarrans by the way they ride. All the same, there is something strange about them. There is a crest on their shields I do not recognize, though I can't make out what it is."

"Skulls," Graedin said, shading his eyes with a hand. "By Ol-rig, I can see them clearly now. They have white skulls painted on their shields."

Tarus glanced over his shoulder. "Commander Paladus had better hurry up. I think we're going to have to fight. Thank Vathris, at least there's only a hundred of them."

"You know little of the knights of Embarr," Durge said, worry shadowing on his brow. "We are over five hundred. It is possible we would win against them. But we would have few men left alive and uninjured if we did."

No, that was one outcome they couldn't afford—it would leave them with too small a force to man Gravenfist Keep. Grace had to find another way out. However, as the knights neared the top of the slope, her mind remained blank.

The main body of knights came to a halt, and a band of six split off, riding up the last yards and stopping before Grace. She knew none of them would stand taller than Durge, but they looked enormous on their chargers, clad in their heavy armor. They wore helms, and visors covered their faces, so that they looked more like machines than men.

"Identify yourselves," said the foremost of the knights, his voice echoing inside his helm.

Here went nothing. Grace nudged Shandis forward. "I am Grace, Queen of Malachor, Lady of the Shining Tower, and Mistress of the Winter Wood." She spoke with all the authority she could muster. *Just pretend you're back in the ED, Grace, and that he's Morty Underwood or one of the other residents asking a stupid question. It's not like that didn't happen often enough.* "You are delaying my journey north. You will remove your men from my path and that of my army at once."

Grace didn't glance over her shoulder, but she imagined Paladus and the rest of her force were in view by now. She was right, given the reaction of the knights. They shifted in their saddles, hands on the hilts of their swords.

"Your words are curious," their leader said. "For we have seen only servants of evil drawn northward these days. And there is another who lays claim to the throne of Malachor."

Grace allowed herself a sharp smile. "I bet he doesn't have this."

With a smooth motion—and silently thanking Beltan and Durge for their lessons in swordsmanship—she drew Fellring from its scabbard and held it aloft. The blade caught the morning light, and the many runes shone as if molten.

Audible gasps escaped the visors of the knights.

"So the tales are true," the leader said. "Fellring has been forged anew."

Grace sheathed the sword again. "You'd better believe it. And I'm heading north not to serve evil, but to destroy it."

"Those are strong words. But if King Ulther's sword is whole once more, then perhaps the other tales I have heard of it are true as well. It is said the sword has been seized wrongfully by a usurper, and that it has been cursed by magic so that the rightful heir of Malachor cannot touch it."

"Really? It wouldn't be much of a sword if it could be cursed so easily."

"And are you not a most powerful witch, Lady Grace?"

She frowned at the knight. "Do I know you?"

"You knew of me once, I believe, as I knew of you."

The knight hesitated, then lifted a gauntleted hand and raised the visor of his helm. He was older than she would have thought, his face deeply grooved, his mustaches streaked with gray. However, there was no mistaking the aura of strength about him. Age had hardened him, not made him weak.

"Sir Vedarr!" Durge urged Blackalock forward, bringing the charger alongside Shandis. "Long have I wondered what became of you since the knights of Embarr were recalled from the Order of Malachor."

That was how he knew her. Sir Vedarr had led the Order of Malachor after its founding just over a year ago. Only then King Sorrin withdrew his knights, and the Order fell apart.

"We had feared the Onyx Knights and the Cult of the Raven were in control of Embarr," Durge said. "Surely this is good news to come upon you here."

"I fear it is not." Vedarr's brown eyes were sorrowful. "While I will have to think on it, it may be I can let Lady Grace continue on her journey, for I have been given no orders concerning her. Regardless, you must come with us, Sir Durge of Stonebreak."

His words struck Grace like a slap. "What are you talking about? What do you want with Durge?"

Vedarr worked his jaw, as if chewing over the words before deciding what to speak. "Our present mission is to ride across the Dominion in search of traitors to the king, and to bring them back to Barrsunder."

"Traitors?" Tarus said, clenching his hand into a fist. "This is madness. Durge is no traitor. He's the most loyal man I've ever met."

Vedarr gave the red-haired knight a hard look. "And loyal to whom?"

Grace cast a frightened look at Durge. "I know what he's talking about. We learned about it in Seawatch, only I never told you, Durge. I was so selfish—I was thinking only of myself, and how much I needed you."

Durge's brown eyes were thoughtful. "What did you not tell me, Your Majesty?"

"His Majesty, King Sorrin, recalled all his knights to Barrsunder months ago," Vedarr said. "Those who have not complied have been branded traitors to the Dominion. It is our mission to find those who have refused the king's call. We have found a few. And now we have come upon another."

Master Graedin cast a startled look at Durge. "What is the punishment for treason?"

"Death," Durge said softly.

"So is that why you painted skulls on your shields?" Lursa guided her donkey forward. There was fear on her face, but defiance as well.

Vedarr glared at her. "This does not concern you, girl."

"All life concerns me. Can you not see I am a witch even as Lady Grace is? And there are many more of my sisters just behind, riding toward us even at this moment."

The other five Embarrans had raised their visors, and now they exchanged uneasy glances. However, Vedarr's stony expression did not falter.

"I say again, why do you wear a sigil of death?"

"Because," Vedarr said, "we are Death Knights, or at least so King Sorrin chooses to call us. It is by his command we carry these shields."

For a moment Vedarr's imperturbable facade cracked, and a recognizable emotion shone in his eyes. It was shame. However, a moment later it was gone.

"Sorrin is completely mad now, isn't he?" Tarus said, shaking his head. "He thinks he can cheat death by pretending to serve it. So he has his men paint skulls on their shields and calls them Death Knights." His lip curled in disgust. "By the blood of the Bull, sir, how can you bear it?"

Vedarr thrust a finger at Tarus. "You will hold your tongue, Knight of Calavan. It is not for you to question the will of my king."

"No, it is for you to do that," Tarus said, his voice edging into a sneer. He was playing a dangerous game, but Grace couldn't think of another tactic. "Only you are too old or too weak or too cowardly to do so. So instead you ride about the land on the whim of a madman while the Onyx Knights control your lord like a puppet on a string and the Raven Cult leads your people to their doom."

The other Embarran knights muttered angry words. Vedarr pounded his thigh with a fist. "I should have your head for those impudent words, Sir Knight, but I will give you all one more chance, though you deserve it not. Deliver Sir Durge to me now, and I will let you ride on if you swear to make straight for the northern border of the Dominion."

Durge nodded. "So be it." He started to guide Blackalock forward.

"Hold, Sir Durge," Grace said. In an instant fear fled, replaced by cold fury. There was so much that terrified her, so many things of which she was uncertain, but there was one thing she was utterly sure of: No one was going to take Durge from her while he still had time left. No one.

Durge gazed back at her, brown eyes startled. "Your Majesty, I beg you. It is the only way. They will let you ride north if I go with them. It is imperative you reach Shadowsdeep." He turned and started again toward the Embarrans.

"I said hold, Sir Durge. That's an order. Or have you forgotten the oath you swore to me?"

This time, when he looked back, his expression was one of horror. "Never, Your Majesty. With every beat of my heart I have served you and only you. Yet again I beg you, you must let me do this thing."

To her astonishment, Grace found herself smiling. But then, fear was impossible when you knew what you were doing was utterly and truly right.

"No, Durge. I will not let you go, not for all the knights in Embarr. You belong at my side and nowhere else."

As he gazed at her, an array of emotions passed across his face. Shock, then outrage, then finally wonder. His drooping mustaches twitched, almost as if they hid a smile.

"As you wish it, Your Majesty," he said, and he guided Blackalock back to stand beside her horse.

Vedarr's gaze was hard, though not without pity. "You have made a dire mistake, Sir Durge."

"No," Durge said. "I nearly did, but I have been saved from it by the grace and goodness of my queen. And if you are yet even a shadow of the strong and wise man I once knew, Sir Vedarr, you would allow her to save you as well."

This seemed to leave Vedarr at a loss of words, and the knights behind him exchanged confused glances. At that moment, Paladus came riding up the slope. The army had come to a halt fifty yards away.

"Do we fight this day, Your Majesty?" Paladus said. There was an eager gleam in his eyes.

"I don't know," Grace said, directing her gaze at Sir Vedarr. "Do we?"

The air was utterly still, as if frozen by the tension that hung between them. One move, and everything would shatter.

"We have our orders," Vedarr said. "And we are loyal to our king. We know what we must do."

Behind him, his men shifted in their saddles. Their expressions were less certain than Vedarr's, but it was clear they would not defy him. Grace knew she had to say something, but Sir Tarus was faster.

"Think, Sir Vedarr," the red-haired knight said. "For a moment don't simply follow orders, but think about what you're doing. You've seen Fellring with your own eyes. Her Majesty Grace is the queen of Malachor. She is above the rulers of all the Dominions, including your king."

Vedarr pressed a fist to his brow. "Stop it," he said, his voice edging into a hiss. "Do not do this to me, Sir Knight. Do not ask me to give up my oath of loyalty."

"I ask you to give up nothing save madness. You speak of loyalty. What of your king's loyalty to you, to your Dominion?

Has he not betrayed you all by casting his lot with the Onyx Knights?" He gestured to Grace. "And here before you is the queen of us all. Is your loyalty not ultimately to her?"

Vedarr shook his head. "If she were the queen . . . perhaps, if she were truly the queen. But how do I know it is true? How can we be certain this is the right thing?"

Before Tarus could speak again, a stunning and impossible thing happened.

Durge laughed.

The knight threw his head back, gazed at the sky, and laughed. It was a deep, rich, booming sound—like the toll of a bronze bell. His body shook with the laughter, and he held his hand to his side as if it would split. All of them stared at the Embarran, mouths agape. He could not have shocked them more than if he had suddenly sprouted wings and flown into the sky. At last his laughter ceased, though his smile did not, and he wiped his eyes as he spoke.

"You search for certainty, Sir Vedarr," Durge said. "That is hard quarry to hunt, but I will tell you what you can be certain of." He slipped from the back of his horse and stood on the frozen ground between the two armies. "You can be certain there is no woman or man in all the world as strong, as wise, and as good as Lady Grace. You can be certain that the blade she carries is indeed Fellring, King Ulther's sword forged again, and that it belongs in the hand of no other. But even if Ulther's blood did not flow in her veins, she would still be better than you or I, than any of us, and worthy of our loyalty. And there is one more thing you can be certain of—that we ride north with little chance of staving off the coming tide of darkness, yet also with the knowledge that someone must stand against it, and so it might as well be us."

At last a breath of wind moved, blowing Durge's hair back from his craggy brow. He gazed northward—not at the knights of Embarr, but past them.

"It is not prevailing against the dark that matters, Sir Vedarr, for every day good and strong men are defeated by hate, fear, anger, and deceit—and by the ones who are slaves to such things." He pressed his right hand to his chest. "It is not defeating evil that makes us good at heart. It is simply choosing to stand against it."

Durge bowed his head, his shoulders stooped, his laughter gone. The only sound that broke the silence was the sigh of the wind through dry grass. All gazed at the knight, unwilling—or perhaps unable—to break the silence. Tears froze against Grace's cheeks, but she could not move a hand to wipe them away, and her heart was so swollen with love that she nearly couldn't bear the agony of it.

A small form slipped from the saddle before Grace, landing lightly on the ground. Tira. The wind tangled through her fiery hair as she padded barefoot to Durge. She coiled her hand inside the knight's and looked up at him with her scarred face.

"Good," she said, then gave a firm nod. *"Good."*

Durge knelt on the ground and hugged the small girl. She threw her arms around him, burying her face against his neck.

Now the wind picked up, rushing over the ridgetop, and it was as if fear and doubt were blown away by it. Grace dismounted and moved to stand above Durge and Tira, a hand on each of them. She looked up at Sir Vedarr.

"So what will you do?" she said.

Vedarr gazed at her for a moment, his eyes unreadable, then he drew a knife from his belt and held it before him. So was that his choice? Death?

Before she could wonder more, Vedarr turned the knife and pressed the tip of it against his shield. With slow, deliberate motions, he scraped away the white paint of the grinning skull. When he was done, he turned his horse around and held his shield aloft. The five nearby Embarrans gazed at him with shining eyes, and a great roar of approval went up from the rest of the knights on the slope below, a cheer echoed by Grace's army.

Vedarr turned his horse around. "We will follow you north, Your Majesty." He glanced at Durge. "Not to defeat evil, but to stand against it."

"Thank you," Grace said. It was all she could think of.

"I'll inform my men of the change in their mission," Vedarr said. He wheeled his charger around and rode back down the slope, his five knights pounding after him.

Grace turned around. Durge had stood, and he held Tira in his arms. His brown eyes were deep and thoughtful.

"You *are* a good man, Durge of Embarr," Grace said softly, and she meant it with all her heart. "Nothing that happens will ever change that." She reached a hand toward him. "You understand that, don't you?"

"Come, my lady," he said, his voice gruff. "It's time to ride north."

PART FOUR

THE GATE OPENS

33.

Dr. Ananda Larsen leaned forward in the desk chair and drummed her fingers beside the computer keyboard. The writeable disk drive whirred as a progress bar crept across the screen. Fifty-seven percent.

"Come on," she whispered, her face bathed in the ghostly phosphorescence of the monitor.

For the last three weeks, she had been timing how long it took the security guard to make a complete round of the building. The average was just over twenty-three minutes with a standard error of two minutes. She glanced at the wall clock. It had been exactly sixteen minutes since the guard had walked past the lab and she had darted in behind him.

It wasn't unusual for researchers to be in Building Five after hours; many experiments, particularly those involving PCR gene sequencing, required observation around the clock. However, regulations required that the researcher notify security first, and she was not about to tell the guard what she was up to.

Her tortoiseshell-rimmed glasses slipped down her nose; she pushed them back into place. Seventy-eight percent.

Maybe she should have chosen a few files instead of copying the entire directory. Except there hadn't been time to sort through everything during the day. Dr. Adler was always looking over her shoulder, curious what she was doing—and no doubt hoping to see something he could use. As far as she could tell, Barry Adler had never had an original scientific thought in his life; all he could do was steal from others.

And that's what makes him perfect for this place, Ananda. Duratek doesn't create anything—you've seen that. All it ever does is copy the work of others, then dispose of the ones who created it.

As they would dispose of her the moment they learned what she was doing. But they would have done it soon enough anyway. After all, if they got their hands on what she had learned today, they wouldn't need her anymore.

The computer emitted a chime, and Larsen nearly jumped from her seat as a tray popped out, bearing a silvery minidisk. She took the still-warm disk, snapped it inside a case, and slid it into the pocket of her lab coat. She typed a command on the keyboard and pressed Enter. A new message appeared on the screen.

Deleting...

They would have archived versions of the files, but the backup programs didn't run until after midnight, which meant they would never be able to recover today's results. And it was the data Larsen had collected that afternoon that had finally convinced her to go forward with her plan.

Last October, after the sudden and violent termination of the project she had been working on in Denver, Duratek had transferred her here, to their facility just outside Boulder, and had placed her on a new project. At first, after what she had witnessed in Denver, research had been the last thing on her mind. However, over the course of the last five months, her need to learn and discover had returned, and she had immersed herself in her new work. No doubt they had been counting on that. It was why they had hired her in the first place.

Until last October, working for Duratek had been the pinnacle of her career. In Denver, Larsen had been part of an incredible project: a member of a team studying two extraworldly beings. True, she had never interacted directly with the being cataloged as E-1. However, she had read the reports, had seen the test results, and had sequenced its blood. It was more than enough to convince her that what they said was true—that this creature was alien to Earth.

Less alien in appearance was the other subject, E-2, with whom she had worked more closely. He had looked like a Viking warrior transported from another century. Only it was another world he had come from, just like the being E-1.

At the time, it appeared all her choices had been vindicated. Even in graduate school, her views had been too radical for the musty world of academia. Her idea to use gene therapy to enhance the mental functioning of nonhuman mammals had made the professors on her committee squeamish. They had granted her a doctorate simply to get rid of her.

However, someone had been interested in her work, for soon after graduation, she had gotten a call from Duratek. Her advisor had told her she was making a grave error going to work for a private corporation instead of staying in the academic world. But the representatives from Duratek had been the only ones who were willing to fund the work she wanted to do.

Even then, she had known that Duratek was not a charity organization, that ultimately they were interested in her research because they believed they could profit from it, but it had been easy to forget that fact in the course of her work. They gave her a lab filled with state-of-the-art sequencing machines and computers—light-years beyond the shoddy equipment she had been forced to scrounge for in graduate school. They had bought her expensive research animals, from the first lemurs and monkeys all the way to Ellie, her chimpanzee.

A sigh escaped her. Ellie had been the culmination of everything Larsen had worked for these last ten years. A pygmy chimpanzee bred in captivity, she had been both curious and accustomed to humans. Ellie had never struggled or fought back as Larsen administered the treatments.

Her progress had been incremental in the beginning, though measurable. Manual dexterity and abstract reasoning test scores rose by over 10 percent. Then Duratek acquired the being E-1, and a whole new world opened up.

Where they had found E-1, she still didn't know. She supposed *he* had brought it to them—the one in the gold mask and the black robe. At first she had thought him some kind of joke, but just standing near him, hearing that hissing voice, made her shudder. And despite the crudeness of his methods, he had known things; it was the gold-masked one who had told them to try using E-1's blood as a delivery vector for the gene therapy.

Skeptical, Larsen had done so—and the results were astonishing. In a matter of weeks, Ellie's complex reasoning skills more than doubled. Intelligence shone like a light in her eyes. Soon she was on the edge of language—real language—and

Larsen had looked forward to the day they could finally speak to one another.

Then everything changed in an instant. Something had placed the secrecy of their research in jeopardy. The order came down to evacuate. However, in the confusion, the human male E-2 escaped the lab, taking Ellie with him. Larsen had watched in horror as Ellie murdered one of the other scientists with her bare hands. Then the guards arrived, and they had shot the chimpanzee.

Ellie was trying to protect him—the man E-2. She jumped in front of the gun.

The experiment had worked. Ellie had finally achieved a human level of consciousness—she had sacrificed her own life to save another. Then, in one moment of lightning and thunder, the gun fired, and all of that work was undone. Ellie lay dead on the pavement, a hole in her chest, the light gone from her eyes.

Despite her shock, Larsen had managed to keep the guards from shooting the human male as well. However, it had all been for nothing. She still didn't know the full story—she never would—but somehow the transport caravan was waylaid on the highway to Boulder, and both of the extraworldly subjects, the being E-1 and the man E-2, had vanished.

In the weeks after, some of her associates whispered it was the Seekers who had stolen the two subjects, but she doubted that. From what Larsen had heard, the Seekers were some sort of scholarly society that sounded every bit as dry and dull as the world of academia. However, she had seen the fierceness in the man E-2's eyes. Whatever world he came from, she could only believe it was a perilous place. More likely it was from there his rescuers had come.

The computer had finished deleting the files. She glanced again at the clock. Twenty minutes had elapsed. She had only one more minute; after that, the guard could return at any second. She switched off the computer, then moved to the door. Just as she touched the handle, the door opened.

A gasp escaped her. This couldn't be happening—she had double-checked the numbers. Statistically, the guard couldn't be here already.

He wasn't. The man who stood in the doorway wore, not a

uniform, but a crisp lab coat. In photographs he would have been handsome, but in person there was a waxy quality to his flesh and a stiffness to his manner every bit as artificial as his shiny hair. He had all the life and charm of a manikin.

"I didn't expect to find you here, Dr. Larsen," he said, baring whitened teeth in a facsimile of a smile.

"I was just leaving, Dr. Adler." She angled her shoulder as if to brush past him, only he didn't move out of the doorway. He was easily twice her size.

Adler kept smiling. "I just saw Mel. He's on security tonight. He didn't tell me you were in the building."

Larsen shrugged, hoping the action hid her trembling. "I suppose he forgot to mention it."

It seemed as if he wanted to frown, but all he could manage was a slight reduction of his smile, though a furrow did shadow his forehead. "Mel never forgets things."

"What are you doing tonight, Dr. Adler?"

He blinked, obviously confused. Maybe he wondered if she was asking him out; he had hit on her often enough those first weeks when they started sharing the lab, before he finally got the hint she wasn't interested.

"Oh," he said, finally getting her meaning. "I wanted to get a new PCR reaction going so I can have the results tomorrow. You got the memo, didn't you? There's a bonus for any researchers who complete their current projects ahead of schedule."

Larsen did her best to mimic his smile. "I'm sure you'll get it, Barry. The bonus, I mean."

She didn't wait for a reply. Instead she turned completely sideways and edged past him. He still didn't move, but she was small and thin—too thin, some people said, but it was difficult to remember to eat when there were so many experiments to perform, so many answers to find—and she managed to squeeze past him into the hall.

"So what was it *you* were doing here tonight, Dr. Larsen?"

Something in his voice made her hesitate. Her hand slipped into her lab coat pocket, and she turned around. "I was just re-working some numbers. I thought I had made some mistakes in a calculation earlier today."

There was a sly light in his eyes now. "You never make mistakes, Dr. Larsen."

"Yes I do," she said softly, clutching the disk in her pocket. "Sooner or later, we all do."

She turned and started down the corridor. Everything was pale in the fluorescent lights, washed of color and life, and she felt dizzy, but somehow she kept going. Only there was no point, was there?

Larsen glanced at her watch. Twenty-two minutes. The guard would be back any second. He would talk to Adler, and Adler was a pathological blabbermouth; he would say he had seen her in the lab. The guard would alert the front gate, telling them to detain her for questioning, and even if she didn't want to, she would tell them everything. Because over the last few months, she had learned that, despite his rigid views, her graduate advisor had been right about one thing. Signing a contract with Duratek had been like making a deal with a devil.

Over the years, she had fooled herself, believing her work would lead to good. She had even been able to rationalize holding the subjects E-1 and E-2 against their wills, even though it broke the most fundamental rules of scientific ethics. After all, one day her research could help to heal those with brain injuries, or give those born developmentally disabled a chance at normal lives. However, she knew now that Duratek cared nothing for such goals.

These last months, she had been performing a different kind of research: observing, listening, trying to understand what it was the company was really doing. As secretive as they were, the managers still let things slip, and while she couldn't be certain—there wasn't enough data to support her hypothesis—she believed she knew something of what they planned. A belief that was confirmed earlier today.

The work we're doing here is going to change the world, Dr. Larsen, said the black-suited executive who had come to the lab that morning to check on the status of her research. *In fact, it's going to change two worlds. Once we can reproduce the alternate blood serum, doors will open for us—doors to entire new worlds, new possibilities. Just think of the potential for profit, Dr. Larsen.*

In that moment, her illusions had finally shattered like a beaker heated too long on a burner. Duratek wasn't interested in her genetic research—they never had been. All they wanted was a complete sequence of the being E-1's blood and a method for synthesizing it so they could somehow use it to gain access to another world. Only there was one compound in the blood that had resisted all attempts at modeling and reproduction.

Until today. For the last five months, every researcher in this facility had been trying to solve the problem. Today, Larsen had done it. She had found the key to synthesizing the being E-1's blood.

And she was going to do everything she could to keep them from getting it.

Larsen made it to the elevator. She pushed a button and stared as the numbers crawled by with maddening slowness. At last the doors whooshed open. Down a long hallway were the doors that led outside, to night and to freedom. She started walking, trying not to imagine what was happening upstairs. Adler talking to the guard. The guard picking up the phone...

She started jogging, then running. White walls slipped by, the doors grew larger. Beyond the glass was nothing but darkness. A feeble spark of hope flickered to life in her chest. Duratek was always talking about destiny—how they could only succeed in their endeavors because fate was on their side. Maybe fate was on her side tonight. She reached out, her fingers brushing the handle of the doors.

White light went red, streaming through the corridor like blood in an artery. An electronic wail pierced the air, causing Larsen's nervous system to spasm, her hand to jerk back. She heard the metallic sound of metal bars slamming home.

"No!" she shouted, throwing her body against the doors. It was no use. They were locked.

The noise penetrated her skull. She had to run, she had to get out. Except she couldn't. All the doors would be locked, and the elevators as well. In seconds they would find her and the disk. Then the questioning would begin. They would use every method available—intimidation, drugs, even pain—and in the end she would tell them everything, including what she had

294 • MARK ANTHONY

discovered today in her lab. She leaned against a wall, resting
her head against the cool paint, and waited for them to come.

"Well, I wouldn't have thought you'd give up that easily,"
said a rasping voice. The voice was low, but somehow she heard
it over the wail of the alarm. "I thought you had a bit more stub-
bornness in you than that, daughter."

Larsen was too frightened to be startled further. She opened
her eyes. A man stood beside her. He was tall and gaunt, dressed
in a dusty black suit that hung on him like old clothes on a
scarecrow. He watched her with black marble eyes.

"Who are you?"

He laughed: a booming sound far louder than the alarm. "I
like you, daughter. You always ask the hardest questions first,
don't you? Yet I fear this one will have to wait for an answer. You
must leave this place."

She shook her head. "I don't know how you got in here, but
the doors are all locked. There's no way out."

"Nonsense. If there's hope, there's always a way out." He
gestured with a knobby hand at the doors. "Go ahead."

"It won't work. I already tried."

"Then try again."

It was ridiculous. She didn't know who this man was. Given
his shabby clothes, he was probably an indigent who had managed to wander in.

*Past the electric fence and motion detectors? Past the armed
guards at the gate and magnetic doors that can only be opened
with a valid identification card?*

Larsen pushed on one of the doors. It swung open. Cold air
struck her face, clearing her head, as the night rushed in. Her
mind searched for a rational explanation but found none. It was,
simply, impossible.

"Go, daughter. Do not fear the guards at the gate. They will
not see you if you move swiftly."

How did you open the locks? she wanted to ask. *And why are
you helping me?* Instead, she said, "Where should I go?"

A smile split his cadaverous face. "A place you can hide. A
place for those with nowhere else to go."

He pressed something into her hand. She looked down and

saw it was a business card. On it was printed an address in downtown Denver, as well as two lines of cheerfully bold text:

The Hope Mission
Come on in—we want to save you!

She looked back up, and her breath caught on her lips. The man in black was gone. The corridor was empty, but not for long. Shouts echoed above the alarm. Boots pounded against hard tiles. She clutched the card in her hand.

They will not see you if you move swiftly. . . .

Then Dr. Ananda Larsen fled through the doors, and the night wrapped her in safe, dark arms.

34.

The sun dipped behind the mountains, casting a blue cloak of twilight over the city, as Travis ran out of the park and past the library. This was beyond him now. He had to tell someone what he had learned—he had to warn them about what was happening. And he didn't have much time.

As he staggered down Thirteenth Avenue, he cursed his own stupidity. He had let himself believe they were a world away, that they couldn't reach him. Only they could. The servants of Mohg and the Pale King were right here. He heard again the mocking words of the young witch he had encountered in the park. The Deadies, Jessie had called them, the Brights. *They'll find you. You can't win against them. That's the one thing I do know. . . .*

She had been weak, her power a fraction of Grace's or Aryn's. He should never have opened the iron box and used the magic of the Great Stones against her. Only he had, and to the wraithlings it would be like a beacon in the night. The first time he had opened the box, when he tried to break the Stones, it would have alerted them he was in Denver. After that, they would have been watching, waiting. Which meant they were already closing in on the park. He had to run.

The blocky outlines of the downtown Denver police station hove into view.

No, Travis, you can't go there. Someone will recognize you, and then even Sergeant Otero won't believe what you have to say. They'll put you in jail.

Travis came to a halt on the sidewalk, staring at the door of the police station, longing to go in. But he couldn't. They wouldn't listen to him, and even if they did, what could they do? The city had signed a security contract with Duratek.

He thought about calling Davis and Mitchell Burke-Favor in Castle City. But he had put the two ranchers in grave peril the last time he had contacted them, and anyway, he didn't know what they could do. Somehow he had to tell everyone in Denver the truth about what was happening here.

All this time, secrecy had been the most potent weapon wielded by Duratek and Mohg; they did their evil work in the shadows where no one could see. However, if people knew the truth, they would rise up against them in outrage, Travis was sure of it. Only how could he tell everyone in Denver what he knew?

He turned his back to the police station and saw it glowing against the deepening purple of the sky: a billboard with four bland, smiling faces plastered across it. DENVER'S MOST WATCHED NEWS TEAM, blared the caption below.

Shock crackled through him, then understanding. Travis shoved his hands in his pockets, hurried east down Thirteenth Avenue, and turned south on Lincoln Street. On the side of an office building hung an illuminated banner with the same four stiffly smiling faces. Atop the building, satellite dishes sprouted like Brobdingnagian mushrooms.

Travis started toward the building, then hesitated. What about Marty and Jay? He had promised to meet them at sundown in Confluence Park, and it was almost full night.

Don't worry about them, Travis. They're probably warm and safe right now in the Steel Cathedral, eating a hot meal, and Jay is laughing at how stupid you are for not coming with them.

He crossed the street, wove his way past a cavalcade of parked news vehicles, and pushed through glass doors into the lobby beyond. After being in the chill of the outdoors all day, the shock of sudden warmth paralyzed him. The lobby was brightly lit, the floor polished stone. Televisions were mounted in each corner, displaying the evening news, but the sound was turned down in favor of generic soft-rock music that drifted from unseen speakers.

"Can I help you, sir?"

Travis wiped his eyes. The lobby was empty except for a receptionist sitting behind a counter. She was young—not much older than the witch Jessie—a gold nose ring accenting her dark skin. Her expression was at once courteous and suspicious. He didn't belong here, and they both knew it.

He shambled up to the counter. "I need to talk to someone."

She smiled, but her eyes narrowed a fraction. "Let me know whom you have an appointment with, and I'll call to tell them you're here." She didn't reach for the phone.

Travis licked his lips. He picked through his brain, searching, but he couldn't remember the names of any of the news anchors, not even the weatherman.

"Sir?"

A name came to him, and he blurted it out. "Anna Ferraro. I need to see Anna Ferraro."

For a moment the young woman's polite facade crumbled, and her eyes darted to one side. Then she spoke in a formal tone. "I'm sorry, sir, but Ms. Ferraro no longer works here."

He stared at her. "What?"

"You have to leave now, sir."

He shook his head, and she looked up at him, her brown eyes imploring. "Please," she said softly. "I don't want to have to call them."

Her gaze flicked again to the left, toward a door labeled *Security*. Travis understood. All the same, he had to try; this was his only chance. He stepped away, tensing to make a dash for the hallway behind the counter.

Motion caught his eye. Outside the plate glass windows, a woman walked across the parking lot, a cardboard box in her hands. She passed through a pool of light, and Travis's heart skipped in his chest. Then he was running. Ignoring the startled cry of the receptionist, he slammed through the doors and pounded across the parking lot. He caught up with the woman just as she set the box on the trunk of a car and began rummaging through her purse.

She turned around, an annoyed look on her face. "You're not going to mug me, are you? Not that it wouldn't be the perfect ending to this complete disaster of a day."

Her tone so completely disarmed him that he could only stare, slack-jawed.

The woman let out a groan. "God, even the muggers around here are incompetent." She dug deeper in her purse and pulled out a set of keys. "Well?" she said.

"Sorry," Travis mumbled. He grabbed the box so she could open the trunk, then set it down inside.

"Thanks," she said as she slammed the trunk shut, then opened the driver's side door.

"Wait," Travis said hoarsely.

She turned around. "For what?"

"I want to talk to you."

She smacked her forehead. "Jesus, you're not a mugger, you're a fan. Just my luck. Well, here's one last news story for you, pal: I'm not giving out any more autographs. Why? Because I just got fired, that's why."

Travis's fear receded. She was older than she looked on TV, more serious. Even in the dim light of the parking lot, the thick makeup she wore couldn't completely hide the lines of weariness around her mouth. On screen, her eyes had always seemed as glossy as her lips. Now they snapped with a sarcastic light. Maybe TV could make anyone look pretty and vapid.

Those eyes narrowed. She gave him a piercing look, then nodded and shut the car door. "So what did you want to talk to me about?"

"Why did you get fired, Ms. Ferraro?"

She crossed her arms across her overcoat and leaned back against the car. "Good question. And call me Anna. Ferraro was my bastard of an ex-husband's name."

"So why do you still use it?"

"Do you really think anyone would hire a reporter named Anna Blattenberger?"

He winced. "Good point."

She chewed one of her fingernails; the stylish red nail polish was chipped. "Not that anyone's going to hire me now, no matter what name I use."

"What happened?"

She looked away. "There was no warning. I was in the editing bay with Kevin, one of the photojournalists. We were cutting together a story we shot this afternoon."

"One about the disappearances among the homeless?"

She looked back at him, her gaze calculating. "Yes, about the disappearances. Only when we were nearly done, Victor came in—he's the news director. He asked Kevin to leave us alone, then he told me to go clean out my desk. That was it. He didn't give me a reason. He just said I had fifteen minutes to leave, and that if I talked to anyone, he'd have security throw me out of the building. So I packed my box. And on the way out, I saw Victor was still in the editing bay, deleting all the footage Kevin and I shot from the video server." She shook her head. "But why?"

The question wasn't for Travis. He answered all the same. "Because he's working for Duratek."

She scowled at him, her makeup cracking. "What are you talking about?"

Travis had to be careful how he worded this; she had to believe him. "Something is wrong in this city, and Duratek Corporation is part of it. They're behind the disappearances."

Ferraro stood up straight. "You have evidence of this?"

"No. I only . . . I know it's true, that's all, and I can prove it to you later. But first we have to get on TV. I have to get a message out to all the people of Denver."

She rolled her eyes. "So that's it. You're just some nutcase who wants to spout off about his manifesto on TV."

No, she had it all wrong. "Please, you've got to believe me. I'm not crazy."

"Really? You sure could have fooled me." She pulled a pack of cigarettes from a pocket, lit one up, and took a drag. "I know who you are, by the way. It took me a minute with the beard and the hair, but we showed your photo enough times on the news last fall. You're the guy the police were searching for, along with that doctor. You're Travis Wilder."

He clenched his hands in his pockets. "So are you going to call the police?"

"I might. But you wanted to talk, so let's talk."

Anger flooded him. "Why? So you can land a big scoop and get your job back? That's all you care about, isn't it—getting the story? That was why you cut off Sergeant Otero when he was trying to talk about the disappearances."

"It's true, I did cut him off in that piece. Do you know why?" She tossed down the cigarette and stamped it out with a heel. "Otero does care about the disappearances, but he's one of the few who does, and I wanted people to get angry, to call the police, to force them to do something. Journalism isn't just about recycling information, Mr. Wilder. It's about getting a reaction out of people, making them care."

His anger cooled into shame. "Did it?" he said finally. "Get a reaction?"

She didn't meet his gaze. "No."

He nodded, then took a step closer. "They're afraid, Anna. The people of this city. Of every city in this country. They're not going to stand up against Duratek, not unless they know the truth."

"Which you do," she said with a skeptical glare.

"No, not completely. But I do know Duratek is linked to the disappearances. And I...I can show you something that might help you believe me." He squeezed the iron box in his pocket.

She sighed. "Fine, let's pretend for a minute that you're not just an escaped mental patient with severe paranoia and a messiah complex, and that Duratek is somehow behind all of this. I can't say it would be a complete shock—journalists have been trying to dig up evidence of shady dealings at Duratek for years, only without luck. But even if you have evidence to prove it's true, there's still no place I can take the story."

"What about another TV station?"

"No go. Victor has a lot of friends in this town. None of the other news directors will even talk to me now. Same goes for the editors at the newspapers."

There had to be somewhere else they could go. "I don't understand." His voice was a croak. "I thought news was about telling the truth."

She laughed, a bitter sound. "You really are crazy, Mr. Wilder. Nothing is what it seems on TV. That's the first lesson every journalist learns. It's all a fantasy. Here's a good example for you: You know the televangelist Sage Carson? He's always preaching about helping others, so I thought he would lend a hand, maybe show some pictures of the missing men and women on his show. But you know what? He wouldn't even return my calls. So much for charity."

Hope turned to dust in Travis's chest. Anna Ferraro had listened to him, but she couldn't help, and he doubted anyone else would believe him.

"Don't look now," Ferraro muttered, "but here comes the goon squad."

Travis turned to see a pair of thick-necked men in blue uniforms walking across the parking lot. For a terrified moment he thought they were police officers. Then he saw the patches on their uniforms; they were security guards. All the same, they carried guns.

"You were instructed to leave the property within fifteen minutes, Ms. Ferraro," one of the guards said as they approached. "You're now trespassing. If you don't leave immediately, we'll call the police."

She glared at him. "Cut the tough guy act, Ben. Believe me, I'm getting out of this dump."

The other guard gazed at Travis, eyes suspicious. "Who are you?"

"A man who was kind enough to help me put my things in the trunk," Ferraro said. "Unlike any of you, Ron."

"You need to go now," the first guard said, his eyes dark, without expression. "Both of you." He reached for the cell phone clipped at his belt.

Ferraro jerked open the car door. "God, Ben, when did you turn into such a creep? You used to be a gentleman."

The guard said nothing as he raised the phone. The logo emblazoned on the device glowed in the light of a nearby streetlamp: a white crescent moon merging into a capital D. A coldness spilled into Travis's gut. There was something about the monotonous way the guard talked, about the flatness of his eyes. Something wrong.

"You have to go, Anna," Travis whispered. "Now."

She met his gaze, then nodded. "Let me just give you a tip for helping me with the box," she said—loudly, for the benefit of the two men. She rummaged in her purse, then pushed a crumpled piece of paper into his hand. He shoved it in his pocket.

Travis stepped away as she got into the car and shut the door. She rolled down the window and looked out. Her expression was still one of annoyance, but Travis saw the glint of fear in her eyes.

"Be careful," she said, glancing past him.

"Don't worry about me," he said with a sudden grin, and he tightened his grip around the box in his pocket.

Ferraro gave a grim nod. She hit the gas, and her car peeled out of the parking lot, speeding down Lincoln Street. Travis felt his grin crumble away, and he turned around.

"Who are you?" the first security guard, the one called Ben, said. His eyes were like black stones.

Travis shrugged. "She told you. Just a guy who was helping her with her box."

"I don't believe you."

"Come on, Ben," the other guard said. "Leave him alone. He's just some homeless guy scrounging for tips."

Ben shook his head. "I have to report this." He punched a button on the phone. The crescent moon logo glowed in the dark, white as bones.

Fear flashed through Travis. He couldn't let them do this. He opened the box in his pocket, and his fingers brushed the smooth surface of one of the Stones—Sinfathisar by its cool touch. He pointed his other hand at the phone.

"Reth," he said.

The phone shattered in the guard's grip. Shards of plastic traced red lines across his face, but he did not flinch.

The other guard did. "What the hell?" He grabbed for his gun with a shaking hand and pointed it at Travis. "I don't know what you just did, but you're coming with us."

"No," Travis said, then spoke another rune. *"Dur."*

The gun flew up, striking the man on the bottom of his jaw. His eyes rolled up into his head, and without a sound he crumpled to the pavement.

The remaining guard, Ben, was watching him with his life-less eyes. "I know who you are."

Travis swallowed the sick lump in his throat. "And I know what you are. You gave it up for them, didn't you? You're not a man anymore, you're a thing. No, don't come closer."

The guard stopped. "There's no point in resisting. The world is changing. A new order comes, and those who resist it will not survive."

"Neither will you," Travis said through clenched teeth.

The guard raised big hands and lunged for him. Travis was faster.

"Dur!"

He directed the full force of the rune not at the man's gun, but at the center of his chest. The guard stopped. A shudder passed through his body, and he lifted up onto his toes, as if something was pulling him from above. His eyes bulged, and a dark trickle of blood oozed from the corner of his mouth.

"Help me ... Master," he choked. "I don't want ... to die."

"Too late," Travis said. "You're already dead."

He made a fist of his left hand, closing his fingers around empty air, then pulled back. At the same moment the thing burst from the guard's chest: a dark lump of metal. It thudded to the pavement and rolled to a stop. The guard stared forward with empty eyes. Then he toppled facefirst, a corpse long before he hit the pavement.

Sound and motion. Travis looked up. A door opened in the side of the building. Several shadowy forms rushed out. In the distance, the wail of sirens approached. So someone had made a phone call after all.

However, it wasn't guards or police officers he feared now. Blue-white light spilled from the mouth of a nearby alley, and a metallic whine rose on the air. Renewed dread pumped energy into Travis's legs. He turned and ran from the parking lot.

"Alth," he whispered, speaking one last rune before closing the box, and shadows gathered around him, cloaking him in darkness as he vanished into the night.

35

"This is perilous, sister," Lirith whispered as the two witches moved as quietly as they could down the corridor. "I do not know why I agreed to this."

"Because you know as I do we have no other choice," Aryn whispered back. She did not spin the words across the Weirding; it was too dangerous to speak that way with so many witches about the castle.

Lirith clutched Aryn's gown, holding her back. "If Liendra or one of her spies sees us here—"

"Then we tell them the truth," Aryn said, trying to sound confident. "We tell them we're going to Queen Ivalaine to try to convince her to help us."

"To help us, yes—against Liendra."

"We'll just leave that last little bit out."

Lirith gave her a dark look. "And don't you think Liendra has ways of getting the truth out of us?"

"Maybe. But if she has the power to pick apart our minds, why hasn't she done so already? Liendra has a hold over the Witches—but I don't think it's as strong as she would like us to believe. We weren't the only ones who joined with the Pattern reluctantly. She has to play her cards carefully."

"As do we," Lirith said. However, she let go of Aryn's gown, and the two women continued down the corridor.

The last two days had been the longest of Aryn's life. Liendra had vowed to watch them closely, and the golden-haired witch had not lied. It seemed at every turn she was there, or one of the young witches who followed her every command as if it were the word of Sia herself.

Except they've shunned the name of Sia, just as they've banned the crones from their covens.

And that was the one thing that gave Aryn hope. Without the older witches and their wisdom, Liendra and her minions were bound to make mistakes. At least, Aryn had to hope so.

That Liendra plotted something to prevent the Warriors of Vathris from marching north to Gravenfist Keep was a given. Even King Boreas seemed certain of that fact. However, exactly what Liendra planned was a mystery—one they had to solve if they were to have any of hope of stopping her. And they had to stop her. Grace was depending on them.

Aryn longed desperately to reach out with the Touch, to fling her consciousness over the intervening leagues and speak to Grace. She didn't dare, of course, and not just because of all the witches in the castle. The Pale King's pylons had been awakened at the command of their master, and their magic tangled through the threads of the Weirding like vipers.

We haven't forgotten you, Grace. Already the Warriors of Vathris number five thousand, and more come every day. Just hold on a little while longer.

She had to pray the words to Sia rather than spin them across the Weirding, but maybe somehow, by the will of the goddess, Grace would get the message.

In the meantime, the best way to help Grace was to learn what Liendra was planning. Whatever it was, it had to come soon. The army of Vathris was to depart on the morrow under the command of King Borcas. Liendra was running out of time.

Which made her behavior earlier that morning all the more strange. They had encountered her at breakfast in the great hall, and she had been all smiles and bright laughter. She had seemed utterly unconcerned that the men of Vathris were ready to march.

"We shall see what weather tomorrow brings," was all the golden-haired witch said. "Storms can come upon one swiftly this time of year, as I'm sure the king knows."

Aryn had dared to relay these words to the king. After all, Liendra couldn't punish her for talking to her liege and warden. At least, she hoped not. However, Boreas had seemed every bit as unconcerned as Liendra.

"Of course Lady Liendra plots against me," the king said, standing before the roaring fire in his chamber. "She's a witch. She can't help plotting." He raised an eyebrow, giving her a piercing look. "No offense intended, my lady."

Despite her fear, Aryn gave him a wry grin. "None taken, Your Majesty." Then she voiced the question that had weighed on her mind these last two days, asking the king why he had allowed Liendra and her witches to stay in the castle.

Boreas laughed. "That's simple, my lady. It's far better to have your enemies near at hand, where you can keep a close eye on them. I do not plan on being caught unawares by any spells Lady Liendra might try to spin."

Aryn wanted to believe that, but she didn't know if she could, and that was why they had to try to speak to Ivalaine. Until recently, she had been Matron of the Witches, and if anyone knew what Liendra intended to do, it was her. There was just one problem: Ivalaine had forbidden Aryn and Lirith ever to try speaking to her again.

The two witches turned down an empty corridor. Ivalaine's chamber lay just ahead.

"What if she's not there?" Aryn said, suddenly uncertain at the wisdom of this.

"She will be," Lirith said. "The servingman I spoke to said the queen takes all her meals in her room."

Aryn reached out with the Touch, but she sensed no threads nearby. She hurried after Lirith to the queen's door. They exchanged one last nervous look, then Lirith lifted a hand to knock.

The door flew open.

"Did I not tell you I would have nothing to do with you?" Ivalaine hissed.

Lirith gasped, and Aryn clamped a hand to her mouth to stifle a scream. The queen of Toloria was barely recognizable. Always in the past she had carried herself tall and straight, her flaxen hair as flawless as her skin, her eyes as clear as ice.

That woman was nowhere to be seen now. Ivalaine stooped over, her shoulders hunched like an old woman's, her gown wrinkled and soiled. Her hair was snarled and dull with oil, and scratches marred her face, as if she had been clawing at it. Her eyes were the same ice gray as always, but they seemed too bright, and they focused on nothing for more than a second.

Lirith recovered first. "Please, Your Majesty. We have to speak with you just this once. After this, we'll leave you alone, if that's what you wish." She reached out a hand.

The queen batted it aside. "I wish you to leave me alone now. I should weave an enchantment—I should make you run away screaming." Her fingers fluttered, then knotted together. "But my spells have fled me. The authority of the crown has fled me.

Love is all I have left, and bitter comfort that is. Would that I had nothing left at all."

She turned from the door and lurched into her room. Aryn and Lirith exchanged startled glances, then they stepped into the queen's chamber.

The smell hit Aryn at once. The air was thick with the reek of spoiled meat. The room was dim—tapestries had been drawn over the windows—but after a moment Aryn's eyes adjusted. Trays of food lay all around, none of it eaten. Aryn glanced at the nearest tray; maggots writhed atop a piece of venison. She clutched a hand to her throat to keep from gagging.

The queen must have sent her maids away along with everyone else. The covers had been stripped from the bed and wadded up on the floor in a kind of nest. The stench of urine rose from an uncovered chamber pot. It was almost too much, and Aryn staggered, but Lirith's grip on her arm held her steady.

"Your Majesty," Aryn said. "Are you well?"

It was a ridiculous question. However, Ivalaine seemed not to hear her. She paced before the cold fireplace, muttering, as if she was the only one in the room.

"I was young . . . so young, and still a maiden. But I did as they asked. I did what they wanted me to do. I sacrificed myself to that bloody bull."

Aryn cast a startled look at Lirith. The witch's dark eyes were locked on the queen.

Ivalaine pulled at her hair as she paced. "A male witch, one of full blood. They needed him for their schemes, and I helped to create him, I gave him up for them." Clumps of hair came away in her hands. "But he is my son. I cannot let them . . . I cannot let her use him. She would . . . in the shadows . . . not alive, and not dead . . . she thinks she can stop me from . . . from . . ."

Ivalaine's words phased into a meaningless hum. She stared with empty eyes, swaying back and forth.

"Now, sister," Lirith whispered. "While her guard is down. You must spin a thread out to her, you must try to glimpse what is in her mind."

Fear paralyzed Aryn. She couldn't.

Lirith squeezed her arm. "You must. You are stronger than I. And we have to know."

Aryn let out a moan, then she shut her eyes and reached out with the Touch. She could see the queen's thread. It flickered like a dying candle, bright one moment, dull the next. Aryn hesitated, then extended a shining hand and gripped it.

Wonder filled Aryn, and terror. She saw everything in an instant. It was all so clear, only it was chaotic, fragmented—like gazing into a shattered mirror. There, in one shard, was Ivalaine as a pretty young maid, no more than sixteen. And there was King Boreas. Only he wasn't a king yet, but rather a man just entering his prime. And there, in another shard, was a woman in a dove gray gown whom Aryn recognized only from paintings. Queen Narenya. A baby appeared in her arms, an infant with dark hair. The broken shards started to align themselves. . . .

Ivalaine had been so young—just sixteen winters old—and newly a witch. She had been willing, even eager, to do as her coven bid her. For many years they had been trying to bring about the birth of a male witch, one as full in his power as any woman who ever touched the Weirding.

To match the men of Vathris, we must have a man of Sia, spoke the wise ones, the crones, the seers of prophecy.

Many of the most powerful witches had used herbs and spells, along with the simpler magics of wine and beauty, to find their way into the beds of strong warriors, but to no avail. A few girl children had been born strong in the Touch, but no males. Until . . .

Aryn could see it as if it was happening before her. Ivalaine had clad herself in one of Narenya's gowns and had waited in a chamber. The king was brought to her, his mind fogged by herbs that had been slipped into his wine. He was rough, but so dull were his wits that he did not hear her soft sounds of pain, did not see the blood upon the sheets.

Yet that was only half the deception, for Narenya had secretly followed the ways of Sia herself. Though she loved Boreas, her duty was to the Witches. Unable to bear his child herself, for she proved barren, Narenya did what she knew she must. With the help of her two handmaidens, both disciples of Sia, she had deceived the king and his court. It had been simple enough to pad her gown a little more each week, and when she was alone with Boreas in their chamber, spells of illusion had made him believe her naked belly swelled even though it remained flat beneath his hand.

Ten moons later, the deception was completed. Narenya told the king the time for their child's birth had come. She ordered all from her chamber save her handmaidens and an old midwife who was Crone of her coven. At the same time, in a room deep in the castle, Ivalaine birthed her own child—a son, fine and healthy. The threads of the Weirding coiled themselves around him like a blanket woven of light. And before she could even kiss his damp head, he was taken away from her and spirited into Narenya's chamber. And that was how Teravian was born.

"Get out!"

The queen's shrill cry pierced the air, breaking the spell. Aryn staggered, clutching a hand to her head as Lirith gripped her shoulders to steady her.

"Get out now!"

Rage twisted the queen's visage. But did she mean get out of the room, or out of her head? Ivalaine picked up a plate, threw it, and it smashed against the wall behind them. Aryn and Lirith stumbled back.

"I see now what I must do." Ivalaine's voice was low, trembling with power. "You would use him just as she would, but there is a way to be certain no one uses him." She shuddered, and a softness stole across her visage. "I am his mother. It is the last thing, the only thing, I can do for him."

With that the queen moved past the two stunned women, through the door, and was gone.

Aryn slumped down into a chair, no longer caring about the stench in the room. Her legs seemed incapable of bearing her; she had to sit for a moment.

"Oh, Lirith . . ."

"Hush, sister." Lirith stood above her. "I touched your thread as you touched Ivalaine's. I saw everything. Sia help us, what cruel treachery. I wonder, when did Boreas finally realize what Narenya had done?"

Aryn didn't know; that had been missing from the shards she had glimpsed. "Whenever it happened, by then it was too late. Boreas couldn't tell the truth—not if he wanted Teravian to be his heir. And I think, even then, he still loved Narenya." However, it surely explained the king's attitude toward Ivalaine and the Witches. They had used him. Just as they meant to use Teravian. Only how?

"I don't know, sister," Lirith said, not requiring magic to understand Aryn's thoughts. "I don't see how using Teravian can help Liendra."

Aryn sighed. "It's broken Ivalaine. She was a queen, and a witch, and a mother, but circumstances wouldn't let her be all three at once. Each required something different of her, and in the end it drove her to madness.".

Sorrow shone in Lirith's dark eyes. "Ivalaine has been a victim of these deeds, just as Boreas and Teravian have."

These words plunged a needle of fear into Aryn's heart. "A victim of these deeds," she murmured. "A victim . . ."

Fear became panic. Aryn leaped to her feet.

"Sister, what is it?"

By Sia, she couldn't be right. Only she knew that she was. "Ivalaine said there was only one last thing she could do, one way to make sure no one used Teravian."

Lirith's eyes went wide. "Sia help us, we have to stop her."

They dashed out the door and careened down the passageways of the castle as servants, knights, and nobles alike hurried to get out of their way. By the time they reached the prince's chamber, they were gasping for breath, their gowns askew.

"My ladies," Duke Petryen said, "what's the matter?"

The duke stood outside the door to the prince's chamber, along with one of Boreas's men-at-arms. Since the attempt on Teravian's life, Petryen and Sai'el Ajhir had taken turns standing guard outside Teravian's chamber. The behavior seemed excessive to Aryn—were not the king's men-at-arms good enough? However, it showed great loyalty on the part of Petryen and Ajhir to be so solicitous of King Boreas's son. Aryn could only hope that loyalty had helped the prince now.

"Queen Ivalaine," Aryn said, fighting to get the words out between gasps for breath, "did she come here?"

"Yes, my ladies, just a minute ago."

Lirith gripped his arm. "Did you let her in? Did you let the queen into the prince's chamber?"

Petryen frowned. "Of course I let her in. The prince was fostered at her court. Why would we deny her entrance?"

They were too late. Aryn couldn't stop shaking. "Is there anyone else in there with him?"

"The Mournish man Sareth came to pay a visit to His Highness," Petryen said. "His company seems to cheer the prince, so we allowed him in. Why do you ask?"

Lirith stared at the door. "By the gods—Sareth!"

A muffled crash sounded from behind the door. The duke gave the women a shocked look, then turned and pushed open the door. Aryn and Lirith rushed into the chamber on his heels. The scene within froze Aryn's blood.

Ivalaine had fallen against the sideboard, upsetting a pitcher of wine. Teravian lay on the floor, his face white with fear. Sareth bent over him, clutching the prince's tunic.

"By Vathris, get your hands off of him, you dog!" Petryen shouted.

Before Sareth could react, Petryen grappled him, pulling him away from Teravian. Sareth tried to break free, but then the man-at-arms was there, and both men held Sareth, knocking his wooden leg out from under him, wrestling him onto the bed.

"Murderer," Petryen said through clenched teeth. "I should have known it was someone the prince trusted, someone who could get close to him. Now you're trying to finish the deed."

Lirith flung herself at the men. "Leave him alone! You're hurting him!"

The two men ignored her cries, and Ivalaine was already moving. She lurched toward Teravian, who still lay stunned on the floor. Something glinted in her hand: a needle, its tip covered with a green substance. She poised the needle above the prince's throat as he looked up with wide eyes.

"I failed once to protect you from them," she said. "I will not fail you again."

Aryn had less than the time between two heartbeats. She reached out and gripped the threads of the Weirding, and as the power of life flowed into her all fear was forgotten. With a single, swift thought, she wove the shining threads into a shimmering new pattern.

Ivalaine cried out. Her feet left the ground, and her body flew backward, as if she had been dealt a blow by an invisible hand. She struck the wall, and the needle flew from her hand. The queen moaned—a sound of fear and rage and pain—and she writhed, but her hands and feet were held fast against the wall, as if bound by ropes no eye could see.

No eyes save Aryn's, for she could see the shining strands of magic that held the queen in place, just as she could sense the way Ivalaine fought against them. However, the queen's power was no match for Aryn's own. Aryn gazed at her hands—the left that was whole, perfect, the right that was twisted and withered. Neither trembled.

"By the Blood of the Bull," Petryen swore. He let go of Sareth and indicated for the man-at-arms to do the same.

Sareth sat up on the bed. He touched his chin gingerly. A bruise was already forming along his jaw. Lirith ran to him, and he held her tight.

"It was the queen," Petryen said, disbelief written across his face. "It was she who tried to murder the prince."

"Twice." Aryn bent down and picked up the needle, taking care to avoid the tip. "This poison would have stopped his heart in an instant."

"But why would she do such a thing?" Petryen said.

Teravian had regained his feet. He gazed at Ivalaine, a hand to his throat, the expression in his eyes unreadable. "Maybe you should ask her."

Aryn knew there was no use in that. Ivalaine had stopped struggling, and she sagged in the invisible bonds. Her eyes were rolled back, her lips wet with spittle. She seemed to be speaking something, only she made no sound.

"Inform the king what has happened," Petryen said to the guard. "And bring more men to carry her to the dungeon."

The dungeon? By Sia, it wasn't right—she was a queen. However, the guard nodded, then turned on a heel and left the room.

Aryn moved closer, laying a hand on Ivalaine's cheek. She shut her eyes, probing with the Touch, but Ivalaine's thread was dull gray, and when Aryn grasped it she could sense no light, no spark of consciousness.

Aryn turned around, tears streaming down her cheeks. "She's gone."

Lirith let out a sob, pressing her face against Sareth's chest. He wrapped his arms around her. Petryen shook his head, his expression one of disgust. Of them all, only Teravian seemed without emotion. His eyes were dark as he gazed at the queen. What was he thinking?

I was thinking about what she said to me.

The prince's lips didn't move, but Aryn heard his voice clearly. She stared at him, astonished by the means of his speech as much as by what he said.

What was it? she managed at last. *What did she say to you?*

Teravian turned his back and walked from the chamber. Then, just as he vanished from sight, Aryn heard his voice in her mind once again.

She said she loved me.

36.

They reached Gravenfist Keep on a cold, brilliant afternoon late in the month of Durdath, just when Grace was sure none of them could possibly walk another step north. As the army entered the mouth of a narrow valley, three eagles flew overhead, their feathers gleaming gold in the light of the westering sun, their cries echoing off the cliffs. Was it a welcome they called out, Grace wondered? Or a warning?

"Well," she said to Durge. "We're here."

"I never doubted for a moment we'd make it, Your Majesty," Durge said through ice-crusted mustaches.

Grace gave him the knight a weary smile. "Funny you should say that. Because I sure did."

They had crossed the frozen waters of the River Fellgrim three days ago, and Grace had not been sorry to put Embarr behind them. It was not just the bleakness of the Dominion that had affected her; it was seeing that desolation reflected in Durge's eyes, and in the eyes of all the Embarran knights. Embarr was the place where they were born, where they had lived their lives. Only by King Sorrin's order it had become a Dominion of ghosts.

It seemed every few leagues the army came upon another abandoned village. All of them were the same. The doors of the hovels stood open to wind and snow; no smoke rose from the chimneys. The only living things were dogs that slunk snarling away between the buildings, tails tucked, ribs showing. And they would not be alive much longer.

The army passed manor houses as well, and stone keeps on hills, all empty like the villages. Once they came upon an entire walled town devoid of people. They had gone in, looking for any items they could salvage, but they had not stayed long. Walking through the town's silent streets had given them all an eerie feeling. Was this what the world would be like if Mohg ruled it? Not a place of shadow, filled with cries of suffering, but rather cold and empty, without sound, without life?

Eventually Grace began to imagine that the entire Dominion was empty, that even if they went to Barrsunder they would find it as sterile as the rest of this land. Then, two days after Sir Vedarr and his knights joined with the army, the Spiders finally reported seeing signs of human life. However, this was not cause for joy, for what the spies had glimpsed was a company of fifty Onyx Knights patrolling to the west.

Aldeth said he hadn't been able to determine the knights' purpose, but Grace knew what it was. They were searching for her. The runelord Kelephon still wanted Fellring, and he still wanted her blood, so he could wield the sword and claim the throne of Malachor Reborn.

However, the Onyx Knights never came nearer to the army than two leagues, Grace didn't know if she had luck to thank for that or Tira. Either way, she amused herself thinking how Kelephon would be drooling with fury if he knew his own knights had come within a few miles of her and Fellring. When Tarus asked her what she was grinning about, she only laughed and hugged Tira. The knight gave her an odd look and rode off, muttering something about the madness of queens and witches.

The next day they crossed the Fellgrim, with only one minor mishap when a horse fell through the ice and was quickly pulled back out. Both beast and rider were cold, wet, and scraped, but not seriously injured.

Once across the river, they found themselves traveling

through a forest. It reminded Grace of the forests of Colorado: light and open, with plenty of space to move between the trees, the ground covered with a carpet of soft needles. Here and there a small evergreen plant grew in clumps, covered with tiny orange-red berries and looking for all the world like kinnikinnick.

However, this wasn't Colorado. The silvery, leafless trees were *valsindar*, not aspen, and the needles of the *sintaren* trees were a feathery purple-green. All the same, they looked so much like ponderosa pine that, as they made camp that evening, Grace couldn't resist walking up to one, pressing her nose to its sun-warmed bark, and inhaling deeply.

"Ice cream," she said in answer to the curious look Paladus gave her. "Where I come from, some pine trees smell like vanilla ice cream."

The Tarrasian commander wore a skeptical look. "And does that one smell like this *vah'nilla*?"

She shook her head. "More like butterscotch."

Tira touched her nose to the tree and laughed.

Paladus hesitated, then followed suit, moving close and sniffing the tree's bark. He turned around, eyes wide. "It smells delicious."

Grace laughed. "So it does."

As the evening wore on, Grace noticed more than one man moving from *sintaren* tree to *sintaren* tree, stopping to smell each one. Despite what lay ahead of them she felt her spirits lifting. While this forest was empty of people, it did not give her the same sense of desolation as Embarr. It was sad, yes, but there was a contentedness to it as well. This land had learned to live alone.

Just like you, Grace.

The next day, as they set out, Durge told her this forest was called the Winter Wood. It stretched across the entire north of Falengarth, and once everything within its borders had been part of the kingdom of Malachor. Maybe that was why she felt less afraid here; maybe she had come home.

Then they came upon the pylon, and the feeling of peace vanished.

It was damaged; otherwise, they would surely have felt its

insidious effects as they had before. As it was, a gloom seemed to descend over the forest, though the sky above the leafless branches of the *valsindar* was clear as a sapphire.

It was Senrael who sensed it first. The crone warned Grace, who instructed the Spiders to scout things out—carefully. Aldeth returned minutes later; he had spotted the pylon in a clearing not far ahead. Tarus gave the commands, and the army veered to the east to give the relic a wide berth. Luckily, the bulk of the force was marching a quarter league back, and so never came near enough for concern.

"I'm not sure what happened to the pylon," Aldeth said. "I didn't want to get too close to it, but it looked to me as if the stone was cracked."

Durge stroked his mustaches. "From years of cold and ice and wind, perhaps."

"Or more likely from this," Samatha said as she approached, holding up a sword. The blade was broken off a few inches above the hilt, but it was enough to see that the sword had been forged of jet-black steel.

Grace took the broken sword in a trembling hand. "Onyx Knights. They were the ones who broke the pylon."

Paladus looked at her. "Why?"

The metal was cold against her bare skin, but she didn't let go. "Kelephon means to betray the Pale King. He wants to gain the Imsari for himself."

"He must have spoken powerful runes to have allowed his knights to approach the pylon," Master Graedin said. He shivered inside his gray robes. "I suppose they broke it to keep the Pale King from spying on their comings and goings."

"Which means Kelephon has unwittingly done us a favor," Durge said. "For the Pale King will not see us either."

Either Durge's theory was right, or luck and Tira's magic continued to protect them, for over the next two days they encountered nothing more menacing than the silver-furred squirrels who made their home in the duskneedle trees, and who scolded them as they marched by.

Then, as suddenly as if a curtain had been drawn aside, the trees of the Winter Wood gave way to a windswept plain at the foot of a range of rugged mountains. A pair of standing stones stood at the entrance to a high-walled valley. They rode between the stones, following a faint road up the defile. Then, as the eagles soared overhead, Grace at last laid eyes on their destination.

"It doesn't look like much," she said.

Seated on his mule, All-master Oragien smiled at her. "Gravenfist Keep is nearly a thousand years old, Your Majesty. We should be glad it's standing at all."

While the main force of the army snaked its way slowly up the valley, Grace rode ahead with the ones who had become her most trusted companions: Durge and Tarus, Aldeth and Samatha, Commander Paladus, Master Graedin and All-master Oragien, and the witches Senrael and Lursa. With them beside her, Grace felt she could face anything.

Well, almost anything.

"We are so incredibly doomed," she murmured as they brought their horses to a halt, then winced, glancing at the others. "Sorry. I meant to just think that."

"Don't apologize, Your Majesty," Tarus said, a pained look on his face. "I think you may be right."

They dismounted and picked their way across the stony ground toward the keep. Tira ran alongside them, flitting from rock to rock on bare feet.

Gravenfist sat at the highest point of the valley, where the cliff walls drew down until they were little more than a hundred paces apart. Grace was no military genius, but she could see this was a highly defensible spot. The cliffs were sheer and unscalable, and the narrow valley would squeeze an attacking force like a stony hand; no doubt that was how the keep had gotten its name. Even a small force such as her own could hold this fortress indefinitely if it was in good repair.

It wasn't. Given the looks of it, the curtain wall that stretched between the two cliffs had once been about thirty feet high. Now in most places it was no more than ten. The wall was cracked and rusty with lichen, heaps of fallen stones piled at its base.

The main keep, which stood behind the wall, was in little better shape. There was a large, square tower from which low barracks reached out to either side, then angled back around to form a courtyard. The barracks looked large enough to house a thousand soldiers, but they were largely roofless, and their doors and shutters had long ago rotted to splinters. The tower, which stood five stories high, appeared solid enough, though its parapets were crumbling like the wall, and no doubt it was as roofless as the barracks.

Grace gazed at the keep, but the tower's narrow windows only stared back at her like bleary eyes. This place had been slumbering for seven hundred years. How could she hope to wake it to war?

"Don't worry, Your Majesty," Durge said. "It's nothing a little elbow grease won't fix."

Grace didn't think there were that many elbows in the world. Besides, even if they could prevent the fortress from falling down, there certainly wasn't time to build the wall back up to its full height. A thirty-foot barrier might be defended. But one that stood ten feet? The Pale King's minions would scale it in seconds. Grace started to tell the others it was hopeless, that they might as well turn around and march back to Calavere.

"Your Majesty!" Master Graedin called out. "I believe you should come look at this." The young runespeaker had scrambled up a pile of stones and now stood atop one of the lowest points along the wall.

The rest of them hurried to the wall, and Aldeth and Samatha nimbly ascended it. There was plenty of room for them to stand alongside Graedin; the wall was a good ten feet thick.

"Oh," Aldeth said.

Samatha laughed, her gray eyes shining. "Well this changes everything."

"I told you so," Graedin said.

All of this suspense was quickly making Grace cross. "Durge, since no one sees fit to tell me what they're seeing, I'll have to look for myself. Help me up there."

Durge knelt and made a stirrup of his hands, boosting Grace up. Aldeth and Samatha caught her, pulling her to the top of the wall. She swayed as the wind struck her.

"Careful, Your Majesty," Master Graedin said, steadying her. "You don't wish to fall that way."

"No," Grace said softly. "I don't suppose I do."

She had imagined the valley sloped away from the keep on the other side, just as it did on this side. It didn't. Instead, the keep stood at the top of a nearly vertical escarpment. While from the way they had come the wall looked to be no more than ten feet high, on this side it plunged down a hundred feet to the valley floor below, sloping out slightly as it went.

It looked as if the wall had at one time been perfectly smooth, but in many places the facing stones had cracked and crumbled. There were enough handholds that a skilled climber—or a nimble creature, like one of the *feydrim*—would be able to scale the wall, but it would be slow going, and an archer could easily shoot anything that tried to climb up. Nor would ladders do much good. Such a tall ladder could be pushed away from the wall before even the fastest climber might ascend it.

"What do you see up there, Your Majesty?" Durge called out to her.

"Hope," she called back. "I see hope."

The restoration of Gravenfist Keep began that day. The first order of business was to clear away hundreds of years of debris from the keep's courtyard and to make a place to set up a temporary camp. As Commander Paladus and Sir Vedarr gave the orders, Grace toured the keep with Durge, Tarus, and Oragien so that they could come up with a plan. There was no way to know how much time they had until the Rune Gate opened; they had to be sure they completed the most important repairs first.

All agreed the wall would be their first priority. There was no need to build it back any higher, but they had to remove the loose stones, square off the top, and add crenellations so that archers could safely stand atop the wall and take aim at any who tried to scale it. Durge also suggested adding a few machicolations, so that fiery naphtha—of which they had many barrels—could be rained down upon the enemy.

The next task would be to clear out the barracks and repair the roofs. On closer inspection, it was not going to be as terrible a task as Grace had feared. The roof beams had rotted away, but there were plenty of trees close at hand to fashion more. Most of the original slate shingles lay scattered on the ground, and more could easily be mined from the walls of the valley, which were made up of the stuff.

The main keep was also in better shape than Grace would

have thought possible. Its roof remained, though with countless holes, as did each of the five floors within, a fact that astounded both Grace and Durge, since they were made of wood. Then All-master Oragien pointed out the symbols that had been etched into the thick beams hewn of *sintaren* trees.

"Every part of this keep—every stone and every beam—has been bound with runes of power," the old runespeaker said. "Great magic yet abides here."

So Falken had said, but how could they awaken that magic to help them? Grace fingered the bound rune in her pocket. If it was really a key, then where was the keyhole it fit? So far she had seen nothing, but surely they would find it as they cleaned out the keep.

By evening, the keep's courtyard had been cleared, and in the barracks the men had swept away a foot of dirt to find solid stone floors beneath. They used the canvas from the tents to fashion temporary roofs, while a corral for the horses had been built outside the keep from freshly felled duskneedle trees.

That night, as stars shone in the sky, they gathered around a great bonfire, and the last casks of wine—which had been saved for just this occasion—were all tapped so that every man and woman could have a cup or two. Some of the men had brought drums and flutes, and they played boisterous music, while others stomped and clapped their hands and a bold few broke into a wild dance.

Grace sat on a log bench on the edge of the firelight, content to watch rather than join in, while Tira slept soundly in her arms. A great whoop rose from the men when a number of the women—the Spiders Samatha and Karthi, and most of the younger witches—picked up the hems of their skirts and joined in the dance. Lursa laughed, her cheeks bright from the fire and exertion, as one of the Calavaner knights whirled her around in strong arms. Grace couldn't help laughing herself. The Witches and the Warriors were supposed to be enemies, but she would never have known it looking at the dancers.

"Do you think it's a good idea to light so large a bonfire, Your Majesty?" said a gloomy voice beside her.

Grace didn't know when Durge had sat down on the log; his charcoal gray tunic blended with the gloom.

"The night's cold," she said. "The fire keeps them warm."

"And the dancing?"

She smiled. "That too. Among other things."

All of the ladies had found a partner in the dance. Lursa was still laughing, her plain face made pretty with mirth, and the knight's eyes were bright with a light that came not just from the fire. Senrael stood not far off, glaring at the couple. Lursa was going to have to be careful if she wanted to remain the coven's Maiden. Then again, there were a few younger witches in the coven who would do just fine. Grace hoped Lursa did what she wanted.

Durge looked back over his shoulder, into the darkness. "The Rune Gate lies but three leagues from here as the raven flies, on the other side of Shadowsdeep. His spies will see the fire. The Pale King will know we've come."

"Good," Grace said, surprised to realize she meant it. "I want him to know I'm here. I want him to be afraid." She gripped the hilt of Fellring, belted as always at her hip. "Maybe he'll think twice before he forces the Rune Gate open again."

Durge shook his head. "He will come. Once the last rune sealing it breaks, the Rune Gate will open, and all the hordes of the Pale King will be upon us."

"That's one thing I don't understand," said a clear tenor, and they looked up to see Master Graedin approaching, along with All-master Oragien. "How is it we've already encountered *feydrim* and wraithlings if the Rune Gate is still shut?"

Grace had actually been thinking about that one for a while. They knew the Pale King had managed to get a few wraithlings to Earth, using Gelthisar to send them through the crack between the worlds—the gap Travis had inadvertently created when he traveled back in time to Castle City and met Jack Graystone. However, Grace doubted the Stone of Ice had allowed Berash to get his minions through the Rune Gate, and they couldn't sail the Winter Sea. The fairy ship had navigated the roiling, icy waters around the northern shores of Imbrifale, but Grace doubted any mundane ship could manage that feat. That meant the Pale King's slaves must have come through the mountains.

She looked up at Graedin. "Falken told me that the Ironfang

Mountains, which border Imbrifale, were woven with perilous illusions by witches long ago."

"That's so," Oragien said. "What's more, the Runelords of old spoke the rune *Fal* over and over, raising the Fal Threndur to great heights and filling them with treacherous chasms. They make a strong prison around Imbrifale."

Grace snapped her fingers. "Right, but no matter how strong it is, no prison is perfect. Say the odds of getting through the Ironfang Mountains, with all their chasms and illusions, were one in a hundred. If the Pale King threw a thousand *feydrim* at the mountains, then ten would make it through. That could explain the creatures we've seen."

"But we've seen hundreds of *feydrim* over the course of the last year," Durge said.

Despite her proximity to the bonfire, a chill gripped Grace. She was a scientist; she knew numbers couldn't lie, and her mind couldn't help doing the math.

"That would mean there are thousands of *feydrim* within Imbrifale," Graedin said, looking ill.

Grace shook her head. "No, tens of thousands."

"You cannot know that for certain, Your Majesty," Oragien said, though his troubled eyes belied his reassuring tone.

However, he was right. They didn't know for certain how great the Pale King's army was. Maybe the odds of getting through the Fal Threndur were not so high as she thought, which meant the Pale King's forces would number far less. She started to speak these ideas, but her words were lost as the bright call of a horn echoed off the cliffs. The music and dancing ceased, and warriors went scrambling for their swords.

Before Grace could move, Samatha was there. "A band of knights in black armor ride up the valley," the Spider said. "There are about thirty of them—at least that we can see in the darkness."

Master Graedin shot Grace a frightened look. "Maybe it's just a small band then. A patrol like we saw in Embarr."

Or maybe it's the vanguard for a larger force, Grace thought. *Maybe Kelephon has found you after all.*

"What should we do?" she said, looking at Durge.

"We cannot hope to hide from them, Your Majesty. Our fire will have given us away. They know we're here."

"Then I'll talk to them."

"You might want to fight first and talk later, Your Majesty," Samatha said, hand on the dagger tucked into her belt.

Despite her fear, Grace gave the Spider a sharp smile. "I find people are much harder to talk to you when their heads aren't attached to their bodies. And I need to find out what these knights are up to." She stood and handed Tira to Master Graedin. "Keep watch over her."

Tira sleepily coiled her arms around his neck. The young runespeaker nodded.

Grace moved swiftly through the camp, Durge, Samatha, and Oragien beside her.

"All-master," she said to Oragien, gently but firmly, "you should stay behind."

The elderly man shook his head. "It was ever the purpose of the Runelords to serve and protect the lords of Malachor, Your Majesty. We Runespeakers trace our lineage back to the Runelords, just as you trace yours to Ulther's heirs."

Grace's instinct was to order him to stay back. Instead she gritted her teeth and nodded. Warriors rushed around her, falling into place as Paladus barked orders. Grace reached the entrance of the courtyard. There was no gate; it had rotted away long ago. Dim shapes moved in the valley below, coming closer, like black moths drawn to the light of their bonfire.

Sir Tarus approached. "Should we attack, Your Majesty? We have every advantage—numbers, a fortification, the slope."

She shook her head. "I want to talk to them. I have to find out what Kelephon is planning. If the Onyx Knights are massing in the valley, we could be fighting a battle on both sides."

"That would cut us off from King Boreas and the Warriors of Vathris," Durge rumbled. "We could not win such a battle."

"Here they come," Samatha said. "There still must be only the thirty of them. Were there more, Aldeth and the others would have seen them by now and warned us."

Unless the Spiders had been captured. Grace stepped forward, chin high, as the troop of Onyx Knights brought their black horses to a halt a dozen paces away. Both men and beasts blended with the night, like things of shadow.

"You are not welcome here," Grace called out.

"Oh, I beg to differ, Your Majesty," said a booming voice. One of the closest knights climbed down from his horse and stalked forward, spurs clinking. He was a huge man—their leader by the three stars on his breastplate. "I think we're welcome here indeed. In fact, I imagine you'll be breaking out the ale for us. You do have ale, don't you?"

Oragien raised his gnarled staff. *"Lir!"*

Silver light rent the darkness to tatters. The massive knight halted, raising a gloved hand before his visor. His black armor was scratched and dented, and not all of the pieces seemed to match.

"Blast it, runespeaker," the knight growled. "Now I can't see a thing. How am I supposed to drink my ale if I can't find the cup?"

As Grace stared in wonderment, a shapeless figure appeared from behind the knights and shambled forward on sticklike limbs.

"Well, don't just stand there like a village idiot," the old hag said, holding out bony arms. "Give old Grisla a hug."

"Get back, witch," roared the enormous knight in black. He tugged off his helm, releasing a wild profusion of red hair. His bushy beard parted in a grin. "If anyone's doing any hugging of beautiful queens, it's going to be me."

Before Grace could move, King Kel caught her in meaty arms, picked her up off the ground, and proceeded to crush her to jelly while his booming laughter filled the night.

37.

Deirdre Falling Hawk stared out the window of her flat as rain drizzled down from a gray London sky.

"Where are you?" she murmured. "Whoever you are, whatever it is you want, I need you to contact me. Please."

Below, a black car sped down the street. Her heart leaped in her chest. Then, with a splash of rainwater, the car swung around a corner and vanished. She sighed, then sat again at the table. The computer the Seekers had given her whirred quietly. Emerald words pulsed on the screen.

What do you want to do?

"I wish I knew," she muttered, picking up the photograph of the clay tablet. The photograph that had mysteriously appeared on her desk after someone had broken into the office she shared with Anders. Her eyes blurred, and the symbols in the photo re-arranged themselves into new patterns, ones she felt she could almost understand.

Only she couldn't. She had some skill with Old English, and she knew a fair amount of Gaelic, but she was no expert on lost languages. That was why she had given a copy of the photograph to Paul Jacoby. He had the reputation as one of the finest classical archaeologists in the Seekers, and he had made a specialty of ancient writing systems.

Luckily, Jacoby had been so thrilled to see the photograph, he had been more than willing to swear an oath on the Book not to tell anyone else about it. Deirdre hoped she could trust him; she thought she could. Then again, she wasn't certain if she could trust anyone right now.

Or maybe it's you that can't be trusted, Deirdre.

Was that really why Nakamura had assigned Anders to be her new partner? After all, it provided a convenient way to keep a former security guard close to her at all times. And gods knew Anders had a way of showing up at her door at odd hours. She had left the Charterhouse early yesterday, grumbling something about having a headache, and he had shown up at her door at half past six with a bottle of porter and another of aspirin.

"If one doesn't solve the problem, the other will," he had said in his incessantly cheery voice.

Every instinct in her had told her to send him away, but it was hard to believe he was really here to spy on her. She had opened the door, and they had sat on the couch—she in baggy sweats, he in the designer suit he had worn to work—watching reruns of *Are You Being Served?* While she wasn't certain if she had the porter or aspirin to thank, by the time Anders had gone, her headache had as well.

It was only after he left that she noticed her computer had been switched on the whole time, sitting on the table next to the folder with the photograph. Had he seen what she was working on? He would have had a few moments to himself while she poured the beer in the kitchen.

Stop it, Deirdre. Farr's the renegade, not you. He's the one they're keeping watch for.

"I wish you were here, Hadrian," she said, setting down the photograph. "You'd know what to do."

Her fingers hovered over the keyboard of the computer, then fell to her lap. There was no point in doing another search. She had tried every possible combination of keywords, but even with Echelon 7 access she had found nothing. Which left only one possibility.

The tablet was part of the Philosophers' private collection.

There was no other answer. Echelon 7 granted her access to everything in the Seekers' catalogues—everything except what the Philosophers kept secret for themselves. Which meant whoever had left the photograph on her desk had access to the vaults of the Philosophers. And that could only mean . . .

"You're a Philosopher yourself," she said, touching the keyboard.

Of course, Deirdre had no evidence that the individual who had spoken to her using her computer was one with the person who had placed the photograph of the tablet on her desk. However, she couldn't believe otherwise.

I know you're out there, she typed on the computer. I know you're watching me. What do you want me to do?

She hit Enter, and the computer let out a chime.

Error. Search request not understood.

Deirdre slammed the computer shut, shoved it into her satchel, and stood. It was long past time to get to work.

She was drenched by the time she reached the Charterhouse. "Good morning, Miss Falling Hawk," Madeleine said. She paused in her typing, peering at the wall clock. "Wait just a moment—there we go. Good afternoon."

Deirdre winced. "I sent an e-mail. I said I was working at home."

"E-mail is for barbarians," Madeleine said. "Where is your umbrella?"

"I don't have one."

The receptionist made a clucking sound. No doubt only barbarians failed to purchase umbrellas when in London.

Deirdre headed down to her office, expecting to find Anders pounding away at his computer, but he wasn't there. Most likely he was out at lunch. It was just as well. This way she could have a bit of quiet to get some work done, though she would miss his coffee. She lifted the pot, but it was cold and empty.

Settling for a glass of water, she sat at her desk, opened her computer, and brought up the files concerning the Thomas Atwater case.

Atwater was the journeyman who, in 1619, had broken the Seventh Desideratum by returning to a former place of employment that the Philosophers had forbidden him to enter. However, as far as she could tell, there was no record of any punitive action. In fact, according to the fragmented accounts she had managed to find, Atwater had quickly risen in the Seekers, becoming a master before his untimely death at the age of twenty-nine.

Deirdre hadn't been particularly excited when Nakamura had assigned her this task, but perhaps he was onto something. Had the Philosophers evolved in their application of the Desiderata over the centuries? If so, understanding the various historical precedents might give the Seekers some power to argue interpretation of the Desiderata with the Philosophers, and that could give them more flexibility in their investigations.

However, over the last couple of days, Deirdre had run into something of a brick wall with regard to the research. There was nothing in the old records that indicated why Atwater hadn't been punished for his infraction. She performed several more searches as the clock ticked away the silent minutes, but to no avail.

She was still staring at the screen when Anders stepped into the office. On reflex she slammed the computer shut. He seemed not to notice, and he shot her a broad smile.

"Afternoon, mate. Glad to see you made it in. Is the head better?"

"Yes," she said, then winced and held a hand to her forehead.

He clucked his tongue and moved to the coffeepot. "Looks like you mean no. We'd better get some caffeine in your system. I imagine the Seekers want your mind in tip-top shape."

Once again she chided herself for being so suspicious of Anders. He had been nothing but friendly and helpful these last days. She opened her computer, and when he brought her a steaming mug, she accepted it with a genuine smile.

By six o'clock, the effects of the coffee had worn off. Deirdre had followed a few more leads in the Thomas Atwater case, but all of them had been dead ends. As interesting as this case was, she was going to have to move on. The fact was, she would probably never know the full story of Atwater's transgression and why the Philosophers hadn't punished him.

Anders put on his jacket and announced he was off to the pub for a pint with some friends. He invited her along, but she declined. After Anders headed out, Deirdre began packing up her own gear. All she wanted was to spend a quiet evening on the couch in front of the television.

A knock on the door startled her. She looked up and saw Paul Jacoby standing in the open doorway.

"Hello, Deirdre. Do you have a moment?"

"Of course, Paul." She noticed the folder in his hands. "Do you have something for me?"

"I think so." He hurried into the room. Jacoby was a small, balding, bespectacled man of around fifty. His graying mustache, crooked bow tie, and worn corduroy coat lent him a comfortable, scholarly look. He fumbled with the folders, pulling out papers and setting them on her desk. "This is fascinating. Quite extraordinary. In fact, I've never seen anything like it."

"Nothing at all?" Deirdre said, her hopes falling.

"Oh, I don't mean this part, of course." He pointed at the photograph of the clay tablet. "The inscription at the top here is clearly written in Linear A."

"Linear A?"

"It's one of the earliest writing systems we know of. It was developed by the Minoan civilization that arose on Crete about three thousand years ago, and it was used to write an early form of Greek. This is a nice example of it. However, it's this inscription that astounds me." He pointed to the runelike symbols on the bottom half of the tablet. "I've never seen writing like this before. I did a full search of the linguistic databases, but there was no match. These symbols are of utterly unknown origin. There is nothing else like them."

Deirdre touched the silver ring on her hand. What would Jacoby think if he knew those same symbols were engraved inside the ring, as well as on the old keystone in the photo she found—the keystone taken from the building that would one day house Surrender Dorothy?

"Can you read the lower inscription?"

Jacoby shook his head. "No, though I might be able to in time. Whoever made this tablet wrote the same inscription twice, in two different writing systems. I was able to translate the passage written in Linear A." He fumbled with more papers. "Here we go. Mind you, this is only my preliminary translation. I'll need time to refine it. But in general, it reads, 'Forget not the Sleeping Ones. In their blood lies the key.'"

Deirdre gripped the edge of the desk to keep from staggering, hoping Jacoby—focused as he was on the papers—didn't notice her reaction. According to the report she had read, traces of blood had been found on the keystone. Blood with otherworldly origins. But what did it mean? And who were the Sleeping Ones?

Jacoby was still talking excitedly. "You don't have access to the original tablet, do you? It would help enormously to get chemical composition data to help place its geographic origin." He flipped back to the photograph and brushed a finger over the lower inscription. "In a way, as different as it is, the two languages appear not entirely unrelated. I can't be certain, but my supposition is that you could actually derive Linear A from this lower language. That would be exciting news. We believed Linear A was the oldest writing system in the Aegean region, but it may be that another system preceded it."

Deirdre took the folder and closed it, forcing her hands not to tremble. "Thanks, Paul. You've been a big help."

He smiled and adjusted his glasses. "You're quite welcome, Deirdre. And I trust you'll be so kind as to inform me if you find any more examples of this new writing system. We'll need more samples if we're to decode it."

"Of course," she said, hardly hearing her own words.

Jacoby nodded and left the room. Deirdre stared at the folder in her hands. An idea buzzed like a bee in her brain, insistent, but too swift to catch hold of.

"So what was that all about?" said a smoky voice.

Deirdre turned around. Sasha stood in the doorway. She wore stirrup pants and a tweed jacket with elbow patches. All she needed were jodhpurs and a riding crop to complete the faux jockey look.

Deirdre sighed. "Sasha. You startled me."

Sasha sauntered into the room. "It's unusual to see Paul Jacoby over here." She ran long fingers through a bouquet of lilies Anders had brought in and bent down to smell them.

"I had asked a small favor of him," Deirdre said, not sure how much she should say. It was just Sasha. Then again, Sasha seemed to know more about what was going on in the Seekers than Deirdre ever did.

Sasha looked up from the flowers. "Paul Jacoby is a specialist in linguistics, right? Only I thought you were researching historical violations of the Desiderata."

"It's a little side project."

Sasha gave her a sharp look. "I thought as much. You have a sneaky look about you."

"I do not," Deirdre said, crossing her arms, hunching her shoulders, and taking a step back. Belatedly, she realized that probably made her look even sneakier.

"Be careful, Deirdre," Sasha said, wagging a finger at her.

"Be careful of what?"

"I don't know. I think..." Sasha cast a glance at the open door. "All I know is they keep watch, all right?"

A shiver ran up Deirdre's spine. "Who's keeping watch? Do you mean Anders? Is that why they assigned him as my new partner—to keep watch in case Farr contacts me?"

Sasha shook her head. "I don't know, and I don't intend to know. And if you're a smart girl like I think you are, Deirdre, you won't start turning up stones that are better left untouched. I've learned it's best to keep your curiosity outside of the Seekers, no matter the access number on your ID card."

Deirdre didn't know how to respond to that. Sasha was attaché to some pretty high-up people in the Seekers. What did she know that Deirdre didn't? Before she could ask, Sasha headed to the door, then glanced back over her shoulder.

"I love you, Deirdre, and I don't want you to come to harm. So be a good girl. I mean it."

Then Sasha was gone.

An hour later, Deirdre stumbled through the door of her flat, cold and drenched once again. Maybe Madeleine was right about the whole umbrella thing. She shucked off her wet clothes and spent the next twenty minutes under a hot shower. As she toweled off, she thought again about what Sasha had said, only it didn't make any more sense than it did the first time around. Besides, Deirdre had other matters on her mind.

Forget not the Sleeping Ones. In their blood lies the key.

Only the key to what? The inscription was important, Deirdre was sure of it. But how? Blood had been found on the old keystone—blood with a DNA signature similar to Glinda's and the other denizens of Surrender Dorothy. Fairy blood.

Connections sizzled—that was it. Travis and Grace had used the blood of the fairy they rescued from Duratek to activate the gate artifact and step through to the world AU-3. Could it be possible the keystone was similar in nature to the gate? Was it part of a doorway—not a door to another room, but one to another world? Maybe. But what did that have to do with anything she was working on now?

The bee in the back of her brain finally buzzed close enough for her to catch it. She had been so focused on understanding why Atwater hadn't been punished that she had forgotten to consider the infraction itself. The place he had been forbidden to return to was an establishment called Greenfellow's. She had assumed it was simply a shop of some sort, named after its proprietor. But what if it was something else?

She threw on a robe and slippers and hurried out to the

dining room. Her computer lay on the table, powered on and waiting. She sat down and typed several commands. Minutes later, she sat back, staring at the screen. Once again she had found a link where she had thought none existed.

A search on the word Greenfellow's had brought up a list of several results. The only one that mattered was a reference to a seventeenth-century London drinking house. She had superimposed the location of the tavern on a modern map, and the result glowed on the screen in front of her.

Brixton. The establishment Atwater had been forbidden by the Philosophers to return to was a tavern located in what was now Brixton. It was the same spot where the keystone had been found. And the same spot where Surrender Dorothy would stand nearly four centuries later, where Glinda and Arion and the others with fairy blood in their veins would die at the hands of Duratek.

But what did it mean? The connection couldn't be random. The Philosophers must have known about the tavern—and the strange nature of the people who inhabited it—for centuries. So why had they kept it a secret all this time? And what did the tavern and the keystone have to do with Linear A and the civilization of ancient Crete?

The phone rang. Deirdre stared as it rang a second time, a third. Then she snatched up the handset.

"Hello?"

A hissing, then a voice spoke. "They're back."

Fear jolted through her, and excitement. She had never heard his voice before, but all the same she knew it was him.

"Who are you?" she said, cupping the phone to her ear. "Why did you give me the photo of the tablet?"

"There's no time for that, Agent Falling Hawk. In a few moments the Seekers will realize I've blocked their wiretapping device and they'll grow suspicious." The man's voice was hollow, tinny; it was being digitally altered. "The ones I spoke of are nearly here, and it's imperative that no one else learns of their arrival. Do you understand?"

She clutched the phone. "Who are you talking about? Who's nearly here?"

There was a *click*, and static filled her ear. At the same moment, a knock sounded at the door. Deirdre was so startled she dropped the phone. She scrambled to pick it up and place it back on the base. Another knock. Clutching her robe around her, she hurried to the door and opened it.

A man and a woman stood on the other side. The man was tall and rangy, with green eyes and longish, thinning blond hair. He wore jeans and a dark turtleneck sweater, but it was easier to picture him in chain mail, a sword at his side. The woman was exotically beautiful, her dark hair slicked back, her gold eyes vivid. Her overcoat could not entirely conceal the sleek black leathers she wore beneath.

Before Deirdre could speak, Vani pushed past her into the flat and glanced at Beltan.

"Shut the door. Quickly."

The blond man stepped inside and closed the door. He eyed Deirdre hopefully. "You don't have anything to eat, do you?"

"Food is not important now," Vani said.

The blond man snorted. "Food is always important."

"Not if you're dead. We must be certain we were not followed." Vani moved to the window, peered out, and jerked the curtains shut.

Deirdre finally managed to speak, her voice hoarse with wonder. "How did you get here?"

Beltan's green eyes shone. "It was the most remarkable thing, Deirdre. We raced through a tunnel beneath this city faster than a horse can run."

Deirdre shook her head. That wasn't what she meant. She looked at the knight, then at the golden-eyed woman, both from another world. "What the hell is going on?"

Vani turned from the window, hands on her hips. "We need your help, Seeker."

Deirdre took a step back and found herself sitting down hard in a chair. "My help? To do what?"

Beltan knelt before her and placed his big, scarred hands over her own. "To find Travis Wilder," he said.

38.

The shadows slipped away from Travis like dirty rags as he stepped into the orange glow of a streetlight. He tried to speak the rune *Alth* again, to conceal himself in shadows once more, but the word was a dry whisper, powerless. Magic on Earth was a thin ghost of what it was on Eldh: a primal river drained and choked and polluted until it was no more than a murky trickle. Touching the Great Stones would have helped, but he didn't dare open the box again.

He leaned against the streetlight, unable to stop trembling. How many blocks had he run since fleeing the television station? It didn't matter. No distance was great enough. The wraithlings would never stop looking for him. He had to find a place he could hide.

He slipped his hand in his pocket, checking the iron box to make certain it was still tightly shut. As he did, his fingers brushed a scrap of paper. He pulled it out. It was the piece of paper Anna Ferraro had handed him just before driving off; a phone number was scribbled on it. Carefully, he put it back into his pocket.

His breathing was less ragged now, and he looked around to get his bearings, only he didn't recognize the street he was on. It was somewhere on the edge of downtown—tall office buildings loomed against the night sky—but east or west? He had lost all sense of direction as he careened through the city. The street was empty, the brick storefronts dark. He walked half a block to the next intersection, but the street signs were so corroded he couldn't read them.

His shaking had become shivering. The cold bit at his hands and feet. Whether or not the wraithlings were following him, he had to get off the street and find a place to stay. He was too weak to speak the rune of fire to warm himself, and without it he would never make it through a night outside. But where could he go?

A neon sign sizzled to life in the darkness. It shone across the street, above an arched doorway. The sign was beautiful: a winged dove rendered against the night in iridescent blue and hot pink. Beneath the dove, orange words pulsed on and off in a spastic rhythm. THE HOPE MISSION.

Travis wondered if he was hallucinating. He had never heard of a downtown mission by that name, and surely Jay and Marty would have told him about it. Jay knew every place in Denver that gave handouts to the homeless.

Dread punched him in the gut. Jay and Marty. He had completely forgotten about them.

You can catch up with them tomorrow, Travis. You know Jay—he'll have figured out someplace for them to stay for the night.

Travis looked both ways, but there were no cars coming in either direction. He stumbled across the street and pushed through the peeling door of the mission. The room beyond was cramped, shabby, and deliciously warm. After the brutal cold, the heat was so intense it knocked Travis silly for a moment, and he could neither think nor move.

"Close the door already," said a gruff voice. "How do you think we heat this place? With magic?"

Shocked into motion, Travis shut the door, then turned around. The room was set up as a sort of reception area. There were several plastic chairs crammed alongside a battered green sofa, and dog-eared magazines strewed the top of a kidney-shaped coffee table. An antique color TV was mounted on the wall, and a potted ivy dominated one corner, tangling its way up a column, growing luxuriously in the near-tropical heat.

"So what are you looking for tonight?"

Travis's eyes focused on the man standing behind the counter. He was short and stocky—late twenties, maybe—clad in a Colorado Avalanche sweatshirt, a wool cap on his head. His eyebrows were thick and dark, and his chin was covered by the bleach blond tuft of a goatee. He looked at Travis with saturnine eyes.

Travis cleared his throat. "I need a place to sleep." He braced himself, expecting to be told there was no more room. After all, it was late. He couldn't expect to find a bed at the shelter.

"I think we might have a bed left," the man said. "I'll have to go check. Can you wait a minute?"

Travis was too astonished to do anything but nod. He hoped

the other took his time. If nothing else, he could get warm while he was waiting.

"You can watch the TV while you wait." The man pressed a button on a remote control, upping the volume, then headed down a hallway. Travis watched him as he went. He walked with an odd, swaying cadence; his legs were bowed inside his jeans, perhaps the result of a childhood disease or a congenital condition.

The other vanished from sight, and Travis sat on the couch. A musty smell rose from it, and he had to shift his rear a few times to find a place where no springs poked up through the cushion, but all the same the act of sitting felt positively decadent. Fear still registered in his chest, but the emotion felt dull and distant through the veil of his weariness. He was safe, if only for the moment.

"And should they come for you, do not fear," said a voice that was thrilling and majestic despite its tinniness. "For know that you have been chosen to be part of God's own army."

Travis craned his neck. On the TV, a man in a white suit strutted back and forth across a stage. His dark hair gleamed, and he moved hands covered with rings in bold gestures as he spoke.

"There's no need to be ashamed if your heart trembles when they appear to you," Sage Carson said. Above him soared the crystalline walls of the Steel Cathedral. "You see, my heart did when they came to me. The Angels of Light are terrible to behold, but they're beautiful as well, so cast aside your fear. Open your arms to the Angels of Light, and know that you are blessed."

Travis sucked in a breath and sat straight up, all thoughts of rest, of comfort, gone. On the television, the scene cut to a shot of the audience. People wept, holding their arms out as if they could see the Angels of Light before them. Outside the glass walls of the Steel Cathedral, the sky was blue.

The scene shifted back to the stage. On it, Sage Carson raised his hands, his splendid words rising toward a crescendo.

"A time of darkness is coming. We see the signs all around us—war, strife, and suffering. Men have forgotten the will of God, and the world is sick and dying. Once before, when evil ruined the world, God knew the only way to save it was to wash it clean and start anew." Carson's voice dropped low. "Such a time draws near again."

An audible gasp rose from the audience, along with wails of fear. Carson swept a hand before him. "No, don't despair, for sometimes the only way to save something is to destroy it first. Our world has been corrupted beyond redemption by the unholy, the unrighteous, the unbelievers. And so God has decided once again to save it the only way He can: by destroying the world and making it anew in His image."

Sickness filled Travis. He wanted to get up, to switch off the TV, but he could only watch.

"So rejoice!" Carson's voice blared out of the television's speaker. "If the Angels of Light come for you, then you have been chosen to prepare the way for His coming. And while the sinners, the evildoers, and the heathens will perish, you will dwell with Him in the new world to come, serving Him as one of his chosen. Hallelujah and Amen!"

The audience erupted into cheers, their fear gone, their eyes alight with fervent joy. Carson smiled, holding his hands out as if in a blessing. However, as the camera panned out over the Steel Cathedral, it couldn't quite hide the men in black suits who stood before the stage, pushing back any who tried to ascend toward the preacher.

Carson waved and walked off the stage, and the camera followed after him. As he reached the curtain at the edge of the stage, it was pulled back by an unseen hand. Carson turned to wave one last time, and in that moment the television showed a glimpse of what lay behind the curtain. Travis could see ropes for operating the curtains, and scaffolding for lights. He also saw a pair of uniformed security guards standing just offstage. One was a large man, but the other was a petite woman with short brown hair. She was young, her prettiness marred by a stern expression.

Travis leaped to his feet. On TV, Carson stepped through the opening, and the curtain fell back into place. The camera panned again to the chanting audience as credits rolled across the screen. Travis couldn't have read them if he wanted to. Instead he stared blindly, his hands twitching at his sides.

Jace. The woman standing backstage was Deputy Jacine

Windom. Only she was no longer a sheriff's deputy in Castle City, and her presence at the Steel Cathedral could only mean one thing.

Travis knew where Duratek had hidden the gate.

"You're in luck," the goateed man said as he stepped back behind the counter. "It looks like we do have one bed left. It's all yours, so come on back."

Travis nodded, too numb to disagree. He shuffled down the hallway after the bowlegged man. Along the way they passed a willowy young woman with a pierced nose and long hair dyed a verdant green. She carried a stack of folders.

The young woman smiled—a beautiful expression. "Welcome to the Hope Mission," she said, then headed through a side door. Travis tried to glimpse what was in the room, but the man gestured for him to keep following.

They came to a larger room filled with a haphazard array of folding tables and chairs. The floor was scuffed tile, the walls a yellow too grungy to be cheerful. Fluorescent lights sputtered overhead. Another TV stood in a corner, but thankfully this one was tuned to the inane babble of a late-night talk show.

"This is the commissary," the young man said. "The men's dormitory is through there. Yours will be the one bed that isn't claimed. There's a bathroom in there if you want to get cleaned up before you go to sleep."

Travis shook his head. How could he sleep, knowing what he did now?

The young man grinned, his teeth slightly pointed. "Don't worry, you don't have to go to sleep hungry. Dinner's over, but there's always soup to be had here in the commissary. You can get a bowl there at the counter—it's self-serve this late. I've got to get back to the front desk, but if you need anything, the preacher should be by soon."

"Preacher?" Travis said, trying not to sound alarmed by the word, though he was.

The young man nodded. "He runs the place, though I suppose he has a little help in the matter. He almost always comes out this time of night to talk to whoever's here. So I hope you don't mind a little sermonizing with your soup."

The young man walked with his odd gait back down the hallway to the front. Instinct told Travis to bolt. After what he had just seen on TV, talking to a preacher was the last thing he wanted. However this place was anything but the Steel Cathedral, and the scent of chicken soup was thick on the air, making his stomach growl.

Travis looked around. There were a dozen people in the commissary. A few spoke in low voices, some watched the TV, and others just stared. Most were men, though there were a couple of women. One—a sharp-faced woman in her thirties—seemed out of place in her smart jacket and slacks. She sat alone in a corner, staring at her clasped hands.

Maybe this shelter isn't only for the homeless, Travis, but for anyone who needs to escape a bad situation.

He moved to the counter and ladled a bowl of soup from a warming pot. A few of the men waved at him, looking for company, but Travis sat at one of the empty tables. He stirred his soup with his spoon, watching as noodles bubbled up to the surface and sank back into yellowish liquid. Jace Windom's presence in the Steel Cathedral could only mean one thing: Sage Carson was no mere televangelist.

Travis shut his eyes. He knew Jace blamed him for the death of Max Bayfield—his business partner and her fiancé. Travis couldn't blame her; in a way it was his fault. The runelord Mindroth had come to Castle City last summer looking for Jack Graystone. Instead he had found Travis, recognizing him as the heir to Jack's power as a runelord. Only Max had gotten in the way. Mindroth had touched him, and he had been burned.

That was when Duratek showed up. They gave Max the drug Electria, using it to ease his pain—and to control him, trying to use him to get to Travis. Only in the end, Max had sacrificed himself to help Travis escape.

Max's death had eaten at Jace, and she had cast her lot with Duratek. Last fall, after she learned from Davis and Mitchell Burke-Favor that Travis had called, she had tipped Duratek off that Travis and Grace had returned to Denver. That act had nearly cost Travis and Grace their lives, and it had almost caused them to lose Beltan. In Travis's mind, whatever pain he had caused Jace was more than repaid. She was Duratek; she was the enemy now. And so was Sage Carson.

"Well, hello there, son," said a slick, rasping voice.

Travis was beyond shock. He only sighed as he looked up into Brother Cy's black eyes. "So you're the preacher that runs this mission."

Brother Cy bared his dingy ivory teeth in a grin. "I have a little help in the matter."

"That's what he said." Travis looked over his shoulder, but the young man with the goatee was nowhere in sight. He remembered the man's crooked legs and wool cap, and the woman's leaf green hair. Yes, Brother Cy had help indeed.

"They're Little People, aren't they?" he said, looking back at the preacher. "He's one of those goat-men, and she's a tree lady."

Cy only smiled. He was clad in the same dusty black coffin suit he always wore, and his visage was more gaunt than ever. All the same, there was something solid and comforting about him.

Travis drew in a breath. "I don't know what to do."

"Then eat your soup," Brother Cy said.

Travis stared at the bowl, then brought a spoonful of the liquid to his lips. It was hot and salty. He ate another spoonful, and another. Warmth spread through him, as well as renewed strength.

"I know what's happening," Travis said when the bowl was empty, setting down the spoon. "I know where people are disappearing to. It's the Steel Cathedral. That's where Professor Sparkman was going before he disappeared, along with that other woman who vanished, Myra. I bet if we could check, that's where every one of them was going."

Brother Cy only nodded. Travis gripped the edge of the table. What had he done? He had sent Jay and Marty to the Steel Cathedral; they were in terrible danger. Only he couldn't think about that, not until he had told Cy everything.

"Jace Windom was there, I saw her on TV, and I know she's working for Duratek. That means Sage Carson has to be working for them, too." He shook his head. "Or working *with* them—I'm not sure which. And that's not all. We learned on Eldh that Duratek is in league with Mohg and the Pale King. So the Angels of Light are really wraithlings. They're the ones who have been abducting people." He sat back in his chair. "Only why?"

"Did not this preacher on the television tell you why?" said a sibilant voice.

Travis turned to see Child Samanda approaching. The girl was clad in the same old-fashioned dress she always wore, and the pale oval of her face was like a cameo set off by the dark frame of her hair. Sister Mirrim followed behind the girl, her dress just as severe, but her hair wild and fiery. She stared with milky eyes, her hands on Samanda's shoulders, letting the girl guide her.

"Yes, he did," Travis said in answer to Samanda's question. "He said he's raising an army for God."

"But which God?"

Travis shuddered. "Mohg," he said, the word bitter on his tongue. "That's who Carson is raising an army for. 'To prepare the way for His coming.' The wraithlings are kidnapping people, turning them into ironhearts to make an army. And once the gate opens, they'll go through to clear the way for Mohg so he can break the First Rune and destroy Eldh."

Samanda nodded, her purple eyes solemn. "Sometimes the only way to save something is to destroy it."

At least Travis felt an emotion: anger. "No, I won't believe that. Destruction can't be the answer. And Mohg wants anything but to save Eldh. If he breaks the First Rune, he'll remake the world in his own image."

"No," Cy said, "he'll remake both worlds. For they are two sides of the same coin—close and getting closer all the time. What affects one affects the other now."

Travis hung his head. This was too much; the weight was crushing him. He couldn't save one world, let alone two. "I can't do this."

"But you will," Sister Mirrim said. "I have seen it, shining like a gem among all the darker possibilities."

He looked up at her. "Can you really see the future?"

Mirrim's porcelain face was stricken. "Which future do mean? There are many, and which one of them will come to pass—dark or light or something in between—depends on many choices. Especially yours, Stonebreaker."

No, he didn't want that power, he never had. Only that was the one choice that wasn't up to him. He hadn't asked for any of this, but that didn't matter. All that mattered was what he did with the choices he had been given.

He gazed at these three otherworldly preachers—these fey, immortal beings who for some reason had taken it upon themselves to help him.

"You say the worlds are drawing closer." He was no longer afraid; with resignation came strange peace. "There's no stopping it, is there? Even if Duratek never finds a way to open a gate, eventually Mohg will be able to cross back to Eldh."

Brother Cy nodded. "That's right, son. And it may be that it's better to face the darkness now, before it gathers yet more strength, than later, when perihelion comes and the gap between the worlds shrinks to nothing. For by then Mohg's army will be great indeed, and he will march to Eldh and make the Pale King bow before him, and all the world will fall under the shadow of the Lord of Nightfall, whether or not he breaks the First Rune."

"But break it he will," Samanda said, "for when that time comes, there will be nowhere on either world where you can hide the Great Stones from him."

"So what am I supposed to do?" Travis said. "If there's no place to hide from him, where can I possibly go?"

Brother Cy laughed, a sound that rattled the walls and caused everyone in the room to stare. Then, as they turned their gazes back to their bowls of soup, Cy pointed at the TV in the corner. The talk show was over; another program was just coming on. The camera zoomed in on a gigantic building that loomed above a river, its glass-and-steel spires soaring like cruel mountains to the sky.

Travis let out a breath of understanding.

"That's right, son," Cy said. "There is still somewhere you can go. Into the heart of shadow itself."

39

Aryn paced before the window of Lirith's chamber as the sky faded to gray outside. The sun had set, and by the time it rose over the world again the Warriors of Vathris would be marching north to Gravenfist Keep.

Or would they? Surely Liendra was not simply going to stand by and wave at Boreas and his army as they set out. But what did she and her witches intend to do?

"Please sit down, sister," Lirith said. "You're wearing out the carpet. As well as my nerves."

"Sorry," Aryn said and flopped into a chair. "I just can't stop wondering what Liendra is up to."

"You're hardly alone in that."

Lirith was tending to Sareth's face while he sat on the edge of the bed. There was a mottled bruise along his jaw as well as a nasty scrape on his cheek where Duke Petryen had struck him.

Sareth winced as Lirith pressed a damp cloth soaked in herbs against his cheek. "I thought you were on my side, not theirs, *beshala*. That stings."

"Then it's working. Hold it in place."

The Mournish man sighed. "You're as bad as my al-Mama. As a boy, every time I was sick, she'd feed me potions that tasted like dung. I've never understood why the cure has to be worse than the affliction."

"Of course you don't," Lirith said with an unsympathetic smile. She turned to mix together more herbs at the sideboard. "Now, be quiet, and I'll brew you something for the—"

Lirith went stiff. A crucible slipped from her fingers, falling to the sideboard with a clatter. She turned around, her eyes wide and dark.

Aryn pushed herself up from the chair. "What is it, sister?"

"Ivalaine," Lirith gasped. "Merciful Sia, it's Queen Ivalaine."

By the time they reached the dungeon, it was already too late.

At first the guard balked at Aryn's request to see Ivalaine, but such was the force of her ire that he quickly reconsidered. He led them down a dank corridor past cells filled with thieves and miscreants culled from the town below the castle, as well as from the gathering army of Vathris. Hands reached out from between the bars, groping at the ladies, but Sareth beat them back; the stench of vomit and urine was thick on the air. A great dread came over Aryn, so that she was shaking by the time the guard unlocked the ironbound door at the end of the corridor.

By the state of things, Ivalaine was not long dead. Her flesh, though pale and stiff as clay, was warmer to the touch than the cell's clammy air. She slumped against the wall, her flaxen hair snarled and matted, her pale eyes wide and staring. A pool of blood had formed on the stones around her, flowing from the long gashes in both of her wrists.

Lirith let out a wordless moan. She would have collapsed, but Sareth held her up, and she pressed her face against his chest. The guard stared at the queen's corpse, slack-jawed.

A peculiar feeling came over Aryn. She felt she should fall to her knees and weep. Instead she remained standing. Everything in the room seemed gray, faded. Ivalaine had been so strong, so vibrant. Surely the very fabric of the Weirding had been torn by her death.

No, it was more than that. Aryn shut her eyes. She could see the threads of the Weirding coiling and stretching, filling back in a dark void in the web of life.

Aryn's eyes snapped open. "Someone else was here!"

Her words jerked the guard out of his stupor. "Impossible, Your Highness. I've stood at the door since the queen was brought here earlier this afternoon. I've seen no one pass."

Aryn had no doubt the man was telling the truth. "Go fetch the king," she said to him. "Now."

The man nodded and hastened out of the cell.

"She did it to herself," Sareth said, his coppery eyes shining with sadness and horror. "She couldn't take Teravian's life, so she took her own."

"Did she?" A strange clarity came over Aryn; she saw everything as if lit by a thousand candles. "And how did she do this to herself?"

The cell was empty, save for a wooden bowl of water.

Sareth shook his head. "Perhaps she used her own fingernails to open her wrists."

Aryn knelt beside the queen, not caring as blood soaked into the hem of her gown. She touched Ivalaine's hand; the fingernails were chewed down to the quick.

"Someone else did this to her." Anger blazed within her, burning away sickness and sorrow. "Someone who feared the queen might yet reveal something in her madness—something others wished to keep secret."

Lirith pushed herself away from Sareth. "But whom do you mean, sister? Surely Liendra would not have done a deed such as this, not even to Ivalaine."

"No, it wasn't Liendra. The guard would not have willingly allowed her to pass, and I don't think her magic is strong enough to have addled his mind." Aryn thought of all she had seen and heard. Again she probed the disturbance in the Weirding, and she recalled Ivalaine's words spoken earlier that day.

She would . . . in the shadows . . . not alive, and not dead . . . she thinks she can stop me. . . .

Who could be alive and dead at the same time?

A shiver passed through Aryn, and at last she realized the answer. "Shemal," she said, standing. "It all makes sense. After Melia left, the Necromancer Shemal must have come back. Those things Ivalaine said to us today—they sounded just like what Master Tharkis said to me in Ar-tolor. Shemal drove him mad, and then she did the same to Ivalaine."

Only the addled fool—who once had been King of Toloria—had been murdered so he could not reveal Shemal's presence. Just like Ivalaine. How long had Shemal been there, waiting in the shadows? From the start she must have seen Toloria as central to her plans. But why?

She felt she almost grasped the answer—then the sense of clarity fled her. A sob rose in her chest. Ivalaine had been a queen, a witch, and—in secret all these years—a mother. More than that, she had been the one who had first introduced Aryn to the mysteries of the Weirding. Only now she was nothing. A cruel despair gripped Aryn; if one so great as Ivalaine could fall, what hope did any of them have?

Lirith bent down and, with a touch, shut Ivalaine's eyes. She kissed the dead queen's brow. "Farewell, fair sister." Then she rose and turned away.

The sound of boots and voices approached down the corridor.

"We must go," Sareth said gently. "The king will wish to speak to us."

He was right. They did speak with Boreas, but only briefly, in his chamber an hour later. He asked them to describe the state in which they had found the queen, and he listened without moving, sitting in his chair, his eyes fixed on the fire. When Aryn began to speak of who she thought had done this terrible deed, the king waved a hand, silencing her, and gave them leave to go.

Aryn hesitated at the door; Lirith and Sareth had already stepped through. "Your Majesty," she said, her voice hoarse from weeping, "will you delay your journey north so that she can be properly mourned?"

Still he did not look away from the fire. "There are many who will depart this life before we see an end. Better we should wait and mourn them all. I leave on the morrow."

Aryn slipped through the door, joining Lirith and Sareth in the corridor beyond.

"I don't understand," Sareth said as they walked. "Why didn't he want to know who murdered the queen?"

Lirith shook her head. "Maybe it doesn't matter to him. If he did know, would it change his plans? I doubt it."

"Maybe," Aryn said, though for some reason she doubted Lirith's theory. She knew the king better than perhaps any other. Though he was given more to action and bluster than thoughtfulness and repose, Boreas was anything but stupid. She couldn't imagine he would not want to gather all information available to him.

Which means he already knows who killed Ivalaine. But how can that be?

She didn't know. But there was one thing she did know. "We have to go talk to Prince Teravian. I know she tried to kill him, but in her mind Ivalaine was protecting him, and now she's dead. Shemal is somewhere around the castle—she might even be inside it. We have to warn him he's in grave danger."

However, when they reached Teravian's chamber, they found the door guarded by Sai'el Ajhir, who refused them admittance. After the second attempt on the prince's life, no one was being allowed in to see him.

"You don't understand, my lord," Aryn said, her frustration so great she shook with it. "We must see the prince. We have to tell him that——" She bit her tongue. What would Ajhir say if she told him a Necromancer, a being of legend, was lurking about the castle? "——I have to talk to him before he leaves."

"You may speak to him on the morrow, my lady," Ajhir said, "before he sets out on the journey north."

That wasn't good enough. Tomorrow could be too late. If Shemal could enter a locked dungeon cell unseen, what was to stop her from stealing into Teravian's chamber?

"Please, my lord," Lirith said in a calm voice, gliding forward. "Sareth and I will wait outside, but surely you will not deny entrance to Lady Aryn. She cannot possibly represent a threat to the prince. She is to be his wife."

Ajhir's dark face was proud and imperturbable. "Is to be, but is not yet. And before this day, would you have said Queen Ivalaine, at whose own court he was fostered, would have posed a threat to him? Forgive me——I know you care for the prince—— but I cannot let any of you pass. I have my orders."

"Whose orders?" Sareth said. "The king's?"

Ajhir crossed muscular arms over his chest. "I have made myself clear. No one shall enter the prince's chamber this night." A smile flickered across his stern face. "None except for one, as Vathris knows."

They implored the southerner for several more minutes, but it was no use.

"Well, that was strange," Lirith said, pouring wine for all of them in her chamber.

Aryn accepted a cup in trembling hands. This day was awful beyond all fathoming. All the same, something told her it was not over yet.

"Very strange," Sareth said. He touched his wounded cheek, winced, and took a sip of his wine. "It's admirable that Ajhir wishes to protect the prince, but under whose authority is he doing so? He made no mention of the king."

Aryn sipped her wine. "And there was something else he said that was peculiar——how no one would be admitted to the prince's room, save for one. What was that supposed to mean?"

Lirith slumped into a chair. "I have no ideas. Save that it

seems to have something to do with the Warriors. 'As Vathris knows,' he said."

"Maybe I should do a bit of asking around," Sareth said, setting down his cup. "I've made a few friends with some of the men of Vathris in the castle. A couple even owe me favors."

Lirith gave him a sharp look. "Really?"

The Mournish man gave her a sly grin. "Let's just say I've been lucky at dice."

"And luckier still I haven't caught you gambling," Lirith said, her eyes narrowing. "Losing only costs you gold; winning might cost you a knife in your back."

"I'll be careful," Sareth said, then headed out the door.

The two women sat in silence, bathed only in the light of the fire. There was no need to speak; both had been shattered by the death of Queen Ivalaine.

After a while it occurred to Aryn that supper was likely being served in the great hall. She knew she should go; it would be her last chance to dine with the king, for tomorrow he would set out on the journey north. Only she had no appetite, and she couldn't shake the feeling that something was going to happen before the Warriors could leave, something terrible. She stared into the fire, hoping for a shard of the Sight as Lirith had. However, though she stared until her eyes were dry and aching, she saw nothing save the flames.

Aryn looked up as the door opened and closed. Sareth drew close to the fire, an odd expression on his face.

"What is it?" Lirith said, sitting up straight. "Did you learn something?"

He hesitated, then nodded. "I think I know who's going to be let in to see the prince tonight. Not the specific individual, mind you, but at least what sort of person."

Aryn frowned. "What do you mean, Sareth? Speak plainly."

The Mournish man shifted from foot to foot. "Lirith, perhaps I should tell you first, then—"

"I am certain whatever you learned is fit for Aryn's ears as well as mine," Lirith said with a stern look.

Sareth swallowed hard, then nodded. "I found one of my warrior acquaintances standing guard in the entry hall. He's a man from Al-Amún, like Sai'el Ajhir, and he owes me quite a few gold pieces. I told him I'd forgive his debt if he told me who was going to be allowed to come to the prince's chamber that night. He didn't know, not exactly, but he knew enough."

"Well, who is it?" Aryn said.

Sareth paused, searching for the right words to say. "From what I gathered, it's a tradition among the followers of Vathris. On the night before a man is to ride into his first battle, it is customary for him to become a man in all ways, if he is not already one."

Lirith leaped to her feet. "They mean to make a man of him!" She gripped Sareth's arm. "They will send a woman to his chamber to relieve him of his maidenhead."

Aryn's cheeks grew hot—and not from the fire. "But Teravian is not a follower of Vathris!"

"Isn't he?" Sareth said. "His father is."

Aryn didn't know how to respond. It wasn't as if she were jealous. However, fate had decreed she and Teravian were to be married. Surely if she was supposed to keep her purity until their wedding day, he could be expected to do the same.

Lirith clenched her hands into fists. "This is dark news. Dark news indeed."

"I imagine it is upsetting for Lady Aryn," Sareth said, giving the baroness a sympathetic look. "But I must say, *beshala*, it is hardly uncommon for a man to have been with a woman before he is married."

"That's not it," Lirith said. "They mean to make a man of him. A full man."

She looked at Aryn, and at last Aryn understood the source of her agitation. Long had the Witches labored to bring about a man of Sia, and with Teravian they had succeeded. He was a male witch, as strong in the Touch as any woman. However, according to Sister Mirda, he would not come into his full power until he was made a man. Quickly, they explained these things to Sareth.

"Liendra," he said in disgust. "Is it she, then?"

Lirith curled her lip. "I doubt Sister Liendra will do the deed, but I have no doubt she is behind this plot, and I must say it is a clever one. She is using the traditions of the Warriors against them."

Aryn's stomach churned; she wished she had not drunk so much wine. "Do you think he will use his power for the Witches?"

"I don't know," Lirith said, holding a hand to her brow. "Perhaps unwittingly."

Aryn stood up; her nerves felt pulled as taut as the strings of a lute. "We have to go to him. We have to warn him about what they're planning."

"I think you've forgotten our friend Sai'el Ajhir," Sareth said with a sour look. "We'll never get a message to the prince."

"What about speaking across the Weirding?" Aryn asked.

Lirith made a sharp motion with her hand. "No. There are too many of Liendra's witches about. Such a conversation would surely be overheard. Besides, there is another way." She glanced at Sareth. "Would you leave us for a moment?"

He frowned at her. "Why?"

"Please, *beshala*." She touched his arm. His eyes locked on hers for a moment, and Aryn thought he was going to protest, only then he sighed and left the chamber.

"What's this all about?" Aryn said after Sareth had left.

Lirith did not turn around. "I will find the maid who is to be sent to Teravian this night, and I will take her place."

"To talk to him, you mean?"

"No, to do what the one sent to him must do. To make him into a man."

Aryn trembled, and a ringing sounded in her ears. Surely she had misheard. "What are you talking about?"

Lirith turned around. Her eyes were dark, haunted. "There is no other choice, sister. One way or another, he will lose his maidenhead this night—Liendra will see to that. I know he fancies me. A boyish crush, to be sure, but better it is me than one of her minions who does the deed. Perhaps, this way, we will keep him from becoming entangled in their snare."

Aryn gripped the back of a chair. "Then it should be me who should do this thing."

"No," Lirith said, her voice hard. "You are pure, sister. You must not give that up, not yet. And with me . . . well, with me it doesn't matter anymore."

This was madness. Aryn couldn't bear the thought of it. "You can't do this, Lirith. You can't."

"Yes, I can." Her expression was stern and cold, then her gaze softened. "Forgive me, sister. I should have told you long ago. Only I was too ashamed."

"You should have told me what long ago?"

"Of the years I spent dancing in the house of Gulthas, in the Free City of Corantha."

Before Aryn could ask what she was talking about, Lirith moved to her and laid a hand on her shoulder. The other woman's shimmering life thread contacted her own. In a single, terrible flash, Aryn saw it all: how Lirith's parents were slain by thieves, how the lost girl was sold into slavery, and how as she grew she danced for the men, scarves fluttering.

Aryn tried to look away, only she couldn't. How many men had paid their gold to Gulthas to lay themselves beside her? How many bright sparks had kindled to life in Lirith's womb only to be extinguished, until no more sparks would kindle there ever again? They were more numerous than the fluttering scarves she wore; Aryn couldn't possibly count.

The last images flickered through Aryn's mind: Lirith's flight on bare, bloody feet to Toloria, her first tentative steps along the path of Sia, her marriage to the count of Arafel, and her rise in the favor of Queen Ivalaine. Lirith's thread pulled away, and Aryn slumped into the chair, weak and sweating.

"I should have told you," Lirith said again, her voice thick with anguish. "Can you ever forgive me?"

Aryn looked up, her eyes full of tears. "Forgive you for what, sister? For being beautiful and noble? For being strong enough to survive in a hell that surely would have destroyed any other of us? Why should I forgive you for these things?"

Tears streamed down Lirith's dark cheeks. She knelt on the floor and laid her head on Aryn's lap, and Aryn stroked her glossy black hair.

"I love you, sister," Aryn murmured. "Now more than ever." Lirith's only answer was a sob.

They stayed that way for a time, then Lirith stood again, and her eyes were dry. "Do not tell Sareth what I do," she said.

Before Aryn could speak, the door opened and shut, and Lirith was gone.

For a time, Aryn simply sat in the chair, staring. Then a strange compulsion came over her, and she stood. She moved around Lirith's chamber, searching, and soon found what she needed: an ivory comb lay on the dressing table. Aryn picked it up, and from the comb's teeth she pulled seven strands of black hair. Quickly, she wove the strands into a slender braid, then knotted the braid into a small circlet.

"What are you doing, Aryn?" she murmured to herself as she sat back in the chair. "What are you doing?"

Before she could answer, she slipped the circlet of Lirith's hair onto her right ring finger and shut her eyes.

The spell worked at once. It was not like the other magic, the one where she had flown through the night, into the garden, and spied upon Teravian and Queen Ivalaine. This magic was subtler. It was more as if Aryn were gazing through a window—one dusted with frost, so that the images beyond were at once crystalline and slightly blurred.

She watched as Lirith stood in a dim corridor, in the shadow of a doorway. For a long time nothing happened, and Aryn's head began to ache. This was wrong, Sia knew it; she should break the spell. Then, just as she was about to pull the circlet from her finger, a figure moved down the corridor.

It was a woman, though Aryn could not see the other's face. She was wrapped in a crimson cloak, the cowl pulled over her head. As the figure drew closer, Lirith stepped from the alcove to stand in front of her.

The hood slipped back, revealing a pretty, slightly plump young woman. Her jaw dropped open, and she stared with surprised brown eyes. Aryn was surprised as well, for she recognized the maiden. It was Belira, one of the young witches who had mocked Aryn at last year's High Coven.

Belira cried out and started to turn away, but Lirith was swifter. She reached out and touched Belira. At once the young woman's eyes fluttered up into her head, and she slumped to the floor. Had Lirith used a spell? Or a needle dipped in some potion? Lirith pulled Belira's limp form into the nearby room.

Then she wrapped herself in the red cloak, shut the door, and hurried down the corridor.

The witch reached the door to Teravian's chamber. It was Duke Petryen who stood guard now. Lirith bowed her head, the cowl concealing her face. A grin split Petryen's beard, but he said nothing. The duke opened the door; Lirith passed through.

For a moment things went dark, and Aryn feared the spell had been broken. Then things grew bright again, and she found herself gazing into the prince's chamber.

It was dim—the only light came from a single candle. Teravian lay on his bed, clad in a white robe bound in front with a sash. His eyes were open, but he stared into space and hardly seemed to see Lirith enter. On the table next to the bed was a wine goblet, tipped on its side. The prince must have drunk most of the contents, for only a few drops had spilled. Lirith touched a fingertip to the spilled wine, then brought it to her tongue. She sucked in a hissing breath.

They've drugged him, Aryn thought. *They don't want any chance of him resisting.*

Lirith drifted close to the bed. She hesitated, then reached toward the prince.

His hand shot up and caught her wrist.

"I know you're there." His speech was slurred, yet there was still an edge to it. "Whatever they put in my wine has blurred my vision, but I have other senses."

Lirith said nothing.

His lip curled in a sneer. "So have you come to finish the job my mother began?"

Deftly, Lirith freed her hand from his grasp. Her fingers moved to the front of his robe and slipped inside.

He gasped and sat up straight in bed.

"Hush," Lirith said, and pressed him back against the pillows.

"No," he whispered. "No, don't do this to me. You don't understand what this will make me."

However, his eyes were dilated like those of a cat in full darkness, and he did not resist as Lirith undid the front of his robe. His chest was smooth, pale, and flat; she ran her hands over it. A soft moan escaped him.

Aryn made a soft sound as well. That Teravian was a man at least in body, there could be no doubt.

You shouldn't be watching this, Aryn. You should break the spell now.

Only she didn't. Lirith let her cloak slip to the floor, followed by her gown. In the candlelight, her body was as smooth and shapely as a figurine of polished ebony. She lay in the bed beside him and drew him close, her arms dark against his milky skin.

"No," he murmured again, but now his eyes were shut, and he was already moving against her. His hands roamed over her body, and he nuzzled her neck, her breasts, with his lips, a look of rapture on his face. Lirith's own expression was unreadable in the dimness, but her touch was gentle, experienced. She reached down, guiding him into her.

The first time was swift—clumsy and over before it had barely begun—but the second was slower, more languorous, as the prince moved with more certainty. All the while Aryn told herself to break the spell, but she could not, and each time the prince cried out, she felt a wave of heat crash through her own body.

At last he was spent, and he dozed for a time, his head cradled against her breasts. Finally, Lirith slipped from the bed. She picked up her gown.

The prince sat up. "Don't go," he said softly. "I would know who you are."

Lirith's back was to him. "No, Your Majesty," she said, her voice low. "You would not."

"Turn around." His eyes were clearer now. "And bring the candle closer. I think I might be able to see you."

Lirith clutched her gown to herself. "Please, Your Majesty. Let me go."

"No." His voice was harder now, commanding. "I am the king's son. You will obey me, woman. If you do not, I will call for the guards, and either way I shall see who you are."

At last there was an expression on Lirith's face: anguish. She drew in a breath, then turned around.

Like the flickering light of the candle, an array of emotions played across his face: shock, wonder, then shame. He lunged for his cast-off robe and threw it over his nakedness.

"By the Seven, what have you done?" He clenched his hands into fists. "What have *I* done?"

Lirith's expression was hard now. "We have done what we must, Your Majesty."

A sound ripped itself from him: half bitter laughter, half moan of despair. "Are you mad? We didn't have to do this. We don't have to do anything—don't you understand?"

Lirith shook her head. "You're wrong, Your Majesty. I had to do this thing, even as you did. Whatever happens tomorrow, you must face it as a man of power."

His eyebrows drew down into a single dark line. "What do you know of that?"

"Not much, I fear, but enough. I beg you, whatever you do, Your Majesty, remember your Dominion, remember your wife to be, and remember your father. Do not betray them, no matter what might be offered you."

The prince's eyes were dark, unreadable.

Lirith reached out a hand. "I bring you a warning as well. There is another in this castle, one whom Liendra is in league with. We believe she is the one who—"

"Go," Teravian said.

Lirith stared at him. His face was pale, and his eyes dark and wide with vision.

"She's coming," he whispered.

Hands shaking, Lirith donned her gown and threw the cloak around her shoulders. She moved to the door, then cast a glance back at him.

"Please, Your Majesty." Her voice shook. "If ever we were friends, and I believe we were, then listen to me now. No matter what happens on the morrow, do not forget who you are."

He gazed not at her, but into the darkness. "I'd go if I were you. She's nearly here."

Lirith gasped, then cast the hood of the cloak over her face, threw open the door, and rushed outside. Aryn jerked the circlet from her finger and opened her eyes. Her palms were slicked with sweat, and her head throbbed.

"Sia help us," she said. "What do we do?"

For a moment her mind was dark and frozen. Then, like a whisper in her mind, it came to her. She hurried from the room and returned to her own chamber. It was dim and silent, lit only by the fireplace. She moved to the wooden chest in which she kept her jewels and other fine things. Kneeling, she lifted the lid, took out a small parcel wrapped in parchment, and undid it. Inside was a scarf. The embroidery on it was only half-finished, and in the center of the white cloth was a dark stain. Blood. Her own blood.

Words came back to her, spoken once by Lady Melia in this very chamber on a rainy day. *Now the cloth contains a bit of your power. It will bring your husband luck in battle....*

Luck, yes. Or what else might it bring?

Aryn took needle and thread, then sat down and, by the light of the fire, began to sew.

40.

Grace stood atop the keep, wrapped in her fur-lined cloak, and gazed out across the vale of Shadowsdeep. She had risen an hour ago, when night still ruled the world, and had slipped from the cot without waking Tira. The sentries had nodded to her as she entered the keep and ascended to the battlements. She wasn't certain why she had come here. Perhaps, if she could look into the distance, she might see the future coming.

However, all she saw were shadows. They reached into the northern sky, higher than the Ironfang Mountains, blotting out the stars. Now, as dawn drew near, she saw the shadows for what they were: great plumes of smoke. The smoke rose up behind the snow-covered peaks of the Fal Threndur, black as ink, writing ominous runes across the sky.

The gate is starting to open, Grace. The rune Travis bound into it at Midwinter over a year ago is weakening. The Pale King will ride soon.

The thought sent a shiver through her, but at least it seemed they would have only one enemy to fight, for King Kel had brought strange news about the Onyx Knights. Grace had spoken with the chieftain until long after midnight. As the bonfire burned low, she listened as he spoke of affairs in the northlands, across which he had traveled these last months.

Much of it Grace knew in part: how the Pale King's pylons had awakened, and how his ravens flew the skies, spying on the lands below. However, there was much that was news to her. Kel described how the pilgrims who marched north in answer to the call of the Raven Cult were amassing in the port town of Omberfell in northern Embarr, as well as in Kelcior, the ancient Malachorian keep north of Eredane in which Kel and his people had made their home until the Onyx Knights drove them out.

"Why?" Sir Tarus had asked. "For what purpose are the followers of the Raven gathering in those places?"

It was Durge who answered. "They're waiting for their master the Pale King to be freed of his prison, so they may serve him."

King Kel let out a massive sigh. "I hate to sound like a gloomy Embarran myself, but I believe you're right in that."

Grace tried to comprehend what this news meant. Last they knew, the Onyx Knights had held Kelcior. Though deluded by Kelephon, the knights of Eversea still believed they worked against the Pale King. They would never have willingly given up their keep to Berash's minions.

When she voiced her confusion about this, King Kel related his most astonishing news. Over the last several months, the Onyx Knights had been preparing for an all-out assault on the remaining Dominions: Perridon, Galt, Toloria, and Calavan. Kelephon would conquer the Dominions under the pretense of serving the Pale King, only at the last moment he intended to betray Berash, seize the Great Stones for himself, and set himself up as the king of Malachor reborn.

Then a fortnight ago, according to Kel, everything changed. The Onyx Knights had fallen into sudden disarray. They had abandoned Kelcior to the pilgrims of the Raven Cult, and they had withdrawn from the borders of Perridon and Galt. Hundreds of the knights had even been seen riding back west along the River Farwander, as if returning to Eversea. What was Kelephon up to?

"Maybe he's gotten distracted," Aldeth had said. "I'm far better at sneaking than fighting, but from what I know wars don't wage themselves. They take a good deal of concentration." The Spider shrugged. "Maybe his mind is elsewhere."

There was no way to be certain, but it was hard to argue with the logic of Aldeth's conclusion. Yet if that was the case, what was distracting Kelephon?

"Perhaps the end comes sooner than he believed," croaked a harsh voice behind her. "Perhaps he was forced to return to his master lest his treachery be discovered."

Grace turned around to see a shapeless figure clad in gray rags shamble toward her across the battlement.

"Grisla," she said, her breath white on the air. She shook her head. "Or is it Vayla?"

The hag batted the air with a bony hand. "Haven't you gotten over that one yet, daughter? It's time you quit asking questions and started finding answers."

Grace reached into the pocket inside her cloak and drew out the rune of hope. "Do you know what I need to do with this?"

Grisla scowled at her. "And why should I know about a thing like that?"

"I saw you." Grace brushed a thumb over the stone disk. "That time in King Kel's camp, I saw you work an augury with runes. Only it didn't make sense. Kel called you his witch. So which are you—a runespeaker or witch?"

Grisla rolled her one eye. "And why are people always so bent on choosing? This or that, left or right, one thing or the other. Don't you see? In the end, we're all just two sides of the same coin."

Quicker than Grace could react, Grisla reached out and snatched the rune of hope. She twirled it in a bony hand, then tossed it into the air. The rune vanished.

Grace gasped, staring in horror. "The key—"

"Is right here, daughter." Grisla reached behind Grace's ear, then pulled her hand back. Between her fingers was the disk of stone. She cackled, then flicked the rune at Grace, who caught it in fumbling hands.

"That's not funny," Grace said. "This is the key to awakening the keep's defenses. Without it, there's no hope."

"Nonsense," Grisla said, clucking her tongue. "There's always hope. You don't need some little chip of stone to give you that. Besides, just because you have a key doesn't mean there's got to be a hole to stick it in."

Grace felt too weary to argue. She gazed again at the distant shadows. "They're counting on me, Grisla. They expect me to find the on switch to the keep's magic defenses, to hold off the Pale King until the Warriors of Vathris get here. But even if Boreas makes it here, we're still destined to lose. That's what the legends of the Warriors say."

Grisla sidled up alongside her. "Well, at least you can say you tried. That's something, isn't it?"

Grace shivered inside her cloak. "What good is standing against darkness if no one's left to remember what you did?"

"There." Grisla pointed at the courtyard below. "He knows that making a stand matters even when you're bound to lose."

Below, a figure clad all in gray walked from the barracks, his heavy shoulders slumped. Durge.

Grace stared at the hag. "What do you mean? Does he know about . . . does he know what's in him?"

Grisla cocked her head. "And do you, daughter? Do you know what's in him—what's in his heart?"

Grace held a hand to her chest, feeling her own heart; it felt so frail. "There's nothing that can be done for him. That's what the forest queen said."

Grisla shrugged knobby shoulders. "Well, I won't go about arguing with the Lady of Gloaming Wood. You'd be hard-pressed to find one in this world who is wiser than she. All the same, even if there's nothing that can be done for him, have you not considered what he might yet do for you?"

Though she did her best to fathom them, Grace couldn't make sense of those words. The task that lay before her was so enormous, and any day—any moment—Durge would be taken away from her. The knight's steadfastness was the only thing that had kept her going all these leagues. She didn't know how she could possibly face this without him.

"I wish Melia and Falken were here," she said softly.

Grisla let out a chuckle. "They are not so far as you might think, daughter."

"What do you mean?"

The hag said nothing. However, her lone eye gazed out across Shadowsdeep, in the direction of the Fal Threndur. Before Grace could speak, a thunderous shout rose from below, shaking the very stones of the keep.

"Where is my witch? Bring me my witch!"

Grisla winced. "It sounds as if His Boisterousness is awake. I suppose I'd better go see what he wants before all his bellowing brings this whole place down." With that, she turned and shambled away, disappearing down the staircase.

Grace gazed again at the dark columns rising into the distant sky. Then she tucked the rune into her pocket and followed after the hag.

Over the next three days, the restoration of Gravenfist Keep continued at a furious pace. Grace doubted this fortress had ever housed quite such a curious army as it did at the moment. There were knights and soldiers from all seven of the Dominions, working alongside witches and runespeakers and Queen Inara's Spiders. What was more, King Kel had brought not only his warriors, but his entire band of followers.

As a result, when stern-faced Embarran knights called for rope or hammers, those things were likely to be brought to them by wenches with frowsy hair and saucy smiles—something which caused even the stolid Embarrans to blink a time or two. In addition, the job of the camp's cooks was made easier by Kel's wildmen, who spent all day scrambling through the underbrush up and down the valley, catching rabbits and quail with their bare hands and bringing them back—usually in their mouths—for the cook's pot.

Despite the motley nature of the army, everyone had their place. The Embarrans were more than stout warriors; they were superb engineers. Under the command of Durge and Sir Vedarr, they made quick work of shoring up the walls. They fashioned sledges that rolled on logs, so that massive stones could be hauled to and fro, then raised into place with levers, and they mixed mortar from limestone and clay found not far from the keep. They also built a series of sluices that brought water from a nearby spring, and they engineered pumps that moved the water to a cistern at the top of the keep, where it could be used to put out fires.

The runespeakers proved invaluable as well. That first day, under Oragien's lead, they went to an abandoned quarry down the valley. There they spoke the rune of stone again and again, splitting slabs of slate into smaller pieces. Soon there were shingles enough to repair the roofs of both barracks and keep. After that, they spent their time inside the keep and along the wall, speaking the runes of wood and stone until their voices were hoarse. Thanks to the power of the spells, even the heaviest beams and most massive blocks remained cooperative as the engineers moved them into place.

The witches wove their own spells, and though they were subtle magics, they were powerful. They blessed the waters of the spring so that they ran clean and pure, and so that a drink would lend a tired man energy and strength. At the base of the great wall grew patches of brambles, and the witches spent long hours weaving the threads of the Weirding, encouraging the thorny bushes to grow thick and to a great height, until soon they were like a wall themselves.

Grace took part in weaving these spells when she could, helping to guide the coven's magic along with Senrael and Lursa—who had managed to retain her position as the coven's Maiden. When Grace asked how she had resisted the advances of the knight she had been dancing with, Lursa had winked.

"He thinks I didn't resist, that's how."

Grace gaped at her. "You mean you cast a spell of illusion on him?"

"A very small one, sister. Sex is more than enough to befuddle the mind of the average man; magic is hardly required. It was simple to make him believe he was getting quite a bit more than he really was."

Senrael let out a cackle. "That's my girl! You deserve a man of peace for a husband, not a man of war."

However, as Lursa and Senrael moved away, Grace noticed how the young witch's gaze traveled across the courtyard, falling upon a knight who was sharpening his sword—it was he. He looked up and waved at Lursa, his eyes lighting up, and a smile touched the young woman's lips. Grace smiled as well;

something told her Lursa did not plan to keep up the illusion forever.

Later that day, Grace found herself speaking with Aldeth. Like everyone, the Spiders had been keeping busy. They had scouted out the keep and surrounding land, and Aldeth had important news: He had found a secret passage.

The entrance lay in the basement of the keep, concealed behind a block of stone cleverly hewn to look like part of the wall. Aldeth and Samatha had followed the narrow passage beyond as it turned and twisted for nearly half a league through the dark. At last they had come upon another door, only it was sealed with a rune, and so they had been forced to come all the way back to the keep to fetch one of the runespeakers.

Master Graedin had traveled back through the passage with them, and he had been able to decipher the runes carved into the door, speaking them to release the spell that locked it. Once it opened, they found themselves looking out over Shadowsdeep.

"The door lets out partway up a steep crag," Aldeth said, "but there looks to be a faint path winding down into the vale. Someone could use this passage to enter Shadowsdeep unseen."

"And someone has," Samatha added. "I saw footprints in the dust near the doorway. At least one man came this way in recent years."

Grace realized she knew who it was. "It was Falken. He came to Shadowsdeep two years ago, when he first began to suspect the Pale King was stirring again. He's not a runespeaker, but I imagine he knows enough about runes to have been able to open that door."

Aldeth dusted cobwebs from his mistcloak. "I believe we'll find the passage useful as well, Your Majesty. There's a clear view of the Rune Gate from the crag where the passage lets out. We'll be able to see the army of the Pale King the moment it begins its march."

Grace supposed that was something. "I'll want one of you Spiders to keep watch at the door at all times. And make sure you always have a runespeaker with you. Once the Rune Gate does open, you'll need to shut that door again."

Despite the dark clouds looming on the horizon, as the days passed, Grace found her spirits lifting. While it was more the result of sweat and muscle than magic, it seemed miraculous how swiftly the keep was taking shape. Soon the wall was strengthened, the crenellations and machicolations built, and all the roofs repaired. After that, the men spent their time gathering piles of large stones that could be dropped on the heads of the enemy, sharpening swords, and fashioning arrows. Everything was coming together better than Grace could have dreamed.

Everything, that was, except for one thing: Though they scoured the keep from top to bottom, they still had not discovered the keyhole into which the rune of hope would fit.

Grace paced back and forth across the keep's main hall as Durge stood nearby. This room had been the filthiest in the keep, being the lowest besides the dungeon, and the men had only just finished clearing out the last of the dirt and debris. Now some of them wiped the floor with rags, cleaning away the last layer of grime. The floor was beautifully crafted, laid out with small pieces of slate of varying shades of gray. More men brought in armfuls of rushes and strewed them over the floor, covering the slate tiles to protect them from the passage of countless boots.

Grace rubbed a thumb over the surface of the rune. "It just doesn't make sense, Durge. If this really is the key to awakening the keep's magic, why would they have put the keyhole in a place where it's impossible to find?"

"They probably didn't," said a ringing voice.

They looked up to see All-master Oragien enter the hall, Master Graedin at his side. The old runespeaker smiled in answer to Grace's look of confusion.

"I imagine that, to the builders of this keep, the keyhole was so obvious they didn't ever bother to write down where it was located. Only to us, seven centuries later, does it seem such a mystery."

Grace supposed he was right. "You said the stones of this keep are bound with runes, All-master. Isn't there a way you can speak runes to awaken the keep's defenses?"

Master Graedin answered before the elder runespeaker could. "I'm afraid not, Your Majesty. Only a bound rune can be used to awaken another bound rune."

Oragien gave the younger runespeaker a sharp glance. "You

are clever, young Master Graedin, but you do not know all things yet." He looked at Grace. "It is true that one cannot awaken a bound rune simply by speaking its name. However, there are other ways a bound rune might be invoked. Their magic may be crafted in such a way that certain things might awaken it."

Grace shook her head. "What sort of things?"

"A bound rune might awaken when touched by water or heated in a fire, or even when the stars stand in a certain position in the sky. Almost anything might trigger the rune's magic. It's entirely up to the one who created it."

Grace chewed her lip. Oragien's words made her think of something Grisla had said. *Just because you have a key doesn't mean there's got to be a hole to stick it in. . . .*

Maybe they had been going about this all wrong. Maybe the reason they hadn't found a keyhole wasn't because they had missed it, but rather because there wasn't one.

"Hope," she murmured, gazing at the rune. "What gives us hope?"

"Life," Graedin said without hesitating. "Where there's life there's hope."

Grace looked at him. "Yes, and what else brings hope?"

Oragien stroked his long white beard. "The coming of spring brings hope. And the sight of an eagle soaring."

"A banner snapping in the wind," Graedin said excitedly. "Men clasping hands in friendship. A field of ripe grain. Holding a newborn baby."

Grace raised an eyebrow. "No babies here, Master Graedin. We need something else."

"Dawn," said a rumbling voice.

They all stared at Durge. The Embarran blinked, taken aback by their sudden attention.

"Forgive me," he said. "I will not interrupt again."

Grace clutched his arm. "No, Durge. You're right. Dawn brings hope. Morning after night. Light after dark."

She had studied the rune countless times, examining the creamy stone and the three silvery lines that marked its surface. However, in all those times, had she ever looked at the rune outdoors when it was daylight? She couldn't remember.

It was afternoon outside the keep, and sunlight shafted through high windows at one end of the hall like columns of gold. Grace drew near one of the sunbeams. It couldn't be this easy. All the same, she held out her hand, so that the sunlight fell full upon the rune, turning the white stone gold.

Nothing happened. She counted ten heartbeats, twenty. Her hand grew warm in the sunlight and began to sweat. She sighed.

"Forgive me, Your Majesty," Durge said behind her. "I did not mean to get your hopes up."

"What's going on in here?" Sir Tarus said, striding into the hall along with Commander Paladus.

"Nothing, unfortunately," Grace said. She pulled her hand back, out of the sunbeam.

On her palm, the rune continued to glow a soft gold.

"But that can't be," she murmured.

Only it was. In fact, the rune was getting brighter. The silver lines glowed like fiery copper now. The rune was hot and heavy against her palm.

"By all the gods," Paladus swore. "It's growing."

The disk had been the diameter of quarter. Now it was twice as large. Three times. It grew so heavy Grace fumbled, and it fell to the rushes on the floor. They gathered around—not too close—watching as the rune grew until it was the size of a dinner plate. It shone so brightly now they had to squint to look at it.

"Look," Oragien said softly.

A shaft of light shot up from the surface of the disk, brighter than the sunbeams that fell into the hall. Dust motes swirled inside the golden column, each one burning like a fiery spark. Then the sparks drew closer to one another, chaos becoming order as they arranged themselves into a recognizable shape.

It was a man. He was tall and proud, his features stern, his robe blazing with symbols of power. Grace had no doubt he was a runelord. Or had been when this magic was created centuries ago.

"Greetings, Lord of Malachor, Bearer of Hope," spoke the image of the runelord. His eyes shone like coals. "As you have been given this rune, so have you been given a most sacred duty, one above all others borne by the heirs of King Ulther. It is your burden to awaken the magic of Gravenfist Keep if times of darkness come again and peril approaches."

"But how?" Grace whispered, staring at the shining figure. "How do I awaken it?"

The runelord wasn't really there; this was only an image—a kind of magical recording made long ago. All the same, his words seemed an answer to her question.

"By our hands, we forged Gravenfist with magic," the image of the runelord spoke on. "We imbued its stones with enchantments of power. And once the stones are awakened, no thing of evil will bear their touch and live. To wield these defenses, you have only to command them. The keep will know the heirs of King Ulther. Ever has the blood of Malachor been the key to hope—so your father and your mother will have told you. May the light of the Shining Tower never fail."

As the sound of these last words faded to silence, the image of the runelord flickered and vanished. The rune lay on the floor, dim and small once more.

Tarus let out a snort. "Well, that wasn't terribly helpful."

"Fascinating," Oragien said, apparently not hearing the Calavaner. "Utterly fascinating! I imagine it was not only the sunlight that awakened the bound rune. Surely its magic required that one of Ulther's line hold it."

Grace bent and picked up the rune; it was cool against her hand. "I suppose the runelord thought he was being clear," she said to Tarus. "Didn't he say something about how my mother and my father would have told me? The runelord assumed I would have knowledge of these things already." Only she didn't; her parents had died when she was an infant.

Durge blew a breath through his mustaches. "For a stone marked with hope, it brings little enough. But perhaps there is some riddle in the runelord's words, one we would be able to fathom if we had long months to decipher it." The Embarran cleared his throat. "Which we don't, of course."

"Can you make the message speak again?" Paladus said.

They could. Each time Grace held the rune in a beam of sunlight, the image of the runelord appeared. However, each time his message was just as mystifying. There was something she was missing, something she was supposed to know but didn't.

Paladus laid a hand on her shoulder. "Do not fear, Your Majesty. It is better to put trust in our skills as warriors rather than in the work of magicians who died long ago. We will hold this keep against the enemy, enchantments or no."

Grace gave the commander a grateful smile. However, as the day went on, her spirits plummeted. Some heir to an ancient kingdom she was. She was already supposed to know how to awaken the magic of Gravenfist. Only she didn't have a clue.

Sunset found her atop the keep once more, watching the gloom gathering in the distance. The columns of smoke were higher than ever, and a sickly greenish light flickered behind them. The sun slipped behind the sharp rim of the mountains. If dawn brought hope, then what did dusk bring?

The sound of bare feet padding against stone approached from behind her. Grace turned around, and despite the thick bands of fear around her heart, she smiled.

"Tira. What are you doing all the way up here?"

As usual the small girl wore only her thin ash gray shift, her arms and feet bare.

"I'm sorry we haven't had much time to play these last few days," Grace said, and she meant it. "But I'm tired of thinking about runes and fortresses. Let's go have some supper, and then maybe we can find something new for your dolls to wear."

Grace expected this to elicit a smile. Instead, while the right side of the girl's face—the scarred half—was as impassive as ever, the left side bore a look of sadness.

Concern rose within Grace. She knelt and touched Tira's thin shoulders. "What is it, sweetheart? Is something wrong?"

Tira reached out and laid her small hands on either side of Grace's jaw in a gentle embrace. A warmth filled Grace, and she sighed. Then Tira lowered her arms, and warmth became a terrible chill. The girl took a step back, and slowly Grace stood.

"You're leaving me," she said.

A tear rolled down the side of Tira's face. In a puff of steam it was gone.

Grace's own cheeks were cold and wet. She was shaking. "I don't want you to go."

Tira gazed at her, then climbed atop the low wall that edged the battlement. The wind tugged at her thin gown.

"Please." Grace was weeping openly now. She held out a trembling hand. "Please, don't leave me."

Tira reached out a chubby hand. The tips of her fingers brushed Grace's.

"Mother," she said.

Then she rose into the evening sky. She ascended swiftly, a spark of crimson light rising up to join the first stars of evening. For a moment she shone among them, like a tiny ruby. Then the light winked out, and she was gone.

Grace staggered, catching herself against the wall. She felt so horribly cold—a husk empty of life. She had known this day would come. However, that did nothing to lessen the bitterness of it. Why had Tira left her?

"She has done what she can here," said a croaking voice behind her. "And she is needed elsewhere. This battle is up to you now, daughter."

Grace turned around, wiping the tears from her eyes with a rough hand. "Is it really?" she said, her voice hoarse with grief. "What about Runebreaker? Isn't he supposed to be the one who decides everything in the end?"

Grisla shrugged knobby shoulders. "And which Runebreaker do you mean?"

A breath escaped Grace. She didn't know how to answer, and it didn't matter. Her place was here, at this keep.

"Are you going to leave me, too?"

The hag let out a cackle. "I think not, daughter. One has to be somewhere when the end comes, and this seems as good a place as any for the likes of me."

The aching in Grace's heart didn't ease, but all the same she felt her fear recede a fraction. At least she wasn't alone. She still had Grisla and Kel, Tarus and Paladus, and the witches and the runespeakers and the Spiders. She still had Durge. For now at least.

Grace turned and gazed out over Shadowsdeep. True to its name, purple shadows filled the valley. "There's no hope, is there? Despite the rune in my pocket, we don't have a prayer of winning." She turned back and faced Grisla.

The hag's face was sad, but there was a glint in her one eye. It was the light of defiance. "Each year, though we wish it not, the sun moves south. Each year, winter catches the world in its cold grip, freezing all life and warmth out it. And no matter how we might rail against it, no matter how we plead or struggle or gnash our teeth, there is nothing we can do to stop winter from coming." She pointed with a withered finger. "We stand before the very gates of winter now, daughter."

Grace shivered inside her cloak. "You mean the gate out there, in Shadowsdeep?"

"No, daughter, I mean the gate in here." Her finger moved, pointing at Grace's heart. "The gate inside all of us."

"I don't understand."

"Then think of it this way, daughter. You cannot stop winter from coming, but is not the coming of spring just as inevitable? Death follows life, and after death comes life again. To the world, to our hearts." She jabbed her finger at Grace's chest. "That's what hope means. Not that you have a chance of winning, but that somehow, even after defeat, life goes on."

Grisla turned and shambled away, her ragged outline merging with the twilight. Grace stood motionless for a time, gazing at the starry sky. Then she headed downstairs to wait for winter.

The next morning dawned colder than any that had come before it. Frost turned swords, armor, and beards white, and the air bit at any flesh left exposed. Even inside the keep and barracks, pails of water had to be thawed over a fire before their contents could be drunk.

For the first hour after dawn, the sun hung red and angry in the eastern sky. Then, as it rose higher, it was swallowed by the great clouds of smoke that rose in the north, casting the world into the half-light of a premature dusk. A stench like the smell of hot iron wafted on the air. By noon, ash had begun to drift down from the sky like fine black snow.

Despite the cold, work on the keep continued. The engineers made their last few adjustments to the walls, creating an overhang of wooden spikes that would make scrambling over the top difficult for anyone who managed to climb so high. Massive timbers were cut and rolled into place along the wall. They could be covered with naphtha, ignited, and cast down on enemies below.

Grace pretended she was supervising the activities, but in

truth she was simply trying to stay out of the way. There was nothing she could do to help—unless, of course, she could figure out how to invoke the keep's defenses. She had lain awake all last night, cold in her cot without Tira to warm her, and she had gone over the ancient runelord's words again and again, but without result. She was supposed to know what to do, only she didn't. Winter would come, and there was nothing she could do to stop it.

"Hello there, Queenie," said a loud voice behind her.

She had been standing outside the main keep, watching the men work on the wall. Now she turned and found herself gazing up at King Kel.

A grin parted his shaggy red beard. "If you don't mind my saying, you look like you just swallowed a mouse."

She laughed despite her dread. "I think it's still crawling around in my stomach." Her smile faded. "I think this day is getting darker, not lighter."

Kel gave her a concerned look. "Don't fret now, Your Majesty. We'll send the Pale King running back through his gate with his tail between his legs, just you wait and see."

"Do you really believe that, Kel?"

The cheerful light faded from his eyes, and his massive shoulders drooped. "No, I can't say that I do. Much as that makes me sound like the doleful Embarran over there."

Grace turned around. She hadn't noticed before—his gray attire blended with the dreary air—but Durge stood on the far end of the wall, gazing into the distance. Grace didn't know why—she didn't have anything to ask of him—but for some reason she wanted to go to him.

"Excuse me," she said to King Kel, who gave her a miffed look, then snorted and headed back to the keep.

When she reached the wall, Grace glanced around, hoping a nearby soldier might be able to give her a hand up. However, all of them seemed to be absorbed in their work, so she headed to one of the wooden ladders and pulled herself up. It wasn't easy in her gown, but she made it to the top without getting too tangled up.

Once there, she had to grip the top of the ladder as a wave of dizziness crashed over her. The valley floor, over a hundred feet below, seemed to pull at her. She waited for the vertigo to pass, then edged her way carefully along the wall.

Durge seemed not to hear her approach. He stood as still as a statue, his gaze fixed on darkness to the north, his right hand pressed against his chest. Alarm flooded Grace. Did he know, then, what lay within his chest?

That's impossible, Grace. There's no way he could possibly know about the splinter of iron. You didn't tell anyone about it except for Mirda, and she's still in Calavere.

She reached into her pocket. Next to the rune of hope lay another object she had carried with her from Calavere: the vial of poison Mirda had given her.

Durge turned around. A look of pain etched his craggy face. She reached a hand toward him.

"What is it, Durge?"

"Something is coming," he said. "I can feel it."

The sound of a trumpet pierced the cold air, then she and Durge were moving. They didn't bother with a ladder. He lowered her to the ground with strong arms, then leaped down behind her. He landed with a grunt, and his knees creaked as he rose, but he waved away Grace's exclamations of concern.

"We must find Tarus and Paladus."

They came upon the knight and the commander in front of the keep. Aldeth and Master Graedin were with them.

"What is it?" Grace said, getting the words out between gasps for breath.

"We managed to close it, Your Majesty," Graedin said, his face pale. "Aldeth drove them back, and I spoke the runes before any of them could enter."

She gripped his shoulders, hard. "Before who could enter?"

"The *feydrim*," Aldeth said. A scratch on his cheek oozed blood. "Thousands of them. We should have seen them coming, but it was so dark from the smoke we couldn't see."

They weren't making sense. Grace turned on the Spider. "You couldn't see what?"

"The Rune Gate, Your Majesty. It's opened."

Durge gazed at Grace with solemn brown eyes. "The Pale King comes," he said.

41

Deirdre hung up the phone, praying to the Great Spirit she had just done the right thing.

It is, Deirdre. You made a promise—no more secrets.

The mysterious Seeker—the one who had been helping her—had said it was imperative no one learned of their arrival. But Deirdre couldn't do this alone, and while she still didn't know if she could trust Anders, she had to trust someone.

"He's on his way," she said, glancing at Vani and Beltan.

"This new partner of yours?" Vani said. She stood by the window, keeping watch on the night with gold eyes.

"Yes." Deirdre forced herself to breathe. "Once Anders is here, you can tell us everything."

Beltan pounded on the buttons of the television remote control. "By the Blood of the Bull, how do you make this thing work?"

Despite her fear, Deirdre smiled. She sat down on the couch next to Beltan and took the remote. "So you like television, eh?"

Beltan's green eyes lit up. "I watched one of these at the hostel where we were staying while Vani searched this city for you. It shows the most amazing things."

Deirdre switched on the TV, and Beltan leaned forward. He seemed to find everything that appeared on the screen fascinating, especially commercials. His mouth opened in horror when a woman spilled red wine on her carpet, then laughed when she used a spray cleaner to remove the stain.

"Is she a witch?" he said.

Deirdre laughed. "Not exactly." She headed to the kitchen and returned with three bottles of Bass Ale. She gave one to Vani, then sat down next to Beltan again, putting the bottles on the coffee table. He had set down the remote; it looked like he had found an old rerun of *CHiPs*.

"So what are Ponch and Jon up to?"

Beltan took a swig of the beer. "A thief has just escaped them. But they can go very fast on their—what are they called?—motorcycles. I have a feeling they will soon catch him."

"I have a feeling you're right."

Beltan took another sip from his bottle and sighed. "With TV and ale this good, why would a man ever do anything else?"

Deirdre grimaced. "A lot of them don't."

"Only we can't just sit here," Beltan said, his expression suddenly serious. He set down the empty bottle and switched off the TV. "We have to find Travis. Now."

Before Deirdre could speak, Vani turned from the window.

"Someone's coming."

It was Anders. Deirdre recognized the broad shape of his silhouette. Seconds later came the knock at the door. She opened it, and Anders stepped in.

"All right, mate, what's going on? You were all hush-hush and mysterious on the phone, and I—oh."

As a neophyte agent, he shouldn't have known anything about the Wilder and Beckett cases. However, the recognition was clear in his blue eyes.

"It's them," he said. "The ones from AU-3."

Deirdre crossed her arms. "How do you know that?"

"I read your and Farr's report." He winked at her. "Well, parts of it, anyway. Most of the text in the copy I had access to was crossed out with black markers. Nakamura gave it to me. He said if I was going to be working with you, I should read it."

Once again, Anders's explanation sounded completely plausible.

Probably because it's the truth, Deirdre. You said you were going to trust him. So trust him already.

"Before we go on, I need you to promise me one thing," she said, locking her gaze with Anders's blue eyes. "I need you to swear it on the Book."

"Anything. You're my partner."

"You can't tell anyone about this just yet. Not Nakamura, not anyone. Understood?"

"Sure, Deirdre, I swear. But do you really think you can avoid telling Nakamura?"

"No, I don't. But I want to do it myself before we leave tomorrow."

He cocked his head. "What do you mean, 'before we leave'? Where are we going?"

Deirdre glanced over her shoulder at Beltan and Vani. "To Denver."

The four of them sat around the dinette table and talked until long past midnight. Deirdre listened in amazement and growing horror as Beltan and Vani told them everything that had happened on Eldh. There was much she didn't understand, especially something about Travis returning to Castle City, only over a century in the past. But what chilled her most was the news that Duratek had somehow sent agents to the world Eldh.

"Crikey, it's a war, isn't it?" Anders said. "Duratek is getting ready to conquer Eldh."

Beltan heaved broad shoulders in a sigh. "They're not the only ones. We've learned the men of Duratek are in league with Mohg and the Pale King."

"Who?" Anders said, confusion plain on his pitted face.

"I'm probably not the best one to explain it," Beltan said, "but Falken's not here, so I'll do my best. One of the Old Gods, Mohg, is trying to get back to Eldh so he can break the First Rune and destroy the world. That way he can make the world anew in his own image. And his servant, the Pale King, is nearly free again. Grace is marching north to Gravenfist Keep with an army to try to stop him, but I don't think even she believes there's much hope of holding the Pale King back." Beltan thumped a fist against the table. "That's why we have to find Travis."

Deirdre held a hand to her aching head. "Wait a minute, Beltan—what can Travis do to stop all of this from happening?"

"Everything," Vani said. She rose, prowling around the table. "Travis has two of the Great Stones, which Mohg seeks, and which are the key to breaking the First Rune. What's more, he is the Runebreaker spoken of in prophecy. It is his fate to be there at the end of the world."

Anders gaped at her. "So you mean Travis Wilder is the one who's going to break this rune thing and destroy the world? But how is that any better than this Mohg person doing it?"

Vani and Beltan answered only with silence.

Deirdre's brain struggled to grasp all these esoteric names and words. It still didn't make sense, but Beltan was right about one thing—they had to find Travis. Somehow he was the key to everything.

"I think we could all use a little more ale," Beltan said.

He stood and headed for the kitchen. Despite his turtleneck and blue jeans, Deirdre would never have mistaken him for just any Londoner. He moved his long, lean body with a predatory grace.

"Forgive my asking," Anders said as Beltan sat back down. "But do you really need our help? You've got the transport device, and from what I read in the report you're both pretty good at taking out Duratek agents. Why didn't you just go to Denver to find Mr. Wilder yourself?"

"We tried." Vani looked at Deirdre. "When we activated the gate artifact, we sought to open a doorway to Denver. However, something . . . happened."

"What happened?"

The *T'gol* coiled a hand beneath her chin. "I am still not certain. It was as if there was some kind of . . . resistance. We were nearly lost in the Void. At the last moment, I envisioned a new destination—this city, London. I journeyed here once during my three years on Earth. The gate responded to my new command, and we found ourselves here."

"So this gate thing can take you anywhere you can picture?" Anders said. "Bloody amazing. But why did you pick London?"

Deirdre gazed at Vani. "You knew the Seekers were here, didn't you?"

Vani nodded. "I learned something of the Seekers in my time on Earth. You have tools at your disposal that could aid us in our search for Travis Wilder. It was my hope you would help us, Deirdre Falling Hawk, so I searched the city for you. It took me some days, but I found the location of the Seeker base. After that, it was a simple matter to follow you here."

Anders raised up a hand. "All right, I'll buy for a moment that wicked gods are helping Duratek to take over Eldh, and that Travis Wilder is the only one who can stop them. But how do you know Wilder is in Denver in the first place?"

"This is how." Beltan reached for his coat—which he had thrown on the couch—pulled something out, and tossed it on the table. "We purchased this in a shop down the street."

It was a copy of yesterday's *Denver Post*. Deirdre picked it up in shaking hands. The headline was something about how the use of the illegal drug Electria had reached epidemic proportions, especially among young people, but Deirdre didn't read the article. Instead her eyes moved to the small photograph of a man at the bottom of the front page. *New evidence suggests fugitive still at large in Denver*, read the caption.

The man in the photo was Travis Wilder.

Deirdre looked up. "We'll catch the first flight we can tomorrow."

Six hours later, Deirdre rose with the smeary gray light of dawn, let the hot water of the shower pound her back to life, and took a taxi to the Seeker Charterhouse, arriving just before eight o'clock. Nakamura usually got in early, and after signing in with Madeleine, she found him already at work in his office.

As she sat down across from the assistant director, Deirdre hoped everything was all right back at the flat. She had left Anders to keep watch over Beltan and Vani.

"You're here early, Miss Falling Hawk," Nakamura said before Deirdre could speak. He took a sip of tea. "Were you aware then?"

"Aware of what?"

"That new orders arrived for you this morning. You've been reassigned. Temporarily, I hope."

Her foggy brain couldn't quite grasp the meaning of these words. "Reassigned? To where?"

"I have absolutely no idea." He picked up a large manila envelope; the flap was sealed with wax. "This just arrived for you. It came directly from the Philosophers. I assume it contains all of the relevant details."

Deirdre took the envelope in shaking hands. Maybe she did understand. Hadn't she decided that he had to be one of the Philosophers? The one who had been helping her.

"It must be about—"

Nakamura held up a hand. "No, Miss Falling Hawk, please don't tell me. If I was supposed to know what your mission was, then I would have been informed."

Lines furrowed the assistant director's usually smooth forehead, and his voice was tight. Was he angry at being kept out of the loop?

"I imagine you'll be leaving immediately. However, do be assured that we'll want you back as soon as we can have you, Miss Falling Hawk."

Not angry. Worried. Nakamura reached across the desk and touched her hand. "Take care of yourself, Deirdre."

"I'll try."

Then, before she broke down, she rose and hurried from his office. Madeleine had a car waiting for her. Deirdre climbed into the back, and as the driver navigated the rain-slicked London streets, she broke the seal on the envelope and emptied the contents onto the seat next to her.

Plane tickets to Denver. Passports. Colorado state driver's licenses. Everything she had planned on asking Nakamura for that morning. There was a set for each of them, including Anders. So whoever the one helping her was, he knew what she had done, and he approved. That was something, she supposed.

The false passports and IDs were of superior quality, each one issued under a new identity. She recognized the pictures of Anders and herself as staff photos on file at the Seekers. By the clothes they wore, the photos of Beltan and Vani had been taken last night with a telephoto lens through the windows of Deirdre's flat. So he had been watching them.

"Who are you?" she whispered, holding up one of the fake passports. "What do you really want?"

It didn't matter. Right now what he wanted was exactly what she wanted. To find Travis Wilder. Deirdre scooped all of the papers back into the envelope as the car eased to a stop.

"Wait for us," Deirdre said to the driver. "We'll be down in five minutes."

"And where will you be going, Miss Falling Hawk?"

"Heathrow," she said.

Their flight left at noon. They made it to the airport with time to spare, and everything on their trip to Denver went without incident.

Mostly, at any rate. There was a moment of panic when Vani was pulled aside at the departure gate for a random security scan. Deirdre feared the assassin was going to break the security guard's neck as he ran the magnetometer wand up and down each of her legs. However, Deirdre locked eyes with her, and Vani stood stiffly until the examination was over.

Vani muttered in outrage as they boarded the plane. "If a man of my people touched an unmarried woman in such a way without her consent, a *va'ksha* would be placed on him, a curse that would make his *thaloks* shrivel like raisins."

Anders winced. "Does *thaloks* mean what I think it means?"

"It does," Beltan said. "So be on your best behavior."

The flight was long, tedious, and frustrating. At least for Deirdre. Vani appeared content to meditate most of the time, and Beltan stayed glued to the miniature television that popped out of the arm of his seat. Occasionally he let out a loud guffaw that caused heads to turn, and once he shouted, "Look out behind you!" at the top of his lungs. Deirdre glanced at his screen in time to see Wile E. Coyote falling off a cliff.

"That is a cruel bird," Beltan said, jabbing a finger at the television.

Once the other passengers stopped staring, Deirdre patiently explained the concept of cartoons, and her words—in combination with the beers the flight attendant brought—seemed to calm the blond man down.

Deirdre readjusted herself in her seat. Across the aisle, Anders was drinking club soda and plowing through a battered paperback copy of *Jane Eyre*. Deirdre's head hurt too much to read, so she spent the rest of the flight shredding cocktail napkins and wondering what awaited them in Colorado.

When they reached Denver International Airport, they found the place crawling with Duratek agents. However, to Deirdre's relief, they breezed through Customs and were approved for entry into Denver. Her fear Vani or Beltan would be recognized was groundless. Whoever her secret helper was, he knew what he was doing; their fake IDs received less scrutiny than the genuine versions carried by actual citizens of Denver.

They showed their approval papers to a security guard—a patch with the crescent moon of the Duratek logo was sewn to his uniform—and he allowed them to get in line for a taxi. Minutes later they sped along the highway as the skyscrapers of downtown Denver grew larger, rising up against the snowy peaks of the Rocky Mountains.

Beltan started to speak in the cab, but Deirdre shook her head, eyeing the driver's radio. There was no telling who might be listening. They rode the remaining half hour to downtown in silence, then got out when the cab stopped in front of the Brown Palace Hotel. Her mysterious benefactor may have been reluctant to reveal his identity, but at least he had the decency to arrange for first-class accommodations.

Whether it was chance, design, or merely irony, they ended up in the same suite she had shared with Hadrian Farr last fall. There was a central living area with a fireplace and bar, and two separate bedrooms.

"Well, we're here," Anders said, tossing down his bag on the sofa. "Now what?"

Deirdre eyed the door of one of the bedrooms. Her back ached from all those hours on the plane. She longed to take a hot bath, then lie down and sleep.

She sighed. "Now we get to work."

They began the search that afternoon. A rental car was waiting for them at the hotel. Anders and Vani took the car to do some reconnaissance of the city, while Deirdre and Beltan headed out to cover downtown on foot. While Deirdre didn't like the idea of splitting up, this way they could cover more ground. Besides, two people asking questions were less likely to draw notice than a group of four.

"So how are we going to find him?" Beltan said as he and Deirdre walked down Sixteenth Street. His expression was hopeful, expectant.

She shoved her hands in the pockets of her leather jacket. She should have brought a warmer coat; despite the blue sky and sun, it was cold.

"I have no bloody idea."

Beltan stopped and stared at her. "That's supposed to be funny, right? Like when the anvil fell on the dog's head?"

"Coyote," Deirdre said. "Wile E. is a coyote. And no, it's not supposed to be funny. I honestly don't know how we're going to find Travis. The Seekers are good for lots of things. We can whip up false IDs and arrange for planes and cars, but it's not like we have an otherworldly traveler homing device."

He let out a groan. "Great. So we're just going to wander around and hope we happen to run into him?"

Deirdre shrugged and gave him a weak smile. "Well, at least it's a plan."

Beltan let out a snort. "And people think *I'm* stupid."

"Do they really?"

"Not anymore, I suppose. And I can't say I'm all that happy about it. Now people expect me to come up with good ideas all the time."

Deirdre hunched inside her jacket. "I know. It's a bloody pain, isn't it? But contrary to what people think, the Seekers don't have all the answers. Not even close."

It was five o'clock, and the sidewalk was filled with people leaving work, getting into cars, catching buses and trains, going home. But Deirdre knew their own work had just begun.

"It's so big," Beltan said, gazing around, awe on his face. "This city is even bigger than Tarras, and that's the biggest city in the world. In my world, anyway. I don't know how we'll ever find Travis."

Neither did Deirdre. All the same, a sudden confidence filled her. "We will, Beltan. We'll find him for you."

He looked away. "Not just for me. For Vani, too."

What did that mean? Before Deirdre could ask, he started down the street, and she had to hurry to keep up with his long strides.

Two hours later, her legs were aching, and she couldn't stop shivering. Night had fallen over the city, and the lights dazzled her eyes, making her jet-lagged head throb. She drank the last swig of the hazelnut latte she had bought a while back at Starbucks. It was ice-cold. She gagged, swallowed the viscous liquid down, then tossed the cup in a trash can.

Beltan threw his own cup into the trash, then held a hand to his head. "I feel like there are bees in my skull and wolves in my stomach."

She allowed herself a smirk. "I told you two was too many."

At Starbucks, the blond man had gotten the largest size mocha they offered, and he had sucked it down so quickly that, when they passed another Starbucks a few blocks later, he had hijacked her and made her buy him a second.

"I guess I have a lot to learn about this world."

Deirdre sighed, regretting her joke. "No, Beltan. You're doing great. Really. No one would ever know you weren't from Earth. You blend in perfectly."

Almost too perfectly, it occurred to her. She knew Vani had spent several years on Earth; the assassin had had time to learn the language and customs. But what about Beltan? He had spent most of his one, brief visit to Earth locked in a laboratory.

"The fairy blood," he said. He must have guessed what she was thinking. "It helps me to know things I shouldn't. Like how to speak the language of this land."

Deirdre felt a tingling in her chest. "What other sorts of things do you know?"

"I'm not sure. The feelings are weaker here than they are on Eldh. Muffled."

"Try."

He shut his eyes. "I know the moon is up," he said after a minute, "but you can't see it. It's behind the buildings. I know there is a storm coming over the mountains, and that it brings snow with it. I know there's a river nearby, even though we have yet to come upon it. It's shallow, and in no hurry to reach the ocean. And I know . . ." His forehead wrinkled in a frown.

She touched his arm. "What?"

"I know there's something wrong in this city. Something terrible and hungry, like a shadow. And it's growing. I know it, just as I know he's here somewhere, not far away. Just as I know he's in danger."

He opened his eyes. They were haunted in the cast-off light of a neon sign.

"Do you think I'm crazy?"

She shook her head.

He sighed. "Neither do I."

"Come on." Deirdre hooked her arm around his. "We've done enough for our first scouting mission. Let's get back to the hotel and get warm."

Together they started up Seventeenth Street. They had covered much of downtown on foot, and while they hadn't seen any sign of Travis, they had discovered some things of interest all the same. Beltan was right about the shadow growing in the city. The clues were everywhere. The newspaper headlines warned of the crashing economy, the rising crime rate. The televisions blared the same bleak news. People moved about their everyday lives, only furtively, with fear in their eyes. And everywhere—stapled to every telephone pole, taped to the side of every fence—were the posters bearing the faces of the missing.

Deirdre had read about it on the plane, but she hadn't realized how serious it was. At first the disappearances had been limited to the homeless—the neglected, the ill, the forgotten. However, over the last few days, others had begun to vanish. The posters that covered the city now showed the smiling faces of well-dressed, healthy people: husbands and wives, sons and daughters. Loved. Missed.

They turned the corner onto Court Street, and Deirdre saw a woman taping a photocopied flyer to the side of a mailbox. The flyer showed the picture of a teenage girl with glasses, smiling. A high school yearbook picture. The woman looked up, her face exhausted, her eyes red and dry.

"I'm sorry," Deirdre murmured, but the woman had already turned away to shuffle down the street, flyers and tape in hand.

When they stepped into their suite at the Brown Palace, they found Vani and Anders already there. The two had driven through downtown and the surrounding industrial areas, and what they had seen confirmed Deirdre's observations: The fear in the city was growing, and that was only helping Duratek to strengthen its hold on Denver.

"I don't know what they're up to," Anders said, "but it's got to be something big. We couldn't turn a corner without running into someone working for Duratek."

"Did you see anything that might give us a clue as to what they're doing?" Deirdre said, shucking off her jacket.

"Perhaps," Vani said, her leathers creaking softly as she paced. "They are careful not to allow anyone to observe their actions, and people are unwilling to speak about anything they might know concerning the men of Duratek. However, it is clear they are amassing a large amount of resources. We saw many vehicles, including transport trucks, moving in and out of warehouse complexes."

"They're getting ready for a war," Beltan said, rummaging through the minibar. He pulled out a canister of cheese puffs. "If you're going to invade a foreign land, you've got to make sure you have an adequate supply chain to fortify your army as it advances."

Deirdre gave Beltan a sharp look. Not stupid indeed.

"How do you open this thing?" he said, turning the canister around and around.

All right, so maybe he still had a few things to learn. Deirdre took the canister from him, popped the top, and handed it back. He grunted, then carefully removed a cheese puff and put it in his mouth.

He looked up. "Is this food?"

"Technically, yes," Deirdre said.

"Just checking." He swallowed a handful of cheese puffs.

A knock sounded at the door. Deirdre turned around, but Vani was already moving. She opened the door in a swift motion.

It was only a bellhop. He carried an envelope for Deirdre. She rose, signed for it, then turned the envelope over in her hands as Vani shut the door.

"What is it?" Beltan said.

"I don't know. Except for my name, it's not marked."

Vani's eyes narrowed to slits. "Be careful."

"She's right, mate," Anders said. "There's no telling who sent that."

Deirdre moved to the window, holding the envelope up to the glass, letting the illumination of a nearby streetlight shine through. However, she didn't see anything out of the ordinary.

"Here goes nothing," she said, and opened the envelope.

There was only a single large sheet of paper, folded into eighths. She unfolded it, then frowned.

"What is it?" Anders said, moving closer.

Deirdre turned the paper in her hands. "I'm not sure. It looks like architectural plans for some building. A big building, by the look of it."

"Anything you recognize?"

"No, there's no outside elevation. It's just floor plans. A theater, maybe?" She turned the paper over. "There's nothing else. No message, no explanation."

"That's strange," Beltan said. His lips and fingers were orange. "Any idea who might have sent it to you?"

A shiver passed through Deirdre. It had come in the same kind of envelope as the IDs and the plane tickets. It was from him, her mysterious Philosopher.

You've got to tell them, Deirdre. They deserve to know he's been helping you all along.

Before she could speak, something outside the window caught her eyes. She glanced down. Moments ago the street beneath the window had been filled with people on their way home. Now it was completely deserted.

No, not completely. A single figure stood in the pool of sepia-colored light beneath a streetlamp. For a second Deirdre wondered if it was *he*. Only it couldn't be. The figure was small—a girl in a dark dress.

The girl looked up, gazing at Deirdre with wise purple eyes her face an ivory cameo framed by hair like shadows.

The paper slipped from Deirdre's hands, fluttering to the floor.

"What's out there?" she heard Anders say behind her.

Deirdre could only shake her head. Below, the girl moved he lips. It was impossible; there was no way Deirdre could possibly have heard her. All the same, the girl's lisping voice whispered in her mind.

Follow me.

42.

For the first time in his life, at thirty-five years of age, Travis fel old. His body ached, and he longed to lay down his head. However, there was to be no rest for him that night. The bowl of sour was empty; it was time to go.

Sister Mirrim and Child Samanda had both retreated throug a doorway, leaving Travis alone at the table with Brother Cy.

"I'm so tired," Travis said softly, still watching the pictures of the Steel Cathedral flicker across the TV. "I don't know how much longer I can keep going."

The preacher squeezed his shoulder with a bony hand. "You'd be surprised, son. You're a whole lot stronger than you think. But take heart. If what Sister Mirrim has seen is true—and I have never known her vision to be false—then your journey is nearly at an end."

Travis didn't know whether to be relieved by those words or terrified. He gazed around the commissary and found that if he concentrated, he could see them as they really were now. Not the men and women who had come to the mission seeking refuge, but the others—the ones who always traveled with Brother Cy, who helped him in his mystery work: goat-men and tree-women, scampering greenmen and ugly little creatures that flitted about the room on butterfly wings.

Who was Travis to talk of being weary? Brother Cy and his followers been traveling on their own journey for over a thousand years now, ever since they helped banish Mohg from Eldh and found themselves trapped beyond the circle of the world. How long had they drifted in the darkness—not merely homeless, but wordless—until Travis went back in time and inadvertently opened the crack in the world Earth with Sinfathisar? That mistake had allowed Mohg to enter this world. But like the box Pandora foolishly opened long ago, it had allowed hope to steal into the world as well, in the form of Cy and his companions.

"Will you ever go home?" Travis looked up into Brother Cy's black marble eyes. "You and Mirrim and Samanda and the others? When this is all over, will you finally get to go home?"

For a moment a light shone in Cy's gaze—a sorrow so vast and deep it was beyond fathoming.

"Home," he whispered in his rasping voice. "You don't know, son. You can't possibly know how sorely tempted I have been to dig my fingers into the crack you made in this world, to strain with all my might and pry it wide open."

He stood, his voice rising into the exultant rhythms of a sermon. "I can envision it now, as clearly as Sister Mirrim might see it. I would march through the gap with my followers behind me. I would stand before the Nightlord and wrestle with him in a battle that would boil seas and shatter mountains to dust. I would wrest the Great Stones from him. And when I arose victorious from the devastation, all the world would kneel before me, and I would tower above, the master of all!"

People in the commissary had stopped to stare, spoons frozen halfway to their lips. Brother Cy was rigid, white and frozen as a statue, staring blindly. Then the preacher sighed, passing a hand before his face, and the moment was over. While he had spoken, Travis had caught a fleeting glimpse of the being he truly was. Majestic, powerful, and terrible: a god. Now he was simply Brother Cy again, gaunt and hunched in his dusty black suit.

"No," he said, his voice a whisper. "I will not destroy my brother only to become him. Such was my choice long ago. Such was all of ours—Ysani, Durnach, and the others. I will help how I can, but that task is not mine."

The preacher looked down at Travis. "There's someone I believe you need to talk to before you go, son." He pointed across the commissary, at the thirtysomething woman in the upscale clothes. Then he walked to the doorway where Mirrim and Samanda had vanished and passed beyond.

A low murmur of noise filled the commissary again as people returned to their soup and their conversations. Travis gazed at the woman in the corner of the commissary, the one Brother Cy had pointed at. Her head was bowed over her hands. Was she praying?

Travis pushed himself to his feet, then headed across the commissary. "Hello."

The woman looked up. She wasn't beautiful—her features were too hard-edged for beauty—but intelligence shone in her eyes, and even grim and frightened as she looked now, there was a wryness to the set of her mouth that bespoke a keen wit.

She looked him up and down, then nodded. "You're the one he said I have to talk to. The preacher."

He sat down across from her. "What are you supposed to talk to me about?"

"About this, I suppose." She opened her hands, revealing silver computer disk. So she had been hiding the disk, not pray ing. "God, I hope this was the right thing to do." Or maybe she had been praying after all.

"You hope what was the right thing to do?"

A laugh escaped her, a slightly mad sound. "I suppose it won't hurt to tell one person. After all, I want to tell everyone in the world about what's on this disk. Besides, I think I can trust him." She glanced at the door where Brother Cy had vanished. "I think I have to."

"Did he bring you here?"

"Yes." She frowned, shaking her head. "No, not exactly. He helped me escape the . . . he helped me to get out. And he gave me a card with this address on it. Only the cab driver couldn't find it, he said the address didn't exist, so I got out and walked, and then I saw the light shining in the dark."

Two of the mission's workers passed nearby—the young man with the bleached goatee and the young woman with the green hair.

"Who are they?" she said, shivering. "They're all so strange, and *him* most of all. Who are they really?"

"Here," he said, reaching out and gripping her hand. "Let me show you."

Before she could pull away, he whispered *Halas*, the rune of vision. It was a weak magic; he was tired, and he had not opened the box to touch the Stones. However, it was enough.

She pulled her hand away and gazed at him with wide eyes. "My God, *what* are they?"

Travis sighed. "That's a good question. And one I don't think we'll ever really know the answer to. But some call them the Little People."

"Little People," she murmured. Already her shocked expression was transmuting to one of sharp curiosity. "But what do they want with us?"

"I think they want to help us."

She brushed tangled brown bangs from her eyes. "Maybe. Or maybe they want us to help them."

"I'm Travis Wilder," he said.

She clutched the computer disk. "I know. You see I work . . . that is, I used to work for Duratek."

He lurched to his feet, sending his chair clattering to the floor as he backed away from the table.

"No." She reached a hand toward him. "Don't go. I told you, I don't work for those bastards anymore. Please, you've got to help me. They'll be looking for me—looking for this." She gripped the disk. "And if they find it, there's no hope of ever stopping them."

The expression in her eyes was earnest, anguished, but it could be she was a good actress. All the same, his heart slowed in his chest. Brother Cy wouldn't have let her in here if she was evil, would he?

He picked up the chair and sat back down. "Who are you? Tell me everything. Now."

"My name is Ananda Larsen. Doctor Ananda Larsen. I used to work at a high-security Duratek facility in Denver. It was the one you and your associates—"

"The one we broke into last fall."

She nodded.

"So what did you do there?"

She fingered the disk. "I was working on a research project investigating the use of gene therapy as a means to enhance animal intelligence. My main work involved a chimpanzee. Ellie. Her progress was amazing. Only then they brought another subject they wanted me to work on. It was . . ." Her voice caught. "It was a human subject. A male."

A sickness spread through Travis, quickly burned away by rage. Until that moment, he had thought he knew what anger felt like. He was wrong. "You were the one who held Beltan prisoner. You were the one who did . . . who did those things to him." He reached a hand toward her. Runes blazed in his mind: spells of mayhem and death.

She clutched the edge of the table, but she did not flinch. "I don't think I'd blame you if you killed me. What I did was wrong. Wrong on so many levels." She shook her head, and her gaze grew distant. "It happens so gradually you don't even notice it. Each step is so small, you think it's just a little slip down the slope, that you're not compromising yourself, that you can always back out later. Only then one day you wake up and realize it's too late—that day by day, bit by bit, they've turned you into a monster, and you let them do it."

Rage burned to ash in Travis's chest, leaving him cold and empty. His hand fell to the table, useless. He knew what it was like to be made into a monster. No rune he could speak, no vengeful magic he might work, could have destroyed her; she was already shattered.

"Why?" he said. "Why did you work for them?"

She laughed as she wiped tears from her eyes. "To help people. At least, that's what I told myself. But deep down, I knew that wasn't the truth. What I really wanted was to prove that I was right, to show everyone who had ever doubted me they were wrong, that my research really could work."

Travis made a decision. He could hate this woman for what she did to Beltan; it would be all too easy. But wasn't that what Mohg and the Pale King stood for? Those who served them gave up their hearts. If Travis gave up his own, if he let hate consume him, he would be no better than they were.

He reached across the table and placed his hand on hers. "I don't believe that, Dr. Larsen. If all you had really wanted to do was to prove you were right, then you wouldn't be here now talking to me."

She stared, astonishment on her face. Then, slowly, she nodded. "All these years, I kept telling myself they would use my research for good. But I know now it is—that it always was—a lie. That's why I stole this." She touched the disk.

Travis leaned closer. "What is it?"

"Everything I need to expose the truth behind Duratek, to show the world what they're really doing." She looked up, her fear gone, her face hard as porcelain. "Everything we need to bring them down."

A shiver danced up Travis's spine, and he cast a glance out of the corner of his eye. The light inside the mission seemed dimmer than before, the walls and floor dingier. Several people in the commissary stared in their direction, and there was no sign of Brother Cy or his followers. Something told Travis it was no longer safe here.

"I think we should leave."

"Why?" Larsen said, eyes startled. "Where will we go?"

Travis stood and shrugged his coat on. "I don't know. Anywhere. Come on."

Larsen rose and put on her coat. They headed down the corridor to the lobby. No one stood behind the counter; the ivy that coiled up the post was brown and shriveled.

"What's going on?" Larsen said.

There was no time to explain. Brother Cy was gone, and so was whatever protection his presence had brought to this place. What if Mohg's slaves had known Cy was here? What if they had been watching, waiting for him to leave?

Travis opened the door, and the cold hit them like fists as they stumbled into the darkness. It seemed like hours had passed inside the mission, but it was still night. They walked quickly down the deserted street, past darkened storefronts. Footsteps echoed behind them.

Larsen glanced over her shoulder. "There are people back there. I think they're following us."

"Keep moving."

"Oh God, they're coming toward us. What do they want?"

"Our money," Travis rasped. "Or maybe our hearts. This way."

He yanked her arm, and they stumbled around a corner. Up ahead, lights shone against the night; the sounds of traffic and distant music drifted on the air. There were people this way, real people—they would be safe. He tightened his grip on her hand, lowered his head, and ran.

The roar of an engine ripped apart the night, and a black car sped from a side street. Tires squealed as the car came to a halt, and both Travis and Larsen had to skid to a stop to avoid crashing into the side of the vehicle. Shouts rang out behind them, but before either of them could move, one of the car's windows slid down.

"Get in," Deirdre Falling Hawk said. There was a *chunk* as the car doors unlocked. Her eyes moved past Travis. "Now!"

He jerked the rear door of the car open, shoved Larsen through, and climbed in behind her. Travis was barely inside before the car started accelerating. He grabbed the door and pulled it shut, then glanced out the tinted glass of the rear window. He saw three shadowy shapes in the middle of the street.

"Are they ironhearts?" Deirdre said.

Travis tried to answer, but he couldn't catch his breath.

"Here, use these," the driver said in a gravelly voice, tossing a small plastic case at Deirdre.

Travis couldn't get a good look at him, but one thing was certain: The man behind the wheel wasn't Hadrian Farr. He was thick-shouldered, his short hair white-blond.

Deirdre fumbled with the case. "What is this?"

"Heat-sensing goggles, mate. They translate thermal patterns into a visual signal."

Deirdre opened the case and pulled out something that resembled a small pair of binoculars. She turned around in her seat and held the device up to her eyes.

"Damn it—how do you adjust these things? Wait, I see them now. They—" She sighed and lowered the goggles. "They're gone. I think they ducked down an alley before I could get a good look at them."

Larsen had managed to right herself on the seat. She swiped her tangled hair away from terrified eyes. "Who are these people, Travis? And what are ironhearts?"

Travis was sweating now, and he couldn't stop shaking. "How did you find me?"

"Child Samanda led us to you," the driver said. "At least, that's what Deirdre told me. Personally, I didn't see any spooky girls lurking about, so I think my partner is positively barking. But I suppose she did find you."

Child Samanda? Yes, that made sense. If any of this could really make sense. "Is there somewhere we can go to talk?"

The driver met his eyes in the rearview mirror. "I'm heading back to the hotel. That's where the others are."

"Others? What others?"

Deirdre turned around in the seat. "Vani and Beltan. They're both there, Travis. They came here to look for you."

A sharp pain stabbed at his chest. They shouldn't have come. It was too dangerous here. They had to go back. All the same, joy filled him.

"Beltan," Larsen said, arms crossed over her chest. "That was what he was called, wasn't it?"

Travis looked out the window. "You never even asked him

his name." He caught the ghost of her reflection in the glass: pale, haunted.

"We didn't . . . I didn't know I could communicate with him. Has he . . . how is he?"

Travis turned to look at her. "Different, Dr. Larsen. He's different now."

She pressed her lips into a thin line and nodded.

They reached the hotel minutes later. On the way, Deirdre introduced them to the driver. His name was Anders, and he was her new partner.

"Where's Hadrian Farr?" Travis asked as Anders brought the vehicle to a halt.

"I honestly have no idea," Deirdre said and got out of the car.

When they reached the hotel suite, the door opened before Anders could swipe the card key through the lock. But then, she was always watching, wasn't she?

Travis gazed into golden eyes. "Vani . . ."

She smiled, then lowered her gaze, as if suddenly shy of him. This astonished Travis. Vani was so strong, so full of danger, that sometimes he forgot how beautiful she was, how small. He coiled her inside his arms, and he could feel her trembling.

"You smell," she said, laughing as she pushed him away.

"And you don't look too good, either."

Travis glanced up, and he was certain his heart couldn't bear the sight before his eyes.

"Oh, Beltan."

The blond man grinned, an expression that transformed his usually plain face. "You didn't think you could get away from us that easily, did you?"

Travis could only shake his head. Beltan's grin faltered, and then he was there, catching Travis in strong arms, holding him so tight it hurt, but Travis didn't care. He returned the embrace with all his might.

Beltan whispered fierce words. "By all the gods, don't you ever leave me again, Travis. Don't you ever leave *us*."

I won't, he wanted to say. *I swear it.* But his throat was too tight; he couldn't speak the words.

At last Beltan let him go. "By the Bull, Vani is right. When was the last time you had a bath?"

Travis scratched his scruffy beard and laughed. "I don't really remember."

Deirdre glanced at Travis. "So, are you going to introduce us to your friend?"

Dr. Larsen stood near the door, her expression uncertain. Travis took a deep breath. How was he going to do this? "Everyone, this is—"

"You!" Beltan roared.

In three strides he covered the distance to Larsen, and before she could react he wrapped his big hands around her neck and squeezed. Her eyes bulged, and her fingers clawed at his wrists, but without effect.

For a moment shock paralyzed Travis, then he was moving. "Stop it, Beltan. Let her go—now."

The blond man clenched his jaw. "No. Not after what she did to Ellie and the fairy. Not after what she did to me."

Larsen's struggling was already growing weaker. Her skin was white, and her eyes rolled up.

"Vani!" Travis shouted. "Help me."

However, the *T'gol* only crossed her arms over her black leathers. Deirdre stared, her expression one of horror. Anders reached into his jacket and pulled out a gun. Travis shook his head. No one was going to die, not if he could help it.

He put his hands on Beltan's arms, not to pull them away, simply to touch them. They were hard and rigid. A light shone in the blond man's eyes: a faint green glow.

"Please, Beltan," he said. "Let her go. Not for her sake, or for mine, but for your own. You said they tried to make you into a killer. Don't show them that they've won."

Larsen was no longer struggling. She hung limply in the big man's arms. For a moment he didn't move, his face as hard as if carved of stone. Then a shudder passed through him, and Larsen slumped to the floor. Beltan stared at his hands. The fey light was gone from his eyes.

"What have I done?" he said softly. "By Vathris, what have I done?"

Deirdre was already kneeling next to Larsen. "Anders, help me."

Together, they pulled Larsen up and sat her on a nearby

chair. Her head lolled back and forth. Panic surged in Travis. She couldn't die. He needed her. They all needed her.

Larsen's eyes fluttered open, and a ragged breath rushed into her.

Travis touched her shoulder. "Are you all right?"

"Yes, I—" She winced, holding a hand to her throat. Her skin was already beginning to bruise. "I'm fine." She looked at Beltan, her expression stricken. "I'm sorry. I know you can never forgive me, but I want you to know how sorry I am."

Beltan tried to say something, but no words came out. He turned and hunched his shoulders. Travis started to move to him, but Vani was swifter. She placed her arms around Beltan. He resisted a moment, then rested his head on her shoulder.

Stunned, Travis simply stared as Anders fetched a glass of water. Deirdre helped Dr. Larsen sit up straight and drink it. Beltan had pushed Vani away. The knight moved to Larsen, kneeling before her chair.

"Ellie gave herself for me. If you made her what she was, then your work could not have been for evil."

Tears streamed down Larsen's cheeks. She reached out a trembling hand and touched Beltan's face, and they stayed that way for a moment before he stood again.

"Well, that was all a bit on the awkward side," Anders said, slipping his gun back inside his coat.

Travis let out a tight breath. "I thought Seekers didn't carry guns."

"They don't." Deirdre crossed her arms and gave Anders a sharp look. "At least, not usually."

Anders winked at her, a grin on his craggy face. "I thought you knew by now I was anything but usual, mate."

Larsen looked up at Travis, new fear registering in her eyes. "Seekers? These people are Seekers?"

Travis nodded. "That they are. And now we're going to have a good long conversation with them."

"No," Deirdre said. "First you're going to have a good long shower. Then we'll talk."

Travis spent the next half hour standing under a jet of hot water, letting it wash away the dirt, the weariness, the fear. As he showered, he thought of Jay and Marty, and he hoped they were all right.

He toweled off, then pulled on a pair of jeans and a sweater that Deirdre had bought for Beltan. They were overlarge for him—Beltan was taller, and Travis was stunned to see how gaunt he had become these last weeks living on the street—but they were warm and clean.

By the time he stepped into the suite's main room, he found the others talking and drinking coffee.

Beltan, who sat on the sofa next to Deirdre, gave an approving nod. "Now that's the Travis we know."

A powerful compulsion rose within Travis to go to the blond man and hold him tight. However, he was aware of Vani standing at the window, her gold eyes locked on him. He poured himself a cup of coffee, then sat in a chair next to Larsen. She was no longer shaking, and color had returned to her cheeks. The computer disk gleamed on the coffee table before her.

Travis sipped his coffee; it was hot and delicious. "So what did I miss?"

"Nothing much." Anders leaned against the back of the sofa. "Just how all the signs point to the end of the world."

"Oh," he said, and took another sip.

They spoke until the small hours of the night, and more than one bleary-eyed bellhop was forced to bring a pot of coffee to their door. Travis listened, at once fascinated and horrified, as Dr. Larsen described in detail her research at Duratek: her work with Ellie and Beltan, and then later her assignment to synthesize the blood of the fairy.

After that, Beltan and Vani took turns explaining what had happened on Eldh since Travis left: how the Warriors of Vathris had begun to arrive at Calavere, and how Grace planned to march north with a small force to prepare Gravenfist Keep for their coming. Her bravery stunned Travis. It was strange to picture Grace as a warrior queen, yet he could.

Finally, Beltan answered the question burning on Travis's mind: How had Beltan and Vani followed him? Grace had figured it out, giving them the bandage she had taken from his arm, stained with his blood. It wasn't much, but it had been enough to activate the gate—a fact which frightened him. Was his blood, changed by the scarab of Orú, truly so powerful?

He could worry about that later. Right now he had to finish what he had come here for. Travis reached out and picked up the computer disk. "What exactly is on this thing, Dr. Larsen?"

"Proof," she said.

Deirdre raised an eyebrow. "Proof of what?"

Slowly, Larsen reached out and took the disk from Travis. "Proof that Duratek is behind the drug Electria. Not just that they created it and are fully aware of its addictive powers, but that they're behind its illegal sale and distribution as well. It's how they've funded so many of their projects, the ones they don't want the auditors to know about. Projects like mine."

Anders let out a low whistle. "I'd say that's enough to bring them down, and then some. They'll be banned across the globe."

"They created Electria for fairies, to keep them alive here on Earth," Deirdre said, twirling the silver ring on her left hand. "That it had euphoric and addictive effects on people was just a happy accident, wasn't it?"

Larsen nodded. "And one they were all too willing to exploit for profit."

Anders pointed at the disk. "If you don't mind my asking, how did you get hold of that information?"

Larsen gave him an ironic smile. "Sometimes they forget that scientists are naturally curious. In their urgency to synthesize the blood of the being E-1, they gave us all the highest security authorization, so that we could quickly access any data we might need. I'm not exactly a hacker, but I'm pretty handy with a computer. I was able to snoop around and collect this information without them noticing."

"But they'll know you have it now," Vani said, crossing her arms. "They'll be searching for you."

Larsen's smile faded. "Yes, they will."

Anders cracked his knuckles. "So how do we keep them from getting the information back?"

"We let the genie out of the bottle," Travis said, and the others stared at him. Couldn't they see it? It was so clear. "Right now the information is on that disk. We need to transfer it, to duplicate it."

"You mean into copies?" Larsen said.

Travis stood up, pacing. "No, I mean into the minds of every person in this city, every person in this country. Once everyone knows the truth, Duratek won't be able to conceal it anymore."

"That's it," Deirdre said, her smoky jade eyes lighting up. "Duratek might deny the report, but there will be investigations. They won't be able to do anything without the government knowing."

"Like launch an assault on Eldh," Travis said. He glanced at Larsen. "Did you know that's what they intend to do?"

She gripped her coffee cup. "One of the executives—I never knew their names—he came to talk to me the other day. He told me there was a whole new world just waiting for us to use, to make a profit." She glanced at Beltan and Vani. "It's your world, isn't it? He said that once they're able to synthesize the blood of E-1, they'll be able to open a door to that world. Only I don't know what that means."

"They've created a gate here in Denver," Travis said. "All they need is blood of power to open it."

Deirdre glanced at Larsen. "Only you destroyed the results of your research, didn't you?"

"Yes," Larsen said. "But I was just the first to realize the solution. Duratek has dozens of scientists working for them. It's only a matter of time until one of the other researchers finds the key like I did."

"So how do we get the truth out there?" Anders said.

"I think I know a way," Travis said, pulling a piece of paper out of his pocket.

Deirdre raised an eyebrow. "What's that?"

"The phone number of Anna Ferraro. She's a TV news reporter here in Denver. She'll do a report on Duratek and Electria for us, I know she will. Only . . ." He sank back to the couch. "Only she was fired from the TV station."

"So she can go to another," Beltan said, his expression hopeful. "There's more than one of these television channels in this city. I know—I've looked at them all."

Travis held a hand to his head. "It's no good. None of the local TV stations will take her. They're all controlled by Duratek.

And we'll never get out of this city, not now. They know I'm here."

They had run out of words. All of them stared at the disk. They had everything they needed to stop Duratek from opening the way to Eldh. Everything except a way to get the message out.

Travis laid his hand atop Deirdre's. "Thanks for coming anyway. You must have broken every Desideratum there is by bringing Vani and Beltan here."

Deirdre bit her lip. "Actually, I'm not sure about that. You see, our orders came from the Philosophers themselves. And there's—"

Anders prowled around the sofa. "And there's what, mate? Remember what we said about no secrets. Is there something you're not telling me?"

Deirdre gazed out the window. "I've been getting help with all this. I'm not sure who he is. He's never told me his name, but he knows things . . . things only one of the Philosophers could know. I think . . . no, I know he's one of them."

"Crikey," Anders said softly, his eyes going wide. "So that's why you've been so mysterious. You're getting all sorts of secret tidbits from one of the Philosophers. I can't blame you for keeping that under your hat."

Deirdre winced. "Yes you can. We promised no secrets, right?" She picked up an envelope off the table. "He was the one who sent me this."

"What is it?" Vani said, stalking closer.

"I'm not sure. Architectural plans of some building." She pulled a large sheet of paper from the envelope and unfolded it. "I suppose he meant for it to help me, but I can't make heads or tails of it."

A buzzing filled Travis's head as he stared at the paper in Deirdre's hands. He had never been inside; he had only seen it on television. All the same, he was certain. There was the stage and the ocean of seats.

"It's the Steel Cathedral," he said, brushing a hand over the plans. "It has to be."

The others gave him confused looks. However, certainty

filled Travis—sharp and cold as ice. *There is still somewhere you can go. Into the heart of shadow itself....*

He stood again, clutching the scrap of paper. "Give me the phone," he said. "I have to call Anna Ferraro. I have to tell her I know how to get her on TV."

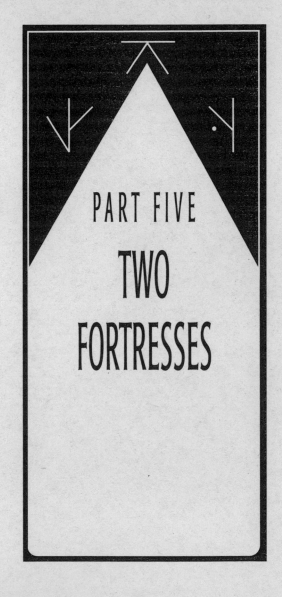

PART FIVE

TWO
FORTRESSES

43.

It is time, sister.

Aryn's eyes snapped open, and she sat up straight in the chair. Her chamber was cold; the fire must have burned out long ago. What was the hour? She had not meant to fall asleep. She had intended to sew all night long, to weave magic into the cloth with every stitch, but she must have dozed off in the end. She glanced at the window. Gray light seeped through the glass.

Please, sister, can you hear me?

"Lirith, is that you?" she croaked, too bleary to simply think the words.

Lirith's familiar voice sounded in her mind. *Thank Sia you're awake. There's no time to waste. Already the Warriors gather on the field below the castle. They will march with the rising of the sun. Sareth and I go now to the upper bailey. Meet us there.*

Before Aryn's foggy brain could fashion a reply, Lirith's presence was gone. Aryn let out a sound of dismay; there was so much she wanted to ask the witch. However, it was too dangerous to speak over the Weirding, as Lirith surely knew; there was no telling who might be listening.

Besides, Aryn, you can't lie when you speak across the threads of the Weirding. So are you going to tell Lirith that you spied on her and Teravian last night? Are you going to tell her how you used magic to watch while they . . .

Despite the chill, a hot wave of shame coursed through her. Or was it another, different sensation of warmth she was feeling? In her mind she saw again the way Teravian's lean, pale body had moved against Lirith's soft, dark flesh.

Aryn shook her head. She did not know how this day was going to unfold, but if things transpired as she feared, she would have to put any thoughts of mercy, of tenderness, out of her mind. The Pale King had his slaves with hearts of iron to serve him. If the Dominions were to have any hope, Aryn would have to harden her own heart—if not into a lump of iron, then at least into a thing of ice.

She touched the scarf that lay across her lap. It was covered with embroidery now, the fine stitches forming intricate patterns of crimson and gold. So skillfully had she sewn that the bloodstain could hardly be seen amid the pattern. In her mind's eye, shimmering green threads of magic shone alongside the mundane strands of red and yellow. However, it was not finished; there was still one section of the scarf she had not managed to embroider, and now there was no more time. She would have to hope it was enough.

You'll have to get close to him, Aryn. This magic is part of you. To invoke it, you'll have to give it to him yourself.

She prayed to Sia it wouldn't come to that. Perhaps they had misjudged him; perhaps the prince was loyal to his father after all, loyal to the Dominions. Perhaps...

Aryn carefully folded the scarf, then rose from the chair, stretched her stiff limbs, and hastily readied herself for the outdoors. She donned a wool gown the color of the winter sky, and over it threw a dark blue cloak lined with fox fur. The light outside the window had changed from gray to silver. She had to hurry.

As she moved to the door, she caught a glimpse of herself in a polished mirror propped in the corner. The woman who gazed back at her looked older than Aryn would have expected, her face pale and regal.

Aryn turned, opened the door, and left her chamber.

The castle was empty as she rushed through the corridors; when she reached the entrance hall she found the doors unguarded. She passed into the upper bailey. Frost dusted the world, making everything a ghost of itself. Clouds scudded across the hard sky above. Already their edges were tinged with copper.

She found Lirith and Sareth waiting for her just outside the king's stables.

"We can speak as we go," Lirith said, her breath white on the air. "We must reach the field below the castle before the Warriors make ready to depart."

"What do you intend to do?" Aryn said as they started across the bailey.

"To watch, and to be ready. If Liendra plans something, it will happen before they begin their march."

Aryn gasped. "You've seen this?"

"No," Lirith said with a rueful expression. "I'm afraid the Sight has abandoned me in this. Yet I'm sure of it all the same. They murdered Queen Ivalaine to keep her out of the way, and then last night they—"

Lirith bit her tongue, and Aryn sucked in a sharp breath. So she had not told Sareth what she had done last night.

"Did you sense something, *beshala*?" Sareth said, touching Lirith's arm. "That's where you were last night, wasn't it? You were out searching for signs of the Necromancer."

Lirith cast a frightened look at Aryn.

Aryn didn't hesitate. "No," she said. "We didn't sense Shemal's presence in the castle. But she's here somewhere. She has to be."

Lirith squeezed Aryn's left hand.

You must not worry, sister, Aryn dared to murmur across the Weirding. *I will never tell him.*

And yet I must, Lirith spoke back, her thread trembling. *I must tell him everything. But not this day.*

They hurried across the lower bailey, past the two ruined towers, and through the castle gates. The road that wound down the hill was more populated; they passed servants carrying bundles and squires dashing back up to the castle to fetch items their lords had forgotten.

As they rounded a corner, the field below Calavere came into view, and Aryn's heart leaped in her chest. Company after company was lined up at the foot of the hill; armor reflected the steely light, so that the army looked like a river flowing into the distance. The number of foot soldiers was beyond counting, and there were horsemen as well, score upon score of them, as well as a fleet of wagons to carry supplies.

Sareth let out a breath of wonder. "Would you look at that. Maybe there's hope for this world after all."

Maybe, Aryn thought, if they could prevent Liendra and her witches from meddling.

They made their way down the hill nearly at a run, and Aryn scanned the army as they went. There were numerous banners, each one bearing the crest of a particular fiefdom: hawks, bears, and serpents. There were other, more exotic banners as well, carried by the lords and chieftains who had journeyed from the far south, bearing the silhouettes of creatures Aryn couldn't name. Then she saw what she was looking for: a banner that stood higher than all others. It was deep blue, adorned with a silver crown of nine points above a pair of crossed swords.

"King Boreas," Aryn said between ragged breaths. "We should go to him."

They left the road behind and made for the king's banner. The sea of soldiers parted, making way for them, and many of the men bowed to Aryn as she passed.

As they drew near, Aryn saw Boreas sitting on his massive warhorse. He wore a mail shirt and an azure cloak trimmed with silver, but his head was bare. He looked big and fierce and terribly handsome. Several lords were gathered around him, but Aryn saw no sign of Teravian. She slipped through the throng of mounted knights, moving to the king, Sareth and Lirith in tow.

"So you've come to bid me farewell after all, my lady?" he said, a grin parting his black beard. "I thought you had decided your sleep was more important than wishing me luck."

Despite her trepidation, Aryn found herself smiling as well. "And who could sleep with all these trumpets blowing, Your Majesty? You're making quite a racket."

"It's all part of our plan, my lady. We'll make ourselves appear so fearsome the servants of the Pale King will take one look at us and run all the way back to Imbrifale."

Aryn laughed. "That's an awful plan."

The king shrugged broad shoulders. "We'll refine it as we go along."

Aryn started to speak again, only her laughter had somehow turned to tears. The king climbed down from his horse and encircled her in strong arms. For a moment, she felt like a small girl again.

"I wish I could come with you, Your Majesty," she managed to say between sobs.

"I wish it were so as well, my lady," he said, his voice gruff.

"Your presence would gladden my heart. But it is a dark road we must travel, to a dark place, and should I never return, there must be someone here to keep the light of hope burning."

Aryn clutched him more tightly. "No, Your Majesty. Do not speak of such a thing. You will return to us, and with Lady Grace at your side."

However, all he said was, "There, child." Then he kissed her brow and gently pushed her away. He climbed back onto his horse. "You'll take good care of her," he said, gazing at Lirith and Sareth.

"With all our might," Sareth said.

One of the knights guided his horse close to the king's. "Any sign of the prince yet?"

Aryn's sorrow receded in the wake of new fear. So they had not seen Teravian either. What did it mean? Before she could wonder more, the sound of trumpets shattered the brittle air. At the same moment, the sun crested the horizon, and the clouds changed from copper to fiery crimson.

"There," the king said, pointing across the field to the east. "Here he comes now, along with Petryen and Ajhir. They were keeping track of him."

The knight grinned. "Perhaps he was a bit groggy this morning after his adventures last night."

Lirith's cheeks darkened, and she turned away. Sareth cast a puzzled look at her. Aryn started to reach for the witch, then murmured oaths rose from the men all around.

"By Vathris," Boreas growled, "what's that they're carrying?"

Something was wrong, but Aryn couldn't see for all the horsemen. She spied a squire holding a horse, probably for a lord who had gone to use the privy trench one last time. Ignoring the boy's protest, she grabbed the saddle and pulled herself up.

The light of the dawning sun tinged countless shields and spears with the color of blood. Aryn shaded her eyes with her left hand and saw three riders approaching from the east. Two of the men rode dark horses; she recognized them as Duke Petryen and Sai'el Ajhir. Between them, on a white horse, rode Teravian. The prince was clad in a red cloak over black armor. A sword was belted at his side, and resting on his brow was a circlet wrought of silver.

Ajhir carried a banner, staff braced in his stirrup, and a breeze caught the cloth, unfurling it. It was a mirror to the banner of Calavan—a crown over crossed swords—only rather than silver on blue, it was gold on green. Petryen carried a second banner, red on white: the shape of a charging bull.

"What does he mean by this?" Boreas roared. "By all the Seven, he had better have a good explanation, or I will have him thrown in the dungeon, prince though he is."

The army fell silent as the prince and the two men rode closer. The air behind them seemed to shimmer with ruby light; the clouds blazed in the sky. The three riders came to a halt, opposite the king and his captains, thirty paces away.

"Hear us, men of Vathris!" Ajhir called out. "Hear us, true followers of the Bullslayer!" His words rang out over the field, impossibly loud, so that every man could easily hear them. Aryn cast a startled glance at Lirith.

It's a spell, Lirith mouthed the words, weaving her fingers together.

With a jolt, Aryn understood. In a way it was like the enchantment that allowed them to speak across the Weirding. Only this magic made it so anyone could hear Ajhir's words. But where were the witches who were casting the spell?

"You have been betrayed, men of Vathris!" Ajhir called out. "You have been lied to by the very man who you now follow— by King Boreas himself."

Murmurs of anger and dismay rose from the army. Men cast shocked looks at the king. Boreas's visage went white, and Aryn knew it was from rage rather than fear. His hand tightened around the hilt of his sword.

Petryen moved his horse forward; his voice rang out like Ajhir's. "He has told you it was the witch Ivalaine who tried to murder Prince Teravian. What he did not tell you was that it was he himself who convinced her to do the deed, using spells to twist her mind—dark magics no true man of Vathris would have dealings with. It was Boreas who did this, so that he might usurp his son's place in prophecy. For it is not King Boreas upon whom Vathris has shone his holy light, but rather upon his son.

The prophecies are clear: It is Teravian who is to lead us in the battle against the darkness of the north, not the traitor and coward King Boreas!"

Now shouts rose from the men, some of protest, but others of outrage. Some of the knights around Aryn appeared as angry as the king, but many more cast odd looks at Boreas, their lips curling in disgust.

It's part of the spell, sister, Lirith's voice spoke in her mind. *The words Ajhir and Petryen speak—they do more than simply pierce the air. They are piercing men's hearts and minds as well, twisting them. Only I don't know how they're doing it. Can you see anything from up there?*

Aryn gazed around, but she saw only the great host of warriors, and the empty plain, and the red clouds that boiled in the sky. The air behind Teravian, Petryen, and Ajhir shimmered as though it were hot instead of bitterly cold.

"This is madness!" Boreas called out. He wheeled his horse around, his eyes casting off sparks. "Do not listen to them! I know not why, but they seek to turn us from our purpose, to prevent us from riding against the darkness."

However, the king's voice sounded small and weak compared to the stentorian tones of Petryen and Ajhir. His words were drowned out by the angry voices of the warriors, though there were shouts of doubt and protest as well.

How can we know if this is true? many of the men called out, and others took up the cry. *How can we know it is the prince who is to lead us? Show us a sign!*

A chant rose from the men, quickly growing in strength as it raced across the army like a wave over the ocean.

Show us! Show us!

Teravian guided his white horse forward, and the chanting ceased as a silence fell over the army.

"I will show you a sign," the prince said, and though his voice was low, every ear heard his words, and every soldier held his breath as he raised his arms over his head.

Aryn clutched the reins of her stolen horse. What was he doing? Then she felt the hum of magic along the threads of the Weirding.

"Show them, Lord Vathris!" Teravian called out, his voice

booming like thunder now. He thrust his hands above his head.
"Show your followers what they wish to see!"

A new sound rose from the army: cries of fear, and of exultation. Men pointed at the sky, and shouts of "Vathris! Lord
Vathris comes!" rang out.

Aryn gazed upward. The molten clouds above the army
roiled, then all at once broke apart. Out of the gap emerged a gigantic shape, as large as castle, as ruddy as the dawn. The thing
charged across the sky, tossing its gigantic head and snorting
fire from its nostrils.

It was a bull, terrifying and beautiful, born of the red clouds
of morning.

44.

A deafening cry rose up from the army. Five thousand men
surged in a crushing tide. At first Aryn thought the soldiers were
fleeing at the sight of the enormous bull floating overhead. Then
she heard Teravian's voice—clear and thunderous—ringing out
over the din.

"To me, Warriors of Vathris! To me, Men of the Bull!"

The soldiers weren't crying out in dread, but in rapture. They
broke from their formations and raced across the field, answering Teravian's call, gathering around him, swords and spears
held aloft to catch the light of the dawn.

In the sky, the bull had wheeled around, and now it halted
above the prince. A morning wind sprang up, blowing the
clouds to the east, but the bull held its place. It was as large as a
mountain now, gleaming red-gold. Wisps of fog curled away
from its body like the steam of sweat.

Some of the knights spurred their horses, racing across the
field toward Teravian's banner. Aryn fought to retain control of
her horse as it was buffeted from all sides. Where were Lirith
and Sareth? They would be trampled.

She caught sight of them not far from the king. He rode beneath his banner, shouting orders, his face as red as the bull in
the sky. A tight knot of men on horse and on foot surrounded

him, and Lirith and Sareth were among them. Aryn pulled on the reins of her mount, trying to guide it toward the king, but men and horses crashed into them. Her mount's eyes were wild with terror.

Get out of my way!

Aryn directed the words along the Weirding with the full force of her will. Men and beasts alike staggered aside; a way opened up before her. She urged her horse, and it sprang forward at a gallop.

"To me!" King Boreas was shouting. "Do not be fooled by witchcraft and trickery! To me!"

A few more heeded the king's call, gathering around him, but they were not many. The shouts of men and the pounding of hooves drowned out his commands, while Teravian's voice continued to ring out as though it issued from the sky itself.

At last Aryn reached Lirith and Sareth. The two gripped the saddle of her horse to keep from being swept away. Aryn tried to speak, but her voice was lost in the din. She abandoned mundane speech in favor of the Weirding.

What's happening? Is it really a sign from Vathris?

No, sister, came Lirith's reply. *Can you not feel it? It has its source in the web of the Weirding.*

Aryn closed her eyes, trying to shut out the noise and confusion around her. The threads of the Weirding were pulled taught, vibrating like the strings of a lute. Something was drawing a river of magic from the great web. Something or someone.

The bull is a form of illusion, isn't it? Aryn spoke in her mind.

Yes, but one forged of enormous power. Last summer, in Falanor, Grace, you, and I were able to part the fog that covered the village green. But this bull is far larger than the cloud of mist we affected, and its shape is formed with great skill. I know of no witch who could have conjured such a thing. There was a pause. *No female witch, at least.*

Aryn clenched the reins of the horse. *It's Teravian. This is why they wanted him to come full into his power last night—so he could do this.*

Remember what Mirda told us—he is more powerful than any witch.

Save for one, Aryn thought. However, she did not spin these words over the Weirding.

She opened her eyes. The greater part of the army had abandoned its position and raced across the field, falling in behind Teravian. A chant of "Vathris, Lord Vathris!" rose from the men, as well as, "Teravian, King Teravian!"

No more than a quarter of the army had remained with King Boreas. In a way, Aryn was heartened so many had stayed at all. The bull still snorted and tossed its head in the sky. What man would not follow in answer to the call of his god? But at least some men had put loyalty before faith.

Only they were not nearly enough. It was to be father against son, warrior against warrior, and King Boreas's side was too small. There was no hope it could win. All the same, the victory over their brothers would exact a terrible toll on the force that had flocked to Teravian. When the battle was over, half the army of Vathris would lie dead on the field, and many of those who remained would be wounded. No more than a small force would be left to march north to Gravenfist Keep—if it marched north at all. Surely that had been Liendra's plan all along.

But where were Liendra and her witches? Aryn gazed over the field, but all she saw were the men gathered behind Teravian. The prince had ridden forward, so that he was now twenty paces before his army. Duke Petryen and Sai'el Ajhir still rode beside him, the banners they held snapping in the wind. Aryn remembered how solicitous of the prince both had been since the first attempt on his life. The two lords must have been in on this treacherous plot from the beginning.

A silence fell over the battlefield. In the sky, the bull lowered itself on one knee, as if bowing to the prince below.

"Hear me, King Boreas!" Teravian's voice rang out over the land. "There is yet hope for you. Throw down your sword and surrender yourself, and you will be forgiven your deeds!"

The prince's words elicited a string of curses from Boreas. The knights gathered around him shook their swords in anger. However, Aryn hardly noticed. A realization came to her, along with a sudden thrill.

Lirith! she said, spinning a thread out to the other witch. *Teravian is powerful, there's no doubt of that. But no matter how powerful he is, he can't be weaving two spells at once. He can't be creating the illusion of the bull and magnifying the sound of his voice as well.*

Understanding flowed back from Lirith. *Someone must be helping him. Someone nearby.*

Aryn gazed again at Teravian. The air behind the prince still shimmered, as though heat rose from the ground. However, despite the rising of the sun, the day was bitterly cold.

Again Teravian's voice boomed out over the field. "What is your answer, Father? Will you obey the will of the sacred bull and surrender yourself to me?"

"I will give him an answer," Boreas roared, drawing his sword. "I placed my trust in him, and he has betrayed me. He is no son of mine. Prepare to charge, true men of Vathris. We will not let our minds be clouded by spells and deceit."

Shouts of approval rose up around the king. Orders were given; the men fell into quick formation. Knights held their lances ready; foot soldiers gripped spears and shields. Their faces were stern, but they were far too few. It would be a blood-bath.

"We'd better get out of the way," Sareth said, looking up at Aryn with wide eyes. "I don't think they're going to stop for anything once they charge."

The cold seemed to crystallize Aryn's mind, and despite the pounding of her heart a resolve filled her. It couldn't be courage, not when she was so deathly afraid. Rather it was a kind of knowledge; she had seen this in a vision, had she not? This was the way it was to be.

A small round shield and scabbard were strapped to the horse's saddle. Aryn looped the shield's strap around her shoulder, so that it covered her withered arm. Then she unbuckled the scabbard and unsheathed the sword, holding it aloft.

Lirith's frightened voice came from below her. "Sister, what are you doing?"

"What it is my purpose to do," Aryn said, and with a thought she urged the horse forward.

She heard Lirith and Sareth cry out behind her, followed by an angry shout she recognized as King Boreas's, but the horse was already cantering across the field. Aryn rode with ease, sitting tall and straight in the saddle, gripping her mount with only her knees. She knew if she could look back at herself, she would see a scene she had glimpsed before: a proud woman all in blue riding away from a castle with seven towers, a shield on her shoulder, a sword in her hand. A queen riding to war.

It was Ivalaine who had first revealed the image to her, in the waters of a ewer, what seemed an age ago. Then she had seen it again, in the card she drew from the *T'hot* deck of Sareth's al-Mama. Both times, Aryn had failed to understand. How could she be riding to war at all, let alone from a castle with seven towers when Calavere had nine? However, two of Calavere's towers were gone now, and so was Aryn's uncertainty. She knew she was not yet a queen; all the same, she would be obeyed.

Aryn brought the horse to a halt before Teravian. Petryen and Ajhir treated her to suspicious glares, hands on the hilts of their swords, but the prince's gray eyes were curious beneath his thick eyebrows.

"Go back to your father, Aryn," he said. His voice was quiet, for her only.

She was aware of Petryen's and Ajhir's angry looks, and of the three thousand men gathered not far behind the prince. All the same, she thrust her shoulders back. "Boreas is my warden, not my father. My place is with you, Your Highness. Am I not your betrothed?"

He blinked, and it was clear her words had startled him. "We can talk about that later. Right now you have to get out of here. There's going to be a battle. I can't stop it."

"Can't you?" Even as she spoke, Aryn probed along the Weirding, tracing the threads of the power.

His visage grew hard. "No, as a matter of fact I can't."

Aryn was still searching. She needed more time. "Why?" she said. "Why are you doing this?"

"You'd never understand."

"I might."

The wind blew the prince's dark hair from his face. He looked older than before, stronger and more serious. His shoulders were no longer hunched. The awkward and uncertain boy she had always known was gone; in his place was a young man.

"I did it because I love him," he said so only she could hear, gazing across the field at the banner of King Boreas.

He was right. Aryn didn't understand. However, there was one thing she did know—the weaving was subtle, skillfully done, but at last she had detected it, hanging like a shimmering curtain behind the prince.

"I will leave you then, Your Majesty," she said. "But first you must let me give you a gift—something to remind you of your wife to be."

Petryen frowned, and Ajhir started to protest, but Teravian waved their words away. "What is it?"

"Only this, my lord." She sheathed the sword, and from her cloak she drew out the embroidered scarf. "It is a small thing, a token I made for you. I ask only that you place it around your neck before you ride into battle."

Teravian hesitated, then reached out and took the scarf. "It's beautiful," he murmured. Carefully, he unfolded it, then wound it around his neck. "Now go, Aryn. Be safe." His words were so gentle she almost lost her resolve.

No, she would not fail. She let the cold air freeze her heart to ice.

"Please," he said. "It's time."

"So it is." Behind the shield, she made a motion with her withered hand.

Teravian let out a choking sound, and his eyes bulged. His fingers fluttered up to the scarf around his neck. He tried to speak a word—it might have been *Aryn*—but no air passed his lips. The prince reeled in his saddle, and shouts rose from the nearest men.

"Your Majesty!" Duke Petryen cried out. He reached for the prince, but as he touched Teravian's arm there was a flash of green light, and the acrid smell of smoke permeated the air. Petryen toppled from the saddle and fell to the ground, dead.

Aryn gazed at the corpse. So the magic she had woven into the scarf was complete after all—a spell of death. It had slain Petryen, and while Teravian was resisting, it would take him as well. As Mirda had said, there was one witch more powerful than Teravian.

Aryn was that witch.

Teravian tilted back in the saddle. His eyes rolled up into his head.

"Harlot!" Ajhir cried, his face a dark mask of rage. "Murderer! What have you done to him? Remove your spell, or I'll strike you down!"

He brandished his sword at her, but Aryn ignored him. A new cry rose from those warriors who had rushed to Teravian's banner: a sound of dismay.

Aryn looked up. In the sky, the gigantic form of the bull wavered, like an image seen through rippling water. The shining beast tossed its head one last time, then a wind struck it, and it broke apart into tatters of mist that quickly scudded away to the west. The cries of dismay became shouts of terror. Men threw down their swords and spears.

Teravian had created the illusion of the bull, only now his magic was failing, along with his life. He clawed at the scarf, but it was wrapped tightly about his throat. Ajhir stared at Aryn, at the prince, at the sky, clearly unable to decide what to do. Aryn knew this was her chance. She imagined reaching out with invisible hands, gripping the curtain of magic that hung behind the prince, and ripping it aside.

New shouts rose from the warriors. As though they had appeared out of thin air, thirty-nine women in green cloaks now stood behind the prince. The young witches gazed around, their eyes and mouths becoming circles of fear as they realized their spell of concealment had been broken. However, Liendra, who stood closest to the prince, wore a look of outrage.

"Shemal!" the golden-haired witch shrieked, turning round and round. "Shemal, show yourself!"

A chill descended over Aryn, and her heart fluttered as a patch of shadow thickened and grew, until in its place stood a figure in a black robe. The robe devoured the morning light, and the figure cast no shadow. By her shape it was a woman, though her face was concealed by the robe's cowl.

The warriors who had flocked to Teravian's banner were now turning and running; the field had become a churning sea as men fled in all direction.

Treachery! the warriors cried. *Witchcraft!*

Liendra stalked toward Aryn's horse. "You deformed runt—you're ruining everything."

Despite the dread in her chest, Aryn's voice did not waver. "It is you who are ruined, Liendra. You did it to yourself long ago, when you cast your lot with darkness."

For a moment the hatred in Liendra's eyes was replaced by another emotion: fear. Then her visage hardened again, and she turned toward the one in black. "Stop her! The horrid little bitch is killing him. Cast the spell back on her."

Shemal glided forward, the hem of her robe not touching the ground. "Such a magic cannot be turned on its maker. If you were not so weak in the Touch, you would know that."

Teravian's lips were blue now. He slumped in the saddle, no longer struggling.

All traces of beauty fled Liendra's face, replaced by the ugliness of rage. "Then do something else! I don't care what it is. Just keep her from killing him!"

"As you wish," Shemal's voice hissed from the cowl. A pale hand extended from the sleeve of her robe. She flicked a finger, and Aryn watched in horror as the embroidered pattern on the scarf vanished, as if the threads had been plucked out. The cloth was white and unmarked. Teravian drew in a gasping breath, clutching the mane of his horse. His eyes were hazed with pain as he looked up at Aryn, but there was life in them. The spell had been broken.

"Sisters, help me!"

The wail pierced the air. Aryn looked at Liendra. So the spell had not been broken after all, only transferred to another.

The same embroidered pattern that had vanished from the scarf now appeared on Liendra's robe—swiftly, as if sewn by a hundred hands. She flailed at the threads, trying to brush them away as though they were insects, but to no avail. The pattern continued to grow until it was complete. Liendra's eyes protruded from their sockets, and she gnashed her teeth, biting her own tongue. Blood ran down her chin. Several of the young witches drew close to her, then as she reached out for them they recoiled, their eyes on Duke Petryen's body.

The golden-haired witch reached a hand toward Aryn. "Die," she said.

Aryn shook her head.

Liendra went stiff, then fell over, a corpse before she hit the ground. The young witches screamed and cried, sinking to their knees. Warriors raced past them in all directions. Many were fleeing the field, but not all.

"Come to me!" Ajhir was shouting. "We must protect the prince. Come to me!"

A few of the men gathered around him, but others kept moving past. The clang of swords sundered the air, along with cries of pain. Somewhere trumpets sounded. Aryn started to turn her mount around, to see what was happening—then froze.

The figure in black glided toward her.

Aryn's horse let out a scream and reared onto its hind legs. She tried to grab the saddle, but she had only one hand; it wasn't enough. She tumbled to the frozen ground, and her breath rushed out of her in a painful gasp. For a moment she was unable to move. Then, with effort, she untangled herself from her cloak and pushed herself to her knees.

The Necromancer stood above her. Despite the wind, Shemal's black robe hung still. From her position on the ground, Aryn could see inside the hood, and what she glimpsed there froze her blood. A smile, thin and sharp as a knife wound, cut across a face as white, as lifeless, as marble. Aryn gazed into black eyes and saw in them an eon of hatred, of death, of suffering. A moan escaped her.

"What an ugly little arm you have. Such a small and twisted thing. How you must hate it."

Shemal pointed a white finger. Aryn had lost the shield in the fall, and her withered right arm was exposed.

Somehow, despite her fear, Aryn smiled. Shemal was wrong. She had done what she had to; she knew who she was. "No, I don't hate it. It's part of who I am."

Shemal's thin lips curled in a sneer. "Really? Well, if you fancy that hideous little arm so much, then I shall mold the rest of you to match."

Aryn's smile shattered as Shemal brushed her cheek with a finger; her touch was like a cold dagger.

"Wither," the Necromancer crooned. "Wither . . ."

Aryn threw her head back and screamed.

45

Aryn had known pain before. Especially during the years of her tenth and eleventh winters, when she had been growing quickly, her right arm had often throbbed with a deep, bone-grinding ache, as if the withered appendage were straining to grow along with the rest of her—and failing. At night she would lie awake, pressing her face against her pillow, so the maids who attended her would not hear her sobs.

That pain was nothing to this: a pinprick compared to the thrust of a red-hot sword. She screamed again as Shemal clenched white fingers into a fist. It felt as if her flesh were clay, her bones wood. She had become a golem, a thing for the Necromancer to mold, to twist into a new shape. To break.

Sister, I am here.

The voice was like cool water flowing over scorched ground. The pain receded a fraction, so that Aryn was able to form words in her mind.

Lirith, is that you?

Yes, Sareth and I are right behind you. King Boreas and some of his men have fought their way close to Teravian, and we followed after.

I can't turn to look at you—I can't move.

It's Shemal's magic that paralyzes you. You must resist it.

The Necromancer's white face filled Aryn's vision like a cold, white moon.

I can't, Lirith. The pain ...

Do not think of it. I will take the pain away. You can do the rest—you have the power. I know it as Ivalaine did. There is none stronger in the Touch than you, sister.

Before Aryn could question those words, the pain vanished, and air rushed into her, revitalizing her. After the agony, the sensation of wholeness was almost too much to bear.

Do it now, sister!

There was something wrong. Lirith's voice had become oddly tight; her thread trembled.

Please, Aryn, before it's too late. You must strike out against the Necromancer.

But how? Shemal was ancient, once a goddess. And she was not truly alive. What power could possibly harm such a being?

Like a whisper in her ear, it came to Aryn—the answer was everywhere around her. Free of the pain, she reached out with the Touch. She gathered the shimmering threads of the Weirding and began to weave them together.

No—that was too slow. She needed far too many threads to fashion this pattern; she could never weave them fast enough.

Remember what Grace did that time at the bridge over the River Darkwine, when the krondrim *approached? She didn't shape the river with the Touch; instead she made herself into a vessel and let the river pour through her.*

Aryn let go of the threads, and she imagined herself as a thing hollow, empty—a cup waiting to be filled. Like an emerald flood, the power of the Weirding poured into her. Even as she felt she must burst with it, she reimagined herself not as a cup, but rather as a pipe: a conduit through which the power of the Weirding rushed. With a thought, Aryn directed all that magic—all the power of life—at the Necromancer.

This time it was Shemal who cried out. Aryn willed her eyes to see through the green veil of magic. Shemal stumbled back, her hands rising before her in a gesture of warding. The smooth marble of her face was scored with lines of pain; her mouth was open in a circle of astonishment.

A strength she had never known, had never guessed at, galvanized Aryn. She rose and held her arms out, drawing the power of the Weirding to her. It came from the men all around, and the witches who still stared and trembled, and even the horses who galloped by. It came from the grass beneath her feet, and from the ground beneath the grass, where even in the frozen depths of winter life endured, waiting to spring forth anew. It came from the sky, where birds flew, and from the waters of the river a league away, where silver fish swam beneath the ice. It came from the trees of Gloaming Wood, which hovered on the horizon, and from the land farther away than the eye could see. To Aryn, it felt as if the entire world was a shining web, and that she stood in the very center.

She pointed a finger at Shemal. The Necromancer bared her teeth, white and pointed against black gums. A hissing escaped her. She strained, trying to reach for Aryn, but the ancient being could not move—a spider caught in the web of life.

I'm doing it, Lirith! Aryn sent the triumphant words along the Weirding. *I'm holding her back!*

There was a pause, then Lirith's reply came back, weak and quavering. *I knew you could do it, sister.*

Fear cut through Aryn's exultation. Something was wrong with Lirith. Aryn sent her consciousness along the Weirding. At first she went too far, swept away by the force of the Weirding, and she was a bird soaring over the battlefield. She could see the chaos as warriors ran from Teravian's banner. There was Boreas, fighting with a knot of men, trying to get close to the prince. Nearby she saw herself and the Necromancer, both standing frozen, and Liendra's fallen body, and the witches in their green robes, clutching one another in fear. Just behind Aryn were two figures. Sareth brandished a sword, keeping Sai'el Ajhir at bay. Lirith knelt on the ground beside him, reeling back and forth on her knees, her eyes clamped shut, her dark, beautiful face wrought into a mask of suffering.

The feeling of ecstasy fled. Lirith had lied; she had not taken the pain of the Necromancer's spell away. She had taken it on herself.

Oh, Lirith...

You must not think of me, came the witch's faint reply. *We each must do what Sia has granted us power to do. I have my task, as you have yours. Now finish it. Destroy Shemal.*

In that moment, Aryn left the last innocent wisps of girlhood behind. She turned from her friend, whom she loved, and instead faced the enemy. She opened herself wider, letting all the power of the Weirding rush through her, into Shemal.

It wasn't enough. Shemal writhed, she clawed at the air, she hissed and spat, but she did not fall. She could not die, because she was already dead; the power of life could not destroy her, because she yet lived. It was no use.

The energy of the Weirding flowed through Aryn, as strong as ever, but she felt herself weakening. The vessel of her body was not made to bear the force of such magic. She felt herself being worn away, as stones over which a river flows. Only what took a river centuries would take the flood of the Weirding only a few more beats of the heart. Emerald light shone through Aryn's skin. Shemal's expression changed, from a grimace of agony to a smile of satisfaction.

I'm sorry, sister, Aryn tried to say, but her voice was lost in the roar of the flood. She felt as transparent and brittle as glass. Another moment, and it would all be over.

"Stand away from her, fiend!" commanded a booming voice.

With the last of her strength, Aryn gazed through the haze of magic. She saw a group of knights on proud chargers, their armor gleaming in the morning light. Their leader leaped to the ground. It was King Boreas, his face handsome and terrible in its wrath. Shemal flicked her gaze in his direction; loathing filled her black eyes, but she could move no other part of her. Boreas drew his sword.

"Heed my command, Creature of Darkness—I said get away from my daughter!"

The king thrust with his sword.

It was forged of mundane metal; the blade should never have been able to pierce a being such as she. However, the magic of the Weirding still crackled around her, through her, binding her. The sword pierced her body, biting deeply as Boreas leaned forward, plunging it through her chest, so that the blade thrust out the back of her robe, slicked with black blood. The Necromancer stared with wide eyes, her white hands fluttering around the sword's hilt embedded in her chest.

"The spell, Aryn!" It was Sareth, shouting behind her. "You've got to break the spell. It's killing her!"

Aryn gazed, not with her eyes, but with the power of the Weirding. Sareth's face was carved with lines of anguish. On the ground before him lay a corpse: Ajhir. Another figure lay beside him as well. It was Lirith, it had to be. She wore the same rust-colored gown; she had the same luxuriant black hair. Only instead of the witch's supple figure, inside the gown was a small thing, dark and twisted. Legs coiled back on themselves like roots; stunted arms reached up from too-long sleeves, ending in fingers thin and gnarled as twigs. Her black eyes gazed, not from a smooth, beautiful face, but from a visage as wizened as one of last year's apples left to dry in the sun.

Aryn let go of the Weirding. Power ceased to flow into her,

but there was still too much within her, and the shell of her body had grown too brittle. The magic would shatter her if she did not direct it elsewhere.

There was no time to consider the wisdom of it. With a thought, Aryn redirected the power of the Weirding away from the Necromancer and into Lirith.

Lirith's crooked jaw opened in a croaking sound. Sareth screamed as well, for Aryn was too weak to properly control the magic. He dropped the sword and fell to his knees, huddling over Lirith, as a cocoon of green light wove around them, so brilliant they were lost to sight.

Aryn staggered—she felt so weak, so cold and empty, now that the power of the Weirding no longer flowed through her. She would have fallen, but strong arms caught her. She gazed up into the king's grim face.

"My lady," he said, his voice hoarse, his eyes bright with concern. "My lady, are you well?"

Words were beyond her, but she managed a nod. She was dimly aware of many knights all around them. The king and his men must have fought through the confusion to her. She was also aware of Teravian standing nearby. Warriors gripped his arms, but he did not struggle. His face was ashen, and his eyes seemed blind as he stared forward.

Those eyes went wide. "Father!" Teravian shouted. "Behind you!"

Boreas whirled around, still holding Aryn, and what she saw sent a spike of terror deep into her heart. Shemal had not fallen to the ground, but still stood. She wrapped white hands around the hilt of the sword and pulled it from her chest. She licked the black blood from her lips, then smiled as she held the sword before her.

"You are a fool," she said, and her lifeless eyes were not fixed on the king, but on Aryn. "You should have finished your spell. You should have sacrificed yourself to slay me. Now look what your error has cost you. For I am not undone. And you will still die."

Shemal thrust the sword toward Aryn's heart.

Boreas roared. He gripped Aryn in strong arms, spinning her

around, away from the Necromancer, then pushed her from him. She stumbled away from the king.

There was a wet sound, followed by a soft exhalation of air, like a gasp of amazement. A silence fell over the field; all the men stared, unmoving, as if a spell had bound them. Slowly, Aryn turned around.

Boreas gazed at her, his mouth open, an expression she had never seen before in his eyes: a look of puzzlement.

"So," the king said, and as he spoke blood bubbled from his lips. He sank down to his knees, then looked down at the point of the sword that jutted from the center of his chest.

Shemal stood behind him, a satisfied expression on her face. "Not what I intended," she said, "but effective all the same." She jerked the sword free.

Blood gushed from Boreas's mouth in a flood. His eyes rolled up, and he fell face forward onto the hard turf.

Like the knights, Aryn was frozen, unable to move. She could only stare at the fallen king. However, Teravian broke free of the men holding him and rushed forward.

"No!" he cried out, throwing himself down beside the king. "Father!"

A smirk sliced across Shemal's face. "You little liar," she crooned. "You loved him after all, didn't you? And yet you've betrayed him. How pathetic."

Teravian bowed his head over the king. Shemal drifted closer. She laid a hand on his shoulder. He flinched but did not pull away.

"Now," she intoned in her sepulchral voice, "weave the spell. Bring the bull back into the sky, and call the Warriors of Vathris to you. They will yet follow you."

He looked up, his gray eyes stricken.

"That's it, my beautiful prince! Weave the magic. You know what you must do."

"Yes," he murmured. "Yes, I do."

The prince shut his eyes and held out his hands. Shemal looked on, gloating.

Aryn . . .

She went rigid as the voice spoke in her mind. It was Teravian.

Aryn, you have to help me.

What? she managed to cast the word back.

Gods, Aryn, don't be so thick, not now. We only have a moment. She can't hear us speak across the Weirding, but she'll get suspicious in a few seconds if I don't conjure the illusion of the bull again. We have to cast the spell.

What spell?

This ...

He abandoned words. Instead, his thread drew close, connecting with her own, and knowledge came to her. Terrible knowledge.

Horror filled her, and regret. How long had he woven alone and in secret, knowing that failure would mean his death, knowing that success would mean the same?

Never mind that, Aryn. I crafted this spell for so long, only today I realized it wouldn't work—I didn't have the power to cast it alone. But you can help me. Do it now. Not for me, for the king.

The words were like a slap, clearing the uncertainty from Aryn's mind. She gripped Teravian's thread, and as he revealed the pattern to her, she wove with all her strength and skill.

Teravian wove with her, so fast she could not keep up with him. His skill with the Weirding was great—greater than her own, greater even than Grace's. But his power wasn't enough; he could not complete the pattern on his own.

Aryn joined her shining hands with his. Once again she opened herself, letting all the magic of the Weirding flow through her, and she felt his astonishment. His skill was great, honed in countless lonely hours, but her power ran deeper, flowing from the well of her soul. With every hateful look at her arm, with every person who had recoiled from her in disgust, she had dug the well a little farther, into the very foundation of of her being. There she had struck bedrock, and a spring from which power welled forth. It did not matter what others thought of her; she knew who and what she was. She was a woman. She was a queen.

She was a witch.

The spell was complete. It shone between Aryn and Teravian:

a net as pure as starlight, holding within it a shadow darker than death.

"I do not see the bull!" Shemal snapped. "What are you doing, boy? You're casting a spell, I can see it. Do not lie to me again, or I'll slit your throat." She clutched his hair with a hand and held the sword against his neck.

Now! Aryn shouted in her mind.

Together, she and Teravian cast the shimmering net at Shemal.

Against the Weirding, the Necromancer appeared as a void, a place of darkness where no threads wove. Then the net struck her, wrapping itself around her, outlining her in light. At the same time the shadow inside the net found the hole in her body made by King Boreas's sword. The shadow entered her; the net vanished. The spell was done.

Aryn and Teravian opened their eyes. Shemal staggered back and dropped the sword. She held up her hands. Thin black lines marred her skin, like cracks in porcelain. Even as they watched, the lines multiplied, lengthened, snaking up her arms. They appeared on her face, turning it into a shattered mask. Then the lines grew darker, thicker.

"What have you done?" she hissed. Her voice rose to a shriek. "What have you done to me, you wretched children?"

"You are neither dead nor alive," Teravian said, his gaze fixed on her. "So we've given you those things you could never have. The gift of life—and of mortality."

"No!" Shemal cried out, and in that sound was such poison, such hatred, that men covered their ears and horses screamed. Like a flock of crows, shadows gathered around the body of the Necromancer, concealing her with black wings, then flew away, leaving only emptiness in their wake. Shemal was gone.

Aryn cast a stunned look at Teravian. "Is she dead?"

"No, not yet at least. She is only fled. But now that she's mortal, she'll feel all the weight of the eon she has dwelled upon this world. She won't come back. Please, Aryn, help me."

He was lifting King Boreas's shoulders from the ground, and Aryn assisted him, and they laid the king's head upon Teravian's lap. Blood still stained Boreas's lips, and his flesh was the color of ashes. His eyes were shut.

"He's dead," Teravian said softly, wonderingly. "He was so strong—I could never be as strong as he was. Only I'm alive, and he's dead."

Aryn only shook her head, unable to form words. Sorrow was like a knife in her heart. She touched the king's face with trembling fingers. Faint but clear, she sensed one last glimmer of life, like the flare of a candle just before it sputters and goes out.

I love you! she cried out to the darkness. *My king, my true father. I love you with all my heart!*

No words came in reply, but she felt warmth, love, pride. He felt no pain; he regretted nothing.

She wept openly now. "I sense him still."

Teravian gripped her shoulders. Hard. "Tell him. Tell him that I didn't betray him." Tears ran down his cheeks. "Tell him I would have given my life for him."

Aryn met Teravian's haunted eyes. "He knows."

The candle flared, went out. The thread, as bright as steel, went dark. Boreas, King of Calavan, was dead.

A chant rose on the air, deep and thrumming. Men had gathered in a circle around them, and they were speaking a lament in low voices.

> *May he dwell in the halls of Vathranan now*
> *May his blood bring life to the land*
> *May he feel the winds of Vathranan now*
> *He sits at the right hand of Vathris*

A gentle touch on Aryn's shoulder. "Sister?"

She turned and gazed into warm brown eyes that looked out from a smooth, dark face. It was Lirith, shapely and perfect as Aryn knew her. She gripped Lirith's slender hand with her own withered one.

"You're whole," Aryn breathed. "By Sia, you're whole."

Lirith smiled. "As whole as I can be. Thanks to you. Your magic undid the spell of the Necromancer."

"I think it did more than that, *beshala*."

They looked at Sareth, who stood above them. He pointed down, to his feet planted firmly on the ground. One foot was shod in leather. The other foot was bare and perfectly formed. The women looked back up. In his hands, Sareth held a length of carved wood. His peg leg.

Lirith leaped to her feet and threw her arms around him. "Sareth—oh, Sareth."

He held her tight, his expression one of wonder. *"Beshala,"* was all he said, stroking her black hair. "My beloved."

Aryn looked down at her hands. The right was still withered. Why had the magic not made her whole like Sareth?

Because you are whole, Teravian spoke in her mind, and he placed his right hand over hers.

She looked up, into his eyes, and nodded.

When their threads touched, she had learned more than just how to weave the spell he had devised to harm Shemal. She had glimpsed his memories as well. King Boreas had known of the Witches' plot to use Teravian against the Warriors of Vathris; it was Ivalaine herself who had told the king, and he in turn had told Teravian. Their counterplot was simple: Teravian would let Liendra and the Witches think they had his allegiance. He would get close to them, learn what they were planning, and reveal it to the king before they could succeed.

Only Boreas and Ivalaine had not counted on the presence of the Necromancer. Shemal had made it clear to Teravian that if he revealed her presence, she would slay his mother and father. Teravian had known she had the power to do it, and so he had been bound, unable to tell the king the full truth. However, even as he did Shemal's bidding, in secret he probed her, sought out her weaknesses, and devised a spell that could do harm to her.

"The spell would have killed you," Aryn said. "You would have poured your whole life into it, and it would have taken you. Only it still wouldn't have been enough."

Despite the grimness of his face, a smile touched his lips. "Only it was enough—because you were there."

He sighed, then laid Boreas gently back on the ground. Around them, the men continued their chant.

"So now what do we do?" Sareth said, still holding on to Lirith, his gaze on the fallen king.

Aryn gripped Teravian's hand. "They will still follow you. The Warriors saw you drive Shemal away, they've seen you weep over your father. They know you were true to him. All you have to do is create the illusion of the bull again."

"No, Aryn." His expression was resolute. "I'll work no more illusions. I think Liendra's cronies have all fled, but the men saw them, and her body is still here. They know I was in league with the Witches. They'll never follow me."

"It's true, I fear," Lirith said. "I've seen what would happen if you take that path. The men would turn against you, the Warriors would lay down their swords and return to their homes."

Aryn looked up at the witch. "Then what can we do?"

"They won't follow me," Teravian said. "But there's another whom they will."

Sareth looked as puzzled as Aryn felt, but Lirith nodded. "I see it as well. There is still one the Warriors of Vathris will follow north to Gravenfist Keep."

This was too much for Aryn. "But Boreas is gone. Who are you talking about?"

"You," Teravian said, touching her cheek. "I'm talking about you, Aryn."

Her mouth dropped open. This was madness. However, before she could speak, ruby-colored light permeated the air. The chanting of the men ceased, replaced by gasps and murmurs. Aryn followed their gaze upward.

Crimson light filled the sky; the dawn had come. Only dawn had already come. How could there be two suns in the sky?

One of the fiery orbs shrank in on itself, descending from the sky, alighting on the ground before Aryn. The light dimmed—but did not vanish—revealing a small girl clad in a gray shift. Her feet were bare, and her tangled red hair blew back from her scarred face.

Despite her sorrow, despite her weariness, wonder filled Aryn. And hope.

"Tira," she said. "How is it you're here?"

The girl laughed and threw her arms around Aryn.

"No!" came a strangled cry.

Fear replaced wonder, and Aryn looked up. Lirith had gone rigid; Sareth gripped her.

Aryn gently pushed Tira away and rose, moving to the witch. "Sister, what is it?"

Lirith's hands curled into claws. Her voice was hoarse, chantlike. "The gates of winter have opened. The Pale King rides forth, his army behind him like a sea of darkness."

The men in earshot let out oaths and made warding motions with their hands. Teravian leaped to his feet.

"It's all been for nothing," the prince said, clutching Aryn's arm. "It will take us a fortnight to march to Gravenfist. Queen Grace will never hold out for so long."

A buzzing filled Aryn, as well as understanding. "You're wrong. It *has* been for something. Grace won't have to hold the keep for long before we can get there."

Teravian looked at her as though she were mad, but Aryn knelt beside Tira. She touched the girl's scarred face. "Have you come to take us to Grace?"

Tira shook her head. "Durge," she said.

46.

It was almost showtime.

Sage Carson, Pastor of the Steel Cathedral, watched in the mirror as the stylist arranged his hair. Her touch was light and deft. With each flick of the brush she coaxed several coal black strands into precise formation, then locked them into place with a puff of hairspray.

He admired her work; it wasn't so different from his own. Find the stragglers and individualists, those who strayed from the flock, and bring them into line. It was those who chose to deviate from the herd that brought unhappiness—to others and themselves. The world would be a better place if everyone followed the same path. The right path. And Carson had spent the last twenty years making sure his path was the one everyone else followed.

A knock came at the door of the dressing room. The door opened, and the head of Kyle Naughton, one of the young assistant producers, popped through.

"Twenty minutes to airtime, Mr. Carson. Everything's ready onstage, and the choir is warming up."

Carson started to nod, then stopped. The stylist was still brushing.

"Thank you, Kyle. I'll be out soon. I think it's going to be a special show tonight."

Kyle grinned and gave a thumbs-up. He adjusted his headset, then retreated through the door, closing it.

Seeing the clean-cut young man now, it was hard to remember that just four years ago Kyle had been a drug addict who had sold his body to whoever would pay in order to buy his next fix. Carson had found him on East Colfax, not long after first coming to Denver. In those days, Carson's show hadn't been what it was now—the number-one-rated television program in all of Colorado. To help get the word out—his word—he would take to the streets, driving through the darkest parts of the city.

When his car stopped, Kyle had climbed in, thinking Carson just another trick. Then Carson had shown him another path; Kyle had been with him ever since. They were all so loyal—his flock, his followers.

"How long have you been with me, Mary?"

The stylist didn't pause in her work, but in the mirror he saw a smile appear on her lips.

"It'll be nineteen years this summer, Mr. Carson."

Mary had been one of the very first to come to him. She had worked for him when he began his first show on a public cable-access channel, taping his sermons in an abandoned gas station outside of Topeka. First people had ignored him, then they had laughed at him. The ministers in their fancy churches had been so proud, so righteous. They had said he wasn't a true pastor, that he was a charlatan. They had thought, just because they had official pieces of paper on their walls, that they were better than he.

Well, he had left Kansas behind, and no one could laugh anymore. He commanded the Steel Cathedral. Two thousand people came every weekday to see him. Hundreds of thousands more watched his show. And his Saturday night broadcasts—like tonight's—were the most popular of all. You didn't need a degree to talk to God, to talk for him. All you had to do was believe.

"You're a good soul, Mary," he said.

Her smile deepened. She was sixty, he supposed, but still pretty. She didn't seem to age anymore. Nor did young Kyle Naughton.

"Thank you, Mr. Carson."

"You can go now, Mary. I'd like to be alone, to prepare myself."

Without a word she set down the brush, then left the dressing room, shutting the door behind her.

Carson removed the towel that covered his shoulders—carefully, so as not to muss his crisp white suit—then gazed at himself in the mirror. He always took ten minutes before the show to himself. This was his time to gather his thoughts, his time to think about what he was going to say to his flock.

His time to listen to the Big Voice.

Carson would never forget the day he first heard the Voice. It had come in his darkest moment, just over four years ago. The unbelievers in Kansas had finally rallied against him. They had seized the cable-access channel that aired his show, claiming it was needed for use by the public schools. And no doubt they would indeed use the channel to teach their lies about evolution, and to show students those lessons in fornication they called sex education.

Despite his prayers, his last sermon was cut off in mid broadcast. He and his followers were escorted out of the recording studio by the police. It was over. As so often happened in this wicked world, the unbelievers had won.

Then the Big Voice had spoken to him.

At first he thought he was going insane. He had become weak in his despair, and he turned to alcohol, which he hadn't touched since starting his ministry. However, still the Big Voice spoke to him: deep, thunderous. Over those next days he had tried to shut it out, but nothing—not cotton in his ears, not loud music, not the pounding water of a cold shower—could stop it. Finally, he had lain down on his bed, and he had listened.

I will gather many followers to you, the Voice said, and though it was only in his mind, it was as clear as if it came over the radio with the sound turned up all the way. *You will have a great flock at your command.*

"How?" he had dared to whisper to the water-stained ceiling

of the motel where he had holed up. His heart had ached with longing; he wanted to believe. "How can that happen now?"

You must believe in me, the Voice said. *And you must do as I tell you.*

He did. The first thing the Big Voice told him to do was to pack his things, to take what few followers would come with him, and to go to Denver, that he would find everything he needed there.

Carson didn't see how that could be true, but he did as he was told. Early on he realized that everything the Big Voice told him was true. It told him men in suits would come to his motel and bring him the money he needed, and the next morning they did. At the time he didn't recognize the name of their company, though he had come to know it and its crescent moon logo well in ensuing years. They were servants of the Big Voice, just as he was.

In return for the money, he gave the men messages from the Voice. The men in suits knew of the Big Voice, but it was hard for them to hear it. Carson found that difficult to believe; to him the Voice was like a trumpet in his head. Yet it was true. The Voice would speak to him, and he would relay its message to others. He was touched. He was a prophet.

But a prophet of whom? In those first months, even years, it had been easy to believe it was God who spoke to him.

Who are you? he would speak into the darkness, kneeling on the floor, hands clasped together.

I am the end, the Voice said. *And I am the beginning. I will be the destroyer of all things. And I will be the maker of all things as well.*

These words filled Carson with dread, but they also brought a quickening to his blood. The world was fouled and corrupted. Was not the only way to cleanse it to destroy it and make it anew?

In Denver, Carson's congregation grew rapidly. The men and women in suits, the ones from the company called Duratek, wrote him check after check. With that money he built a church, and the followers poured through the doors to listen to him preach. Then the owner of one of the Denver television stations called him and gave him a show. More people came through the doors of the church, rich and poor, young and old, all looking for an answer to the emptiness in their lives.

Soon the church was too small, and he drew up plans for a cathedral, one so high it would rival the mountains, and so strong nothing could shake its foundation—a cathedral of steel. He felt fear when he went to Duratek; he knew it would cost an enormous sum of money. However, the Duratek lawyers wrote the checks, and building began. Carson chided himself. He should never have doubted.

Except, deep in the most secret recesses of his heart, he did doubt. As time went on, as the cathedral climbed ever higher toward the sky, a fear grew in him.

It was all so good. Too good. The Big Voice had given him what he had always wanted—a great flock to follow him—but what did it want in return? He relayed the words of the Voice to the agents of Duratek Corporation on a regular basis, but that was hardly a burden. Like the Voice, they seemed to want little of him; they never asked to be mentioned as a sponsor of his show in exchange for the checks they wrote him. It didn't make sense; surely the Voice wanted more of him. However, when he asked, it never told him what.

Gather your followers unto you. That is all I ask.

For now, Carson would add to himself. But what would the Voice seek later in return for what it had granted him? That seed of doubt sprouted in him, blossoming like a dark flower, and in time he began to fear that the Big Voice was not truly the voice of God, but rather the voice of Satan.

It seemed impossible. The Voice in his head was deep and ancient and beautiful. But was not Lucifer the fairest of the angels before he was cast out of heaven? Did not the Devil tempt with sweet words and promises? He brought people to him not with fire and sword, but by giving them what they most wanted.

For over a year, Carson had struggled with this fear, though he did not show any outward signs of it. Even those in his inner circle didn't sense his doubt. His show climbed in the ratings, and construction of the Steel Cathedral proceeded according to schedule.

At last his new church, his new house, was completed. On that day Carson at last understood the truth, and it was even more terrible than his darkest fears. The Big Voice was not God, and nor was it Satan. It was something else, something other. More real, more present, and more powerful than anything dreamed of by the hearts of men.

It was not God.

It was *a* god.

The day draws close, the Big Voice spoke to him that night he stood on the empty stage of the Steel Cathedral and imagined the audience that would fill the ocean of seats for the first time the next day. *Soon the gate will open, and I will leave this forsaken world. My exile will be over, and I will return. The world will tremble beneath my feet, and night will fall forever.*

The world. When the Voice spoke that word, a vision formed in Carson's mind, only he saw not the world he knew, this Earth, but a different place, one distant, yet strangely close at hand. A world of possibility.

He began to understand, though not completely. In that moment he realized how far beyond him all of this was. Yet he probed where he could, asking what questions he dared of the agents of Duratek. He would color the words of the Big Voice he was to relay to them, or even speak small falsehoods to see how they reacted. That was how he came to know he was right; the world the Big Voice spoke of was not this world. It was another world, a world from which the Voice came. A world to which Duratek intended to go.

When at last he learned this, it occurred to Carson to flee back over the dusty plains to Kansas. Except that was impossible. He couldn't give up what he had wrought here; no matter how it had come to him, he loved his cathedral and his followers. Besides, if they sensed his doubt, it would all be over. They would discard him and find someone new, another prophet to raise in his place.

Or they would find a way to make him obey.

It had begun not long after he started preaching in the Steel Cathedral. *Your flock has grown great in number,* the Big Voice told him. *It is time for you to offer up a lamb on the altar to the one who brought your followers to you.*

At first it was just one or two at a time. Carson culled them from his congregation with care. He chose those least likely to be missed: the homeless, the lonely, or the elderly who had been abandoned by their families. The Angels of Light came and led them away.

He was terrified the first time the Angels appeared, but the Big Voice told him not to fear them. Still, he did. They were tall and beautiful to behold, thin as wisps inside the halos of silvery light that followed them. Their eyes were like large jewels, and they had no mouths. Nor did they have wings. Weren't angels supposed to have wings?

What was done to the people after the Angels of Light took them away, Carson didn't know, at least not at first, but when he saw them again they were ... different. Their faces were smoother, calmer. Harder. A fervent light shone in their eyes.

Their hearts are strong now, the Big Voice told Carson when he asked what had been done to them. *Their doubts have been taken away.*

As time passed, Carson began to think it was something else that had been taken from them, something warm and human. Then, one night, he grew bold enough to follow the Angels of Light. He watched what they did with an old homeless man in a chamber deep beneath the cathedral, and he learned the truth. Iron. They were given hearts of iron.

He had fled, and had not said anything about it. He didn't dare, not if he didn't want his own doubts, his own heart, to be taken by the Angels of Light. Soon it was not one or two at a time, but three or four or five. Every day, the Big Voice asked for more, and every day it grew harder to find people in the congregation who would not be missed.

Finally, over the course of the last week, Carson had grown desperate. The homeless people of Denver had grown wary; there were no longer enough who could be lured to the cathedral with the promise of charity. Carson no longer cared if those he selected had husbands and wives, sons and daughters. Any who seemed weak and lost enough, who could be persuaded that something better than this life awaited them, were led to the Angels of Light. The reports of the missing were all over the news.

"Speak to me," Carson whispered, gazing at the mirror.

The man gazing back had an ageless, slightly plastic quality, as if the thick makeup he had worn all these years had been bonded to his face by the hot stage lights.

"Please," he whispered. "Tell me what to do."

Silence. He stared at the mirror. There—Mary had missed a lock of hair. It stood out. He picked up the brush, but his hand trembled. More hairs strayed from formation, falling out of line. He would have to call Mary back.

More, spoke the Voice in his mind. *I want more.*

The brush slipped from his hand and clattered to the floor.

"I can't," he murmured. "The police are getting suspicious. I received a phone call from an officer yesterday. A Sergeant Otero."

The men of Duratek will deal with this Sergeant Otero. The end of all things comes soon. You have nothing to fear, as long as you are faithful to me.

Carson clenched the arms of the chair. "I have always been faithful to you."

Yes, so do not fail me now, when my time is close at hand. A great battle comes, the likes of which this world has never seen. Soon my servants will open the way for me, and when they do, I must have an army to march at my side.

There was a pause, a blessed silence. Then, *The Angels of Light come. Have more people for them to take. Do not make them take you instead.*

A roaring sound filled his ears, and he leaned over in the chair. Nausea clenched his gut, and his head spun, as it always did when the Big Voice was done talking with him.

When the dizziness had mostly passed, he sat up and turned the chair toward a closed-circuit television in the wall. It displayed a camera shot of the half-full auditorium; his flock was already gathering. He fumbled for a remote control and pressed a button.

The scene on the TV changed, showing another view of the auditorium: smiling people, their faces expectant, hopeful. No, they looked as though they were loved, as if they would be missed. That wouldn't do. He couldn't risk more interest from the police, no matter what the Big Voice said. Carson pushed the button again, and again.

He stopped. Now the TV showed a pair of unshaven men in

mismatched clothes sitting near the back of the auditorium: a small, pudgy, bald fellow whose face was wrought into a permanent glare, and a gaunt man, perhaps Native American, his face placid, his big hands folded in his lap.

Carson set down the remote control. Relief washed through him, and he shut his eyes. *Those two fellows,* he spoke to the darkness inside his mind as he pictured the two homeless men. *Take those two.*

His eyes opened. That was it. Ones with hearts of iron would approach the two in the audience, would tell them they had been chosen for a special meeting, and would lead them away. They wouldn't resist; no one ever did. After all, who wouldn't want to meet an angel?

Carson lifted a fluttering hand, trying to smooth his mussed hair back into place, but he only made things worse. Sweat beaded his makeup; it was beginning to run. Mary would have to powder it. Yes, he had to call for Mary.

Carson reached out, but instead of picking up the phone, he opened a drawer. Inside was a large envelope. He opened it and pulled out a sheet of film. He held it up to the lights that surrounded the mirror.

It was an X ray. He could see his spine, his ribs, his heart, and the pale outlines of his lungs like the wings of an angel. Only one of the wings was marred by a dark blot.

The doctors had first detected it a year ago. They told him they had to do a biopsy, that the rate at which it was growing suggested it was malignant. He had told them no, that it was up to God to heal him. However, each time he went to the doctors, the blot was larger—a shadow reaching out to replace his own heart. God had not healed him. Soon, God would call him home.

Or would God cast him down into the fiery pits of Hell for what he had done?

Forgive me, he prayed. Not to the Big Voice, but to something purer, more distant. *Please forgive me. Show me how I can redeem myself before you take me.*

No answer came to him, but the silence was as sweet as a benediction. Man's mortal ears were not fit for the voice of God. He knew that now, if he knew anything at all.

Another knock at the door. "Ten minutes, Mr. Carson."

He bent down and picked up the hairbrush, clenching his fingers around the handle until they no longer trembled. Then Sage Carson brushed his hair.

47.

The streets of Denver slipped past the windows of the car; the tinted glass cast the world into premature night.

Travis sighed. Was that what the world—both worlds—would be like if Mohg stepped through the gate to Eldh? He was the Lord of Nightfall. If he ruled, would the sun ever rise again? Or would all things be forever shrouded in gloom?

"What is it, Travis?" Vani sat beside him on the backseat of the car, Beltan next to her. She hesitated, then touched his hand. "Are you afraid of what we do?"

He turned from the window and grinned despite the churning of his stomach. "How could I be afraid of anything when you and Beltan are here?"

"Hey," Anders said in a wounded tone, turning around in the front seat. "What are Deirdre and I—chopped liver?"

Travis laughed. This was completely absurd. It was five of them against a fortress of steel. Then again, he couldn't think of five other people in the world—in any world—who would have a better chance of getting in there than they did. That was, if they had any chance at all.

Outside the windows, sharp towers jutted into the dusky sky. The car came to a halt.

"Do you have the videotape?" Deirdre said to Anders.

He slapped the breast pocket of his suit coat. "Got it right here, safe and sound."

Deirdre switched off the ignition. "All right, everyone, put on your most pious faces. Remember, we're just a group of audience members. We love Sage Carson's show, and we can't wait to speak a few prayers."

Beltan gave an enthusiastic nod. "I'll speak my prayers to Vathris."

Anders cleared his throat. "Wrong god, mate."

"Nonsense," Beltan said. "Vathris is the god of warriors. What other god would I speak my prayers to?"

"Well, the thing is, according to these folks, there's only one god."

Beltan scowled. "That hardly gives a person much of a choice."

"I think that's sort of the point," Deirdre said. "Entire nations have gone to war to prove not just that their god is the right one, but the only one."

The blond knight let out a breath of exasperation. "I've never heard of such foolishness. Why shouldn't people be able to follow the god that best suits them? I'm beginning to think this is a very silly world."

"I won't argue with you there," Anders said, and got out of the car.

They joined the crowds of people hurrying across the gigantic parking lot, huddled inside their coats. It was too cold to talk, but there was no need; they had spent all day back at the hotel going over the plan. Such as it was.

"I was right," Anna Ferraro had said after she showed up at their suite last night. After he told her what they wanted to do. "You really are a complete nut, aren't you?"

Travis had laughed. "You still came."

Some of her annoyance changed into astonishment. She nodded, and he closed the door behind her.

For the next several hours, he and the others had watched while Ferraro spoke with Dr. Larsen. At first the reporter was skeptical; investigative journalists had been trying to pin all sorts of misdoings on Duratek for years, only to no avail. Then Larsen popped the disk into Deirdre's computer, and all of them watched the evidence flicker across the screen—the memos, the reports, the results of the tests performed on human subjects. Doubt wasn't an option; not only had Duratek created Electria, they were behind the entire trade in the illegal drug.

Ferraro pulled a small digital video camera out of a bag, a glint in her eyes. "Let's get to work, Doctor. We've got a multinational corporation to bring down."

They had done the interview there in the suite. Ferraro had

wanted to bring Kevin, the photojournalist she had worked with at the television station, but Travis had told her to come alone, so she set up the shot herself. She interviewed Larsen on the couch for over an hour. They had printed out some of the most damning pieces of evidence, and Larsen held them up for the camera as she spoke in precise sentences.

Once they were done, Deirdre downloaded the video to her computer, and Larsen cut the piece together, muttering an almost constant stream of profanities.

"I'm a reporter, not an editor," she growled and lit another cigarette.

She kept working, and by midnight it was done. They exported two copies out to tape. One for Ferraro, and one for the rest of them. In addition, Deirdre duplicated the disk. After they were done, Travis looked at Ferraro.

"So, do you think this will save your career?"

The reporter picked up one of the tapes. "Screw my career. This will save lives." She slipped it into her camera bag.

"I'm sorry in advance for bringing it up," Anders said, "but what's going to happen to the doc here?" He glanced at Larsen, who sat motionless on the couch. "After all, she took part in some illicit activities herself at Duratek."

"Immunity," Ferraro said, turning toward Larsen. "The government will give you immunity in a heartbeat if you promise to testify for them. You'd be wise to take it."

Larsen's eyes were frightened; she nodded.

The weekday edition of Carson's show, *Hour of Salvation*, aired in the afternoon. However, tomorrow's show was the Saturday edition, which was broadcast in the evening. Ferraro made a phone call—she was jobless, but she still had friends in the business—and scored five tickets to the production.

"Thank you," Travis told her before she left, not knowing what else to say.

She hesitated at the door. "Air that tape. Tell the truth about those bastards. That's all the thanks I need."

Then the door shut, and she was gone. Ferraro had taken Dr. Larsen with her. The two women were going to hole up in Ferraro's apartment, then they were heading straight to the police once the story broke. If the story broke.

The five of them reached the doors of the Steel Cathedral. Spires of glass and metal soared overhead, like claws raking the darkening sky. They waited their turn in line, held out their tickets, and passed through.

As they entered the cathedral, Travis kept waiting for an alarm to sound, for a voice to blare over the loudspeaker. *Alert! Unbelievers! Infidels! Alert!*

However, nothing happened, and they moved along unnoticed with everyone else. It was a varied crowd. Upscale, working-class, jobless. Small children in strollers and elderly hobbling on canes. The only common denominator was the look on their faces: desperate, empty, searching. These were people who needed something, anything to believe in, and Sage Carson had given it to them: hope, salvation. Too bad all of it was a lie.

Travis craned his neck as they passed through the soaring lobby, trying to see if there was any sign of Marty and Jay. By now the two men probably thought he had abandoned them, and he supposed he had. However, he wanted them to know why, to know how important this was.

There was no sign of them. Travis sighed, letting the crowd jostle him forward. He was being swept toward the doors that led to the auditorium. Beltan gripped his arm, pulling him aside. He found himself and the others pressed close to a wall, behind a group of potted trees.

"Well, we made it in," Deirdre said, her smoky jade eyes serious. "Then again, that was the easy part."

Their plan was simple: get to the control room that housed the show's production facilities, take over, put in the videotape, and play it on the gigantic television screen that dominated the back of the stage where Sage Carson preached. There was just one problem with simple plans—they never seemed to stay simple for long. According to the blueprints of the cathedral, the control room was backstage; there were bound to be security guards. Besides, there was something else Travis intended to do while he was here.

"You've got the radios?" Anders said to Vani and Beltan. "And you're sure you know how to use them?"

Vani's eyes flashed gold. "We know." The assassin wore

slacks and a loose-fitting blouse, but Travis could hear the faint creak of her leathers beneath.

Anders held up his hands. "Just checking, sweetheart. No need to think about stabbing anyone."

"Vani doesn't need knives to kill people," Beltan said with a cheerful grin.

"No, just a look," Anders muttered.

It was time to go into action before their nerves got the better of them. "It's fifteen minutes until showtime," Travis said. "We'd better get moving." He looked at Beltan, then Vani. "Good luck." It was all he could think to say.

"We'll see you soon, Travis," Beltan said.

Vani only gazed at him, then the two turned and disappeared into the crowd.

"Come on," Deirdre said, touching Travis's arm.

The plans of the Steel Cathedral that Deirdre's mysterious Philosopher friend had sent were shockingly detailed. The drawing showed a guard station at the main entrance to the backstage area. There was another way to get backstage, through a smaller maintenance corridor. There was a guard station there as well, but the plans noted it was staffed by a single guard. That was the direction Travis, Deirdre, and Anders headed.

It was easy to blend in with the crowds of people buying souvenir pins, T-shirts, and CDs before heading to their seats. Travis caught sight of several security guards; patches with the crescent moon of the Duratek logo were sewn to their dark blue uniforms. However, the guards never even looked in their direction. It seemed odd there were so few of them, yet it made sense. What was there to guard up here?

The gate is below the cathedral, Travis. The blueprints showed a whole complex of rooms down there. This building is far larger than it has to be to hold two thousand people. It wasn't built this way to catch God's attention; it was built to hide what they're doing.

They ducked down a narrow side corridor.

"All right, partner," Anders said. "If the map your spooky little Philosopher chum gave you is spot on, the maintenance corridor is right through there."

"It is," Deirdre said, approaching a door.

"Wait," Travis said, panic rising. "That sign says an alarm will sound if the door is opened."

Anders winked at him. "Don't believe everything you read, mate." He pulled a small black device—about the size of a quarter, but thicker—from his pocket. He pressed it to the door, and some adhesive held it in place. A red light on the device flashed.

"It's activated," he said to Deirdre.

She pushed through the door. Travis hunched his shoulders, bracing for the wail of an alarm. There was only silence.

"Hey there, Travis, what are you waiting for?" Anders said, and followed Deirdre through the door.

Travis let out a tight breath and headed after them. He caught up to the Seekers on the other side. The door shut behind them.

Travis looked at Anders. "What was that thing?"

"An electronic scrambler. It sends out electromagnetic pulses over a small area, pretty much befuddling any electronic gadget in range—including the motion sensor on that door. Pretty handy, eh?"

They moved down the corridor, and Deirdre raised a small black device to her ear.

"Vani, Beltan—can you hear me?"

There was a crackle of static, then a voice emanated from the radio, tinny but familiar. Vani. "We can hear you."

"We're in position," Deirdre spoke into the radio. "Can you see the main guard station?"

"We can. There are two guards. One stands at attention, while the other watches a number of screens that show pictures of places in this building. One of the screens shows a guard station in a narrow corridor; I believe it is the corridor you are in now. There is one guard there, a woman. She does not look very large or strong."

"Good work," Deirdre said. "Are you and Beltan ready?"

"Do not fear—we will not fail you."

"I hope we can say the same." Deirdre slipped the radio into her pocket, then looked at Travis and Anders, her cheekbones sharp. "Let's go. If Vani and Beltan do their job right, we won't have to wait long."

They moved down the corridor, Deirdre first, Anders last.

The walls and floor were bare cement; fluorescent lights shone overhead at distant intervals, so that the passage alternated between light and shadow.

Travis tried to imagine what was happening at the entrance to the backstage area. It was Beltan and Vani's job to pose as overeager fans trying to get Sage Carson's autograph. The real intent was to distract the guards and get them away from the video monitors so they wouldn't see as Deirdre, Anders, and Travis entered the control room.

There had been some debate as to who would engineer the distraction. Anders had pointed out that, as Beltan and Vani weren't from this world, it might be hard for them to convince the guards they were simple fans. However, there was no telling what sort of equipment they'd find in the control room; Deirdre and Anders had the best shot of any of them at making sense of it and getting Larsen's interview on-screen.

Anders held up a hand, halting them. They were near the backstage area; the guard station would be just ahead. Vani had said there was only a single guard, but it was going to be tricky all the same. They had to take out the guard before she sounded an alarm.

Anders drew his gun. Together, the three edged around a corner. Just ahead, in a pool of light, was a desk beneath a bank of video monitors.

The chair behind the desk was empty; there was no one in sight. Travis shot Deirdre and Anders a puzzled look. Wary, they moved forward. One of the video monitors showed the guard station at the main backstage entrance. A pair of guards blocked the way as two figures tried to push through.

It was Vani and Beltan. They were both smiling maniacally, waving pens and pads of paper. In their Earth clothes they looked exactly like what they were supposed to be—zealous fans of Sage Carson. The guards were gently but insistently pushing them back. Travis couldn't help grinning. What would the guards do if they knew those two people were capable of taking them out with their bare hands?

"Those two are a couple of naturals," Anders said. "They've got the guards completely bamboozled."

Deirdre glanced around. "Yes, but what about the guard who was here? Vani said she saw one on the video screen."

"Maybe that was a different corridor," Travis said, though they all knew it wasn't.

"We'd better get moving," Anders said. "Beltan and Vani have to back off soon if they don't want to raise suspicion."

Deirdre started down the corridor, Anders after her. Travis didn't move. The Seekers stopped and turned around.

Deirdre held out a hand. "Travis, we have to get to the control room."

He shook his head. "No, *you* have to get to the control room, Deirdre. You and Anders. I won't be any help there."

"That's not true," Anders said, scowling. "We don't know how many people are in there."

Travis eyed the Seeker's big, capable shoulders. "Whatever's in there, I'm sure you two can handle it. I have something else I need to do."

"The gate," Deirdre said softly. "You're going to try to find the gate." She touched the yellowed bear claw at her throat. "It's below the cathedral, isn't it?"

Travis met her eyes. "I didn't want to tell Beltan and Vani. They would ... they would just worry too much."

"Worry about what?" Anders said, shaking his head. "What are you going to do, Travis?"

It was Deirdre who answered. "He's going to destroy the gate."

"It's the only way." Travis should have felt afraid, but instead a calmness stole over him. "Once you get that videotape on air, Duratek is finished. They'll never be able to build another gate. But as long as this one still exists, Eldh is in danger. There's no telling who could open it, and if they did, Mohg could return to Eldh."

Tears shone in Deirdre's eyes, and a hundred questions. The one she asked was, "Will we ever see you again?"

Travis had opened gates before, had passed through them. What would happen when he destroyed one? Professor Sparkman had said breaking things was a dangerous business.

"I don't know," he said with a faint smile. "I honestly don't know."

"Good luck, mate," Anders said, his craggy face somber. "And here's hoping we see you on the other side."

The two Seekers moved down the hallway, then passed out of sight. Travis was alone. He stood frozen for a moment, then he gripped the iron box in his pocket, turned, and headed back down the corridor.

48.

He spoke *Alth*, concealing himself with a cloak of shadow, and *Sirith*, so that his footsteps made no sounds.

It was draining to speak runes. There was so little magic left in this world; he had to draw the energy from himself. Though he longed to, he did not dare open the iron box and touch the Great Stones for power. The moment he did, the wraithlings would know he was here, and so would Duratek. He kept muttering the runes through clenched teeth as he continued on. He had to get down to the complex of rooms beneath the building.

Just ahead, a security guard opened a door with a magnetic card and passed through. Travis hurried after, slipping through the door before it closed and locked. No eyes saw him, no ears heard him. The corridor ended at a pair of elevator doors. The guard swiped his card again; the doors opened.

"Hey there!" a voice called out.

Travis shrank back against the wall, trying to press himself into an alcove. Another guard, a portly man in need of a shave, waddled down the corridor like a duck whose tail feathers had caught fire. "Hold on, Jackson. It looks like we still need you up here."

The guard at the elevator turned around. His eyes were flat, lifeless. "What is it?"

The heavyset guard halted, breathing hard. "We're having some problems with overeager fans. They keep trying to get backstage to see Mr. Carson. We need an extra hand."

Jackson glanced at the elevator with his stony eyes. For a moment he stood without moving, like a machine waiting to be operated. Then he turned and started back down the corridor.

Travis only had a moment. He dashed into the elevator. The doors whooshed shut behind him.

He turned around. There were no buttons on the elevator's control panel, no way to open the doors. The elevator whirred into motion. He felt light; it was going down.

The elevator stopped, and the doors slid open. Beyond was a white room illuminated by fluorescent lights. A row of hard plastic chairs stood against one wall, opposite a desk with a computer terminal. A guard stood beside the entrance to a corridor; a gun was holstered at her side. Her eyes were as hard, as dead as those of the man Jackson.

Those eyes flicked toward the elevator. The guard squinted, taking a step forward. Travis muttered the runes again and again under his breath. He was shaking; he didn't know how long he could keep this up.

"Is someone there?" the guard called out.

The computer on the desk beeped. She moved a few steps back and glanced at the screen. Travis didn't hesitate. He lunged forward, past the desk, into the corridor.

He was silent and virtually invisible, but his passage must have stirred the air, for the guard turned around, and her hand moved to the gun. However, Travis kept racing down the hallway, and he doubted she would be able to leave her post to follow him. At least, that was what he told himself.

The corridor branched. Left or right? He tried to picture the plans of the cathedral in his mind, but all he saw now were a jumble of lines, like runes he couldn't read. Footsteps echoed down the right-hand corridor; he went left.

Doors lined the hall to either side, all of them unmarked save for numbers that meant nothing to him. He tried one of the doors. It was not locked.

Beyond was a windowless office. Books lined the shelves and papers cluttered a desk. Travis moved on.

He tried several more doors. All revealed offices or labs empty like the first. It seemed this was the place some of Duratek's researchers did their work. But where were they?

Maybe they don't need the scientists anymore. Maybe their work on the gate is done, and they've all been reassigned to other projects.

Or maybe another use had been found for them.

The corridor turned and widened. Travis passed another guard station, but it was abandoned. Why would they leave this place unguarded? It didn't make sense.

Silver light oozed into the corridor, and a coldness crept over him. Maybe it made sense after all that the area was abandoned. No living person would freely choose to be near the wraithlings, and though they served the same master, even the ironhearts hated them.

The silver light grew brighter. Instinct screamed and snarled inside him, a frightened animal desperate to flee. Travis edged past the desk. As before, doors lined the corridor, but they were made of glass, and the rooms beyond were not offices. They contained steel operating tables, IV racks, trays of scalpels, clamps, and forceps, and machines whose purposes he could not guess. He thought of Grace and wished she was here, but she was a world away.

All of the operating rooms were dim and empty, all except the last. Light streamed through the glass door. Travis drew even with it and peered inside.

It took his eyes a moment to adjust to the light. This room was larger than the others. There were two of the steel beds, and he could see a form—a man—lying on each one. The men were held down with straps. One of them was short and pudgy, the other tall, gangly.

Travis's eyes adjusted; terror turned his body to ice. The men strapped to the beds were Jay and Marty.

Two other beings stood in the room. One looked like a man, but Travis knew that was only illusion, that the human-shaped husk was a shell that housed a thing of evil powered by a heart of iron. His dead eyes gave it away. The ironheart wore a white lab coat; in his gloved hands was something dark and heavy the size of a fist.

The other being in the room was a wraithling. Its spindly body was a shadow wreathed in a silvery corona, and its eyes were dark jewels. It drifted closer to one of the beds—the one in which Jay was strapped down.

The little man squirmed, straining against the straps. "Let me

go, you freaking weirdos! I told you, all we were doing was
looking for a little food, a little charity. Let me go!"

His voice was muffled by the glass, but the terror in it was
clear. The wraithling moved closer. Jay turned his head, looking
over at the other bed.

"Come on, Marty, wake up," Jay moaned. "Wake up
dammit. You've got to get us out of here, you big oaf."

Marty lay still, his eyes shut. Had they drugged him? Travis
had to get them out of there. He reached for the iron box—then
froze. If he opened it, Duratek would know where he was. They
would keep him from reaching the gate.

"Oh, God, no!" Jay choked. "Don't let that thing touch me.
Please." His shirt was open. The wraithling reached a slender
hand toward his chest.

The ironheart smiled. "Don't be afraid. It will only hurt
while you live. Once the Angel takes away your weak, mortal
heart, I will make you strong."

Jay went limp, his face ashen, all the fire, all the anger gone
from it. He stared at the wraithling hovering over him. Its
spindly fingers brushed his skin, then dug in.

Jay screamed. The sound broke Travis's paralysis. He opened
the box, gripped the Stones, and shouted a rune.

"Reth!"

The ironheart turned just as the door shattered and glittering
shards flew into the room. Splinters of glass sliced across his
face and hands, cutting skin to ribbons. He howled and stumbled back. The lump of iron slipped from his bloody fingers.
Travis snatched it up and threw it at the wraithling with all his
might.

The Pale One screamed—a sound at the edge of hearing. It
fled away from Jay, its fingers fluttering up to its breast. There
was a dark hole in the corona of light that surrounded it. The
Little People could not bear the touch of iron, and nor could this
thing, for it had been a fairy before the Necromancers corrupted it.

Though wounded, the wraithling was not slain. Neither was
the ironheart. The dead man rushed toward Travis. His face was
a bloody ruin; strips of flesh hung from his hands.

"Dur!" Travis said.

The man lurched once. A gurgling sound escaped his lips. Then the lump of iron that served as his heart burst from his chest. With a flick of his hand, Travis sent it spinning through the air at the wraithling. Again the fey being cried out. It slunk back against the wall.

Now, while the thing was weak, this was his chance. He drew one of the Stones from his pocket. Sinfathisar—he knew it by its cool, familiar touch. A hungry light ignited in the wraithling's jewel-like eyes. It reached out toward the Stone.

"Be what you were," Travis said, and clenched his hand around the Stone.

A new light filled the room, soft gray rather than hard silver. When it dimmed, the pale one was gone. In its place was a slender, putty-colored creature. It lay on the tile floor, naked and dim, its thin arms coiled around its oblong head. Two dark blots marred the smooth gray skin of its chest. It gazed up at Travis, sorrow and pain in its ancient eyes. And gratitude. It shuddered once, then went still. The light faded from its eyes; the fairy was dead.

Travis lowered the Stone, and sickness filled him. He hadn't meant to kill the wraithling, but rather to heal it, to make it back into the fairy it was.

You did heal it, Travis. It was Jack's voice in his mind. *But this is not its world. Its kind cannot live here, not without the drug the men of Duratek call Electria. Yet the fairy was grateful for what you did. It would not have chosen differently.*

He understood. All the same, horror filled him.

"Travis?" said a faint voice. "Holy crap, is that really you, Mr. Wizard?"

Travis turned. Jay's eyes were open, gazing at him. Travis stepped over the lifeless body of the ironheart and moved to the side of the bed.

"It's me, Jay."

"Hell's bells, so Marty was right. I thought you'd ditched us for good, but he said you'd come back."

"And here I am. Like magic." Travis forced himself to smile, despite what he saw.

There was a hole in Jay's chest. Blood oozed from the opening, though only a little, as if the wound had been cauterized by the wraithling's cold touch. Jay's heart was exposed; the organ beat with a spastic rhythm. Travis covered the hole with Jay's shirt.

"So where have you been, Mr. Wizard?" Jay's words were hard to hear; there was little breath behind them.

"Nowhere important."

"Jerk. I figured as much."

Travis wiped his eyes and laid a hand on Jay's bald head. His skin was cold.

"So guess who I saw today," Jay said. "Old Sparky."

Travis sucked in a breath. "You saw Professor Sparkman? Here in the Steel Cathedral?"

"That's right. And get this—the old professor was walking. It was like some freaking miracle in an old movie about lepers and orphans and crap like that. The angels . . . the angels must have cured him. They must have given him new legs." Jay's forehead wrinkled. "Only they weren't really angels, were they?"

Travis said nothing. But Jay was wrong. Professor Sparkman hadn't been cured. He was dead, and Travis would never have another chance to talk to him about endings and beginnings, and about how you could destroy something and save everything at the same time.

"Marty," Jay said, his voice barely audible. "You've got to promise to take care of Marty for me. That big goofball doesn't know anything about anything."

"I promise," Travis said, and he could no longer pretend that he wasn't crying.

Jay grinned, and despite the pain in his eyes, it was his same wicked, impish expression. "And you'd better collect your share of cans or I'll . . ."

There was no more. Jay's grin faded as his face went slack. His eyes stared upward, empty. Travis leaned over the bed. One more. One more person had died because of him. How many more would there be before it was over?

Maybe a whole world of people.

"Travis?"

He jerked his head up. Marty was looking at him with his placid brown eyes.

"Travis, help me. I can't get up."

Marty was still alive. His shirt was buttoned up; the wraith-ling hadn't gotten to him yet.

Travis rushed to the other bed. His fingers fumbled with the straps, then they came free. Marty sat up. The tall man's face was as serene as ever.

"Jay is dead," he said, looking at the smaller man.

Travis nodded. "Come on, Marty. I have to get you out of here, and there isn't much time."

Marty nodded. Travis swung the other man's legs around and helped him stand. Then he turned and started for the door, Marty behind him.

Travis halted. A woman stood in the open doorway. She was petite, though too stern for prettiness. Her brown hair was short as he remembered it, and her uniform wasn't so different than what she used to wear in Castle City, though it was the uniform of a security guard now, not a sheriff's deputy. A crescent moon was sewn just above her left shirt pocket.

Broken glass crunched under her boots as she took a step forward. She held a gun in her hands.

"Hello there, Travis," Jace Windom said, and pointed the gun at his chest.

49.

Fires burned in the distance.

Durge stood atop the wall, peering through the gloom that filled Shadowsdeep, trying to see what they were doing. It had been twelve hours since the Pale King's army had withdrawn from the wall, and they were gathering themselves again for an-other assault, he was sure of it.

A league out into Shadowsdeep, a column of green flame rose up to the clouds. It blazed for a moment, rending the shad-ows, then went out. They were formulating some new deviltry, only what could it be? Never had there been so long a pause be-tween their attacks on the keep. Yet as sure as water flowed and stone cracked, they would come again.

Five times the army of the Pale King had thrown itself

against the high wall of Gravenfist Keep, and five times Queen Grace and her men had turned them back.

Durge had lost count of the hours—or was it days?—that had passed since the Rune Gate had opened and trumpets had sounded, calling the men of Gravenfist to arms. Clouds filled the sky, black as ink, blotting out sun and stars, so there was no way to know whether it was day or night, and acrid smoke hung on the air, burning lungs and making eyes water, casting a perpetual gloom over the world. While torches burned inside the keep, behind curtained windows, they could not light torches atop the wall, lest they make easy targets for the enemy.

Not that the arrows of the opposing forces could reach so high, but they had other darts at their disposal: balls of red sparks propelled by magic. The balls wove back and forth through the air until they struck a man. Once they did, they burned into his flesh, and the only way to stop them from digging deeper was to cut them out.

In the second wave of attacks, one of the fiery balls had struck a Calavaner who stood atop the wall near Durge. It had hit the man in the foot and had quickly burned its way upward. Durge had swung his greatsword, lopping the man's leg off at the knee to stop it. Only then another one of the orbs had struck him in the face. Durge had never heard a man scream like that before. He had clawed at his eyes as sparks shot out of them, then his writhing carried him to the edge of the wall. Durge had tried to grab for him, but he slipped in the blood from the stump of the man's leg. The Calavaner had fallen over the edge, his screams merging with the jabbering of the horde below.

It was Master Graedin who discovered, during the third assault, that the fiery orbs were attracted to motion, and that if one stood still the things would fly past. Once the balls flew over the wall, the runespeakers were able to speak the rune of breaking, directing the force of the magic at the orbs so that they burst apart and vanished.

Where the balls of sparks came from was still a mystery, but while it was difficult to get a good look in the gloom, Durge had seen more than *feydrim* among the Pale King's army. There were men among them as well. No doubt many of them were ironhearts, and some had to be wizards. Logic dictated that if the runespeakers could dispel the fiery orbs, then it was rune magic that had created them.

That there were men in the Pale King's army was a startling and horrible realization. They must have dwelled in Imbrifale for a thousand years, since the last ride of the Pale King. Durge could not help wondering what had happened to them in the centuries since. Were any of them still truly alive? Or were they given new hearts, tiny lumps of iron, the moment they emerged from the womb?

Another gout of green fire leaped up toward the black sky, then died back down. Durge pressed a hand to his chest. The pain was constant now, jabbing between his lungs, though at times, when the *feydrim* surged against the wall of the keep, it became fiercer yet, setting his entire body afire, so that Durge would think he had been struck by one of the fiery orbs.

You should throw yourself over the wall, Durge, as that Calavaner did. It was no accident he went over the edge; he knew he was doomed, and so do you . . .

"Sir Durge, there you are."

Durge lowered his hand and turned around. A shape appeared in the gloom: Sir Tarus, walking along the top of the wall.

"Yes," Durge said. "Here I am."

Tarus halted beside him. There was a bandage on the young knight's cheek. In the fourth wave of attacks, while their attention was focused on the enemy below, another threat had descended from the sky. Hundreds of ravens had swarmed down from the clouds. They were great birds, their wingspans as long as a man's arm. They had pecked with beaks and clawed with talons. In the confusion of beating them back, several men had fallen from the wall, and more might have done so had the witches not woven a spell that outlined the ravens in shimmering witchlight, making them easy targets for the bowmen. The ravens had come again in the last assault, and one had clawed at Tarus's cheek. Durge had seen it: a dirty, ragged gash.

"How is your wound?"

Tarus touched his bandaged cheek. "Sister Senrael said that women will find the scar alluring. I told her that was something I really wasn't concerned with." He frowned. "She seemed to find that funny for some reason. She was still cackling away when I left her."

It *was* funny. Tarus had heard the Call of the Bull. The thought of women chasing after the handsome knight was an amusing one, and Durge found himself grinning. It was strange; for so many years he had thought he had forgotten how to smile. Why was it now, when things were at their most hopeless, that he had suddenly remembered how?

Tarus groaned. "Not you, too."

"Do not fear," Durge said. "I am certain not only women will favor your new countenance."

The red-haired knight peered into the murk. "Can you see what they're doing out there?"

"The smoke is too thick on the air."

"Maybe the Spiders will see something. Queen Grace has sent them back to the secret door, to open it a crack and peer out. Don't worry—she sent All-master Oragien with them to seal it back up if any *feydrim* try to get through." Tarus took a step closer. "So you know why I'm here, don't you?"

Durge pretended he didn't.

"I have orders from Queen Grace. You're to return to the keep at once and get some rest."

"I will rest later."

Tarus let out a frustrated growl. "She's your queen just as she's mine, Durge. You have to obey her. Besides, she's right— you have to rest. You're stronger than any of us, I won't argue that, but even you can't go on forever."

His hand crept back up to his chest. No, he couldn't go on forever, could he?

Tarus gave him a sharp look. "Brother, are you well?"

"I'm fine," Durge said. "And I will do as our queen orders. I will go rest—until the next assault begins. But before I leave the wall, tell me the state of our men. Have you spoken to Commander Paladus?"

"Not long ago. He was in the barracks, going among the wounded to lend them heart. Although I have to say, I think King Kel has him bested at that." Tarus laughed. "Did you see him in the last assault? He was grabbing ravens out of the air and breaking their necks with his bare hands. Then one of those fire balls struck him, right in the beard, and set it ablaze. I've never heard such cursing in my life, but Kel's hag was there, and she jumped forward and cut his beard off with a dagger, quick as that. Needless to say, he was less than pleased—I gather he hasn't cut his beard since it started growing—but he got off with no more than a scorched chin, so I'd say he's lucky. The witches were putting salve on it while I was there, and he was telling jokes that would make a sea captain turn red. Needless to say, he had all the men roaring."

Durge was glad to hear that. Laughter would help wounds mend faster. And many of those men, despite their injuries, would soon be called upon to return to the walls.

"How many?" he said. "How many have we lost so far?"

Tarus's smile vanished. "In all the attacks, fourscore and eight. We've gotten better at dodging the orbs, but not perfect, and the ravens have made it all the harder. And I think the enemy has other spells at work as well. I've seen men drop dead without a mark on their bodies. All-master Oragien says they may have runespeakers uttering the rune of death down there. It's a long way for their magic to reach all the way up to the wall, but apparently some of their wizards have succeeded."

"Fourscore and eight gone," Durge said. "And how many wounded and unable to fight?"

"At least twice that number, though the witches are working on that, and Queen Grace herself. She's in the barracks, healing those with the gravest wounds. When she's near, it's like a light shining in the dark. The men love her. They would give their lives for her."

"I imagine she would rather they keep them," Durge said. He considered the knight's words and made the calculations in his mind. "So we cannot hold out much longer, then. Two more assaults, perhaps three. After that our defense of the wall will go thin. We're already out of naphtha to rain down on them, and we cannot cast enough stones to crush them all. We'll not be able to push their ladders back as fast as they raise them. When that happens, all is lost."

Durge knew he had a reputation, like all Embarrans, for being overly gloomy, but he did not think he was overstating the facts, and from his expression neither did Sir Tarus.

"Commander Paladus and Sir Vedarr have said much the same thing. If King Boreas and his warriors don't arrive soon, the enemy will swarm the keep. The Pale King will ride across all of Falengarth. There'll be no stopping him."

As if to punctuate Tarus's words, more flames erupted into the sky, igniting the clouds with sickly light. It was hard to be sure, but for a moment Durge thought he saw spindly shapes casting long shadows across the vale.

"Come," he said, "let us obey the wishes of our queen."

However, as Durge lay on his cot in the darkness of his cell, he could not shut his eyes. Instead he stared at the darkness, and it seemed he could see things there. He saw the livid green fires, and the shapes of ravens swooping, and in their midst a tall figure clad in black steel. Spikes rose from his armor and from his great horned helm. Around his neck was an iron necklace in which shone an ice-blue stone. Eyes like coals burned in a lifeless face. The figure reached out a pale hand. . . .

Durge sat up, sweating despite the bitter cold. It was a dream, it had to be. He must have fallen asleep. His pulse thudded in his ears. He groped beneath his tunic, feeling his chest. His heartbeat was rapid, but strong and even. Only for how long?

"It is time, Durge of Embarr," he whispered to the dark. "You should do as that man from Calavan did. You should throw yourself over the wall before it is too late."

Lady Grace believed he didn't know about the splinter of iron in his chest. However, old as he had gotten, his ears were still sharp. He had heard Grace speaking with the witch Mirda in Calavere; he knew what had been done to him two Midwinters ago, though all these leagues he had done nothing that might cause Grace to think otherwise.

This duplicity gnawed at him, but she had never asked him what he knew, and so he was not bound to tell her, and it seemed to ease her mind to think he was unaware of what was happening. That was reason enough to keep it from her.

Or was it something else that compelled him to keep silent?

What a fool you are, Durge of Stonebreak. What a prideful old fool.

Two Midwinters ago, he had allowed himself to believe he

had slain the *feydrim* which attacked him that night while he waited alone in an antechamber—even though afterward he couldn't fully remember how he had done it. However, it wasn't his memory that had failed him that night; it was his heart.

You should have died that night, Durge. Perhaps you even did, before they put the splinter into you.

However, the wicked magic had kept him alive. That it had not taken him immediately was only a small and bitter consolation. In the time since, the splinter had worked its way steadily toward his heart. When it finally pierced that weak and mortal organ, he would suffer a fate far worse than any death. He would become a thing of evil, a slave of the Pale King.

Only, the strange thing was, he couldn't quite make himself believe that. And that was what kept him from going over the edge of the wall.

It wasn't that he doubted Lady Grace; never in the time he had served her had he known her to be wrong. All the same, he couldn't help doubting. For even when the pain stabbed at it like a hot knife, his heart felt true.

Durge loved Lady Grace as his noble mistress; he could no more imagine betraying her than lopping off his own head with his sword. And there was another he loved. Not as he loved Grace, who was his queen. Rather, he loved this other with a tenderness he had not thought himself capable, not since he was a young man. Not since he had buried his wife and son in the cold ground. Only he was wrong; such feelings were still possible for him, as he had discovered the moment he first laid eyes on her brave, beautiful face.

Only you'll never see Lady Aryn again, and it's just as well. She has an affection for you, yes, but as for a favored uncle and no more. And even if you're wrong, even if somehow she could have loved one so old and worn as you, what would she do if she knew what lies in your chest?

No, it was better he never saw the horror in her eyes. For that, more certainly than any splinter of enchanted iron, would break his heart.

The shadows still swirled above him. A pale face leered at him out of the dark. He could almost hear a voice, whispering in his ear. . . .

Durge threw aside the covers and stood up. Staying abed was pointless. He could not sleep; there was only one rest left to him, and he was not ready for that. By all the gods, he was not ready yet. There was too much to do.

He picked up an object from the table next to the bed: a silver star with six points. It was the deputy's badge he had worn in Castle City—a symbol that represented his vow to protect others. He tucked the badge inside his tunic, then strapped his greatsword on his back and headed out the door.

As the wind struck him, he remembered he had left his cloak in his cell, but he did not turn back for it. These last years, since he had passed his fortieth winter, the cold had seemed to bother him more and more, seeping into his joints and bones. Now he suffered the cold not all. Bits of ice danced on the air, scouring his cheeks, but he did not feel them.

A group of foot soldiers passed him, marching toward the wall. They clamped their fists to their chests in salute.

"Have you seen Queen Grace?" he asked them.

"She left the barracks an hour ago, my lord," one of the men said. "Perhaps she has returned to the keep."

Durge headed that way. The wind hissed in his ear. It seemed he could almost hear a voice in it.

The guards at the door of the keep nodded to him, and he passed down a corridor into the main hall. There he found, not Grace, but rather Master Graedin.

"Hello, Sir Durge," the young runespeaker said, his voice cheerful, though his homely face was smudged with dirt and lined with weariness.

Durge came to a halt in the center of the hall. The rushes that strewed the floor crunched under his boots; they had turned dry and brittle. The torches seemed to throb. Durge held a hand to his head.

Graedin cocked his head. "Is something the matter, Sir Durge? Were you injured in the last assault?"

Durge shook his head. "Where is the queen?"

"I think she has taken a brief respite in her chamber. The guards said she would return shortly. I hope she does—I have something important to show her."

Despite his excitement, Graedin's voice sounded dull and

distant. Durge licked his lips; his mouth had gone dry. "What is it you wish to show her?"

"It's quite promising," Graedin said, his eyes lighting up. "I've been observing the balls of flame the enemy has sent over the wall, trying to fathom how they are created. I think I've gotten close to discovering the secret. At first I thought they must be bound runes, but I don't believe that's the case. I think they're created by speaking several runes—fire, air, swiftness, and others—in a single incantation. Here, let me show you."

Before Durge could question the wisdom of it, Graedin held out both hands, then uttered several arcane words in rapid sequence. A ball of sparks, not unlike those that the enemy conjured, appeared between his hands. Graedin smiled—

—then cried out in dismay as the orb burst apart. Sparks flew in every direction, whizzing across the hall and bouncing off the stone walls. Dozens of them fell to the floor, and in seconds flames sprang up all around. The dried rushes had caught fire. Graedin stared, jaw agape.

"Water!" Durge cried as the flames leaped higher, running in search of a bucket. "We need water."

"Sharn!" spoke a commanding voice.

Like rain from a clear sky, water precipitated from thin air and poured down on the floor. There was a hissing of steam, and when the air cleared Durge saw that the fire was out.

"What are you doing, Master Graedin?" Oragien intoned in a stern voice as he strode into the hall, leaning on a wooden staff. "Do you mean to do the enemy's work for them and burn the keep down from within?"

Graedin's gray robe was blackened in several patches. "No, All-master," he stuttered. "I was just trying to conjure a ball of fire as the enemy has, to use against them. Only I think perhaps I got the order of the runes wrong."

"Evidently," Oragien said, then his face grew a fraction less stern. "I am glad you seek to find a way to help the queen in battle, but perhaps next time you could see fit to do it outdoors."

"Yes, All-master," Graedin said, hanging his head. "I won't do it—by Olrig!" He jerked his head up, eyes wide.

The anger on Oragien's face was replaced by concern. "What is it?"

"Look," Graedin said, pointing at the floor.

In the center of the hall, a large patch of the rushes had been burned to ash and washed away by the water, and the floor showed through. The stones were pale and smooth, but something had marred them at some point in the past; there were five deep gouges in the stone, arranged in parallel.

"That's it," Oragien said, wonder on his ancient face. "It's the key."

Durge shook his head. It felt as if his skull were filled with fog. "What are you talking about?"

"This." The All-master pointed at the floor with his staff, touching each of the five gouges in turn. "I would that I or one of the other runespeakers had set foot in here before they covered the floor with rushes. It's a rune. The rune of blood."

" 'The keep will know the heirs of King Ulther and Queen Elsara,' " Graedin murmured, repeating the words spoken by the image of the runelord which had sprung forth from the rune of hope. " 'Ever has the blood of Malachor been the key to hope.' "

Oragien laughed, and he gripped the younger runespeaker's shoulder. "We should have known! That's the key to awakening the keep's ancient defenses. 'The keep will know the heirs.' "

Graedin nodded, his eyes shining. "We must find Queen Grace at once and—Sir Durge, what is it? Your face, it's pale as a ghost's."

Durge held a hand to his chest, certain he would find a dagger stuck into it, the pain was so great. He felt old and so terribly weak. A rushing filled his ears, and a gray veil descended over his vision. Graedin held his arm, and Oragien started to speak, but at that moment Samatha appeared in the doorway and rushed into the hall.

"Where is the queen?" the Spider said between gasps for breath. "I have news for her."

"Is it the Pale King?" Oragien gasped. "We have yet to see Berash himself approach the wall."

"It's not that. Karthi saw them first—even now they're marching up the valley from the Winter Wood."

"Who?" Graedin said, confusion on his face.

"The Warriors of Vathris," Samatha said, her eyes bright.

"Hundreds of them. Thousands. They march under the banner of Calavan. I must go tell the queen!" Before they could ask anything more, Samatha dashed from the hall.

Oragien gripped his staff. "This is auspicious. Hope arrives not once, but twice. Come, we have our own news to speak to the queen."

The elder runespeaker started to turn away. Durge gripped his staff, stopping him.

"What is it, Sir Durge?" Oragien said.

Durge felt a moment of sorrow, of regret, of bitter loneliness. Then he let out a sigh, and with that final, living breath, all those things passed from him. In his chest, his heart shuddered—then began to beat with a new rhythm.

Strength shimmered through his limbs. The pain was gone, and the fear and doubt. A certainty filled him, and a purpose, bright as fire. The gray veil lifted from his eyes, and he saw clearer than he ever had in his life. Yes, this was for the best. Why had he resisted so long?

The voice whispered in his ear, and Durge spoke the answer in his mind. *I hear you, O King, and I obey!*

Durge pulled the staff from Oragien's hands. The All-master began to cry out in protest, but in a swift motion Durge spun the staff. There was a loud crack as it contacted Oragien's skull. The old man's cry was silenced; his frail body crumpled to the floor like a bundle of sticks. Durge raised the staff again.

"No!" Graedin cried out. The young runespeaker threw himself to his knees, shielding Oragien's body.

Durge watched him with disinterest. "You cannot be allowed to tell her what you've found."

Tears ran down Graedin's cheeks. "By Olrig, what's happened to you, Durge? What's wrong with you?"

Those words made no sense. Nothing was wrong with him. The error of his ways had been shown to him, and he had been corrected.

"Get away," Graedin said. He raised his hands and began to speak a rune.

That could not be permitted. Durge swung the staff, and Graedin's words ceased. The runespeaker slumped over Oragien's body, motionless, blood oozing from his ears. Durge threw down the staff and turned away from the bodies of the runespeakers. He tilted his head, listening to the whisper in his ear.

Then he smiled and walked from the hall.

50.

Grace lay on her cot, staring into the darkness of her chamber. She knew she needed to rest while she had the chance. All the same, sleep was impossible.

He's coming for you, Grace. The Pale King. It's only a matter of time until—

A knock sounded at the door—hard, urgent. For a moment terror gripped her, then she threw back the blanket. When she opened the door, she found herself gazing at the excited faces of Samatha and Sir Tarus.

"He's come at last, Your Majesty," the Spider said, her nose twitching, making her look even more mousy than usual.

Fear pierced Grace's chest. Was this it, then? "You mean Berash?"

Tarus laughed. "No, Your Majesty! She means King Boreas and the Warriors of Vathris. They ride up the valley to the keep even now, five thousand men strong."

Were it not for the speed of Sir Tarus's reaction, Grace would have fallen. The room spun around her, and her knees buckled, but the knight gripped her arm, holding her upright.

"What is it, Your Majesty?" Samatha said with a frown. "Do you not feel joy that King Boreas is finally here?"

Joy? Did she feel joy?

After the Rune Gate opened—how many hours, how many days ago?—when the hordes of the Pale King swarmed toward the keep, she had thought she would be filled with horror. Instead, a grim resolve had come over her. She had gripped Fellring in her hand, had raised the blade above her head, and had called for her men to defend the keep.

She had seen the same reaction countless times in the ED at Denver Memorial Hospital, on the faces of cancer patients when she was forced to tell them their remission was over, in the eyes of burn victims who knew they were too damaged to live. There is a calmness when there is no hope, a peace. What is there to fear when death is certain? No, she didn't feel joy that the Warriors were here; she felt terror. Because now they had a chance.

"You can let go of me, Sir Tarus," she said through clenched teeth. "I think I can stand now."

"As you wish, Your Majesty, but don't blame me if your face hits the floor."

"I'm the queen. I'll take responsibility for my face. Sam, where are Sir Durge and Commander Paladus?"

"Paladus is on the wall, keeping watch. The enemy is holding back for now. It looks as if they're fashioning some new weapon, and I doubt they'll attack again until it's ready."

"A weapon? What is it?"

"We're not sure. They're too far away to make out what they're doing, though Aldeth is still at the secret door, trying to get a closer look."

Grace nodded. "What about Durge?"

"I saw him a couple of hours ago," Tarus said. "I gave him your orders to get some rest, and last I saw he was headed back to the barracks."

Good. He was going to need his strength. They all were. "Send word to both Paladus and Durge," she said to Samatha. "Tell them to meet me outside. I want them to be there when I greet Boreas. Once the king is here, they'll be following his orders, not mine."

As the Spider left them, Tarus gave Grace a questioning look, but she raised a hand before he could protest. "King Boreas is the leader of the Warriors of Vathris, not me. I'm just the warm-up act. They've been waiting a thousand years for this day. This is their Final Battle. And yours, Sir Tarus."

His grin was gone, replaced by a stricken look. "I follow you, Your Majesty."

She touched his shoulder. "Vathris is your god, Sir Tarus. I'm just a woman."

"No," he said, his eyes serious. "You're not just a woman, Your Majesty."

Grace was suddenly afraid what else he might say. She

brushed past him, through the door. "Come on, Sir Tarus. Let's go meet our salvation."

A bitter wind rushed up the valley, and Grace was forced to clutch her cloak around her as they hurried across the yard between the two wings of the barracks.

"I can't see them," she said when they reached the gates of the keep. The gloom hung thick on the air.

"Perhaps the Spiders were mistaken," Sir Vedarr said. The grizzled knight had been standing guard at the gate with several of the Embarrans. "Perhaps their eyes were tricked by some wizardry of the enemy."

However, at that moment, another gust of wind raced up the defile, and suddenly—for the first time since the opening of the Rune Gate—a ragged-edged gap appeared in the clouds. Beyond the gap was a shard of blue sky, and a shaft of sunlight, heavy and gold, fell through.

So it was late afternoon out in the world; night had not yet fallen over the land. And perhaps it wouldn't after all, for just as Samatha had said, a host marched up the valley toward the keep. The sunlight glinted off breastplates and helms like five thousand sparks of fire.

Trumpets sounded, sending a thrill through Grace. Banners snapped in the wind, and the tallest of them were the two at the fore of the army. One showed a crimson bull against a white field, while the other bore a crown above a pair of crossed swords: the crest of Calavan. Only the crest was different than Grace remembered. The crown had seven points, not nine. Did the king intend never to rebuild the two towers that had fallen?

She could ask about it later. Suddenly she wanted nothing more than to look upon King Boreas's fierce, familiar, handsome face. While it probably wasn't very queenly, Grace picked up the hem of her gown and rushed through the gate. Two others already stood on the rocky slope outside the keep—the witches Lursa and Senrael. Grace gave them a questioning look.

"We came out here to gather *sintaren* sap," Lursa said. "It helps stop bleeding when applied to a bandage. Then I looked up, and I saw them coming. I thought surely it was another one of my visions."

"No, deary, it's no vision," Senrael said, wonder on her wrinkled face. "The Warriors have come, as foretold by the seers long ago."

Grace faced into the wind, and her hair—so much longer than when she first came to Eldh—tangled back from her brow. Boreas had done it. Against all odds he had brought the Warriors to her. They could hold Gravenfist Keep for weeks now, perhaps months. And after that, if the hordes of the Pale King kept coming? She didn't know. But Travis Wilder was still out there somewhere. He still had two of the Great Stones, and they had just bought him some time.

"By the Blood of the Bull," Paladus swore. The Tarrasian commander stood beside her now, along with Tarus, Vedarr, and several other knights, though there was no sign of Durge. The army was close now, its vanguard no more than a hundred paces away. The horses tossed their heads, and the foot soldiers marched with swift precision, as if none of them felt the burden of the long journey north.

"Where is the king?" Tarus said, squinting.

They had dwelled so long in the darkness that the sunlight dazzled Grace. She lifted a hand, shading her eyes. Two figures rode beneath the banner of Calavan, but both were too slight of build to be the bullish king. One rode a white horse, while the other's mount was jet-black. Then the riders drew closer, and Grace staggered.

This was impossible. She couldn't be here. Only she was, and now Grace did feel joy—true, boundless joy.

"Aryn," she gasped. Then louder, her voice ringing out over the valley. "Aryn!"

The young baroness urged her mount into a gallop. She was clad in royal blue, and she looked proud and regal astride the white horse. Strapped to her right shoulder was a shield, and in her left hand, a sword. She raised the sword, and its tip caught fire as the sunlight struck it. At that moment a roar rose up from the army behind her, echoing off the walls of the valley. *Queen Aryn the Fair! Queen Aryn the Fair!*

Grace's mind spun. What did that chant mean? And where was King Boreas? The figure on the black horse was riding hard after Aryn, and Grace saw it was Prince Teravian. None of this made any sense. Both Aryn and Teravian should be in Calavere, not here—not at the end of all things.

Aryn brought her horse to a halt a few paces away. She sheathed the sword and slipped out of the saddle with an easy motion before any of the knights could hurry forward to help her. Grace tried to say something, to find words to express what she was feeling, but Aryn was faster. She rushed forward and threw her good left arm around Grace, catching her in a fierce embrace. The shield made the gesture awkward, but no less warm. Grace returned the embrace with all her strength, holding on tight to the young baroness.

Or was she still a baroness? *Queen Aryn*, the men of Vathris had called her, and there was no sign of King Boreas. An edge of fear cut through Grace's joy.

Gently, firmly, she pushed the younger woman away. "Aryn, what's happening? How can you be here? And why have you brought the prince instead of the king?"

Aryn's blue eyes were solemn. "I have brought the king, Grace. The king of Calavan."

Teravian had caught up to them now. The prince climbed down from his horse. His face was graver than Grace remembered it, and he was clad all in black and silver, just like his father always wore.

Just like his father . . .

Grace took a staggering step back. She looked at Aryn, at the prince, then at Aryn again. It felt as if someone had jabbed a needle into her heart. In the sky, the gap in the clouds closed; gloom settled back over the world.

"Boreas is dead," Grace said.

Aryn nodded, and gasps of dismay rose from Tarus, Paladus, and the other men around Grace.

"How?" Grace clutched Aryn's arm. "You have to tell me how."

Aryn shook her head. "There's so much, Grace. I don't know where to begin."

"Then you might want to save this little chat for later," Samatha said, flicking her mistcloak back over her shoulders. "I've just come from the wall. It looks as if the enemy is preparing to advance again."

Grace felt so cold. "Was Durge there, Sam? Did you see him at the wall?"

The Spider shook her head. "He wasn't in the barracks either."

"We have to find him," Aryn said. "We have to find Durge right away."

Grace stared at her. "Why?"

"Because Tira spoke his name to me."

Grace's heart was too frail to bear this. "Tira?"

"She appeared to us three days ago. It was just after Lirith had a vision of the Rune Gate opening. It's impossible that we've journeyed so far in so little time, but I think that's why Tira came to us—to help us reach you before it was too late."

Three days. So that was how long it had been since the Rune Gate had opened. Just three days. It seemed like a lifetime.

Grace gazed past Aryn. "Where is she? Where's Tira?"

"She's gone," Teravian said, finally speaking. "She was riding in the saddle in front of me. Then, when we started up the valley, I looked down and she was . . . gone."

Grace turned her face up to the sky, certain if the clouds were gone she would see it there, shining in the south: a red star.

"The enemy will approach the wall soon," Paladus said. "What are your orders, Your Majesty?"

The men looked at her, their faces expectant. What did she do? She needed to know more before she could decide.

Aryn, she said, spinning a quick thread across the Weirding. *I have to know—I have know everything that happened. And there's no time for words.*

The young woman's voice came back, clear and strong. *I understand, Grace.*

Her sapphire life thread drew close, entwining with Grace's strand. There was a flash as the two threads contacted, then, in an instant, Grace understood everything. She saw—no, she lived—all of it. Ivalaine's descent into madness. The scheming of Liendra and the Witches. The treachery on the battlefield, pitting father against son.

It was too much. Grace tried to stop the river of knowledge rushing into her, but the force of it overpowered her. Liendra was dead. Ivalaine was dead. Boreas was dead. All should have been lost, but somehow Teravian and Aryn had joined together, and they had wounded the Necromancer Shemal, driving her away. Then, from the sky, a tiny figure descended—a girl with red hair.

Despair filled Grace, and horror. The Warriors had come, but at what cost?

He loved you, Grace. Aryn's voice was gentle, soothing the fresh wounds in her mind, in her heart. *King Boreas. He would have made you his queen, if he could have. Only he knew it was never to be.*

How, Aryn? she managed to spin across the Weirding. *Boreas was the one who called the Warriors of Vathris to war. He was the one they followed, and he's gone. I know Teravian did what he did to try to stop the Witches, but the men wouldn't have known that. How did you convince them to follow him?*

She didn't, spoke another voice in her mind, and while it was wiser than she remembered it, the sardonic edge had not entirely left it.

Teravian?

Yes, Your Majesty, it's me. And to answer your question, it wasn't me who the Warriors followed north.

Grace saw it as Teravian brought his silvery thread closer: He and Aryn standing in the middle of the battlefield as a priest of Vathris placed her hand in his.

Yes, it was the only way. The Witches had created a rift between father and son. With the father dead, there was only one way to heal it—for the one who had remained true to the king to accept the one who had betrayed him.

You're married, Grace said, spinning the words out to both of them. *You didn't wait for the Feast of Quickening.*

We had no choice, Teravian spun back. *I'm King Boreas's heir, but after what I did, the men would never have followed me. And while they loved Aryn for her loyalty to Boreas, they couldn't follow her north, not unless—*

Not unless she was the queen of Calavan, Grace finished. *So you're a queen, Aryn, just as in the vision you saw. And they followed you. The Warriors of Vathris followed you here.*

"Your Majesty?" Paladus said.

Grace opened her eyes. In all, the exchange across the

Weirding had taken no more than a minute, but it had changed her forever.

The commander gazed at her, concern on his face. "You must give us your orders."

Boreas had been so strong, but he was gone. It was up to Grace, and Aryn, and Teravian to be the strong ones now. She set fear and uncertainty aside. When she spoke, it was with the authority of a queen.

"I need you to see to the wall, Commander Paladus. Keep watch on the movements of the enemy. Sir Vedarr, I want you to make preparations for the arrival of the reinforcements."

"And what of me, Your Majesty?" Tarus said.

"Do whatever King Teravian asks of you."

Tarus looked as if he was about to protest, but Grace laid a hand on his shoulder. "He is your liege, Sir Tarus."

The red-haired knight met her eyes. Then he turned and bowed before Teravian. "How can I serve you, Your Majesty?"

Teravian's gray eyes were thoughtful. "It turns out I'm rather new at all this kingly business, Sir Tarus, and I really don't want to muck it up. People think little enough of me as it is. I could use some help getting the army properly situated in the keep, and many of the knights will be glad to see a familiar face."

Tarus called for his horse, then rode with Teravian back toward the army. Grace noticed that Aryn followed the young king with her gaze, though the expression in her blue eyes was unreadable. Samatha had vanished, and Paladus, Vedarr, and the other men went to see to their duties, leaving only the four witches.

Senrael hobbled up to Aryn. "You've grown since I last saw you, deary."

Aryn laughed. "I'm sure I'm exactly the same height I was at the High Coven, Sister Senrael." But of course that wasn't what the old witch had meant.

Lursa hesitated, then shyly gripped Aryn's left hand. "It is good to see you again, sister. And tell me of Sister Lirith? Did you bring her with you?"

"I'm afraid Lirith remained in Calavere." Aryn glanced at Grace. "I asked her and Sareth if they would keep watch over the Dominion while we were gone. They weren't happy about being left behind, but Teravian and I needed to leave someone we trusted to help Lord Farvel in our absence. Not all of the enemy's forces are here in the north."

Lursa sighed. "I'm sorry she's not here. Our coven could have used her. She is stronger in the Sight than any I have ever met." The young witch glanced at Grace. "What would you have us do, sister?"

"Keep healing the wounded," Grace said. She touched Lursa's arm. "And you're stronger in the Sight than you believe. If you see anything..."

"I will come to you at once, sister," Lursa said, and she and Senrael passed back through the gate of the keep. Aryn and Grace were alone.

A smile curved Aryn's lips despite her troubled eyes. "Do you remember the day we first met in Calavere? We all thought you were a queen, only you said you were just a doctor. But it turned out we were right all along. You *are* a queen."

Grace started to protest out of habit, then stopped herself. Perhaps Malachor was a dead kingdom, but she was alive, and she had King Ulther's sword at her side. "I suppose you're right at that. Come on, let's go find Durge."

They hurried across the yard, asking if anyone knew the whereabouts of the Embarran knight. They found a soldier who had seen Durge walking toward the keep's main tower some time ago, and the two women headed that way.

"Did Tira say why you had to find Durge?" Grace asked Aryn as they hurried across the yard.

"No, she just spoke his name. But it has to be important, doesn't it? After all, Tira has hardly ever spoken. What do you think it means?"

Grace didn't answer. However, a note of dread cut through the joy she felt at Aryn's arrival. Tira had helped Aryn to hurry north. Why? To reach the keep before it was too late? Or to reach Durge?

You have to tell her, Grace.

She started to reach out to Aryn's thread, only they had come to the tower, and she pulled back. It could wait a little while longer; let Aryn see Durge one last time without knowing what lay in his chest.

They headed down a corridor, toward the doors to the main hall. The doors were shut, and no guards stood outside, which seemed odd. Then again, it was not the inside of the keep that needed guarding, but rather the outer wall. No doubt Paladus had ordered all of the men on duty there. Grace pushed open one of the doors, and she and Aryn entered the hall beyond.

"Oh," Grace said, stopping short.

Aryn pressed her hand to her mouth, too late to stifle a gasp. The sharp scent of smoke hung on the air. There had been a fire; some of the rushes that strewed the center of the hall were burned. The stone floor was wet and slicked with soot. However, Grace saw all of this in a flash. It was the two forms sprawled on the floor that held her gaze. Ashes smeared their gray robes, darkening them.

"Sia help us," Aryn breathed. "Are they dead?"

Shock gave way to motion. Grace rushed forward and knelt beside the two runespeakers. Blood matted Oragien's white hair and trickled from Graedin's ears. She laid her hands on them and reached out with the Touch.

They were alive. However, both had taken severe blows to the head, knocking them unconscious. Each of them had a concussion, yet the injuries were not fatal. Whoever did this didn't intend to kill, just to neutralize, and he had known exactly what he was doing. Less force and they would have awakened by now, more and their skulls would have been crushed. Who had such skill with weapons?

"They're alive," Grace said, looking up at Aryn, who stood beside her now.

Aryn's face was pale. "Thank Sia, but who would have done this?"

"I don't know. We have to get them to the barracks where the witches can care for them."

She rose, ready to send Aryn to find men to help, but at that moment one of the hall's side doors opened, and a familiar form clad in smoke gray stepped through.

Thank the gods. Grace let out a sigh of relief. However, before she could speak, Aryn dashed toward him.

"Durge!"

The young woman threw herself against the knight, wrapping her good arm around the neck, kissing his craggy cheek. "I've missed you, Durge. I've missed you so much."

Grace felt a bittersweet joy. She didn't know if Aryn felt for Durge as he did for her. Aryn and Teravian were married now, and Grace had seen the way her gaze had followed after the young prince. All the same, that Aryn loved Durge was clear. Only as a man or a fond friend?

That question would have to wait. Right now, they had to understand what had happened here. "Durge, I'm so glad we've found you," Grace said. "There's an enemy in the keep. Whoever it is, they've attacked All-master Oragien and Master Graedin. We have to get them to the barracks, then find whoever did this."

Durge said nothing. He had not raised his arms to return Aryn's embrace. He stared forward, his brown eyes—always so full of kindness—blank and empty.

Relief gave way to fear. Grace tried to speak, but her mouth had gone suddenly dry.

Aryn pulled back from the knight. "What's wrong, Durge? Aren't you glad to see me?"

"Glad?" he said in his deep voice, as if the word were alien to him. His skin was pale; dark circles hung beneath his yes.

Grace didn't want to do this, but she had to. She shut her eyes and reached out with the Touch, toward Durge's thread. It was gray as ash. A moan escaped her.

"Grace?" It was Aryn, her voice quavering. "Grace, what's wrong?"

The thing in all the worlds Grace had cherished most had just been taken from her, but she had to put that aside. She had to forget how much she loved him if they were going to live.

"Get away from him, Aryn."

Confusion hazed the young woman's blue eyes. "What are you talking about, Grace? It's Durge."

"No, it's not." Grace slipped a hand into her pocket, feeling the vial of barrow root. There was no way to get him to drink it, but the toxin was potent. If she could cut him, could get it into the wound, the poison would still do its work.

The young witch stared at Grace, then at Durge. Rarely in

the time they had known the knight had he ever smiled. Now he did, a grin cutting across his face, and it was a terrible sight. There was hatred in that smile. Death.

Aryn screamed.

Durge shoved her away, and she fell tumbling to the floor. He crossed the room in swift strides to stand before Grace. She searched his familiar, craggy face for any trace of the man she knew, the friend she loved.

There was nothing she recognized there. No life, no expression. He smelled of smoke.

"Are you going to kill me?" Grace said softly.

"That is for the Master to do," he said, his voice flat. "They will bring you to him."

A sound vibrated on the air: low, guttural. Grace glanced at the main door of the hall; it was still ajar. She gauged the distance, calculating how long it would take to run to it. Only she couldn't leave Aryn, and it didn't matter anyway. She knew she would never make it.

The sound grew louder, rising into a hungry chorus of growls. Aryn scrambled on the floor, eyes wide, backing away from the side door through which Durge had come. Lanky shadows moved beyond.

"Listen to me, Durge," Grace said. "I know you're still in there—you've got to be. Please, don't do this."

"Shut up, Malachorian whore," he said and struck her cheek with the back of his hand.

There was a crunching sound inside Grace's skull. Pain sizzled outward from her jaw. She reeled, then caught herself and looked up to see spindly gray forms stream through the side door into the hall, one after the other. *Feydrim.* There were *feydrim* inside the keep.

Gravenfist was lost.

51

Travis opened his mouth, but whether to speak a rune, or to tell Jace he was sorry, he wasn't sure. It didn't matter; either way he was too slow. Jace gripped the gun in a small, steady hand and fired.

Thunder roared through Travis's skull, then rolled away. Before him, Jace lowered the gun. Travis lifted a hand to his chest, groping, but there was no blood, no gaping hole.

Jace's eyes gazed past him. Travis turned around. Marty sprawled on the floor, his gangly limbs tangled together, his brown eyes dull, empty. The bullet had torn a fist-sized chunk of bone and brain from his skull.

Travis staggered around, staring at Jace. Why? He didn't manage to speak the word, but Jace answered all the same.

"He was an ironheart." She lowered the gun and holstered it with a precise motion.

Travis looked back at Marty's corpse. He knelt and unbuttoned the man's shirt. A thick bandage was taped to the center of Marty's chest. Travis pulled it aside, revealing a long incision just to the left of the breastbone. The wound was fresh, but it had been neatly sewn together.

Travis shut his eyes. *I was too late, Jay. I should have taken care of him, but I was too late.*

It wasn't the usual placidness Travis had seen in Marty's brown eyes. It was the flatness of death. Marty—or the thing that had been Marty—would have killed him. If it hadn't been for Jace.

He opened his eyes and turned around. Jace still stood in the doorway. Her expression was stern, but there was something in her eyes—a haunted light—that made his breath catch in his chest.

"I don't understand," he said.

Jace took another step forward. "I saw Deirdre Falling Hawk on the monitor at my guard station. Just for a moment, but it was enough, and I knew if she was here, you had to be close by. So I left my station to look for you."

So Jace had been the woman Vani had seen on the monitor, standing guard at the station in the maintenance hallway.

"You were following me," he said.

"I wanted to see what you were up to. I thought maybe I had an idea of what it was."

"So why aren't you stopping me?"

Her hand did not move back to the gun at her side. "Because someone has to stop them, and I'm pretty sure you're the only one who can do it."

It was too much. Travis had to catch the wall to keep from falling. The last time Travis was in Denver, Jace had betrayed him and Grace to Duratek, and it had nearly cost them their lives. What she had just said made no sense.

Jace tucked a lock of hair behind her ear; the gesture made her look vulnerable despite the uniform and gun. "I don't expect you to understand, Travis. I'm not sure I do myself. Nothing made sense to me after Maximilian died. It was as though the world had been turned inside out, and all the rules and laws that had mattered one moment didn't the next. I blamed you for that, for bringing that madness into Castle City. And when they came to me, they offered a way for me to find order again. They gave me a new set of laws to follow."

Travis clenched a fist. "Duratek."

She looked away. "For a little while it was enough. If I followed their rules, if I didn't think about them, it was almost like the world made sense again." Jace looked back at him. "Only it was all a lie. Duratek wasn't interested in following the law, but in making their own laws. Deep down I knew Maximilian would have been angry with me."

Sympathy welled up in Travis. It was as much Travis's fault as anyone's what had happened to Max, what had happened to her. He was the reason the runelord Mindroth had come to Castle City, and the reason Duratek had come as well. All the same, until a moment ago Jace had been the enemy. It was not easy to realign his thinking.

"How much do you know?"

Her gaze moved past him, to Marty's corpse. "Not even close to everything, but enough. I know the things they call angels come from another world—the world you've been to, Travis.

And I know they give people hearts of iron and make them slaves. Only slaves to who I'm not sure." She crossed her arms. "I suppose I'll find out when they make me into one of them."

Travis cast aside his suspicion. Whatever she had done, she was trying to help now. He touched her arm. "No, Jace. Never. You won't become one of them. I'll make sure of it."

She looked up at him. Tears shone in her eyes. "There's only one way to be sure, Travis."

Before he could speak, a burst of electronic static broke the silence. The static came again, along with a familiar voice. "Travis, can you hear me?"

He reached into his pocket, fumbling for the radio he had forgotten was there. "Deirdre?" he said, pressing a button. "Deirdre, is that you?"

"We're in the control room." Her voice was clipped but understandable. "Anders is very good at persuasion, and the three producers in here have agreed to help us out. No one outside knows anything is going on in here. At least not yet."

He let out a sigh. "What about Beltan and Vani?"

"They've retreated and are lying low."

"That's good."

"Yes, but this isn't." Urgency sounded in Deirdre's voice. "The show's about to start, and we've got the videotape in, but there's a problem—we can't get the tape to show on the big screen onstage. Anders and his gun convinced one of the producers to tell us why. It turns out there's a panel onstage that Sage Carson uses to control the big screen. Unless that panel is activated, we can't show the tape."

Fresh dread blossomed in Travis. If they couldn't air the tape, then all their effort had been for nothing. Even if he destroyed the gate, Duratek would remain. There would be nothing to stop them from constructing another gate. It might take them time, but they would do it.

"Travis?"

Jace. He lowered the radio and looked at her.

"I don't know what's on the tape," Jace said. "It sounds important."

"If we air it, it will bring Duratek down."

"So it is important then. But you'll never get to that control panel. There are guards positioned all around the stage. I'm not sure, but I think some of them are ironhearts. Their mission is to keep everyone away from Mr. Carson."

"Why?"

"I'm still not sure. He matters to Duratek, that's all I know. If you try to get onstage, they'll stop you. And once they realize who you are, they'll kill you."

"I have to try, Jace."

"I had a feeling you'd say that. You'd better follow me. I know an access stairway that will get us close to the stage before we're seen."

Amazement filled Travis. He lifted the radio. "I'm on it, Deirdre. We'll flip that switch for you."

Before she could reply, he turned off the radio. "We've got to hurry, Jace. The wraithlings know I'm here. They'll tell Duratek."

She headed through the broken doorway. Travis cast one last glance at the bodies in the room. The ironheart who once had been a man, the crumpled form of the fairy. Jay and Marty.

It wasn't just that evil killed. Death was terrible, but in the end it came to everyone. Rather, it was that evil took good people and made them its own. That was its greatest crime; that was why he had to stop it.

Travis followed Jace. At the end of the corridor was a doorway. Jace drew a card from her pocket and inserted it into a slot. There was a *click*, and she pushed against the door. Beyond was a stairwell.

Jace glanced at her watch. "The show's about to start."

They raced up the stairs, Jace moving lightly, Travis lumbering after, up flight after flight, until his lungs burned and his legs quivered. Finally, they reached another door.

Jace placed her hand on it, then hesitated and glanced at him. "Are you really what they say you are?"

He fought for breath. "What do they say I am?"

"Dangerous."

He rubbed his right hand. "I guess even they tell the truth sometimes."

"Let me go first," she said, and opened the door.

They were in an access corridor. Jace moved forward, and

Travis followed. The corridor opened up into a long, narrow space. Metal scaffolding rose to a ceiling so high it was lost in shadows. Ropes dangled like spiderwebs, and spotlights shone like eyes in the gloom above. To the left was a cinder-block wall, while on the right a gigantic velvet curtain cascaded from above like a deep blue waterfall.

Various show personnel rushed in every direction, speaking into their headsets. A choir dressed in white robes huddled in a circle, engaged in breathing exercises. Several people sat in a row of chairs, looks of wonder and fear on their faces. Some clutched canes and crutches, others stared with blind eyes or hunched over as if in pain.

Jack kept moving, and Travis followed, but they had gone no more than ten steps before a pair of guards—two men—spotted them and approached. The crescent moons on their uniforms glowed in the dimness.

"Who is this man?" one of the guards said to Jace.

"One of today's sufferers," Jace said matter-of-factly.

The other guard eyed Travis. "Where's his clearance badge?"

Jack licked her lips. "He's a last-minute addition. There wasn't time to laminate a badge for him. That's why I've escorted him here myself."

The second guard's eyes narrowed in suspicion, but the first one's face was hard, implacable. His hand rested on the grip of the pistol at his hip. "No guest is allowed backstage without a badge, Ms. Windom. You should be aware of that policy."

Jace drew a breath. Travis wondered what she was going to say. Before he could find out, a woman holding a clipboard rushed up to them.

"What's going on here?" Her hair was slipping out of the tight bun it had been drawn into. "It's five minutes to airtime. The backstage area has to be cleared of all nonessential personnel."

Jace was faster than the other guards. "This man is another sufferer."

The woman's eyes lit up. "Thank goodness. Why didn't you say so? The little kid with the seizures is out. His parents decided to take him to the hospital instead, so we're one short." She grabbed Travis's arm and started pulling him along.

"Wait a minute," the guard with the flat eyes said. "He doesn't have a badge."

The woman glared back at the guards. "Badge? All I care is that he has an affliction."

She led Travis away. The two guards started to follow, but Jace stepped in front of them. She glanced at Travis and gave an almost imperceptible nod.

"So what are you suffering from?"

Travis turned his head to stare at the woman. What she was talking about?

She let out a groan. "Please, don't let it be idiocy." She stopped in front of the bank of chairs, then spoke slowly. "What is your affliction? What do you want Mr. Carson to cure?"

Travis looked at the people in the chairs: crippled, thin, hunched over in pain. Finally, he understood.

The woman was looking at him expectantly. What did he say? *I can do magic—magic that kills people. Cure me of that.*

Instead he said, "I'm dyslexic."

She frowned, then gave a resigned sigh. "Well, I suppose that's something. You're sure you don't have epilepsy?"

"Sorry. Just the dyslexia."

"Well, I guess beggars can't be choosers." She pointed to the last empty chair. "Sit right here. The show will begin with a medley of hope sung by the choir. While they're singing, Mr. Carson will come out and talk to each of you to get your story. You're to answer his questions as quickly as possible, and don't even think about asking for an autograph. When the healing segment begins, I'll come back to lead you and the other sufferers onstage, where Mr. Carson will cure you."

"Just like that?" Travis said.

The woman gave him a tight smile. "Just like that." She scribbled something on her clipboard, then hurried away.

"He can do miracles, you know."

Travis looked at the woman next to him. Her eyes were rimmed with red, and shadows gathered in the hollows of her cheeks.

"What?" Travis said.

The woman smiled. Her neck was so thin he could see her larynx moving as she spoke. "Sage Carson. I've seen him do it on TV. He's cured all sorts of afflictions with just a touch. I'm sure he'll cure you, too."

Travis didn't want to ask the question, but he found himself speaking all the same. "And what about you?"

"The doctors say I need chemotherapy, but I've seen what chemo does. They have to kill you just to try to save you. I'd rather put myself in God's hands." She cast her eyes upward. "I know he'll take away the cancer. My daughters need me."

Anger blossomed in Travis's chest. How many people had died because of lies like that? A tumor couldn't just be waved away with a wish and a prayer. However, radiation could shrink it, could stop it from growing back. The trick was finding a dose that would kill the cancer without killing the patient.

The woman's eyes were shut now; she was humming a hymn under her breath. Travis looked down at his hands. Could he find a way to remove Eldh's affliction without killing the whole world in the process? He didn't know, but he wasn't going to just sit here and pray that somehow everything would work out.

From the other side of the curtain, a roar of applause sounded, then a triumphant chorus of voices burst into song. Travis looked up. The choir had gone onstage; the show had begun. A guard stood at either end of the curtain, but neither of them was Jace. Panic gripped him. Had she set him up? Had she led him here so they could capture him?

"Hello, there, son. Tell me what ails you."

Hope surged in Travis. The voice was smoother—a bell rather than a rasp—but it carried the same rich cadence, the same promise of power and redemption.

He turned in the chair, and hope became ash in his heart. The preacher standing above him was clad, not in dusty black, but in tailored white. His shoe black hair was shellacked into a perfect wave, and a thick layer of makeup lent his face an inhuman smoothness.

"Speak up, son." Sage Carson's smile broadened, sending cracks through his makeup. "The show's begun, and there are other sufferers to whom I need to speak."

The other people in the chairs gazed at Travis, some with less-than-friendly expressions.

Travis looked up into Carson's eyes. "I think you already know what my affliction is."

Carson's smile vanished. Confusion clouded the preacher's gaze—followed by understanding. Before he could speak, Travis stood, clamped a hand on his arm, and steered him away from the row of chairs.

"Hey!" one of the sufferers called out after them. "They told us no autographs."

Travis turned his back to them. He could feel Carson trembling under his grip. The preacher's eyes were fearful, alive. He was no ironheart.

"So you recognize me," Travis said. "I figured you would. They seem to like to show my picture to everyone."

Carson swallowed. "Is this the end, then? Are you here to kill me?"

His words stunned Travis. What had Duratek told the preacher about him? More lies, he supposed.

"I'm not going to kill you," Travis said. "If you don't believe me, call out to your guards. Go ahead—I won't stop you. They'll take me away, and you can go on with the show."

The preacher shook his head. "What do you want from me?"

"I want you to listen to what I have to say."

"Why?"

"Because something is happening here. Something terrible, and I don't think you know what it is."

All at once Carson's trembling ceased, and he grinned. Shocked, Travis let go of his arm.

"I know more than you think, Mr. Wilder." The preacher smoothed away the wrinkles Travis had left on the sleeve of his suit coat. "I know what the Angels of Light really are. I know what they do to the men and women I send to them. And I know they come from the world you've been to, the world Duratek seeks to claim for its own."

Travis recoiled; he had made a terrible mistake. He had allowed himself to think they were using Carson, taking advantage of his blind faith to mislead him, that if he knew the truth about what was happening to his followers, he would help Travis. Only the preacher knew exactly what they were doing.

"You're one of them," Travis croaked. "Duratek."

A new emotion seeped through the thick layer of pancake on Carson's face: anger. "You're wrong. They need me, that's all. I give them things they cannot get for themselves."

Travis fought for understanding. "What things?"

However, Carson only shook his head, his eyes distant.

They were running out of time. Travis tried a different tactic. "Why? Why are you giving them whatever it is they need from you?"

"For this, Mr. Wilder. I wanted a great house of worship for my flock." He looked up, his expression sorrowful, fond. "I love it so much, my Steel Cathedral. It's everything I've ever dreamed of." He lowered his gaze. "And when I am no longer of use to them, they'll take it all away and dispose of me."

Travis's mind raced. He didn't understand everything Carson was saying, but there was something strange about Carson—a sadness, a resignation. And a power. Why hadn't he called the guards? It was as if he was the one who was afflicted, the one who needed to be cured. And maybe Travis was the one person who could cure him.

"There's a way out," Travis said, trying not to rush the words. He had to make every one of them count. "There's a way to stop Duratek. All you have to do is switch on the big screen onstage."

Carson held a hand to his temple. "I don't understand."

The voices of the choir rose into a final crescendo. Time was almost up.

"The big-screen television," Travis said, his words urgent now. "I can't get to the panel that controls it—the guards will never let me near it. All you have to do is turn it on and watch it. Then you'll understand everything. Duratek will be finished for good. They'll—"

The woman with the clipboard hurried over. "Thirty seconds, Mr. Carson. Have you talked to all the sufferers?"

Carson was silent for a moment, then he looked at her. "The healing segment is canceled for today."

The woman's eyes turned into circles of shock. "But Mr. Carson, it's in the script."

"Not anymore. It's been replaced with another segment." He glanced at Travis. "It's a surprise for my congregation, and all my viewers at home. Now run along, Karen."

The woman looked as if she wanted to protest, then she clamped her jaw, gripped her clipboard, and scurried away.

"You'll be looking for the gate, I imagine," the preacher said to Travis. "Keep going down until you can go no farther. You'll find it there. But it will be protected."

Travis searched for words to speak but found none. Was Carson really going to help him?

The preacher cocked his head. It was as if he was listening to something. Then a shudder passed through him, and he looked at Travis.

"Perhaps it would have been better if you had come here to kill me after all, Mr. Wilder." His hand crept up to his chest, and his eyes seemed to peer into some other space. "But the end will come soon, and perhaps this will be enough. Perhaps it will make amends for what I've done."

Travis didn't know what these words meant. Was Carson seeking salvation? Or merely death?

The preacher started toward the curtain.

Travis held out a hand. "Can I trust you?"

Carson hesitated, then glanced over his shoulder. His eyes were unreadable in the dimness. "I don't know, Mr. Wilder," he said. "I honestly don't know."

The preacher stepped beyond the curtain, and the thunder of applause shook the air.

52.

Travis raced down the stairwell, hurling himself around the corner at each landing, every flight taking him deeper beneath the Steel Cathedral. He pulled the radio out of his pocket and mashed the button with his thumb.

"Deirdre, are you there?"

It was Anders's gravelly voice that crackled through the static a second later. "We're here, mate, though it looks like we're in a bit of a pickle. The show's started, thanks to the production lads here cooperating so nicely, but we still can't get the video up on the big screen, and I think security is starting to get suspicious something's going on in here."

Travis threw himself around another landing. "Just hang in there. You'll be able to play the video in a minute. Sage Carson is going to activate the panel."

"Say again, Travis? There was too much interference. It sounded like you said Carson is going to activate the screen."

"That is what I said."

It seemed insanity to believe Carson would help them; if that video aired, it would be the end of Duratek as well as the preacher's funding. The doors of his precious cathedral would close forever. Then again, if Travis's hunch was right, there wasn't going to be a cathedral at all soon. Besides, Travis couldn't shake the feeling that Carson was really going to do it.

The end will come soon enough. . . .

Sometimes even a wicked man wanted absolution when his time drew near.

"Travis, what's going on?" It was Deirdre's voice buzzing from the radio now. "What do you mean Carson is going to activate the panel?"

"Just trust me on this one." He pounded down another flight of steps. "I don't have time to explain."

There was a pause, then Deirdre's voice came again, a sharp edge to her words now. "Where are you, Travis? What are you doing?"

"You'll know when I do it. Just air that video as soon as you can, and when it's done, pull the fire alarms. You've got to evacuate everybody from the cathedral as fast as you can."

Before Deirdre could reply, he switched off the radio and shoved it back in his pocket. He hit one last landing and skidded to a halt. This was the level with the laboratory where he had found Jay and Marty. There was a door to his left; that was the one he and Jace had used to enter the stairwell. Another door was closed before him. Through a small glass window he could see more stairs going down. The light on the card reader next to the door glowed red.

Travis laid his left hand on the card reader, and his right hand slipped into his pocket and opened the box. There was no use fearing the wraithlings now; they were already coming for him.

"Urath," he said. A rushing noise filled his head, and the light on the card reader changed from red to green. Travis hunched his shoulders, waiting for an alarm to sound, but none did. With a push, the door opened; he started through.

"Hold it right there."

Travis went stiff, then turned around. The sound of magic had deafened him for a moment; he hadn't heard the door behind him open. A guard stood in the doorway; the gun in his hands was leveled at Travis's chest.

"Don't move," he said.

Travis knew he could speak *Dur* to yank the gun out of the guard's hands, but then what? The man's eyes were stern but not dead. Travis couldn't be sure—not after Marty—but he didn't think this man was one of *them*. The rune of iron wouldn't stop him.

Then speak Krond, *Travis,* Jack's voice said in his mind. *Fire will do the trick.*

No, he had made a vow. An ironheart was one thing; it was already dead. But Travis would not speak runes against a living man, even one who pointed a gun at him. He clamped the iron box shut in his pocket.

The sound of footsteps echoed down the corridor behind the guard. More were coming.

You must speak the rune, Travis. Reaching the gate is more important than one man's life. And he serves the enemy.

"Take your hand out of your pocket," the guard said. "Do it slowly."

Travis's fingertips brushed the box; all he had to do was open it again, to speak the word. *Krond.*

The man tightened his grip on the gun. "I said take your hand out of your pocket."

Now, Travis. Do it!

Travis opened his mouth to speak.

A gunshot ripped apart the air.

The guard cried out, and the gun clattered to the floor. He fell back through the door, sprawling to the tiles, and clutched his knee, moaning. Blood oozed from between his fingers.

Travis looked up. A figure darted down the stairs, a gun in her small hands. Jace.

"Go, Travis," she said as she reached him.

Shouts rang out now along with footsteps. The wounded guard groped for his gun, but Jace kicked it away.

Travis stared at Jace. "More guards are coming. You can't stop them all."

She slammed a new magazine into her pistol. "Maybe not, but I can hold them off for a while. Those stairs will take you down to the primary research area. The gate is there."

"Oh, Jace . . ."

She looked up at him, her brown eyes solemn. "They were the ones who took Maximilian away from us, Travis. You've got to stop them. Please."

Pain welled up in his chest. He ached to tell her how sorry he was, and how proud Max would have been of her, but words fled him. All he could do was nod.

Her mouth curved in a wavering smile. "Good-bye, Travis."

She turned and stood in the doorway, gun before her. Travis launched himself down the staircase. The door closed above him with a *boom*. Or was it the sound of gunfire? The noise was drowned out by the pounding of his own feet against the metal steps. Jace had sacrificed herself to give him a chance; he wasn't going to waste it.

Travis rounded another corner, then skidded down the last few steps and came to another door. It wasn't locked from this side. He pushed through and found himself at one end of a long corridor.

The corridor was dark, the gloom interrupted only by a small circle of light every ten feet. If this was the main laboratory facility beneath the cathedral, it should have been filled with people. Instead it was empty. He held his breath, but all he heard was the thrum of his own pulse.

Travis started down the corridor, moving between the pools of light. He passed openings that led to rooms and hallways, but this corridor was wider than the others; instinct told him he'd find what he was looking for at the end of it.

Something glowed silver-blue in the dimness ahead. It was hard to be sure, but it looked as if the corridor ended in a larger space. He heard the soft whir of machines. Travis quickened his pace.

A fist shot out of the darkness, punching him in the right kidney. Hard.

The air whooshed out of Travis in an exhalation of pain. He tumbled to the floor and rolled into one of the pools of light. There was a clatter as something hard skittered away from him.

A boot kicked into the circle of light. Travis rolled away, and instead of his skull the boot contacted his right shoulder. There was a crunching noise, and more pain. Travis looked up, but he couldn't see his attacker in the shadows.

"Lir," he said through clenched teeth.

A faint glow hovered on the air, then dissipated like fog. The rune was feeble; he was too tired. He slipped his hand inside his pocket. It was empty.

"Get him," snapped a male voice.

Hands shot into the circle of light, groping for Travis's throat. He twisted away from them—then his heart ceased to beat. Ten feet away, lying on the floor in the center of another bright circle, was the iron box that contained Sinfathisar and Krondisar. It was shut.

Travis started to crawl toward the box, but fingers closed around his ankles, yanking him back.

"I've got him." A woman's voice, shrill and hard. "Tie him up, and gag him, too. This one's words are dangerous."

Travis looked up, over his shoulder. A figure stepped into the light above him—a man in a blue suit. On the street he might have been unremarkable: just another businessman heading to the office. Except the suit was disheveled, and his close-cropped hair greasy. In his hands was an electrical cord.

"The Pale Ones were right. They said you were here, that you'd try for the gate. They'll be along in a minute. In the meantime, we can have a little fun together."

Panic shredded Travis's heart. He kicked and bucked against the hands that held him, but they gripped his legs with unnatural strength. The man grinned, pulled the cord taut, and bent over Travis.

"Dur!"

Travis shouted the word, but it was no use without the touch of the Stones. He had no energy of his own left. The man grimaced, staggering for a moment, then his face twisted in rage.

"No more tricks," he hissed, and pressed the cord against Travis's neck.

Sparks exploded before Travis's eyes. He clawed at the cord, but he couldn't get his fingers underneath it. A buzzing filled his head.

"Don't kill him, you idiot!" the woman said. "The Master wants this one alive."

"Shut your trap. I'm not going to damage him. At least not permanently. I just want to try a few experiments before—"

His words ceased as his head abruptly turned to one side. The pop of bones breaking echoed off hard tiles. The man slumped to the floor next to Travis. His arms flopped against the tiles, then went still.

A shriek of outrage cut through the darkness. The hands holding Travis's legs let go. He saw the woman as she entered the circle of light. She was short and dumpy, dressed in a bag lady's shabby clothes. Her long gray hair was snarled, and her yellowed teeth were bared in an expression of hate. However, it was not Travis she was looking at.

The darkness rippled, unfolded. A lithe form clad all in black stepped through.

Vani stood with her hands on her hips, her gold eyes shining in the dimness. The ironheart curled her hands into claws and lunged, but the assassin didn't move. Fear stabbed at Travis. Wasn't Vani going to fight?

Something flashed out of the darkness. The bag lady's head tilted at an odd angle, then fell to the floor with a *thud*. Her body collapsed into a heap like a pile of rags. Beltan stepped into the light, an axe in his hands, its edge wet with blood.

He knelt beside Travis, concern in his green eyes. "Are you all right?"

"I think so." Travis sat up. There was a hot line across his throat, and his side and shoulder ached. Blood trickled from a scratch on his hand, but that was all. He eyed the axe. "Where did you get that?"

"It was in a glass box in the wall." Beltan grinned. "The sign said it was for use in an emergency. I think this qualifies."

"Can you stand?" Vani said.

She helped Travis to his feet with strong hands. The iron box still lay where it had fallen. He retrieved it.

"Not that I'm complaining or anything, but how did you two find me?"

Vani turned her gold eyes on Beltan.

"I got lucky," the blond man said with a shrug.

"I would hardly call it luck. You made not a single misturn." Vani looked at Travis. "He knew right where to find you. Just as he knew you were in danger."

Beltan looked away and said nothing, but Travis understood. It was the fairy blood with which Duratek had infused Beltan. Sometimes he knew things it seemed impossible he should know.

"There were guards at the top of the stairs," Travis said. "She was going to hold them back. Jace."

Vani raised an eyebrow. "You mean the female guard? We found her dead, along with the other three."

Travis shut his eyes. He didn't know if he could believe Jace and Max were together at last, but he wanted to with his entire being.

Vani sucked in a breath, and Travis opened his eyes.

"Do you hear it?" the *T'gol* said.

Beltan nodded, his face grim. "They're coming. Ironhearts. And there's another with them."

A metallic buzz drifted on the air. Silver light oozed like fog from the stairwell, into the corridor.

"A wraithling," Travis breathed. He gripped the iron box.

Beltan laid a hand on his shoulder. "We know what you came down here to do, Travis. Deirdre told us on the speaking device. You have to go."

Travis felt sick. "I can't leave you. I can stop them with the Stones."

"That would only draw more of the Pale Ones to you," Vani said, standing beside Beltan. "We can hold them back while you go to the gate. You must destroy it. From all we have seen, they have created an army of ironhearts in this place. They must never be allowed to reach Eldh."

No, Travis couldn't leave them. How could he, if he truly loved them both?

Beltan hesitated, then touched Travis's cheek. "They want you to stay and fight, I can sense it. They want to keep you from the gate as long as possible, to give more wraithlings time to come—more than even you can stop. Don't give them what they want." He grinned. "Besides, we'll be fine."

In that moment Travis knew the answer to his question. If he loved them both, he had to leave them. Because if he didn't destroy the gate, there was no hope for them. For any of them.

Despair hardened into resolve. "The artifact of Morindu," he said, turning toward Vani. "Do you have it?"

She handed him the onyx tetrahedron, then glanced over her shoulder. Shadows moved down the corridor.

"What are you doing, Travis?"

He removed the top of the artifact and pressed his hand against it. Blood oozed from the scratch into the reservoir within the artifact. When it was full he replaced the top.

"Hold them off as long as you can, then get out of here. If I'm right, this whole place is going to go." He pushed the artifact into Vani's hands and met her eyes. "Promise me you'll use it. That you'll both use it."

Vani nodded. "We promise."

"Now, Travis." Beltan gripped the axe in big hands. "Get out of here."

Travis hesitated. There was so much more he wanted to say, so much more he wanted to tell them.

Silver light poured from the stairwell. Travis turned and fled down the corridor.

After fifty yards the passage turned. At the corner was a guard station with a bank of closed-circuit television screens. There were no guards in sight.

One of the screens showed a shot of the audience in the Steel Cathedral. The volume was turned down, but even if it wasn't, Travis knew no sound would have come from the TV. The audience stared, mouths open, horror written across the faces. The screen next to it showed a shot of the stage. Sage Carson stood motionless, arms spread wide in a gesture of supplication, eyes cast upward. Playing on the gigantic screen behind him was the videotape of Anna Ferraro's interview with Dr. Larsen. A pair of security guards huddled over the podium on the left side of the stage, frantically jabbing at buttons, but to no effect. Carson must have jammed it.

Travis grinned at the televisions, then he ran on.

He was halfway down the corridor when crimson lights flashed and the wail of an alarm pierced the air. At first he thought he had triggered some sensor, then an electronic voice droned out of loudspeakers in the ceilings.

"This is an emergency. Please follow the illuminated signs to the nearest exit. This is an emergency. . . ."

The Seekers had done it; they had pulled the alarms. Travis ran on. The corridor ended in a pair of double doors. He gripped the Stones in one hand and held the other hand before him.

Urath!

He didn't even speak the word. With a thought, the doors blew off their hinges and clattered to the floor. He walked over them, into the space beyond. The chamber was large and domed, like an astronomical observatory. Banks of computers lined the walls. In the center was a raised platform, and on the platform was the gate.

It was simple and beautiful—a parabola fashioned of dark metal jutting up from the platform, about twelve feet high and four feet wide. Plastic tubes wrapped around the arc of metal; clear fluid bubbled in them. With his eyes, Travis traced the tubes back. They originated in a tank at the edge of the platform.

He approached the gate, casting his gaze back and forth, the Stones gripped in his hand. He expected the darkness to explode in rage and fury at any second, but the room was empty. The computers blinked, performing unknown calculations. The red lights of the alarm played across the walls, but he heard the siren only from a distance, through the broken doors.

Where are they, Travis? Where are all the scientists?

Gone. They had finished their work; the gate was ready. All they needed was blood of power to fuel it, and they were frantically trying to synthesize it even now.

And what about the guards?

He understood that as well. They had cleared out on purpose; they had let him reach the gate. There were no doors here. They believed they had trapped him. Only there was still one way out.

Travis raised his hand. The scratch had crusted over with dried blood, but he could open it again. There was no way Duratek could know what ran in his veins. The blood of the god-king Orú. Blood of power.

Travis stepped onto the platform and moved to the tank. It was made of Plexiglas; clear fluid bubbled within. On top of the tank was a plastic vial with a cap. It looked as if the vial could be filled, then pushed down into the tank. He removed the cap from the vial.

It took a minute to get the blood flowing from his wound again, and another few minutes to fill the vial. He replaced the cap.

Another sound melded with the distant wail of the alarm—a metallic buzzing. Travis looked up. The crimson light flickering through the open doors was tinged with silver.

He fumbled in his pocket for the radio and pulled it out. "Deirdre, can you hear me?"

The only answer was static. "Deirdre, please, come in."

The silver light was brighter. The metallic drone drowned out the blare of the siren. The wraithlings were coming, and the army of ironhearts with them. Vani and Beltan had used the gate artifact. Either that, or they were—

A burst of static phased into words. "Travis? I think it's you. I can hardly hear you, but. . . ."

More crackling. Travis clutched the radio. "Deirdre, talk to me. I have to know if everyone is out. Have all of the people gotten out of the cathedral?"

He counted five heartbeats, but all that came from the radio was a hiss. He was about to press the button when Deirdre's voice came again, clearer than before.

". . . that the last people have just made it out. The cathedral is clear, though no one has seen Carson. And it's already begun. The story is on all of the national news channels. They're running the tape nonstop, and several senators are already calling for an investigation. Duratek is finished."

Travis couldn't help smiling. "That's good, Deirdre. That's really good."

A pause. Then, "Travis? Where are you—?"

He pushed the button. "Good-bye, Deirdre. And thank you. You've been a true friend."

He switched off the radio and set it on top of the tank. At the same moment, brilliant light flooded through the open doors. Figures moved within, spindly arms reaching out for him.

"Come on," Travis said, raising the Stones in his left hand. "Come get them if you can."

He sensed them quicken, like a grove of trees in a wind. They surged toward him. Travis grinned, then pressed on the vial, slamming it into the tank. Blood spread through the clear plasma, tinting it crimson, flowing through the tubes.

A sheet of blue fire crackled into being inside the arc of dark metal. Duratek's scientists had done well; they had learned much from the sorcerer and from their research. The gate looked exactly like the one conjured by the artifact of Morindu.

No, not exactly. The gate wavered at the edges, and it seemed to flicker, growing dim then bright again.

They haven't perfected it, Travis. The gate isn't stable.

The flickering grew more erratic. There was no more time. The wraithlings reached the platform, encircling it. Men and women flooded into the chamber behind them, eyes dead and full of murder. Ironhearts. Hundreds of them. The wraithlings reached out slender, deadly hands.

Travis tightened his fingers around the two Stones and threw himself forward, into the blue fire of the gate. As he jumped, he shouted a single word.

"Reth!"

High-pitched cries sounded behind him, a chorus of rage, of hatred, of despair. Then the screams were drowned out by a sound like shattering glass. Shards of blue magic flew in all directions, slicing apart the darkness, then were gone, and nothing remained but the Void.

Travis's mind was already shrinking. The coldness of the Void froze him. All the same, he felt one faint, warm spark of satisfaction.

You did it, Travis. You've destroyed the gate. Mohg will never use it to get to—

The Void was no longer empty. A sound thrummed through it, far louder than the sound of the gate shattering. It was like the rending sound of an earthquake, only there was no land in this place, nothing to break apart.

Travis felt a deep wrenching sensation. At the same moment a crack appeared in the Void, a jagged line of gray light. Even as horror filled him, the crack snaked across the darkness, growing wider as it went. Travis felt himself being sucked toward its center. He fought, but there was no resisting. The crack yawned like a mouth; through it he saw a valley surrounded by knife-edged mountains.

Vani! He tried to cry out. *Beltan!*

He had no voice. The crack swallowed him, and Travis fell through a hole in the sky.

53.

Durge stood rigid and unblinking as the *feydrim* slunk into the hall. Grace searched his face, looking for any trace of the man she knew, any sign that she might still reach him.

There was nothing. His features were the same as they had always been—craggy and careworn—only vacant of the nobility that had always resided there, like a castle where the kindly lord no longer lived, where only shadows now dwelled.

Aryn let out another cry as several of the *feydrim* sidled toward her, talons scraping against the floor. She retreated until her back was to the wall, then thrust out her withered right hand. The two closest beasts fell back, snarling and whining, biting and clawing at their own flesh. Grace didn't know what spell Aryn had cast, but it had worked. However, more of the creatures poured through the door until the hall was a sea of writhing gray fur. Hisses and growls echoed off stone.

I don't understand, Grace. Aryn's frightened voice sounded in her mind. *What's wrong with Durge?*

There was no time for words. The Pale King wanted Grace alive, to torture and corrupt; the *feydrim* might harm her, but they wouldn't kill her. They had no such orders regarding Aryn. Grace gathered everything that had happened since the day she and Durge rode into Gloaming Wood together and wove it into a single, shining globe. She sent it spinning along the Weirding toward Aryn.

Oh, came Aryn's astonished reply. And then again, only this time as a sound of sorrow, of horror. *Oh...*

Aryn knew now. She knew what lay in Durge's chest. She knew what he had become. And she knew that he had loved her with all his heart.

Another scream ripped itself from Aryn, only this one was not a sound of fear, but of fury. She thrust out with both hands, and the air rippled like a pool into which a rock had been thrown. Grace felt the threads of the Weirding go taut as power was pulled from them. The six *feydrim* closest to Aryn shrieked, then fell over, brain and blood oozing from their snouts.

Wary now, the creatures retreated from Aryn. She rose to her feet, her face a porcelain mask, her eyes brilliant as gems. Power crackled around her, and tears streamed down her cheeks.

Some of the *feydrim* now turned their attention on the unconscious forms of Oragien and Graedin. They began to paw at their bodies. Grace drew Fellring and swung it with all her strength. Most of the *feydrim* were quick enough to scramble out of the blade's reach, but one was not; its head rolled away across the floor, trailing blood.

The blood shimmered, then vanished as if evaporating.

No, that wasn't it. Rather it was as if the blood had been absorbed into the stones of the floor. However, there was no time to think about it.

"The Master knew you would resist," Durge said, his voice hollow and empty as his gaze. "Yet there is no use in it. I have dealt with those who stood guard at the secret door. The way is now open. Already the servants of the Master work to enlarge it. They will pour into this keep like a dark river, and all your men will perish in the flood."

Aryn looked up from the corpses of the *feydrim* around her. She stepped over them and walked across the hall, toward Grace and Durge. The creatures scuttled out of her way; they knew her touch was death to them. Grace tried to call out to her to stay back, but she couldn't form the words. Blood flooded her mouth, and fragments of a tooth.

The young witch stopped before Durge. She reached out her left hand, as if to touch his cheek, then pulled back. "What have they done to you, Durge?"

His eyes were stones. "They have made me perfect, my lady."

Grief lined Aryn's face. "No, Durge. You *were* perfect." A broken smile touched her lips. "Only why didn't you tell me that you loved me? Why did you keep it a secret?"

Durge's cheek twitched, and it seemed an expression—a flicker of pain?—passed across his face. Had Aryn somehow gotten through to him?

No. Durge's lip curled back from his teeth. "It matters not. Love is a weakness—an affliction of which the Master will cure the world."

Aryn shook her head. "You're wrong. Love is the only thing that ever had the power to save us. 'Love shall yet defy you.' That was what the witch Cirsa said when Mohg betrayed her. And I say it to you now, Durge, and to the Pale King." She raised her withered hand and pointed at the center of his chest. *"Love shall yet defy you."*

Durge turned away from her. A sizzling sound rose on the air, and silver light welled from the side door. The *feydrim* hissed and cowered.

"He comes for you now," Durge said to Grace.

The light grew brighter; the sizzling rose to a metallic whine. *Now, Grace. You have to do something now.*

There—on Durge's right hand was a scratch. He must have received it in the struggle at the secret door. It was shallow but still oozed blood. It would be enough. She slipped a hand into the pocket of her gown, found the vial of barrow root, and unstopped it with her fingers.

She stepped forward, closing the gap between her and Durge. "If your precious master wants me so badly, why don't you give me to him yourself? Surely you'll get a reward."

She reached for him, and—as she had hoped—he snaked out his right hand and caught her wrist. He squeezed, and a gasp of pain escaped her as the bones of her wrist ground together. However, she let the pain clear the fear and anguish from her brain. This thing was not Durge. In a motion of surgical precision, she pulled out the vial with her free hand and splashed the purple elixir over his wound.

Durge let out a roar. He reeled back, clutching his right hand, his eyes filled with hate. "What have you done to me, witch?"

The words were a hiss of rage, but slurred. Already his muscles were beginning to spasm; the cords of his neck stood out. He tried to strike at her, but he stumbled and fell to his knees.

Aryn stared, her mouth open. *By Sia, what have you done, Grace? You're killing Durge.*

Each word of Grace's reply was like a dagger in her own heart. *No, I'm saving him.*

Durge fell over onto his hands. Foam boiled from his mouth; his body shook as if beaten by unseen hands.

"Grace!"

Aryn's frightened shout did not come across the Weirding. Grace looked up. The side door was a rectangle of blazing silver. Then a silhouette appeared against the brilliance. It drifted into the hall: tall, slender, deadly.

The *feydrim* howled and pissed on the floor as the wraithling drifted across the hall toward Grace. Its lidless eyes were like black jewels. It had no mouth, but all the same she heard its voice, and the words froze her blood.

You will be the Master's bride. You will be the Queen of Ice, pale and beautiful and terrible. Together you and the King will rule forever....

No, Grace wanted to say, but she couldn't speak. She tried to reach for Fellring, sheathed at her side, but she couldn't move. She heard a *boom* as the main doors of the hall burst open, but the sound was oddly muffled.

It seemed Aryn called out, and the sound of swords being drawn rang on the air. A group of men were trying to fight past the *feydrim* and into the hall. Were Sir Tarus and Commander Paladus among them? Grace couldn't be sure; she saw them only dimly, as if they were shadows. The wraithling drifted closer, the silver light blinding her.

A strange peace came over Grace. Yes, there was nothing to fear when all hope was gone. She would wed the Pale King. He would take away her frail, human heart and all the pain that went with it, and he would give her a new heart of enchanted iron, a heart that would never feel pain or sorrow or fear again.

Or love. Or laughter. Or joy.

"Get away from her!"

Grace blinked, trying to see through the glare. Aryn rushed forward, both of her hands, whole and twisted, weaving together in a spell. The threads of the Weirding hummed with the power of it. She cast the spell at the wraithling. It threw its hands up, letting out a mouthless cry of agony. The silver corona of light wavered—

—then grew strong again. Before Aryn could weave the strands of the Weirding into another spell, the pale one lashed out with spindly arms.

This time it was Aryn who screamed. The sound of the young witch's agony shattered Grace's torpor, so that she perceived everything with perfect clarity. Aryn's eyes fluttered shut, then she slumped to the floor. Her body was still, her flesh as pale as snow.

Grace started to reach out with the Touch, to try to grasp Aryn's thread, to see if she yet lived, but there was no time. The wraithling drifted toward her. However, there were dark gaps in the corona of light surrounding it. Aryn had wounded the thing with her spell.

"Tell the Pale King this is my answer," Grace said.

She drew Fellring and thrust it into the wraithling. The blade passed through the being's slender body. Bitter cold numbed Grace's arm, but she ignored it and twisted the blade.

The wraithling's cry ceased; the corona of light winked out. The thing slipped from Grace's sword and fell to the floor, dark and thin as a bundle of burnt sticks. It was dead.

Durge wasn't. Grace sucked in a breath as the knight rose to his feet. He held out his arms and gazed at his hands. The spasms had ceased. He looked up, and the pain was gone from his face.

That was impossible. The amount of barrow root she had poured on his wound would have dropped a horse. It should have stopped his heart cold

But it's already stopped, isn't it, Grace?

She should have known. He wasn't a truc ironheart—it was

only a splinter of metal in his chest—but the effect was the same. He felt pain, but not for long, and no poison could kill him. Because Durge was already dead.

Grace held Fellring before her, then the tip drooped back to the floor. It was no use; what strength she had possessed had fled her. Tarus and Paladus and the others were making headway against the *feydrim*, but they would never break through in time. Aryn lay on the floor, as still and pale as if carved of ice. In a moment, Grace would join her.

"I can't do it, Durge," she said softly. "I know what you are, but I still can't do it." Fellring slipped from her fingers and clattered to the floor. "I can't kill you."

Durge gazed at Aryn's motionless form. "Love is a weakness." A shudder passed through him, his shoulders shaking with it. Was that one last effect of the barrow root?

It didn't matter. The tremor passed. Durge pulled a knife from his belt and clenched the hilt, his knuckles going white.

"Forgive me, my lady," he said.

Before Grace could wonder at these words, Durge stabbed her with the knife.

A voice shouted out in anger. Grace thought perhaps it was Sir Tarus, she couldn't be sure. The sound of swords and the screams of *feydrim* echoed off the walls. Another figure appeared in the side door, all in gray. At first she thought it was another wraithling, only there was no silver light. Something hissed through the air. Suddenly an arrow stuck out from Durge's side, then another, and another. The knight fell to the floor. Blood flowed from the wounds.

Then, just as before, the blood vanished. The stone floor was smooth and unstained.

"Your Majesty!" a voice cried out.

The figure in gray was moving from the door, fighting past the *feydrim*. Dozens of the creatures lay sprawled on the floor. The men were breaking through. It was almost over.

Almost over . . .

Grace looked down. She expected to see the hilt of the knife jutting from the center of her chest. Instead, the blade had pierced the fabric of her gown just above her left collarbone. The blow had gone far wide of her heart, nor was it deep. Even as she touched the knife it slipped free, and blood welled forth, smearing her fingers.

Blood. Like Durge's blood, which the stones had seemed to drink. Grace sank to her knees. She gazed at the floor, cleared of the rushes. Five parallel marks gouged the stones, too sharp and precise to be accidental. She had seen the same pattern before, on Kelephon's ship, when he had tried to steal her blood so he could wield Fellring.

At last Grace understood. She started to reach her hand toward the floor, then halted.

Durge was looking at her. He sprawled with limbs twisted, his cheek pressed against the floor, the arrows jutting from his body. His brown eyes were fixed on her. One was dead and lifeless, but the other shone with a familiar light, gentle and true. She had not felt the pain of the knife wound, but she felt this pain, and it was unbearable.

"Do it, my lady." Durge's voice was a croak, but it was not flat, not dead. It was he. It was really he. "Awaken the defenses of the keep. Slay the servants of the Pale King."

Tears trailed down her cheeks, bitter as they touched her lips. "It will kill you, too, Durge."

"I am already dead, my lady. I died over a year ago, on Midwinter's Eve. That I was granted so much time after that to serve you was a reward I did not deserve, though it was one I cherished beyond measure. But now all I deserve is death. I have betrayed you. And I . . . I have slain Lady Aryn."

"No," said a soft voice, "you haven't."

Aryn knelt beside Durge. Her face was ghostly and tight with pain, but her blue eyes were as brilliant as sapphires. She lifted his head, cradling it on her lap.

Durge wept, though from only one eye. "No, my lady. I beg you, do not do this. Do not show me such tenderness, not after what I have done."

She smoothed his hair from his brow. "You should have told me, Durge. You should have told me you loved me."

"I did not wish to bother you, my lady."

Despite her tears, Aryn laughed. "And how could it possibly have been a bother, to be loved by a man as noble and good as you, Durge of Embarr?"

"I am not so noble, my lady. And you could never have returned such a love."

Her eyes went distant. "I might have," she said quietly. "I might have."

His body jerked. "You must go, my lady. I can feel it, digging deeper. In a moment I will be lost again."

"No, Durge," Aryn said, gazing into his eyes. "You will never be lost to us. Never." She hesitated, then bent down and pressed her lips to his.

Aryn lifted her head. A sigh escaped Durge, and a stillness came over his body. The lines that had always rendered his face so grim were smoothed away. His eyes stared without seeing.

"I am a lucky man," he said, his voice soft with amazement. "I am such . . . a lucky man."

Aryn wept silently. Durge groped with a blind hand toward Grace.

"Tell me, my fairy queen, what is your command?"

Grace kissed his brow. "Sleep, my sweet knight," she murmured. "Sleep."

Then she pressed her bloody hand to the floor.

54.

Grace straddled a gap in the line of sharp-toothed peaks. Her arms braced against the cliffs to either side, so that her broad shoulders guarded the pass. And her head reached up toward the sky, so that she could gaze for leagues around.

She could see—could sense—the small sparks of life that moved within her. Hundreds of men stood atop the high wall that skirted her, and a thousand more gathered behind, ready to take the place of those who fell. More men moved in the yard between her encircling arms, fletching arrows, sharpening swords. She was pleased; not in seven hundred years had she hosted a force so proud as this.

Thunder shook the air like the sound of drums. Dark clouds churned in the sky. Grace turned her gaze out over the vale of Shadowsdeep. Three leagues away, outlined by a livid glow, were the sharp spires of the Ironfang Mountains: the walls of the prison in which the Pale King had been trapped for a thousand years.

Trapped no longer. There was a shadowy hole in the Fal Threndur. The Rune Gate—forged by the same wizards who had bound Grace's stones with magic—had opened. The army of the Pale King streamed forth. Gouts of fire shot up to the black sky. The army marched toward the keep.

Let them come. She was ready.

But what was this? Servants of evil already prowled within her. Dozens of them were in the main hall at her very heart, though most them were already dead. However, hundreds more slunk down the passage leading from the secret door that opened into Shadowsdeep five furlongs from the wall. The way had been widened by brute force and the power of runes. The enemy sought to take the keep from within.

Grace would not allow that. Countless runes carved into the stones that made up her body blazed to life with blue-white fire. A sound like the call of a thousand trumpets rang out, echoing off the cliffs, so that the warriors stopped what they were doing and looked up, while across the vale the river of darkness halted for a moment, the flood becoming a trickle.

The runes carved into her stones brightened, until a shining nimbus encapsulated Grace. A pillar of light shot up from the tower at her center, piercing the clouds like a glowing sword, so that the stars and moon shone through.

Inside the keep, creatures of evil died.

They writhed and shrieked as the touch of the keep's stones became like burning knives. They leaped from the floor, trying to escape the cruel bite, but there was nowhere they could flee, no surface they could touch that did not strike at them. The *feydrim* gnashed their teeth, clawed themselves and each other, and perished. Their bodies shriveled to charred husks, and the cinders blew away.

The wraithlings fared no better. Their mouthless keening ceased; their silvery light winked out. They dissolved into puffs of foul-smelling smoke. The men with hearts of iron died as well. The lumps of metal caught fire, turning molten, searing holes in their chests as they fell. The fires kept burning until their bodies were consumed.

Grace felt satisfaction as the slaves of the Pale King were destroyed. None of them could escape her power, granted to her by the Runelords of old. None who touched the stones of the keep could survive. None. . . .

Grace.

The voice was faint, but all the same it cut through the deafening chorus of trumpets. She felt herself shrinking inward, so that she was small again, not built of stone, but molded of flesh and bone.

Oh, Grace. . . .

She opened her eyes. Grace knelt on the floor of the hall, in the center of the rune of blood. Aryn knelt close by. Tears stained the young witch's cheeks. On the floor before her was a thin layer of ashes cast in the vague outline of a man. Amid the ashes lay an Embarran greatsword. There was something else as well—a silver star with six points.

A gust of wind rushed through the open doors. The ashes blew away, stinging Grace's eyes.

Aryn gazed down at the sword. "He's gone," she said.

Grace forced her limbs to move, though it was effort. A moment ago she had been so massive, so strong—a fortress made of stone. Now she was simply a woman: bony, shaky. She crawled to Aryn, then laid her hand over the young woman's heart.

"No, Aryn. He's here." She took Aryn's hand and pressed it to her own heart. "And he's here."

Aryn said nothing, but she nodded.

"Your Majesty! Are you well?"

She looked up to see Sir Tarus rushing toward her, Commander Paladus on his heels. The other soldiers stared in wonder at the cinders that swirled on the air—all that remained of the *feydrim* they had fought a moment ago.

Was she well? It was a meaningless question. Durge was dead; she would never truly be well. However, she was alive, and she was far from ready to surrender.

"Help me up, Sir Tarus. This battle isn't over yet."

"You're right about that, Your Majesty," Aldeth said. He

limped toward her as Paladus and Tarus hauled her to her feet, slinging his bow over his shoulder.

So it was the Spider who had shot Durge. But he couldn't have known. To Aldeth it had seemed Durge was trying to kill her with the knife. He couldn't have understood what she had finally realized—that Durge had saved them all.

Paladus gave the Spider a hard look. "What have you seen?"

Aldeth reeled, as if he might fall, but Paladus caught him. Blood trickled from a wound on the Spider's temple.

"Engines," the Spider said. "The enemy has great siege engines, a hundred feet tall, built of iron not wood, and powered by fire and magic. Leris and I dared to venture out through the secret door, to draw closer to the enemy and spy upon them. When we returned to the entrance, we found the runespeakers had been struck down, as well as the warriors who guarded them. Then the traitor attacked us as well, and he was too strong. We couldn't fend him off." Aldeth reached a hand toward Grace. "Your Majesty, it was Sir Durge. He was a servant of the Pale King all this while. He betrayed us."

Tarus's face was ashen. "King Teravian sent us here while he stayed at the wall to keep watch. He said he sensed treachery in the keep, Your Majesty. By Vathris, I never would have thought it would be Sir Durge who turned against us. His betrayal almost doomed us all. Only you've done it, Your Majesty. You've awakened the magic of Gravenfist."

Grace gazed down. "No, it wasn't me. It was Durge. He was the one who saved us."

Grace looked back up. The men stared at her, and by their startled expressions she knew her face was hard and white, at once terrible and beautiful.

"You will listen to me now," she said, her voice low, commanding. "And you will not dare to doubt what I say. Whatever battle any of us may fight against evil this day, it will be nothing to the battle Sir Durge fought and won. He was braver, and stronger, and truer than any man. And if we have any chance now, any hope at all, it is because of him, because of his sacrifice. Do you understand?"

Still the men stared at her.

"I said, do you understand?"

Her words echoed off the stone walls. As one, Tarus, Paladus, Aldeth, and the others nodded, their eyes wide. Grace was satisfied. She crouched beside Aryn.

"Can you stand?"

Aryn's tears were gone, her cheeks dry. "I must. My king needs me."

Together Grace and Aryn stood.

"All right, gentleman," Grace said. "Aldeth tells us the Pale King is coming with his new toys. So let's get ready to play."

Stretchers were called for and brought, and the still-unconscious forms of Master Graedin and All-master Oragien were carried to the barracks where the witches would care for them. More men were dispatched down the passage to the secret door to see how the runespeakers and warriors there fared. The report came back that all of them lived, though they had been knocked unconscious. In their haste to enter the keep, the *feydrim* had not molested them further.

Grace felt relief, as well as amazement. Despite what had been done to him, Durge hadn't succumbed to evil, and neither would she. The beginnings of a plan formed in her mind.

"Your Majesty," Aldeth said, holding a rag to his wounded forehead, "you must send more runespeakers to the secret door at once. We must close it, and quickly."

"No," Grace said. "We're not closing the door."

The Spider staggered. "Then what are you going to do?"

She gripped the hilt of Fellring. "I'm going to send my army through it."

Grace described her plan to Tarus and Paladus, and the two soldiers raced from the hall to relay the orders. Grace started after them, then stumbled. Her jaw ached, and her head felt light. She touched her shoulder; the wound still oozed blood.

Aryn caught her elbow, steadying her. "You must go see Senrael, sister. You must not lose any more blood."

"Not yet, at least," Grace said, gazing at the rune embedded in the floor.

Aryn spoke to Aldeth. "Take the queen to the barracks. And have your own wound seen to." She met Grace's eyes. "Don't worry, sister. I'll tell Teravian what you plan to do."

"And will he agree?"

"He may be the king of Calavan, but you're the queen of Malachor. You outrank him." Despite her haunted eyes, Aryn smiled. "I know he's not his father, but he's a good man."

Grace nodded. "I believe you."

She and Aldeth made their way to the barracks. Clouds swirled in wild circles above; the air smelled like snow and ash.

Lursa met them as they entered the infirmary. Scores of soldiers had been laid on cots, and on blankets on the floor when the cots had been filled. The most common wound was from the balls of runic fire the enemy had sent over the walls.

"We've created a salve that soothes the burns and helps them heal," Lursa said.

Senrael clucked her tongue. "But we can hardly brew it quickly enough. I have blisters from stirring the pot!"

Lursa sat Aldeth down and examined the wound on his head, while Senrael started to lead Grace away toward a private chamber.

"No, treat me here, where the men can see me."

Senrael gave her a sharp look. "As you wish, sister."

Grace didn't want the wounded men to think she was getting better treatment; there were no finer healers on this world than these witches, and Grace wanted her followers to know that. However, she did allow Senrael to raise a sheet as a curtain while she unlaced Grace's gown and dressed the wound in her shoulder.

"Don't bind it too tightly," Grace said, and though Senrael gave her an odd look, the old witch did as instructed.

When it was done, Grace asked how Oragien and Graedin were doing. The All-master slept now, but Graedin was conscious. The young runespeaker sat up on his cot as Grace approached. His face was pale, but his eyes were clear.

"Your Majesty," he said. "I've been trying to go to you, but they wouldn't let me leave."

"For good reason, I'm certain."

"No, you don't understand, Your Majesty. The key to the magic of Gravenfist—I know what it is. It's the rune of blood in—"

"In the hall in the tower." She smiled at his shocked expression. "I know, Graedin. Durge showed it to me."

He frowned, then winced and touched his head. "There's something I feel I should remember about Sir Durge, but it's all so foggy. I can't quite recall what happened after I saw the rune in the floor."

There was no need for him to. "Rest now," she said.

"But I've heard the trumpets. The enemy comes."

She pushed him back down to the cot. "Your part in this battle is done, Master Graedin. Without you, we'd have no hope at all, but your only duty now is to rest."

He started to protest, but whether it was something the witches had given him, or some power in Grace's voice, his eyes fluttered shut. Grace rose and saw Aldeth approaching, a bandage wrapped around his head.

She touched his arm. "Are you sure you're well enough to go out there?"

"No, the blow to my head has clearly knocked me silly." He bared his rotten teeth in a grin. "I should be terrified at the thought of fighting the Pale King. Only I'm not."

Grace wasn't either. "Don't worry, Aldeth. I think we've all gone a bit mad. I think it's the only thing that gives us any sort of a chance."

55.

It was the most terrible day of Grace's life; it was the most glorious day. The glint of fire on steel, the banners bright against the dark sky, the sharp tang of smoke, the call of trumpets echoing off the mountains—all of these things were clear and vivid. It was as if she had never really seen, had never really lived, before that day.

She stood upon the wall and watched the enemy march toward the keep—a force far larger than those of the previous five assaults combined. There were *feydrim*, and pale wraithlings, and lumbering creatures like gorillas, only larger. Their fur was thick and white, and yellow tusks curved down from their jaws.

The beasts were trolls, King Kel said. He laughed and raised his bow—a massive weapon as tall as a man, and which none besides Kel had strength to pull—and released an arrow. It flew with such speed that it struck one of the trolls two full furlongs from the wall. It passed through the beast, felling it. The army trampled over the corpse as it advanced.

There were men among the army as well—wizards in crimson robes who conjured the blazing orbs of fire and sent them up and over the wall. There were women with them, witches in black who had learned to twist the power of the Weirding, to pervert it to their cruel will. All of them, men and women alike, were dead, hearts of iron in their chests.

Like a dark tide surging toward a shore, the army marched toward the keep. Then, just when Grace was certain there could be nothing more, the stones of the wall shook beneath her feet, and a rumbling noise drowned out all other sounds.

Out of the smoke and gloom, three towers appeared. The towers were fashioned of iron, not wood, and lit from within by fire, so that Grace could see a confusion of gears and pulleys moving inside them. Each one was a hundred feet high—as tall as the wall—and they belched steam as they lurched forward, rolling on great wheels that crushed to a pulp any not swift enough to get out of the way.

Balls of sparks shot through the air. The men raised their bows, ready to fire, waiting for Grace's command. She did not give it. She had to wait until they were close, until all of the Pale King's army had entered the sharp-walled defile below the keep. Kel's arrows might reach them, but the bows of the other men would not. However, it was more than that. The only way they could win this battle was to lose it first. The enemy had to reach the keep.

The siege engines lurched closer. Shouts rose from the dark army—jeers and taunts meant to boil the blood. Still Grace's men held.

More of the fiery orbs shot over the wall. A dozen soldiers fell, blazing like shooting stars. Others dropped dead where they stood; it was not the wizards who worked that terrible magic, but the witches in black. One by one they sought out the threads of men who stood on the wall and cut them short.

However, their task was made difficult by the coven of witches behind the wall. Lursa, Senrael, and the others stood in a circle, doing what they could to unravel the weavings of the dark witches. Grisla stood with them, so that their number was thirteen. Grace could feel the magic that radiated out from the circle—the shimmering, wholesome power of life.

The towers rolled close to the wall, grinding *feydrim* beneath their wheels. Bridges extended from their summits, reaching toward the top of the wall. Still Grace raised her arm, holding her men back. The gap between the bridges and the wall closed. Below, the dark ocean of the Pale King's army surged against the walls.

"Now!" Grace called, lowering her arm.

Feydrim rushed over the bridges to the top of the wall with wraithlings behind them, and the warriors loosed a storm of arrows. The air was thick with the shafts, buzzing like angry insects. Hundreds of the gangly *feydrim* died, their carcasses falling onto their brethren below. More swarmed up the siege towers to take their place. Already the creatures had reached the wall and were beginning to force the men back from one of the bridges. In minutes all would be lost.

"Hold them back!" she called to King Kel and Commander Paladus. "Keep them on the wall but don't let them get past it!"

The two men nodded, then turned back to the battle. Grace climbed down a ladder and raced toward the keep's main tower. As she passed inside, she slipped her fingers beneath the bandage on her shoulder and dug them into the freshly scabbed wound. There was pain, then blood flowed.

She burst through the doors of the main hall. Men were waiting, forming a circle around the rune of blood, guarding it. They let her pass to the center. Grace knelt on the floor and looked at her hand. It was wet with blood.

Now, Aryn! she called out across the Weirding. *Now, Teravian! Ride forth—drive them toward the keep!*

She thrust her hand against the rune of blood.

This time she was ready for it. She was the keep again; its power was hers to wield. With a thought she lashed out. The runes embedded in the stones of the keep blazed to life. Creatures of evil screamed, burned, died. The *feydrim* and wraithlings atop the walls perished, as did those who were pressed against the wall below by the force of their kin pushing behind them. The creatures stopped prowling across the bridges from the siege towers; the dark army started to pull back from the wall.

Trumpets rang out. The slaves of the Pale King turned around, and they saw an army behind them.

Grace could see everything as if she were an eagle flying above. A thousand horsemen thundered toward the defile, quickly cutting off the enemy's retreat into Shadowsdeep. Three thousand foot soldiers marched behind, spears lowered, driving the enemy back toward the wall. The warriors had made it through the secret passage in time and had come upon the Pale King's minions from behind, flanking them.

Two figures rode at the fore of the army. One was a grim-faced young man on a black horse, but it was the young woman the warriors looked to. She shone in the gloom on her white horse. A shield was strapped to her right shoulder, and in her left hand she held a sword. She pointed the sword at a knot of *feydrim*, and the creatures flew back as if tossed by invisible hands.

Shouts rose on the air, louder than the din of battle. *Aryn! Queen Aryn!*

Again the trumpets sounded. The army of warriors pressed forward, pushing the Pale King's slaves back toward the wall. Once the creatures touched its stones, the keep's magic took them, burning them to ashes. It was like a hammer crushing the enemy against an anvil.

Wave after wave of monsters were pushed against the wall where the magic consumed them. Some of the warriors fell, from claw or arrow or deadly spell, but more marched through the secret entrance to take their places. Sir Tarus rode with them, and Grace watched the three fight together. Tarus was skilled with his lance, using it to drive the *feydrim* before him. Teravian was not unskilled with his sword, but he gave it up in favor of wielding the power of the Weirding. He and Aryn wove a net of power between them, using it to force the enemy back against the walls.

Finally, the heap of ashes before the wall was a drift ten feet high. Soot choked the air. Still the warriors pushed the enemy back against the wall, and still the monsters perished, thousands upon thousands of them.

The end was in sight. Shadowsdeep was empty; all of the enemy lay in the defile between keep and warriors. There were but a few hundred of them now. The siege engines stood empty, their fires burnt out, their gears still. The call of trumpets sounded again as the men realized victory was at hand.

Weary, dizzy, Grace pulled her hand away from the floor. Her vision collapsed back inward; she was a woman again. Before her, the rune of blood still shone. The magic of Gravenfist had been awakened from its slumber; it would not cease until the enemy was no more. Grace staggered to her feet.

"What will you do now, Your Majesty?" one of the men who had stood guard asked her.

"I ride into Shadowsdeep."

Grace made her way to the secret passage, where a horse was waiting. She rode down the tunnel and out into the vale. She glimpsed the silver-and-blue banner of Calavan and urged her mount into a gallop, pounding across the battlefield. Cheers rose up as the men saw her. One of the guards rode behind her, bearing the banner of Malachor.

Grace reached Aryn and Teravian. Tarus was with them, a grin on his face. The young king and queen were more somber; all the same, their eyes shone.

"We've done it, Your Majesty!" Tarus said. "The Pale King's army is no more."

It was impossible, but it was true. The warriors circled around the last knot of *feydrim*. They didn't bother to drive the creatures against the wall, but instead slew them with lance and sword. It was over. The blue sheen faded from the wall of the keep; the magic of Gravenfist was quiescent again. A great roar rose from the army, echoed from the keep above.

"Your plan was a sound one, Your Majesty," Teravian said. His gray eyes were thoughtful. "King Boreas would have been proud of you."

Aryn glanced at Teravian. "He would be proud of all of us. And so would Durge." She looked older than Grace remembered. All traces of the mild, tentative girl she had been were gone. She was a woman now, a queen. Yet she was still Aryn.

"So now what do we do?" Teravian said.

If she hadn't been so exhausted, Grace might have laughed. For so long, all her thought, all her being, had been focused on fighting this battle. Only now did she realize she had never expected to survive it, for she had no idea what came next. She opened her mouth, unsure just what she would say.

It didn't matter. A deafening sound rent the air, like the call of a horn, only at once more shrill and more thrumming. The air trembled. All around, men held their hands to their ears. Slowly, the sound faded to a low sound of rumbling; the ground vibrated like the skin of a drum. The men turned toward Shadowsdeep, confusion on their faces. Then confusion gave way to a new emotion: fear.

Sir Tarus's grin vanished. Teravian and Aryn stared, eyes wide. An unseen hand squeezed Grace's heart.

She was a fool. How could they believe they had fought all of the Pale King's army when they had not seen the Pale King himself? Her hand sweated around the hilt of Fellring.

He's coming, Grace. He's coming for you.

The army that marched toward them made all the others that had come before it seem no more menacing than a swarm of flies. It advanced across Shadowsdeep like a black wave, stretching from wall to wall of the vale. There were not ten thousand creatures, but ten times ten thousand. And still they kept coming, pouring out of the Rune Gate, as though it were a mouth breathing a fog of darkness.

A hundred siege engines jutted up from the churning sea, fire spurting in gouts from their summits. *Feydrim*, trolls, and men all marched under the black banners of the enemy. The sound of drums shattered the air, and the gloom was sundered by the light of a thousand wraithlings.

The Warriors of Vathris stared, unmoving. The cheers had turned to silence. No orders were given, no swords and spears were raised. It was they who had been caught this time, between army and keep, between hammer and anvil. Already the vanguard of the dark force had come level with the entrance to the secret passage. There was no retreat, and against this force they could not prevail.

The prophecies were true. The Warriors of Vathris would fight gloriously in the Final Battle. And they would lose.

"What do we do, Grace?" Aryn said beside her. Her voice was not panicked. Instead it was quiet.

Grace shook her head. There was nothing they could do, save die. *We're coming, Durge!* she called out in her mind.

A fear such as she had never felt before pierced her. At the head of the army, on a black mount twice the size of a horse, rode a terrible figure. Spikes jutted from his armor, and on his snowy brow was a crown wrought into the twin shapes of antlers. In his hand was a scepter of iron.

The scaly mount tossed its head and snorted fire. It stamped its hooves, sending off sparks as it turned in Grace's direction. So it had seen her. The Pale King rode toward Grace, his eyes two hot coals in his white face. An iron necklace hung against his breast, and in it was embedded . . .

. . . nothing.

A note of confusion sounded in Grace's mind. Shouldn't there have been a stone in his necklace? A Great Stone?

Fear dulled her brain; she couldn't think. Fellring. She had to draw the sword—it was her only hope—but she couldn't move. Beside her, the others were frozen. Even the horses stood still. The dread majesty of the Pale King paralyzed them all.

The dark army jabbered and jeered. The beast the Pale King rode drew near. Berash raised his iron scepter. His crimson eyes burned into Grace, and she bowed her head. Who was she to stand against one so great?

There was a booming sound, like a clap of thunder. The sound struck Grace, ringing in her head, and for a moment she wondered if that was it, if the Pale King's scepter was shattering her skull.

New shouts rang out: the terrified cries of men. And of monsters.

Dazed, Grace raised her head. The Pale King still held the scepter above her, but now he gazed up at the sky. Grace looked up as well.

Above Shadowsdeep, the clouds boiled, then parted, revealing a cold blue sky. Dawn had come at last—only there was something wrong. A dark line ran across the sky from east to west, like a jagged crack. Men cried out. *Feydrim* barked and whined. The Pale King's eyes blazed with a new hatred.

Grace didn't know what it meant. All she knew was she had one chance. With his scepter raised, his steel breastplate had pulled upward a fraction. Beneath its lower edge was a narrow chink in his armor.

There's only one operation that will cure this, Doctor, spoke the dispassionate voice in her mind. *Make your incision now.*

Grace drew Fellring and thrust the sword upward with all her might. The tip of the blade found the gap in the Pale King's armor—then passed through it. The sword shone with silver light as it plunged deep into his chest. There was resistance as the blade met something hard—then clove it in two.

With a flash, Fellring shattered in her hands.

There was a scream, a terrible sound of fury and anguish that should have frozen the marrow of her bones. However, Grace hardly heard it. A coldness came over her, freezing blood and brain. Dimly, she realized she was falling. There was a crunching sound as she struck the ground, and she saw a shadow above her, crowned by antlers. The iron scepter descended toward her head.

Then came another clap of thunder, and the sky broke open.

PART SIX

THE
LAST RUNE

56.

It was a hooting noise that woke Travis.

The sound was soft, like the calling of doves at day's end, only deeper, so that he could feel it as a thrum through his body. Though toneless, the sound seemed to weave a shroud of music around him, warming his ice-cold body, breathing breath back into air-starved lungs.

Gentle hands touched his legs, his arm, his chest. Travis opened his eyes and stared up into strange brown faces. He tried to move, but pain tingled up and down his limbs, paralyzing him. Had his bones been crushed to splinters when he struck the ground? He had fallen what seemed like forever.

Fingers fluttered across his forehead. The face above him came into focus, and a queer, wrenching feeling filled Travis. It was like looking into a mirror only to see a stranger's visage gazing back. Yet despite the differences, the face was not so alien compared to his own. It was a human face.

The man studied Travis with brown eyes, small and wise beneath a thick, jutting brow. A leather thong held shaggy hair back from a sloping forehead; his nose was flat and broad, and his cheekbones as sharp as the chipped planes of a stone axe. A scraggly beard covered his jaw, which was chinless and receding but delineated by bulging muscles on either side. He wore simple clothes cut of aurochs hide, colored rust orange with ocher.

Others knelt in a circle around Travis, watching him with gentle brown eyes: men and women, and even a few young ones. All of them had the same jutting browridges, the same flat noses, the same chinless jaws. However, unlike the man who touched Travis's forehead, their aurochs hide clothes were not colored with ocher.

"Who are you?" Travis asked. The words came out as a croak.

The man in the ocher-stained hides made a series of sounds.

To Travis's ears they were a stream of toneless hoots, clicks, and guttural purrs. However, in his mind he heard words; the magic of the silver half-coin was at work.

We are the ones who waited.

"For what?" Travis said, and the words were still hoarse but louder now.

More hoots and grunts. *For you to fall from the sky. We knew you would come. The end of all things is near.*

Travis tried to remember what had happened. He had spoken the rune of breaking, and he had felt the gate shatter around him. His last thoughts had been of Beltan and Vani, and he had fallen into the Void. Only then something had happened. A crack opened in the Void between the worlds, and it had pulled Travis in, swallowing him.

He gazed upward, past the faces of the strange people. Above, sickly gray clouds swirled in wild circles, cauterized by forks of red lightning. The sky. There was something wrong with the sky.

Again he tried to move, and this time he succeeded. His body was not shattered, just stiff as if it had been frozen. However, warmth radiated from the people leaning over him, seeping into him, and it was this that caused the pinpricks of pain. Strong hands helped him sit up. His skin was unbroken, but his clothes had been torn to rags.

Mountains loomed all around, black as iron, raking at the bleeding sky.

"What is this place?" he murmured.

The place where hope ends. The man pointed to the bone talisman that still hung around Travis's throat. *The place where hope begins.*

Travis didn't understand. Or did he? With a shaking hand, he gripped the rune of hope the hag Grisla had given him what seemed so long ago now. First came birth, then life, then death. Then birth again, as the circle went round and round.

The strange people reached out, removing the last remnants of his clothes with gentle motions. He shivered but did not resist, too weary to be ashamed of his nakedness. With deft motions they clothed him again in garments of soft, warm aurochs hide, and soon his shivering subsided. A leather cup was pressed into his hands; it held water laced with some bitter herb. He drank it down, and he felt his mind clear and strength flow into his limbs.

Travis stood with the help of several strong, brown hands. He was taller than they; even the men stood no higher than his chin. However, all of them—men and women alike—were powerfully built, their shoulders rounded and heavy.

They were in a narrow valley between two toothy ranges of mountains. The valley was barren of life, its floor covered with a deep layer of ash, its air cold and metallic on the tongue. A few twisted shapes that might once have been trees jutted up from the ground, their blackened limbs cracked and splintered. An eerie feeling of familiarity came over Travis. He had seen these mountains once before, only from the other side.

"This is Imbrifale," he said softly. "This is the Pale King's Dominion. But that's impossible. The only way in and out is through the Rune Gate."

The man in orange gestured with his hands. *We know other ways through the mountains, ways unknown to the servants of He-Who-Wields-The-Ice. Or to most of them, at least. We knew we would be here when we found you, and so we came.*

Again Travis was struck with wonder. "Who *are* you?"

"I think they're the Maugrim," said a familiar tenor voice behind him.

Travis turned around, and a feeling of joy almost too powerful to bear came over him. "Beltan!"

He ran to the big man, and they caught each other in a fierce embrace.

"By all the gods, I thought I'd never see you again."

"So did I," Travis said, and held him tighter.

At last Beltan pushed him away.

"Who are they, Beltan?" Travis said, aware of the people gathered behind him. "Maugrim—I've heard that word before, I think."

Beltan glanced at the brown-skinned people. "Falken told us about them. They're the first ones, the people who were here when the Old Gods dwelled in the forests and fields. The stories say they vanished long ago. Only King Kel said the Maugrim still existed. It looks like he was right."

Finally, Travis understood—that was why they had seemed familiar to him. He had seen paintings of them in books, had seen dioramas in museums where wax facsimiles of them had held spears or squatted over fires, working bone and flint. According to the textbooks, on Earth, the Neanderthals had vanished over thirty thousand years ago.

Only maybe they didn't vanish, Travis. Maybe they went somewhere else.

Beltan touched the hide jerkin they had given Travis. "They've dressed you in orange. Just like their shaman."

Shaman? Travis glanced over his shoulder. The man who had spoken to him, the one whose hides were stained with ocher, gazed at him, his eyes unreadable.

Travis turned back. "How can you be here, Beltan?"

"We used the gate artifact," Beltan said, brow furrowing. "As we stepped through, we pictured the city of Omberfell in our minds. It was the only place both of us had been to before that was close to Gravenfist. Vani said it's safer to choose a destination you can envision clearly." He shook his head. "Only something went wrong. There was a crack in the Void, and we fell through. It seemed like we fell a thousand leagues."

Travis crossed his arms. "I saw the crack in the Void, too. It pulled me in, just like it did you. But why did we end up here, in this place?"

Because this is where it was broken, the Maugrim man said in his alien language.

Travis shivered. "Where what was broken?"

The shaman gazed up at the tortured sky.

Dread spilled into Travis's gut. He looked at Beltan. "Where is Vani?"

Beltan's green eyes were troubled. "I think you'd better come."

Beltan moved across the dusty plain, and Travis followed, the Maugrim shuffling behind. They crested a rise, then came to a rough half circle of stones that offered some protection from the wind. In the center, a fire burned in a pit. Travis didn't know where they had found the wood—maybe one of the few withered trees—but the fire drew him forward like a moth. A group of women clustered near the fire; he saw Vani in their center.

He ran the last remaining steps. "Vani . . ."

She looked up and smiled. The expression broke his heart. Her face was lined in pain, as gray as the ashes on the ground. She wore aurochs hide clothes like Travis and Beltan, and another hide, fur side in, over her shoulders.

The Maugrim women drew back, and Travis knelt beside her. "Vani, what is it?"

She only shook her head; tears ran from her golden eyes, snatched away by the dry air.

"There's something wrong with the baby," Beltan said.

Vani drew in a sharp hiss of breath. Travis looked up. What was Beltan talking about?

"How long?" Vani said, her voice trembling. "How long have you known I am with child?"

Beltan's face was sad, thoughtful. "Since the white ship. It wasn't hard to figure out, even for me. Your sickness in the mornings gave it away."

She bowed her head. "I wanted to tell you."

"I know," he said.

This didn't make any sense. How could Vani be pregnant? Travis and she had never been together, not that way. He looked from her to Beltan, and all at once the sorrow on both their faces made the answer clear.

He staggered to his feet. "How?" It was all he could say.

Vani shook her head.

"It was the Little People," Beltan said, not meeting his gaze. "On Sindar's ship. They tricked us. We came upon each other in an impossible garden, only we each thought . . ."

Travis clutched his arm. "You thought what?"

"We each thought the other was you," Vani said, looking up at Travis, her gold eyes anguished. "We lay together, and only when we awoke did we know the truth. Why the Little People did this to us, we know not. Only that they did."

A tide of emotions surged in Travis: shock, betrayal, jealousy, dread. Vani and Beltan had made love? He fought for comprehension. Only it didn't matter if he understood. The Little People were ancient, and they were not human; their purposes were a mystery. Besides, all that mattered was that Vani was with child. With Beltan's child. And that child was in danger.

Travis took all feelings save love and put them aside. He sank again to his knees, hesitated, then laid his hand on her stomach. Vani tensed but did not resist. He could feel it: the first swelling of her belly.

"What's wrong?"

"I don't know." Vani grimaced in pain as a spasm passed through her.

One of the women pushed past Travis. She was old, her face as soft and wrinkled as her robe of aurochs hide. The robe was marked with several bright ocher handprints. She brushed knobby fingers across Vani's stomach and made hooting and grunting sounds deep in her throat.

The cold of the Void has harmed the child. Its hold upon the mother's womb has been loosened.

"What can we do?" Travis said.

The woman looked him up and down, her eyes like hard pebbles. She jabbed a finger at Travis's chest. *You are a wizard. Cold has frozen the child, and only fire can warm her. You must use the Stone.*

Travis stared at her. No, that couldn't be the answer. Fire couldn't save, it could only burn.

"What is it, Travis?" Beltan said. "I could almost understand her, but not quite."

He reached into his pocket and pulled out one of the Imsari. Krondisar, the Stone of Fire. "She said the cold has harmed the baby, that only fire can save her."

"Her?" Vani clutched her stomach. "The child is a girl? But how can she know?"

The old woman let out a chortling sound. *She is awake already. It is too soon, but she speaks to me all the same.*

Travis relayed these words, though he did not really understand them.

Vani's eyes were frightened. "Travis, please. Do what she tells you. I do not . . . I do not wish to lose her."

"You can do it, Travis." Beltan laid a hand on his shoulder. "I know you can."

For so long, he had been afraid of what he was, of what he could do. Afraid of hurting others. In that moment—for the first time since that stormy October night when Jack gripped his hand beneath the Magician's Attic and made him a runelord—Travis set fear aside. Power was not evil in and of itself, he knew that now; it was what the wielder chose to do with it that shaped it for good or for ill. He hadn't asked for this power, but it was his to wield, and he was going to use it how he chose. Not to destroy life, but to preserve it.

Travis gripped the Stone of Fire in one hand and pressed the other to Vani's stomach.

"Krond," he murmured.

He spoke the rune, not in panic or rage or despair as he had in the past, but gently, out of love. There were no flames this time. Instead, a soft red-gold glow sprang into being around his hand, spreading out over Vani's belly—then sinking into it. Vani gasped, her eyes going wide, her back arching. A shudder passed through her, and color crept back into her skin. Then a strange thing happened. It seemed a voice, tiny and innocent, spoke in Travis's mind.

Hello, Father.

Travis snatched his hand back. Vani and Beltan stared at him. "What happened?" Vani said.

Travis shook his head. The voice had been so clear, so full of joy and love. But that was impossible.

The old woman moved close to Vani, touching her body with probing fingers. At last she let out a grunt.

It is well. The child's roots are stronger now, and it grows again in her womb. Her eyes narrowed as she gazed at Travis. *It grows quickly, in fact. Too quickly. But then, this child has not one father, but two.*

"What's she saying now?" Beltan said.

Vani looked at him expectantly. Travis opened his mouth, unsure just how to tell them.

A sound pierced the air, like the keening of cold wind over sharp stones. It was a cry of hatred, of fury, of utter despair. The sound was far off, but not so far that all of them didn't shiver as it faded to silence.

"By the Blood of the Bull, what was that?" Beltan said, his face pale.

Before anyone could answer, a column of gold sparks shot up to the roiling sky, plunging into the clouds. It emanated from behind the spine of a low ridge a half league away, near the base of the mountains. The column blazed against the darkness for several heartbeats, then ceased.

A tug on Travis's arm. It was the man with the wise brown eyes—their shaman.

Come now, he said in his hooting language. *The end has begun.*

Travis looked at Vani and Beltan. "I think we have to go. Toward that light we saw."

Beltan helped Vani to her feet. "Can you walk?"

"Let's go," the *T'gol* said.

57.

They followed the man in the ocher-stained hides as he set out across the valley. The old woman who had told Travis to use the Stone of Fire came with them, but they left the other Maugrim behind. They did not speak as they walked. Ash swirled on the air, stinging their eyes and making their throats ache.

They reached the ridge, which sprawled like the carcass of a dragon at the foot of the mountains, and scrambled up its flanks. Loose stones littered the slope, their edges sharp as knives. Crimson lightning stabbed at the clouds as they climbed. The sky seemed to boil now, like a pot of some vile liquid. A sickness came over Travis every time he looked up; he kept his eyes on his feet.

They had nearly reached the summit of the ridge when a hot bolt of pain shot through Travis's chest. He staggered and would have fallen and gone skidding down the slope were it not for Beltan's strong hands steadying him. A sound thundered in his skull, like a thousand voices speaking a single word in chorus.

Bal.

Death. It was the rune of death.

"Travis, what is it?" Ash made the knight's face a gray mask

The voices in Travis's mind faded to silence. The pain in his chest was gone, but his right hand itched. "I don't know. I felt something, only it's passed now."

Vani touched his cheek. "Your face, it's so pale. What is it, Travis?"

The wizened Maugrim woman pulled at his sleeve. *You will see,* the coin translated her grunting speech. *Come, now.*

They continued on, and after a few more steps they reached the top of the ridge. Travis blinked the grit from his eyes, then stared in disbelief.

Thirty paces away, on the flat top of the ridge, stood three figures. Travis knew two of them well: Falken and Melia. The third was a tall man, powerfully built, though his white hair and time-etched face spoke of age. The man wore a black robe embroidered with scarlet runes. His fingers twitched around the blade of the sword that pierced his chest. Falken's sword. The bard gripped the hilt in his silver hand.

The white-haired man opened his mouth as if to speak, but all that came out was a gush of blood. Tears traced lines through the layer of ash on Falken's cheeks.

"For Malachor," he said and jerked the sword out of the other's chest.

The white-haired man fell to the ground. His robe fluttered. He was dead.

Falken bowed his head. Melia moved to him and laid a hand on his arm. "It is over at last, dearest one."

Travis's paralysis broke. He shouted—a wordless sound of joy—and ran over the broken ground toward Melia and Falken. The bard and the lady looked up, astonishment shining in their eyes. Then Melia was running as well, and Travis caught her in his arms, lifting the small woman off the ground.

"Am I dreaming?" Melia murmured.

Travis held her tight. "I'd think we both were, only I'd choose a happier place for my dream than this."

"It is happy with you here, sweet one."

All the same, she was weeping, and it did not seem all her tears were ones of joy. Travis set her down. Falken was there now, and Beltan and Vani. It seemed so strange, to be embracing one another in such a lifeless place. All the same, it filled Travis with warmth.

The Maugrim man and woman nodded to Melia and Falken,

and the bard and lady bowed in return. Curiosity glinted in Falken's eyes, but Melia smiled.

"It is long since I have had the pleasure of meeting the *Gul-Hin-Gul*," she said. "I am honored."

Falken shot her a sharp look. "You mean you've met the True People before?"

"Once. It was over a thousand years ago, just after we banished Mohg from the world, just before they vanished into the mists of the deepest forests and wildest mountains."

"You mean all this time you knew the Maugrim still existed?" Falken said, his expression stunned.

Melia gave the bard a fond smile. "I know lots of things, dear one."

The Maugrim man spoke to Melia in his strange language. *The honor is ours, ancient ones. We saw you come through the pass into the land of He-Who-Wields-The-Ice. We would have greeted you then, but we knew the one we waited for was coming.*

Melia turned her golden eyes on Travis. "And now he is here, in this place."

"So this truly is the end, then," Falken said. He gazed at the bloody sword that lay on the ground.

"Kelephon," Beltan said, glancing at the dead body of the man. "You've killed him, Falken."

So that was who the white-haired man was. Travis pressed his hand to his chest, remembering the pain he had felt a few moments ago. Kelephon had been the last of the Runelords. Now there was only Travis. Or was that true? Was there not one other who could yet break runes?

With his boot, Falken nudged Kelephon's arm, and the runelord's dead fingers fell open, revealing a Stone. It was smooth and spherical, its surface a mottled snow blue. Travis heard a hum, like the sound of metal against dry ice.

"Gelthisar," he said, standing next to the bard.

Falken nodded. "Kelephon tried to use the Stone of Ice against us, but I don't think he had time to fully master its power. It had been long centuries since he last held it, and its touch seemed to freeze him. For a moment he couldn't move, and it was enough for me to put my sword in him."

Travis shook his head. "Why did he have the Stone? And how did you find him here?"

"It was Shemal," Melia said, her eyes going hard. "She led us here."

While the wind moaned over the ridge and silent lightning flashed above, they listened to Melia and Falken tell how they had come to this place. After leaving Calavere, the bard and the lady had set out on Kelephon's trail and soon found the runelord in Embarr, where—in the guise of General Gorandon—he was amassing his Onyx Knights for an all-out assault on the remaining Dominions. Falken and Melia had not been able to get close to him, but then they had spied one of the Pale King's ravens, and in a daring ploy they had caught the attention of the bird. They had convinced the raven to spy on Kelephon, and to take news of what it saw back to the Pale King.

Shortly thereafter, more ravens had flown from the direction of Imbrifale, and then Falken and Melia had seen Kelephon riding north, cloak flying, a look of fury on his face. It had worked—the Pale King had grown suspicious and had summoned his runelord to him. Kelephon had had no choice but to go and feign loyalty, not if he didn't want his treachery revealed. Without his presence, the spell with which he held the Onyx Knights in thrall weakened. The order began to crumble; many of them began the long journey back to Eversea in the far west.

"I don't understand," Beltan said. "Why did Kelephon go back to Imbrifale right when he was ready to attack? Why didn't he just turn against the Pale King then?"

"That's why," Travis said, pointing to the Stone on the dead runelord's hand.

Falken nodded. "He always intended to steal Gelthisar back from the Pale King. I suppose he lusted after it all those years. He had known its touch once, before he surrendered it to Berash, and he wanted it back." The bard knelt beside the corpse. "I imagine he convinced the Pale King not to take the Stone into battle, to keep it safe in his fortress in Fal-Imbri instead. Once Berash rode through the Rune Gate, Kelephon absconded with the Stone. He was trying to escape through this hidden pass when we came upon him."

"I thought there was no way in and out of Imbrifale," Beltan said with a frown.

Falken stood. "So did I. I suppose this way has been here for centuries—from the very beginning, perhaps. My guess is, when the Runelords raised the Fal Threndur, Kelephon created this pass in secret, keeping it concealed from his brethren. I'm not sure even Berash himself knows about it, though it's clear the Necromancers did."

Melia picked up the tale then, telling how after they saw Kelephon ride north, they had turned their attention to Shemal. They had searched for the Necromancer without luck. Then, only a day ago, Melia sensed her presence, fleeing north.

"She was wounded and unguarded," Melia said. "That was why I was able to discover her so easily. We followed and came upon her here. I believe she was seeking to enter Imbrifale even as Kelephon was fleeing it, though what her purpose was I do not know." A shiver passed through her. "I feared I would not have the power to face her."

Falken laid a hand on her shoulder. "But you did."

Melia gazed at a scorched circle on the ground. "She was severely weakened. How Shemal came to be wounded, I don't know, but it was the reason I was able to stand against her. Somehow she had lost her immortality. She still had her magics, but in the end she was too weak to work them—she could no longer hold on to her mortal form. She is . . . dissipated."

"Dead, you mean," Beltan said. "Shemal is dead."

"More than dead. Her spirit is gone, as dust before a wind. Just like poor Tome and the others." Melia bowed her head.

Vani knelt beside the scorched circle on the ground. "There are strange tracks here, like those of some great cat." She looked up. "Did you see such a beast?"

Neither Falken nor Melia answered.

"So now what do we do?" Beltan said.

The Maugrim man made a breaking motion with his hands. *The end must be made to come.* He pointed to the Stone resting on the dead runelord's palm.

A sick feeling filled Travis. That couldn't be the answer; there had to be something else they could do. "The Rune Gate."

He looked at Falken. "You said it's opened again, that the Pale King has ridden through."

Falken nodded, his face grim. "Grace rode to Gravenfist Keep to stand against Berash, and to await King Boreas and the Warriors of Vathris. Although whether she has held or the keep has fallen, there's no way to know."

"Yes there is," Travis said, his voice shaking. "We can go to her. We can go to Gravenfist Keep right now and help her fight until King Boreas gets there."

Melia turned her amber gaze on him. "Can we?"

These words were like a blow; Travis staggered. "What are you talking about?"

Melia looked up at the roiling clouds.

"The sky," Beltan said softly. "Something's wrong with it."

"It has been broken," said a voice behind them.

The voice was sharp-edged but haggard—a man's voice. They turned to see a figure in a black robe appear from behind a boulder, walking down the last few feet of the hidden path toward them. The man moved slowly, as if weary beyond imagining. He came to a halt a dozen paces away. The heavy cowl of his robe concealed his face. Vani crouched, ready to spring.

Travis tried to moisten his lips, but his tongue was dry as sand. "What do you mean?"

The man held out his hands. On it were the fractured pieces of a disk of creamy stone. Travis could still make out the symbol that had been embedded in the disk: a curved line over a single dot. *Tal*, the rune of sky. The broken pieces of the rune slipped through the man's fingers and tumbled to the ground.

Anger and sorrow tore at Travis's heart. "You. It was you we saw at the Black Tower. You're the one who killed Sky—you're the other Runebreaker."

The man said nothing, and the others stared, shock written across their faces—all except for the two Maugrim, whose brown eyes were as calm as ever.

Bitter laughter rose in Travis's throat. "So, have you come to take the Stones from me? They're all here. I have Krondisar and Sinfathisar, and here's Gelthisar." He pointed to the Stone resting on Kelephon's dead hand. "It's everything Mohg needs to break the First Rune." He drew the two Stones from his pocket. "Have you come to take them to him?"

"No," the man in the black robe said. "I will not take the Imsari from you, Master Wilder."

Travis clenched his hand around the Stones. "But you broke the rune of sky. You opened the way for Mohg so he can return to Eldh and break the First Rune."

"You're wrong."

The man pushed back his cowl. Intelligent eyes gazed from a face that was a shattered mask crisscrossed by white scars. His lips twisted in a sardonic smile.

"Mohg will not break the First Rune," Master Larad said. "Because you will, Master Wilder."

58.

Travis knew he should do something, that he should speak a rune to save them. Master Larad was the other Runebreaker. He was in league with Shemal.

He had slain Sky.

The last time they had seen Larad, the runespeaker had been leaving the Gray Tower, banished by All-master Oragien. In the months since, he must have found the Necromancer Shemal, must have cast his lot with hers out of bitterness at his exile. He had journeyed to the Black Tower, and he had murdered Sky— sweet, voiceless Sky, who had somehow been both man and rune. Larad had made off with the rune of sky, taking it back to Shemal. And now he had broken it.

Do it, Travis! Jack's voice—and a hundred other voices— roared in his mind. *Speak* Krond. *He cannot match your strength, Runebreaker though he may be.*

Travis gathered his will. However, before he could speak the rune, an animal snarl sounded to his left, and a shadow streaked toward Larad. For a stunned moment Travis thought it was Vani, but the *T'gol* stood next to Beltan, and this thing moved on all fours.

It was a panther, its eyes gleaming like gold moons. Dimly,

Travis noticed that Melia was no longer beside Falken. The panther crouched low before Master Larad, growling deep in its throat, ready to spring. The runespeaker staggered back a step and held up a hand. It was stained with blood.

"Please, listen to me," he said, his voice tight with pain and fear. "Kill me after you hear these words. I don't care, for I imagine I'm dying anyway. But first you must listen to what I have to tell you, Master Wilder."

The rune evaporated on Travis's lips. It had been hard to see against the black fabric, but now Travis did: There was a dark, wet patch on the right side of Larad's robe, and it was growing.

"Stand back," Falken said, his voice stern.

The panther snarled again, its tail twitching.

Falken made a fist of his silver hand. "I don't care what you think he did. It can't be chance he's come upon us in this place, and we're not going to kill him before we listen to what he has to say. Now stand back, Melia."

The panther let out a complaining growl, then a nimbus of azure light sprang into being around the great cat. Its form shimmered, changed, and a moment later Melia stood in its place. She smoothed her black hair with a hand as the nimbus faded, and her amber eyes gleamed with anger and suspicion.

Beltan appeared nonplussed at this transformation, and Vani looked on in curiosity, but Travis forgot Master Larad and instead stared at Melia.

"Have you always been able to do that?"

She gave him a sharp smile. "It's my little secret, dear. Although I suppose that cat's been let out of the bag, if you will." Melia turned her gaze on Larad, and all traces of her smile were gone. "For some reason I cannot fathom, Falken seems to be of a lenient mind. I am not so merciful. You killed Sky in the service of Shemal. Why should I not kill you now?"

Larad sighed, a sound of weariness and sorrow. "Because I didn't serve the Necromancer, much as she believed I did, and I didn't kill Sky. He gave himself of his own free will."

Beltan snorted. "That's not how it looked to us at the Black Tower. We saw you stab him. I'm with Melia. I say we kill you right now."

The runespeaker did not look at him. "As I said, do what you wish. Just hear what I have to say first."

Travis hesitated, then moved closer. At the Gray Tower, it had been largely because of Larad's machinations that Travis had been sentenced to die at the null stone. However, Larad had also helped to arrange Travis's escape from that fate, and as they had learned, he had done the things he did to help the Runespeakers find purpose again.

"How?" Travis pointed at the shattered fragments of the bound rune. "How did you manage to break the rune of sky? The art of Runebreaking is lost."

Larad's expression was part grimace, part smile. "Not lost to you, Master Wilder. And nor to me, now." He wiped his right hand against his robe, cleaning away the blood, then held it out. A silver symbol shone on his palm: three crossed lines. The rune of runes.

Travis clenched his right hand into a fist; if he were to speak a rune, the same symbol would appear on his own palm.

"By Olrig," Falken swore, his faded blue eyes wide. "You've become a runelord. But how?"

Larad's eyes were thoughtful in his shattered face. "And if I told you it was Olrig One-Hand himself who made me into this, would you believe me, Master Falken?" He lowered his hand. "No, don't answer, for it matters not. There is no time for this. I have broken the rune of sky. The circle of the world has been cracked open. Mohg, Lord of Nightfall, comes."

Melia balled her small hands into fists. "It took all of us gods working together, Old and New alike, to banish Mohg from the world. Such an alliance will never come again. And now you have opened the way for him." Tears shone in her eyes. "Why?"

Larad met her gaze. "Two worlds draw close to one another. They move nearer every day—our world, and the world from which Travis Wilder comes. Once they draw close enough, the way will be bridged, and Mohg would be able to return no matter what any of us might do."

"But it could have been years before such a thing took place," Falken said, his wolfish face haggard. "We could have had more time to prepare."

"And so could the enemy," Larad snapped.

He winced, pressing his hand to his side, then spoke more softly, so that they had to move closer to listen to him.

"Do you not see it? Sooner or later, evil will return to Eldh. By breaking the rune of sky, I have made it so that evil comes sooner, when it is ill prepared. If we waited until Mohg had gathered his strength, until he marched from that world to this with a vast army at his side, we never would have been able to stop him. We still may not be able to now, but at least we have a chance, however small it may be. Sky understood that. He found me not long after my exile from the Gray Tower, and he convinced me it was the only way. That was why he sacrificed himself at the Black Tower. The only hope for the world was to allow Mohg to return to it."

Sorrow shone in Falken's faded eyes. "And now that Mohg has returned, he'll break the First Rune and remake Eldh in his own shadowed image."

"Not if Master Wilder breaks it first," Larad said, his voice ragged.

All of them stared at the runespeaker. Above, bloodred lightning hissed across the churning sky.

"No." Sickness filled Travis, and dread. "No, I won't do it. It's not my fate. I have no fate."

Larad waved the words aside with an angry motion. "Fate is what we choose, Master Wilder, not what is chosen for us. The end is here, you can't change that—no one can now. The First Rune *will* be broken. There *will* be a Runebreaker. It can be Mohg—or it can be you. That is your fate. That is your choice."

Travis couldn't move. For so long he had run from this destiny. He had done everything he could to keep it from coming to pass. Only all this time he had been running, not away from it, but straight toward it.

"Go, Master Wilder," Larad said, and blood flecked his lips. "Take the three Imsari. Go to the Dawning Stone." He nodded toward the two Maugrim, who had stood silently a short distance away. "They will help you. They know the way."

Travis reeled. Once again Larad had worked to purposes unknown to them—unknown to anyone, save for Sky, it seemed. Shemal must have thought him her slave, another Runebreaker she could manipulate to her own ends, a tool she could use to bring about victory for her master. But the Necromancer had been wrong.

"So you betrayed Shemal," Travis said.

Larad gave him a rueful look. "I have betrayed us all, if you do not do what you must, Travis Wilder. Shemal was..." A shudder coursed through him. "No, I will not speak of my days with Shemal. It is enough to say I used her even as she thought she was using me, and somehow, though I never expected to, I have survived. Somehow she was wounded in Calavan, and she sought to flee back to Imbrifale for protection. I followed, knowing that was my chance to gain Gelthisar. Then, quite to my surprise, we came upon Kelephon, and he had the Stone of Ice with him. When I saw that was so, I knew the time to act had finally come."

"So you began the end of the world," Travis said softly. "And now you want me to finish it."

"It is not my choice such a task should be given to you, Master Wilder. I still believe you are given to foolishness and impracticality, and that your knowledge is insufferably lacking." Larad hesitated, then despite the pain on his face, he grinned. "But I also believe that you are good at heart, and that there is no one in this world stronger than you."

Travis was aware of the gazes of the others on him. He could only shake his head. Larad was wrong; he had to be.

With stiff motions, Larad moved to Kelephon's dead body, bent down, and picked up Gelthisar. "I am a runelord now. I can touch the Great Stones and live. But I have not your skill with the Imsari, Master Wilder. I could not wield them, not like you, even were I not wounded. This power is new to me. I have found it... difficult to control properly. That's why this happened when I broke the rune of sky." He touched the dark spot on his robe.

Travis understood. It was hard to control something you had been given all at once, something that should be earned over time, gradually, and through hard work.

But you have worked hard, Travis, Jack's voice spoke in his mind. *You've learned much. More than you think you have. Larad is right. Only you can do this.*

"You are losing blood," Vani said, eyeing Larad's robe. "You should let us see to your injuries."

Anger crossed his scarred face. "There's no time for such unimportant things." He limped toward Travis. "You must take the Stones, Master Wilder. You must go to the First Rune. That is what I had to tell you, and now I have." He held out his hand. Gelthisar shone blue-white on his palm.

Thunder rolled across the world, shaking the ground. A wind sprang up, rushing from the mountains, slicing through cloth and into flesh like a bitter knife. Forks of lightning tore apart the clouds, and the air deepened into dusk, as if a shadow had fallen across the world.

"The Lord of Nightfall comes!" Larad shouted above the moan of the wind. "Mohg will be upon us in a moment, and he will wrest the Imsari from us." He thrust the Stone of Ice forward. "Take it, Runebreaker. Go, before it's too late!"

Melia and Falken gazed at Travis, their faces pale, their eyes imploring. The wind blew ash into his eyes, stinging them. When he blinked the grit away, he saw Beltan standing before him. It was impossible, but the blond man was smiling.

"I know you're afraid, Travis." Beltan took his hand and squeezed it tight. "We're all afraid, too. I can't really see how all this can possibly work out. But maybe it's like the guard tower at Calavere after the explosion. Sometimes, to save something, you have to destroy it first."

If Travis had added up all the grief, all the sorrow and despair—and all the love—he had ever felt in all the years of his life, it would have been nothing compared to what he felt in that one, single moment. He tried to speak, but the only sound he could seem to make was a sob. Over the knight's shoulder, Vani was looking at him, her gold eyes filled not with fear or doubt, but with hope. She held both of her hands to her stomach, and she was smiling at him.

Beltan kissed his brow. "Go."

For a moment Travis stood frozen. Then another crack of thunder rent the air like the sound of a great and terrible whip. The shadow deepened, stretching out over the world. Travis turned and took Gelthisar from Larad's hand. It was not cold against his skin as he had expected, but rather cool and smooth as glass. He drew the other Stones from his pocket and held all three in his hand. They glowed softly, one blue-white, one fiery red-orange, and one as gray-green as twilight in a forest.

The two Maugrim—the shaman and the gnarled witchwoman—had drawn close. Travis looked up at them. "Take me to the Dawning Stone."

The man pointed with a thick-knuckled finger, toward the mountains, and made a low grunting noise in his throat.

This way.

59.

Travis did not look back.

If he had, he was afraid he would fall to his hands and knees, that he would crawl back over the dusty ground to Melia and Falken, to Beltan and Vani, that he would clutch them and beg them not to make him go.

Instead he kept his eyes forward and clenched his jaw as he followed after the Maugrim. They moved quickly across the valley, walking with a strange, loping gate, and he had to hurry to keep up with them. The cold, dry air knifed at his lungs, and the metallic taste of blood spread through his mouth. How far would they have to go? Was it even possible to reach the Dawning Stone before Mohg?

The sky grew darker. The lightning had ceased, but the wind blew harder, howling down from the Ironfang Mountains, blowing away the clouds to reveal a jagged line running across the sky.

Grit clawed at Travis's eyes. By the time he blinked them clear, he had lost sight of the Maugrim. He turned in circles, calling out to them, but the wind snatched his voice away. He was lost, and this was the end of everything.

A strong hand gripped his arm and pulled him to the side. The buffeting of the wind ceased, though Travis could still hear its keening. He rubbed his eyes and saw he was in a cave. Walls of rough stone pressed close, only the force was comforting rather than oppressive. In one direction lay the mouth of the cave; dust swirled beyond. In the other direction lay . . . what? Travis wasn't sure. It was as if a gray curtain hung over the back of the cave, its fabric billowing as air moved past it. A faint silver light hung on the air.

"Do you live here?" Travis said, his voice echoing off the stone walls. "Is this your home?"

The man—the shaman—shook his head. *We make our homes in such places, in the sheltered spaces of the ground. But not here. Not under the watching eyes of He-Who-Wields-The-Ice.*

The witch-woman let out a cackle. She pointed at Travis. *Now this is He-Who-Wields-The-Ice. And He-Who-Wields-The-Flame-And-The-Gloom.*

Travis clenched his hand around the Stones. Their touch was solid and reassuring, lending him a small measure of strength. He moved deeper into the cave. The gray curtain undulated. Soft tendrils curled away from it, evaporating.

It wasn't a curtain at all; it was a wall of fog. Only there was something queer about it—about the way it remained cohesive despite the air moving through the tunnel. He started to reach a hand toward it, then pulled back.

"What is this?" he said. "Is this a way into the Twilight Realm?"

The way can be found anywhere, the man said in his hooting language. *Atop any lonely mountain, beneath any ancient tree, in the dim heart of any hollow hill. You have only to look for it.*

A cool tendril brushed Travis's face. "But what kind of place is the Twilight Realm? I've heard Falken talk about it, about how the Old Gods and the Little People retreated there a thousand years ago, but I don't really know what it is."

The old woman clucked her tongue. *The Twilight Realm is not a place. It is a time. A time when the world was not so weary as it is now, when trees ruled the forests and clouds the mountaintops. A time when silence was the sweetest music, when the air had never been sundered by the sound of a smith's hammer against a forge, or by the cries of men dying on the swords of other men. A time when the gods were everywhere—in every hill and river and stone. A time of wildness, of beauty.*

Sorrow shone on her strange yet human face, and joy. Her hands fluttered to her breast, and she sighed.

It was . . . it is . . . our time.

Travis breathed. He didn't understand, not with words anyway. All the same, he could feel it in his heart: an ache, a longing, too deep and ancient to be expressed in such a recent and human invention as language. It was a peace, a power. A sense of belonging. For a moment he almost caught it, almost knew what it would be like not to try to master the world, but simply to be part of it—a single strand of the shining web that connected all things.

Like the fog, he could not grasp it. The moment passed. The Stones weighed heavy in his hands.

"How do I find the Dawning Stone?" he said.

The Maugrim man pointed at the Imsari. *They will know the way.*

The witch-woman nodded toward the wall of fog. *Go.* Tears ran down her weathered cheeks. *Be the end of all things.*

Travis could find no words to reply. He gripped the Stones and stepped into the fog.

In a heartbeat he was lost. The mist coiled around him, left and right, above and below. Something was wrong; he hadn't passed through. He had to go back.

Travis stumbled in what he thought was the direction he had come from, but his hands didn't find the rough stone of the cave, just more cool fog. He called out to the Maugrim, but the mist filled his mouth, muffling his voice. This place was empty except for the fog and himself.

No, there was something else here. A roar echoed through the mist: low and distant, yet drawing nearer. The fog swirled, agitated. The gloom deepened as a shadow drew closer.

Mohg. He was here in the Twilight Realm. Or wherever this place was. Another cry sounded all around—hateful, longing. He was looking for Travis.

Travis pressed forward, but it was no use; the mist and the shadow lay in every direction. The fog shuddered as another groan passed through it. The Lord of Nightfall was coming. He would find Travis, he would wrest the Stones from him. . . .

The Stones. Travis had forgotten about the Great Stones. He

brought his right hand close to his face, until he could see them glowing softly in the gloom. The Maugrim had said they would show him the way to the Dawning Stone. Only how?

His right hand jerked, as if something tugged at it. Startled, he let go of the Stones. The three Imsari hovered before him, shining in the fog. Then they began to move.

Travis was too surprised to do anything but follow. The glowing spheres floated swiftly, like tiny comets. The fog pushed against him, trying to hold him back, but he forced his way though it.

"Krond," he said, not trying to speak against the mist, but rather whispering with it. *"Gelth. Sinfath."* The Stones knew their names. Their light brightened, driving back the fog, and Travis found he could move more freely.

Again he spoke the names of the Imsari, and in so doing he caught a glimmer of knowledge. For so long Travis had resisted the power of the Stones; he had locked them away for fear of those who sought them, and for fear of the havoc he might wreak because he did not understand them. Only now that he had finally dared to speak their names, he realized he did understand them, at least a little.

The Great Stones were everything. Creation, permanence, destruction—the Imsari combined all of those things, just as the Runelords had combined the arts of Runespeaking, Runebinding, and Runebreaking into one. However, while the magic of the Stones was like rune magic in a way, it was not the same. It was deeper, older. Fire, ice, twilight—these essences had been infused into them by the craft of the dark elf Alcendifar long ago. The runes *Krond*, *Gelth*, and *Sinfath* colored their powers. However, at their core, each of the three Stones was the same— a part of a whole greater than any one rune. Together, they might perform wonders. Or horrors.

It was too late to stop them. The Stones raced forward, swifter now, as if they sensed what it was they sought. Travis hurled himself after them.

The fog ended. Travis blinked and found himself in a forest. He turned around, expecting to see the curtain of mist behind him, but all he saw was trees marching away in silent ranks.

In a way, it was like his first journey to Eldh. He had fallen through an impossible billboard, and had found himself in a forest with no sign of the portal, no way to get back home. However, while the gray-barked trees of this forest looked like *valsindar*, they were taller than the trees of the Winter Wood, and there was no sign of Falken Blackhand.

"Hello?" Travis called out.

The word echoed away among the trees. No reply came back. The three Stones whirred around Travis's head like insects. He held out his hand, and the Imsari settled onto it.

"Which way do I go?"

They glowed on his palm but did not move.

Travis looked up, trying to see the sky, to see if it was broken in this place as in the world outside, but there was no gap in the leafy canopy. A drowsy green-gold light permeated the air, making him think of an afternoon in late summer, and he caught the cool sound of water flowing. A desire came over him to seek out the stream, to drink from its waters, and to lie down on its bank and doze. This was a peaceful place, an ancient place. Travis started toward the sound of the water.

"Now is not the time for rest," said a piping voice. "You will not find what you seek that way."

Travis turned around. A tiny man clad in a green jacket and yellow breeches sat on a fallen log ten paces away. His face was as brown as the forest loam, and his eyes as bright as river pebbles.

Travis was beyond astonishment. "Trifkin Mossberry."

The little man stood on the log, doffed his feathered cap, and bowed.

Travis took a step forward—slowly, afraid that if he moved suddenly the little man might vanish. He had first encountered Trifkin Mossberry and his troupe of curious actors in King Kel's keep. Then, on that fateful Midwinter's Eve more than a year ago, Trifkin had helped Travis and Grace to uncover the conspiracy of murder in Calavere. The next day, the little man had been gone. Travis had not seen him since.

Until now.

"Who are you?" Travis said. "Who are the Little People, really?"

"A wordless song no longer sung. A memory of a time long

lost except in the minds of forgotten gods. A dream." Trifkin shrugged small shoulders. "Even we don't know who we are, and the world could not tell us, for when it came into being, we were already here. Just as we are here at its end."

Travis felt so heavy. The Stones seemed to weigh him down, as if they had grown larger. However, they still fit snugly in his right hand.

"Does it have to end?"

The tall trees swayed, as if a wind stirred their tops, though the balmy air of the forest was still.

Trifkin sighed. "It has already ended. More times than there are trees, the world has been made and unmade and made anew. Always there is a Worldsmith. And always there is a Worldbreaker. Just as night follows day. You cannot change that. You can only choose what the world will be."

The trees danced in slow circles. Travis felt the first stirring of a cold wind. Always before, facing into the wind had brought a sense of limitless possibility to him. However, now it brought . . . fear. A low rumble shook the air, like the sound of thunder. The gold light dimmed.

Travis's hand sweated around the Imsari. "What do I do?"

"You know what you must do. Go to the Dawning Stone."

"But I don't know where it is."

Despite the sorrow in his eyes, Trifkin clapped his small hands and laughed. "Why, it's right beneath your boots."

This was too much for Travis. "What?" he croaked.

Trifkin hopped down from the log. "Think, mortal man. You already know the answer. What happened at the making of the world?"

It was hard, but Travis thought back to the stories the rune-speakers had told him. "The Worldsmith spoke the First Rune, the rune Eldh, and the world came into being. Then he bound the First Rune into the Dawning Stone, so that the world would know permanence and endure."

"Yes," Trifkin said. "Permanence." He knelt and pressed his hands against the ground, digging his fingers into the soil.

For a moment Travis stared, not comprehending. Then it struck him like a bolt of lightning. All this time he had been picturing the Dawning Stone as a piece of rock with a rune in it, like one of the creations of the Runebinders of old. But that was ludicrous. The Worldsmith was far more than a mere mortal wizard, and Eldh far more than a simple disk of stone.

"The world," Travis said softly. "The whole world Eldh is the Dawning Stone."

Trifkin held up his dirty hands and smiled.

Travis staggered. "That doesn't make sense. Falken said the Dawning Stone was hidden in the Twilight Realm."

Trifkin cocked his head. "And have you not found it here?"

Travis knelt and pressed his left hand to the ground. He felt it—the force of the rune Eldh, binding the world, holding it and everything on it together.

And so the First Rune shall also be the Last Rune, spoke Jack's voice in his mind, *for when it breaks, the world shall end, and in that instant all things will cease to be.*

The gold light dimmed. Dusk stole among the trees, as if carried on the wind.

"Night comes," Trifkin said.

Then the little man was gone, and Travis was alone.

No, not alone. He could feel it drawing closer. A shadow—a thing forged of fury and hate, its heart consumed by a dragon and replaced by cold, hard iron.

Mohg, Lord of Nightfall.

The forest was dark now; the only light came from the Imsari. Travis laid them on the ground.

"I don't know what to do," he said simply.

Yes you do, Travis, Jack's voice spoke in his mind. *You are the Runebreaker. There is but one thing you can do.*

"No, Jack." He clasped his hands together. "I don't want to destroy the world. I want to save it."

By the Lost Hand of Olrig, don't be so dim! Haven't you figured it out by now? Worldmaker and Worldbreaker—they're the same thing. You can't be one without being the other. Mohg knows that—that's why he wants to break the First Rune. Not to destroy the world, but to remake it in his own image.

The trees rocked wildly under the force of the wind. Their trunks cracked and splintered as they fell over. One tree came crashing down beside Travis. A few feet more to one side, and it would have crushed him. He stared at the three Stones and dug his fingers into the dirt beside them. Jack was wrong, he had to be. Creation and destruction—they couldn't really be the same thing, could they?

Except they were, and Beltan was right. Sometimes the only way to save something was to destroy it first.

A shadow streaked toward Travis: vast, malevolent, unstoppable. The wind verged into a shriek. Trees burst apart in deafening explosions. The darkness was complete, save for the glow of the Stones. Silhouetted by their light, Travis saw a figure: tall and powerful beyond mortal imagining, a single, blazing eye staring from a face both beautiful and terrible. A maw opened, revealing fangs like daggers. Hands reached out, extending talons toward the Imsari.

Mine, intoned a voice as deep as a midnight ocean.

Travis looked up, into the one fiery eye, and a sharp smile cut across his lips.

"Too late," he said.

The blazing eye widened. The talons lashed out, only too slow. Larad was right. Despite an eon of exile, this moment had come sooner than Mohg had expected; he was not prepared.

Travis was. He lifted his muddy hands from the ground, pressed them on top of the three Stones, and cried out the word with all his being.

Reth!

Travis braced himself for terrible thunder, for a blinding flash. He waited to feel the ground buckle and crack beneath him, for fire to rain down from above, to feel his body being ripped to shreds. Instead there was . . .

. . . nothing. Nothing at all.

It didn't work, Jack, he called out in his mind. *You were wrong—I'm not the Runebreaker after all. It didn't work.*

He tried to laugh, only he could make no sound.

Jack?

Travis heard nothing, not even the beat of his own heart. All was silence. The forest was gone, and he drifted in some sort of fog. Was this the mist that bordered the Twilight Realm?

No, it was different. Even then, he had been able to see different shades of gray swirling in the mist. Here, everything was the same color, though exactly what color it was, he couldn't say. It was neither white nor black, neither light nor dark, neither warm nor cold. It was nothing.

And it was everything at once.

He had always feared the end of the world because he had imagined it as a violent happening: a time of boiling seas and crumbling stone, of screams cried out in pain and fear, of blood and mayhem. Of death. But he had been so absurdly wrong.

For when it breaks, the world shall end, and in that instant all things will cease to be. . . .

The words were a whisper in his mind, though whether they were spoken by a voice or a memory of a voice, he couldn't be sure.

Jack?

Again there was no reply. He was alone. Truly alone. The world was gone. Eldh was no more. He was the very last being in all of existence.

Or the very first.

That was when he sensed it, like the first whisper of a wind in the stillness. It made him think of Castle City, of standing on the boardwalk outside the Mine Shaft Saloon and turning to face the wind as it raced down from the mountains. Waiting to see what it would blow his way.

He felt it now—the sweet ache of endless possibilities. The old world was no more. The new world was yet to be. And it could be anything he chose to make it. Joy filled him, and power. Like a billion doors, the possibilities opened before him—a different world beyond each one. What should he choose? A world without hatred, without fear, without violence?

Yes, there was such a world. He reached toward it . . . then recoiled. The people in that world huddled in mud huts, staring with listless eyes at smoky fires, their bodies filthy and covered with sores. They spoke no stories, sang no songs, made no music. They had no fears, no cares, no worries. And no hopes, no desires, no dreams.

Did such things have to go hand in hand? He had chosen the wrong door, that was all. Travis moved toward another, toward a world without hunger, without pain, without sorrow.

He saw a modern city, not unlike Denver, but its lines

cleaner, sharper. In it, a mother walked down a street. She stared at the dead child in her arms, then let it fall to the gutter as she continued on. Nearby, a man had been struck by a car. He flopped in the street, confusion on his face, not agony. No one stopped to help him. He dragged himself to the edge of the street, trailing shattered legs, then died. A street sweeping truck drove by, scooped up the bodies, and drove on. The sky was dark with soot; no one looked up.

No, that wasn't what he had meant. Travis turned away and flung open another door. In this world, there was no such thing as death. He saw a village like that below Castle Calavere, its dirt streets littered with bundles of sticks.

Horror blossomed in him. They weren't sticks, but people— withered, decrepit people. They raised desiccated arms, staring with milky eyes, opening toothless mouths in moans of suffering, begging for release. Passersby stared at them with hate, then hurried past.

Travis fled. That wasn't it. A world of peace, of joy, of beauty, that was what he wanted. He found a door beyond which people danced and laughed, smiles on their simple faces. Yes, this was right. Then he drew closer and saw more. At night, monsters dragged the children from their beds and ate them. The people made it a game; they never spoke of the ones who went missing. They simply danced and clapped their hands as shadows prowled just beyond the lights of their small, happy towns.

A thousand doors he opened, and Travis glimpsed a thousand terrible worlds beyond them. He cried out into the nothingness, but there was no one to listen to him. It wasn't supposed to be like this. There had been such sorrow in the old world. War and hatred and violence. What was the use of being the Worldsmith if he couldn't create a world without these things? He wanted a world without pain and suffering, without despair. A world where Beltan and Vani's daughter had a hope of growing up ...

Travis stopped, letting himself drift in the fog. He reached up to touch the bone talisman at his throat, but of course, like all things, it did not exist.

Yet it could.

He knew a world where there had been pain, and sadness,

and death, and where all the same people kept on going, kept on fighting, kept on living. Because they had hope. Hope that they and the ones they loved could someday be happy. Hope that, after night, another day would come.

Yes, he knew a world where there was hope.

Travis searched, and he saw it at once among all of the other possibilities. It seemed so dim and imperfect. No wonder he hadn't noticed it before; surely there were far better worlds to choose than this. Maybe, if he had been a god, he could have found those worlds. But Travis wasn't a god. He was a man. A man who loved and hated. Who laughed and wept. Who feared. And who hoped.

Even as he wondered how to make his choice, he did.

Eldh, he whispered to the mist. *For the world to be, I choose the world that was.*

Somewhere, there was a sound like a door shutting.

And then.

60

Beneath a flawless cerulean sky, Grace Beckett, Queen of Malachor, opened her eyes.

For a time she simply lay there without moving, nestled in the embrace of the ground, content to gaze upward. The sunlight was like a warm caress on her cheeks, and there wasn't a cloud in sight. She couldn't remember ever seeing anything so beautiful as this sky in all her life.

"Over here!" a man's voice shouted, breaking the silence. "I've found her—over here!"

More shouts came in reply, though too distant for Grace to make out what was said. She heard the thud of boots draw closer, followed by the jingle of chain mail as someone knelt beside her. She couldn't see who it was; the sky filled her gaze.

"Your Majesty, can you hear me?" said a man, the same one who had shouted. "Are you well?"

What a strange question! She felt no pain, no fear, no sorrow. Why shouldn't she be well? Nothing could possibly be wrong when you were already dead. She would lie here in the embrace of the ground and watch the sky forever.

The sound of more boots, as well as lighter footsteps and the soft swish of wool. This time it was a woman's voice who spoke. "What is it, Sir Tarus? Oh, by Sia, she's not . . . ?"

"No, her eyes are open, thank the Seven, but she won't answer me. Your Majesty—lend me a hand."

Strong hands reached down, gripping her, pulling her upward, and the sky tilted. Black shapes hove into view, jagged as teeth. Mountains. She gasped as the hands sat her upright, and cold air rushed into her lungs.

"Lay me back in the ground," she murmured. "I'm dead. Lay me back down."

"I'm sorry to have to disappoint you, Your Majesty," the man said with a laugh, "but you're very much alive." Amazement stole into his voice. "Somehow we all are, though I don't have the foggiest idea how that can be."

Grace blinked, and three faces came into focus before her.

Tarus and Teravian held her shoulders, and Aryn knelt before her, relief in her sapphire eyes.

"Thank Sia you're alive," the young witch said. "We've been searching the battlefield for hours, but we couldn't find you, and night comes soon. Only we didn't give up hope."

"We must have walked right past this place a dozen times," Teravian said. The wind blew his dark hair from his brow. "We were certain you fell somewhere near here, Your Majesty, only we couldn't sense your thread. The Weirding is a tangle of life and death here."

"It was this blasted crack in the ground," Tarus said. "She was wedged down inside of it. There was no way to see her unless you were three paces away." The red-haired knight grinned at her. "And I still wouldn't have found you, Your Majesty, if it hadn't been for your breath. It's getting colder, and I saw a white puff rise up from the ground."

Aryn threw her left arm around Grace. "We were near you when it all happened, only we lost track of you in the chaos. We saw you strike down the Pale King. Then everything went mad."

Piece by piece, the shards of memories came together in Grace's mind. She remembered ancient eyes, burning with hatred in a face as pale as frost. "He was about to strike me down with his scepter. I couldn't stop him. Only then the sky... there was a terrible sound, and something happened to the sky. Berash looked up, and I saw a gap in his armor. I thrust at it with my sword." She looked around. "My sword..."

"There, Your Majesty," Teravian said, pointing into the narrow pit in the ground from which they had pulled her. "I'm afraid you won't be wielding Fellring again."

She must have fallen on top of them in the pit: several shards of steel. The sword ended in a broken stump just above the hilt. It had done what it had been forged to do; she would not need it again.

Thank you, Sindar, she whispered in her mind.

The shadows of the mountains stretched out over the vale, and Grace shivered. Somehow the world was still here, and she wasn't dead after all.

"I think I'd like to stand up now," she said.

Wanting and doing were two different things, but with the

help of the two men Grace got her feet beneath her. The feeling of wellness was gone. Her sword arm ached, and she couldn't feel her right hand at all.

"It's cold as ice," Aryn said, touching Grace's hand.

She murmured a spell, and Grace felt the warmth of the Weirding flow into her. The pain in her arm receded, and her hand burned with a thousand hot pinpricks. She concentrated and found she could move her fingers.

Turning, Grace gazed out over the vale toward the Rune Gate, which yawned like a dark maw. The Gate stood open, but she saw no sign of the enemy—only the abandoned siege engines, which hulked like gigantic scarecrows over the battlefield. The floor of the vale was white in the gloaming. Had it snowed while she was asleep?

Another shiver passed through her. It wasn't snow that covered the ground. It was a layer of bones, stretching all the way to the foot of the mountains.

"The Pale King's army," she said, clutching Tarus's arm. "What happened to them?"

"They're dead," the knight said.

"But how?"

Together, Tarus, Aryn, and Teravian did their best to describe what had happened, though it was hard for them to put into words exactly what they had seen. What they told her fused with what she recalled herself, and an amalgam of the truth began to form in her mind. It was dim and incomplete, but she thought perhaps she understood.

The *feydrim*, the wraithlings, the ironheart wizards and witches—even, it seemed, the trolls of the Icewold—all had been created by the dark magic of the Necromancers, who themselves had been forged by the will of the Pale King. When Berash perished, so did everything he had created.

A thousand years ago, in this same vale, when King Ulther plunged Fellring into Berash's chest, shattering the Pale King's iron heart, the Necromancers had been there; they had managed to pour some of their essence back into Berash, sustaining him until his heart could be reforged.

This time, there were no Necromancers to save the Pale King. Shemal was the last of her kind, and wherever she might be, she had not shown herself in this place. When Fellring shattered his heart, Berash had died—truly, finally—and so did everything he had brought into being with his dark enchantments. Only the bones remained.

Tarus moved to a jumbled heap of armor. It was forged of black metal; spikes jutted from it. "You did it, Your Majesty. You slew the Pale King." With the toe of his boot, he kicked at a helm crowned by antlers of iron. The helmet rolled over; it was empty.

Grace stared at the fallen armor, pressing her aching arm against her chest. It seemed impossible. He had been a figure of dread majesty, and she was a skinny mortal woman. All the same, she had defeated him. She should have been relieved, only she wasn't. Something nagged at her. Then, as the sun touched the tips of the mountains, she had it.

"Mohg," she said, staring at the dying sun. "The Pale King wasn't the real master of these creatures. Mohg was. He created Berash, just as Berash made the Necromancers and they made the *feydrim* and wraithlings. These things shouldn't have died when the Pale King did."

Teravian shrugged. "Maybe Mohg's power couldn't sustain them. After all, he's still banished beyond the circle of the world."

Grace looked up at the sky. Cerulean had deepened to cobalt. "Beyond the circle of the world," she murmured.

"Can you walk, sister?" Aryn said, touching her arm. "It's growing colder. We should return to the keep."

Tarus nodded. "Sir Paladus and Sir Vedarr are in charge of things there at the moment, but I imagine they'll be more than happy to turn command over to you, Your Majesty. There are many who are wounded, and the sight of you alive will lend all the men heart. I know Master Graedin and All-master Oragien in particular will be glad to see your face."

"Wait a moment," Teravian said. "We won't want to forget these." He took off his cloak, then laid the broken shards of Fellring on it. He wrapped them up in the cloak and held the bundle toward Grace.

She gave him a wan smile, then gestured to her right arm.

"Would you do the honors, Your Majesty? I don't think I'll be carrying any swords, broken or not, for a while."

The four of them moved slowly toward the passage that led back to the keep. Though the light was beginning to fail, men still combed the battlefield, looking for any survivors they might have missed, and gathering the bodies of their comrades who had fallen. The Spiders Aldeth and Samatha were directing the search, and the witches Senrael and Lursa assisted them, seeking out the life threads of any who still lived.

It was grim work, but according to Tarus it was nearly done. Of the five thousand men that had marched to Gravenfist Keep, over a thousand were lost forever, and many hundreds more would never fully recover from their wounds, but that they were not all dead was a miracle Grace still could not comprehend.

They had nearly reached the door to the secret passage when a massive figure strode over the battlefield toward them. It took Grace a moment to realize it was Kel. His bushy red beard had been shaved off, and without it the petty king looked younger and jollier—more like an overfed monk than a warrior-chieftain.

"Your Majesty!" he cried out, clamping big arms around her and lifting her off the ground. "By Jorus, you're alive!"

Grace gritted her teeth. "Not for much longer if you keep that up."

Kel set her back down. "Sorry about that." He turned his head, gazing from side to side.

"Have you lost something?" Tarus said.

"As a matter of fact, I have," Kel said with a grunt. "I've lost my witch. Somehow I managed to misplace her during the fray, and now I can't find her."

"Maybe she's back at the keep," Aryn offered.

Kel scowled. "I've already tried there, but no one's seen her. This is most bothersome. I need her to look at her runes and tell me whether it would be auspicious to grow my beard back or not." He clenched a meaty fist. "The wretched hag is hiding from me somewhere."

"How about right in front of your face, Your Obliviousness?" croaked an acidic voice.

As one they turned to see a ragged form shambling toward

them on stick-thin legs. Grisla halted before Grace and bared her lone tooth in a grin. "Greetings, Queen of Malachor."

The hag bowed low, and Grace was so flustered she started to bow in return until Tarus caught her arm.

Kel glared at the crone. "What about me, hag? Aren't you going to show me proper obeisance? And where have you been all this time?"

She thrust her hands against her lumpy hips and rolled her one bulbous eye. "I've been seeing to more important things than the fur on your face, Your Hairiness. I've been searching for stragglers on the battlefield. In fact, I've just found some." She gestured with a knobby hand.

Grace and the others looked up. Five figures walked toward them—slowly, as if exhausted beyond imagining. At first they were only silhouettes in the gloom. Then one last stray beam of sunlight found its way through a gap in the mountains to fall on the battlefield, illuminating their faces.

There is a joy that is beyond expression in words. It is experienced, not by the heart or by the mind, but by the soul—a sudden sense of *rightness* so clear and perfect that man's fleeting glimpses of it are surely what first gave him the idea of heaven.

Grace felt such a joy now. The sunlight made their faces shine, as if illuminated from within, so that each of them was more fair than she remembered. Melia and Falken. Beltan and Vani clad in strange, primitive leathers. And . . .

"Travis," she whispered, and then louder, with all the force of her joy. "Travis!"

She staggered forward, then he was running. He caught her in his arms, holding her with gentle strength. Her right arm wasn't much use, but she gripped him with the left, holding on with all her might. Like Vani and Beltan, he wore clothes made of aurochs hide, though his were stained orange with ocher.

The others reached them, and Grace was being held by Falken and Melia at once, and she was dimly aware that both the bard and the lady were weeping. Before she knew it, Beltan scooped her up in his arms, and she didn't care—she couldn't feel pain, not now. Then she found herself gazing into gold eyes.

Vani. She embraced the *T'gol*, and as she did Grace felt the faint swelling of the other woman's stomach.

After that Travis was there again, and he held her hands in his own. He looked older than she remembered. There were lines she hadn't seen before around his mouth and eyes, but they made him look handsome and wise.

"How?" she said. "How can you possibly be here?"

His voice was soft with wonder. "I'm not sure I know myself, Grace. I'm not sure any of us do."

"And is that true, Runebreaker?" Grisla said. She let out a cackle. "Or should I say, Worldmaker?"

Grace gave Travis a questioning look. He pulled his hands away from hers.

"Travis, what is it? What's happened to you?"

Grisla hobbled toward him. "I'll tell you what happened. He did it. He broke the First Rune."

An edge of terror cut through Grace's joy. "That's what happened to the sky, isn't it? It was the other Runebreaker. He broke the rune of sky, and Mohg returned to Eldh to break the First Rune, but somehow you stopped him."

"No," said a sardonic voice. "He didn't."

There was one more figure they hadn't seen; his black robe blended with the twilight. He approached Grace—slowly, hand pressed to his side—and the webwork of scars on his face glowed in the half-light.

"Master Larad?" Grace stuttered, completely confused. "How are you here?"

He said nothing, but only gestured to his black robe.

Confusion gave way to cold understanding. "You," Grace said softly. "You're the other Runebreaker. You broke the rune of sky and let him back into the world. That was the shadow that fell over us, right before the end. It was Mohg."

"Yes," Larad said, pain twisting his face. "It was."

"But you stopped him, Travis." She clutched his arm. "You must have, or none of us would be here. You stopped Mohg from breaking the First Rune. Only how?"

A queer light shone in Travis's gray eyes.

"I'll tell you how he did it," Grisla said with another cackle. "He broke the First Rune himself, that's how." She jabbed a bony finger at his chest. "Bones and stone, that showed him, lad! Mohg wasn't ready for that."

Grace stared at Travis, trying to understand. Only maybe she didn't need to. Travis was here, and so were the rest of them. So was the world. That was all that mattered.

"The witches were right," Aryn said to Travis, her blue eyes wide. "You really were the Runebreaker. Yet if that's so, how are we still here?"

"He chose the world that was!" Grisla said gleefully. She capered about in a circle and chortled as if this all were a grand joke. "For the world to be, he chose the world that was! He's the Worldsmith now!"

Grace reached up and touched his face. His beard was coming in, copper and gold flecked with gray. "Is it true, Travis? Did you really choose this world?"

He gripped the bone talisman that hung against his neck. "Hope. I chose hope, Grace."

It was growing colder and darker; all the same none of them could move from that place. More questions were asked. In quick words Melia, Falken, Vani, and Beltan explained what had happened to them, and Aryn, Teravian, and Tarus did the same. On Eldh, Shemal and Kelephon were dead, along with their master the Pale King. On Earth, Duratek was doomed. However, there was one thing Grace didn't have the heart to speak of yet; she didn't tell them about Durge.

"What about Mohg?" Vani said, gazing up at the deepening sky. "Is he dead as well?"

Grisla gave Travis a piercing look. "Well, lad. Is he?"

Travis seemed to think for a long moment, then he sighed. "No, he's not dead. But he's . . . dispersed. He was right there when it happened, when the—" He swallowed. "—when I used the Great Stones to break the First Rune. I think he was torn apart by the force of it."

"That he was, my lad," Grisla said. "Mohg remains in the world, but only his spirit, not his hatred, not his will. Never will he gather himself again." She looked up at the darkening sky. "Night still comes. There will always be darkness in the world, there will always be evil. But dawn will come again, at least tomorrow."

Grace smiled at Travis. "Hope," she said.

Though the expression was tentative and fragile, he returned her smile.

Falken moved to Grisla, giving the old woman a sharp look. "If you don't mind my saying, you seem to know an awful lot for a simple hag. How did you know Travis broke the First Rune?"

She shrugged knobby shoulders. "It was a lucky guess, Your Nosiness."

"I think not," Melia said, gliding forward, her catlike eyes gleaming. "You were not there in Imbrifale with us. So how could you know?"

Kel roared with laughter, slapping his thigh, the sound of his mirth ringing out over the vale. "Well, it looks as if the bard and the moon lady have finally got you, hag. Don't you think it's time you finally told them who you really are?"

She scowled at the petty king. "What are you talking about, Your Deludedness? I'm Grisla, your witch."

Kel's laughter subsided, and his face grew unusually thoughtful. "In one of your guises, yes. But you are other things to other people, are you not? Don't look at me that way. I am not quite the simpleton you take me for."

Grace didn't know what Kel was talking about. Or did she? She held a hand out toward the hag. "Vayla?"

Grisla was silent for a moment, then she sighed. "It's time for me to go," she said softly. "I suppose there's no harm in it now." She hobbled toward Grace, and as she did she changed. In the place of Grisla stood another old woman, still gnarled and withered, but she wore a brown robe rather than motley rags.

"Greetings, my queen," Vayla said, bowing. She turned toward Aryn. "And to you as well, child."

As she spoke these last words, Vayla was gone, and in her place was a striking woman of middle years clad in a rainbow-hued gown, her jet hair marked by a single streak of white, her almond-shaped eyes accented by fine, wise lines.

Aryn's eyes went wide. "Sister Mirda!"

"Yes, sister," the beautiful witch said. "It is I."

"But how?" Aryn gasped.

Mirda smiled. "Does she not have many faces to wear? Crones. Mothers. And Maidens."

With this last word, her form shimmered again, and in her place was a radiant young woman Grace had never seen before. Her hair was like flax, her lips as red as berries.

Falken staggered, clutching his silver hand to his chest. "You!" the bard said, his voice hoarse. "For so many centuries I've searched for you."

She laughed, a sound like water over stones. "And you found me, only you didn't know it. Yet I would always know you, Falken of Malachor." She reached out, taking his silver hand. "Tell me, has it suited you?"

He gazed at her, amazement on his weathered face. "It has. Thank you. It's served me better than my own hand did."

"I am glad," the young witch said. "For I know what it is like to lose a hand."

Now the flaxen-haired woman was gone, and in her place stood a tall man, his face stern and imposing, but softened by kindness and wisdom. His left hand was missing at the wrist. He held up his right hand, and a silvery symbol shone on his palm: three crossed lines.

"The rune of runes," Travis murmured. "So that's who you are. You're Olrig Lorethief. You're an Old God."

"More than that," Master Larad said, limping closer. "You're the one who made this world. You're the Worldsmith."

"I *was* the Worldsmith," the one-handed man said. He turned his ancient gaze on Travis. "You are the Worldsmith now, Runebreaker."

Travis shook his head. "I chose the world that was. This is still the world as you made it."

The man's eyes were thoughtful. "So it is," he said. "So it is."

Master Larad held out his right hand. The rune of runes shone faintly on his palm. "The rune of sky has been broken. I don't need this anymore, and somehow it seems I'm not going to die after all. You must take it back."

The bearded man shook his head. "I cannot. Once a thing is made, it cannot be unmade without breaking it."

Larad lowered his hand. "Like Sky, you mean. You made him, didn't you? He was your servant."

"I gave him the form you knew, that he might do my work upon the world, yet I did not make him or any of the other runes. I spoke them at the beginning of the world—this world—and I bound them so they would not fade. But the runes were first wrought by an even older Worldsmith than I."

Larad closed his right hand into a fist and lowered it by his side.

Aryn hesitated, then stepped forward. "You're not just the Worldsmith, are you? You're Sia as well."

The man smiled, and in his place stood a woman, though what she was—maiden, mother, or withered crone—it was impossible to say. The features of a thousand different women flickered across her face. "Sia and the Worldsmith are just two names for the same thing, daughter. Why people insist on believing otherwise, I cannot say."

Aryn smiled, and Grace did as well. She wished Master Graedin was present. What would he think to learn that his mad idea, that the runespeakers and the witches were not so very different, was in fact the truth? Olrig. Sia. They were one. Magic was magic—it all sprang from the same source.

It was almost full dark now. Grace couldn't stop shivering. They could talk more tomorrow. Tomorrow, when the sun rose again. Until then, they should return to the keep.

"Will you stay?" Grace said to the woman with many faces, though she wasn't certain if she meant here, at Gravenfist, or if she meant *in the world*.

The woman's face blurred, and she was Grisla again. She grinned, baring her one tooth, but there was sorrow in her eye. "Perhaps I'll stay for a time, Your High-And-Mightiness. But my children have already gone on before me, back into the Twilight Realm. This time, when we go, we shall never return, and I think the Maugrim shall come with us. No one will remain who knows the way through the mists. Our world, our time, will be removed from yours forever."

Grace wept. "Why? Why are you leaving us?"

"There, there, daughter." She brushed the dampness from Grace's cheeks. "I am old. We are old. And the world has newer gods. Look—here comes the newest of them all even now."

They turned as ruby-colored light pushed back the gloom.

Three figures walked toward them from the direction of the keep, hand in hand. One was a man with coppery eyes, a grin on his handsome, familiar face, though he walked on two feet, not one. The other was a beautiful woman with black hair and eyes and skin like polished ebony. Between them was a child clad only in a gray shift, her hair wild and fiery. It was from the girl that the light emanated.

"Lirith!" Aryn called out. "Sareth!"

But Grace called out another name. "Tira!"

The little girl slipped her hands free and dashed forward on bare feet. Grace knelt and caught Tira in her arms.

"You came back," she said, even though she knew she hadn't. All the same, it felt good to say it. She stroked the girl's wild hair.

"I love you," Tira said in a solemn voice.

The crimson light grew stronger, encapsulating Grace in warmth. Then it dimmed and Grace held, not her warm little body, but shadows. She stood and looked up. A star shone in the southern sky, bright as a ruby. A fierce ache throbbed in Grace's chest, but it was a good pain. It meant that somehow, after all that had happened, her heart was still there.

It meant she was alive.

"Come on, Grace." It was Travis. He touched her arm. "It's getting cold. We should go inside."

They started back toward the keep, and as they went Grace noticed how Travis and Beltan stayed close to Vani's side. Though they had not spoken of it, it was clear both men knew the *T'gol* was with child. Grace wondered what would happen to them, but for now the three seemed content to walk close together. As for what the future held—if Fate would allow them to stay together—that could wait for tomorrow.

Other things could not wait, and as they walked Grace finally told them about Durge, though Aryn had to help her, and when one was too overwhelmed by grief the other would speak for a time. However, neither Grace nor Aryn mentioned what Durge had revealed to them: how he had loved Aryn. It was a private thing. The young baroness had married Teravian out of duty, and she had not resisted. However, the knowledge that Durge had wanted her not for her position, but simply for herself, was like a secret jewel she could treasure in lonely times to come.

Then Grace saw the way Teravian's hand brushed against Aryn's, and despite her sorrow she smiled. Perhaps there would not be so many lonely times in Aryn's future after all.

"There's one thing I don't understand," Beltan said as they drew near the secret passage. It was lit with torches against the night, and guards stood at the entrance.

"What is it?" Grace asked him.

The blond man scratched his chin. "Well, Travis broke the First Rune, just as prophecy said he would. But prophecy also said the Warriors of Vathris were destined to lose the Final Battle."

"We did," Sir Tarus said. "The army of the Pale King had us trapped in front of the keep's wall. They were about to crush us. Victory was theirs."

"We could not have defeated them," Teravian agreed.

Aryn glanced at Travis. "Only then the Pale King died, and without Mohg to help them, so did his slaves."

Grace thought about this. "That doesn't change the fact that we lost." She sighed, gazing at Aryn, Teravian, and Tarus. "It was Travis who saved the world. I suppose, in the end, we didn't really matter."

"That's not true," Travis said, his gray eyes intent upon her. "You did matter. You all did. If you hadn't held Gravenfist Keep, the forces of the Pale King would have had time to overrun Eldh. They would have killed thousands upon thousands of people. The Dominions would have been laid waste." He gripped her hand. "Without you, Grace, there wouldn't have been a world for me to save, a world for me to choose."

Tarus grinned at her. "It looks like we did good after all, Your Majesty."

Grace lifted a hand, touching the bandage on her right shoulder. "Durge did good," she said firmly.

Together they stepped into the passage, leaving night to rule over the world. For a time.

61

It was after midnight.

Deirdre Falling Hawk sat at the dinette table in her South Kensington flat, gazing at the screen of her computer. She had spent the last three hours performing search after search in the Seekers' databases using her Echelon 7 clearance, but she had turned up nothing more relating to the Thomas Atwater case. She lifted a glass to her lips, but it was empty, and so was the nearby bottle of scotch.

Deirdre set down the glass, then leaned back from the table and rubbed her aching neck. An image shone in the center of the screen: the keystone taken from the location that had housed the tavern Thomas Atwater had been forbidden by the Seekers to return to. The same location that centuries later would house Surrender Dorothy, along with Glinda and its other half-fairy patrons. But what did it mean? Who was Atwater really? And what was the true purpose of the keystone?

Maybe it didn't matter now. She pushed aside the computer and picked up the copy of today's London *Times*, which lay on the table. Anders had brought it to the office that day, and she had stolen it before heading home. DURATEK INVESTIGA-TION CONTINUES, the headline read, NEW ATROCITIES UNCOVERED. Another headline caught Deirdre's eye, in smaller type near the bottom of the page: MORE DURATEK EXECUTIVES FOUND DEAD. The first sentences of the article described the mystery around the deaths. It seemed, when they were found, all of the executives had been missing their hearts.

A sharp smile cut across Deirdre's lips. "I hope you're seeing this Hadrian, wherever you are."

She wondered where in the world he was just then. If he was even still in this world. Would she ever see him again? She didn't know, but she hoped so. Just as she hoped one day she would see Travis Wilder and Grace Beckett again. She gripped the yellowed bear claw that hung around her neck. That was the funny thing about hope. It kept you going, even when the odds seemed impossible.

Her computer let out a chime, and her gaze snapped back to

the screen. The picture of the keystone was gone, and crimson words pulsed in its place.

> Open your door.

Deirdre leaped up, moved to the door, and jerked it open. The hallway outside her flat was empty. On the doormat lay a small parcel wrapped in brown paper. She looked both ways, then picked up the parcel, closed the door, and sat at the table. Fingers trembling, she unwrapped the package.

It was a sleek wireless phone. She hesitated, then opened it up and held it to her ear.

"I'm glad to see you're taking a break," a man's voice said. "Are you enjoying the newspaper?"

She sucked in a breath and stood, looking out the window. The street below was dark and empty, but he was out there somewhere, watching her.

"What do you want?" she said, snatching the curtains shut.

Soft laughter emanated from the phone. "Don't worry, Miss Falling Hawk. This is merely a social call. I wish only to see how you are faring after your trip to the United States. Tell me, did you enjoy today's headline?"

She glanced again at the newspaper. "Our plan worked," she said, amazement lowering her voice. "It's over."

"You're wrong about that, Miss Falling Hawk. A great darkness has been averted, yet other shadows remain. Duratek is finished. They will never reach the world called Eldh. But there are others who would go there. And some from that world who would come to this one."

She sank again into the chair at the table. "But that's impossible. Travis Wilder destroyed the gate. There's no way to cross between the worlds now."

"I hate to appear rude, but once again you're wrong. You see, Earth and Eldh draw closer to each other every day. One day, sooner than you think, perihelion will come. And with it will come great peril as well."

Her head throbbed, and the scotch burned in her stomach. "What do you mean? What sort of peril?"

The computer let out another chime, and an image appeared

on the screen. Deirdre's eyes locked on it. The image was dark and grainy. It showed two figures in black prowling down a narrow urban street, moving toward the camera.

"This photograph was taken three days ago," came the smooth voice through the phone.

Deirdre touched the screen. "What is it?"

"Allow me to magnify it for you."

The image expanded to take up the entire screen. Deirdre saw them clearer now. The two figures wore black robes that fluttered behind them like shadows. The final pixels rearranged themselves, and Deirdre clutched the phone.

Instead of faces, masks were nestled within the cowls of their robes. The masks were made of gold, like those stolen from a sarcophagus in a mummy's tomb, gazing forward with serene, deathless expressions.

"He's dead," she said into the phone, voice hoarse. "The sorcerer. I saw the *gorleths* tear him apart. He's dead."

"And now more have come to take his place."

"But what do they want?"

A faint hiss emanated from the phone. For a terrified moment she thought he was gone, then his voice spoke again.

"I am not yet certain what it is they want. However, it has something to do with the approaching perihelion. They are waiting for something, planning, though for what I cannot say. Only one thing is certain: This is all far from over."

Deirdre could sense it—he was going to hang up. "Please," she gasped. "Tell me more."

"Not just now. I am at great peril telling you what I already have."

"Why are you in peril?"

A pause. Then, "There are those who would not be pleased if they knew I was aiding you. You must be wary of them. They could have agents anywhere."

Deirdre stood again, running her free hand through her hair. "Who do you mean? Please, help me."

"Good-bye, Miss Falling Hawk," came his polite, accentless voice through the phone. "It may be some time until we speak again. But when the time comes, I'll be in touch."

There was a click as the phone went dead in her hands. At the same moment the image of the figures in black robes and gold masks vanished from the computer screen, replaced by the picture of the keystone. Deirdre set down the phone with a shaking hand, then moved to the window and pulled back the curtains. She gazed into the night, but all she saw was darkness and her own ghostly reflection staring back at her.

Here ends *The Gates of Winter*, Book Five of *The Last Rune*. The ultimate secret of the connection between Eldh and Earth will be revealed in Book Six, *The First Stone*.

ABOUT THE AUTHOR

MARK ANTHONY learned to love both books and mountains during childhood summers spent in a Colorado ghost town. Later he was trained as a paleoanthropologist but along the way grew interested in a different sort of human evolution—the symbolic progress reflected in myth and the literature of the fantastic. He undertook this project to explore the idea that reason and wonder need not exist in conflict. Mark Anthony lives and writes in Colorado, where he is currently at work on the next book of *The Last Rune*. Fans of *The Last Rune* can visit the website at http://www.thelastrune.com.

On Earth, Duratek Corporation has been shattered, while on Eldh the Pale King and his wicked master Mohg are no more. Evil has been defeated on two worlds. For both Grace Beckett and Travis Wilder, it is a time of peace and simple joys. Until...

The sands of ancient Amún stir, and knowledge long buried comes to light once more: Morindu the Dark, lost city of sorcerers, has been found. At the same time, dread news flies on a dragon's wings: a dark rift has appeared in the heavens, a ravenous void that threatens not only Earth and Eldh but the very fabric of existence itself.

Now final perihelion approaches. Two worlds draw near. Together, Travis and Grace must embark on one last perilous quest: to reach the lost city of Morindu before forces of darkness can seize it, and to discover once and for all the ultimate secret of the connection between Earth and Eldh. In the final reckoning, all of existence will be saved... or nothingness will rule forever.

So be sure not to miss

THE FIRST STONE

the explosive conclusion to

MARK ANTHONY'S

epic saga

The Last Rune

Coming in summer 2004 from
Bantam Spectra

Here's a special preview:

The dervish stepped from a swirl of sand, appearing on the edge of the village like a mirage taking form.

A boy herding goats was the first to see him. The boy clucked his tongue, using a yew switch to prod the animals back to their pens. All at once the goats began to bleat, their eyes rolling as if they had caught the scent of a lion. Usually a lion would not prowl so near the dwellings of men, but the springs that scattered the desert—which had never gone dry in living memory—were failing, and creatures of all kinds were on the move in search of water and food. It was said that in one village not far away, a lion had crept into a hut and had stolen a baby right from the arms of its sleeping mother.

The boy turned around, and the switch fell from his fingers. It was not a lion before him, but a man covered from head to toe in a black *serafi*. Only his eyes were visible through a slit in the garment, dark and smoldering like coals. The man raised his right hand; its palm was tattooed with red lines. Tales told by the village's elders came back to the boy—tales about men who ventured into the deepest desert in search of forbidden magics.

Obey your father and your mother, the old ones used to tell him when he was small, *or else a dervish will fly into your house on a night zephyr and steal your blood for his craft. For they require the blood of wicked children to work their darkest spells.*

"I need..." the dervish said, his voice harsh with a strange accent.

The boy let out a wordless cry, then turned and ran toward a cluster of hovels, leaving the goats behind.

"...water," the dervish croaked, but the boy was already gone.

The dervish staggered, then caught himself. How long had he been in the Morgolthi? He did not know. Day after day the sun of the Thirsting Land had beaten down on him, burning away thought and memory, leaving him as dry as a scattering of bones. He should be dead. But something had propelled him on. What was it? There was no use trying to remember now. He needed water. Of the last two oases he had passed, one had been dry and the other had been poisoned, the bloated corpse of an antelope floating in its stagnant pool. But he would find water here; the spirits had told him so.

He moved through the herd of goats. The animals bleated until the dervish touched them, then they fell silent. He ran his hands over their hides and could feel the blood surging beneath, quickened by their fear. One swift flash of a knife, and hot blood would flow, thicker and sweeter than water. He could slake his thirst, and when he was finished he would let the blood spill on the ground as an offering, and with it he would call spirits to him. They would be only lesser spirits, to be sure, enticed by the blood of an animal—no more than enough to work petty magics. All the same, it would be satisfying. . . .

But no, that was not why he was here. He remembered now; he needed water, then to send word, to tell them he was here. He staggered toward the circle of huts. Behind him, the goats began bleating again, lost without the boy to herd them.

This place was called Hadassa, and though the people who dwelled here had now forgotten, it had once been a prosperous trading center, built around a verdant oasis and situated at a crossroads where merchants from the north coast of Al-Amún met with traders of the nomadic peoples who lived to the south, on the edge of the great desert of the Morgolthi.

However, Hadassa was not immune to the plague that affected this land, and over the decades the flow of its springs had dwindled to a trickle. The merchants and traders had left long ago and not returned; the city's grand buildings were swallowed by the encroaching sand. Now all that remained was this mean collection of huts.

When he reached the center of the village, the dervish stopped. The oasis, once a place of sparkling pools and shaded grottoes, was now a salt flat baked by the sun and crazed with cracks. Dead trees, scoured of leaf and branch, jutted up like skeletal fingers. In their midst was a patch of mud, churned into a mire by men and goats. Oily water oozed up through the sludge, gathering in the hoofprints. The dervish knelt, his throat aching to drink.

"You are not welcome here," said a coarse voice.

The dervish looked up. The water he had cupped dribbled through his fingers. A sigh escaped his blistered lips, and with effort he stood again.

A man stood at the other edge of the mud. His yellowed beard spilled down his chest, and he wore the white robe of a village elder. Behind him stood a pair of younger men. They were thin and stunted from lack of food, but their eyes were hard, and they gripped curved swords. Next to the man was a woman of middle years. In youth she had likely been beautiful, but the dry air had parched her cheeks, cracking them like the soil of the oasis. She gazed forward with milky eyes.

"The cards spoke truly, Sai'el Yarish," the woman said in a hissing voice, pawing at the elder man's robe. "Evil flies into Hadassa on dark wings."

"I cannot fly," the dervish said.

"Then you must walk from this place," the bearded man said. "And you must not come back."

The dervish started to hold out his hands in a gesture of supplication, then stopped, awkwardly pressing his palms against his *serafi*. "I come only in search of water."

One of the young men brandished his sword. "We have no water to spare for the likes of you."

"It is so," the old man said. "A change has come over the land. One by one, the springs of the desert have gone dry. Now ours is failing as well. You will not find what you seek here."

The dervish laughed, and the queer sound of it made the others take a step back.

"You are wrong," he said. "There is water to be found in this place."

From the folds of his *serafi* he drew out a curved knife. It flashed in the sun.

"Do not let him draw blood!" the blind woman shrieked.

The young men started forward, but the mud sucked at their sandals, slowing them. The dervish held out his left arm. The knife flicked, quick as a serpent. Red blood welled from a gash just above his wrist.

"Drink," he whispered, shutting his eyes, sending out the call. "Drink, and do my bidding."

He felt them come a moment later; distance meant nothing. They buzzed through the village like a swarm of hornets or a vortex of sand, accompanied by a sound just beyond hearing. The men looked around with fearful eyes. The blind woman gnashed her teeth and swatted at the air. The dervish lowered his arm, letting blood drip from his wound.

The fluid vanished before it struck the ground.

He clenched his jaw. The flow of his blood quickened as if the hot air gobbled it.

"Water," the dervish murmured. "Show me the water you said was here."

A moment ago they had been furious in their hunger. Now they were sated by blood, their will easy to bend to his own. He sensed them plunge downward, deep into the ground. Soil, rock—these were as air to them. He felt it seconds later: a tremor beneath his boots. There was a gurgling noise, then a jet of water shot up from the center of the mud patch. The fountain glittered in the sun, spinning off drops as clear and precious as diamonds.

The village elder gaped, while the young men dashed forward, letting the water spill into their hands, drinking greedily.

"It is cool and sweet," one of them said, laughing.

"It is a trick!" the blind woman cried. "You must not drink, lest it cast you under his spell."

However, the young men ignored her. They continued to drink, and the man in the white robe joined them. Others appeared now, stealing from the huts, moving tentatively toward the spring, the fear on the sun-darkened faces giving way to wonder.

The blind woman stamped her feet. "It is a deception, I tell you! If you drink, he will poison us all!"

The village folk pushed past her and she fell into the mud, her robe tangling around her so that she could not get up. The people held out their hands toward the splashing water.

Quickly the dervish bound his wound with a rag, stanching the flow of blood lest the bodiless ones come to partake of more. *Morndari,* the spirits were called. Those Who Hunger. They had no form, no substance, but their thirst for blood was unquenchable. Once, he had come upon a young sorcerer who had thought too highly of his own power, and who had called many of the *morndari* to him. His body had been no more than a dry husk, a look of horror on his mummified face.

The flow of the fountain continued. Water pooled at the dervish's feet. He bent to drink, but he was weak from hunger and thirst, and from loss of blood. The sky reeled above him, and he fell.

Strong hands caught him: the young swordsmen's.

"Take him into my hut," said a voice he recognized as the village elder's.

Were they going to murder him then? He should call the *morndari* again, only he could not reach his knife, and he was already too weak. The spirits would drain his body dry of blood, just like the ill-fated young sorcerer he had once found.

The hands bore him to a dim, cool space, protected from the sun by thick mud walls. He was laid upon cushions, and a wooden cup pressed to his lips. Water spilled into his mouth, clean and wholesome. He coughed, then drank deeply, draining the cup. Leaning back, he opened his eyes and saw the bearded man above him.

"How long will it flow?" the old man asked.

The dervish licked blistered lips. "For many lives of men, the spirits say. I do not doubt them."

The old man nodded. "All the tales I know tell that a dervish brings only evil and suffering. Yet you have saved us all."

The dervish laughed, a chilling sound. "Would that were so. But I fear your seeress was right. Evil does come, on dark wings. To Hadassa, and to all of Moringarth."

The other made a warding sign with his hand. "Gods help us. What must we do?"

"You must send word that I am here. You must send a message to the Mournish. Do you know where they can be found?"

The old man stroked his beard. "I know some who know. Word can be sent to the Wandering Folk. But surely you cannot mean what you say. Your kind is abomination to them. If they find you, your life is forfeit. The working of blood sorcery is forbidden."

"No, it isn't," the dervish said. He looked down at his hands, marked by lines tattooed in red and fine white scars. "Not anymore."

It was the quiet that woke Sareth.

Over the last three years he had grown used to the sound of her heartbeat and the gentle rhythm of her breathing. Together they made a music that lulled him to sleep each night and bestowed blissful dreams. Then, six months ago, another heart—

tiny and swift—had added its own note. But now the wagon was silent.

Sareth sat up. Gray light crept through a moon-shaped window into the cramped interior of the wagon. She had not been able to make it any larger, but by her touch it had become cozier. Bunches of dried herbs hung in the corners, filling the wagon with a sweet, dusty scent. Beaded curtains dangled before the windows. Cushions embroidered with leaves and flowers covered the benches on either side of the wagon. The tops of the benches could be lifted to reveal bins beneath, or lowered along with a table to turn the wagon into a place where eight could sit and dine or play *An'hot* with a deck of *T'hot* cards. Now the table was folded up against the wall, making room for the pallet they unrolled each night.

The pallet was empty, save for himself. He pulled on a pair of loose-fitting trousers, then opened the door of the wagon. Moist air, fragrant with the scent of night-blooming flowers, rushed in, cool against his bare chest. He breathed, clearing the fog of sleep from his mind, then climbed down the wagon's wooden steps. The grass was damp with dew beneath his bare feet—his two bare feet.

Though it had been three years, every day he marveled at the magic that had restored the leg he had lost to the demon beneath Tarras. He would never really understand how Lady Aryn's spell had healed him, but it didn't matter. Since he met Lirith, he had grown accustomed to wonders.

He found her beneath a slender *ithaya* tree on the edge of the grove where the Mournish had made camp. A tincture of coral colored the horizon; dawn was coming, but not yet. She turned when she heard him approach, her smile glowing in the dimness.

"Beshala," he said softly. "What are you doing out here so early?"

"Taneth was fussing. I didn't want him to wake you." She cradled the baby in her arms. He was sound asleep, wrapped snugly in a blanket sewn with moons and stars.

Sareth laid a hand on the baby's head. His hair was thick and dark, and his eyes, when they were open, were the same dark copper as Sareth's. But everything else about him—his fine features, his rich ebony skin—was Lirith's.

The baby sighed in his sleep, and Sareth smiled. Here was another wonder before him. Lirith had believed herself incapable of bearing a child. When she was a girl, she was sold into servitude in the Free City of Corantha, in the house of Gulthas. There she had been forced to dance for men who paid their gold—and do more than simply dance. Countless times a spark of life had kindled in her womb, only to go dark when she consumed the potions Gulthas forced on all the women in his house. Then, in time, no more sparks had kindled.

Lirith had wept the night she told him this, thinking that once he knew he would turn away from her. She was wrong. Knowing this only made him love her more fiercely. That she could endure such torture and yet remain so good, so gentle showed that there was no one in the world more deserving of love.

Even so, he had wept as well. For even if she could have conceived a child, he could not have given her one. Or at least so he believed. When the demon below Tarras took his leg, it had taken something else—something intangible but no less a part of him. Since that day, no woman, not even Lirith, could cause him to rise as a man should. He could love her with all his heart, but he could not make love *to* her.

Until Lady Aryn's spell.

And now, here was the greatest wonder of all: little Taneth, dark and sweet and perfect.

Lirith sighed, turning her gaze toward the east.

Sareth touched her shoulder. "Are you sure it was because of Taneth you came out here, *beshala*? Is there not another reason?"

She gazed at him, her eyes bright with tears. "I don't want you to go."

So that's what this was about. He had thought as much. Last night a young man from another Mournish band had ridden hard into the circle of their wagons, bearing ill news.

"I do not wish to leave," Sareth said. "But you heard the message Alvestri brought just as I did. A dervish has come out of the desert, or at least one who claims he is a dervish. He must be seen."

"Yes, someone must go see him. But why must it be you?"

"You know why the task falls to me. I am descended of the royal line of Morindu."

Lirith's dark eyes flashed. "So is your sister Vani. She is the one who was trained at Golgoru. She is the *T'gol*. It is she who should be doing this thing, not you."

Sareth pressed his lips together. He could not argue that point, for Lirith was right. Two thousand years ago, the sorcerers of Morindu the Dark had destroyed their own city lest its secrets fall into the hands of their foe, the city of Scirath. The people of Morindu, the Morindai, became wanderers and vagabonds, known in the north as the Mournish.

After their exile, the Morindai forbade the practice of blood sorcery, until such time as Morindu should be raised again from the sands that swallowed it. However, there were those who defied that law. Dervishes, they were called. They were renegades, anathema. The silent fortress of Golgoru had been founded in part to train assassins who could hunt down the dervishes and destroy them with means other than magic.

Sareth stepped away to the edge of the grove. "It's true. This task should be Vani's. But my sister is gone, and the cards do not reveal where, though al-Mama has gazed at them time after time. I know of no way to find her, unless you think Queen Grace may have heard some news."

They had last seen Vani in Malachor, in Gravenfist Keep. Then, just before the Mournish arrived there three years ago, she vanished.

Lirith shook her head. "You know I have not Aryn's strength in the Touch. I cannot reach her over the Weirding, let alone Grace. They are too far away." She frowned. "Indeed, it seems my ability to reach out over the leagues grows less these days, not more. The Weirding feels . . . I'm not certain how to put it. It feels tired to me somehow."

"Perhaps it's you that's a little tired, *beshala*," Sareth said, touching Taneth's tiny hand.

She smiled. "Perhaps so. Still, it is strange. I will have to ask Aryn about it the next time she contacts me."

While Sareth did not doubt Lirith was happy living among the Mournish, he knew she missed her friends. The Mournish had journeyed to Calavere—where Aryn and Teravian ruled over both Calavan and Toloria—only once in the last three years, and they had not returned at all to Gravenfist Keep, where Queen Grace dwelled. Still, the three witches could speak from time to time using magic, and that was a comfort. However, the last time Lirith had spoken to them so, neither had heard any news of Vani.

An idea occurred to Sareth. "Why don't you go to Calavere, *beshala*?"

She stared at him.

He laughed at her surprise. "Go on. Take Taneth. Be with Aryn. It will not take you long to journey there, and the roads are safe these days. Aryn is to have her own child soon, is she not? I am certain she will enjoy seeing our little one. And when I am finished with my work in the south, I will come to you both there."

"I believe you are trying to distract me," Lirith said, giving him a stern look. However, she could not keep it up, and she laughed as she hugged Taneth to her. "I confess, I long to see Aryn with my eyes, not just hear her voice over the Weirding. And if I stayed here, I imagine I would do nothing but fret and worry about you."

"Then it's settled," Sareth said. "You will go to Calavere at once. I will ask Damari to accompany you." He scratched his chin. "Or maybe I'd better make that Jahiel. He's much less handsome."

"Damari will do just fine," Lirith said pertly. Then her mirth ceased, and she leaned her head against his bare chest, Taneth between them. He circled his arms around them both.

"Promise me you won't worry, *beshala*."

"I will be waiting" was all she said, and they stayed that way, the three of them together, as dawn turned the sky to gold.

He left that day, taking only one other—a broad-shouldered young man named Fahir—with him. Word had been sent to the fastness of Golgoru, in the Mountains of the Shroud, but there were few *T'gol* these days, nor was it likely one of them would reach Al-Amún sooner than Sareth. From this place, it was only a half-day's ride to the port city of Kalos, on the southernmost tip of Falengarth, at the point where the Summer Sea was at its narrowest. Sareth hoped to reach the city by nightfall and book passage on a ship the next day.

Before he left, his al-Mama called him into her dragon-shaped wagon and made him draw a card from her *T'hot* deck. His fingertips tingled as they brushed one of the well-worn cards, and he drew it out. As he turned it over, a hiss escaped her.

"The Void," she said in a soft rasp.

There was no picture on the card. It was painted solid black.

"What does it mean? Do I have no fate, then?"

"Only a dead man has no fate."

He swallowed the lump in his throat. "What of the *A'narai*, the Fateless Ones who tended the god-king Orú long ago?"

She snatched the card from his hand. "As I said, only a dead man has no fate."

His al-Mama said no more, but as Sareth left the wagon he glanced over his shoulder. The old woman huddled beneath her blankets, muttering as she turned the card over and over. Whatever it portended, it troubled her. However, he put it out of his mind. Perhaps the dead had no fate, but he was very much alive, and his destiny was to return to Lirith and Taneth as soon as possible.

They reached Kalos that evening as planned and set sail the next morning on the swiftest ship they could find—a small spice trader. Fahir, who had never been at sea before, was violently ill during the entire two-day passage, and even Sareth found himself getting queasy, for the Summer Sea was rough, and the little ship ran up and down the waves rather than through them, as a larger vessel might. The ship's captain remarked that he had never seen such ill winds so early in the year before.

Fortunately, the voyage was soon over, and they disembarked in the port city of Qaradas, on the north coast of the continent of Moringarth, in the land of city-states known collectively as Al-Amún. Sareth had traveled to Al-Amún several times in his youth; it was a custom among the Mournish of the north that young men and women should visit the southern continent, where most of the Morindai yet dwelled. Qaradas was just as he remembered it: a city of white domed buildings and crowded, dusty streets shaded by palm trees.

"I thought the cities of the south were made of gold," Fahir said, a look of disappointment on his face.

Sareth grinned. "In the light of sunset, the white buildings do look gold. But it is only illusion—as is much in Al-Amún. So beware. And if a beautiful woman in red scarves claims she wishes to marry you, don't follow her! You'll lose your gold as well as your innocence."

"Of the first I have little enough," Fahir said with a laugh. "And the second I would be happy to dispense with. This is my first trip to the south, after all."

They headed to the traders' quarter, and Sareth examined the front door of every inn and hostel until he found what he was looking for.

"We will be welcome here," he said with a grin. In answer to Fahir's puzzled look, Sareth pointed to a small symbol scratched in the upper corner of the door: a crescent moon inscribed in a triangle. This place was run by Morindai like them.

Inside, Sareth and Fahir were welcomed as family. After they had shared drink and food, the hostel's proprietor suggested a place where camels and supplies for a journey could be bought at a good price, and Sareth went to investigate, leaving Fahir with orders to rest and not even think about approaching the innkeeper's lovely black-haired daughter.

"By her looks I think she favors me," Fahir said proudly. "Why shouldn't I approach her?"

"Because by her al-Mama's looks, if you do, the old woman will put a *va'ksha* on you that will give you the private parts of a mouse."

The young man's face blanched. "I'll get some rest. Come back soon."

They set out before dawn the next day, riding on the swaying backs of two heavily laden camels as the domes of Qaradas faded like a mirage behind them. At first the air was cool, but once the sun rose into the sky heat radiated from the ground in dusty waves, parching their throats with every breath. Despite this, they drank sparingly. By all accounts it was a journey of six days to the village of Hadassa, where the rumors of the dervish had originated.

During the middle part of each day, when the sun grew too fierce to keep riding, they crouched in whatever shade they could find beneath a rock or cliff. They were always vigilant, and one would keep watch while the other dozed. Thieves were common on the roads between the city-states of Al-Amún.

Nor was it only thieves they kept watch for. Ever were the sorcerers of Scirath attracted to news of a dervish. While the Scirathi had suffered a great blow in the destruction of the Etherion more than three years before, where a great number of them were consumed by the demon, recently the Mournish had heard whispers that their old enemy had been gathering again, regaining its former strength. Even after two thousand years, the Scirathi still sought the secrets lost when Morindu the Dark was buried beneath the sands of the Morgolthi. Because the dervishes sought those same secrets, where one was found, the other could not be far off.

The days wore on, and water became a hardship. The first two springs they came to had offered some to drink, though less than Sareth had been led to believe. However, after that, every spring they reached was dry and they found no water, only white bones and withered trees. Doing their best to swallow the sand in their throats, they continued on.

Fahir and he never spoke of it, but by the fifth day of their journey Sareth knew they were in grave danger. There were but two swallows for each of them left in their flasks. It was said that Hadassa was built around a great oasis. However, if that was not so, if its spring had gone dry like the others, they would not make it back to Qaradas alive.

You could cast a spell, Sareth thought that night as he huddled beneath a blanket next to Fahir. Once the sun went down the desert air grew chill, and both men shuddered as with a fever. *You could call the spirits and bid them to lead you to water.*

Could he really? The working of blood sorcery was forbidden among the Morindai; only the dervishes broke that law. True, the elders of the clan had allowed Sareth to use the gate artifact to communicate with Vani when she journeyed across the Void to Earth. However, that had been a time of great need, and it was not a true act of blood sorcery. Sareth had spilled his blood to power the artifact, but he had not called the bodiless spirits, the *morndari,* to him as a true sorcerer would.

Besides, Sareth asked himself, *what makes you believe you could control the spirits if they did answer your call? They would likely consume all your blood and unleash havoc.*

Yet if he and Fahir did not find water tomorrow, what choice did he have but to try?

The next day dawned hotter than any that had come before. The white sun beat down on them, and the wind scoured any bit of exposed flesh with hard sand. They were on the very edge of habitable lands now. To the south stretched the endless wastes of the Morgolthi, the Thirsting Land, where no man had dwelled in eons, not since the land was broken and poisoned in the War of the Sorcerers.

The horizon wavered before Sareth. Shapes materialized amid the shimmering air. He fancied he could almost see them: the high towers of the first great cities of ancient Amún. Usyr. Scirath. And the onyx spires of Morindu the Dark . . .

A shout jolted Sareth from his waking dream. He sprawled on the sand as his camel plodded away from him. Fahir slumped over the neck of his own camel as the beast followed its partner toward a cluster of square shapes. That was no mirage; it was a village.

Sareth tried to call out, but his throat was too dry. However, at the same moment he heard voices, then shadows appeared above him, blocking the sun. Voices jabbered in a dialect he couldn't understand, though he made out one word, repeated over and over: *Morindai, Morindai*. Hands lifted him from the ground, and he could not resist.

He drifted in a dark void, then came to himself as something cool pressed against his lips. It was a clay cup. Water poured into his mouth. He choked, then gulped it down. Greedily, he clutched the cup and drained it.

"More," he croaked.

"No, that's enough for now," said a low, oddly accented voice. "You have to drink slowly or you'll become sick."

Sareth blinked, his eyes adjusting to the dim light. He was inside a hut, lying on a rug, propped up against filthy cushions. A man knelt beside him, holding the cup. He was swathed from head to foot in black; only his dark eyes were visible.

Fear sliced away the dullness in Sareth's mind. Was this one of the Scirathi? They always wore black like this. He remembered how he had been tortured by the sorcerer who had followed them through the gate to Castle City. That one had enjoyed causing Sareth pain.

No, they always wear masks of gold. The masks are the key to their power. This is no Scirathi.

Fresh dread replaced the old. What manner of creature was this? Sareth pushed himself up against the cushions, knowing he was too weak to flee.

"What have you done with Fahir?" he said.

"Your friend is being cared for in another hut," the dervish said. "You need not fear for him."

Sareth licked his cracked lips. He had planned to come upon the dervish unaware, so that the other could not cast a spell. But now he was in the dervish's power. He tried to think what to say.

The dervish spoke first. "You're her brother, aren't you? Vani, the assassin. We knew she was in communication with her brother through the gate artifact, and the resemblance is clear enough."

Confusion replaced fear. How could the dervish know these things? And why did his accent, strange as it was, seem familiar?

"Who are you?" Sareth demanded.

The dervish laughed. "That's a good question. Who am I indeed? Not who I was before, that much is certain." The dervish pushed back his hood. His pale skin had been burnt and blistered, though now it was beginning to heal. "I used to be a man called Hadrian Farr."

Sareth clutched at the cushions. "I know who you are! Vani told me of you. You're from the world across the Void. How can you be here?"

The other made a dismissive gesture. "That's not important now. All that matters is that you take word back to your people."

"Take word of what? And why don't you tell them yourself?"

The dervish moved to a window; a thin beam of sunlight slipped through a crack in the shutters, illuminating his sunravaged face. "Because once I am done here, I must go back. Back into the Morgolthi. After all these ages, it has finally been found."

"What are you talking about?" Sareth said, rising up—angry at not understanding, angry at his fear. "What has been found?"

The dervish—the Earth man named Hadrian Farr—turned and gazed at him with haunted eyes.

"The lost city of Morindu the Dark," he said.

Outside the hut, the wind rose like a jackal's howl.